Festive Fakes

Festive Fakes

The Complete Collection

BY
KEIRA ANDREWS

Written and published by Keira Andrews
Illustrations by Ignacia Ibarra Black
Cover by Dar Albert
Formatting by BB eBooks

Omnibus Contents

The Christmas Deal

BY
KEIRA ANDREWS

Acknowledgements

Many thanks to Anara, DJ, Mary, Leta, and Rai for their friendship and assistance with Logan and Seth's story. Ho, ho, ho! <3

Chapter One

WHEN THE PHONE rang again, Logan allowed himself a flicker of hope before snuffing it out. No, it wasn't the warehouse manager calling back to say he had the job after all. No Christmas miracle was coming.

He stared at the screen, dread sinking through him. It was Rencliffe Academy, which meant his balls were about to be busted because the kid had fucked up.

Again.

Logan shivered on the side of the bed in his skivvies, the battered parquet floor freezing under his bare feet since he'd put the heat down as low as possible in hopes of paying the bill. Fuck, he was tempted to huddle under the blankets and go back to sleep, dealing with whatever crap this was later.

But Veronica's disappointed face filled his mind. As foolish as the choice had been, he'd married her, and her son was his responsibility now. He swiped the screen and answered.

"Mr. Derwood? It's Assistant Headmaster Patel calling." She spoke calmly and smoothly in a British-type fancy accent. Logan braced himself. She said, "I'm afraid there's been another incident. Can you join us this morning for a get-together?"

He wasn't sure why Rencliffe insisted on making it sound as if they were inviting him over for finger foods and Chardonnay or some shit. "Yeah. I'll be there in—" He groaned to himself, remembering his Ford was broken in the shop. Because of course it was.

After a pause, she prompted, "Mr. Derwood? This is really quite urgent. Connor's behavioral issues—"

"Yeah, I know. I'll be there as soon as I can. Thanks." He hung up, bile rising in his throat. The only silver lining to apparently being unemployable was that he didn't have to take time off work for yet another school visit. Too bad his disability benefits had run out. That sure made being jobless a real son of a bitch.

Merry fucking Christmas.

There was nothing else to do but text Jenna:

Can I drive u 2 work and take the car? Will pick u up at 3.

His sister was working short days Monday to Thursday after having her second kid, and hopefully he'd caught her in time. The typing bubbles appeared on the screen, and she replied:

No prob. Just leaving day care. Everything okay?

He barked out a laugh in his empty bedroom. He couldn't even remember what *okay* felt like. Forget *good* or *great*. Those feelings were distant memories. He typed back:

Just have to run errand. Thx. They had to order a new part for the pickup.

A new part he couldn't afford, but he left that out. He also didn't mention Connor because it would only make Jenna worry, and she had enough on her plate. Shit, her plate had been overflowing since she was fourteen.

When the cancer finally got their mom, Jenna was the one who'd taken care of their father and the house while Logan had been in Iraq. He was seven years older than his baby sister, but she was the one who kept them all afloat.

She worked her ass off to include Connor in family stuff, and at least he tolerated her. For a moment, Logan considered whether he should ask Jenna to come with him to the school, but no. She had work, and she had to save her emergency time off for her own kids. Connor was his responsibility. Logan was thirty-eight years old, and he should be able to unfuck his own life.

He stood, wincing at the stiff ache in his muscles and the phantom twinges in his formerly broken bones. After being in traction, he'd never take moving his body for granted again, but goddamn, everything felt tighter than it used to. Of course, he hadn't done his stretches, so what did he expect?

There was no time to shower and shave, but he splashed his scruffy face, ran a comb through his cropped dark hair, and scrubbed a wet towel under his arms. He sniffed five shirts before finding a fresh-enough gray Henley and pulling it on over his jeans and combat boots. Maybe he should have dressed up a bit, but the folks at Rencliffe knew who he was. Putting lipstick on a pig wouldn't change anything.

After Jenna picked him up, he listened to her good-natured complaints about her kids and husband and Christmas shopping. She chattered nonstop until they reached the six-story, glass-fronted office building in a corporate park on the outskirts of Albany.

There was a puke stain on her shoulder, but Logan didn't tell her. She'd call it "spit-up," but from what he could tell, it was puke. But it was already dry and too late for her to change anyway.

Putting the SUV in park by the front of the building, she gave him a gleaming smile, dimples appearing in her cheeks. Logan and Jenna shared the same greenish-hazel eyes, but she'd been the only one to inherit their mother's sunny smile and optimism. "I haven't let you get a word in edgewise. Sorry." Her smile faded. "You sure everything's okay?"

"Yep. Have a good day at work."

But Jenna stayed put behind the wheel. "Look, I know it's still too soon to think about dating again—"

"Yet you're bringing it up anyway."

She sighed. "I just hate seeing you so miserable—and don't bother telling me you aren't. I know you don't like me worrying, but newsflash: I worry anyway. And maybe dating would help."

"It wouldn't." The thought of meeting a woman and trying to impress her, getting to know her, inviting her into the shit show of his life—it was exhausting.

Hell, Logan hadn't even had the energy to hook up with guys beyond a half-hearted hand job in a bathroom stall at the mall a few weeks ago. It had been quick and rough, the way Logan liked it with men. No kissing, no hugging, no need to be tender and concerned about feelings.

That's how he knew he was straight. He only wanted that other stuff with women. Men were for getting off and nothing more.

Jenna sighed again. "You're right. I don't know why I said that."

He gave her a small smile. "Because you're desperate to fix things for me." Because Jenna was good and kind. He didn't deserve her. "Don't worry about me, all right? You'd better get inside or you'll be late."

"Oh, did you hear about the warehouse job?"

He shrugged. "Not yet." He'd put in a bunch of applications other places, so maybe one of them would call. For now, there was no point in worrying Jenna more by telling her he'd failed yet again.

"I'm knocking on wood." She rapped her knuckles on her head, then leaned over the console and pressed a kiss to his cheek. "Have a good day."

He walked around the vehicle, waving to her before she disappeared inside. Logan had a good foot on his baby sister, and as he adjusted the driver's seat and mirrors, his phone rang again. He pulled it from the pocket of his leather jacket, his stomach dropping. The landlord. He let it go to voicemail. He didn't need to hear Mrs. Politano tell him again that the rent was overdue.

He hadn't been able to afford the rent on Veronica's house after her death, and he'd moved into a tiny bungalow in a rundown neighborhood. Even if he'd had the money, the thought of sleeping every night in the room where Veronica died had been unbearable.

"Fuck," he muttered as he drove out toward Rencliffe. It was about forty-five minutes away, and Logan wished he could just be there already to get this over with.

He jabbed at the presets on the radio, and every one played commercials or Christmas songs with sleigh bells and peace on earth by a warm fireplace. He left it on a station blaring an ad for extended Black Friday deals. From what he could tell, Black Friday went for about six weeks at this point.

If that warehouse job had come through, maybe he'd have a hope of a decent Christmas. He could've at least bought Connor some presents. But the job hadn't come through, because no one would hire him once they found out he'd been fired from the railway and blamed for the accident.

No matter that he'd served his country for four years in the Marine Corps after 9/11 and earned a commendation medal. *Thank you for your service, but you're a useless sack of shit now.*

He struggled to take a deep breath, the low ache in his sternum that had never fully gone away flaring hot. Logan tugged at his seatbelt. His broken bones had healed, but sometimes he just couldn't fucking breathe. Usually it was only when he exerted himself, and he knew right now it was probably all in his fucked-up head, but it still hurt.

The sign marking Rencliffe's curving driveway was freshly painted in gold and navy, proclaiming:

Rencliffe Academy
The Brightest Minds Since 1909

Logan followed the driveway through the towering trees, only a few red, gold, and shit-brown leaves left hanging as winter quickly approached. Visitor parking was empty but for a silver Audi. Birds chirped almost desperately as he walked up the path to the main gray-brick building, which was decorated in massive red-ribboned holiday wreaths and lights that were currently off.

The school was a sprawl of five or six buildings, including the dorms. A newer addition had been constructed in the same style with big arches and turret-type things on the top like a castle. Veronica had called it Gothic, which apparently didn't actually mean scary, although Logan found it all pretty creepy. Rencliffe was definitely the type of place where a crazed murderer would strike in the movies.

He walked into the vaulted foyer of main building, his boots thudding. He stopped in front of a massive Christmas tree decorated in white lights and old-fashioned wooden ornaments shaped like birds, pinecones, and angels. Probably all made by the students.

The hush hanging over the polished wood and marble foyer made him think of church. They'd been Easter-and-Christmas Catholics when he was growing up, but he hadn't even done that much in years. Though Rencliffe wasn't a religious school, he still half-expected a priest or nun to appear to greet him. Instead it was an older woman, who led him down the eerily quiet hallways to Mira Patel's book-lined office.

She was surprisingly young—probably thirty. According to the framed diplomas behind her desk, she'd attended the University of Delhi and Oxford, so clearly she was pretty freaking smart. Her black hair was tied back in a twisty bun, and she had big eyes behind her gold-framed glasses.

If they were in a porno, she'd be about to let down her hair, take off her glasses, and rip open her cream blouse to reveal big tits. She'd hike up her skirt and—

"Thank you for coming, Mr. Derwood. It's good to meet you." She sat in the padded leather chair behind her desk as Logan took one of the guest chairs and shoved away the stupid porno thoughts. "The headmaster's absent on personal business, so I'm handling Connor's case for the moment."

"Right. I'm sorry if the kid's been acting up again."

"Mmm." She leaned forward in her chair, folding her hands on the shiny wood desk, her nails gleaming with pale polish. "I hope you don't mind if I go back over the particulars with you?"

"Um, the particulars?" Jesus, he felt like he was back in high school about to fail an exam he hadn't studied for.

"Connor's background. How we've gotten to where we are now. I understand you were a recent addition to his life before his mother passed away?"

Dull pain throbbed in his chest, and he forced a breath. "Uh-huh. Veronica and I met about a year and a half ago. I was in an accident at work and had to be in the hospital for a few months. Veronica was my nurse."

A memory flashed—*the wedding march playing on someone's phone at the hospital chapel, Logan dragging an IV and Veronica still in her purple scrubs, her fellow nurses throwing confetti made of paper from the shredding bin.*

Clearing his throat, he added, "My life was shit, and she was the one good thing." He shifted on the hard-backed chair. "Um, excuse my language."

Ms. Patel smiled. "Shit happens. You're recovered now?"

"Mostly. If I push too hard, I get out of breath. But it's fine."

She nodded. "So you and Connor's mother married quite quickly?"

"Yeah. Within a couple months. Dumb, I know. But I loved her and was so sure we'd be together forever." He snorted. "Then, you know. Reality smacked us upside the head. She brought me home from the hospital, and in a few weeks we were driving each other crazy. Living with someone's not all roses and unicorns."

"No, it certainly isn't." Ms. Patel smiled wryly. "Compromise isn't easy."

He shifted, hot trickles of shame in his gut. "We tried, though. We did. We really cared about each other, even if we didn't fit."

"Of course."

"And I've tried with Connor. I really have." He cringed internally at his defensiveness.

She eyed him sympathetically. "I know you have. It's a challenging situation. Thirteen can be a tough age already, and Connor's faced a traumatic loss and major life changes. Plus, you've suddenly found yourself a single father. It's an adjustment, to say the least."

A single father.

It was so weird to think of himself that way. He wasn't qualified to be anyone's dad, let alone a single one. Logan nodded. "Yeah."

"What was your relationship like before his mother's passing?"

Passing. As if she'd drifted off down a lazy river in the sunshine. Logan hated when people didn't just call it what it was. Veronica hadn't *passed* anywhere—she was rotting in a hole in the ground. He choked down the resentment. Ms. Patel was only being polite.

"We didn't really have a relationship. He was pissed when I married his mom, and I can't blame the kid for that. He hardly talked to me when he was home on vacations from school, and I didn't know what to say to him anyway. Things got very tense with me and Veronica. Then she died."

"It was an aneurysm? That must have been quite a shock."

He tugged at a loose thread on the cuff of his Henley. "Yeah. I'd spent the night on my sister's couch since Veronica and I had been going at each other all day. They said even if I'd been home, it wouldn't have mattered." *But maybe the docs were wrong. If I'd been there…*

"Then Connor discovered her in the morning since he was home for the summer."

Hearing Ms. Patel say it out loud was a steel toe to Logan's nuts, guilt surging through him. Jaw clenched, he nodded. A clock ticked on the wall, each second louder than the last. His mind filled with red flashing lights, the sympathetic—yet definitely suspicious—cops escorting him inside his own place, a sheet over Veronica on the bedroom floor, waiting for a body bag. The poor kid sitting in the kitchen with a female cop.

Connor hadn't been crying, and Logan hadn't seen him shed a tear since. The kid was empty, although when Logan had clumsily tried to squeeze his shoulder, Connor had exploded with rage. It was apparently all he had left.

Ms. Patel quietly stated the fucking obvious. "It was extremely traumatic for him. We've endeavored to give Connor the support he needs, but he's simply not cooperating. His biological father isn't in the picture at all?"

Logan huffed. "Waste of space. Took off down to Florida years ago. Every once in a while he shows up with expensive presents and a bunch of bullshit stories. For a smart kid, you'd think Connor could see through him. The guy has zero interest in being a father."

"When was the last time you were in touch with Mr. Lisowski?"

"Dunno. After Veronica died. I don't know if Connor's talked to him."

"A few texts, apparently. You don't feel he can be any help in this situation?"

"Fucked if I know." He winced. "Excuse my language again."

She waved off his apology. "I'd need your permission to speak to Mr. Lisowski about Connor since you're the legal guardian. I understand Connor's mother had been a foster child? No family?"

"Right. If you think he can help, call him, but he probably won't answer. Mike couldn't care less about the kid if he tried."

She picked up a gold and silver pen and wrote in a leather-bound notebook. Logan watched her pen making loops and swoops before she capped it and looked back at him. "I understand you're currently out of work?"

Anger flared, a hot burst in his veins. What she meant was: *I understand you're a useless sack of shit?* He barked, "Look, are we going to talk about whatever Connor did, or what?"

"Yes, of course." She folded her hands again, calm as anything. "You know that Connor's full scholarship is incumbent upon him keeping his grades at a minimum of a B average. And even more importantly, it requires him to behave in an orderly, respectable manner. To not put himself or any of his classmates in harm's way."

Fuck. "What did he do?"

"Connor dropped his backpack down the gap in the stairwell from an upper floor."

"Oh." That didn't seem so bad? "Did he break something?"

"The bag hit another student in the lower leg and caused significant pain and bruising. If it had hit him in the head, it very well could have killed him. This is no laughing matter or a 'boys will be boys' situation. Perhaps that recklessness would fly in a public school, but this is Rencliffe, Mr. Derwood."

All he could do was nod like he was back in the principal's office. "I understand. It was a stupid thing to do. It won't happen again."

She sighed, sitting back with a squeak of leather. "I sincerely hope not. We've attempted to engage him repeatedly, but he's sullen and uncooperative. Connor has a brilliant mind. He used to be one of our best students. We've been cutting him a lot of slack, but he needs to curb this destructive and harmful behavior. Not only toward his classmates, but himself."

Logan went very still. "What do you mean? Is he, like, cutting himself or something?"

"Not that we know of. But he's skipping classes, showing up late, and not completing assignments. Getting into fights, as you know from your discussion with Mr. Howard a few weeks ago. Connor's going to fail his courses, and we know it's not because of his intelligence. The term exams are next week, concluding on Friday, December twenty-first, followed by the holiday break."

"Right." The colorful ceramic tree in the corner of Ms. Patel's office seemed to mock him with its cheery lights and glossy snow. The holidays were supposed to be a magical time for kids, and what would Logan be able to give Connor? A roof over their heads if Logan was lucky.

"If Connor performs at a B level on his exams—which should be infinitely doable for him even without studying a word—and if he stays in line, he's welcome back in January to turn things around."

"And if he doesn't?" Logan gripped the arms of the chair.

"Then I'm afraid Connor's tenure here at Rencliffe will end. You should investigate the public school options in your neighborhood, although I sincerely hope it won't be necessary."

My neighborhood.

Where was that, exactly? The rented house he was about to be evicted from? He rubbed a hand over his face, a week of scruff scratching his palm. "Okay."

"Mr. Derwood, I assure you we want Connor to succeed. It would truly be a shame if he squanders his limitless potential. He's had a full scholarship here for two years because we believe in him. But he has to meet us halfway. It's been months of acting out, and while we're very sympathetic, we have to think of the other students. Connor has been too disruptive for too long."

"Yeah. I get it." He pushed to his feet. "You've been fair. Thank you." He stuck out his hand, and she shook it firmly.

"Connor's waiting in the atrium. I can take you there."

"I know the way. Thanks."

When he reached the high-ceilinged greenhouse down the hall—all glass and flowering plants and even a tinkling fountain, Logan found Connor tossing stones from a rock garden into the pool of water. Two stone fish were twisted together in the middle, water spouting out of their open mouths.

Connor didn't turn, instead plonking a rock right at one of the fish heads. His navy uniform jacket was stretched tightly across his narrow shoulders, gray pants a bit too short.

If he gets kicked out, I guess I don't have to pony up for new uniforms.

That wasn't much of a silver lining. "Hey," Logan said, jamming his fists in his pockets. Shit, he never knew what to say to this kid.

Connor ignored him, bending to scoop up more rocks. Logan stood there and let him finish that handful before he said, "Are you going to knock off the crap you've been pulling? You're smarter than this."

Another rock dinged off the stone fish's head. "You don't know anything about me. You're not my father."

"I know. But I'm…" Logan didn't know. In the eyes of Ms. Patel, he was a single dad, and he felt like such a fake. But he was all the kid had left.

"You're just the asshole loser my mom married because she hated being alone."

It shouldn't have hurt, yet Logan's chest tightened the way it did when he exerted himself too much, his breath coming short. Right now it was completely in his head, and he reminded himself of that as he forced in a gulp of air. He was sorely tempted to leave Connor to his sulking misery, but he had to be the grown-up.

"You took forever to show up." Connor turned, narrowing his dark gaze. The kid was maybe five-two, a full foot shorter than Logan and probably a hundred pounds soaking wet. Still, he internally cringed as Connor sized him up. "Bet you were hungover."

Logan breathed out evenly, ignoring the tug in his chest. *I'm the adult here. He doesn't really know me at all.* "I wasn't hungover. I had to borrow Jenna's car. Mine's in the shop."

"Sure. Bet you were out late screwing sluts, just like you were before my mom died."

"Hey!" Logan clenched his jaw, imagining they were being watched through all the glass windows, the heat of hidden eyes crawling on his skin. He gritted out, "First off, don't use that word. Second, I never cheated on your mother. Never."

Connor muttered, "Yeah, right."

"I didn't." Christ, he'd barely jerked off since she died. Didn't even wake up to morning wood anymore—even his dick knew how useless he was. "Listen to me—"

"Why?" Connor's sandy hair was a shaggy mess over his ears, which was probably a dress code violation or something. Was Logan supposed to take him to get his hair cut?

Connor's lip curled as Logan stayed silent. "You're such an idiot. No wonder you barely graduated high school."

Logan didn't argue for his own intelligence since the kid had a point. Look at the mess Logan had made of his life. But he was all Connor had, so he stood there and took it.

Veronica had loudly questioned his faithfulness a few months before she died. Logan didn't really blame her—he'd stayed out later and later to avoid their fights about everything from doing the dishes to which way to put the damn toilet paper. She'd assumed the worst about his absences, although he wasn't a cheater.

In the small house, of course Connor had heard all their shouting matches. Logan wanted to comfort Connor in his grief—*their* grief—but everything was poisoned between them. He had no clue how to fix it.

Summoning patience, Logan unclenched his hands. He spoke calmly but firmly—the way the parenting vids he'd watched on YouTube advised. "Listen to me. They're going to expel you."

Connor rolled his eyes. "They won't go through with it. No way."

"They will. You're here on their good graces, and they've had enough of your shit. Ask Ms. Patel. You could have put that kid in the hospital with your prank. Why would you drop your bag like that?"

With a jerk of a shrug, Connor said, "Dunno. To see what would happen." He added defensively, "No one was down there when I let go! Then stupid Tim walked out."

"You know it wasn't his fault. But listen—Ms. Patel told me you're out if you don't get a B on your exams and stop acting up. This is serious. They're going to expel you. She told me to look into other schools."

Connor's perma-scowl evaporated as his brown eyes went wide. In a heartbeat, he looked so fucking young, his voice breaking. "Really? She said that?"

The poor kid was angry and hurt and surging with confusing new testosterone on top of it all. Logan tried to soften his voice. "Yeah. And if you get kicked out of here, you're stuck with me full time. So hit the books and cut the shit, okay?"

The bluster returned in an instant, and Connor raised his chin. "I'll go live with my dad in Florida. I'm sick of the cold anyway."

No, you won't, because your dad doesn't give a goddamn about you.

Forcing an even tone, Logan said, "Your mom always talked about what a genius you are. That she knew it from the time you could barely talk."

Connor's brows drew together, and he fidgeted with his fingers, shifting from foot to foot. "She… She did?"

"Yep. She was so proud of you, getting a full ride to Rencliffe out of elementary school. She used to smile so big when she talked about you. You know, how her eyes got squinty and her nose would crinkle?"

Connor nodded, biting his lip. Even with the pimples and attitude, he looked like a baby sometimes. Logan wanted to tell him everything would be okay and give him a hug the way kids deserved to be hugged, but the few times he'd awkwardly tried anything like that, it had resulted in Connor shoving him away.

Logan sighed. "I know you hate me. I don't blame you." He laughed hollowly. "There's plenty to hate. But you've got a good thing here. They want to help you. So let them. Okay? You can get a B on your exams in your sleep. Stop skipping class and screwing around. Make your mom proud."

After a few moments, Connor nodded, his jaw tight. He toyed with a plaid scarf hanging around his neck, and Logan eyed it. "Is that the one Jenna gave you at Thanksgiving?" They'd always done one gift for everyone at Thanksgiving in Logan's family for some reason. He didn't even know how the tradition had started.

Connor scoffed. "Dunno. I guess." He whipped it off and stuffed it in his uniform jacket pocket. "I was cold."

"She says hi, by the way."

"Whatever. Tell her hi back." He shrugged. "I don't care."

"Okay. I'll see you at the end of next week when school gets out." *Assuming you don't get expelled in the meantime.* Logan could only pray he'd somehow land a job so he could afford rent and food and maybe a few presents for the kid. If there was ever a time for a Christmas miracle, it was now.

Connor rolled his eyes. "Can't wait."

Ms. Patel appeared before Logan had to think of anything else to say. She smiled warmly. "Connor, are you up for a talk before you go back to class?"

Thank Christ the kid nodded and followed her out. Logan gave her a tight smile and made his way back through the main building and out to the parking lot. The birds still chirped, the sun peeking out from steel clouds. His phone buzzed, and this time there was a text message from Mrs. Politano:

Without rent I can't eat. Time's up. Changing the locks in two days, so get your stuff out.

Logan tasted bile. That was a definite no-go on the holiday miracle. He climbed behind the wheel of his baby sister's shiny SUV and tried not to cry like the pathetic, useless sack of shit he was.

Chapter Two

W HEN THE STAFF email hit his inbox, Seth rolled his eyes at the all-caps *"URGENT!"* in the subject line and went back to his spreadsheet. To the receptionist/office manager, everything was *URGENT!*, including—but not limited to—running out of mochaccino coffee pods in the break room too quickly, overusing staples, and the minimum length of shorts on casual Fridays in summer (eleven-and-a-half-inch inseam).

At her desk a few feet away in their pod, Jenna gasped. "She's here! Oh my God."

"Hmm?" Seth glanced over as Jenna whirled around on her chair, her hand catching a garland and sending a bright pink ornament rolling across her desk.

Jenna's side of the pod was an explosion of life and holiday cheer. After Thanksgiving, she'd strung colored fairy lights over the top of her monitor, and sparkly red garlands snaked between framed family photographs on both sides of her desk, ornaments nestled throughout.

Seth had no such photos since he had no family at all—at least not any who would actually talk to him. The jagged edges of that particular pain had dulled after twelve years, but as another lonely Christmas approached, he had to force away the memories more than usual.

Jenna hissed, "Angela Barker is here!"

His heart skipped. "Wait, what? Why?"

"Surprise visit." Jenna pressed a hand to her chest. "What if they're doing a re-org? But the CEO wouldn't be the one to come and fire people. Right?"

"They promised our positions were safe when BRK bought us out." His stomach dropped. He'd moved to Albany. He'd bought a house. He'd been dumped by his boyfriend—was his job next? "They promised," he repeated weakly. Of course, everyone knew what a corporate promise was worth these days.

I'm going to have nothing but a half-finished house to my name.

"Why did she have to come the day I have spit-up on my blouse?" Jenna rubbed despairingly at the mark on her shoulder, which she'd dabbed with Seth's Tide pen when she'd arrived.

There was no denying the green blouse was stained, but Seth said, "It's not noticeable at all. Can barely see it now."

"You're a liar, but a sweet one." Jenna opened her top drawer and pulled out a compact. She blotted at her nose and then tugged her blond curls loose from her customary ponytail and squinted at her reflection in the little mirror. "Nope," she muttered before tying her hair back up again. "Frizz city."

"It's fine," Seth said. "You look great." He glanced down at himself. He wore a standard work outfit—pressed gray slacks, button-down shirt in blue, and a navy tie. His black Oxfords were polished. He ran a hand over his short, thick, brown hair, which he kept neatly combed back. "Do I look okay?"

Jenna didn't even glance up as she examined the stain on her blouse with her compact mirror. "Of course. You look perfect as always. I should have done my hair this morning, but the baby was being so fussy, and Ian refused to wear long sleeves even though it's supposed to snow today."

As she grumbled about what a pain in the butt five-year-olds were, Seth adjusted the knot on his tie half an inch higher before smoothing a palm down the subtly patterned silk. He snorted mentally. *Perfect.* Jenna always insisted he was classically handsome ("*like Jimmy Stewart!*"), but if he was so perfect, why had Brandon left him?

Nope. Abort. Focus on the current crisis.

He stopped himself from tumbling down the rabbit hole of *why*, a question he knew he'd never really answer. Brandon was gone. The end. It had been more than a year for Pete's sake.

Because I wasn't enough. That's why.

"Focus," Seth muttered to himself as Matt's head appeared over the partition that separated Seth and Jenna's desks from the next pod.

Matt's ruddy face was flushed even more than usual beneath his pale, shaggy hair. "Guys. I've got the scoop." Jenna wheeled her chair over to Seth's with one push, bumping into him. The other two desks behind them in their pod were empty since the interns had finished for the semester.

Matt glanced around and whispered over the partition, "They're implementing a new structure. Allegedly no one's getting fired, but we'll see. Angela's picking five new directors herself. It's this thing she does. You know how she's all about the company being like family?"

Jenna said, "Uh-huh. 'Family values' to the point where people married with kids get ahead more."

"What?" Seth sputtered. "But that's not fair."

Jenna and Matt stared at him like he had three heads. Matt said, "How do you not know this already? I sent you the link to the subreddit on Angela and BRK Sync when they bought us out last month." He fiddled with the collar of his suit jacket, which he wore over a T-shirt. There were undoubtedly dark suede sneakers on his feet instead of dress shoes, but since he was the graphic designer in the communications department, everyone let it go. Young creative types and all that.

"That message board?" Seth asked. "I've been busy working."

Matt rolled his eyes. "Well, this has happened at every other company BRK has absorbed. Married with kids gets you ahead. Becky said Angela's going to be here all week, and she's taking us on some family Christmas retreat next weekend, so cancel your plans. Her way of welcoming us to the clan."

Matt was sleeping with Becky, the alarmist receptionist/office manager, so Seth had no doubt the intel was good. Seth muttered, "Is this a corporation or a cult?"

"Little bit from column A, little bit from column B," Matt said. "It's batshit, but she's the boss, so…" He leaned closer, his head all the way over the partition. He clearly hadn't shaved in a few days. "Director of systems training is one of the roles. Everyone knows that should be yours, dude."

Seth's whole body clenched. "They're finally creating that role?"

"About time," Jenna said. "You've been doing the job since you transferred here."

He had. He *had*, and that job was *his*. He'd done the job without the title and raise he'd deserved, hoping that he'd be rewarded eventually. He'd uprooted his whole life to come to Albany—after very careful consideration—with the promise that he'd move up in the company. Now that BRK had bought them out, this was his chance.

Too bad about his utter lack of spouse or family. He hardly even had friends after the breakup. There were some people back home in Georgia he saw on Facebook and never actually *talked* to anymore, and acquaintances at work. While Jenna had been on maternity leave, Seth had realized how friendless he was.

He'd thought about joining some kind of club—although definitely not the pretentious wine tasting group he and Brandon had attended before Brandon dumped him.

But *which* club? Seth had been researching it for, well, almost a year. There were variables and pros and cons to consider! He didn't want to choose the *wrong* club. What if he ran into Brandon and Brandon's new boyfriend? The thought was horrific. In the end, every weekend he'd wound up staying home. Alone.

Bitterness swelled. "Guess I'm not getting the director position. Single and gay won't cut it." He wasn't sure who he resented more—Brandon for leaving or himself for being so pitifully alone and indecisive. If he didn't deserve happiness in love, maybe he didn't deserve it at work.

"She doesn't care about the gay part." Matt's face lit up. "In fact, she's all about LGBTQ inclusion. Thinks everyone should experience the joy of having kids and all that shit. And she's got a real lady boner for showing off how open-minded she is. So just, you know, get married to some guy, stat. Tell her you're going to adopt a starving orphan. She'll love it." He jerked his head around, then hissed, "Here she comes!" before ducking back to his desk on the other side of partition.

Angela Barker's Texas accent and nasal tone preceded her as she made her way through the maze of pods. Jenna shoved a stack of paper into a desk drawer, then pawed at the stain on her blouse, muttering, "Why today of all days?"

Pulse racing, Seth straightened his little area, scooping a few stray paper clips into the jar by his keyboard. His pen and pad of sticky notes sat in their usual place by his phone, and his notebook rested on the other side of his computer. He adjusted the thumb tack pinning the calendar over his desk to make sure the December snowy sunrise landscape was centered on the bulletin board.

Said board also held a corporate lunch-and-learn schedule and a coupon for twenty percent off at Bed, Bath & Beyond Jenna had passed along to encourage him to buy more furniture for his house. He should have put up something Christmassy. He bet Angela loved Christmas.

Compared to Jenna's desk, Seth's looked hardly lived in. His black and white mug stated: "I really love my ~~boyfriend~~ cat." Considering his ex had given it to him as a birthday gift weeks before leaving him, Seth probably should have tossed it instead of adding a splash of masochism to his daily cup of coffee.

Especially since his cranky old calico, Agatha, had died a few months after Brandon left. Jenna had asked him once why he kept using the mug, and he'd said it was because it was the last thing Brandon had given him.

She'd tilted her head, mouth pulled down in pity. *"He's not dead. He dumped you, and he's dating a gym bunny from Schenectady. Which is what you should be doing. Get out there and hook up! You're only thirty-seven. You're still young!"*

Too bad the thought of hooking up left him feeling even emptier than Brandon's absence. Seth wished he was one of those guys—apparently every other man who walked the earth—who could have casual sex and not feel guilty and bleak.

Heck, he still felt guilty when he masturbated—although it didn't stop him when the need was too much. He hadn't been to church in years, yet he couldn't seem to completely let go of the strict rules he'd grown up with.

He straightened the ridiculous mug.

"Well, it's good to meet you, Lin!" Angela was a few pods away. Getting closer.

Seth's pulse raced. He'd been the de facto leader of the systems training team for three years. He planned worldwide training sessions for clients who purchased Greenware's corporate telecommunications system.

Now they were Greenware Sync after the takeover from BRK Sync, but the equipment and systems hadn't changed. Jenna didn't technically report to him, and neither did the revolving door of interns who helped with the sessions, but they should have.

When Seth had transferred to Albany from Atlanta a year and a half ago, it had been with the promise of a promotion and manager title. A pay raise. Yet he'd received excuse after excuse. And now he'd be out of consideration for the director role because he wasn't married with kids? It just wasn't fair.

He muttered to Jenna, "I'm going to get screwed, aren't I?"

"And not in the way you need to get screwed."

"Hiya, Matt!" Angela Barker was right in front of their pod. Seth glimpsed the top of her poufy bleached hair over the partition. As she talked to Matt and a few other people, Seth's mind spun. He wanted the promotion. He needed the promotion. Most of all, he *deserved* the promotion.

He rolled over to Jenna and whispered, "Too bad I don't have a magic wand to create an instant family." He pushed off the thin beige carpet and rolled back to his spot, clicking on his spreadsheet as he tried to look both busy and casual at the same time. It was what it was. There was nothing he could do to—

A framed picture suddenly appeared on the left side of his desk, Jenna diving back to her chair just before Angela popped into the wide entry to their pod.

Angela grinned. "Well, howdy!"

Before Seth could process the new addition to his desk, he had to stand and meet Angela's firm grip. Around fifty, she was petite and slim, her gray pantsuit neatly pressed, a fuchsia scarf knotted around her throat. Her earrings were delicate little silver Christmas trees decorated with what was probably Swarovski crystals or even diamonds.

He said, "I'm Seth Marston."

Jenna shook Angela's hand next. "Jenna Derwood-Kim."

"Hiya," Angela said. "Not sure how much you know about me, but a few years ago, I took over the family business. My daddy built BRK Sync from the ground up in the eighties, and as technology and the times have changed, so have we."

Seth wondered how many times she'd delivered the spiel. Probably millions. He said, "It's wonderful to meet you, Ms. Barker."

"Oh, I'm a proud missus, but you can call me Angela." Her gaze went to Jenna's colorful desk, and she neared it to peer at the photo frames. "And who do we have here, Jenna?"

"That's my husband, Jun-hwan—but he usually just goes by Jun—and our two boys. Ian's five and Noah's almost six months."

"Jun. Is that Korean?" Angela asked.

Jenna smiled. "It is! His parents moved here just before he was born."

"Wonderful. I hope you're transitioning back to work all right after the baby?"

"Yes, I came back part time a few weeks ago. It's been a much better transition with the extended maternity leave option you introduced. Thank you."

"Oh, my pleasure, sugar! I know how tough it can be as a working mom."

Jenna said, "Seth's been carrying so much of the workload. He's incredible. The training department would fall apart without him!"

He cringed internally as Jenna laid it on but kept a smile on his face as Angela turned her attention back to him and his desk—with the new addition from Jenna.

Angela leaned over the framed photo, which Seth realized was a new picture Jenna had put on her desk after Thanksgiving of her brother and his stepson. It was framed in cheery, multicolored wood squares, but Logan and the boy were barely smiling, their spines stiff as if they were lined up in front of a firing squad instead of posing for a family snap by the newly decorated Christmas tree.

Jenna's brother was handsome in that craggy, Daniel Craig kind of way. The kind of rough-and-tumble guy Seth's mother would have called a "bruiser" with a disapproving sniff. His wife had died suddenly in the summer, and Jenna worried a lot about him and the boy. It was all very sad from what Seth knew.

"And who's this?" Angela asked.

Before Seth could hope to formulate a response to explain the picture, Jenna said, "That's Logan, Seth's fiancé, and their son, Connor. Seth has such a lovely little family."

Angela clapped her hands together, appearing genuinely delighted. "Isn't that something? You know I've always said gay folks are just as the good lord made 'em."

My parents and their church would strenuously beg to differ. Seth kept smiling robotically. *Say something!* "Uh, yes. Thank you?"

"Families are at the heart of our biggest successes in this world. Too many people try to go it alone." Angela shook her head sadly.

Seth wanted to argue that single people could certainly be just as happy and successful—his own miserable single life notwithstanding—and that some people were thrown out of their families, but he just nodded and smiled.

Angela beamed. "When's the big day?"

"Oh, uh… We haven't set the date yet."

Jenna said, "They're thinking next summer."

"I look forward to seeing the wedding pictures." Angela eyed Seth speculatively. "Now, Seth—if I recall correctly, your name's come up for one of the director roles we're fixin' to fill."

"Has it?" he asked, trying not to look too excited. But maybe he didn't look excited enough? "I'd love to discuss it further with you." *And if I pretend to have a fiancé while you're around, what's the harm if it helps me get the promotion?*

"Seth's really been holding down the fort for systems training since he came here," Jenna said. "He'd be an excellent director."

"Good to hear it! Seth, we'll have to sit down soon and have a confab." Angela checked her gleaming Rolex. "I've got to get going now—duty and lunch call."

As if summoned from thin air, a short, slight young man with dark skin stepped into the pod. He wore a suit and glasses and spoke in a deep murmur. "I'll alert the driver that you're on your way down."

"Thank you, Dale." Angela motioned to him with a wide smile. "My right-hand man. Wouldn't know if I was comin' or goin' without him." Before Seth or Jenna could reply, she chuckled as she glanced around. "Now I told y'all I didn't need an escort while I toured the office, but darned if I'm not turned around."

Dale opened his mouth, but Seth quickly offered, "We'll walk you out!" Between beige partitions, he could feel the eyes of coworkers, the floor unnaturally hushed as he and Jenna guided Angela and Dale back toward reception.

"How did you and your fiancé meet?" Angela asked as they passed Becky's immaculate desk and approached the glass doors leading to the elevators. Becky sat almost comically straight, smiling with gleaming white teeth.

"We—Uh, we met through Jenna, actually." Seth debated whether to dart ahead and open the door for Angela. Was that anti-feminist? Or rude not to? Dale wasn't opening it for her. Should Seth—

In the time he was trying to decide, Angela had already pushed open the glass door. "Oh, here's your fiancé now!"

As Seth attempted to process the cheery, absolutely *horrifying* words ringing in his ears, he stared at Logan Derwood. Logan was all scruffy and— wow, *gorgeous*—in his black leather jacket, somehow standing there in the flesh. In real life.

Seth prayed the polished tile beneath his feet would open up and swallow him whole in one merciful gulp.

Chapter Three

AS THE ELEVATOR doors slid shut behind him, cutting off the damn cheery instrumental version of "Jingle Bells," Logan gripped Jenna's car key in his pocket, the metal digging into his palm. At least if he dropped off the key early and bussed it back, he wouldn't have to make conversation and pretend everything was fine and that he wasn't about to be homeless.

"Oh, here's your fiancé now!" a woman exclaimed. Small and aggressively blond, her teeth flashed in a blinding smile. Beside her was a tall, slim man with dark brown hair and blue eyes gone comically wide. The vaguely familiar man gaped at Logan as the woman stuck out her hand. "Logan, wasn't it?"

He automatically shook her hand. "Uh, yes. Logan." That part was right, although he sure as hell wasn't anyone's fiancé, least of all this stuffed shirt's. Clothes perfectly ironed and tucked in, not a hair out of place. Although at the moment, the man's face was bright red, and he looked as if he might puke all over the woman's fancy stilettos.

Jenna and another man trailed them, Jenna's frozen expression of horror making Logan tense. He hated seeing her upset. That's when it clicked into place—the tall guy was Jenna's co-worker. Her boss, maybe? Logan recognized him from the odd Facebook post.

Since Jenna and her boss didn't seem able to do anything but stare mutely, and the short man only came to stand beside the blond woman with a passive expression, Logan was forced to speak. "Um, good to meet you…"

"Angela Barker from Dallas, Texas. President and CEO of BRK Sync, which owns Greenware now. I'm getting out in the field and meeting the family, like your fiancé. Seth was telling me about your wedding plans."

"Was he?" Logan asked. Behind Angela, Jenna nodded frantically at him, making a rolling motion with her hand, gaze imploring. Logan tried to smile, glancing at this Seth, who appeared close to hyperventilating, his chest rising and falling rapidly.

What the fuck is all this?

Angela beamed. "I think it's so wonderful you two will be creating a family with your son. Family first, I always say. Gay or straight!"

My son? He wanted to scoff as he thought of Connor's hunched shoulders and hateful scowl. Shit, Logan just wanted to be alone, but Jenna pleaded with her eyes, and he couldn't deny her anything.

He bit down the knee-jerk denial that he was gay and kept what he hoped was a friendly expression on his face. Clearly he'd been roped into some kind of weird scheme, although for the life of him he couldn't guess what the hell it was about. Seth stood beside Angela with a rigid smile.

"And what do you do, Logan?" Angela asked.

There it was again, the shame somehow jaggedly icy yet burning as it ripped through him. *I don't do anything. I'm a useless waste of fucking space.* He cleared his throat and said, "Railway work." At least it had been true for more than ten years.

"Oh, how fascinating!" A gleam entered Angela's eye. "You know, I have been on the road so much lately, and I would kill for a home-cooked meal." She glanced at Seth. "What would you two say if I shamelessly invited myself over for dinner while I'm in town?"

Logan would say he had no fucking idea what was going on, but he only raised an eyebrow at Seth, who said, "Uh, th—that would be wonderful, Angela! It would be our pleasure."

To the short young man in the suit, who was probably her assistant, Angela said, "Talk to Seth and schedule something for next week before the retreat." She turned back to the rest of them. "I hope you're as excited about the retreat as I am! Going to be fun for the whole family. I know I'm springing it on y'all, but I hope you can make it."

The tinny notes of a pop song echoed from Angela's dark-pink purse, and she exclaimed, "I'm so sorry, but that's my daughter's ring tone. She loves that Shawn Mendes." She swiped to answer. "Hey, sugar! Hold on a sec." To Logan and Seth, she smiled widely. "So wonderful to meet you. I look forward to seeing you both again soon! Don't worry, I'm not a fussy eater!"

Logan took the opportunity to turn and press the elevator call button so he wouldn't have to say anything else. Thank fuck it had parked on the floor, and the doors opened immediately. He nodded and tried to smile as Angela stepped on with her assistant, chattering to her daughter about a dog named "Pom-pom" who was pissing on the furniture.

Jenna twisted a loose curl from her ponytail around her finger the way she did when she was stressed as hell. As soon as the elevator doors shut, she and Seth exhaled loudly. Seth rubbed his face, mumbling, "This was a terrible idea." Then he hissed to Jenna, "This was a terrible idea!"

Jenna glanced around the empty foyer, and Logan looked as well. To the right, through glass doors, a young redheaded woman at reception watched them with sharp-eyed interest.

Jenna whispered, "I was just trying to help!"

"Someone want to fill me in on what the hell's going on?" Logan asked.

Seth winced. "I'm so sorry. Thank you for playing along."

"Anything for my fiancé," Logan said dryly. "Seth, is it?"

"Seth Marston." He extended his hand. "I work with Jenna."

Logan shook Seth's sweaty palm. "Right. And how did we get engaged? Neat trick since we've never met and I'm not gay."

"Let's discuss this in a breakout room," Jenna said, leading the way into the carpeted main area past the redhead, who didn't try to hide her curiosity as they went by. Jenna chose the first of the rooms that ran down a long wall. After knocking and poking her head in, she ushered them in and closed the door.

Jenna stood by the oval table in the middle of the narrow, windowless room. "I thought you were coming to pick me up at three?"

"Got done early. I'll bus it back. Sorry to mess up your little plan, whatever the hell it is." Logan crossed his arms and glared at Seth. "You in the habit of telling people I'm your boyfriend?"

"No! I swear I'm not. I'm sorry. Jeez, this is messed up." He tugged at his tie as if he couldn't breathe.

Jenna sighed. "It was all me. Spur of the moment thing. We found out Angela was here, and she's going to be choosing new directors in the company. Seth *so* deserves a director role, but he's single, and Angela has this thing about families. Nine times out of ten she always promotes someone married with kids."

"That's fucking weird," Logan said.

"It is, but it's her company, and thanks to even more deregulation lately, she can hire, fire, and promote however she wants. Anyway, I framed that pic I took of you and Connor at Thanksgiving. You know, after we put up the tree?"

"Uh-huh." Logan remembered Connor's bony, rigid shoulder beneath his palm, Jenna trying to get them to smile, her cheeks rosy from a glass of wine. He'd been surprised Connor had even agreed to pose, but Jenna had that way with people.

"Well..." She grimaced. "I put the picture on Seth's desk at the last second and told Angela you're Seth's fiancé. It was all me. Seth had no choice but to go along with it or it would have been awkward and bizarre."

Logan said flatly, "Good thing we avoided that."

"I didn't expect you to show up!" Jenna actually looked indignant.

"So it's *my* fault?"

"Let's not argue." Seth looked between them, holding up his hands. "It's definitely Jenna's fault."

Logan tensed, his protective instinct kicking in even though Seth was on his side. It was one thing for Logan to say his sister was wrong...

But Jenna huffed out a laugh and lightly slapped Seth's arm. "Okay, yes.

It's my fault. Obviously I didn't have time to think through all the ramifications. I thought it could just be a little white lie to help Seth get the promotion."

"And I went along with it," Seth said. "I'm sorry. It was wrong to involve you and your son."

"Stepson." Connor's voice echoed in Logan's head. *"You're not my father! I hate you!"* That had been after Mike had said he didn't want custody, giving Connor a load of excuses and empty promises about how Mike would be in a better position "soon."

Jenna frowned. "Not that that matters. He's part of the family."

Logan snorted. "For now. He'd never see me again if he had his way." People might act like Logan was his dad now, but Connor sure wasn't fooled.

"He's thirteen." She shook her head. "Connor doesn't know what he wants. Don't be butt-hurt over a teenager acting out."

"I'm not." Fine, maybe he was. He wished like hell it didn't bother him. For so many years he'd avoided big emotional commitments, and this bullshit was why. He'd been better off alone. "Speaking of family, what's this retreat Angela mentioned? It sounded like she expected me there?"

Jenna and Seth shared a glance, frowning. Jenna said, "We actually don't have the details yet. Let me just… I'll be right back." She jerked her thumb toward the door, leaving and closing it behind her.

Logan and Seth stared at each other. Seth dropped his eyes to his fingernails and leaned against the edge of a white board that had bullet points on it about meeting goals or some shit.

Aim high!
But be realistic
Ask for help when needed
Work as a team
Manage stress
We're all in this together!
What a load of crap.

Seth cleared his throat. "Are you back at work on the railway? Jenna never said. I remember when you were in that terrible accident. I'm glad you're better now."

His cheeks going hot with shame, Logan stared at the ugly beige carpet. "Nah. Never going back. I'm looking for something else, but it's a pain in the ass explaining it all to strangers."

"Ah. I understand. I'm sure you'll find something soon."

Logan only shrugged, still unable to meet Seth's gaze. Seconds ticked by in awkward silence, and thank Christ, Jenna returned quickly. She leaned back against the door and bit her lip.

"Well, the good news is that the company is paying for us to have a weekend in Lake Placid. Staying at a lodge, winter activities, etc." She grimaced, and Logan braced and waited for the rest. She said, "The bad news is that they want our spouses and kids to come."

Seth frowned. "When is it? Not this weekend but next? The weekend of the twenty-second?" When Jenna nodded, he half-laughed disbelievingly. "On such short notice? That's ridiculous. People have plans—especially at the holidays. They have lives."

Jenna gave Seth a wry smile. "Yes, some of us do."

"I have a life!" Seth insisted. "Regardless, I'll just say we can't make it. Surely not everyone is going to drop everything and attend because Angela Barker wants us to jump when she snaps her fingers. Obviously we're not going to ask Logan and his stepson to come on this retreat and play fake family for a weekend."

Logan said, "Good. Can I go? If you want to tell the boss lady I'm your boyfriend, feel free. Just leave me out of this. I have enough crap on my plate right now." He made a move toward the door, but Jenna blocked his path, her forehead creasing.

"Wait, what happened?"

He tried to laugh it off. "Nothing. Just stressed about the job situation. You know." He had to figure out a plan before he dumped the latest disasters from his garbage life on her.

But Jenna didn't budge. "I know that tone. Something's wrong."

There was a knock at the door, and she turned to open it, ushering in a shaggy-haired guy who whispered, "What's going on? Becky said you guys were talking to Angela by the elevators and now you're hiding in here." He nodded to Logan and stuck out his hand. "Hey, man. I'm Matt. You're Jenna's brother, right?"

Logan shook his hand. "Right. I was just leaving."

Matt gave him a quizzical look. "The weird thing is that Becky thought she heard that you and Seth are getting married?"

Seth groaned. "That means everyone will know in the next ten minutes."

"No, it's okay," Matt said. "Becky's holding it in for now. I figured I should buy you some time. So how exactly did you two end up engaged? I mean, *mazel tov*, but this is a surprise."

Jenna quickly filled him in, then added, "We can just make up an excuse about why Logan and Connor can't attend the family retreat."

Matt winced. "Word is that when Angela springs these retreats on people, you'd better go unless there's a life-or-death excuse. It's completely unreasonable, but basically it's a test. She's paying for everything, which is generous, but the catch is that we only get 10 days' notice, and we have to prove we're BRK team players whether we're single or married or whatever. And if you have kids, you should definitely bring them. I guess it's not such a big deal when it doesn't fall near the holidays. But it's happening, and if she thinks Logan and Seth are together..."

"Which we aren't," Logan said. "Can I go now?" He needed to find another place to live before the landlord locked him out, and definitely before the kid got off school for the holidays. Had to find some way to put down a deposit. Crashing at Jenna's would be the last resort.

Jenna groaned, ignoring him. To Matt, she said, "Angela also invited herself over to Seth and Logan's for dinner."

"Whoa. This is…" Matt grinned, which was bizarre. "This is *awesome.* It's, like, a *caper.* Who doesn't love a caper?"

Logan stared at him, wondering what planet Matt was from, as Seth said, "*Me.* And I can't have Angela over for dinner regardless. My kitchen's not finished. I don't have a dining table. There's so much to do. I don't even know where to start."

"But the demo's done and the drywall's up," Jenna said. "Don't you have all the cabinets and stuff sitting in the garage? It would only take a couple days to fix it up. You know, our dad was a contractor. If you can find the muscle, Pop could supervise. Would give him something to do other than watch TV all day—and get him moving at least a little. He still refuses to do his exercises."

Seth shook his head. "This is crazy, Jenna. Even if I could fix up the house in time, why would Logan want to pretend to be my fiancé?"

An idea popped into Logan's head, accompanied by a flash of unfamiliar emotion that left him a little breathless. Was it…*hope?* This whole situation was batshit, but maybe there was a way to temporarily solve his problem and Seth's.

What the fuck do I have to lose?

Jenna was saying, "Logan, I know it's so much to ask, but…"

He spoke before he could talk himself out of it, a twist of acid in his gut reminding him he and Connor were about to be homeless. "I could do the renovation stuff. Would need a hand to carry things and get it all in place, but I worked with Pop when I was a teenager. I can do it. The thing is…"

He hesitated. The itchy heat of Jenna, Seth, and Matt staring at him, waiting, made him sweat. Humiliation prickled the back of his neck, and he considered just shutting up and telling them to forget it.

Jenna stepped closer, concern softening her face. "What's going on?"

Logan spit it out, afraid he might puke at the same time. "I was evicted. Connor and I need a place to stay. Not for long—just over the holidays until he goes back to school. I'll find a job in January for sure." Had to. There was no other option.

"*What?*" Jenna grabbed hold of his arm, awful sympathy shining from her eyes. Logan was so sick of his baby sister feeling sorry for him. Being worried about him all the time since he was a mess. She said, "Why didn't you tell me?"

He scowled. "You have enough going on with the kids and Pop. You don't need me on the couch, and what about Connor? There isn't enough room. Besides, it just happened this morning. I have to be out by Friday, and I *did* hear from the factory. I didn't get the job." He shrugged, dislodging Jenna's hand and pretending he didn't care. "It's fine."

There were a few beats of awkward silence before Matt exclaimed, "Guys, this is perfect." He quickly added, "Not that you're getting evicted, man. That sucks. But Seth needs a fake boyfriend, and you need a place to stay. Two birds, one stone." He made a motion like he was dunking a basketball. "Nothing but net."

As Seth and Logan looked at each other dubiously, Jenna bounced on her toes. "Yes! You guys can finish the kitchen with Pop this weekend. Have Angela over for dinner, and then play happy family next weekend on the retreat. Seth's been alone out there in that house too long anyway."

Seth shot her a glare. "I have not."

Jenna gave him an impatient, disbelieving look Logan had seen many, many times. She said, "Seth, I know you'd prefer to make an extensive pro and con list and examine it for a week before committing, but there's no time. You deserve this promotion. What do you have to lose?"

"My job if she finds out this was all a lie?"

"Oh, right." Jenna made a face. "Valid point. But she won't. Think of how many employees Angela Barker has. BRK has offices around the world. We won't see her again for years."

"What about everyone else you work with?" Logan asked.

Jenna shrugged. "We'll just say I set up you and Seth, and it's been a whirlwind romance."

"Everyone will definitely believe Jenna played matchmaker," Matt said. "Less believable that you didn't tell every last person here about it, including the janitor."

Logan wanted to defend her, but, well… Jenna huffed. "I can keep a secret! I knew for months you and Becky were hooking up before you went public."

"Fair enough." To Seth and Logan, Matt said, "Well? You two ready to make a deal?" He grinned.

Seth fidgeted, cracking his knuckles. "It does seem like it would be a mutually beneficial arrangement?" He looked to Logan, his expression creasing. "But I know you're grieving, and if it feels inappropriate, I'd completely understand."

Logan shifted uncomfortably, aware of being watched by everyone in the room. "It's fine."

Yes, Logan did grieve Veronica's death, but he missed the awesome, caring nurse he'd known before it had all gone to crap. And that probably made him a complete shit-brick to not miss her as his wife, but he couldn't make himself feel something he didn't. Maybe he was just broken.

Seth said, "You'd be welcome to stay through the holidays and until you can figure out something in the new year."

"I'd earn my keep." The thought of taking any charity had Logan defensive.

"Of course!" Seth agreed. "Trust me, there's plenty of work for you." He laughed incredulously. "This is completely insane, but maybe it could work?"

"Caper, caper, caper!" Matt chanted, raising a fist in the air.

Jenna bit her lip. "Might take some convincing to get Connor on board."

Logan grunted. "We'll deal with that. Things aren't great at school. I'll fill you in later."

"And you know you're both always welcome at my house," Jenna insisted. "We'd make it work. It's not even a question."

Warm, familiar affection for her flowed through Logan. "I know. But if we could pull this off, maybe it's not the worst idea ever."

"Caper, caper, caper," Matt whispered, pumping his fist again.

Logan looked at Seth, and they shared a laugh. Logan hadn't imagined smiling on this crappy day, let alone laughing. That little flare of hope burned brighter. The plan was nuts, but it was all he had.

With a rueful smile, Seth asked, "It's a deal, then? Think you can pretend to be in love with me for a couple weeks?" He held out his hand.

Logan sure as hell didn't do *love* with men, but it had to be easy enough to fake. He grasped Seth's palm firmly. "Deal."

Chapter Four

THE NEXT DAY after work, Seth made the drive over to the suburb where Logan lived. Apparently neither of them had regained their right minds, and they were actually going to stick with the crazy deal they'd made. Granted, Logan was being evicted and didn't have much choice. Seth couldn't exactly back out and leave the guy out in the cold.

Light snow fell in the early darkness after five p.m., and he shivered, turning up the heater. He wasn't sure he'd ever get used to northern winters. Where he'd grown up in Georgia, if there was even a hint of a flurry everything ground to a halt. Of course, they didn't have snow tires down south, and now his SUV was fully equipped for the worst Mother Nature could—and would—throw at him.

So far there was just a dusting of snow over everything, and as Seth turned off the main road and into a residential area, colored Christmas lights gleamed on houses and wrapped around trees, the snow making everything magical. "I'll be Home for Christmas" played on the radio, and though Seth braced for the pang of longing, it still stole his breath when it hit.

Christmas had always been his favorite time of year, with the lights and music, the smell of fresh cookies baking, and presents under the tree. Friends and family gathered together to celebrate that holy holiday. He'd actually liked going to church around Christmas, singing carols joyfully until his voice was hoarse, no one minding that he couldn't carry a tune to save his life.

He snapped off the radio. It would definitely be only in his foolish dreams that he would ever be home for Christmas again. He didn't even own decorations. Brandon had never been keen on celebrating, and after the terrible holiday twelve years ago, it had all seemed poisoned to Seth. Christmas wasn't for him now.

Following his phone's directions, Seth turned down a few streets, the houses getting a little more rundown and ramshackle. Number eighty-two was a small bungalow and didn't have any holiday lights or decorations. He recognized Jenna's SUV outside and parked behind it, his headlights illuminating the boxes already packed high inside.

Snow crunched under Seth's boots as he got out and walked up the driveway, keeping his bare hands in his coat pockets. The wind was calm, fat snow drifting down peacefully. However, that peace was broken by the shouts exploding out of the house like the *rat-tat-tat* of gunfire even though the front door was closed. Seth stood on the stoop, debating whether to knock.

"That's my shit! Don't touch anything else!"

Logan's rough voice rumbled. "I'm only trying to help."

"You had no right to touch *anything* of mine!" a young voice screeched. That had to be Connor, the stepson.

"For fuck's sake, I only packed the clothes hanging in the closet. I could have just moved all your stuff without telling you, but I didn't want to invade your privacy. Now hurry up, because whatever you don't get into these boxes in the next half hour is staying behind. You've wasted enough time arguing."

"Fuck you! I'm not going anywhere."

Logan's voice rose. "Yes, you damn well are. We're moving our shit over to Seth's, and then I'm taking you back to school before curfew. So get a move on."

Listening to the foul language in shock, Seth decided he'd better knock instead of eavesdrop, so he rapped his knuckles against the door. He knew he was laughably repressed when it came to cursing, but Logan and Connor just sounded so horribly angry towards each other.

When the door opened, Connor was still complaining loudly, but Seth blocked it out and focused on Logan, who ushered him in with a grimace. He wore a black T-shirt and jeans, the cotton hugging the firm, broad muscles of his chest and back. And jeez, his arms were nothing to sneeze at either. Seth had always thought Logan looked handsome in Jenna's pictures, but in person he really was…*wow*.

"Hi. Sorry, it's a bit…" As Connor screamed more curses, Logan winced, rubbing a hand over the scruff on his face with an audible rasp. Seth wondered what that would feel like against his own face.

"Chaotic?" Seth offered. "Moving always is." He peered into the living room, which was still furnished with a plaid couch and a wooden coffee table. "You said the furniture isn't yours?"

"Right. Rented a furnished place." He glanced over his shoulder, dropping his voice. "When Veronica died, there were a lot of bills, and that was on top of what I still owed for my insurance copay on my hospital bills after the accident. Had to sell just about everything."

Seth nodded, shame that he'd been ogling Logan twisting in his gut. *The man's wife died barely six months ago. Have some decency.* "I understand. Well, I put the back seats down, so should be plenty of room for what's left."

"Thank you." Logan winced at a thump from the direction of what had to be Connor's room. "There's still time to back out."

A little voice did pipe up saying that Seth was biting off more than he could chew, but he couldn't exactly leave Logan high and dry, now could he?

He tried for an easy smile. "Nah, we made a deal. You're helping me out just as much."

Logan snorted. "Not sure if that's true. But thanks." He glanced down the hall. The cursing from Connor had faded. Logan still spoke softly. "I didn't want to go through his stuff, so I picked him up after school to tell him in person. Give him a chance to pack up his things so he wasn't completely blindsided."

"Sounds like it's been a barrel of laughs." This earned him a sardonic smile from Logan, and Seth tried to ignore the sexy little dimples that appeared in Logan's cheeks. Before Seth could say anything else, a gangly boy who needed a haircut appeared down the short hall. He wore uniform slacks and a white dress shirt, the sleeves rolled up to his bony elbows, his tie missing. He scowled at Seth.

"Oh, hello," Seth said with a smile. "You must be Connor. I work with your Aunt Jenna. It's nice to meet you."

"She's not really my aunt," Connor muttered, crossing his arms.

"*Connor*," Logan warned.

Seth smiled awkwardly. "Well… It's still nice to meet you."

"Whatever. I'm calling my dad, and he's going to fly me to Florida for Christmas, so I'm not staying with you."

Seth glanced at Logan, who only shrugged, his face impassive as he said, "Okay. Go ahead and call him."

Connor glared. "I did. I left a message. He'll call me back any minute. He's probably still at work. He actually *has* a job since he's not a loser like you."

Waiting for Logan to scold Connor for the rude insult, Seth bit his tongue. But Logan didn't rise to the bait, only saying, "In the meantime, keep packing." He picked up a box in the hallway. "Seth, there isn't too much to go into your SUV. It'll mostly be Connor's stuff."

"Right. Uh, okay." Seth fished out his keys and opened the front door for Logan, following him out into the snow. Flakes caught in Logan's dark hair, his wide shoulders rigid as he walked out. At the SUV, Seth opened the back and said, "Don't you want your coat?"

Logan's muscles flexed as he pushed the box into the back. He straightened and blew out a long breath, his exhalation clouding in the cold air. "I'll grab it in a sec. Just had to get out of there before we got in another fight."

"Understood. I didn't realize his father was still in the picture?"

Logan shook his head derisively. "He's not—selfish piece of shit is what he is. He probably won't even call back for days, and when he does, he'll be full of excuses. But I try not to say a bad word about him to Connor."

"Right," Seth repeated. "That's smart. Let him figure it out for himself."

Logan shivered, rubbing his bare arms. Jenna'd mentioned that Logan had worked hard to get back in shape after recovering from the accident, and

Seth couldn't imagine how good he'd looked before it, although his brain stubbornly tried.

Logan said, "For a smart kid, it's sure as hell taking him a while to get the message."

Seth thought of his own parents—his mother's round face and big eighties-style curls, his father's balding head and wire-framed glasses—wondering what they would do if he actually called. "It can be hard to accept." He knew without a doubt his parents would hang up on him, yet he still thought, *Maybe…*

"Although the kid's right that his asswipe father does have a job, at least."

"Hey, it's not your fault you're out of work."

"That's not what the railway says. Worked there more than a decade, and I'm out with nothing. I wasn't speeding, and I know I braked in time. I *know* it."

He was obviously referring to the accident. "I'm sure you did."

"Doesn't matter anyway. Except for the fact that I can't seem to get another job without a reference since I worked there so long." He headed back to the house. "Anyway."

Seth followed him inside, standing in the doorway as Logan put on a black leather jacket and gloves. It was quiet from down the hall, and Seth hoped that meant Connor was packing. "In the new year, something will turn up."

"Let's hope so. For both our sakes." Logan grimaced. "But don't worry, I'll figure something out. The deal is just until January and we'll be out of your life. Thanks again."

"Hey, you really are doing me just as big a favor."

"What favor?" Connor asked. He must have been listening, and now he neared them in the foyer, his socked feet slapping on the parquet.

Seth's heart sank at the thought of explaining it, embarrassment prickling his skin. He glanced at Logan, who sighed and mumbled to Seth, "Hadn't got there yet." Logan faced Connor. "It's no big deal. Seth needs to pretend he's getting married so he gets a promotion at work that he really deserves. So I'm going to be his fake fiancé."

Connor's face creased with confusion and possibly disgust. "What the fuck?"

It was entirely strange for Seth to hear a kid swear the way Connor did without being reprimanded. Seth would have been belted if so much as a "damn" or "hell" slipped out. Even "darn" or "jeez" or "heck" had been forbidden since they were clear derivatives of curses. Logan seemed to swear regularly, but he was an adult, at least.

Seth cleared his throat. "I'm sure it sounds a little confusing to you." He tried to smile. "It's a little confusing to us as well. It started as a white lie and snowballed into this…*caper*, I suppose you could call it."

Connor stared at Seth, then Logan. To Logan, he hurled, "You're gay now?" as if it was a barbed accusation.

"No. I'll just be pretending for a little while. It's not a big deal."

Grunting, Connor shifted his focus to Seth, eyeing him up and down, his lip curling. "So you're a fag no one wants to date?"

Seth flinched, not sure whether the slur or the accurate assessment of his love life hurt more. "Uh…"

Logan stared at Connor in apparent disbelief before drawing himself up even taller and barking, "What the hell kind of word is that? Jesus Christ, you know better."

Connor opened his mouth as if to shout back, but then his pimply face flushed, his gaze dropping to his feet. He muttered, "Sorry."

"What would your mother say, hearing you talk like that?"

In a flash, the defiant rage returned, Connor's head snapping up and his eyes flashing. "She wouldn't say anything. She's dead. Because of you."

Seth blinked in surprise. From what he recalled, it had been natural causes—an aneurysm, perhaps? Heart attack? But guilt definitely flinched across Logan's face, his shoulders hunching as he muttered, "You know she'd hate to hear you talk like this anyway."

To Seth, Logan added, "Sorry. Look, if you want to back out, I don't blame you." His gaze flicked up to Seth's and then away miserably.

Resisting the urge to reach out and touch Logan's arm, to give some kind of comfort, Seth shook his head. "No. We had a deal. Trust me, I've heard worse."

Logan's nostrils flared. "Well, you shouldn't have to. And you *won't*, at least not from Connor." He raised an eyebrow at the boy. "Since when do you call gay people names? Isn't your buddy Jayden gay?"

Connor fidgeted, his expression miserable. "Yes." Then panic seemed to seize him, and he sucked in a breath and pleaded with Logan, eyes wide. "Don't tell him I said that word!"

"I won't," Logan assured him. "I think it would hurt his feelings a lot."

Exhaling, Connor nodded. To Seth, he added, "I didn't mean it. I'm really sorry. I don't know why I said it."

Because you're angry and confused and lashing out. Seth gave the kid a little smile. "Apology accepted. I'd really like to be friends. What do you say?" He extended his hand. Connor peered at it suspiciously before shaking it briefly, his small hand damp.

Fortunately, Connor was quiet after that, finishing packing his room and helping to carry the boxes without any more complaints. They piled up the back of Seth's SUV and drove back to Saratoga Springs, Logan and Connor following in Jenna's vehicle.

Turning into his hundred-foot driveway, Seth glanced at the retro metal mailbox by the curb, his stomach tightening at the flyers sticking out. He hadn't checked the mail for two weeks. He should just bite the bullet and face what was likely inside, but…

I'll look tomorrow.

After parking at the top of the drive, he followed the unshoveled brick path and climbed the two steps to the front door. The outdoor light had switched on automatically, and it illuminated the fluffy snow that was still drifting down. Logan and Connor approached, both gazing around.

Logan whistled softly. "Real beautiful home you have. Lots of land."

"Thanks." He pointed left and right. "You can see the lights of the neighbors through the trees. They're close, but not too close, which is perfect for me." He ushered them inside, all of them stamping their feet on the mat and taking off their snowy boots in the little foyer.

Seth pointed up the stairs, which extended back on the right-hand side of the house. "Two bedrooms and bathrooms up there." To the left, he led them through the little sitting room area, which currently only held an armchair. "Uh, you can tell I haven't finished furnishing the place yet." He laughed awkwardly and continued on into the kitchen on the left and empty dining space to the right.

Logan examined the kitchen. "Did you demo some walls and open this up when you moved in?"

"Yes." He winced, looking at the wide island and counters that were still covered in plywood, and the complete lack of cabinets. At least the medium hardwood flooring that ran through the whole main floor was done, although the walls where the blue-tinted subway tile back-splash would go were still bare.

"As you can see, it still needs some work. The pantry's finished in the corner, so I've been storing food and whatnot in there." He glanced to the bare room on the right. "Still need the dining table and chairs. When we moved up from Georgia we were going to buy most things new."

Connor, who had poked his nose into the long pantry, asked, "Who's 'we'?"

Logan looked like he was about to chastise him, but Seth spoke before he could, keeping his tone light. "Well, 'we' was me and Brandon. We met in Atlanta at my first job out of college. Both worked in HR back then. We were together a long time, and when I was transferred here about a year and a half ago, I bought this house and Brandon came with me." His throat got tight, and he cleared it. "But it didn't work out. We broke up last October."

"That sucks," Connor said, going back to the pantry. He seemed to be eyeing the little collection of Halloween treats Seth had bought at half price on November first and hadn't finished yet. He'd hidden up in his room on Halloween instead of shelling out, although he wasn't sure any kids would have come by anyway.

Seth asked, "Are you hungry? Help yourself to whatever you like."

Logan swore under his breath. "Forgot about dinner."

"I'll order a pizza." Seth pulled out his phone. "What do you guys like?"

"No, I'll order it. You already went out of your way to help us move our crap." Logan took out his own phone.

Seth shook his head. "I insist. You can get the next pizza." Of course he had no plans to let Logan pay for anything. For goodness' sake, the man was jobless and evicted. He joked, "Trust me, there will be plenty of opportunities. I don't cook as much as I should." When it was just him, it didn't seem worth the bother.

"Pepperoni and extra cheese," Connor said. "Um, please. Thanks." He held up a snack pack of Doritos. "Cool if I have these?"

"Absolutely," Seth said. "Logan, what's your pizza order?"

He shrugged. "Anything." He examined the kitchen. "You said you have the cabinets and the counters already?"

"Yep. It's all in the garage." Seth tapped in an order for one pepperoni pizza and one sausage and mushroom, both with extra cheese. "Think it's doable?"

"Definitely." Logan glanced at the dining space. "You're definitely going to need a table and chairs if the boss lady's coming for dinner. It's all painted, at least."

"Right. Yes." The white trim was done along with the pale gray walls. Seth groaned. "I shouldn't have put it off so long."

"We'll figure something out. Don't worry."

"Whoa!" Connor's exclamation echoed from beyond the short little space, barely a hall, that led to the great room at the back of the house.

Seth smiled as he and Logan joined him, taking the two steps down into the room. This was the space Seth could actually be proud of—a vaulted white ceiling with wood beams, tall and wide windows, a sleek gas fireplace stove in one corner and a massive TV in the other. A curved black leather sectional with chaises on both ends dominated the right side, facing the fireplace and the TV. On the far side of the room there was a sliding glass door to the patio.

"This is dope," Connor said, gazing around in apparent awe.

Seth felt ridiculously pleased to have impressed him. "Thanks."

Logan seemed equally awed. "Wow." He walked across the thick area rug, which was a navy and gray diamond pattern, and cupped his hands around his eyes to peek out the sliding door. "Is that a built-in barbecue?"

"Yep. We had a gas line put in, so figured why not?" He'd barely used it, and shifted guiltily. "There's a fire pit back there too. The outdoor space was a big selling point. And this room, of course. Got them to vault the ceiling and put in new windows. It was small and dim before, and now it's, well, this. An improvement, I think."

Logan gave him a look. "You could say that. Anyway, we should bring in the boxes. Have to get Connor back to school by nine."

Mouth full of Doritos, Connor said, "Yeah, you'll be in shit if you don't."

It was still jarring to hear the way Connor and Logan cursed freely around each other, but it wasn't Seth's place to say anything. Logan didn't seem to think anything of it, but of course he'd been in the military. Seth imagined he'd become inured to obscenity.

They put their boots back on and went out, unloading the boxes and bags into the foyer. Between the three of them, it didn't take long. There were some boxes of kitchen and miscellaneous items that Seth left in the empty sitting room before they took Connor's things up to the spare room. It was a nondescript guest room—a double bed, dresser, closet, and generic art of a sailboat and a country road up on the pale gray walls.

Seth cleared his throat as Logan and Connor came in. "So, there's only the one extra room. I figured two bedrooms would be enough since I don't have any family and Brandon's are real homebodies who don't travel much. There was another small room, but we sacrificed it for the great room ceiling."

Connor frowned. "Why don't you have any family?"

"Don't be nosy," Logan snapped, a little harshly in Seth's opinion.

Before Connor could retaliate, Seth said calmly, "It's all right. I don't mind talking about it." It wasn't pleasant, but he tried to be matter of fact about it when it came up. "My family cut me out of their lives after I told them I was gay. It was twelve years ago now. They're very religious, and their church is quite homophobic. They believe I'm choosing a life of sin and all that kind of stuff." He shrugged tightly. "I knew this could happen when I came out, but I'd hoped for the best anyway."

Connor and Logan seemed to be taking it in. Logan shook his head and said, "Sorry, man."

"It's okay." Seth forced a laugh. "I mean, it's not *okay*, but it is what it is. I couldn't stay in the closet. I like to believe in a God who made people the way they're supposed to be."

Connor was watching him silently. Then he said, "Your family are dicks, huh?"

Seth had to laugh for real this time. "They are." Of course guilt slammed him immediately, and his smile faded. "I shouldn't say that. They're good people—they just have their beliefs."

"That gay people are going to hell?" Connor asked, eyebrows shooting up. "That's bullshit. Good people shouldn't think that. And good people shouldn't choose to never see their own kid again because of the way they were born."

Logan said, "Hard to argue with that."

"My friend Jayden? His parents are awesome. They love him the way he is. That's what parents are supposed to do."

Guilt still lingered, leaving sticky trails like gum on the bottom of Seth's shoe, stuck in the crevices. He simply said, "Anyhow, we should get the sleeping arrangements sorted out."

"Right. I'll sleep on the couch if that's okay?" Logan asked. "Connor, this can be your room while we're staying with Seth."

"You could stay in here while Connor's at school." Seth knew the couch was comfy, but he felt like a bad host regardless.

Connor stared at the wood floor. Logan said, "No, I'll be good on the couch. Connor, why don't you unpack a bit? We'll bring the rest up before the pizza gets here."

"Yes, should be soon," Seth said. "The place I order from takes a while, but it's worth it." He gave Connor a smile and went back downstairs with Logan.

In the foyer, Logan glanced up behind him and whispered, "Hope it's okay if I stay on the couch? He already had to move after his mom, and now this. I think it'll help if he has his own space without me in it at all."

"Of course. That makes perfect sense. He's been through a lot of upheaval."

"Thanks for getting it. And we'll be out of your hair ASAP. I'm job searching every day, and either way we'll be out in January." He grimaced. "You're sure it's okay to be here over the holidays? You probably have plans."

That would require having a life. "No, actually. I'm not really big on Christmas."

"Oh." His brow furrowed.

"What?" Seth shifted uneasily, trying to smile.

"You just seem like you'd be into all that wholesome holiday stuff."

He probably finds me incredibly lame. Seth admitted, "I was, but…"

Understanding seemed to wash over Logan's stubbly, handsome face. "Right. The family thing."

"Yeah. Will you and Connor be with Jenna on Christmas? I know she loves it." Poor Connor. His first Christmas without his mother, and he didn't have a proper home.

"On Christmas Eve, I guess. She'll be with her husband's family on Christmas Day." He waved a hand. "But we'll do our best to stay out of your way. Thanks again for this." Logan clapped a calloused hand on Seth's shoulder, and Seth tried to ignore the tingle that spread through him at the strong, warm touch.

They went back to work, taking the rest of Connor's boxes upstairs. The pizza arrived, and they all sat on the couch in the great room, the pizza sitting on the iron and wood coffee table on top of tea towels Seth spread so the grease didn't seep through. He realized he was out of napkins, but they didn't seem fazed by using paper towels.

He and Logan let Connor pick something on the TV, and he went for *Mythbusters* on one of the streaming channels, complimenting Seth on the surround sound from the home theater speakers he'd had installed. Seth sipped a Sprite and put a coaster under Connor's cola.

He'd ordered a six-pack of soda since he realized he only had water, coffee, and tea on hand. He should make a list of what they liked and stock up, especially for Logan since Connor would still be at school before the family retreat.

Seth had to choke down his bite of pizza at the reminder of the retreat, the extra cheese almost lodging in his throat. Could he and Logan really fool everyone—and Angela in particular—into believing they were a *couple*? Was Connor going to behave? Would he even agree to go?

Maybe it was best if he didn't, but Angela was so keen on families that it would probably help if he did. Assuming he didn't blow their cover, of course. Seth wasn't above bribing him handsomely.

They ate and watched a segment about whether drifting a car around a corner was faster than just slowing down and re-accelerating. It turned out to be a myth that drifting was faster. Seth said, "Guess no one gave Vin Diesel the memo."

Logan chuckled, wiping his mouth with a paper towel. "To be fair, that's the only *Fast and the Furious* movie he's not in."

Connor huffed. "He is too. He has a scene at the end." He shook his head as if Logan was a complete idiot, and it set Seth's teeth on edge.

But Logan only shrugged. "Yeah, okay."

Seth supposed Logan had learned to pick his battles, but Connor's bursts of hostility just seemed so…unnecessary. Seth knew the boy was grieving and hurt, but it was a shame he was dedicated to regarding Logan as the enemy.

After they ate, they drove in tandem to drop Connor off at school, where he slouched away without a wave goodbye, and then to Jenna's to drop off her SUV. Seth had gotten a bit behind when he was caught at a yellow light, and he was surprised to see Logan waiting for him on the curb. Jenna's modest house was alight with golden Christmas lights and Santa decorations beyond him.

And if Seth's gut tightened with a spark of lust as the headlights caught Logan's tall, muscular frame, that was no big deal. So Logan was hot and looked like a classic bad boy in his leather jacket and combat boots. Nothing wrong with Seth enjoying the view. Yes, Logan was a widower, but looking was harmless.

I'm allowed to be attracted to other men even if I'm not in love with them!

Yet no matter how many times he told himself that, guilt lingered. With Brandon, Seth had assured himself it wasn't sinful because they'd loved each other. But now Brandon was long gone, and Seth should be able to admire another guy without feeling like he was doing something wrong. It was…

Well, it was a work in progress.

Logan climbed into the passenger side. He opened his mouth, but then his rough face creased. "You okay?"

"What? Oh, yes! I'm fine." Seth's cheeks flamed hot, and he was glad it was relatively dark in the SUV. "Uh-huh."

"I gave the keys to Jun. Jenna's busy getting the kids down, and I don't feel like talking to her right now."

"Oh. Sure." Seth headed down the street. Truthfully, it was getting late, and he didn't much feel like talking to her either.

"Not that I don't love my sister. She's amazing. But sometimes she's…"

"A little exhausting?"

Logan smirked. "Damn right." He quickly added, "But she's the best."

"Absolutely! She's been so kind and supportive of me since I moved here." Seth stopped for a red light, glad the snow had tapered off. "I don't know what I would have done without her last year after Brandon… After we split."

"Right."

Silence fell, and Seth was about to flick on the radio when Logan asked, "It was only a few months after you moved here that you broke up?"

Seth's fingers tightened on the wheel before he fiddled with the wipers even though the windshield was clear. "Yes. Four months. The renovation had been dragging on, and it was stressful for both of us on top of moving across the country, but it was almost finished. Things hadn't been great, but I thought the light was at the end of the tunnel. We'd been together so many years."

He sprayed fluid on the windshield, the wipers thumping across before he turned them off and tried to laugh. "Turns out he'd blasted a hole through the side of the tunnel and made his escape with some guy he met at the gym who's not even thirty yet." Seth winced at how bitter he sounded.

"Fuck. That's brutal."

"Yeah." Seth did flip on the radio then, scanning past endless Christmas songs until he found someone talking about global warming. "This okay?"

"Whatever you want."

The planet's doom should have been more depressing than his failed relationship with Brandon, but Seth decided it was a tie. It was strange to be with Jenna's brother driving back to the house—which wasn't really *home* the way Seth had dreamed it would be when he'd planned the renovation.

He should have known back then that Brandon had one foot out the door. Brandon had let Seth make all the decisions, like he'd known deep down he wouldn't be around to live in the final product.

As the people on the radio talked about islands of plastic in the ocean, Seth turned onto the 87, careful of the slush that was accumulating. He peeked at Logan from the corner of his eye. Odd to think that Logan would be staying at the house.

Odder still to think that they'd be posing as loving partners. How were they going to pull it off? He supposed they should come up with a plan, but he stayed silent.

How much PDA do we need to make it look real?

Heat flowed through Seth, very much in a southerly direction. Logan was like his secret young fantasies about Dylan McKay come to life, but minus the nineties hair and sideburns.

Seth swallowed through the pang of hurt as he remembered huddling late at night with his big sister, Christine, the volume down low on their secretly recorded VHS episodes of *90210* after everyone had gone to bed.

Now she won't even acknowledge I'm alive.

He exhaled sharply, annoyed at himself for thinking about Logan and PDAs and teen fantasies in the first place. This was a deal he and Logan had made, and he had to stay…professional, for lack of a better word. Logan was going to be sleeping in his house. Seth had a responsibility to be a good host.

Does he sleep in underwear or pajamas? Or maybe in nothing at all… And what kind of underwear does he wear? Is he hairy?

No. It was wrong for Seth to be thinking about that, even if it was only in his screwed-up head. He shifted, blowing out a long breath. Yes, Logan was handsome—fine, incredibly gorgeous and sexy—

"You okay?" Logan asked.

"Huh?" Seth said too loudly. "Oh, yeah. Just frustrated about all this plastic in the environment. It's terrible."

"Oh. Yeah."

Seth turned up the volume and put all thoughts of Logan, leather jackets, and *especially* underwear firmly out of his mind.

BOXER BRIEFS.

Black and clinging to a spectacular rear and meaty thighs. Seth stood frozen atop the two steps down into the sunken great room, gripping the mug of coffee he was bringing Logan.

Logan was sprawled on his belly on the couch at the far end, his left arm stretched out on the chaise, the sheet twisted beneath him and duvet pushed down to his feet. He'd asked about putting on the gas fireplace, and Seth had told him to feel free. Now it was overly warm, condensation glistening on the windows.

"Need to set the maximum temperature so it shuts off and doesn't get too hot." Seth realized a second later that he'd said the words aloud. His heart raced as he tried to focus on anything but the lust sizzling through him at the sight of Logan's half-naked—more like three-quarters—and splayed body.

Jenna was right. Seth was ridiculously pent-up and needed to try dating before he humiliated himself and tented his slacks in front of his guest.

Grunting, Logan pushed himself up. "Huh? What?" He peered around in a daze, his sexy voice sleep-scratchy.

Yep. Hairy chest. Would it feel rough under Seth's fingers? He tore his gaze back up to Logan's bleary face. "Sorry! I'm so used to talking to myself I apparently don't even realize I'm doing it." He waved a hand around at the fogged windows. "It got too hot, huh? I can set the fireplace so it turns off after it hits a certain temp." His other hand was still gripping the mug, which he thrust forward. "Coffee? This is black, but I have milk and sugar if you want?"

"Black's great. Thanks."

Seth crossed to the couch, concentrating on breathing. He put the mug on the table, afraid he'd spill it on all that exposed skin if he tried to pass it to Logan directly.

Mmm, hair on his legs and arms too.

Standing upright, Seth backed away. What was the matter with him? He encountered attractive men all the time and kept his libido in check. Was it that he'd been alone and celibate so long now that he was cracking under the pressure? Or was it that there was something undeniably intimate about having Logan sleeping under his roof? In his boxer briefs?

As Matt would say: *Little bit from column A, little bit from column B.*

"I'd better get to work. Have a good day! Make yourself at home. Oh, let me get you some towels." He spun to escape before Logan could reply and tried not to think of Logan naked and wet in the shower.

He failed badly, but at least he tried.

Chapter Five

"**I**'LL PAY YOU back."

Expertly balancing the car seat with a sleeping Noah inside, Jenna opened her front door and called, "Hi, Pop!" To Logan, she said, "I know. I heard you the first three times."

Logan nodded and kicked the door shut behind him, his hands occupied with canvas grocery bags. He'd had to borrow the money from Jenna to pay for the repair on his truck. The garage had been impatient for him to pick it up right away, and if Logan was going to be staying out in Saratoga Springs, he needed wheels.

Friday was Jenna's temporary day off until she went back to work full time in the new year, so she'd picked him up at Seth's and taken him to the garage.

He took off his boots and leather jacket and followed her through into the kitchen. Noah was somehow still fast asleep in the car seat, which Jenna put on the kitchen table. Logan took things out of the bags and put them on the island for her.

"Seth's house is so beautiful," she said for the hundredth time, tightening her ponytail. She wore sweats with a dark stain of something that had dripped down her chest. Peering around her beige and pink kitchen with a miserable expression, she sighed. "God, this is so nineties. All this laminate. Ugh."

"It's nice."

Jenna narrowed her gaze. "Don't shit a shitter. I'm dying for a new kitchen, but these kids keep wanting to eat and stuff, so." Her face lit up again. "But wow, Seth's great room looks incredible now. I only saw it once, back before Brandon sleazed off and I'd shamelessly invited myself over. It's gorgeous now."

"Yeah. Slept like a baby on that couch." The wide leather had been soft, yet firm, and Seth had given him a pillow with cool foam in it. Logan had gotten more sleep than he had in weeks even though it had gotten too hot with the fireplace on.

He was a jobless loser who couldn't afford rent, but Seth had brought him a steaming mug of coffee and acted like he was a real guest, not just a freeloader. They'd made a deal, but Logan was sure as hell getting more out of it.

He'd found himself thinking about Seth a lot. Seth wasn't like most people he knew. He was…fancier. Not arrogant, though. But the way he didn't swear, and how he did everything so neat and orderly…

For some weird reason it reminded Logan of his grandma's sitting room, with fake flowers in vases and plastic on the couches. Which probably sounded like an insult even though he didn't mean it that way. He'd always wanted to rip the plastic off those couches and bounce on them.

Logan asked, "He's a good boss?"

"Oh yeah, the best. I mean, he's technically not my boss, but he should be. *Will* be after this caper." She grinned, waggling her eyebrows and adding fresh bananas to the fruit bowl by the toaster. "I still can't believe you're doing this."

He snorted. "Me either. Not a lot of options."

Her face softened. "I know. But Seth really is so great. Kind, generous, patient. He deserves this promotion so much. I'm really glad you're helping each other. I can't tell you how many times he covered for me when I was pregnant and puking. Picked up so much of my slack. I just wish he wasn't so tough on himself. I think it's because of his upbringing."

"Right. Crazy religious parents?"

Jenna grimaced. "Yup. I mean, we grew up with standard-issue Catholic guilt, but his family's evangelical church took it to a whole new level. Seth's always been a bit reserved, but when Brandon dumped him, it was a big shock. Really did a number on him."

"What happened there?" Logan had already decided this Brandon was a fucking idiot.

"Ugh." She opened the fridge and loaded up the crisper drawer. "I guess Brandon was already having doubts before they moved, but he thought the change of scenery would fix their problems or something. Like a fresh start would make him fall back in love with Seth. That's apparently what he told Seth when he was leaving. Obviously that never works, so when he met another guy at the gym, he bailed. That was over a year ago now, and Seth seems…stuck."

She opened a cupboard and pulled out a jar of natural peanut butter, taking a spoonful and saying through it, "I think this caper will do wonders for him. At least he'll finish his house." She held out the jar, the spoon inside.

Logan filled his mouth with the sticky peanut butter, pondering what Jenna had told him. When he swallowed, his tongue still coated with thick residue, he asked, "Seth's not seeing anyone else?"

"Not that I know of. Of course, I don't want to pry."

"Of course not," Logan said dryly.

She smirked. "Shut up. But as far as I can tell, he hasn't dated at all the past year. He's such a catch! Handsome and sweet. Don't you think?"

Shrugging, Logan said, "Sure." He didn't usually think of men's looks or personalities that way since that stuff didn't matter when it came to simply getting off.

But yeah, Seth was in good shape and had a nice smile and blue eyes. And a lot of people would have backed the hell out of the deal after Logan and Connor started going at it, but Seth had been patient with them.

"I'm sure he could get laid easy," Logan said.

Jenna sighed. "He could if he wanted to, but I think he's got some hang-ups about casual sex. When I suggested he try Grindr, he almost choked on his tongue."

Logan had to laugh. "Do you ever mind your own business?"

"Nope."

"You know, I was wondering about the house. Seth said *he* bought it, not *they* bought it."

"Yeah, apparently Brandon's never been good with money." She swirled the spoon around the peanut butter jar. "It's a blessing that Seth was smart enough not to put the house in both their names. Honestly makes me think he had his doubts too, even if he hadn't admitted it to himself."

"I guess." Logan thought of that voice that had told him marrying Veronica was nuts and that they barely even knew each other. But his life had been garbage, and there she was, beautiful and kind and taking care of him.

"Do you think Connor's going to agree to go on the retreat next weekend?" Jenna asked. "And, more importantly, that he'll behave?"

"Maybe. Guess he won't have much choice. And he'll be stuck with me all the time if he doesn't get in line at school." Logan hesitated. Might as well just spit it out. "He's getting kicked out if he doesn't."

The spoon clattered to the counter. "Shit."

"Yup."

"But he's a genius. I remember Veronica saying he practically had a photographic memory."

"Yeah, but he's been skipping class and blowing off assignments. Being an asshole to other kids. Acting reckless. He has to do good on his exams next week, or else."

"Maybe it would help to supervise him this weekend. Make sure he studies."

Logan unpacked a jumbo box of bran cereal. "Maybe."

"I think Seth can be a good influence on him. And you."

"Me? I ain't studying for jack shit." He slid some jars of baby food across the island. "Thank Christ. You know school wasn't my strong suit."

She rolled her eyes. "I mean just that you and Seth could, you know." She shrugged. "Become friends."

The back of his neck prickling, he shrugged. "I'm going to go say hi to Pop."

"No, no, no." She blocked his path and stared at him, hands on her hips. "You always blow me off when I bring this up. You used to hang out with your buddies from the railway all the time. But when was the last time you talked to them? Saw them? Liked one of their Facebook posts?"

He huffed. "You know I hate that shit."

"Yes, I'm well aware you and social media are not on the same wavelength. But you used to go out drinking and watching football games with those guys every week. Why don't you call them up?"

His lungs tightened, and he forced a jagged breath. "Just leave it alone."

"But those guys—"

"Those guys never came to see me in the hospital." He raised his voice, clenching his fists. "Okay?"

She blinked, jutting her chin forward. "What?"

"The bosses said the accident was my fault. Huey went along with it—said he couldn't remember anything. Everyone knew I was taking the fall for faulty equipment, and since it happened in the train yard and not out on the line, and no one got killed, there was no investigation. Maybe they paid off the feds, I dunno. But they said Huey got hurt because of me. I was poison after that. I haven't fucking seen my friends once since I woke up broken on a ventilator."

Jenna opened and closed her mouth. Then her eyes glistened with tears, and Logan felt like a piece of shit. He begged, "Don't cry. It's fine. Really."

"It's not fine! I should have known!" She hugged him fiercely, standing on her tiptoes. She smelled like Vaseline and spit-up, and Logan held her tightly. Voice tight, she whispered, "It makes so much more sense—why you moved so fast with Veronica."

No sense in denying it. "Yeah."

"I should have known." She stepped back and shook her head. "Why didn't I know?"

"Because I never told you?"

"I should have realized."

"You can't read my mind. You've spent your whole life taking care of other people. What do I ever do for you?"

She slapped his arm. "You do plenty. You're my big brother. Remember when you terrified that asshole Billy Morgan after he made fun of my training bra? Not that I condone the threat of violence, of course."

Laughing softly, he swiped at her tears with his thumb. "Haven't done much for you lately."

"True," she joked with a wink. "Think you can keep an eye on Noah for half an hour or so before I have to pick up Ian from his half day of preschool?"

Logan was more than happy to stop talking about all this emotional shit. "Sure." The kid was still fast asleep, so it would be simple enough.

"Awesome. I know eventually when Ian is Connor's age and wants nothing to do with me that I'll long for these days when he wants to be with me every second he can, but sometimes it's just so nice to go to the bathroom by myself. Maybe even have a shower all alone."

"Go nuts. Noah and I'll be fine." Then he frowned. "If you need help with the kids during the day, I can come over. It's not like I have a job." He should have offered ages ago and kicked himself silently. *Useless sack of shit. Can't even babysit.*

"No, no, we're fine. Jun helps before and after work. I shouldn't complain."

"Why not? Wanting to drop a deuce in peace isn't exactly asking for the moon."

She grimaced. "Must you use Pop's old classics? And I know, but the kids already spend time away from me at preschool and daycare. In January, I have to work full days. I'm lucky I've been able to ease back part time."

"If boss lady's got such a hard-on for families, she should pay for more maternity leave."

Jenna smirked. "Indeed. But she gives a lot, comparatively. I was damn lucky to get almost six months off because BRK took over—it was barely a month with Ian. Okay, if he gets fussy, just shout." Smiling down at Noah, she ghosted a kiss over his forehead before straightening. "And just… I'm sorry I pressed. I only want you to be happy again."

"I know. Now go read Facebook and take your dump." He kissed her cheek and waved her off before easing out a chair at the round kitchen table. Sunlight beamed in over the sink, which was full of dirty dishes. Logan wondered if he could wash them quietly enough.

The TV murmured distantly from the den, Pop watching some morning game show by the sounds of it. Noah was still fast asleep, making little whimpers from time to time, opening and closing his round little mouth. His dark hair was spiky the way Ian's had been.

It was strange to imagine Ian and Noah at Connor's age, and just as hard to imagine Connor ever being so small and peaceful. Of course he had been—Logan had seen the pictures. Veronica had said Connor was a happy, easy baby, and a good toddler until his father had abandoned them.

As Noah fidgeted, kicking out his little boot-covered foot and grasping the air with tiny fingers, Logan wondered if Connor would ever be happy again. God, he hoped so. He wanted to help, but he was so unqualified to be a father figure. And had Mike bothered to return Connor's messages? Sometimes it took weeks.

He gave Noah his finger to grasp, the baby gripping on with surprising strength and blinking blearily. Logan tried to imagine actually abandoning your own kid and couldn't. There was a special place in hell for cowardly fucks like Mike.

When Noah started kicking harder and whining, Logan carefully unbuckled him and lifted him out, taking off his coat and boots and holding him. The kid seemed to settle a bit when Logan walked around with him, patting his back and making soothing noises the way Jenna and Jun did.

Logan headed into the den as Noah gurgled against him wetly. The blinds were shut, probably to avoid glare on the TV. The Christmas tree was lit with gold in the corner, strands of silver decoration stuff all over the carpet. There weren't any presents under it yet.

"Hey, Pop," Logan said, walking closer to the tree with Noah still in his arms.

On his ancient stuffed armchair, slippered feet up on the matching orange footstool, Pop grunted. He'd never been much of a talker, but after the stroke, he talked even less. He *could* after a lot of speech therapy Jenna paid for, but chose not to most of the time, especially when watching TV. On the screen, a contestant played Plinko.

"Anyone guess an exact price today?" Logan asked, peering at the tree's glass balls and icicle ornaments along with the old decorations he remembered from his childhood. He smirked at the butt-ugly beagle he'd made in Boy Scouts, its tongue too long and ears too short. He didn't know why Jenna had hung on to all that stuff, but he had to admit it wasn't bad to see it every December.

"Pop?"

"Nah. These guys are guessing for shit." Pop took a sip from his mug of coffee, which was probably stone cold by now. He folded his hands over his gut, the TV reflecting in his glasses.

He was only sixty, but after the stroke five years before, he'd stopped dyeing his thinning hair, and it had gone completely gray now. His glasses slid down to the end of his nose, and he was constantly pushing them up.

Shifting Noah to his other arm, Logan reached up to the treetop to brush his fingers along the fringed bottom of the old angel's dress. His mom had loved that angel with her gold-flecked halo that got bent one year in storage. It was still bent, but the angel beamed like everything in the world was perfect.

"Getting big already," Pop said.

Logan rocked Noah gently. "He is."

"How's Connor?"

"Fine," Logan lied, lowering himself and Noah to the worn couch carefully.

Pop grunted, watching the TV again. They sat in peaceful enough silence until the next commercial break. "Jenny says you need help finishing a kitchen."

"Yeah. The bones are all in place. Just needs the finishing touches." Truthfully, Logan probably could have done the work himself as long as there were enough extra hands to carry the heavy pieces. But it would be good to get Pop out of his chair. "Could really use your help."

He grunted again. "If it'll make you and Jenny happy." Pop was the only person allowed to call Jenna anything but her proper name.

"Thanks. Maybe we can go over and take a look. See what equipment or materials we need."

The grunt was accompanied by a shrug this time. "After the Showcase Showdown."

"Sounds good."

"It's Jenny's boss's kitchen? She said you're staying over there."

"Yeah. Just temporarily." They'd decided there was no need to tell Pop about the deal Seth and Logan had made. It would probably just confuse him. Mostly Logan didn't want to go there. His father had never seemed to have an issue with gay people, but… Yeah. Just didn't want to go there.

"That warehouse job fell through?"

Shame simmered in his gut, and he braced for Pop's judgment. Yet Pop only grunted when Logan nodded. After a few moments, Logan added, "I'll get a job soon." Noah gurgled and squirmed, and he rocked him. "I'm trying."

Pop actually looked away from the TV, bushy eyebrows drawn tight. "'Course you are. Those bums at the railway fucked you over. Sons of bitches. You always tried hard. Skinned your knees raw, but you rode a bike before any of the other kids."

Logan blinked. He couldn't remember the last time Pop had talked about something from the past. After the stroke, just getting him to talk about *The Price is Right* had been a massive win. He tried to think of something to say, a swell of emotion sticking in his throat.

Pop turned back to the TV and farted. Smiling to himself, Logan settled back on the couch. Maybe he wasn't good or great, but he hadn't felt so *okay* in a long time. He still didn't have a job, and his stepson still hated him, but at least thanks to this deal with Seth, he wasn't homeless.

He watched the Showcase Showdown with his Pop, yelling at the contestants for their stupid bets, and let Noah suck on his finger until the kid started screaming for the real thing.

Chapter Six

"L EFT!" BILL DERWOOD barked, leaning on his cane.

Straining, Seth, Logan, and Jun shifted, trying to line up the quartz counter just right on the island. When Bill gave them the okay, they lowered it, and Seth exhaled and rolled his wrists when he could let go.

From where he was playing with a toy dump truck in the would-be sitting room, Ian clapped. Strapped in his car seat, Noah kicked and gurgled. Jun raised his palms, and Seth and Logan high fived him.

Jenna's husband was on the shorter side, wore round glasses, and had a build Seth's mother would have called "husky," with the implication that "fat" might not be far behind if he wasn't careful.

Why he still cataloged people's appearance through the prism of his mother's judgment, Seth wished he knew. Maybe because when he looked in the mirror, deep down he was still imagining how she might judge him.

She'd always favored short, trimmed hair, clean-shaven faces, shirts tucked in, and slacks creased down the middle. Brandon used to tease Seth about how he ironed his pajamas.

Seth squirmed with embarrassment now as he looked at how he was dressed—polo shirt tucked into his khakis and Oxfords since Bill had insisted everyone wear sturdy shoes while the work was being done. Bill, Logan, and Jun were all in jeans and old tees, Bill with a ratty cardigan over top, and work boots.

Seth tried not to stare as Logan bent over, denim stretching tight over his firm butt as he examined something near the base of the island.

Now if I could find a rear end like that on Grindr, maybe I'd swipe right. Or left, or whatever you're supposed to do.

Scoffing to himself, Seth turned away and ran his palm over the new counter around the rectangular apron sink. The hard, cold truth was that he was too terrified to try any of the gay hookup apps. Partly because of his hang-ups about casual sex, and partly because he hadn't been with anyone but Brandon and it was…daunting. The whole reason he was lusting after Logan was because it would never happen in a million years.

"Hi!" Jenna's voice rang out. "Wow, you guys have been busy!" Leaning in the front door beyond the little sitting room, she kicked snow off her boots on the edge of the top step. "Hi, baby!" she exclaimed as Ian hurtled toward her, grabbing her around the legs as if it had been days since he'd seen her instead of a few hours.

She shuffled inside with difficulty, and Connor appeared behind her at the top of the makeshift ramp they'd constructed to wheel the cabinets and quartz inside.

"Connor!" Seth smiled, saying a little prayer that there wouldn't be any screaming arguments. "So glad to see you."

Shoulders practically up to his ears, Connor regarded Seth dubiously. Jenna had apparently taken him for a haircut, since it was clipped neatly. "Hey." His gaze skittered over to Logan. "She said you needed my help."

Logan glanced at Jenna, seemingly at a loss for words, so Seth jumped in. "We do! All hands on deck. We'll be putting Noah to work any minute." Fortunately, Jun laughed at the lame joke as he plucked Noah out of the car seat.

Jenna gave Connor's shoulders a big squeeze, Ian still attached to her legs. "We always need you around."

Connor rolled his eyes, but Seth noticed he couldn't hide a tiny smile, and he wasn't trying to get out of her grasp. He mumbled, "Sure," glancing at Logan.

Unfortunately, Logan said, "Are you sure you shouldn't be studying for your exams?"

Now Connor did squirm away from Jenna. "I've studied more in the past couple days than you probably have in your whole life." He reminded Seth of a stray dog who wanted so desperately to be loved but would bark and bite out of fear.

"Good," Logan bit back, his jaw clenching.

Jun had Noah in his arms, and he beckoned Ian over with the lure of cookies. Bill had plonked down into a folding chair Seth had brought out from the garage and seemed to be staring off into nothing.

Jenna kept her tone low and even as she said, "Logan, I know you're just concerned about Connor's future. Right?" She glanced at Connor, who scowled, his hands jammed in the front pockets of his jeans.

"Right," Logan said. "Of course."

She smiled, her voice soothing. "You both want the same thing—for Connor to ace his exams and go back to Rencliffe in January. Connor and I talked about how important it is for him to do his best." She glanced at her father, her voice still low. "We also talked about how important the family retreat is next weekend. He understands, don't you?"

"Yeah," Connor muttered. "I won't screw it up."

"Thank you," Seth said. "I really appreciate your help." He looked to Logan, who was watching the exchange warily, as if ready for Connor to act out. When Logan didn't say anything, Seth added, "We both appreciate it very much."

"Yeah." Logan nodded.

"Am I getting lunch soon?" Bill asked loudly.

"Yes!" Seth was happy for an excuse to do something to break the awkward moment. They'd moved the fridge over into the sitting room, and he hurried to take out the sandwich fixings.

They had lunch in the great room, Jenna managing to keep the conversation flowing and noncombative. They all laughed as she told a story about an explosive diaper incident with Noah. It might not have been the best topic while they ate, but if there was one thing that could unite most people, it was embarrassing poop stories.

As they howled with laughter, Jenna standing now to animate her story, Seth realized it had been so long since he'd heard true laughter in the house. Not just the odd chuckle when he was watching *The Good Place*, but full-throated, belly-busting *laughter*. It echoed off the high ceiling, filling him with cozy warmth.

He knew that come January, once their caper was done and Logan moved on, that he'd be alone again, but at least Seth could enjoy having a family around him for the moment. Even if they weren't *his* family, there was something profound and beautiful about three generations together, sharing food and jokes.

After lunch, Seth and Logan left the others relaxing in the great room for the time being, Jun reading Ian a story before he had his nap, Jenna nursing Noah with her feet up on the chaise and a blanket draped across her, Bill dozing on the other side of the couch.

Seth and Logan put on their boots and coats, and Seth impulsively asked Connor to come along. He shrugged but followed without complaint.

In the garage, which ideally would soon hold Seth's SUV instead of the unfinished renovation materials, they had to take the cabinets out of their crates and load them onto a dolly. Logan said to Connor, "Hold the dolly still once we get the cabinets out."

Connor rolled his eyes. "I can do more than that."

"Oh, for fuck's sake," Logan snapped. "Can you just do as you're told for once?"

"Screw you! I knew you didn't really want me here." With a dramatic huff, Connor spun on his heel and marched off down the driveway, snow crunching under his boots.

Seth stared after him in shock, boggled at how quickly that had gone south. Everything had been fine, and then *bam*. Logan and Connor couldn't seem to communicate at all without anger and resentment exploding between them. Over nothing—although Seth knew it wasn't really about the dolly.

He cleared his throat. "Should I go after him?"

Logan's face was flushed, his nostrils flaring. "No. Just let him sulk." He muttered something under his breath and got to work, taking a crowbar to the crates with gusto.

Seth tried to help but mostly stayed out of the way since Logan was apparently working off his frustration, prying open the crates, removing the cabinets, and loading them on the dolly. But when a grunt morphed into a gasp, Seth reached for him.

"Okay?" Seth asked. Logan's face was an alarming red, and his arms shook where he held a cabinet. Seth tugged it free and thunked it down onto the garage floor, his heart skipping. "Logan?"

Panting now, Logan pressed a palm to his chest as if he couldn't breathe. Seth's own breath caught as Logan dropped to his knees on the concrete, his shoulders heaving. Squatting, Seth checked to make sure Logan wasn't wearing a medical alert bracelet or necklace he hadn't noticed.

"Is it asthma? Do you have chest pain?" Seth asked. Logan shook his head, but his eyes were wild and he still couldn't seem to breathe. "I'm calling 911. I'll be right back!" Seth jumped up, but Logan caught his wrist in an iron grip.

Logan shook his head. He gasped out, "Will…pass."

He still had hold of Seth's wrist, his strong, callused hand freezing. Seth sank back down, letting Logan hold on, angling himself so he could tentatively reach out with his other hand and stroke Logan's back. Not thumping—that didn't work for choking, let alone whatever this was. A panic attack? Seth prayed it wasn't actually a heart attack and that Logan wasn't just being a stereotypical tough guy by insisting he was fine.

"What's wrong with him?"

Seth looked over his shoulder to see Connor with one foot in the garage, his eyes wide as he stared at Logan. Logan released Seth's wrist, sucking in a breath and wheezing out, "It's nothing." He pushed to his feet, still breathing hard, sweat glistening on his brow despite the frosty air, his exhalations clouding.

Seth added, "Everything's okay. It was just a little…" He had no idea what, and grasped for a word, landing on the one his gram would have used. "Just a little turn."

Connor stared at them, his gaze jumping back and forth between Logan and Seth. To Seth, he said, "He's supposed to be better now." He bit it out like an accusation, but Seth could sense the terror beneath it. The poor kid had lost his mother suddenly and been through so much upheaval. Seth managed a smile and approached him.

He hoped he wasn't lying when he said, "He is." He squeezed Connor's shoulder, and he could feel little tremors despite Connor lifting his chin and putting on a careless tone.

"Fine. Whatever."

Seth ignored that. "I'm glad you came back. We really do need your help."

"I didn't have my phone," Connor replied flatly.

Heh. Should have known. "Right. Well, I'm still glad. How about you help me get these first few cabinets inside? I'll push and you pull." Seth motioned to the long dolly. He glanced at Logan, who nodded, gratitude clear in his brown eyes.

It gave Seth a satisfied little flush of warmth to help Logan. He grasped the cold metal handles, yelping. "Yikes! We need to get our gloves when we go in. Think we can tough it out?"

Connor nodded as Seth hoped he would, glancing at Logan as he took hold of the dolly's handles at the other end and pulled. *Wants to prove he's tough*, Seth thought. He bet Connor wanted Logan's approval far more than either of them realized.

Nodding encouragingly, Seth pushed, and they made their way out of the garage and along the front walk over the temporary plywood path. It wasn't too heavy, and they were able to get up the ramp without too much struggle on Seth's end, his thighs flexing as he dug in and shoved.

Inside, he asked Connor, "You want to help Jun unload these and warm up for a minute? I'll be back." Seth grabbed his gloves and hurried out. He exhaled in relief when he saw Logan standing in the garage, his color back to normal and seemingly breathing okay.

"You all right?" Seth asked as he neared. He rubbed Logan's arm, the leather of his jacket and Seth's gloves creaking. Wait, was he being too familiar? He dropped his hand.

Logan nodded and rasped, "Thanks."

"What happened?"

"It's fine." Logan shrugged. "No big deal. Let's get back to work."

Seth stayed put. "I thought you were having a heart attack. It was a pretty big deal."

Logan rubbed a hand over his face, making that scratchy sound that sent a thrill down Seth's spine. "I guess I pushed a little too hard. Docs have a fancy word for it: dyspnea. Just means shortness of breath. Because of the accident."

"Ah." Maybe he was being nosy, but Seth's curiosity got the better of him. "It was a derailment?"

"Yeah." Logan's jaw tightened, his gaze on the concrete. "I was driving the engine, just moving it to the other side of the yard. The conductor had released the other cars, thank fuck. It would have been much worse. They said I was going too fast, being a hotshot or something. I know I wasn't. The brakes failed. I wasn't speeding, and I braked in plenty of time, but it was just..." He shuddered. "Screeching metal like you've never heard before."

"My goodness," Seth whispered. He could only imagine the terror.

"Track curved, and we went over. Last thing I remember was my buddy Huey screaming, and this punch to my chest, like being stomped by an elephant."

Logan swallowed hard, raising his head and looking off somewhere beyond Seth, unfocused. "One of the monitors had come loose, and it hit me square in the chest. Massive pulmonary contusion. My lungs were so bruised, I needed to be on a ventilator to breathe. Woke up like that—tube down my throat."

Seth shuddered. "That must have been horrendous."

"Yeah." His gaze was still distant. "Dislocated my shoulder and broke my arm, and it had to be in traction. Cracked ribs. Everything was just…broken." He inhaled and seemed to give himself a shake, meeting Seth's eyes. "Anyway. Once in a while I get short of breath. I guess it's in my head sometimes, but today I just pushed too fast. Connor must think I'm pathetic." He looked away. "You too."

"What? No, not at all. I'm just relieved there's an explanation. I can't imagine how much work you had to do to recover the way you have. I'd never know you'd been so badly injured."

"The physio helped. Having a goal. And Veronica…" He shrugged. "She helped a lot."

"Connor's mother? I'm so sorry for your loss."

"'*My loss*,'" he muttered darkly. "I always feel like shit when people say that."

"Oh. I'm sorry." Seth tried to think of something better to say.

"No, it's not your fault." Logan lifted his hands out to his sides before dropping them. "It's just that we were done. It was over between us. So I feel like an asshole acting like she was still…mine. You know what I mean?"

"Yes, I understand that. I didn't realize."

"Not that I'm *not* sad she's dead. I did love her. She was a good woman, but we were a mess together. I wish I could change a lot about what happened." He shrugged tightly. "I guess that's life. She dropped dead at thirty-four, and I can't fix it. Connor got the shit end of the stick, that's for sure."

"The poor boy. It's heartbreaking." Seth frowned, going back to what Logan had said before. "But you know, I don't agree that Connor thinks you're pathetic, or that he truly dislikes you. He was scared to see you like that."

Logan scoffed. "He'd probably be thrilled if I dropped dead."

"You can't really believe that? As much as he may want his biological father to be in the picture, you're the one who's here. If you two could stop butting heads for five minutes…"

Logan was silent a few moments. "But he's never liked me from the day we met. I try not to lose my temper, but he just—" He made a stabbing motion with his index finger.

"Pushes your buttons. I noticed." Seth glanced out of the garage to make sure they were still alone. "I don't think you should take what Connor says to heart. I realize that's easy for me to say. But he's lashing out and angry at the world. You're a convenient target."

"Yeah." Logan gave Seth a rueful smile. "And since I'm not thirteen, I should try to be the adult, huh? Not fly off the handle."

"Right," Seth agreed gently. "Praise him. Try to build up his confidence."

"But he doesn't care what I think."

"I'd argue he cares very much what you think. Despite what he might say."

Logan seemed to ponder that. "I guess so. Shit, Jenna and Jun are so good at this stuff. I'm useless."

"Doesn't Jenna…talk to you about this kind of thing?" He tried to phrase it delicately. "She's usually eager to…help."

Barking out what sounded like a genuine laugh, Logan scratched his head. "That's a polite way to put it. She does help, but she's always given me more credit than I deserve. And she's got so much with the kids and Pop and working. When our mom died…"

"You were teenagers, right?"

"Jenna was. Fourteen. I was twenty-one and in the Marines. Pop only had the stroke five years ago, but when Mom died, he needed taking care of. Hell, I don't think he could even use the microwave. Jenna stepped up, like she always does. She barely had the chance to move out after college. Pop had the stroke, and he ended up moving in with her and Jun. He'll be there until he has to go in an old-folks home or they take him out feet first."

Logan took a deep breath and blew it out. "I was working long hours on the railway. On call, never knowing exactly when I'd have to go in, and for how long. Just depended on the shipments and where they had to go. I'd be away a couple days sometimes since we had to wait at least ten hours in the bunkhouse upstate before we could come back. Regulations and all. Pop needed stability."

Seth tried to assure him. "Of course. It's not your fault you couldn't be the primary caregiver. And with Connor, you're still learning. From what I gather, parenthood takes practice."

Logan scowled. "That's just it. It's not like I'm a *parent*. I'm totally fucking unqualified for that."

"But…you are. A parent, I mean. Whether you're ready or not, Connor needs you." Seth thought of his mother and father with a pang of longing, a bite of pain quick on its heels. "His mother's gone, and his father's MIA. He needs a dad he can depend on. Who will look out for him, no matter what. Being rejected by your parents, it's… I wouldn't wish it on anyone. Let alone a confused kid."

After a moment, Logan softly said, "Parenthood," as if he was trying out the word, weighing it on his tongue and in his heart. "The lady at the school called me a 'single father.' It's weird as hell to think of myself like this. Me actually being…a *parent.*"

Footsteps approached, and they turned as Connor pulled the long dolly back into the garage, wearing gloves now. For a moment, no one said anything. Then Connor frowned and glanced at the dolly. "Did I do it wrong?"

"No, not at all," Seth quickly assured him.

Logan cleared his throat. "You did a great job. Thanks."

It was silly for Seth to be proud and pleased that Logan had taken his advice, but he was nonetheless.

Connor watched Logan warily. "Okay." Then he waved a hand toward him. "Are you…?"

"Oh yeah, I'm fine. It's nothing to worry about."

Connor glanced at Seth, as if looking for affirmation, so Seth nodded and smiled. "Let's get back to work! Team Caper needs to finish this kitchen, right?" He held up his palms for high fives, which was probably a nerdy thing to do, but he'd never pretended to be cool.

After a moment, Logan and Connor dutifully slapped his palms, and Seth grinned as they got to work.

ALONG THE MAIN street in town late on Sunday afternoon, fluffy flakes of snow drifted down, the sun already setting by four-thirty, the trees glowing in white Christmas lights. Red-ribboned wreaths hung from the old-fashioned streetlight poles, and other shoppers popped in and out of the antique stores and gift shops.

"I think that's the one," Seth said. "I can't imagine we're going to find another dining table in store without waiting for a custom build or warehouse delivery." Although it made him a bit nauseous to think of buying a major piece of furniture without looking in *all* the stores in the area. And online. And after making an exhaustive list of the pros and cons.

Logan said, "Looked good to me. A table's a table, right?"

Seth laughed. "You just want to finish shopping, don't you? Your eyes glazed over in the second store two hours ago."

"Guilty as charged." Logan gave him a sexy little smirk.

Stop thinking about how sexy he is.

The struggle was real. As much as Seth tried not to think about how hot Logan was, his sexiness was *right there.* And aside from the way he looked, it was very attractive that Logan had gone furniture shopping with him and not complained once, even though all the talk of wood grains and rustic vs. classic vs. modern had surely bored him to tears.

Seth might have pretended once or twice that Logan *was* his boyfriend, and when a few shopkeepers had made the assumption, he hadn't corrected them. He'd told himself it was only for practice purposes, but he was full of it. If he only cared about faking it, he wouldn't be imagining what it would be like to hold Logan's hand as they walked down the street.

Or what it would be like to steal a kiss under one of the boughs of mistletoe that hung outside the bookstore. Their lips cold and noses red in the frosty air… How they'd warm each other up, Logan's arms strong around him and pulling him close…

Seth cleared his throat. "Okay, let's look in one more store down here and—" Breath punching out of him, he staggered to a halt, almost tripping over his own feet.

Oh, merciful lord.

Or cruel and not merciful at *all* as the case may be, because there was Brandon. Seth blinked, willing the nightmare to end. But no, that was definitely, one hundred percent Brandon standing twenty feet away looking in a store window, snow catching in the bushy hipster beard he'd grown that year. Which Seth only knew about from stalking public Facebook posts.

He closed his eyes and opened them. Still Brandon.

Of course—because the horror had to be complete—Brandon was talking to Peter, who even at a distance in a parka was clearly still climbing ropes and lifting cars one-handed or whatever people did at CrossFit.

They were with Bethany and Jake—no, Joe—from the wine club, which shouldn't have bothered Seth at all—he hadn't even liked the pretentious wine club in the first place. Why should he care that Brandon had kept going with Peter? Why had he been Facebook stalking in the first place?

That Seth had been dumped and replaced, seemingly without missing a beat, *hurt.*

His feet felt locked in ice. "You've got to be kidding me," he muttered. With Logan stopped beside him, clearly confused, Seth had never wanted to make a run for it so badly in his life.

Chapter Seven

SQUINTING DOWN THE sidewalk, Logan tried to see what was making Seth look like he might puke, his face going red the way it had when Logan had shown up unexpectedly and met Angela Barker.

Seth's mouth was open as he stared at four people nearby peering in the window of a store that looked like it sold candles and oil and that kind of froufrou stuff Logan's long-ago ex Jacinta had loved. If Logan never smelled lavender and that sandalwood shit again it would be too soon.

Grabbing Logan's arm, his fingers digging in through the leather, Seth took a step back. Then he froze as one of the people glanced over and did a double-take. She was a blonde around thirty and had a nice rack under her tight jacket.

Her eyes went wide for a moment as she and Seth stared at each other, and then she slapped on a fake-looking smile and called, "Oh my God, is that you, Seth?"

Seth dropped Logan's arm like it was burning and laughed shakily, calling back, "Hi, Bethany. Joe." He paused as the other people looked over. "Brandon."

Oh fuck. Logan wasn't sure which of the three men was Brandon, but he assumed it was one of the guys who immediately linked hands and put on bullshit smiles. The two couples approached, Seth still frozen beside Logan, his breath clouding the frosty air in shallow bursts.

He looked scared shitless, and Logan wondered if he'd looked like that himself in the garage when he couldn't breathe. Fuck, he hated when he was like that—so helpless and…bare. Seth had been good to him, and seeing his fear now, Logan wanted to protect him.

Hell, they were supposed to be pretending to be engaged—that was the deal, wasn't it? Might as well get in some practice.

He slung his arm around Seth's shoulders, squeezing when he felt how Seth was trembling. This breakup had kicked Seth in the nuts, and Logan wasn't going to let any shit-brick ex make him feel worse. In a world full of assholes, Seth was good.

Putting on his own bullshit smile, Logan said, "Hey there!" He stuck out his free right hand to the closest guy. "Logan Derwood. Seth's boyfriend."

The man's eyebrows shot up so far they might never come back down. He looked between Logan and Seth, his smile faltering. "Oh! Wow! Uh, hi." He had to let go of his boyfriend's hand to shake Logan's. "Brandon Templeton."

Logan squeezed. Hard. "Great to meet you." He let his eyes drop down over Brandon—short, teeth too big for his mouth, and one of those bushy beards that must be making up for a small dick.

Then he looked away dismissively, moving on to shake the hand of Brandon's boyfriend, Peter—thick neck, probably took steroids but could kick Logan's ass—and the male/female couple whose names Logan forgot as soon as he heard them.

Brandon gave Seth an uneasy smile. "Babe, I didn't realize you were seeing anyone."

What an asshole. He had no right to call Seth any names like that—and right in front of Logan! The fucking nerve. Sure, they were fake boyfriends, but Brandon didn't know that. Seth was rigid against Logan's side, and Logan willed him to unclench.

"Uh-huh," Seth managed, his voice higher than Logan had heard it.

"That's great, babe." Brandon tilted his head and touched his hand to his chest. "I'm so happy for you."

Would Seth be mad if Logan punched the condescending prick? Logan wished he was a better actor. He couldn't think of anything to say that wasn't telling Brandon, his hipster beard, and tiny dick where they could go.

But it got easier when Seth exhaled and slipped his arm around Logan's waist. Maybe it should have felt weird, but it was reassuring. They were faking this together.

Seth said, "I'm happy for us too," his voice calmer.

Act like Seth's your boyfriend!

Logan tried to think of something cheesy and in-love sounding. He went with "Me, three," and leaned close and pressed a slow kiss to Seth's smooth cheek, just the hint of five o'clock shadow under his lips.

He made it a lingering kiss—a kiss promising more once they were alone. A tremor vibrated through Seth, and he turned his head to meet Logan's gaze.

His blue eyes were dark, and he licked his lips. Logan looked down at the movement and then back into Seth's eyes, a bolt of lust shooting to his balls and waking up his dick.

Whoa.

The woman laughed awkwardly. "Well, I guess we should leave you lovebirds to it!"

Tearing his eyes away from Seth's, Logan looked at her like she was incredibly boring, which she probably was. "I guess you should." He didn't even glance at the others as he strode forward with Seth at his side, forcing them to move out of the way or be stomped on by his combat boots.

He could feel them watching—the back of his neck practically sizzled with it—and he knew they were whispering even though he and Seth were too far away now to hear. It was in the air, swirling with the snow.

Seth matched his strides, arm snug around Logan's waist. "Wow."

"Oh, look, pookie—that kind of chair would be perfect for our new table," Logan said, stopping in front of a furniture shop's window. He added under his breath, "Smile and play along, but don't look back, whatever you do."

"That *is* a great chair!" Seth exclaimed, pointing at it. He whispered, "You think they're still watching?"

"You bet your ass they're watching." He needed to do something else a boyfriend would do, so he brushed some fresh snow from Seth's dark hair. He leaned in and murmured, "Think I should grab your ass?"

Seth swallowed so hard Logan could hear it. "Okay."

Slowly, Logan ran a gloved hand down Seth's straight back, keeping their faces close as if they were nuzzling. Seth's jacket was one of those pea coats, and Logan stroked his nice, round ass and slipped up under the hem of his coat, gripping the firm flesh.

He whispered in Seth's ear, "Imagine I'm saying something really dirty."

Seth made a sharp little sound that had to be a laugh. He reached around Logan, grabbing his shoulders before stroking one hand over Logan's head. He teased the back of Logan's neck and ran his blunt fingernails over the short scrub of Logan's hair at the base of his skull, sending sparks through Logan and getting his dick interested again.

With guys it was always fast and rough—this was different. Logan figured it was definitely boyfriend-like. He had to hold up his end of the deal, so he'd do what it took.

Besides, he liked Seth, and that ex was a fucking idiot for dumping him for the thick-neck who probably also had a tiny dick thanks to steroids. Seth deserved a hell of a lot better from where Logan was standing, and it was satisfying showing Brandon that Seth didn't miss him one little bit.

Then he wondered if Seth *did* miss him. "Do you wish he hadn't left you?" he asked before he could tell himself to mind his own damn business.

Seth was toying with the ends of Logan's hair, sending nice little shivers through Logan. He stopped, resting his bare hand on the back of Logan's neck, warm and heavy.

"You know what? No." A smile lifted his mouth, his lips wide. He laughed like he couldn't believe it. "Seeing him now made me realize how much I *don't* miss him. Not that we didn't have good times over the years. We did—a lot of good times."

"I'll take your word for it."

Laughing, Seth said, "We did. But it seems so long ago. Seeing him now, it was the strangest thing. I've looked him up on Facebook and found pictures, but it's been over a year since I saw him in person. And he's so familiar to me—aside from that ridiculous beard. I knew him so well. So…intimately. I think I recognized his body before his face. But now he's someone different. I wouldn't want him back. I *don't*."

"Good. He's a shit-brick." Logan realized his hand was still resting on Seth's ass, but he didn't move it, just pressed firmly.

Seth was breathy as he asked, "Think they're still watching?"

"Maybe. Let's go a bit longer to make sure." If they were going to do a job, they should do it right. He massaged Seth's ass and nipped at his jaw, scraping with his teeth and grinning at Seth's gasp.

"Okay, I'm going to look," Seth murmured, his breath hot across Logan's mouth. A moment later, he sighed and eased away. Logan dropped his hand, and Seth did the same.

"All clear," Seth said. He squinted at the store window. "You know, that chair really is great. Let's see how many they have."

Logan shoved his hands in his pockets, suddenly not sure what to do with them. "Sure."

As Seth opened the door, a bell tingled. He glanced back at Logan. "Thanks for all that, by the way." He laughed, his cheeks going red. "You were very convincing."

"Sure," Logan repeated, feeling his own face go hot. "Anytime."

Chapter Eight

"*I* MAGINE I'M SAYING *something really dirty.*"

Although Seth's imagination when it came to sex was admittedly lacking, that hot gust of a whisper echoed through his head endlessly the next day, accompanied by wisps of thrilling, forbidden words. Like *suck* and even *fuck*. Or *co*—

"I haven't seen Logan smile so much in a long time."

Seth jumped so violently at Jenna's words that his knees rattled the keyboard tray. She laughed and said, "Sorry. Didn't mean to interrupt your deep thoughts."

He spun in his chair. "My thoughts aren't deep!" He winced at how strange he was being. "I mean—yeah. Um, I was miles away." *Thinking dirty thoughts that are probably pathetically tame by most people's standards.* "What did you say?"

"Oh, that Logan was smiling for once on the weekend." She kept her voice low, rolling closer on her chair.

Seth's heart skipped, thinking of Logan's grin when he'd called Seth "pookie." "Oh, well… That's nice."

"I mean, obviously his problems aren't magically fixed, but he's been so beat down. It's a relief to know he'll have a few weeks with you. I think you'll be a good influence. You handle Connor really well."

"Has that relationship always been so…fraught?"

She crossed her legs, her foot swinging as she made a face, the low pump hanging off her foot. "Oh yeah. From day one, it was snippy comments and butting heads. Connor was deeply suspicious of Logan, and I can't say I blame him considering how quickly Logan and Veronica got married. I mean, Logan was still in the hospital. He hadn't even met Connor. I can imagine that was a shock for a kid."

"A heck of a shock."

Jenna smiled briefly. "A heck indeed. And when Veronica brought Logan home with her, it went to hell fast. They really seemed to love each other, and he needed her so much. I think she *needed* to be needed. If that makes any sense? But once he healed, that connection faded. It was like, the Florence

"

Nightingale syndrome or something. Nurses and patients falling for each other." She laughed. "I don't think that's what it's called. I need to apply more coffee."

Seth smiled. "I understand what you're saying." He passed her his ridiculous cat mug, and she finished the last few gulps of dark roast with a grateful smile.

"Anyway. He just seemed a bit unclenched this weekend. He's been wound tight for a long time. And you're wound pretty freaking tight yourself, if we're being honest."

He could only laugh. "Which apparently we are. Yes, I'm wound tight. I can't deny it."

Jenna tilted her head. "You're both uptight in different ways, but maybe together you can loosen each other up." She laughed, slapping a hand to her forehead and whispering, "Oh my god, listen to me! I'm talking like you two are really a couple and this isn't a fake relationship."

Seth laughed, then blurted, "We ran into Brandon and Peter yesterday."

She sat up comically straight, eyes wide. "What? How? Where?"

"Saratoga Springs. We were shopping for a table and chairs."

Jenna's eyebrows sailed north. "Okay, I need a minute to process the idea of my brother…*antiquing.*"

"He was a good sport. In more ways than one."

After a pause, Jenna poked Seth's arm. "What happened? Tell me already."

Seth gave her a quick version of events. "So he pretended to be my boyfriend, and we walked off like… Like Brandon and Peter and the others didn't matter at all."

"Yes!" She pumped her fist and whispered, "I love it."

He had to grin. "It felt pretty good." *So did your brother's hand on my butt.* Seth imagined he could still feel the pressure of Logan's palm and fingers, firm against the swell of his backside.

She asked, "Hey, did Dale set up the dinner?"

"Oh. Let me check." Seth typically checked his work email at home in evenings and over the weekends in case of anything urgent, but realized he hadn't.

His brain helpfully supplied a collage of images of what he'd been doing instead—seeing Brandon and Peter, Logan's hot breath and scruff against his face, his hand on Seth's rear…

"Imagine I'm saying something really dirty."

"You sure you're okay?"

"Yep!" Seth could feel Jenna's gaze on him, his skin prickling as he clicked the mouse too hard to open his email. There it was:

Sender: Gupta, Dale Subject: Dinner with Angela Barker

Seth double-clicked and read the short message. To Jenna, he quietly said, "Thursday night, seven p.m."

She scanned the email, leaning in close, smelling like apples and Tide. "Okay. This works."

He took a deep breath. "Dinner Thursday. Then we leave Friday after work for the retreat."

Jenna said, "It is blowing my mind to think of Logan…canoodling with you."

"Well, we are in a committed fake relationship," he murmured. "He did a great job. I admit I was surprised." He quickly added, "Not that I thought Logan was a homophobe or anything. He just comes across very macho, I guess."

"Yeah, between the Marines and the railroad, he's not used to being in touch with his feelings or anything. Not that all gay men are in touch with their feelings." She eyed him speculatively. "Speaking of which, I'd expect you to be moping today, and probably pining after seeing Brandon. Ruminating at the very least."

Huh. She was right. "How do you know I'm not?"

"Not what?" Matt's shaggy head appeared over the partition between their pods. "What are you whispering about?" He mouthed, "*Caper?*"

Jenna nodded and waved him over impatiently. In his usual sneakers and dark jeans, Matt came around and wheeled over one of the desk chairs the interns had used, spinning it to sit backwards and lean his forearms on the top of the backrest. Under his suit jacket, his graphic T-shirt had the image of a guitar and the name of a band Seth had never heard of.

After Jenna filled him in, Matt grinned. "Oh, man. How much do I love that you got to rub your hot new boyfriend in that douchenozzle's face?"

"Fake boyfriend," Seth whispered. "Well, fake fiancé, actually."

"Whatever. Douchenozzle doesn't have to know that." Matt's brow furrowed. "But yeah, I'm shocked you're not brooding about the whole thing."

"Again, how do you know I'm not?"

"No fidgeting," Jenna said. "It's your brooding-about-Brandon tell. You fidget endlessly, like you want to climb out of your skin."

Matt said, "I can hear your chair when you do it. *Squeak, creak, squeak.*"

"Oh." Seth was taken aback. He shifted then, recrossing his legs, feeling dangerously exposed. His chair *creak-squeeeeeaked.* He froze. "Uh. Guilty as charged, it seems."

"Oh, don't forget decorations for your house!" Jenna said. "Angela loves the holidays."

Ugh. "Oh. Right. I'll have to buy some stuff." It was silly to dread decorating. "It's not really my thing."

Matt's eyebrows rose. "Seriously? Huh. I thought you'd be all about hanging stockings by the chimney with care and visions of sugarplums."

I don't deserve Christmas.

The thought filled his mind, but fortunately was blocked before it could reach his tongue. The swirl of memories of Christmases past made him ache—his family's stockings hanging from the mantel cluttered with his mom's ugly Christmas figurines and nativity scene, the paint chipped on the three wise men.

Jenna said, "I'll arrange a tree and talk to Logan about what to get. Our cousin manages a tree lot, so he'll give us a great deal."

"Uh, okay." Seth's head was spinning. He was going to have a real Christmas tree. He'd only ever known his parents' artificial one, which had become rather threadbare the last time he saw it. Years ago, of course. Surely they had a replacement by now. There were probably lots of things different at home now.

Home.

"Ho-ho-ho!" Tara from accounting appeared at the entrance to the pod, her Santa hat slipping down over her forehead. She shoved it up, the bell on the end making a faint *ding*. "Have you contributed to the food bank collection? We want it to be the biggest donation ever this year! Angela will be in on Friday when the volunteers come to collect."

They all agreed to bring in more cans of tuna and jars of peanut butter, guilt tugging at Seth that he actually hadn't contributed at all yet. He'd been meaning to stop by the grocery store and stock up, but admittedly had wished he could just write a check or give cash instead.

Matt returned to his pod, and Jenna wheeled back to her desk. Seth tapped his keyboard and scanned a few new emails—this time checking to see what Becky had deemed *URGENT!* It was something about printer toner.

As Seth scanned another email, his gaze drifted to the framed photo of Logan and Connor on his desk. Logan really was handsome and…masculine. He remembered the sensation of Logan's hand on his butt, then imagined Logan in his boxer briefs, sprawled on the couch with the blankets shoved down…

Clicking his mouse, Seth cleared this throat. He realized Jenna was right—he really wasn't brooding over Brandon. Running into Brandon and Peter would have sent him into a tailspin in the past, yet he'd barely thought of them at all. Instead, his mind had been occupied with Logan, and that secret whisper in Seth's ear.

AS SETH PULLED into the driveway in the early darkness, his heart skipped to see Logan up on a ladder in front of the house. The jolt wasn't specifically because he was on a ladder, but just that he was there, period.

Seth eyed the already-familiar shape of his broad shoulders in the leather jacket, the way his jeans clung to his rear, on display as Logan reached up to attach a section of Christmas lights to the edge of the slanted roof.

There was no denying the flutter in Seth's belly or the excitement that spun through him. He grinned to himself as he parked on the driveway and turned off the engine. So maybe he had a little crush. It was a heck of a lot better than mooning over Brandon. Maybe a little crush was exactly what he needed to move on.

Seth left the bags of canned goods in the back of the SUV and juggled the other cloth bags while he locked the car with a *chirp*. On the walkway, he called up, "Looking great!" His face went hot even as his breath clouded in the frigid air. Should he clarify that he meant the lights? Although the lights weren't even on yet, it was just a dark string of bulbs. Why had he said that?

"Should be okay," Logan replied. He looked down and gave Seth a pleased little smile that softened his face, and despite his best efforts, Seth's heart foolishly swelled.

As Logan strung another few feet, stretching precariously to his right, Seth inhaled sharply. "Be careful up there!" He dropped the bags on the shoveled walk and held the ladder.

Grunting, Logan climbed back down before shifting the ladder over. "It's fine. One more section to go." He frowned down at the groceries. "Those are getting wet."

"Right! I'll just…" Seth grabbed the handles and carried the bags inside, stamping his feet and taking off his boots, the door still open.

A colorful wreath made of glittery ornaments now hung on the front door, a mix of traditional holiday colors as well as pinks and purples. He'd admired similar wreaths while driving through the neighborhood, and it gave him a pulse of pleasure to have his own.

But this is just for Angela. For show. It's not really mine.

Seth leaned outside. "The wreath is gorgeous."

"Yeah? Jenna said to get an ornament wreath, and that one looked good."

"It's perfect." *It's not really mine. This is all pretend. I don't get to have this.*

"Can you flip the switch?" Logan called down.

Seth turned on the switch by the front door and leaned out. Multicolored lights adorned the lines of the roof, fat snowflakes drifting down to make it even more perfect. "It really does look great!"

Logan climbed down the ladder and stood back on the edge of the snow-covered lawn, craning his neck. He nodded. "This works."

"You must be freezing! Come inside. I'll make dinner. Well, I'll nuke the rotisserie chicken and cheesy mashed potatoes I grabbed from the ready-made section."

Logan grinned. "I'll just put away the ladder and shit."

"Right. I love the wreath too, by the way. Thank you."

"Yeah? I wasn't sure if it had too many colors. But it looked pretty. Jenna gave me a list of indoor stuff to get too, but I only had time for outdoor today. Had to take Pop to a doctor's appointment."

"I hope everything's okay?"

He shrugged. "Same old shit. Pop won't listen about cutting out the junk. Not to mention red meat and scotch."

"Ah. I admit I enjoy a good scotch myself."

"Yeah? Although I don't think Pop drinks the good stuff." He grabbed the ladder and carried it back to the garage.

Seth hurried to unpack the groceries, trying to ignore persistent flutters of excitement. It was a crush! No one had to know. He and Logan didn't have a real relationship, but Seth could enjoy his company. He could enjoy not being so terribly alone.

As he opened the pantry, he stopped. This was the part when he typically would have thought of Brandon with a pang of loss that was at turns dull or deathly sharp. But tonight…

Nope. It wasn't there. He didn't miss Brandon. Maybe he hadn't actually missed Brandon for a long time.

"Need a hand?"

He jumped, whirling around and dropping a bag of macaroni, which rattled. "No. I'm good."

Logan eyed him warily. "Okay."

Seth needed to say something else, and he cast about for a topic as he bent to grab the pasta. "How's Connor doing?"

After a pause, Logan said, "Um, fine? I guess."

"You haven't spoken to him today?" Seth went back to unpacking.

Brows drawing together, Logan said, "No. We don't really… He doesn't want to talk to me."

"Right. I hear what you're saying."

"But?" Logan snorted. "Go ahead. I can take it."

"Well, I know you two tend to butt heads, but…" Seth tried to find a way to say it without offending. "The thing is, if you don't make the effort with him, he'll think you don't care. Even if you end up arguing, I think it still helps to reach out. He's angry and scared and difficult, but if you keep trying, he'll surely come around."

Logan frowned, seeming to ponder it. "I don't want to bug him. You know?"

"Right. I get that. It doesn't have to be a big thing. Maybe send him a text every day asking how he's doing. Or it could be something like talking about sports or sending him a link to a funny video. Just…contact. Show him you're thinking of him. That you care."

"That makes sense." Shaking his head, Logan rubbed a hand over his short hair, smiling ruefully. "Told you I'm useless at all this."

"You're not useless. It's new. You're learning."

"You don't have kids. How are you so good at it?"

"I'm not an expert by any means." Still, he flushed pleasantly at the compliment. "I'll heat up dinner. And how about a drink?" The thought of imbibing on a Monday felt ridiculously rebellious.

He really did need to get a life, didn't he?

Logan said, "Yeah, thanks."

"We might as well live dangerously, right?"

"Sure," Logan agreed with a rumbling laugh.

Seth tried very, very hard not to think of what Logan would say if he talked dirty to him.

Chapter Nine

SETH MUTED THE TV as another batch of commercials blared before the post-game. Logan had been surprised when Seth had suggested watching the Monday night football game with their dinner. Now they were relaxing on the couch, bellies full of chicken and cheesy potatoes. They'd moved on from beer to an after-dinner scotch.

Logan sipped his drink, enjoying the smooth burn. Seth could apparently afford the fancy stuff, and Logan wasn't complaining. Instead of a harsh, hollow aftertaste, he was left with a spicy richness that made him think of his grandma's fruitcake.

On the silent TV, dogs played basketball in a commercial for insurance or some shit. It was snowing, and if he squinted, he could see it piling up on the deck through the sliding doors. The gas fireplace made the room perfectly warm.

He definitely needed to get a tree and stuff before the boss lady came for dinner. And Logan had to admit the room would look great all done up, even if it was just for show and not a real family's decorations.

Seth had gone quiet, although it wasn't awkward. It was weirdly nice, sitting on the big couch and listening to the hum of the flickering fire.

"I need to—" Seth cut himself off, taking another swallow of scotch and swirling the ice in his glass. "It's ridiculous."

"Uh… What is?"

"Oh, sorry. My brain won't shut its trap, and I'm used to talking to myself."

"About what?"

"Everything. Oh, you mean now?" He chuckled and rubbed his face, his five o'clock shadow making a scratchy sound against his palm.

"You don't have to tell me." Although Logan was strangely eager. "Unless you want."

"Maybe it'll do me good to get some advice."

"I dunno if I'm any good at that. That's Jenna's department."

Seth swirled the ice in his glass, smiling. "Whether we like it or not."

"Heh, yeah." Normally Logan would bristle at the slightest criticism of

Jenna, but Seth's smile was nice. What was the word? Affectionate. "Well, go ahead if you want my dumbass advice."

After frowning, Seth said, "I came out to my family twelve years ago because I couldn't hide anymore. I couldn't pretend Brandon was just my roommate and that I hadn't met the right girl yet. I hated lying so much."

He stared toward the TV, but his eyes were unfocused. "The lying started to feel more sinful than being gay. And here I am, over a decade later, and I still feel guilty for wanting to…" He sighed. "You know."

Logan frowned. "Huh?"

"Uh, physical needs."

"Are you talking about getting laid?"

Seth looked at him and laughed. "Yes, I am. I can't even *say* it. It's not that I don't like…sex. I do! Very much."

"Okay." Logan swirled his own ice cubes and watched Seth from the corner of his eye. Seth was wearing slacks and a dress shirt. He'd removed his tie, rolled up the sleeves to his elbows, and slouched a bit, his legs parted.

Logan thought about how firm Seth's ass had felt the day before when they'd gotten cozy for the asshole ex, and now he was thinking about Seth having sex. With another man. Not just hand jobs or hard screws with a nod and thanks after. But full-on sex with kissing and all that. *Real* sex.

It was weird. Also weirdly hot.

Getting off with men had never been about that for Logan—about hotness or whatever. Not the way it was with women and how beautiful they were, how sexy. He couldn't remember thinking of a guy as *sexy*.

He glanced at Seth and the sprawl of his legs, and the way his shirt was unbuttoned at the top exposing his throat.

Until now, apparently.

Gulping his scotch, Logan stared at the TV and some replay of a hard tackle. Seth was quiet again, so maybe he'd drop it and—

"I loved Brandon, and he loved me. Until he didn't." Seth shook his head like he was still in shock, a little smile tugging on his mouth. "And since finally seeing him again, I've realized I truly don't love him anymore. That I'm not *in* love with him. Which is good."

Logan nodded, trying not to stare at Seth's full lips. "It is." That asswipe didn't deserve Seth.

"I dated a few guys before him, but nothing serious. I never…" He flushed light red, shifting and tapping his fingers on his glass. "I didn't do much at all with the other men. I felt like I should be in love. You know— to—to have sex."

Logan tried not to gape. "*Why?*"

Huffing out a laugh, Seth rolled his eyes. "I know. It's stupid. But it was drummed into me at church and at home. That sex was only for marriage. Since Brandon and I couldn't get married back then, I made this…deal, I guess. With myself. With God. I needed it to be an expression of love, and then I was allowed.”

“Religions sure fuck up a lot of people. Uh, no offense.”

Seth laughed, tipping his head back for a moment, showing his long throat. “None taken, I assure you. It really is ridiculous, the knots I’ve tied myself in all these years. Why should I feel guilty for, for…*getting laid?*” He said it like they were cuss words.

“You shouldn’t.”

“No, I shouldn’t! I’m a grown man. I can do what I please.” Seth was fidgety now, all worked up. Logan imagined Seth’s cheeks would feel warm to the touch.

Logan frowned. “Are you drunk?”

“No!” He laughed again. “A little tipsy, maybe. It’s nice. I’m tired of being miserable and alone. Why am I punishing myself by being celibate? Why do I think if no one loves me I don’t deserve sex? It’s not a sin to have sex if there’s no love. Is it?”

“Definitely not. All that sin crap is bullshit.”

“It is, isn’t it? Why should I sit around here waiting for…what, exactly? Prince Charming? Mr. Right?”

“Are you telling me you haven’t gotten your rocks off in over a *year?*”

Seth drained his glass and thunked it onto a coaster on the wooden table. “That’s what I’m telling you. Been afraid to try dating again.” He screwed up his face. “The whole…rigmarole of it. It’s exhausting to contemplate. Now there are these apps, and I’ll probably do it all wrong. Do you use them?”

Before Logan could answer, Seth inhaled sharply. “Although you and your wife didn’t break up, she…” He covered his mouth before dropping his hand, face even redder. “I’m sorry. I didn’t mean to draw a comparison. That was incredibly thoughtless.”

“It’s okay.” Maybe Logan should have felt worse, but Veronica was gone. He felt like shit most of the time for a lot of reasons, and he was so *tired* of it. “Like I told you, our marriage was a bad idea from the start, and it was already over. I can’t change any of it. But hey, you can get back out there. Back on the horse.” He needed to take his own advice.

“Right.” Seth repeated, “Right,” murmuring almost to himself, “I need to conquer my fear.”

Man, Seth really *was* wound tight. “It’ll be like riding a bike.”

“Seeing Brandon yesterday, I was terrified.” He shook his head, exhaling a little huff of air and half-smiling. “I’m sure you could tell.”

“I might have picked up on it.”

Seth shifted to face Logan, his right leg bent on the leather couch, his eyes bright and earnest. “But you helped me. Having you there… None of this is real, but Brandon doesn’t need to know that. Seeing him, it feels like I crossed a raging river, and I’m finally on the other side. You know what I mean? If I run into Brandon and Peter again, I can just smile and wish them well, and that's that. I'm over the hurdle. I can't tell you how liberating that feels. Thank you."

Satisfaction flowed through Logan. He was so fucking useless most of the time, and being needed warmed his veins even more than the scotch. "You're welcome." He shrugged. "I like helping you," he said without thinking. It was the truth, and as Seth beamed at him, his blue eyes so damn sincere, an idea popped into Logan's head.

A crazy fucking idea.

He might be no good to anyone most of the time, but getting off? That he could help with. Maybe it was the beer and scotch—although he'd barely had three fingers—or Seth talking about sex, but the idea rocked through him with a bolt of adrenaline.

Maybe Seth would turn him down flat, but... Shit. Logan really, *really* wanted to help make this all better. Wanted Seth to look at him again like he was special and *good.*

Before he could lose his nerve, he blurted, "Here's another deal for you. I'll help you get off. Get over your hang-up about it."

Seth's eyes widened, and he stared, his mouth opening and closing. "You'll... What did you say?"

Logan shrugged even though excitement pinballed through him. Maybe this was stupid, like most of his ideas, but his dick was coming alive at the thought. "We could mess around. But if you don't want to—"

"I didn't say that." Seth licked his lips, leaning closer over the space between them on the couch. His eyes were bright, the earnestness replaced by clear hunger. "But you're straight. Aren't you?"

"So? Doesn't mean I don't want to just get off sometimes. Men are less complicated. We know what we want. Don't have to worry about feelings and all that shit. It's easier."

Seth stared at him. Holding up a hand, he squeezed his eyes shut, then opened them. "You're telling me... Are you saying that you have relations with other men?"

"You mean sex? Sure, once in a while. In the Marines, you'd help a buddy out. Or in the bunkhouse at the rail yard sometimes. Sometimes do it quick in a bathroom. If someone gives me a look and offers to suck my dick, I'm not gonna say no."

"I..." Seth was staring at him like he had two heads. "I never would have guessed. Huh. *Huh.*" He was quiet a moment, biting his lip. "Have you ever done it? Been the one doing the...?" He waved his hand.

"The sucking?" At Seth's red-faced nod, Logan answered, "A few times when I was in Iraq. Fair's fair. But it's mostly hand jobs, or I'll fuck someone's ass if they want it. Like I said, it's just about getting off." He shrugged. "Not that there's anything wrong with sucking cock. I don't look down on you or anything."

Seth's eyebrows rose. "Ah. Good to know. So… Have you ever been…on the bottom?"

"No. That would be way too… No. Not into it." He could admit he'd never tried, and that the idea of being fucked was way too…much. *Too gay*, although he didn't say that out loud. There wasn't anything wrong with it. It just wasn't for him.

And maybe he'd thought about it sometimes, and he'd been curious once or twice, but hell no. Letting a guy do that would be… Hell, he didn't know what, but it was better to keep it simple with men.

"What about kissing?"

He screwed up his face. "No. That's too…" He took another gulp of scotch, warmth spreading through him. "I'm probably sayin' this shit all wrong. With guys it's just quick and easy."

"But you're not gay."

"Exactly." Now Seth was getting it.

"Or bi?"

Logan scoffed. "Isn't that just being wishy-washy or pretentious?"

"No." Seth's brows drew together, and he was quiet a few moments. "You know, it's perfectly valid to be attracted to both men and women. Bisexuality is real." He clasped Logan's shoulder, a current of heat sparking down all the way down to Logan's fingertips. "It really is okay."

"Sure. Nothin' wrong with it. That's just not me. I'm straight. I've been with women since I was fifteen. I love fucking them. The stuff with guys is different. Separate."

"Huh. I read something about this. Men who have sex with men, but who don't necessarily identify as gay or bi or somewhere on the LGBTQ-plus spectrum."

"Spectrum?" Logan echoed. He had no clue what Seth was talking about. He was straight, and sometimes he got off with dudes. He didn't need to get all fancy or hippie or whatever about it.

Seth's hand was still gripping Logan's shoulder, and he looked down at it like he wasn't sure how it had gotten there. He didn't move it, though, and Logan didn't complain. The grasp was warm and strong. Logan's dick sure liked it, and he rubbed the heel of his hand over himself through his jeans without thinking.

Seth's gaze zeroed in on Logan's crotch, his Adam's apple bobbing. "Are you…? Do you want to…?"

"Yeah." It was the first time in months he'd been turned on, and he realized maybe it wasn't so strange for Seth to have gone more than a year. Maybe he'd felt as dead inside as Logan. But now, Logan's blood was pumping, and he wanted release.

Even more than that, he wanted to help Seth.

Seth said, "I think this is the most surreal conversation I've ever had. Wouldn't it be strange? For us to…"

"Why? It's just getting off. Doesn't mean anything. We're guys. Sometimes I just need to bust a nut. Don't you?"

"I…" Seth licked his lips, staring between Logan's face and his crotch. "You know what? Yes. I usually analyze everything to death. Analysis paralysis," he muttered. Then, louder: "Yes. Sometimes I need to get off. Damn it."

"Ohh. Watch your language," Logan teased. His heart raced, lust building in his veins. He could see it on Seth's face, that determination and growing confidence, and it turned him on big time.

With a grin, Seth shoved at the coffee table so there was enough room for him to drop to his knees in front of Logan. Seth was breathing shallowly as he muttered, almost to himself, "I'm going to do this. I want to do this. There's nothing wrong with this." His gaze was locked on Logan's crotch.

Logan unzipped his jeans and shoved them down with his skivvies, yanking his left foot free so he could spread his legs wide. He gave himself a few tugs as Seth watched like a starving man.

"Go to town," Logan said.

Seth started without touching Logan's dick at all, running his palms up and down Logan's hairy thighs and dipping his head to nose around his belly. His breath was hot, but sometimes he blew it colder over the tip of Logan's cock, sending shivers through him. Seth's hands weren't as callused as some men's, but they were big and definitely rougher than a woman's. Not better or worse, just different.

When he drank alcohol, it usually took a while for Logan to get fully hard, but shit, Seth knew what he was doing for a guy with hang-ups. Foreplay was something Logan identified with women. In his experience, most of them liked to take their time. There was no foreplay with men in a bathroom stall or getting off at the bunkhouse.

But hell, as Seth ducked farther and licked at his taint, Logan sure as shit wasn't going to complain. Seth circled his blunt nails over Logan's thighs, and goosebumps spread. Logan was rock hard. Damn, it really had been too long.

When Seth finally sucked him into his mouth, Logan moaned loudly. It was so tight and wet, and Seth was doing something with his tongue behind the head that had Logan practically hitting the ceiling. "Fuck, you're good at this," he muttered.

Seth pulled off with a spit-soaked *pop* and smiled up at him, his hands spread wide above Logan's knees, thumbs stroking the soft flesh of his inner thighs. He wasn't just smiling—sunshine was shooting out of him like laser beams, and Logan had to smile back. Seth ducked his head again and sucked him deep.

Even though he'd already said way more than he usually would to another guy—grunts and nods were all it took most of the time—Logan found himself wanting to see that smile again. Seth was a good man. Maybe he could be an actual friend, and clearly he needed the ego boost. Plus, he sucked cock like a *champ*.

As Seth licked up and down his shaft, spit dripping into Logan's pubes, Logan said, "You're fuckin' born for this." He could feel Seth smile around him before sucking hard, hollowing his cheeks.

Logan jerked up his hips involuntarily, and Seth briefly choked before he pressed harder with his hands, fingers digging into Logan's hips.

Logan grunted. "Sorry."

Apparently all was forgiven since Seth was still sucking him like there was no tomorrow. Logan moaned, all the tension draining out of him. The bad tension, anyway. The good kind had pleasure sparking through him.

He could see their reflection in the dark, wide windows, and it gave him a jolt to see himself like that—legs spread and breathing hard with Seth sucking him off. Watching the reflection, he ran his hand over Seth's head, caressing his thick hair. Seth seemed to like it, making happy little noises.

Shit, Logan *loved* that. He wanted to make Seth happy. He mumbled, "Gonna make me come so hard. You want it?" Some guys didn't like swallowing—not that Logan blamed them. But he had a feeling about Seth, and sure enough, Seth gazed up at him, eyes eager as he gave a little nod, his mouth still stuffed with Logan's dick.

The way his lips stretched wide around Logan's meat, his blue eyes looking like he was begging for it, had Logan's belly tensing, his balls tight. "Yeah, you want my cum, don't you?" Not thinking, he reached out and traced a finger around Seth's wet, swollen lips. "Gonna swallow it all?"

Seth reached down to massage Logan's balls, their eyes locked, his nostrils flaring as he slurped harder. The tight tingling in Logan's nuts surged into an orgasm, and he shot down Seth's eager throat with a groan, fingers tangling in his thick hair.

"Fuck yeah," he mumbled.

Seth pulled off Logan's twitching cock, gasping, his chest heaving. White semen dribbled out of his mouth, and Logan impulsively swiped at it with his finger and fed it to him. Eyes closing, Seth sucked his index finger the way he had his cock. The sight had Logan pulsing again, a final few drops escaping his softening dick.

Seth's cock was anything but soft, tenting his dress pants. Logan leaned forward and urged him closer, tugging Seth up fully on his knees. "Come on, get it out."

Breathing hard, Seth blinked at him, shoving down the gray pants and his boxers until his cock sprang free. It was cut and thick, straining, almost purple and leaking. Logan wrapped his palm around it and stroked, spreading the liquid from the tip.

Balancing with a hand on Logan's thigh, Seth moaned low in his throat and curled forward against him. Fiery, wet breath tickled Logan's neck under Seth's open mouth. In his left hand, Seth's dick was an iron rod, hot and ready to blow.

Seth whimpered. "Oh. *Oh*, I…"

"What does it take to get you to swear?" Shit, Logan wanted to find out. He wanted Seth to truly let go—wanted to help him get there. Seth was good. He deserved it. "You're close, aren't you?"

After a few more strokes, Seth's fingers dug into Logan's thigh so hard they'd leave bruises, and with a cry, he came. It whipped through him like a gunshot, his body rigid as he spurted over Logan's hand. It was warm and sticky, dripping on Logan's knuckles.

Logan let go of him and relaxed back, arms at his sides. Seth followed, slumping against him, his face pressed to the side of Logan's neck. Their harsh breathing and the drumming of Logan's heart filled his ears.

He blinked at the muted TV, where the post-game guys were apparently talking about passing stats according to the graphic on the screen. Logan waited for Seth to move, even though he liked the warm weight of him.

Logan was about to run a hand through Seth's hair, but he stopped himself. This wasn't how it went with guys. *It's just getting off. Doing us both a favor. A bonus to our deal.* Logan was about to nudge him when Seth sat back on his heels, breathing heavily, his face flushed. He smiled again, that grin full of sunshine and puppies or some shit.

Logan had no clue what to say, but then he was biting back a moan as Seth dropped his head and sucked Logan's hand clean, his tongue dipping into the V between fingers, lapping up his own jizz.

It probably should have been gross, but a fresh coil of desire unleashed in Logan's gut. He was reaching out again to touch Seth's head, the urge to sink his fingers into that soft, thick hair too much to resist, when Seth pushed to his feet, yanking up his slacks.

"You're right. I needed that. Thank you." Seth looked like he wanted to say more, but after a few seconds he grabbed their glasses off the table. "Another round?"

Logan nodded, watching him disappear toward the kitchen. For a few moments, he could only sit there with his legs spread and his dick out, Seth's spit drying on it. He ordered himself to move and managed to get his foot back through the leg hole in his underwear and jeans before tugging them up and zipping.

Seth whistled softly as he came back in. "Do you think they'll trade Williams?" He held out Logan's glass.

Logan took it. "Huh?" As Seth got settled on the far end of the couch, stretching his long legs out to cross his ankles on the chaise, Logan tried to remember a single thing about Williams and the Patriots. "Dunno." It was the truth, at least.

"I don't think they have the depth without him. It might give the team a short-term gain, but in the long run? Bad move." He un-muted the TV, and the talking heads filled the surround sound.

"Yeah." Logan nodded and repeated, "Yeah."

What the fuck is my problem? Snap out of it.

Seth seemed fine, engrossed in the football talk on the TV while Logan's heart thumped. He felt like he'd been riding roller coasters, his stomach and head all swoopy. All he could think was:

That was one hell of a blow job.

Chapter Ten

LOGAN WAS RIGHT—CASUAL sex was *fantastic*.

As he showered the next morning, Seth found himself grinning. He was positively giddy, thinking about Logan filling his mouth—salty and *male* and powerful.

He tugged at his hard cock, tempted to go downstairs and wake Logan by sucking him again. Rubbing against him and feeling his body, kissing him—

Seth squeezed his shaft painfully. He needed to stay in control. Because, fine, perhaps he hadn't quite gotten the hang of the *casual* aspect yet of the sex they'd had. It had been incredible to taste Logan, to be filled with him, and Logan had clearly enjoyed it, shooting down Seth's throat in long, ropy spurts.

But, *oh*, to then feel that callused hand around his…his *cock*, had made Seth tremble. Embarrassed, he laughed at himself, reaching for the shampoo. Even after all the years of sex with Brandon, he still hesitated to even think of explicit words.

It was ludicrous that he could perform all the acts but then blush to think of his penis as his *cock*. He took hold of it again, stroking, a shudder running through him as he remembered the dirty things Logan had said.

Seth and Brandon had never talked much during sex. Over the years they'd settled into a routine, and it had been good. Seth had always loved going down on Brandon. But now, a new world of possibilities was opening. He inhaled deeply, the steamy air and hot water loosening his muscles. All the things he and Logan could do…

This is just casual, though.

Right. It was only "getting off," as Logan had put it. Seth let go of himself and rinsed the shampoo from his hair. He couldn't get carried away. But how he'd ached to kiss Logan, to feel that stubble against his face and breathe him in. It would have been crossing a line, since Logan said he only kissed women. He'd been clear in his boundaries.

It had taken all of Seth's will power to peel himself off Logan and stand, to act normal and offer him another drink. He'd longed for Logan to take him in his strong arms and just hold him in the afterglow, but that was clearly beyond the parameters of their arrangement.

Seth's knees had been shaking so much he was surprised he'd been able to walk to the kitchen without tripping. He'd splashed scotch over the new gray quartz counter and had stood there deep breathing for a long minute before going back into the great room and feigning casualness with football talk.

He and Logan had a deal, and Seth would hold up his end. He still couldn't believe Logan had sex with men even though he said he was straight. It certainly wasn't Seth's place to label anyone else's sexuality, but he wondered what it would be like if they didn't live in a society teeming with toxic masculinity. Growing up, any boys who didn't fit the traditional mold were deemed lesser and called the F-word.

What was the incentive for a man like Logan to acknowledge bisexuality? Growing up in a working-class family in the Albany suburbs, joining the Marines out of high school, then working most of his adult life on the railway… Likely not the most positive, open-minded environments.

Seth laughed harshly, closing his eyes as he stood under the hot water. Of course he knew what that was like. He'd grown up trying so hard not to be different.

But he'd never been attracted to women, and it had proved impossible to compartmentalize his attraction for men, or his love and affection for them. Logan apparently only felt those kinds of tender feelings for women, and who was Seth to question that?

Logan did say he'd topped men occasionally. *What would it be like?* Seth shuddered, boldly touching himself, trying to push aside the automatic guilt that flared. Was it really less of a sin to have sex when you were in love? Why shouldn't he be able to fantasize?

Taking a deep breath, he let his mind go, letting the explicit words flow, along with matching images.

What would it be like to have his cock in my ass? He's nice and thick. He'd stretch me open, pound into me, fuck me so good—the way I need it.

Seth's breath caught as he jerked himself hard, already splattering the gray granite tiles white as he imagined Logan coming inside him, whispering deliciously filthy things in his ear.

As the guilt threatened to return, he shoved it away. He murmured, "Why shouldn't I feel good? Why shouldn't I enjoy sex? I don't have to be in love to get off. Why would God have made orgasms if we weren't supposed to use them? Have them. Whatever."

He laughed derisively and shut off the water. "I really do talk to myself too much."

On the fuzzy bathmat, he rubbed his head with a towel. It was fortunate that he'd masturbated and taken the edge off. He needed to keep his cool around Logan and remember that the sex was only about physical pleasure. Logan did those things with strangers and didn't have any feelings involved.

That's what it was supposed to be.

Yes, Seth was going to conquer his fear and stop making sex such a big deal. He was on the other side of the river. Maybe he should install Grindr on his phone and hook up with some random guy.

But he shuddered unpleasantly at the thought, reaching for his bathrobe and tying the belt tightly around his waist. Although he'd only known Logan less than a week, he trusted him—unlike the unknown men he might meet online.

Taking that bold step and kneeling between Logan's legs to suck him had been terrifying—and exhilarating since Logan had made him feel safe.

Just as he had standing on the street in Saratoga Springs, big and strong at Seth's side, helping him face Brandon and the others. Of course Logan was only being kind—only holding up his end of their deal for a fake relationship—yet his support had felt genuine.

Maybe it was his friendship with Jenna that allowed Seth to trust her brother so quickly. Yes, they had an arrangement, but that didn't mean they couldn't be genuine friends. Seth had seen Logan vulnerable and shaking in the garage when he'd exerted himself too much, and he'd shown Logan his own vulnerability.

You can only be friends. You're not allowed to want more.

He wiped condensation from the mirror and picked up his electric razor, staring at his reflection. He looked the same as he did every morning, and he laughed at himself softly. Had he expected to look different? He and Logan had shared orgasms, but that was all.

Logan was sleeping on the couch as he had every other night since he'd moved in. *Temporarily* moved in. Nothing had changed between them, no matter how much Seth had wanted to bring him up to bed and sleep naked together, touch him from head to toe, rub against his hairy body and muscles. Kiss him for hours.

They had a deal, and *that* wasn't part of it. Seth wasn't allowed to fall for Logan. This was only pretend. He nodded to his reflection.

No ifs, ands, or buts.

He dressed, his pants enjoyably warm from the trouser press in the corner of his room. He chose a dark tie with a subtle purple diamond pattern and surveyed himself in the closet-door mirror.

After fiddling with his hair, he realized he was acting like he was going on a date or something, not to the office. Yes, Logan was downstairs. No, Seth didn't have to impress him with the sharpness of the crease in his pants.

The coffee maker had started brewing automatically, and Seth inhaled gratefully as he went downstairs and rounded the corner of the sitting room. He stumbled to a halt, blinking at Logan standing there by the fridge. Shirtless. Thank goodness he was wearing track pants, although now that Seth knew what his cock looked—and tasted like—he could imagine it so easily…

"Morning!" Seth said too cheerily and loudly.

Logan leaned a hip against the counter. "Morning." A mug in one hand, he smiled tightly. "Hope it's okay that I helped myself."

"Of course! Make yourself completely at home." Seth stood there across the island, trying to think of something else to say. He came up completely blank. Logan looked back at him, and an awkward silence built until Logan turned away.

He poured another mug of coffee and held it out, and Seth forced his feet to move. "Thanks!" His tone was still too cheery. Their fingers brushed, and the instinct to kiss Logan swelled. *Uh, no. He's not your boyfriend. No sleepy-sweet morning kisses.* Seth drank a mouthful of coffee even though it was too hot.

Stop looking at his chest.

Logan laughed uneasily and crossed his arms. "Scars are ugly, I know."

"Huh?" Seth blinked up at him, then back at his chest. He realized there were marks snaking through the dark hair on Logan's sternum. He'd been too distracted by the reddish discs of Logan's tight nipples to even notice. "Oh! No, not ugly at all. I didn't notice them."

He forced his gaze away, wincing at his false tone. He really hadn't noticed, but Logan would think he was lying, not ogling his nipples. It was still dark outside, and in the window's reflection over the kitchen sink, he could see Logan's broad back, which wasn't any less distracting.

Seth asked, "What are you up to today?"

Logan nodded toward the sink. "I'll put up the backsplash tiles and grout it all."

"Oh! Right." Seth had chosen the pale blue glass tiles so long ago he'd almost forgotten about them. "Hope I still like them."

"It'll look good." Logan scratched his chest, the sound of his nails on his hairy flesh drawing Seth's attention despite himself. His pecs were wonderfully furry. Not too much, not too little. Just right.

You're not Goldilocks. Stop it.

"Great! Thanks. Did you have breakfast? There are eggs in the fridge. Please help yourself."

"Cool. Um, thanks." Logan turned and opened the fridge, poking around the shelves.

Seth went to the pantry and blindly reached for something. *Casual. Be casual.* He blinked at what he was holding—baking soda. Quickly putting it back, he picked up a box of gingersnaps and read the nutritional info. From the corner of his eye, he could see Logan leaning against the island again, the fridge door closing with a soft *thwack*.

After a moment, Seth could sense Logan's gaze on him. His neck went hot, and he imagined he could feel Logan's eyes roaming over his body.

Which was ridiculous! So Seth glanced over, telling himself Logan would definitely not be looking at him.

But he *was*.

And when their eyes met, they both startled and turned away, Logan returning to the fridge as Seth came out of the pantry and grabbed his coffee and gulped.

Seth cleared his throat. Casual. This wasn't a big deal. Logan bent over the crisper drawer, the track pants stretching over his rear. Seth's balls tightened, desire coiling deep in his belly as he imagined pushing inside Logan's body.

"Okay, I'd better get on the road. Have a great day!" Seth ran for it. He could buy breakfast. And lunch.

"Hey, are we cool?" Logan asked as he turned from the fridge.

Seth stopped and faced him. "Hmm?" His heart drummed. "Uh-huh. Great. Thanks again for helping me…get over the hump. So to speak."

Logan smirked. "Anytime." He sipped his coffee. "Well… Have a good day at work."

"Yes! I will. Thanks. Uh, you too!" Seth gave a wave because he was a complete dork. He escaped to jam on his boots, throw on his coat, and slip his way to the driveway through the fresh snow. He turned on the SUV's engine in the garage and waited a minute while it warmed.

The guy who mowed his grass also came in winter to plow the long driveway, and it was freshly cleared. Seth threw down salt on the pathway so Logan wouldn't slip and got on the road, his pulse racing for a good few miles.

A peppy Kelly Clarkson Christmas song played on the radio, and for once, Seth didn't turn the channel. Instead, he upped the volume with the button on the steering wheel, pressing with his thumb.

His mind wandered to Logan—and masturbating in the shower. A thrill shot through him at the memory of the stretch of his lips around Logan's shaft, and then bringing himself off this morning.

"It's okay," he said aloud, interrupting Kelly. "I had casual sex, and this morning I…*jerked off*, and it's all okay. I'm allowed. There's nothing wrong with it."

The plows and salters had been out, and the drive into work was smooth. Especially since Seth spent it grinning to himself, thinking about seeing Logan again that night. Wondering if they'd get off again.

"Casual sex is awesome." He repeated his new mantra, tapping the wheel as another pop holiday song came on.

He was still grinning when he pushed open the glass door to the office. Becky gasped excitedly when she saw him, practically bouncing in her chair behind reception, her red hair swirling in waves.

She exclaimed, "Seth Marston, you sly devil! It's always the quiet ones."

Seth's grin froze as he jolted to a stop. Matt had said he'd contain the rumors at work, but it was Tuesday, and apparently the containment could only last so long. "Uh…"

She crooked her finger and beckoned him closer to her desk. "Don't worry, I haven't told anyone."

Seth resisted the urge to snort in derision. "Thanks." If everyone didn't already know about his fake engagement, they would soon.

Becky whispered, "Strong work bagging Jenna's hot bro. I didn't even know he was gay!"

He's not, despite the fact that I sucked his cock last night and then he gave me a hand job. Just thinking the words sent a secret little shiver through him. "Uh, yeah, we just hit it off. Anyway, I should get to it. Have a great day!" He rushed away before Becky could launch into a real cross-examination.

Seth was normally in before Jenna, but he skidded to a stop as he rounded the corner of their pod. She sat at her desk, blotting at her pants above her knee with his Tide pen.

She glanced up, clearly exasperated. "Honestly, how does this baby manage to get spit up on my *leg*?"

"It's a talent." Seth laughed, and it came out too high. Looking at Jenna, strange guilt boiled up in him.

I had your brother in my mouth last night.

Her brows drew together. "Everything okay?"

"Uh-huh! Why wouldn't it be?" He yanked out his desk chair, the wheels knocking into his foot. He could still feel Jenna's curious gaze on him.

"Is Logan behaving himself?"

A strangled laugh brayed out as visions of Logan spread-legged—hard and leaking—danced through Seth's mind. "Uh-huh."

Jenna groaned. "God, don't tell me he's leaving his sweaty gym socks out or farting."

This time, Seth's laugh was genuine, and he looked over at Jenna, who was wincing. He lowered his voice. "I assure you he's being a model guest. No dirty socks or passing gas."

She laughed and whispered back, "Okay, good. To be fair, I haven't lived with him since he was a teenage boy, and you know how gross they can be. Not that you were."

"Of course not." He lifted his chin haughtily. "I've never even broken a sweat."

"You know, you're so neat and orderly I can almost believe that."

Matt's shaggy head appeared atop the partition. "What are we whispering about?" His eyebrows rose. "Caper?"

"Yes!" Jenna hissed. "Keep your voice down."

Matt leaned closer and murmured, "Don't worry. This is all under control."

"Easy for you to say!" Seth rolled his eyes. "But it should be fine. New furniture's coming today. We still have time to get everything in place."

Matt asked, "How's the boy toy?"

Heat washed through Seth like a tidal wave, and he jerked his eyes to the computer screen, the words jumbled and meaningless. "He's not my boy toy."

Matt huffed. "You'd better fake this better for Angela. I'm just saying. What are you going to make her for dinner?"

Dread joined the hot swirl of guilt and embarrassment. "I have no idea." Seth shook his head, his voice raising. "I have no idea!"

"Shh!" Jenna and Matt hissed in unison.

Matt winked. "I'll get Becky on the case and find out what Angela's favorite foods are. Don't worry, man. You got this." He pumped his fist and mouthed, "*Caper!*" before disappearing behind the partition.

Sighing, Seth hoped Matt's confidence wasn't grossly misplaced.

AS HE PULLED into the driveway, a fresh layer of snow crunching under the tires, Seth was momentarily puzzled by the warm glow of lights from inside the house and the silhouette of a man on the walkway leading to the front door.

His heart skipped as he blinked at Logan, who paused in his shoveling to give a wave. The garage door stood open, and Seth eased in and killed the engine.

The moon had emerged from behind clouds, and at the end of the driveway, Seth could see that the distant mailbox was crammed full, flyers poking out the end, the flap unable to close now. He should just empty it. He knew what was likely inside, and not looking wouldn't change a thing.

Yet he turned onto the walkway, breathing through the tightening in his gut and focusing on Logan—which sent a spiral of jittery excitement through him.

We had sex yesterday. Is it going to happen again today? Does he want me the way I want him?

Out loud, Seth said, "You don't have to shovel. Leave it for me."

Breath pluming in the cold air, Logan said, "Happy to do it."

Seth stopped a few feet away on the walkway. He cocked an eyebrow. "Really? *Happy?*"

Logan chuckled. "Believe it or not, I am. I like working. Feeling useful." In the yellow glow through the front window, his cheeks were ruddy.

"It's not too much exertion?" It had honestly been frightening when Logan had been unable to catch his breath that day in the garage.

This was clearly the wrong thing to say, since Logan scowled and muttered, "Nope."

"Okay. You should wear a hat. You'll catch a cold." *Great, act like his mother. That's really sexy.* But should he be attempting to be *sexy*? They were only friends. Barely that—still mostly strangers.

Although the little quirk of Logan's crooked smile was already becoming familiar, and Seth wanted to see it again and again. Wanted to see everything. Wanted to learn all the shapes and sounds of Logan.

Logan's laugh was throaty, and the sound sent lust spiking through Seth. Logan pulled his black woolen hat from his pocket and tugged it over his ears. "You're the boss."

Seth laughed, although unease prickled his skin. "Let me get the other shovel and help." He didn't want Logan to feel like they weren't equals.

"I just have the steps to finish." Logan squinted at the driveway. "Didn't think there was enough fresh to warrant shoveling all of that as well. But I can if you want."

"No, no. Like you said, there's not enough. The SUV gets through it no problem, and if there's too much, a guy comes to plow the drive."

Logan nodded, then bent to push a shovelful of light snow off the walk. "I'll be done in a minute. Why don't you check out the backsplash?"

"Oh! I almost forgot. Thank you." Seth climbed the few steps and stamped his boots before going inside. On the indoor mat, he tugged off his boots, carefully stepping onto the hardwood in his socks and trying to avoid the wet spots.

After hanging up his coat, he padded through the still-empty sitting room and into the kitchen, gasping softly. The pale blue subway tiles gleamed, brightening the space immeasurably and making the white cabinets really pop. It all looked so clean and crisp and inviting, and Seth was suddenly eager to cook. And not just prepackaged stir fries and bacon and eggs. This was a kitchen he wanted to spend time in.

Grinning, he admired it, running his hands over the shiny gray quartz counters. The rhythmic scrape of the shovel on the walkway outside was strangely soothing. Seth had been rattling around the half-finished house all alone for more than a year, and having Logan there helping and doing things for him made Seth feel…

It was silly, but it made him feel cared for. Comforted and peaceful, even though it was only part of their deal. It wasn't *real.* It was only temporary. Soon enough he'd be shoveling his own walkway and he'd be alone again.

His smile faded, his pleasure over the finished kitchen diminishing. Yes, he'd still make better use of it and cook for himself in the new year, but a hollow void cracked through the swell of comfort that had filled him.

"Enough of that," he muttered to himself. Logan was with him now, and he'd make the best of it.

Before long, he had chicken breasts cooked and pasta boiling, and he was grating an old hunk of Parmesan after cutting off the questionable bits. The sauce would have to be jarred, but it was a decent organic brand. He smiled to himself as he listened to Logan come inside the house and take off his winter gear.

"Something smells good," Logan said as he rounded the corner.

"The boiling water?" Seth joked.

"Yep, that must be it."

"The kitchen's so gorgeous I had to start cooking immediately, even though I'm not much of a chef. Thank you. I can't tell you how much I appreciate it."

Logan shrugged, but his smile was definitely pleased. "Glad you like it." He rubbed a hand over his cold-red face, the scruff rasping. The sound went straight to Seth's groin. Logan wore a sweatshirt over his jeans, and he pulled it over his head, his T-shirt riding up and exposing his belly and the dark hair that pointed down to what was under his waistband.

"Do you drink wine?" Seth asked Logan too loudly. "I have a nice Pinot. Well, I think it's nice. Hopefully."

"Sure. I'm not fussy."

Seth busied himself grabbing the bottle from the pantry. "I should get a proper wine rack. Instead of keeping the wine beside the Bran Flakes."

Logan filled the pantry door with his broad shoulders. "Should be easy enough to do. Where do you want it? I'll get the dimensions and ask Pop what he thinks. He was here today supervising." He stepped closer, peering around Seth at the corner of the pantry. "If he tells me what to do, I could probably build one pretty easily."

"Oh, you don't have to do that!"

Logan shrugged. "I want to."

They stood a foot apart, and Seth suddenly could barely breathe. When he did, he inhaled the faint fresh scent of Irish Spring soap. Then he was imagining Logan naked and wet in the shower, lathering himself, sudsy and slippery…

"Seth?"

The timer for the pasta beeped in the kitchen, and Seth plastered on a smile as Logan backed out of the pantry to let him by. Seth hurried to place the colander in the sink and dump the pasta into it.

He asked Logan, "Do you want to open the wine? I think the glasses are in that box in the corner. Still need to get all the cabinets sorted."

"Sure. And yeah, I figured you'd want to organize it yourself. I'm not the best at that shit. Not like Jenna. And you seem like you enjoy things…neat."

"That's a generous way to put it." Seth shook his head and stirred the bubbling sauce. "Hard to believe I've lived with this half-empty disarray for so long."

Soon they were in front of the TV, watching *Brooklyn Nine-Nine* and laughing. The pasta was hearty and tasty enough, and the red wine went down too easily for a weeknight. Seth clucked his tongue as he splashed a drop of sauce on his gray shirt.

"You don't usually change into sweats or whatever when you get home?" Logan asked from his end of the couch, the middle cushion between them.

"Oh, I usually do, yeah." He dabbed at the spot.

"Well, you don't have to do anything different because I'm here. It's your house."

"Right." He laughed softly. "I suppose I'm not used to having anyone here, so I'm in 'guest mode' or something."

"Well, make yourself at home," Logan joked.

After dinner, Seth did go upstairs and change into a tee and sweatpants, as well as thick, fuzzy socks since his feet were perpetually cold in winter. He also spritzed himself with a woodsy cologne he hadn't worn in ages and fussed with his short hair as if he were going on a date. In his own living room. With an almost-stranger he'd had his mouth on the day before.

Situation normal.

They watched a new Netflix show on home renovations that seemed well-timed, and Seth turned on the fireplace. It was cozy and weirdly comfortable to hang with Logan in near silence aside from the odd comments from both of them on paint and sofa choices.

Logan had changed into his sweatpants too and didn't wear a shirt. Which was perhaps slightly distracting, if Seth was being honest.

Around ten, Seth paused a new episode and said, "I guess I should get to bed."

"Right. How'd you sleep last night?"

"Uh, good! Good." The mention of last night had Seth on red alert, memories sparking fresh lust. He tried to watch Logan from the corner of his eye. Was Logan simply asking an innocent question? Sitting there shirtless and sprawled and sexier than he had any right to be?

Logan held a glass of water, and he toyed with it, his hand moving up and down, gathering condensation. "Yeah, I find getting off helps. With sleep."

"Uh-huh!" Seth all but squeaked.

"But if you want to go straight to bed—"

"No, I'm good. I mean, I can… We can… If you want…"

The rumble of Logan's laughter was warm. "C'mere."

Seth forced himself to move slowly instead of launching at Logan like an attacking predator. Their knees knocked as he settled himself, and before he could formulate a sentence, Logan was cupping him through the cotton with a strong hand, and Seth was almost instantly hard.

He lifted his hips so Logan could tug him free, and he concentrated on breathing and staring at the paused TV, their reflection moving over the image of a rundown bungalow.

The urge to turn his head and shove his tongue down Logan's throat positively burned, but he kept his lips pressed together tightly, his nostrils flaring as pleasure built.

"Doesn't have to be a big deal," Logan murmured, his voice gone gravelly. He rubbed at himself—at his *cock*—through his sweatpants as he stroked Seth, pausing to spit on his palm a few times.

That's probably how he does it in bathroom stalls, with just spit.

For some reason it excited Seth, the rough drag of Logan's callused hand and the dirtiness of using spit. The rawness of it. It was illicit somehow. Seth leaned into him, Logan's left arm flexing between them as he stroked Seth.

"Not awkward? Using your left hand?" Seth asked. The strokes were so measured and sure, so skillful.

"I'm left-handed."

"Oh!" Seth's breath caught, turning the sound into a long moan. "*Ohhh.*" It felt so good, and Seth was going to come soon, and he wanted Logan to feel as good as he did.

Taking a shaky breath, he spit into his right hand, licking it a few times before reaching toward the bulge in Logan's sweats. "Should I…?"

"Fuck yeah."

So there they sat, hands down each other's pants, knees and elbows bumping as they brought each other off. Their harsh inhalations and exhalations filled the air, heads leaning closer together as their movements became more frantic.

Seth wanted to devour Logan, inhale him and feel that rough stubble on his lips and face, taste tomato and garlic on his tongue and kiss through their orgasms.

But he didn't cross those last several inches. Logan didn't want that. He'd set his boundaries, and even though Seth had Logan's throbbing cock in his hand, the spongy, flushed steel in his grasp so alive and powerful, that was as far as he could touch.

Still, as Seth came, spurting over Logan's knobby knuckles, he imagined that kiss, closing his eyes and letting himself go, his head thrown back and spine arching.

Logan wasn't far behind, and his groan as Seth milked him was delicious. Pulling his sticky hand free, Seth wiped it on a stray napkin. They breathed hard, and Seth mumbled, "Thanks. That was…"

"Yeah."

"I… Thanks." Before he could stop himself, Seth nuzzled at Logan's cheek. Not kissing him, but almost…

Logan inhaled sharply, shuddering. Then he cleared his throat and sat up straight, breaking contact. "All part of the deal, right?"

It was like a splash of cold water, and Seth tucked himself into his sweatpants, nodding. "Right. Yes. Okay, good night!" He balled up the napkin in his fist and made a hasty retreat.

All part of the deal. Nothing more.

He repeated the words to himself like a mantra as he went to bed and stared at the ceiling far too long.

Chapter Eleven

"Shoot!" Seth tightened his arm around the cardboard box full of wine bottles, feeling it slip as he turned the key in the lock.

His front door sprang open, and he almost sprawled flat on his face. He would have if not for Logan's strong hands on his arms. Logan took the box, easing it onto the floor by the mat. "Close one. You almost cussed."

Seth laughed as he closed the door, the warmth of the house beckoning. Not to mention Logan. A pang of longing filled him—the urge to pull Logan into a hug, to kiss him hello the way he would a lover. A partner. He had to remind himself that this was all pretend.

Well, aside from the orgasms.

Those were very, very real. The night before, Seth and Logan had eaten Thai delivery in the great room while watching TV. After some time for digestion, Seth had blown Logan, on his knees between Logan's legs, glad of the thick throw rug.

Logan hadn't offered to do the same yet, and Seth hadn't asked. He was getting off powerfully just with the touch of Logan's rough hand, the hot puff of his breath on Seth's cheek, the press of their thighs and shoulders when they sat close. In those moments, Seth could almost forget that it was only a bargain between them.

"Table's here," Logan said.

"Oh, thank goodness!" There had been an unexplained delay, and Seth had devised a backup plan. "Glad we won't have to throw together an IKEA special."

"Me too. It looks great. Boss lady'll love it."

Today was the big day when Angela came to dinner, and Seth had taken a few of his banked personal hours to pick up the groceries and start cooking. His stomach tightened. "I can't believe Angela Barker is actually coming to my house for dinner."

It was time to stick to business and remember their deal and why they were doing this in the first place. It was time to be professional and keep his head about him.

"You'll do great. Jenna said that floppy-haired guy got the dirt on Angela's fave food?"

"Matt, yeah. His girlfriend is the office manager, and she knows every-thing. And Jenna looked up recipes that should fit the bill."

"Bet she gave you a very specific shopping list too." Logan's lips quirked into a smile.

Oh, how Seth wanted to kiss that mouth. Wanted to get completely naked with Logan and feel the whole press of his body, skin-to-skin from head-to-toe. He wanted to make Logan moan and sigh and be *happy*. Seth wanted to take that heaviness shrouded around him and make him smile all the time.

"Gee, how'd you know?" he joked, and Logan smiled wider.

And *fine*, maybe it was more than lust sparking in Seth. But he had to keep it in check, because affection and *feelings* weren't on the menu. Logan identified as straight, and he'd made his boundaries clear.

Even if he'd ended up caressing Seth's hair when Seth had gone down on him again, groaning before he'd reached out, as if he'd been giving in somehow. It didn't mean anything, and Seth needed to remember that this was all simply part of their deal.

He nodded to the wine and grocery bags as he yanked his feet free from his winter boots. "Pricey Bordeaux and rib-eye steaks. Guess I'd better figure out how that grill out back works."

"You ain't used it before?" a gruff voice asked, feet shuffling toward them in cheap slippers.

"Mr. Derwood!" Seth felt nervous and embarrassed that he'd just been thinking inappropriately about Logan. "I didn't realize you were here."

The man grunted. His shoulders were stooped and his face lined, belly large and fingers stained with tobacco. He wore track pants and a striped sweater. Seth had been shocked to learn he was only in his sixties. Bill said, "Got yer wine rack in."

"Oh! Thank you so much."

Logan added, "Hope it's okay. And I wasn't sure how you wanted to do the decorations and tree, so I won't be offended if you move stuff."

"I'm sure it's all wonderful. Thank you again."

The sitting room now held two wingback chairs by the window with a small table between them, a glass coffee table separating a new beige couch that had been in stock at one of the local stores. The area rug was a fluffy white, navy, and tan.

These items had been delivered the day before, and it was nice to have the space filled. Seth honestly wouldn't really use the room much, but the back of the couch served as a good separator between the front room and the kitchen.

A ceramic Christmas tree lit with golden lights now sat on the table between the chairs, a real pinecone and fir candle arrangement on the coffee table, red holly berries bright and cheerful. Seth had to touch the berries to see if they were real since the plastic was so convincing.

On the new dining table off to the right beside the kitchen, there was a similar holiday centerpiece. It suited the big rustic table, and Seth found himself smiling.

"The chairs really do fit well, don't you think?" he asked Logan, heat rippling through him as he remembered standing in front of the store window, Logan's hand on his rear and that sexy whisper…

"*Imagine I'm saying something really dirty.*"

Logan's father was right there, and Seth was officially out of control. He didn't even hear Logan's reply, but assumed it was an agreement. The wine rack had been built into one end of the island, a criss-cross of wood painted white that matched the cabinets perfectly.

"Wow," Seth breathed. "You built this?"

Logan shrugged. "Sure. Pop told me what to do. You've lost some storage space in the island, but with the cupboards and huge pantry, I don't think you'll miss it."

"This is perfect. Thank you so much." He turned to Logan's father. "Mr. Derwood, I'd like to pay you for your consultation."

"Sure. I'll stay for dinner and have a steak."

Seth froze. "Uh…" He glanced at Logan, who seemed equally at a loss for words. First there was Angela to impress, although maybe she'd appreciate the family aspect? But Seth and Logan also had to pretend to be a couple, and what would Logan's father say about *that*?

Bill laughed, a rough, rasping bark, his shoulders shaking. "Just messin' with ya. You don't want me around at your fancy dinner. Besides, I don't wanna watch my boy pretendin' to be a fairy."

Seth jolted. Wait, when had Bill discovered the plan? He stammered, "Oh, um—I… Well…" He looked to Logan, who shifted uneasily and jammed his hands in his pockets, his neck flushed red.

Logan mumbled, "I didn't think Jenna was telling you about that part."

Bill snorted. "Jenny didn't need to tell me. I'm not deaf. My ears are one of the few things not breakin' down. You're all not as clever as you think you are."

Seth had to chuckle ruefully. He certainly couldn't argue that point. A line of tension between his shoulder blades made his neck ache, and he rubbed at the nape, wishing he could disappear.

He supposed "fairy" wasn't the worst thing Bill could have called him. Logan was a wall of tension, and Seth needed to say something, but his tongue felt too thick.

"Look, you seem like a decent fella," Bill said. "Been real good to my Jenny. And Logan." He grunted. "None of my business what you get up to. Don't make sense to me, but…" He grunted again. "In my day, folks didn't…" He raised weathered hands and lowered them dismissively. "Look, you need to season that grill. Got oil?"

"Uh, yes." Seth nodded and hurried into the pantry, relieved at the abrupt change of topic. He imagined that in Bill Derwood's day, most "folks" stayed locked away in the closet. Still, at least the man hadn't said anything truly hateful. Hadn't called Seth an abomination.

He fetched his winter gear and headed toward the back of the house, carrying his boots so he didn't track snow and salt on the floors. He jolted to a stop as he entered the great room. The decorations in the sitting room were nothing compared to the veritable explosion of Christmas here.

"Goodness," Seth breathed.

Logan had strung colored lights and garlands across the back wall along the metal divider in the arched glass above the sliding doors and blinds. More candle/holly/fir displays sat on the side tables and coffee table, red bows neat and bright.

The *pièce de résistance* was a massive pine tree standing between the TV and black fireplace, strung with colored lights, garlands, and ornaments, dangling silver icicles making it positively shimmer. A lit silver-gold angel sat atop, and beneath, wrapped presents crowded.

Seth deeply inhaled the fresh, woodsy smell, gazing around in wonder. The room had never seemed so cozy and warm—so much like a *home*. And suddenly he was blinking back tears.

For so many years, he'd told himself Christmas wasn't for him. That he didn't deserve it somehow. Standing in front of the tree, surrounded by holiday glitter and color, he ached down to his bones for this home to truly be his and not only for show.

Yet it wasn't.

The charmingly clumsily wrapped presents were surely empty. Only window dressing for the life he was pretending was real for Angela's sake. It was *all* window dressing—the new furniture and decorations, and Logan himself. Come the new year, Logan would be gone, the decorations would come down, and Seth would be alone again.

"Is it not good?"

Seth hadn't heard Logan's approach, and he jumped, managing an awkward laugh, glad that he'd kept the tears from falling. Not meeting Logan's gaze, he forced a smile, looking all around the room. "It's fantastic!"

"Yeah? Jenna told me what to do, so…"

When Seth made himself look at Logan, Logan was watching him warily. Seth was able to smile genuinely this time. "It really is wonderful. Thank you."

"Okay. Cool." Logan carried his own boots, his father shuffling up behind him.

Bill sat heavily on the far end of the sofa and groaned as he bent to tug on his boots. Logan made a step toward him, but his father snapped, "I can do it!"

So Seth and Logan stood awkwardly by the sliding door, waiting. Seth said, "I'll shovel a path," and escaped outside. He'd left a spare shovel on the porch and went to work gladly.

Even if this was all for show, at least his house would be finished. His grill would even be seasoned! And at least he'd gotten over his hang-up about casual sex. Hadn't he? Even if he craved more with Logan, he wasn't going to get it, and that was simply the way it was.

Yes, in the new year, Seth would start dating. He'd install the apps and go out with a bunch of men, and maybe he'd eventually meet someone who wanted more with him. Something real. In the meantime, he could enjoy the holidays with Logan, couldn't he?

Well. After tonight's dinner and the weekend retreat tomorrow. After they convinced Angela they were madly in love. Piece of cake.

Fortunately, Mr. Derwood was a wealth of information on barbecuing, and he seasoned the grill and taught Seth how to use it, giving him cooking times and techniques. Seth took out his phone and tapped notes, his bare fingers icy. Logan finished shoveling the rest of the back deck, even though there wasn't really a need.

Time was marching on, and Logan drove his father home while Seth set the steaks marinating and prepped the creamy, cheesy scalloped potato ingredients. When Logan came home—came *back*—he mumbled an offer to vacuum and mop, keeping his gaze anywhere but meeting Seth's eyes.

Brandon had wanted a sound system wired through the main floor, and Seth had reluctantly agreed. He'd never actually used it, but after a while, he went to the stereo set back in a little alcove between the dining room and great room and turned on a Christmas channel on one of the streaming networks.

Judy Garland's rich, soulful voice filled the main floor. As Seth obsessed over the thickness of his potato slices and ensuring consistency, Logan fiddled with a fresh pad on the steam mop. It seemed very likely it was his first encounter with such a device, but he didn't ask for help.

It was all very…domestic, and Seth tried to pretend it didn't make his heart swell.

But this isn't real. Logan is your fake boyfriend. Remember that.

"This is a pretty song," Logan said. "A little sad, though."

"Oh, the mention of 'muddling through' in this version is nothing compared to the original lyrics. Most depressing Christmas song ever."

"Really?" Bent over the mop, Logan grumbled something under his breath.

Seth had to laugh. "Are you ready to declare defeat and ask me how to get the pad on?"

Logan glared, but there was no heat to it. He stood back with his hands on his hips. The black Henley that stretched over his chest and arms clung to his muscles. He looked like he belonged on the back of a motorcycle rather than steam mopping.

He's doing it for me.

Seth reminded himself that it was all part of their deal as he showed Logan how to release the mechanism and slip on a new pad. To distract himself from Logan's muscles, he rambled on.

"Yeah, the original version of 'Have Yourself a Merry Little Christmas' posits that this Christmas might be our last, so enjoy it while we can. Which isn't untrue, but it was less 'seize the day and grab happiness' and more a 'life sucks and then you die' vibe. They rewrote it, and then it was tweaked again for Sinatra's version. That's the most common one. All happiness and sweet nostalgia."

"Huh. That's interesting."

Seth stood and handed over the mop. "You're being kind. I used to love all things Christmas, and apparently still retain useless, boring facts in my brain."

"It's not boring." Logan bent to plug in the mop by the edge of the kitchen, dark denim accentuating his spectacular backside. "Maybe you can love Christmas again."

"Maybe." He went to the pantry and stopped short. "What's this?"

Logan looked embarrassed, scratching his head and fidgeting. He switched off the mop. "I know you bought a fancy dessert, but I thought the boss lady might like homemade. Might taste like crap. Probably does since I made it."

Seth stared at the dark cake sitting on a stand under a glass dome. It looked like chocolate, and sure, it was a little lopsided, but that only made it more charming. "I… It's perfect. Thank you. I didn't know you could bake."

Logan scoffed. "I can't."

"Clearly untrue since I'm looking at the fruits of your labor."

"It's an easy recipe." He shrugged, toying with the mop handle, running his rough hands over the molded plastic.

Seth's groin tightened. He wanted those hands on his body. *Stop thinking about sex!*

"It was our mom's favorite. We always had it for Christmas. She said pie was for Thanksgiving, and cake was for Christmas, but not that gross fruitcake. She said chocolate was way better. I used to help her with it when I was a kid."

Guilt for his inappropriate thoughts flared as Seth watched Logan smile, a sad little lilt of his lips, his eyes distant, looking lost in a memory. Seth said, "I'm sure it's delicious."

"Yeah. She'd always give me one of the beaters to lick while she kept the other. We'd get chocolate on our noses and chins trying to get it all."

Stop thinking about Logan licking something else! This is an innocent story! Seth cleared his throat. "I can't wait to try it. Thank you." There was a battered metal box sitting beside the cake stand, which had to be Jenna's. Seth stepped forward and picked it up, opening it to find lined index cards inside separated by tabs in neat block letters reading: *Salads, Appetizers, Mains, Sides, Cookies & Bars, Various Desserts*, and *Cakes!*

"Cake was her favorite," Logan said from the door of the pantry.

Smiling at the exclamation mark, Seth thumbed through the cards. The recipes were written in neat, looping cursive, and some were stained with faded remnants of tomato sauce or drops of oil. He knew which cake recipe Logan had made when he came to it, the ink faded in places and chocolate stains abundant, the corners ragged from use.

Seth reverently held the recipe and imagined Logan bent over a mixing bowl creaming butter and sugar. For an insane moment, he thought he might burst into tears, and he didn't really know why.

"Uh, sour cream is the secret ingredient," Logan said.

"Right!" Seth replied too brightly. "It sounds delicious!" He scanned the ingredients. "My mom used applesauce in just about everything she baked." His throat was too thick again. "Still does, I'm sure." He hadn't let himself even glance at the mailbox when he'd come home, though the flyers were probably littering the snowy ground now.

Seth carefully returned the recipe card to the *Cake!* section. He ran his fingers over the metal box, which was a dull silver with a faded, mishapen daisy painted on the side.

"Made it in shop class in ninth grade," Logan said sheepishly.

"It's lovely. Truly."

He shrugged. "Mom stored the recipes she called 'keepers' in it. Her frosting's the best. Oh, here." He disappeared, the fridge door opening before he returned with a small bowl, which he thrust out. "There was extra. Try it."

Seth stared at the bowl of chocolate frosting, swirled ridges hardening from the fridge. "Should I just…?" He lifted a finger.

"I can get you a spoon if you really want," Logan said dubiously.

Laughing, Seth scooped up a finger-full and sucked it into his mouth. He closed his eyes and moaned. "Oh my goodness. That is incredible." He licked his finger, opening his eyes.

Logan watched him with a hooded gaze, his voice gravelly as he said, "Yeah?"

"Um…" What would Logan do if Seth kissed him right now?

"You've got…" Logan motioned at Seth's mouth, and Seth licked the side of his lips, his groin tightening. Then he dipped his finger in the bowl again and sucked it clean, his eyes locked with Logan's, their breathing harsh in the quiet of the pantry, the air thickening as they leaned closer—

Beep-beep-beep!

They sprang apart, and Logan barely kept hold of the bowl. He backed out, and Seth followed to jab at the timer on the counter. "First part of the potatoes is done!" Seth exclaimed too loudly. "Better get back to work. Showtime's in a couple hours." He had to keep his wits about him.

"Right. You worried about it?" Logan asked as he returned to the mop, the bowl of leftover frosting back in the fridge.

Seth certainly had been earlier, and now it rushed back. He tried to shrug it off. "A little, I guess. It's fine. I should get moving so I can change before Angela and Dale get here." She'd invited her assistant along to make it a foursome for dinner, which made sense.

"Oh, shit. What am I supposed to wear?" The mop was hissing again, and Logan peered down at it suspiciously.

"Just a dress shirt and slacks? Maybe a tie?" Seth asked hopefully.

"Uh…" Logan experimentally pushed the mop, seeming pleased when the wet pad slid across the floor. "I have a set of nice clothes I wear to job interviews somewhere. Haven't needed to dress up, so I probably shoved them in one of my bags. I put all my stuff in your room, by the way. Pillow and blanket too. Do you have an iron?"

The idea of not having an iron was like not having a refrigerator, but Seth only nodded. "I do. And a trouser press. I'll show you after we finish here."

Soon they had Logan's slacks pressing, and Seth ran the iron over the cheap white dress shirt. He wished Logan could wear one of his, but his shoulders were too broad. Logan said, "Got it!" as he extricated a crumpled tie from a duffel bag.

"Er… Would you like to borrow one of mine?" *Please borrow one of mine.*

Logan laughed. "Sure. Boss lady has expensive taste. In the closet?"

"Yes, there's a rack."

A low whistle sounded. "Is there ever. You have a shit-ton of ties."

"I suppose I do. Here, let me see. Put this on."

The dark green tie had silver highlights, and it complemented Logan's hazel-y eyes. As Logan fiddled with the knot, Seth found himself reaching up and gently knocking Logan's hands away. He fixed the knot and straightened Logan's collar, Logan's breath puffing across Seth's face.

"There," Seth said, his voice hitching. He cleared his throat. "Suits you."

"I'll try not to spill on it. And don't worry—it's going to be fine." Logan squeezed Seth's shoulder, sending warmth spiraling through him. "We can fake it."

The warmth fled, and Seth backed away, nodding. He bumped into the wall. "Yep! I'll go check on the potatoes."

He escaped to the kitchen, all beautiful and gleaming now thanks to Logan, and tried to focus on the meal. Yes, it was time to be professional. This was for his career, and Logan was right.

We can fake it.

Chapter Twelve

"IT IS SUCH a treat to be in a real-live *home*." Angela tinkled with jewelry as she walked, her sparkly earrings Christmas wreaths this time with diamonds and rubies and emeralds—or really shiny fakes, but Logan figured they were the real deal.

She'd also changed from her high-heeled boots into a pair of red-soled stilettos that tapped the wood floors with her confident strides through Seth's sitting room and into the open kitchen.

Fiddling with his tie, Logan stared at the shoes, trying to remember what they were called. When he looked up, he realized Angela had noticed. Laughing awkwardly, he said, "Uh, nice shoes. Are they French or something?"

"You have an eye for fashion, huh?" Angela beamed. "The gays often do! They're Loubou-*tin*."

Dale cleared his throat, looking like he wanted to say something, but after a second, he just smiled without teeth. Since Seth was by the kitchen island looking like a deer in the headlights, apparently already freaking out having the boss lady in his house, Logan needed to say something.

So because he was a moron, he said, "My wife wanted a pair of those. She saw them on TV or something."

Angela's shiny red lips formed an O before she tilted her head sympathetically. "I understand she passed."

He choked down his irritation at the wording and nodded. "Uh, anyway."

Seth asked too loudly, "Can I get you both a drink?"

"I'll have a G and T," Dale said—whatever that was. He'd arrived wearing a dark suit but had left the jacket of it hanging with his coat.

Angela was still fixed on Logan. "I think it's remarkable that you've been able to find happiness again. And with a man! Love is love."

He nodded, not looking at Seth. Not thinking about how much happier he really had been the past week or so. "Thanks." He thought of Veronica again, guilt bubbling up.

Seth toured Angela and Dale around, and Logan was pleased that they complimented the holiday decorations. He had to say that the tree looked damn good, tall and glittery with colorful lights and balls and everything. It made the great room really cozy, especially with the gas fire burning. He'd debated between a star and angel on top, and decided Seth was an angel type of guy.

Once Angela and Dale had their cocktails, complete with fancy stir sticks, Seth put out trays of little appetizers on the great room's coffee table, and they sat there talking about BRK and Angela's kids and cheerleading. Angela was like one of those old toys that you wound up, and Logan was more than happy to nod and smile and let her yammer on. Seth and Dale seemed to be too.

After finishing a beer that Seth had poured into a glass for him, Logan shrugged into his coat to go fire up the grill, more than happy to escape the small talk. Angela had informed them the driver was arriving at nine since it was a "school night," and Logan figured the guy would be right on time. He had to make sure dinner wasn't late, and even though Pop had taught Seth the basics, he'd asked Logan to handle the barbecue.

"So you're the manly meat griller?" Angela asked with a weird wink.

"Yep." Logan had decided to just agree with everything she said.

She took a bite of a cracker with cheese. "Do you find the bisexual men are usually like that?"

At the sliding door, Logan shoved his feet into his boots. "Sure!" He escaped outside and turned on the gas, hoping the snowflakes drifting down wouldn't get any thicker. He probably should have grabbed his gloves, his fingers going numb, the freezing air harsh.

His lungs hitched, and he fought back a flare of panic before exhaling in a plume of frost. He could still breathe. Everything was fine. It was all in his asshole head.

Bisexual.

Logan poured more oil, brushing it onto the grill. It was fine that Angela had assumed it about him. Shouldn't bother him if she thought that. It wasn't him—he'd always been straight. But it was fine.

The oil sizzled on the metal, and he poured more, sloshing too much and getting it over his freezing hand. Snowflakes caught on the oil and melted.

Sure, he and Seth were getting off. And Seth wasn't the first dude Logan had hooked up with. But that didn't make him *bisexual.* That was for pretentious college kids trying to be adventurous or some shit. Didn't apply to him.

He brushed on more oil, drops splattering all over the place. Maybe he was looking forward to being alone with Seth later, but it didn't mean anything. Seth was awesome at sucking cock—which made sense since he was a real gay guy. Logan was only doing him a favor, but there was nothing wrong with enjoying it.

"How's it coming?"

Logan jumped the way Jenna did when Pop came up behind and tickled her. Seth said, "Sorry to sneak up," as he closed the sliding door behind him, his parka unzipped. He rubbed his bare hands, blowing into them. "Should it be smoking like that?"

"Shit," Logan muttered. "Nah, bit too much oil. But it'll burn off." He'd messed up a simple job. *Typical.* "Sorry."

"It's okay. I'm sure you've got it all under control. You manly creature, you."

Logan adjusted the barbecue's shelf, his smile hurting his cheeks. "Right. I guess that's me."

Seth took Logan's shoulder, strong and comforting and weirdly warm, even through the bulk of Logan's jacket. "You okay? I know Angela is a bit...much with all her questions." He smiled, and gritted out, "And I'm pretty sure she's watching us now. It's like she's never seen a same-sex couple in their natural habitat." He dropped his hand and whispered, "Not that we're..."

Logan murmured, "I get it." He could feel Angela's gaze on them as well. Dale was probably bored shitless. Giving Seth a wink and a sly smile, Logan drew him closer, his arm slipping under Seth's parka. He spread his hand on Seth's waist and nuzzled his cheek.

Seth's laugh was a little high-pitched. He whispered, "Should I pretend you're saying something really dirty?"

Logan chuckled as he leaned back. "Always." There were fat snowflakes caught in Seth's dark hair, and Logan automatically brushed them away. Seth glanced up at the dark sky, and when he lowered his head, there was a flake right on his lower lip.

And Logan kissed it away before it could melt, barely a little press of his mouth on Seth's. It was nothing—only a split second—but Logan couldn't believe he'd just done it.

Chest too tight again, he dropped his hand from Seth's back as he turned to the grill. He said too loudly, "Meat."

Seth seemed frozen in place, more snow catching in his hair, the lips that Logan had just kissed parted. Blinking, Seth said, "What?" Then he nodded. "Steak. Yes! I'll get the steak. We need to—yes, right. Dinner! I'll get the meat." He whirled around and almost tripped in his unlaced boots. He waved, and Logan realized Angela was definitely watching them.

She was smiling like a maniac, her hands pressed to her chest and shaking her head. Was she going to cry or some shit? As Seth opened the door, Logan could hear her exclaim, "Sugar, it's so beautiful to see you two together. Like I always say, love is—"

The glass door slid shut, cutting her off. Logan fiddled with the grill, his heart pounding. It was all part of the act. Kissing Seth like that wasn't anything. They had a deal. And Angela was eating it up, so it was working. That promotion was as good as done. Logan breathed a little easier. He wanted Seth to get the promotion. Seth deserved good things.

And in the new year, Logan would unfuck his life. He'd figure out a way to get a job, and he'd take care of Connor. He wasn't sure how, but first things first. He had to concentrate on helping Seth. This was something he could accomplish.

Seth returned with the steaks. "So far, so good. Thanks again for all this. I know it must be…" He motioned with his hand. "Anyway, thank you."

"All good," Logan said, focusing on the grill and the steaks, getting the temp just right. "We've got this." He bumped Seth's shoulder, and Seth leaned back into him.

Once they had dinner on the table, Angela and Dale praised the food, and Logan had to say it was all delicious. He had to stop himself from shoveling it in too fast, and said, "The potatoes are amazing."

"Thanks, hon," Seth said with a smile from the other end of the table, and Logan smiled back. A Christmas carol played softly in the background, sung by one of those big church choirs with pretty voices.

Logan's phone buzzed. "Shit, sorry." He grimaced as he pulled it from his pocket to switch it off. "Uh, sorry for the language too."

Angela laughed, almost a cackle. "*Shit*, sugar, I've heard far worse." She winked. "Might've said worse too. Go ahead and check it. Might be your boy."

"Oh. Right. Yeah. Says he did well on his last exam." Logan snorted. "And that the joke I sent was stupid." He quickly typed back: *Good job. And that joke was hilarious.* Connor's immediate reply was an eye-roll emoji, but for some reason it didn't feel like he really meant it. Logan smiled and slipped the phone back in his pocket.

Angela swallowed a bite of steak. "He's thirteen? Get ready for that attitude for years to come. All our jokes are lame and we're clueless. They've got all the answers."

Seth laughed. "That sounds about right with Connor."

Logan smiled at Angela tentatively. "So it's not just me who doesn't know anything?"

"This is all part of having a teenager, trust me. My girls think they know every darn thing there is to know."

"So how do you stay patient?" Logan asked.

Angela lifted her glass. "Lots of Merlot. But really, it's hard sometimes. You just want to shake them and stop them from making mistakes you can see coming a mile away. I remind myself that it's my job to love them through all their mistakes. Hug them when they need it, and especially when they think they don't. Because they sure need all the hugs and patience we can give them. Even when they're bein' assholes. Especially then."

Logan's throat suddenly tightened thinking of Connor's regular scowl and crossed arms, how he kept himself an angry little island. Logan had to get through to him. He had to make it better. Nodding, he said, "Thank you," to Angela and meant it.

"Connor's a real challenge, but Logan's doing a wonderful job," Seth said. "Parenting isn't easy. I'm so proud of him." He smiled at Logan, and it was probably just bullshit for Angela's sake, but damn if Logan didn't want so badly to make Seth proud for real.

"Sugar, you just have to keep trying. I was probably the same as a teenager, although my daddy had the patience of Job." She smirked. "Momma, not so much." Her face softened. "But with Connor's momma gone, it must be real hard on him. Especially at Christmastime."

Logan nodded, pushing his roasted squash and parsnip around his plate. "First Christmas without her."

Seth cleared his throat in the silence and said, "But we're determined to give him a wonderful holiday. The retreat will be the perfect start."

"It's going to be fabulous," Angela said. "Isn't it, Dale?"

Dale nodded and actually spoke more than a few words. "There'll be sleigh rides and snowman-building contests. Sledding and skating. Crafts and lots of food, and there's a big indoor pool as well. A Santa's coming with toys during lunch. We think the children will be thrilled."

"Wow," Seth said. "How did you plan all this last minute?"

Angela winked at Dale. "Dale's my little miracle worker. Don't ask him how the sausage gets made—just enjoy the taste. Speaking of taste—Seth, you and Logan have hit it out of the park."

"Oh, thank you," Seth said. "I'm so glad you're enjoying it."

Logan noticed Dale's smile seemed a little tight, a twitch in his cheek before it smoothed out again. How the sausage was made probably involved a fuck-ton of work for Dale with no complaining.

Seth added, "Logan's dad helped with the grilling. I admit I'm a newbie."

Angela beamed. "Isn't that one of the best things about family? Passing on traditions and recipes and old-fashioned how-to. Imagine how much would be lost if gays were all cast out? Everyone needs family. I've said it before and I'll say it again."

She lifted her wineglass for a toast, and they all followed suit. Logan could tell Seth's smile was fake, although he wasn't sure how he knew. Probably because Seth's family were shit-bricks, and it must suck even more at Christmas.

Angela said, "Here's to Seth and Logan and your lovely little family. I can't wait to meet Connor this weekend." After she drank, she added, "And Logan, a little birdie tells me you baked your momma's famous chocolate cake for dessert?"

"Oh, yeah. I hope it doesn't suck." He gulped too much of the red wine, which was a little sweet and went down easy. "I mean, if my mom had made it, it definitely wouldn't suck. But I followed the recipe exactly."

He wondered what she would have made of all this with him pretending to be Seth's boyfriend. The only image that came to mind was her lopsided grin and the devilish spark in her blue eyes. She would have played along really well.

"It's going to be delicious," Seth said. "I may or may not have tasted a tiny little bit of the frosting. Mmm." He gave Logan a wink, and then seemed shocked by himself, his cheeks going red.

It was *adorable*, and Logan grinned.

"So, what do you do on the railway?" Angela asked him.

The warm, cozy feeling exploded like a grenade. Logan squeezed his fork, the reminder that he was a total failure slamming him back down to earth. He should have just lied again, but for some fucked-up reason, he found himself saying, "Actually, I had a bad accident last year. I can't do that work anymore. I'm looking for something else, but..." *But I'm a useless sack of shit.*

She gasped, and Dale made sympathetic noises. Angela said, "I'm so sorry to hear that, sugar! Are you all healed up now?"

He didn't feel like he'd ever be, but Logan said, "Mostly."

"Logan's a veteran as well," Seth said. "He served a tour as a Marine. I really think more should be done to support vets in finding employment."

"Thank you for your service," Angela said to Logan very seriously. "And I could not agree more, Seth. Dale, make a note to look into job opportunities for Logan."

Oh, fuck no. "I don't want charity!" He shifted on Seth's new wooden chair, barely stopping himself from shoving back from the table. "I can do honest work for honest pay." His face felt hot, and he wasn't going to be able to breathe in a second.

But Angela didn't seem bothered by his outburst. "I assure you it wouldn't be charity. I expect damn hard work from every one of my employees. Or from anyone I recommend to business partners. I'm making connections in Albany, and you never know what jobs might come up. This is how it works. Nothing wrong with getting a foot in the door. Then it's up to you to walk through it and not get tossed out on your butt. I make no bones about inheriting my company from my daddy on a silver platter. But I've worked my tail off to expand it and make it even more of a success. I will continue to work hard. It ain't charity."

Logan realized he was gripping the edge of the table, and he exhaled, sitting back and dropping his hands. "I... I see what you're saying. I'm sorry."

"Don't be." She gave him a kind smile. "And don't be a dumbass with too much pride either."

Logan had to laugh. "That's good advice."

Seth laughed too. "Words to live by." He added, "Logan's quite handy and has experience as a contractor. He built that wine rack into the kitchen island."

"I was admiring that!" Angela exclaimed, and it didn't seem like bullshit.

"He finished the kitchen as well and helped with all the decorating," Seth said, and Logan supposed it was true.

"What a beautiful home you boys have built together." Angela lifted her glass again. "Here's to your first Christmas here as a family, and many happy and healthy years to come."

Logan drank, not meeting Seth's eyes. Wishing—just for a crazy minute—that it could all be true.

Chapter Thirteen

"WELL." SETH CLOSED the front door and leaned against it. "We did it."

They'd stood shivering in the doorway waving as Angela's driver had backed down the long drive and out onto the snowy street. Logan rubbed his hands, enjoying the warmth and the relief. He loosened his tie and pulled it off over his head.

Seth laughed softly. "Been dying to do that, huh?"

"Yep."

"Thank you. I know it couldn't have been easy tonight. And that cake really was delicious. I just might have another piece to celebrate our success." He pushed off the door, and Logan followed into the kitchen, pleased that Seth liked the cake so much. With a smile, he watched Seth pour a glass of milk and then lift the carton in question.

Logan said, "A celebratory glass of milk? Not scotch?"

Seth wrinkled his nose. "Milk goes way better with cake. You want?"

"Sure. Cake too. Glad you like it."

"Mmm." Seth cut off two big wedges and ran his finger along the dull part of the knife, licking up the frosting. "So creamy. Sweet, but not cloyingly so. It really is an excellent cake." His tongue darted out to grab a stray bit of chocolate from the corner of his mouth. "Logan?"

"Uh-huh." He realized he'd been staring as Seth licked his finger clean. "Um, thanks."

They stood by the island, eating cake and sipping milk, a Christmas song filling the air with a gentle melody about snow and mistletoe. Logan didn't want to think about it too much yet, but he couldn't help saying, "That was nice of her—about jobs. Might not lead to anything, but..."

"But it just might! I think we have every reason to be optimistic. If anyone can get something done, it's Angela Barker."

Logan watched Seth lick milk from his upper lip. *We.*

Seth frowned at him. "I know you're afraid to hope, but I really think you can look on the bright side here."

"Yeah," Logan said. "We'll see. But thanks." He ate a big forkful of cake and gulped his milk, wiping his mouth with the back of his hand. "Should turn off the lights outside."

His socks were quiet on the hardwood as he returned to the front door and flipped the switch. In the sitting room, he leaned over the golden little tree in the window, switching it off. He could see the car tracks down the driveway being filled in already with fresh snow, the mailbox in the distance with a fluffy lid of flakes.

"Oh, that reminds me," he said, walking back into the kitchen. He opened one of the drawers on the island where he'd stuffed the mail. "When I came in earlier, I noticed the mailbox was overflowing. Probably mostly fliers and crap, but here you go." He dropped the pile on top of the island with a *thwap* and took his last bite of cake.

Seth was frozen with his fork halfway to his mouth, staring at the mail with a strange expression. Logan watched, swallowing his cake with a gulp. He realized it was *fear* on Seth's face, clear in the shallow breaths he was taking and the way his gaze was locked on the mail as if Logan had dropped a big hairy spider there.

"What is it?" Logan asked. He eyed the flyers and letters, trying to see the problem and wanting to fix it. He didn't like seeing Seth like this. Not at all.

Seth tried to smile, ripping his gaze away and blinking at Logan. "Hmm? Oh, nothing." His voice was high and tight.

"Bullshit. Tell me what's wrong." Logan looked at the mail again. He still had no fucking clue what it could be. "Are you expecting bad news or something?" Most mail these days was junk anyway. Did anyone still write bad news that wasn't delivered online or over the phone first?

Seth closed his eyes for a moment and exhaled heavily. He shook his head and pushed away his plate before reaching for the pile. Part of Logan wanted to move closer and touch him—maybe squeeze his shoulder or something— but he stayed put. Best not to crowd him.

"It's silly," Seth mumbled. He stood straighter and determinedly leafed through the flyers, a few envelopes sprinkled throughout. His hand froze, and his bitter smile sent a shiver of dread down Logan's spine. Seth lifted the square, red envelope.

Logan could see the delivery address had been crossed out, and *return to sender* had been scrawled across the front in huge letters. It looked like a Christmas card or something. He couldn't make out who it had been sent to.

Seth answered the unasked questions. "My parents." He flicked through the mail, drawing out two more identical red envelopes. He held them up. "My brother and sister." Dropping the three cards on the island, he added, "I don't bother trying with my grandparents or my aunts and uncles and cousins anymore. But every year I still send these three. Hoping…"

"Fuck. I'm sorry." He should have just left the mail alone. *Stupid.*

Shaking his head, Seth attempted a laugh. "It's the definition of insanity, right? Doing the same thing and expecting a different outcome?" He ran a fingertip over one of the red envelopes. "The cards have always come back on the same day, as if my family has marched to the mailbox together to return my pathetic little olive branch in tandem disgust." His gaze ran over the pile of mail. "Not sure which day it was this year. I haven't checked the mail for two weeks. Last year…"

After a few dull thuds of his heart, Logan quietly asked, "What?"

Seth picked up one of the envelopes, staring at it. "They came back on the twenty-third. I'd almost convinced myself it would be the year my family kept the cards. It would be the year that maybe we could find a way to have some peace between us. Even if they'd just kept the cards, at least I'd be able to believe they don't wish I was dead." He dropped the envelope back to the counter with a soft slap.

"I'm sure they don't wish that." They were fucking assholes if they did. Even more than Logan had thought.

Seth laughed, and Logan hadn't realized how much he liked the usual gentle baritone of Seth's laughter until he heard this ragged bark that set his teeth on edge.

"Oh, they definitely wish I was dead."

"I'm sure—"

"No, *I'm* sure. Here, I'll prove it." He pivoted and strode to the stairs, thumping up them without waiting to see if Logan was following. Which he was, his pulse racing. This was all so wrong, and maybe he could still fix it.

In his bedroom, Seth flicked on the overhead light and marched to his dresser to open one of the top drawers. He pulled out a square leather box, dark brown and expensive looking. Logan waited in the doorway, wary. He should have kept his damn mouth shut and just left Seth alone.

Seth was practically shaking with tension or maybe fury. Logan wasn't sure. He only knew he hated it.

Whipping around, Seth held out a folded piece of paper. "Here." It sounded like he'd swallowed sand.

Logan didn't have a choice but to come inside and take the paper, which was bent a bit at the edges and seemed to have been read many times. When Logan unfolded it, the crease down the middle was deep. It was typed, which he wasn't expecting for some reason. He blinked at the words that ran in a narrow column down the page.

MARSTON, SETH
October 2, 1981—December 24, 2006

Seth Michael Marston passed away suddenly. Seth was raised in the loving arms of Christ by his parents, Mary and Stephen; grandparents Doris and John, and Sarah (reunited with Christ 1998) and Michael;

alongside his loving siblings Christine (David) and Paul (Bethany).

Seth tragically chose the abominable path of the devil, sinning without shame And choosing the wicked homosexual lifestyle. He broke the hearts of his family, who weep for his loss and take solace in Jesus Christ our Lord.

There will be no service. Memorial donations gratefully accepted at The Church of Christ's Grace in Macon, Georgia.

Logan stared at the words, first with confusion, then disbelief. Then the horror slammed into him, his throat painfully tight. He had to swallow twice before he whispered, "They wrote your obituary?" The paper shook in his hand. "Jesus fucking Christ."

Seth laughed harshly. "Indeed. They published it too, in the local paper. I'd have never thought they'd want a soul to know the truth, but this way, I guess they were in control. They probably knew rumors would run rampant, and this way, they were the righteous victims. And I think they expected me to be so humiliated and ashamed that I'd repent my sins and beg forgiveness. But I didn't. Couldn't."

"Shouldn't!" Logan stared down at the hateful words dressed up in religion. "This isn't what Christians should do. Jesus wouldn't do this."

Seth smiled thinly, taking the paper back. "I don't think so either. There are many accepting churches out there, but mine wasn't one of them, to put it mildly. *Everyone* knew—all my old friends, extended family. No one ever talked to me again."

He folded the piece of paper back into the box and closed it away in the drawer. "I think maybe they still expect me to beg forgiveness and repent. Crawl back to them."

Logan wondered why Seth hung onto that piece of paper at all, let alone in a fancy box like it was something precious, but he kept his trap shut. "That's fucked up."

Tense from head to foot, Seth nodded. "I'd been living in Atlanta with Brandon for three years after college. In a studio apartment. I mean, I thought they might piece it together when they came to visit one summer, but apparently not. So I decided that year to tell them all when I came home for Christmas."

He paced a few steps, his fingers digging into his arms where they were crossed. "I told them I was gay and in love with Brandon. That I knew I'd never be able to change, no matter how much I prayed. That… That I didn't *want* to change. That this was the way God made me."

Seth jerked his shoulders in a shrug. "The next morning, my dad and my brother dragged me out of the house. Threw my suitcase after me. Then my mom gave me that piece of paper with the obituary they'd written. My sister and grandparents were there too. They watched from the porch. Everyone was crying and praying. They turned their backs on me and locked the door. That was it."

"Unless you changed your mind?"

"Right. Obviously that's not going to happen." He paced again, shaking his head. "And every year I send them Christmas cards and tell them about my life as if I think it will make any bit of difference. They're bigots. They're not going to change. But I keep hoping anyway. I'm an idiot. Pathetic."

"Hey, stop that." Logan stepped closer. "You are not. Don't be mad at yourself. Be mad at them. They're the assholes." *Fucking cowardly pieces of shit who don't deserve you.*

Seth stared at him, and as the silence stretched out, Logan was afraid he'd gone too far even though he'd choked down most of what he'd wanted to say. Then Seth lunged toward him, clutching at Logan painfully. Trying to breathe, Logan didn't know what to do, standing there with his arms at his sides and Seth attached to him.

He'd never *hugged* another guy—at least not like this. There was no back-slapping, and it went on and on, Seth hanging on like his life depended on it, his arms in a vise around Logan, face pressed against Logan's neck, wet and warm.

Shit, he was *trembling*, and Logan wrapped his arms around him. "Shhh," he murmured, since that's what he would have done with Veronica or one of his old girlfriends. Not that Seth was a woman, but he was upset and clearly needed comforting.

They were practically the same height, and Seth was stooped with his face in Logan's neck, still clinging to him. Logan didn't think he was crying, just hanging on real tight. Instead of slapping Seth's back, Logan stroked it tentatively and said, "It's okay."

"I'm sorry," Seth mumbled, his breath hot on Logan's neck. "Thank you."

"Don't worry about it." They were pressed together, and Logan had to admit it felt good. Warm and solid. They stood there, and it probably should have been really awkward or weird, but...it wasn't.

"I need..." Shaking, Seth kissed Logan's throat, his hands tightening and sliding down to his hips. Sparks flared as Seth rocked their bodies together. "I want..." He exhaled sharply. "Shit."

It was the strongest curse word Logan had heard from Seth, and it sparked something in Logan. He couldn't fix Seth's terrible family, but this? This he could do.

He smoothed a palm down over Seth's ass. "You want me to fuck you?"

Logan could hear and feel the sigh of relief that washed through Seth. "Yes. Please. Please do that."

Seth didn't seem able to say the words, but Logan had the feeling he liked hearing them. That it was what he needed. "That's what you want? My cock inside you?"

Almost whimpering, Seth nodded against Logan's neck, rutting his hips forward.

"How do you want it? Want it rough?"

Groaning, Seth broke away. "Yes." He opened a drawer beside the bed and took out a bottle of lube and an unopened box of condoms, dropping them on the neatly made bed. He jerked off his clothes with shaking hands and left everything in a pile on the carpet.

Logan was still kicking off his slacks as Seth yanked down the duvet and crawled onto his hands and knees on the sheets. Struggling with his skivvies, Logan realized he was hard as rock, lust roaring in his veins. His breath was short, but his chest didn't hurt.

He squirted lube all over the place, managing to get some on his fingers before kneeling behind Seth. He stared at Seth's firm, amazing ass and grabbed hold.

"Fuck, you're hot." The words were out before Logan could stop them. A distant voice hissed that there was something different about this than the other times he'd gotten off with guys.

He and Seth were completely naked together, and although he'd fucked guys before, it had never been on a bed. He'd never said any of them were hot.

"Please," Seth begged, his head hanging low, body shaking.

"You want my cock? Want me inside you?" Logan's words made his own balls tingle and tighten. With guys there usually hadn't been any talking aside from maybe a "thanks, man," once they'd gotten each other off.

But the way Seth moaned and let go, the words turning him on and giving him what he needed—what he couldn't say—that made Logan crazy horny.

"I'm going to fuck you so hard, baby." *Baby? Where the hell did that come from?*

Seth cried out, pushing back against Logan's hands and widening his knees. "Please."

When Logan had fucked guys before, the men had usually prepared themselves, or they'd just used spit. Hadn't always been a lot of options in Iraq or the bunkhouse. But now he was tentative, pushing the tip of one finger inside Seth, not wanting to hurt him. *Never* wanting to hurt him.

Seth squeezed around Logan's finger, and holy shit, he imagined what that would be like on his dick. *Amazing.* He pushed in farther, making sure his finger was dripping with lube. "You like that?"

"*Yes.*"

Logan was dying to bury himself in Seth, but he went slowly, eventually easing in another finger as Seth trembled. Then another.

"Please just do it. I need it." Seth moaned as Logan inched in. "Need you."

Logan tried to ignore the way those two words made his chest feel light and his dick even harder. "You want it now?" He could not screw this up. He asked again, "Rough?"

"Yes, yes—like that."

After unrolling a condom and slathering on lube, he spread Seth's ass and inched into him. It had to hurt, although Seth didn't complain, only grunting and groaning along. Logan tried to soothe him with gentle touches over his head and shoulders.

Whimpering, Seth bore down, muttering encouragement Logan couldn't quite make out—more noises than actual words. Then he clearly pleaded, "Harder."

"Fuck, you're so tight. So good." Logan thrust fully into him, making it rough but glad of the lube. He didn't want to risk really hurting Seth. "You like that? You wanna come on my dick?"

"Yes," Seth panted. Sweat beaded between his shoulder blades already, and Logan bent to lick his salty skin. Seth said something else he didn't hear, and Logan lifted his head. There had been an urgency in his tone.

"What did you say?" Was he going too hard? He slowed his thrusts, running his hand over Seth's head, fingers sliding through that thick hair. "You okay?"

"Yes!" It came out almost like a sob. "I said I'm a queer. It's what I am." He pushed back against Logan, turning to look over his shoulder with wild, defiant eyes, his cheeks red and hair sticking up. "It's what I am. I'm not sorry. I'll never be sorry. Even if they never talk to me again, I can't be sorry."

"That's right, baby. Fuck them. They're the ones going to hell, not you. You're perfect like this." To punctuate his words, Logan pulled almost all the way out and slammed back in, their skin slapping together.

Sweat dampened Logan's forehead, and he breathed hard, his chest tight, but not in the danger zone. Even if it was, he wouldn't stop. He was going to give this to Seth. He was going to fuck him and make him come harder than that piece of shit Brandon ever did.

Holding Seth's hip with one hand and reaching below him with the other, Logan stroked Seth's straining cock. He was leaking, and Logan smeared the liquid with his thumb, muttering, "You got more of this for me? You want to come? You like being fucked like a dog? Baby, you take my dick like you were born for it."

"Yes!" Seth gasped, his whole body jerking. "There. That's—"

Logan angled to get more pressure on just the right place, and Seth unloaded with a shout, shaking and clamping down. Logan jerked him through it, Seth's cock throbbing and twitching. He loved the feel of it in his hand, so alive and strong but vulnerable at the same time. It made his balls ache. He shoved his face onto the side of Seth's neck, lips open and pressing, feeling a wild pulse.

Seth's arms gave out, and he collapsed to his elbows, breathing loudly, his ass still up in the air, beautiful and tight. Logan took hold of his hips, still going hard, chasing his own orgasm.

"Fuck, you feel so good," he muttered. "Going to come hard. Seth…" Holding Seth's hips, he unleashed, wishing there was no condom so he could come inside him until it was dripping out.

"Fuck," he groaned, the pleasure so pure and deep he twitched, Seth squeezing around him perfectly, more intense than any sex Logan could remember.

He breathed heavily, but his chest felt loose and easy. He ran his hand down Seth's spine, kissing the top knobs before easing out as gently as he could, both of them moaning. After he got rid of the condom in the bathroom, Logan wet a washcloth and returned to the bedroom.

Seth was sprawled on his belly, boneless. Normally, Logan would have tossed the cloth and said thanks before leaving. He stood at the foot of the bed, the overhead light bright on Seth's flushed skin, his long limbs lean and strong.

Even though he'd gotten off, the urge to touch remained. Logan's fingers itched. He was crawling beside Seth on the bed before he could talk himself out of it. Gently, he wiped Seth's asshole, then urged him to roll over. He cleaned what he could with the cloth, and Seth's eyes flickered open, a sweet smile tugging up his lips.

"Thank you." He trailed his fingertips over Logan's cheek, and Logan turned his face into that touch, letting himself be drawn down.

Then Seth kissed him.

Their mouths met before Logan could process it. The stubble on his chin rasped against the hint of Seth's, but their lips were soft, pressing together like they fit just right.

Like they'd kissed a thousand times, like it made perfect sense to breathe the same air, tasting sweetness that was more than chocolate cake. This was nothing like the peck by the barbecue with Angela watching.

Their mouths opened, but as their tongues met, Seth jerked and shoved Logan away, scrambling back. "I'm sorry!"

Blinking, Logan tried to focus. His pulse raced, and he wanted nothing more than to roll on top of Seth and taste him completely. Kiss him until they couldn't even breathe, rub their naked bodies together and pull the covers over their heads.

But Seth was staring at him like he was seeing a car accident, and Logan's chest seized up tight, a dagger of pain returning.

Seth ran a hand through his hair, clutching at it. "I'm so sorry. That wasn't part of the deal."

Right. The deal.

"No." But… Fuck, Logan had never kissed another man before tonight, and now he wanted to kiss Seth more than anything. *Needed* it. Maybe it was gay, or bi, or whatever the fuck, and right then, he didn't care. He didn't care that Seth was a guy. All he cared about was kissing him again.

Before Logan could even try to find the right words to say any of that, Seth was up and tugging on his clothes even though it was time for bed. His fingers shook as he did up the buttons on his wrinkly shirt and said, "You've helped me so much, but I think we should keep things strictly business from now on. We just need to pretend through the retreat. A few more days. No more of…this." He shook his head, gaze on his trembling hands. "I really do apologize. Clearly this was a mistake."

Logan had to say something, but the tightness in his chest increased, cramping pain radiating outward. Seth thought it was a mistake? Hell, he was probably right. Logan's mind spun like an old record player with the needle stuck.

"I hope you'll accept my apology." Seth stood stiffly by the bed. His shirt was even tucked into his slacks.

Logan was still naked, and he needed to reassure Seth that he wasn't angry. That he…he was… *Glad.* But that made no sense. He'd always been straight—he'd never *liked* a guy. It was just supposed to be casual, but now Seth was so shaken, and Logan wanted to make it right.

"It's okay," he said, because he was useless.

Seth nodded tightly and walked out of the room. *His* room, and now Logan was sitting there naked on Seth's bed trying to figure out what the fuck was happening.

He had no clue where to begin, so he stumbled up and yanked on his clothes. Seth was downstairs. "Baby, It's Cold Outside" echoed up from the speakers they'd left on before it was switched off.

In the silence, Logan tiptoed into the bathroom adjoining the guest room, closing the door. He leaned over the sink and splashed his face with cold water.

This was all supposed to be fake.

While he leaned against the counter, taking deep breaths and trying to understand, he heard a door close. Peeking into the hall, he saw it was to Seth's bedroom. Should he go knock? What the fuck was he going to say? Maybe he should give Seth time alone. Seth seemed to want it, so he shouldn't push.

He crept downstairs. The great room was lit by the Christmas tree—soft blue, green, red, yellow, and pink lights that reflected on the tall glass windows. Logan pressed his forehead to the sliding door, watching the snow drift down and inhaling the fresh pine in the air.

Everything was silent. Peaceful. But in his head, he heard Seth on a loop.

"That wasn't part of the deal."

"Clearly this was a mistake."

It was after midnight when Logan accepted that Seth wasn't coming back down. Should he go up? They should probably talk about it, as much as Logan dreaded the thought. Would Seth be glad if Logan went up and got into bed with him?

He huddled under the blanket on the couch, closing his eyes and trying not to think about kissing Seth, wishing he knew the right thing to do for once in his damn life.

Chapter Fourteen

S ETH TOLD HIMSELF again that he needed to stop talking.

He'd been nattering on during the entire drive to Connor's school, Logan mumbling agreements every so often as Seth sermonized about global warming, the abysmal state of world politics, and a recent scandal involving one of the judges on a baking show. As if Logan cared in the least about baking shows!

Although he had made that cake.

As Seth exited the freeway, his belly flip-flopped, a sweet spike of warmth filling him. That adorably lopsided, delicious cake that had been Mrs. Derwood's favorite. That Logan had baked it for him filled Seth with such gratitude and affection, which was insane since it had all been for show.

It was only part of the deal. Nothing more.

It felt like more, though. Just like last night had. Seth's bottom was sore, but in a pleasing way that gave him a forbidden thrill every time he shifted on the heated seat. It had been so long since he'd experienced sex like that. He'd been abstinent for over a year, but even before that with Brandon, the fire had petered out long before.

With Logan, he'd felt consumed. Mastered and taken care of, *known* in a way that made him want to weep with pleasure and gratitude. Logan had called him *baby*, and Seth had felt loved, even though he knew it was impossible. But he could fool himself in the moment.

Then he'd gone and ruined it all by kissing Logan. Logan had been kind not to shove him away. Kinder than Seth deserved after breaching their agreement. Logan had said no kissing, and Seth had to remember that none of this was real.

The whole idea had been to engage in casual sex to get him over his hang-ups. Not to saddle Logan with his family issues and have a sort of breakdown. Seth should have been ashamed of how he'd unloaded all of it on Logan and then begged for sex.

Yet when he remembered the hot growl of Logan's voice in his ear, it thrilled him.

"Baby, you take my dick like you were born for it."

"It's coming up on the right," Logan said in the here and now.

"Okay!" Seth replied far too loudly, his voice pitched up and cheeks feverish. He made the turn onto the curving drive to Rencliffe, the bare trees standing sentinel, fresh snow clinging to their branches, the sun peeking out from clouds.

The drive had been plowed and salted, and when they reached the gothic buildings, the closest lot was full of vehicles and parents picking up their sons.

Seth parked and climbed out of his SUV, walking in silence next to Logan, their boots crunching in the snow. Seth stopped short. "Oh, wait. Would you rather I stayed in the car?"

"Nah. Connor will probably be nicer if you're here." Logan's hands were in the pockets of his leather jacket as they walked on, and Seth thought he should really be wearing a hat.

Before he could stop himself, he asked, "You brought winter gear, right?" *I sound like a nag.* "Just don't want you to be cold this weekend," he added lamely.

"Yep," Logan said. He lifted his chin. "There he is."

Connor waited under a vast stone arch, his arms crossed and shoulders hunched. He wore a bright red ski jacket that was too short in the sleeves with a striped scarf that looked handmade. A stuffed duffel bag sat by his boots. As Seth waved, a pretty woman appeared, saying something to Connor.

She called, "Good afternoon, Mr. Derwood! Happy holidays."

"Hey," Logan replied. "Thanks. Um, you too, Ms. Patel."

She smiled at Seth, clearly waiting for an introduction. There was an awkward silence for several moments until she said, "Hello, Mr...?"

"Oh! This is my—" Logan cut off, floundering. "Seth."

"Seth Marston." Seth stuck out his hand. "I'm a friend of Logan's."

"Mira Patel." Her hand was soft, but the grip strong. To Logan she said, "Could we have a quick word?"

Logan gave Connor a sharp glance, frowning, then nodded and followed her inside the school. Seth smiled at Connor. "You must be glad school's finished." Then he remembered Connor had been threatened with expulsion. "For the holidays, I mean. I'm sure your exams went very well."

Connor shrugged, his arms still crossed. He needed a hat too, his ears red from the cold. Seth adjusted his own beanie, wondering if it would be weird to offer it.

"Did everything go well?" Seth asked tentatively. *Please don't let this boy be expelled.* Seth could imagine how devastating it would be. And what on earth would Logan do? Seth had promised he and Connor could stay until the new year but had been too swept up in—well, in Logan and the amendment to their deal—to really think about what exactly Logan would do come January. Or even how he and Logan and Connor would spend

Christmas.

He felt queasy at the uncertainty of it all and prayed Angela would come through with some kind of job connection. And in the meantime, he had to focus on getting through the weekend retreat.

Connor rolled his eyes. "Yeah. I got an A on every exam."

"That's wonderful! Congratulations. Logan will be so proud. I'm proud too, although I know I just met you."

The surly veneer cracked a bit, and Connor smiled slightly. "Thanks."

"We'll have to celebrate this weekend in Lake Placid. What's your favorite treat?"

"Dunno."

"Well, we'll think of something. Thank you again for agreeing to this. I can't tell you how much I appreciate it."

"Sure." Connor shrugged, but gave Seth a bigger smile.

So perhaps he liked feeling useful. Who didn't? Seth vowed to find ways to encourage it. As Logan returned, Seth exclaimed, "Connor tells me he aced his exams!"

Logan grinned—a real smile that lit up his worn face. "I know. He can come back in the new year. Good job." He clapped a hand on Connor's shoulder and said exactly what Seth was silently urging him to. "I'm real proud."

"I told you I could do it," Connor said, but without heat.

"You did," Logan agreed.

It was possibly the friendliest exchange between them that Seth had witnessed. He hoped it boded well for the weekend. "We'd better get going. The bus leaves the office at two."

Angela had allowed everyone attending the retreat—which was nearly all staff except those who had unchangeable travel plans—to leave work at noon to collect their families and luggage. As they drove into Albany, Seth peppered Connor with questions about his schoolwork, and Connor seemed willing enough to answer, warming up to the topic of computer science.

"You still like robots?" Logan asked.

"Yeah," Connor answered warily. In the rear-view mirror, Seth could see his gaze narrow and shoulders hunch. "It's not just kid stuff, you know."

Logan opened his mouth as if to bite back a response, then snapped his jaw shut. When he spoke, his voice was even. "Yeah, I remember that amazing robot you built."

"That wasn't from scratch or anything. I had instructions from the internet." Still, Connor seemed pleased.

"You got it to wake up your mom one morning, and she screamed so loud I dropped the coffee pot."

The tentative peace was shattered, Connor visibly retreating into his shell. "Surprised you were even there that morning."

Logan opened and closed his mouth again, pressing his lips together. This time, he stared out the window and said nothing more, probably thinking silence was better than an argument.

Seth flipped on the radio, and "I Saw Mommy Kissing Santa Claus" filled the SUV. Cringing, he jabbed the button on the wheel with his thumb, changing the station until he found one playing regular music. It was "Highway to Hell" by AC/DC, a song that had been forbidden to him growing up.

He sincerely hoped they were on a highway to a far better destination this weekend.

At the Great Adirondack Lodge, Santa had come early. The man himself greeted the BRK Sync buses, passing out Lindt balls with a hearty "Ho-ho-ho!" In the early dusk, Lake Placid was a winter wonderland, its quaint, shop-lined main street aglow with holiday lights and wreaths, the snowbanks still fluffy and white and not splashed with mud and grime yet.

The lodge sat at the foot of the main street on the icy shores of Mirror Lake, the actual Lake Placid apparently nearby, but outside of its namesake town. The Olympic center was across the street, and Logan motioned to it.

"Pop would love to come here. The US beat Russia in hockey at the 1980 Olympics. One of his favorite moments in life."

"Oh!" Seth said. "Yes, I've heard of that. We should take a look tomorrow. What do you say, Connor?"

Through a mouthful of chocolate, Connor mumbled, "Whatever."

He'd sat in the back with some other kids on the two-and-a-half-hour bus trip. Logan had offered Seth the window seat, and he'd stared out at the snowy landscape, trying not to think about the occasional touch of Logan's thigh against his, and how their shoulders brushed, the leather of Logan's jacket smelling rich and enticing. Logan had leaned back and closed his eyes, although he hadn't seemed to actually sleep.

Not that Seth had been sneaking glances at him or anything.

They trooped into the lodge, where a hotel staff member went through the list and handed out room keys. It took a while, and Seth was aware of the curious glances from his colleagues as he stood next to Logan. Connor had his face buried in his phone again, and Jenna was busy bouncing crying baby Noah while Jun wrangled Ian.

A shiver zipped down Seth's spine as Logan leaned in, his strong hand finding the back of Seth's neck above the collar of his unzipped parka. Logan whispered right in Seth's ear, his lips almost brushing.

"People are real curious, huh?"

Seth nodded, not trusting himself to speak without squeaking.

Logan chuckled. "Pretend I'm saying something funny."

Of course, in Seth's mind he'd heard the echo from that day they'd run into Brandon, and he laughed slightly hysterically as he tried very hard not to think of Logan saying anything dirty. Now more people were looking at them, and Seth caught Angela's eye across the crowd. A grin splitting her face, she waved and winked.

It's all an act. All part of the deal. Now play along!

He did, he and Logan laughing at nothing and acting like they were engrossed in some secret conversation. Connor shot them the odd frown and eye roll, but Seth supposed that played right into their ruse, as most teenagers were embarrassed by their parents.

For a moment, as the hotel woman called out, "Marston family!" Seth let himself imagine what it would be like if Logan really was his fiancé and Connor their son. He had to catch his breath at the swift punch of longing and cursed himself for being a fool.

Their room was on the third floor of the lodge, and they rode the elevator in silence, Connor's thumbs still flying over his phone screen. Once inside the room, he suddenly came to life.

"I get my own bed!" Connor launched himself at the bed by the window, throwing his duffel on top and then sprawling on the mattress. A little saying from childhood came to mind, and Seth half-expected Connor to add, "*No take-backs!*"

Standing in the entryway, there was a bar fridge, microwave, and coffee machine to the right, then a bathroom, and beyond that, the beds were to the right in the room, a long dresser with TV atop to the left.

Seth and Logan eyed the near bed uneasily. It was a queen, at least, but still. Seth shifted and cleared his throat. "I'm sure we can get them to bring up a cot."

Connor looked over his shoulder where he was sprawled on his belly, screwing up his face. "Wouldn't that seem weird if you guys are supposed to be getting married?"

"Well..." Seth was going to say no one had to know, but considering his luck, Angela herself would be in the hallway as the cot was wheeled in. "Good point."

Connor glared at Logan. "What, you think it's catching or something? I've slept in the same bed with Jayden. It's no big deal." He rolled his eyes. "I'm sure Seth isn't going to try anything."

Logan unzipped his leather jacket and opened the mirrored closet in the narrow entryway. "Obviously. It's fine," he said gruffly. "Of course we can sleep there."

It was interesting to Seth that after using the other F-word when they first met, now Connor was implying Logan was the one with homophobic issues. Seth gave the kid the benefit of the doubt that he'd been thoughtless that first night, lashing out blindly. He just wished Connor would stop attacking Logan. He wanted to scold him, but would that be overstepping? Surely it would.

"Better get changed for dinner. It starts early."

Logan and Connor stared at him. Logan glanced down at his jeans and Henley. "Changed into what?" Alarm creased his handsome face. "Was I supposed to bring something fancy?"

"No, no. I'm sure the dress code is casual." He was wearing his usual dress shirt and tie with slacks. "I'll probably be the one overdressed. I should change."

He bustled around, unzipping his small suitcase and hanging up the clothes he'd brought. Logan sat on the bed and flipped on the TV, going through the channels while Connor was back into a game. Seth had brought a forest-green cashmere sweater that he thought would look good over dark jeans. Yes, that would do nicely.

He almost took the clothes into the bathroom to change but decided that would seem ridiculously prudish and likely strange to Connor. Not that Connor had so much as blinked, entirely engrossed in his game and paying Seth no mind. After taking off his tie, Seth began unbuttoning his shirt.

Logan was watching.

Butterflies flapped in Seth's stomach. It was from the corner of his eye, but yes, Logan was *definitely* watching. Seth pretended he hadn't noticed, trying not to fumble with the buttons. He sucked in and peeled off his shirt, puffing out his chest a bit. Hoping he didn't look like a fool.

Standing in his boxers, Seth hung up his shirt, looping the tie over the neck of the hanger. He could feel the heat of Logan's gaze on his bare skin like a caress. Without meaning to, he thought of the night before, being on his hands and knees for Logan, being filled by him.

He remembered the rough caresses of Logan's hands on his flanks, his hips, his thighs. His...

Cock.

Oh good lord, Seth was getting hard. He bit the inside of his cheek, still facing into the closet. Thinking of his old cat Agatha did the trick, the ache of missing her flushing out the burst of lust. He finished dressing quickly and escaped into the bathroom to splash cold water on his cheeks.

Dinner was a buffet of comfort food—definitely not fancy. Which was actually a relief, and Seth dug into the mac and cheese with gusto. He, Logan, and Connor sat with Jenna, Jun, and the boys, and Jenna kept up most of the dinner conversation.

Matt and Becky were at the next table, and Matt gave Seth a thumbs-up and mouthed, "*Caper, caper, caper!*" Seth promptly spilled gravy on his sweater and excused himself to the bathroom to blot at it with a paper towel.

When he re-entered the corridor off the hotel restaurant, Jenna was there bouncing a fussy Noah. She groaned. "I just want to eat all the carbs and go to sleep. Kids are exhausting."

Seth whispered, "Don't complain about motherhood too loudly with Angela around. Actually, that's not fair. She had good advice for Logan last night."

Jenna stepped closer. "How did it go? You barely answered my nosy texts." Since Friday was her temporary day off from the office, this was the first chance Seth had had to speak with her privately.

He whispered, "Really well, I think? Seemed to, at least. She was all smiles."

"And Logan performed?"

It was an innocent question, but Seth's brain immediately supplied the memory of Logan *performing* extremely admirably in Seth's bed. The echo of grunts and moans and slapping skin filled his head, and he swore his butt twinged. "Uh-huh!"

Jenna groaned. "Oh no. What did he do? What aren't you telling me?"

"Nothing!"

"You're a terrible liar, Seth."

He rubbed his face. "I know! That's why I should never have agreed to any of this!" But the thought of not getting to know Logan the past week or two was a gut-punch, shocking in its sudden severity. Seth exhaled shakily. "But I'm glad I did. Logan's been terrific. Really."

Jenna raised her eyebrows. "Yeah? Okay, good. You guys seem to be faking it really well. I almost believe all the longing glances between you two."

It truly shouldn't have hurt—but, oh, it did. Seth told himself it was ridiculous, yet his heart ached anyway, and he could only manage a strangled half-smile. He hadn't even realized he and Logan had been glancing at each other during dinner, and especially not with longing.

Part of him wanted to insist that it wasn't fake at all, that the sex he and Logan were having *had* to mean something. Of course he couldn't say that to Jenna since she had no idea her brother was anything but straight. At least not that Seth was aware, and there was definitely no good way to casually probe to see if she had an inkling.

Jenna touched his arm. "It seems like you guys have become friends? I'm so happy about that. You're both wonderful people, you know that?"

His smile this time was genuine. "So are you." He hugged her briefly, careful not to squish Noah, who had settled. "And yes, I'd like to think we've become friends through this deal. Logan's so hard on himself. He and Connor both."

"Hopefully this weekend will be good for them. And you." She glanced around. "We'd better get back. Angela's probably going to make a 'BRK is one big happy family' speech any minute."

Sure enough, Angela did just that. Seth clapped in the right places and nodded and smiled as he tried not to look at Logan. It was a relief when they could escape back to their room after a performance by a local choir.

"Santa Claus is Coming to Town" was stuck on a loop in Seth's head as he changed into his flannel pajamas. He was aware of Logan's gaze and looked up as he finished the buttons on his top. Logan stood by the side of the bed in his black boxer briefs.

And nothing else.

"Oh," Seth murmured without meaning to. Connor was in the bathroom, so it was just the two of them for the moment. Seth looked down at his plaid PJs. He felt stupidly prim and overdressed.

"I should probably…" Logan unzipped his duffel and pulled out a plain gray T-shirt. He pulled it on, covering his sexy, hairy chest. "Ugly, I know."

Seth jolted, realizing he was staring, and that Logan meant the scars. "No. Not at all. That wasn't…"

Connor re-emerged, wearing an oversized T-shirt and boxers. He yawned widely as he shuffled by, pimple ointment dotted over his face. He huddled under the covers and didn't bother saying goodnight.

In their bed, Logan crawled over to the left side, which was against the wall separating the bedroom area from the bathroom. Seth stretched out on the edge of the mattress, in danger of rolling off and cracking his head on the side table. He reached up and snapped out the light, murmuring, "'Night."

"Sleep well," Logan whispered from behind him. Only inches separated them, and Seth imagined he could feel the heat of Logan's muscular body.

He could still feel it an hour later, sleep stubbornly elusive. As gently as possible, Seth rolled over, facing Logan. In the white glow of the digital clock on the side table, he could see the lines and shadows of Logan's face, and the rise and fall of his shoulder as he breathed softly.

When Logan opened his eyes, Seth had to bite back a gasp, his heart skipping. They stared at each other, and Seth's body responded, his breath shallow, blood flooding south as he got shamefully hard. He reminded himself Connor was in the other bed and that even if he wasn't, this connection with Logan wasn't real.

They stared at each other, only inches apart. It would be so easy to lean a bit closer, to kiss Logan again and breathe him in, just for a minute before they slept. He could feel the heat from Logan's body and wanted to climb into his skin…

Seth rolled away, squeezing his eyes shut as he curled on the very edge of the bed. He swore he could sense Logan watching him, and willed himself to think of something else—anything else!—so he could sleep and this night would be mercifully over.

Chapter Fifteen

A THUD AND muffled curse woke him, and Logan was instantly alert. He sat up, blinking at Connor near the foot of the bed in the gloom, hopping on one foot.

The alarm clock on the table between the beds gave off enough light to see. It was just past seven. Beside Logan, Seth curled away from him under the comforter. Logan could see enough of his slack face to know he was still asleep.

Connor was in his swimming trunks and a concert T-shirt from a rapper Logan could remember him blasting from his room when he and Veronica had argued.

Connor whispered, "I'm going swimming with some other kids." He nodded to a folded piece of paper on the bureau by the TV and said defensively, "I left a note," as if he was expecting Logan to get mad. His chin was jutted out. Always ready for a fight.

Logan smiled and nodded. "Have fun," he whispered. "You've got your card?" He tugged at the neck of his tee, not used to waking up wearing anything but his skivvies.

Connor eyed him warily but held up the plastic key card. With his other hand, he waved awkwardly, then tiptoed into the foyer. In the mirrored closet, Logan could just make him out sliding on his flip-flops and easing open the door. The yellow light from the hallway flared bright, and then was gone as Connor closed the door silently.

Logan sat listening to Seth's steady breathing and cute little murmurs as he shifted onto his back. His lips were parted, and he drew up one arm over his head. What would he do if Logan woke him with a kiss? Would he like it? Or would he get all uptight?

Would I like it?

He'd never thought of another guy as "cute" before. There was something about Seth that gave him all these weirdly…soft thoughts. Not that Seth wasn't manly. He was. Even in his grandpa button-up plaid pajamas. Logan wanted to unbutton him and rub his hands over Seth's hairy chest, roll on top of him and kiss him awake, feel the scratch of his stubble…

The wall was to Logan's left, and he carefully crawled to the bottom of the bed so he could go piss and stop thinking about stupid shit that would ruin everything. Sure, Seth had kissed him after they fucked, but then he'd seemed horrified. Maybe it was because he didn't want to kiss a loser like Logan.

After switching off the bathroom light, he opened the door and crept back out—and almost banged right into Seth. Seth jumped back, and they both laughed. Weak daylight was glowing around the edges of the curtains now, and Logan could see Seth's spiky bedhead.

And his morning wood tenting those plaid PJs.

Seth's eyes went wide like someone in a dumb movie, and it was so damn *cute*. He was probably about to make some stammering apology, and Logan couldn't remember the last time he'd simply *liked* someone so much. He laughed again, and Seth blinked at him, a hopeful little smile tugging on his lips.

Logan wanted to take care of him. He wanted to say a bunch of stuff, but he had no clue where to start—he'd always been crappy at words. But fuck, he burned with it, and he was moving, pushing Seth against the striped wallpaper. Dropping to kneel at his feet.

Seth gasped, his hands clutching at Logan's shoulders.

Being on his knees, looking up at Seth—at his chest rising and falling quickly under the buttoned-up PJ top, his tongue licking his lips—made Logan horny as hell. He rubbed his cheek against Seth's hard dick through the soft flannel.

It had been years since Logan had returned the favor of a blow job. It had been rushed, and yeah, he'd liked it. He'd enjoyed the power of it, even though he was the one kneeling.

But with Seth, it was so much more. Seeing buttoned-up Seth come undone made him excited and stupidly proud. It made him want to do anything—everything—to give Seth what he needed.

Maybe it was what Logan needed too.

He tore down Seth's pajama bottoms and swallowed him as deep as he could, loving how Seth bucked his hips and gasped again. Logan choked and pulled back, keeping the head in his mouth as he breathed through his nose. He sucked hard, tonguing the slit. He probably wasn't very good at it, but Seth didn't seem to mind.

In the hush of the room, their grunts and groans seemed really loud, and it made Logan's dick rock hard in his boxer briefs. He loved the way Seth was holding his head now, his fingers flexing, digging in one second, and then rubbing the next.

It was probably weird, but he loved how Seth was still buttoned in his pajama top while underneath he was bare, getting his dick sucked. He tasted musky and male, and Logan licked desperately, taking him too deep again, spit dribbling out of his mouth as he choked.

His head spun, whole body tensing as he sucked like his life depended on it. Making Seth come felt like the most important thing in the world.

Logan fondled Seth's balls, and that did it. He shot his load with a rumble of moans and whimpers, palming Logan's head. Logan swallowed as much as he could, not caring about the bitter taste, sucking him through it until Seth's trembles turned to jerks and it was obviously too much.

Logan released Seth's dick, and his mouth felt messy, his lips swollen. He pushed to his feet, and Seth reached for him, rubbing Logan's shaft through the cotton of his skivvies.

Seth was wrecked, his mouth open and face bright red in the pale light. Logan moaned, thrusting against Seth's palm, leaning against the wall, his hands on either side of Seth's face.

He'd only have to lean in a few more inches and they'd be kissing.

And *fuck*, Logan wanted to kiss him for real. Wanted to shove his tongue into Seth's mouth and kiss him until they couldn't breathe. Would Seth freak out if he did? He groaned as Seth pulled him out of his shorts, and—

The slide of a key card in the door echoed as loud as a gunshot, and Logan stumbled back. He and Seth stared at each other in horror, everything feeling like slow motion as the door handle went down.

Logan dove back into the bathroom, kicking the door shut and crossing the tile floor so Connor couldn't hear him panting. The T-shirt was too tight on his neck, and he tugged it off.

He heard Connor say, "I forgot my goggles. We're diving for pennies."

"Cool!" Seth said, his voice really loud and fake, but farther away. He was probably back in bed with the covers up.

"Um, yeah," Connor said, and Logan could picture his face creased in his *"you're a weirdo"* expression that was usually reserved for Logan. After a few moments, Connor said, "Later," and all was silent again.

Slumping against the towel rack, his head against the tile wall, Logan exhaled. He was still achingly hard, and he automatically reached down to stroke himself, shoving his underwear to his hips to free himself.

The bathroom door opened, and Seth appeared, wearing his pajama bottoms again, the top still buttoned neatly. They stared at each other, and Seth opened his mouth to say something, probably an apology or whatever, but then snapped his jaw shut, gaze flicking from Logan's face to his dick in his hand. Even though he'd just come—the taste of it lingering in Logan's mouth—Seth's eyes went dark, and he licked his lips.

Spreading his legs, Logan jerked himself. The scars on his chest surely looked too ugly in the bright light, but Seth didn't seem to mind judging by the way he stared.

As he worked himself, Logan watched the hitch in Seth's breathing. It made him so hot the way Seth looked at him like that.

He wanted to talk dirty and get Seth hard again—because he bet he could, without even touching him. But words were all twisted up in Logan's head, and he could only grunt, the slap of his hand on his dick echoing.

Maybe none of this had been part of the casual sex addition to their deal, because as Logan came, he arched his back, his toes curling on the tile, displaying himself for Seth in a way that was very, very gay—or bisexual or whatever the hell people wanted to call it. Sure as shit, none of it felt *casual*.

Breathing hard, he slumped against the towels. They stared at each other.

Finally, Seth said too loudly, "You want first shower? We should get ready for breakfast. Time to put on a show, right?"

Logan had been panting so much his voice was raspy. "Yeah. Don't worry, we'll fool everyone." He tried not to be embarrassed about the show *he'd* just put on.

Under the hot blast of the shower, he wondered who the fuck they were actually fooling.

"NO. NO WAY." Seth crossed his arms, staring down the hill. "We're going to kill ourselves."

Logan laughed. "That's half the fun of sledding." He'd climbed up without his chest hurting, and even after the awkwardness of breakfast—trying to make boring small talk and not think about getting Seth's dick in his mouth again ASAP—he was excited to sled. It had been years.

They stood at the top of a big wide hill outside of town. There were lots of people sledding, locals and BRK staff climbing up on the sides of the slope and then blasting down the middle. It was a mostly cloudy morning, the snow thick around their boots.

They wore wool hats and thick gloves, and Logan had looped a red scarf around his neck over his leather jacket. Jenna had knit it for him, and she and Jun, Ian, and Connor were all decked out in more of her creations in all sorts of bright colors. Noah was being cared for with some other kids who were too young or didn't want to sled.

She nudged Seth playfully. "Come on, where's your Christmas spirit?"

"Since when is Christmas spirit about hurtling down an embankment and breaking our necks?"

"The spirit of Christmas is giving," Jenna said. "And you'll be giving us a huge amount of amusement to watch you sled down this hill, Southern boy. Preferably screaming all the way."

Connor laughed. "Savage." Jenna gave him a wink, and he grinned.

"You're supposed to be my friend!" Seth huffed. "What if there's an avalanche?"

They all laughed, and Jun said, "We're at the top of the hill, and this isn't a mountain." He pointed in the distance at the jagged gray peaks, snow covering the Adirondacks. "Those are mountains."

"Feels like a mountain," Seth muttered, holding up his round plastic sled. "And we're supposed to ride down on *this*?" He rubbed at the back of his neck.

Logan's smile faded as he realized Seth was actually nervous. More than that—he was afraid. "Hey, it's okay." He stepped closer and squeezed Seth's shoulder through his puffy parka. "You can walk down."

Seth groaned. "I'll look like such a wimp in front of everyone. And we're so…high. It didn't look this high from down there."

Shit, was he afraid of heights? Logan said, "I'll walk down with you."

"But you want to sled." Seth sighed. "I'm being a big baby."

"You're not." He rubbed Seth's back up and down, up and down, and Seth leaned closer to him. "We'll walk down together."

"Or sled down together," Connor said, looking at them with his forehead creased like it did when he was trying to figure out some hard math thing. "Logan knows what he's doing. Right?"

It was possibly the first time Logan had ever heard Connor say anything like that. He tried not to be too happy since the kid would probably be telling him he was an idiot in a minute. Logan was still rubbing Seth's back, and he thumped it now.

"I do. Jenna and I grew up with these flying saucers."

"Flying?" Seth shuddered. "No flying, please." He kicked at the plastic. "There's no way two of us can fit."

"Oh, you totally can," Jun said. "My brothers and I used to get four of us stacked on one."

Logan positioned his sled near the edge and flopped down, getting his butt wedged in at the back. He spread his legs. "Come on."

For a second, Seth just stood there, his face going beet red, breath clouding out in little bursts. Then he mumbled something under his breath, looking up as if saying a prayer.

Gingerly, he squatted and got into place, and Logan yanked him back so he was snug between his thighs. Logan had worn his long johns with waterproof pants over top, and the material squeaked as Seth squirmed into place.

The pom-pom of Seth's beanie was in Logan's face, so he hooked his chin over Seth's shoulder. "Lift your arms over my legs." Now Logan could wrap his arms tightly around Seth's middle. "Lean back into me and keep your feet up. That's really important, okay? Feet up."

Jenna bent with her hands on Logan's shoulders, and Logan said, "No spin."

"Okay, okay," she grumbled. "Don't worry, Seth. Logan'll take care of you. We're coming right behind!"

Logan tightened his arms, pressing his cheek against Seth's, the skin freshly shaved and warm with Seth's blush even in the cold air. "Feet up!"

Then they were sailing down the hill, the wind whipping, Seth's feet jutting up perfectly straight in the air like a solider obeying orders. The world fell away and everything was the two of them locked together, soaring so fast.

Adrenaline spiked, and Logan made a "Wooooo!" noise as they flew down. Seth dug his gloved hands into Logan's thighs, making little gasping, squeaking noises that were so fucking cute Logan could hardly take it.

They slowed at the bottom, sliding along the flat ground toward a tall snowbank that had been built up to make sure no one went into the thick pine trees beyond. They skidded to a stop, breathing hard, the shouts of Jenna and Jun and the kids echoing as they neared the bottom as well.

"See?" Logan said, squeezing Seth with his arms. "All in one piece."

Panting, Seth leaned back against him, his hands gripping Logan's knees. "That was… Goodness. Wow."

The others skidded near, Connor spinning and tumbling out with a laugh. More people were coming down all the time, and they needed to get out of the impact zone, but Logan wished he could just stay all snug with Seth for a while longer.

Jenna held up her hand for Jun, who tugged her to her feet. She grinned at Seth. "Well?"

"It was absolutely terrifying." He turned his head to look at Logan, his blue eyes lit up. "Let's do it again."

They all laughed, climbing up the hill and zooming back down several more times. Seth didn't want to go down alone, and Logan was happy to share his sled.

When they were tired out, it was time for hot chocolate and donut holes set up near their bus on folding tables. Dale really had thought of everything. Logan wanted to tell him he'd done a real good job, but wondered if it would seem like kissing ass since Dale was supposed to be finding work for him.

As he poured hot chocolate into a paper cup from a big plastic container, thumbing down the spout, excitement skittered through him. Would Dale actually be able to get him a job? Obviously Logan had to do an interview and prove himself at whatever it was, but if he could actually get money coming in, it would be such a relief.

He popped a sugary donut in his mouth. It would be more than a relief to have a job again. It would feel so damn good to not be useless anymore. He could get a place and stop freeloading off Seth, and save money for Connor and be worth something again.

Although he had to admit that the thought of moving out of Seth's house wasn't as happy as it should have been. Probably because even with a job, he'd never be able to afford something as nice as Seth's place. And with

Connor at school, he'd be alone most of the time. But that was fine. Maybe he and Seth could still hang out. Maybe…

Shoving another donut in his mouth, Logan told himself to stop being such a moron. He might not even get the job even if Dale could help him, and that was a big if anyway. And he and Seth… It was stupid to think about. They had a deal, and that was it. It was temporary.

"I thought you were just faking it with Seth?"

Stomach dropping, Logan gripped his paper cup a little harder and took a gulp, burning the roof of his mouth. "I am."

Holding his own cup, Connor was watching him suspiciously, his eyebrows almost meeting. "Really?"

"Of course." Logan forced a laugh.

"Because you look at him the way you looked at my mom, back at the beginning. When I thought maybe things wouldn't suck."

Logan tried to figure out what Connor was saying. It didn't make any sense. "When you thought… But you hated me from day one."

Connor looked down at the donuts, shrugging. "You weren't so bad, I guess." He picked out a chocolate one and ate it.

"I…" Logan had no clue what to say. "Oh. Thanks?"

Connor huffed, eating another donut and mumbling, "Anyway, Seth seems into you. But you're just pretending. Right?"

"Don't talk with your mouth full." Logan glanced at where Seth stood off with Jenna and Jun, drinking their hot chocolate and laughing about something.

Connor rolled his eyes, licking crumbs from his lips. He looked up at Logan, apparently waiting for an answer.

Heart thumping, Logan chugged his hot chocolate, wiping his mouth after. "Guess we're both good actors." Sure, he and Seth were screwing, and they were into it, but that's all it was. That was the deal—casual.

"Guess so."

Logan tried to think of something to say. "You looking forward to lunch with Santa?"

There was that familiar scowl. "I'm not some little kid."

"I know. But it's Christmas. My mom used to say we all get to be kids at Christmas." He hadn't thought of that in years, and for a moment, he missed her so damn much.

This was Connor's first Christmas without Veronica, and he wanted to tell him that it would be okay, and that it would get easier over time. Or at least it would be different. It would still hurt like hell sometimes, but not all the time.

But he didn't say any of that because Connor was already gone with a handful of donut holes, off to hang with some kids around his age. Shit, Logan really needed to get presents for Connor to open. Jenna would surely be getting some for Christmas Eve at her place, but they'd be at Seth's on Christmas morning.

And shit, he needed to get Seth a present too. More than one. With no money, he'd have to borrow from Jenna and Jun, and what if he didn't get a job after all? He was suddenly afraid he'd puke up hot chocolate all over the snow.

"Okay?" Seth asked as he walked up. "Don't tell me all that sledding has made you green around the gills and not me." He squeezed the back of Logan's neck over his scarf, and Logan concentrated on deep breaths, a stab of pain in his chest flaring and then easing.

He almost said he was fine and shrugged Seth off but let Seth ground him until he could give him a real smile.

Chapter Sixteen

"WELL, IF THAT isn't the moony face of a man in love!"

Seth jolted as Angela's twangy voice rang out from alarmingly close by. He realized he'd been too busy staring at Logan rolling the base for a snowman. And at Logan's firm backside as he bent over to perform said task, his short leather jacket riding up, jeans clinging to his butt and thighs.

Squirming, he tried to laugh. "Guilty as charged." He raised his gloved hands. *Ha, ha, ha. Hilarious.*

The pom-pom on Angela's fuchsia beanie wobbled as she joined him at the railing of the large stone patio where Seth stood watching the snowpeople being created in all shapes and sizes on the hotel's back lawn.

Ice covered the empty lake beyond, but Seth assumed it was still too thin to skate on since they were skating later at the Olympic center. Sunlight beamed down, glaring off the snow, the sky having cleared to a perfect blue, the air absolutely frigid.

"It really is festive here," Seth said, nodding at the decorations strung between light poles.

"It is. I love the holidays. I think no matter what your background, you should be able to enjoy Santa and Rudolph if you want. It's a treat to get all the snow, even if it's colder than a penguin's pecker."

Seth laugh-choked, coughing hard. "That's one way to put it."

Angela laughed. "I speak it like it is." She eyed Connor in the distance where he stood with crossed arms, watching Logan roll the massive snowball, little Ian joining in beside Logan. Connor was saying something.

Angela snorted softly. "Probably telling his daddy he's doin' it all wrong."

Seth laughed ruefully. "Most likely. Connor can be a handful." He was acting like he hadn't just met the boy and guilt nagged at the deception. Still, he had gotten to know Connor a bit and would be spending the holidays with him. He rolled his eyes internally. *As if that makes this lie less of a whopper.*

"Logan was his stepfather, right? His biological father's not in the picture?"

"Not much at all. He lives in Florida and is hardly in touch."

She shook her head, pom-pom waving. "That'll really do a number on a kid, especially after losing his momma."

"Yes." Seth thought of his own parents. He'd been grown, but it had undoubtedly done a number on him to be rejected and ignored.

"It'll be good for him once you and Logan are married. Give him stability. I realized I plumb forgot to ask about the wedding details when I came for dinner. When's the big day?"

Uh-oh. Was she angling for an invitation? Seth stammered, "Um, well—you see—uh, I—" He snapped his jaw shut, feeling his ears go hot under his wool hat.

Well, *now* he had Angela's attention. Her sculpted eyebrows met. "Is there a problem?"

"No! It's just… I need to find a church."

"Oh! Surely there are some open-minded houses of worship up here? New York State doesn't get much bluer. Heck, you might be pleasantly surprised by some of the churches in Texas. Not all of 'em, I grant you, but I suppose that's true everywhere." She sighed heavily. "I'll just never understand why we can't love our fellow man the way the good lord made 'em."

"I'm sure my parents would have some thoughts on the matter." Seth cringed as soon as he said it. "Anyway, I'm sure we'll find something soon." He fiddled with the fringe on his plaid scarf. "So we're going skating later, right? Can't wait!"

But Angela didn't answer, instead watching him with clear sadness, her mouth pulled down. "Your parents aren't supportive of you and Logan?"

"No. Well, they don't know Logan exists. It's been years since I had any contact with them. One Christmas, I told them I was gay and had a boyfriend, and they showed me the door." He shrugged, going for careless and surely failing.

"Oh, sugar." Angela squeezed her gloved hand over his where Seth gripped the balcony railing, the icy stone cold even through insulated leather. "That just breaks my heart. I hope you know you're not alone."

Seth nodded, a lump in his throat almost choking him. Come January, he *would* be alone again. Sure, he'd see Jenna at work, but he'd come back to his finally finished house every night and there'd be no one else. Not even Agatha.

He missed her with a sharp pang. He'd felt too guilty about "replacing" her, but he really had to get another cat. And after saying it aloud, he realized he *did* want to find a church.

He found himself saying, "After my family turned their backs on me, I stopped going to church. I should have found a place in Atlanta, but I told myself I had a private relationship with God. And I do, but it would be nice to find a congregation where I could be myself." He shook his head. "I'm sorry. I don't know why I'm telling you all this."

Angela winked, her long lashes heavy with mascara. "Because I'm a nosy broad."

"I'm not sure whether I should agree or not."

She laughed throatily. "I get plenty of people blowin' smoke up my backside. Now tell me about your ideas for your department. No pressure, even though I'm putting you on the spot."

"Oh! Right. No problem." For a horrifying moment, his mind was completely blank. But he watched Logan rolling another snowball with the kids and caught his breath. "I'd start with tweaking our initial approach."

They stood by the railing discussing Seth's ideas, Angela asking sharp, intelligent questions before she was called away by Dale. Before she left, she winked at Seth and told him HR would be in touch in the new year about his promotion, and he almost did a cartwheel right there on the snow-covered stone.

When they all trooped over to the Olympic center for skating, he couldn't wipe the grin off his face. Logan leaned in, his breath gusting warm over Seth's cheek. "What's got you so happy?"

Everything. The promotion. You.

"Pretty sure I got the job," Seth whispered.

Logan grinned, and his craggy face was beautiful in a way Seth had never imagined when they'd met. It seemed impossible it had been less than two weeks ago. As Seth lined up for skates, he checked his math.

Yes, eleven days. But that was another reason why whatever this was between them was only casual. They barely knew each other, and they'd made a mutually beneficial arrangement.

A successful one! Seth had apparently snagged the job, Logan might get a job out of it himself, and he'd had a place to stay while helping Seth get over his hang-ups about having sex without being in love. Seth was surprised to not feel particularly guilty about the hookups.

That's because they aren't just hookups.

His traitorous mind immediately supplied images of Logan on his knees that morning with his mouth full of... Well, of Seth. He shivered with pleasure just to think of it—and what had followed. Seeing Logan touching himself had been shockingly electric. The silence between them during the act had made it feel even more secret and special.

Although now Seth could imagine what Logan would say about it.

"You liked seeing me jack myself, hmm? Bet it makes your cock hard to think about watching me. Want to watch me again? Or do you want to get down on your hands and knees so I can fuck you and come—"

"Size?"

For an awful moment at the head of the line, Seth could only think about penises. Then he managed, "Eleven and a half," and the bored girl behind the counter thunked a pair of skates on top. Seth added, "And a ten and a half, and a six. Please."

The skate pairs were tied together by their laces, and he carried them hooked over his fingers to where Logan and Connor waited on one of the benches lining a white wall.

He was very glad his parka went to mid-thigh, and he forced his mind back to the present. Skating. With countless children present. No sex going on, casual or otherwise. He jammed his socked feet inside the skates and focused on lacing them.

"You need to tie those tighter," Logan said a minute later. He and Connor had their skates on already and were standing waiting. Logan knelt at Seth's feet to retie the laces, which was so sweet, yet spectacularly unhelpful in regards to Seth's partial erection.

The black skates were big and clunky and apparently made for hockey, although Seth wasn't sure how exactly they differed from figure skates. As he stood, he clutched Logan's arm. "Whoa. I don't know if I can walk in these, let alone go out on the ice."

"You've never skated before?" Connor asked.

"I'm from a small town in Georgia. I think there might have been a rink, but I never went there." Too busy with countless church activities.

Connor said, "It's just like walking, but you know. Faster or something."

"Right. No problem." Seth squared his shoulders and walked assuredly. There. He could do this.

His confidence evaporated the moment the thin blades touched the ice. He clung to the boards beside the entryway, where others waited behind him to get out on the rink. His knees shook, and he took a baby step forward, trying just to get out of the way.

He immediately overbalanced and landed on his knees and bare hands. He'd stupidly left his gloves with his shoes since it was chilly in the arena, but quite comfortable compared to outside.

"Whoa!" Logan was there, his hands also bare as they grabbed around Seth's waist and lifted him to his feet. Seth leaned too far back against Logan, his skates making little slicing motions. But Logan was a rock behind him, chuckling softly as he pushed Seth to the safety of the boards and the railing around the rink.

"You're like Bambi," Connor laughed, his eyes crinkling.

"This was a mistake. I can't do it." Seth gripped the wide top of the boards. His whole bottom half felt out of control, although at least his inappropriate erection had vanished.

Other people whizzed by, everyone circling the rink counter-clockwise. On the loudspeaker, someone sang about rocking around the Christmas tree. "You guys go ahead. I'll wait on the bench. Just help me get there."

Logan laughed too, taking Seth's hand after prying it loose from the boards. "Come on. One lap around."

Connor nudged Seth's other side. "We won't let you fall. If you do, you'll take us all down." He nudged Seth again. "Let go."

Saying a quick prayer not to break any bones, Seth released the boards and took a tiny step. Then another. Connor's small hand took his right, and with Logan on the left, Seth tentatively walked across the ice. He had their hands in a death grip, but they didn't complain.

The skates hurt his feet, and his thighs burned from the strain of keeping steady, but he was making progress. Jenna, Jun, and Ian whizzed by with a wave, Ian between them.

"I'm like the five-year-old," Seth grumbled. "Except Ian's much better at this."

"It's okay," Connor said. "We all have to learn stuff sometimes. Try pushing off some." He demonstrated, gliding on his right foot and pulling Seth along. "It's actually easier to go faster."

Seth tried to mimic the smooth stride, almost pitching over onto his face. They patiently pulled him upright, and he tried again. And again. And again. As the Madonna cover of "Santa Baby" played, Seth was practically skating.

"I'm doing it!" he exclaimed, and then pitched forward, over-corrected back, and smacked onto the ice on his butt, yanking down Logan and Connor too with gravity's help.

The three of them sat on their rear ends laughing, families skating by around them. "I'm sorry!" Seth shook his head. "Oh my lord, how am I going to get up?"

Connor was already on his feet, and Logan rolled to his knees and pushed upright. He said to Connor, "Dunno. Maybe we should leave him here."

Connor blinked as if surprised to be in on a joke with Logan. He shrugged with forced nonchalance. "I guess. We can pick him up again after a few laps. He'll still be here."

It made Seth's heart so glad to see them bonding, even if he was the butt—no pun intended—of the joke. He harrumphed theatrically. "Go on. Abandon me here to my fate."

Matt and Becky skated by, and Matt howled with laughter, pointing at Seth, Becky rolling her eyes.

"Nah," Connor said, and they took Seth's hands again, pulling him to his feet and keeping him steady. "It's more fun with you."

Hand-in-hand, the three of them set off again, and Seth managed half a lap before slipping and pulling them down in a heap of laughter.

DINNER WAS OVER, but it seemed Angela had one more activity planned. Or least Dale did, as he instructed volunteers in setting up two rows of chairs in the middle of the open space in the dining room as hotel staff cleaned up the buffet tables.

Beside Seth, Logan eyed the game setup suspiciously. "What's this, musical chairs or some shit?" He took another sip of red wine.

The room still smelled like roast beef and gravy, and Seth was stuffed. Connor had gone off with the other kids for a screening of *Home Alone* in a conference room, Angela promising them bean bags and candy and a popcorn machine.

"Logan!" Dale trotted over with a smile. "Been meaning to tell you that I sent your resume to Bob Ricci. He owns a statewide contracting company that's done some work for Angela in New York City. He's going to call you later this week after Christmas. He's eager to do more work for Angela, so unless you royally screw up the interview—and I mean *royally*—he'll have a job for you in January. He said he's starting a new office renovation in downtown Albany. It's perfect timing."

"Wow." Logan shot to his feet and stuck out his hand, pumping Dale's vigorously. "Thank you."

Seth grinned, barely resisting the urge to hug Dale for making this happen. Logan was beaming with joy, and Seth's heart clenched to see it.

Logan said, "I promise I won't take a dump on his desk at the interview."

Dale tipped his head back and laughed. "You remind me of Angela. You both say exactly what's on your mind. And remember, even though she got your foot in the door, you're the one who's going to walk through." He nodded to Seth. "Merry Christmas. It's been a pleasure meeting you both."

Seth stood to shake his hand, and he and Logan shared a grin when Dale left. Seth squeezed the back of Logan's neck, wanting to pull him close and kiss him, wanting to whirl him around in celebration even though Logan was probably too heavy for him to lift.

At the next table, Jenna bounced in her chair, she and Jun giving them a thumbs-up since they'd clearly overheard Dale's news. Ian had gone to the movie, and Noah was with a hotel sitter for a few hours. Jenna had been sniffing her glass of wine loudly, apparently savoring every sip.

Logan sat back down heavily, smiling in a daze. "I might have a job."

Seth squeezed his wrist, almost taking Logan's hand. "You'll nail the interview. I know it."

Of course, if Logan got a job, there'd be no reason for him not to move out in January like they'd agreed. That splashed cold water on his happiness, although Seth really did want Logan to get the job. He wanted Logan to get…everything. Absolutely everything.

He wanted to share everything with him.

We made a deal. Casual. No feelings. Stop making it into more.

Folding his hands in his lap, Seth tuned back in as Angela stood by the rows of chairs holding a long branch with red ribbon tied on it and a sprig of berries dangling off the end as if it was a fishing rod.

Waving the branch, she said, "Y'all know what this is, right? We're going to play a fun little game for the grown-ups. It's like musical chairs, but whoever's left standing gives their sweetie a kiss under the mistletoe. Don't worry, BRK is a family company and this is strictly PG. Maybe PG-13 if someone's feelin' saucy. Maestro?"

"Have a Holly Jolly Christmas" filled the air, and couples rose to circle the chairs, some clearly reluctant, others skipping along. Seth laughed as Matt dragged Becky up, but his smile froze as Angela pointed right at him.

She shouted, "Come on now! We need some diversity up here!"

Jenna and Jun tugged on Logan and Seth's arms. Jun muttered, "If we have to do this, you have to do this."

They made their way to the double row of back-to-back chairs. Seth gave Logan an apologetic smile, and Logan shrugged, smiling back as they joined the group circling the chairs.

The silence was sudden, followed by shouts and laughter as they scrambled for the chairs. Logan and Seth ended up a few apart, but both safely seated. Left standing, Miriam from IT pulled up a man Seth presumed was her husband and kissed him soundly as Angela held the mistletoe over their heads with her branch.

Everyone applauded, and the song started again, Burl Ives's kind voice telling them to have a cup of cheer and kiss under the mistletoe. The game went on, Seth's heart racing as they circled, waiting for the shock of silence to dive for a chair.

When he missed, it was Matt who grabbed it before him, his shaggy hair flying. He whispered, "Caper!" with a big grin. Logan stood and joined Seth, and Angela whipped the mistletoe over their heads with eagerness she didn't try to hide.

"Now let's hear it for our lovebirds!" she exclaimed.

Everyone clapped and hooted, and Seth felt like he was blushing all the way down to his feet in his leather shoes. Fidgeting, Logan's smile was too tight.

Seth laughed nervously and stepped closer, giving Logan a lightning-quick peck on the lips. More clapping, and Seth waved and laughed, ready to escape back to the table.

Then Logan was blocking his way.

Then Logan was taking Seth's face in his work-rough hands.

Then Logan was kissing him.

Then Logan was kissing him for *real.*

Not a peck. A genuine kiss—sweet and soft and sure all at the same time, pressing their lips together like there was nothing else in the whole world but the two of them. Nothing casual about it.

Head spinning, Seth clutched at Logan's waist. His heart was thunder in his ears as the kiss went on, their mouths fused and his knees actually going weak. Logan smelled like musky earth and pine, and Seth melted into him.

When he gasped for air, he realized the thunder wasn't only his heart—it was stomping feet and palms on tables, a swell of applause and support from everyone in the room. Seth's skin prickled with the heat of so many eyes on him, but Logan's warm gaze was the only one that mattered.

What's happening?

Seth couldn't look at anyone as he and Logan returned to their table. His heart pounded, his body thrumming with adrenaline and stubborn joy. And when Logan tugged his wrist, Seth followed him out of the dining room and into the elevator. Neither of them spoke, staring straight ahead.

The kiss had felt so real. But Logan was probably regretting it, fleeing to their room because he was done with this charade.

The hotel room was dimly lit and silent as the door shut behind Seth with a *click*. His heart thumped as Logan turned to regard him seriously in the narrow entryway. Logan opened and closed his mouth, frowning.

Then he kissed Seth again, this time his tongue thrusting past Seth's lips as he grabbed him. Seth could only moan, meeting Logan's tongue, wet and insistent, tasting of gravy and wine and perfection.

"Want you," Logan muttered against Seth's mouth, their kisses broken only by little gulps of air.

"Oh!" He hummed with desire, and as Logan dropped to his knees like he had that morning, Seth thumped back against the door, already hard, and—

He gasped and jerked up ramrod straight, his fingers digging into Logan's shoulder, staring in horrified disbelief at Connor, who'd appeared by the end of the far bed. They'd left the bedside lamp on before going down for dinner, and it partly illuminated Connor now, half of his face creased and confused, the rest in shadow.

"What are you doing?" Connor asked.

Logan shot to his feet. "What are you doing here?" he asked too sharply. "I thought you were watching the movie."

Jaw tight, Connor said, "Seen it a million times. We decided to go swimming again. I came up to get changed." He still wore his jeans, long-sleeved T-shirt, and sneakers. He asked again, his voice harder, "What are you doing?"

"Nothing!" they answered in unison, as if they were the kids and Connor the adult.

Fists clenching, his shirt sleeves too short, Connor marched toward them, glaring daggers at Logan. "You're lying to him like you did to my mom, aren't you? Aren't you!" His face creased. "I should have known. I thought maybe I was wrong, but I'm not."

Logan seemed stunned into silence. Seth said, "Connor, everything's okay. I know this must be confusing, but—"

"He's playing you!" Connor shouted. "Can't you see that? He's telling you everything you want to hear. He's a liar. Don't believe what he says. He doesn't really like you!" He sneered at Logan. "You're not even gay, but you'll do anything to get what you want. You don't really care about him. Or me. I bet you'll take all Seth's money."

"I didn't marry your mother for her money," Logan said quietly. Seth prayed his restraint would continue.

"Yeah, the joke was on you because she didn't have any," Connor spat. "But you needed a place to live, so you made her think you loved her. It was all a lie, wasn't it?"

"No!" Logan's chest rose and fell with a sharp breath. "I really did love her, and she loved me. We got caught up in a stupid dream of helping each other, and we moved way too fast. We never should have got married. But I didn't lie when I said our vows. It was way too good to be true, but I wanted to believe we could be happy."

Logan looked to Seth, his eyes beseeching. "And maybe I'm being a dumb fuck all over again, but I really like you."

Seth took his hand, squeezing Logan's rough fingers. "I like you too."

Red-faced, Connor gritted his teeth. "But I asked you this morning, and you told me it was all fake!"

"I didn't know what to say," Logan said. "It *is* supposed to be fake. That was the deal."

"And now you're suddenly gay?"

"No." Logan rubbed his face with his free hand, the other clinging to Seth's. "I honestly don't know what I am. Apparently more bisexual than I thought. What I know for sure is that I like Seth more than I've liked anyone in a long, long time."

Connor looked between them, his pimply face creased. He glared at Logan. "But you'll ruin everything! Seth's awesome, and you'll fuck him over!"

Seth kept his voice even. "Okay, let's sit down and take some deep breaths, and we can talk about this."

"He's using you! What's there to talk about? Fuck this." Connor shoved past them with surprising strength, wriggling behind Seth and out the door before they could stop him.

"Shit!" Logan was hot on his heels, and Seth followed, jogging down the carpeted hall past wooden doors.

Connor went for the stairs, and they chased him down and right outside through a fire exit, Seth grimacing as his leather shoes filled with freezing snow that came up to his shins.

"Connor, get back here!" Logan shouted. But Connor ignored him, running hard through the snow at the back of the hotel, weaving around snowmen and out onto the lake. Seth's lungs burned in the freezing air, but he didn't slow.

"Get back here! Get off that ice!" Logan yelled. "Now!"

"Fuck you!" Connor slid forward, his arms outstretched as if he was on skates instead of sneakers.

Seth tried for a gentler approach. "Connor, please! Just come back and we can talk."

Connor ignored him, continuing away from the shore. Seth wasn't even sure exactly where the land ended and the lake begun.

Logan bellowed, "I swear to God, if you don't get back here now—"

Connor spun around. "What? What are you going to do? I hate you! I'm going to live with my dad in Florida."

"Have you spoken with him?" Seth asked loudly after coming to a stop. None of them had jackets on, and it was too cold to be outside. Connor faced them from about thirty feet away.

After sputtering, Connor insisted, "He's busy! He has a hard job!" In the moonlight, tears glittered on his cheeks even at a distance, a stifled sob making him gasp. "But he's my dad, so he has to love me. He *has* to."

Logan exhaled sharply in a white plume. In a calmer tone, he called, "Come inside and we'll talk about this."

He glanced behind, and Seth realized they'd garnered some attention, faces at windows and a few people in open doors, shivering and watching them.

Logan called again, "Please come back."

Connor sneered. "Afraid of what people will think? They should know the truth. You used my mom and now you're using him too." A fresh surge of rage seemed to erupt. "Go to hell!" He turned and slip-stepped across the ice, the wind having blown away the snow from some patches.

There was no dramatic *craaaack!* or warning sign. One second Connor was there and the next he disappeared into a pit of darkness with only a splash that echoed in the night.

Seth's heart slammed against his ribs, and he sprinted onto the lake, shouts echoing in the distance, Logan's fingers clutching at his sleeve. Seth lurched forward, shaking off Logan.

"Wait!" Logan shouted. "You'll—"

The ice crumpled beneath him, plunging Seth into the icy depths. The cold punched the breath from his lungs, his limbs locking, muscles rigid. His brain shouted at him to kick and resurface, but his body wouldn't— couldn't—obey.

Lungs burning and body frozen, he sank.

Fingers tugged his hair upward, and he barely felt it. As he broke through the water, he sucked in a deep, desperate breath. Logan was on his belly hauling Seth out, saying something Seth couldn't understand.

Then Logan was gone, and there were other people slithering across the ice on their stomachs, reaching for him and dragging him to safety.

But Connor! Seth tried to speak, but it was only a garbled grunt. From behind him, he heard a cry, weak and high-pitched, an animal sound that sent a shiver through his soul, his limbs jerking in spasm.

People were talking at him, tugging at him, wrapping a blanket around him. Seth's lungs stuttered, and he screamed at his body to cooperate.

Finally, he was able to turn his head to look for Connor and Logan. They weren't there.

Panic rocketed him to his feet. Had he been sitting on the ground? He stumbled back toward the lake, ignoring the voices around him and hands trying to stop him. Didn't they understand? Logan and Connor were out there! Seth had to find them!

Someone grabbed his shoulders, right up in his face. Seth blinked at him, realizing it was Matt. Matt was saying something. Seth felt like he was trying to get a radio station but was a few degrees off, the words distant and staticky.

"Okay," Matt said.

Seth put everything into focusing on Matt. "What?" he rasped.

"They're okay. You're all safe." Still grasping Seth's rigid shoulders, he looked behind him. "See?"

Blinking, Seth made out the cluster of people beyond, Logan and Connor at the center. Relief coursed through him, and he staggered, shivering violently now, his body finally responding to his commands. With Matt's arm around his shoulders, he stumbled to them. A siren wailed distantly.

There were so many voices, but they were static again as Seth reached for Logan, slumping against him. There was only soaked cotton between them as Logan hugged Seth tightly, his arms trembling. Connor huddled against them, people wrapping blankets around him.

Then paramedics were there with bright lights and very loud questions, poking and prodding. Someone was saying they were lucky they were so close to the hotel and the town, and that they'd only been in the water a very short time.

"I want my mom."

Connor's words cut through the rest of the noise, so horribly plaintive that everyone seemed to stop short. Connor said it again, his anguished wail piercing Seth's heart.

"I want my mom!"

Seth and Logan reached for him together, Connor thrashing for a few moments before collapsing against them, weeping with gasping sobs that seemed far too big for his skinny little body to contain without shattering completely.

Holding him safe between them, Seth and Logan clutched each other with frozen fingers as Connor cried for the mother he'd never have again.

Chapter Seventeen

"WELL, *THAT WAS* quite a scene tonight."

Sitting on the side of the hospital bed, Logan looked up to find Angela standing in the open gap in the curtain around his ER berth. Hands on hips, lips pressed tight, she shook her head gravely, fancy dangling earrings catching the washed-out fluorescent light.

Logan cringed. The last thing he wanted to do right now was act more. "Sorry," he rasped, his throat still dry.

Her face softened, and she reached for his hand, giving it a kind squeeze. "Sugar, I'm messin' with you. Thought I'd lighten the mood. There's nothing to be sorry for. We're all just relieved you, Seth, and Connor are okay."

"Oh. Uh, thanks." One of the worries that had been jabbing at him spilled out. "You're not going to fire Seth?"

She scoffed. "What on earth gave you that idea? You think I have time to find another new director of systems training? Tomorrow's December twenty-third, and I'm flying home when we get back to Albany. Besides, he's the man for the job. No question about it."

"Thank God," Logan muttered, relief pouring through him. He'd still been shivering in his hospital sweatpants and sweatshirt, and now he relaxed a bit. He hadn't fucked it up for Seth after all.

"So what's with the glum face?" Angela let go of his hand and hoisted herself up to sit beside him on the bed, her short legs dangling, leather high-heeled boots knocking together. Logan was only wearing thick socks, but his feet brushed the linoleum floor.

"Dunno. I'm worried about Connor and Seth. Jenna said they're fine. She's been going back and forth. I tried to stay with Connor, but he didn't want me there." Logan ached from it, but it wasn't about him. If Connor needed Jenna right now, that's who he'd get.

"Yep, just getting their walking papers like you have."

"Good. I don't know what's wrong with me."

"I'd say it's a touch of shock."

"Yeah. That's what the doc said."

"Taking an unexpected ice bath will do that. Not to mention seeing your son and your man go under. That must've been the fright of your life."

His son. His man.

A thick, sticky burst of emotion punched him in the gut. Logan wanted it to be true. He wanted a family. *This* family with Connor and Seth.

"I never thought I could love a man like this." He flattened his hand on his chest, almost able to feel the scars through the cheap cotton sweatshirt. "With—with my whole heart." He had to watch his mouth and not give the game away to Angela.

But it didn't feel like a game at all anymore.

He shuddered violently. "I thought they were gone."

Angela slipped her arm around his shoulders with a surprisingly strong grip, and Logan let himself lean into it. Then he found himself talking again, his brain shouting to be careful.

"I can't get it out of my head. Seeing them disappear." He rubbed his hands up and down his thighs, nervous energy pinballing through him. "They were there, and then they were gone. I don't think I was ever that scared before. Even fighting in the desert. Maybe that's just faded over the years. But this was like I was choking. Sometimes I have trouble breathing because of the accident I had, and it was like that, but so much worse. I thought I was gonna die too if they were dead."

Saying it out loud was fucking scary, but it felt good at the same time.

"You yanked out your man and jumped right in after your boy like a big darn hero."

His brain replayed it: Connor being gulped up by the lake, Seth running after him—not knowing to drop to his stomach to spread out his weight since he grew up in Georgia without ice. The bone-deep relief when he'd pulled Seth out and the terror that Connor would be out of reach.

He snorted. "I'm no hero. I'm the reason Connor ran out there in the first place. I messed up. Again."

When Logan had taken a huge breath and plunged into the water to get Connor, part of him had thought it must be a nightmare. The idea of losing Connor—of failing him so badly, of never having a chance to be the dad he needed—was un-fucking-bearable.

Angela squeezed his shoulders. "Show me a parent who says they never messed up, and I'll show you someone crooked as a dog's hind leg."

Logan had to laugh, which felt good. Then the guilt crashed in. He'd fucked up and Connor and Seth had almost died. He shouldn't be laughing.

Angela said softly, "That poor boy, crying for his momma. That's a hurt you can't fix."

"If I'd been there the night she died, maybe I could have saved her. We were breaking up, and…"

Angela sighed. "Life sure can be a kick in the crotch. You wish you could turn back time and make it right somehow. But the only thing you and Seth can do is be there and give him all the love in the world. And I know you will."

Will we? Can we? Logan wanted it so bad, the constant ache inside him surging and taking his breath away. It wasn't only that he didn't want to be alone. He wanted Seth—and Connor. He wanted to make a family with them.

A real one.

"We haven't known each other that long," he blurted, because he was an idiot.

But Angela didn't seem suspicious and only shrugged. "So? I knew my husband was the one the first time I met him. Rosebud county fair, nineteen-eighty-four. I was sweet sixteen."

"Rosebud?"

"Yep, south of Waco. Paul was taking tickets at the Ferris wheel—rickety old thing, let me tell you. My girlfriends refused to ride it, so I went on my own. I was always the adventurous one, and Paul was just too cute to pass up. He was a shy one, but he stammered out a few sentences, and every time I came around the bottom, I waved to him, and he waved back. When my time was up, he let me keep going. I rode that old wheel for an hour, and then the fair was closing, and he took a spin with me. His buddy stopped it at the top, and we sat up there talking—mostly me talking and him listenin'—and I never wanted to come down. When you know, you know."

"I thought I knew with Connor's mom. Veronica." Logan scrubbed his face. "That's a lie. I knew we were kidding ourselves, but I went along. I don't want fuck up again with Seth. It feels different, but what if I'm wrong?"

She shrugged. "Only one way to find out."

Logan was quiet, listening to machines beep and murmured conversations beyond the curtain. "It's happened real fast with Seth." He didn't say quite *how* fast. "But seeing him and Connor go through the ice. Seeing how they could be taken away just like *that*." He snapped his fingers dully. "That's what happened to Veronica." He snapped again.

"Then you know how precious life is. Grab on to the people who make your heart happy and don't ever let go. And to hell with anyone who doesn't like it."

"Is that what you did?"

"Yes, sir. We waited until after high school to get hitched—I knew, but I was no fool either. It's been *mumble-mumble* years now." She laughed. "But he still listens to me until I'm tired of talkin'. Every word."

"I want that."

"Ain't a thing wrong with that."

But what did Seth want? Logan believed Seth liked him, but it was all so new. What if this really was a mistake as well?

Only one way to find out.

IT WAS PAST midnight when they trooped into the hotel room, all of them wearing the gray sweatsuits from the hospital and cheap flip-flops, their shoes still soaking wet.

Jenna said to come down the hall and wake her the second they needed something, but what they needed was rest. They took turns in the bathroom and changed into PJs.

Logan watched Seth shiver as he buttoned up his grandpa pajamas. He wanted to kiss him so bad. He didn't want Seth to ever be scared or hurt again. Hell, he didn't want Seth to even be cold.

Connor sat up against the padded headboard of his bed, his big tee pulled up to his chin along with the thick comforter. Seth asked, "Should I turn up the heat more?" Connor shook his head. Seth sat on the other bed. "We should get some sleep, huh?"

Connor nodded but didn't move. The lamp between the beds cast a low golden glow. Shivering himself in his T-shirt and boxer briefs, Logan sat beside Seth, brushing against him and the flannel, resisting pulling Seth onto his lap just to hold him.

They sat in silence, Seth giving him a worried glance. Logan figured Connor wanted to talk or he would already be asleep. Or be pretending or something. But he sat up still.

"I miss my mom," Connor whispered. His eyes were still red and puffy from earlier, and he seemed so small in the big bed. Would Logan mess it up if he tried to hug him?

Logan cleared his throat. "I know. I wish I could bring her back for you. I wish I could go back and be there and change it."

After a few beats of silence, Seth murmured, "I thought they said there was nothing anyone could do."

"But I *was* there!" Connor's lip wobbled, tears filling his big brown eyes. "I was up late playing video games even after she told me to turn it off and go to bed. I used my headphones, and eventually I fell asleep with the game still going. If she—what if she called for me? What if she asked me for help?"

Logan shook his head. "With that kind of aneurysm, there was nothing you could have done. It was over in a few seconds." He snapped his fingers. "Like that."

He wasn't sure if it was exactly true—docs could guess, but no one would ever know for sure how long it had taken and if she'd suffered. But he wouldn't let Connor blame himself. Connor was a kid, and he needed sure things. He needed Logan to be sure. What was that saying? *Fake it 'til you make it.*

"But what if it wasn't?" Connor whispered. "What if she laid there with her brain exploding and I didn't hear her? What if she was scared? I was right next door, and she told me to stop playing. I didn't listen, and then I couldn't hear her!" He sobbed raggedly. "Don't you get it? It's my fault!"

"*No*." Logan was on his feet, and he stood there uselessly for a few moments before sitting by Connor's feet, Connor's knees still pulled to his chest under the covers.

Don't fuck this up.

Logan said, "It wasn't your fault. You didn't do anything wrong. You know your mom would say the same thing. She loved you more than anything in the whole world. She would never blame you. Not in a million years."

"I wanted her to make breakfast." Connor sniffled loudly, wiping his nose with his hand. "Because I was too lazy to do it myself. I was an asshole. That was why I went to find her. Not because I was worried. I should have been. I should have noticed the coffee pot was still upside-down on the side of the sink from when she washed it the night before. But I was only thinking about myself."

"You're a kid," Logan said. "That's what kids do. You think I appreciated everything my mom did for me? No way. Took it for granted until I joined the Marines. And pretty soon she was gone, and I didn't even get to say goodbye."

Connor blinked at him, fresh tears streaking his flushed cheeks. "Really? I didn't know that."

"Yeah. It sucked. It sucked real hard. I got to talk to her on my CO's computer, but it's not the same. She looked so pale and…small. I couldn't understand how she'd gotten so small, so fast."

Connor shivered. "Mom was all gray," he whispered. "Waxy, like she was fake. But it was her. And then they put a sheet over her like she didn't mean anything. She was everything!"

Logan put his hand over the mound under the comforter where Connor's knees were. "I know. Your mom and I made a mistake getting married, but I'm so glad I met her. And you."

Wiping his eyes, Connor snorted. "Yeah, right. You're just stuck with me."

"That's what family's about. Being stuck with each other." Hand still on Connor's knees, he looked at Seth sitting on the other bed. "And sometimes your birth family sucks and they throw you out like Seth's did. Or they don't take care of you the way they should, like your dad."

Logan held his breath, waiting for Connor to freak out and defend his asshole father. But he didn't. He nodded, sniffling loudly. "My dad sucks." He looked at Seth. "Your family sucks too."

"Yeah," Seth said. "But you know, we get to pick our families too. You and Logan get to pick each other. Your mom brought you together, and you can choose to embrace it." He smiled wryly. "Maybe give each other a break?"

Logan and Connor looked at each other, and they smiled too. Logan's chest went warm and gooey. "Yeah, that sounds like a plan, huh?" He jostled Connor's knees.

"Okay." He wiped his eyes. "Thanks for rescuing me."

Logan thought of how bony and fragile Connor had felt under his frozen hands as he'd pushed him up onto the ice. How breakable. He couldn't let Connor break. Maybe he wouldn't always do or say the right thing, but he was going to try his hardest every day.

He was going to be the best dad he could.

Logan cleared his throat. "Anytime. Although let's not do that again. And let's not… Look, I'm sorry I lied to you about me and Seth. I should have told you the truth, even though it was confusing. Confusing to me, I mean."

He glanced at Seth, who gave him a little smile. Logan went on, his heart drumming. "Because this was all supposed to be pretend, and it doesn't feel like that now. It feels real. And I want it to be real. I really like Seth a lot."

He was still looking at Seth. Seth's smile grew wider, and he was so pretty and sweet, and yep—Logan wanted to kiss him over and over. He wanted to kiss Seth until their lips hurt. Logan smiled back before looking at Connor again.

Connor eyed him with his brows drawn close. "You really mean it?"

"I do. I'm not trying to steal Seth's money or anything like that."

Connor's cheeks went pink, and he looked down. "I know," he mumbled. He snaked one hand out from under the covers and pulled at a loose thread on a seam. "Did you cheat on my mom?" He looked Logan straight in the eyes.

"Never." Logan didn't have to fake the confidence in what he was saying. "I didn't cheat on her. We weren't meant to be together in the long run, but I never even looked at other women." He hesitated. "Or men. I'm a lot of things, and I sure ain't perfect, but I'm not a cheater."

Connor nodded. "I believe you. I think… I think I always knew that." He dropped his head, then blurted, "I'm sorry I called you stupid so many times. I—you're not stupid. I just get so mad." His thin shoulders hunched.

"I get it," Logan said gruffly. "It's okay. How about a clean slate? Like Seth said, we can give each other a break."

"Yeah. Okay." Connor wiped his nose. "I'm tired. Can I sleep now?" When Logan nodded, Connor curled away toward the dark window, the drapes firmly shut.

"We should all sleep," Logan said, getting up and crawling across the mattress past Seth. He shimmied under the covers and stretched out on his back.

Seth got settled and switched off the lamp. "Sleep tight, Connor."

In the darkness, he turned toward Logan, his palm warm and comforting on Logan's chest. He whispered, "How's your breathing?"

"Good," Logan whispered back. *Better now.*

"It was so hard to breathe after being in that freezing water. Must have been worse for you." He rubbed his fingers lightly over the spot where Logan's scars were beneath the cotton.

"Didn't even think about it. All that mattered was you and Connor. You both disappeared. It was only a few seconds, I guess, but it was fucking forever."

Seth shivered, and Logan shifted them until he was spooning Seth, pressed against his back. There was nothing sexy about it—certainly not with Connor a few feet away. But it was just right.

Despite the warmth in the room, Logan could hear Connor's teeth chattering. In the faint light of the clock, Logan and Seth shared a worried look and sat up. Connor was still curled toward the window, his shoulders shaking.

"Still cold, Connor?" Seth asked.

A small, chattering voice said, "Yeah."

Seth met Logan's gaze and pointed down at their bed. Logan nodded, and Seth asked, "Do you want to sleep with us? We're all freezing."

The silence lasted several dull thuds of Logan's heart, and then Connor whispered, "Okay."

He got out of bed and stood hugging himself as Logan scooted over to the wall. Seth pulled up his legs, and Connor crawled between Seth and Logan and got under the covers.

Connor said, "It's too quiet."

Seth reached for the remote and turned on the TV, the screen flickering blue in the darkness. He kept the volume low and switched channels until he landed on *Elf.*

There was something soothing about the soft murmur of the TV, although Logan's brain still turned itself over. There was so much he wanted to say to Seth. They liked each other, but… Now what?

Now you sleep, asshole.

As much as Logan ached to feel Seth in his arms, snuggling under the covers with Connor between them was comforting in a way all its own. As the characters in the movie sung "Santa Claus is Coming to Town," Logan drifted off and let himself believe.

Chapter Eighteen

SETH HAD WOKEN with Connor's knobby knee in his back and an arm half across his face, and the three of them had grumbled about it being way too hot in the room.

But there hadn't been any real fire to the complaints, and although it was a little awkward and stilted, they'd gotten ready for breakfast in companionable-enough silence, the TV still on and playing the Mormon choir singing carols.

Breakfast was spent smiling and nodding at all the well-meaning inquiries into their well-being, and Seth was relieved when they boarded the buses back to Albany. Connor sat with Ian and buried his nose in the games on his phone, and Seth drowsed next to Logan, their arms brushing.

The fragile peace continued as they drove back to Seth's house after bidding Angela farewell. The next day was Christmas Eve, and the office was closed until the twenty-sixth. Seth was relieved to have the time off, although his stomach fluttered thinking about the conversation he and Logan had to have. And would Connor's quiet calm hold?

It had snowed more, and the midafternoon skies were gray. Seth's long driveway had been freshly plowed by the man he hired. Inside, he dropped his bag and looked around in foolish surprise at the new decor. He blurted, "I almost forgot that it's finished now."

Logan chuckled as he unzipped his leather jacket and hung it in the closet. "Still like it?"

"Yes." Seth smiled as he walked through to the kitchen, flipping on lights. "Definitely."

Connor followed, peering around. "Wow. Looks awesome."

"It was all Logan," Seth said. "He did an amazing job." *Please be nice*, he willed Connor.

Standing in the entrance to the great room, where the decorated pine tree waited, Connor nodded. "It's really good."

Logan's smile was shy and tentative, and Seth wanted to kiss him so badly he felt like a swooning teenager. Logan gruffly said, "Thanks."

"Can I hang out in my room?" Connor asked Seth. "I mean, like, upstairs."

"Of course. We'll order something in for dinner in a few hours. Any requests? Chinese or Thai or pizza and wings? Or anything you like."

"Sweet and sour chicken balls and fried rice would be cool. Can I have Coke?"

"Absolutely," Logan said.

A little while later, Connor locked away upstairs, Seth and Logan took what had become their places on the couch, the middle cushion between them. They watched football, the colored lights of the Christmas tree reflecting on the glass as the afternoon grew dark early.

There was so much to say, but maybe they both needed some quiet before they said it. But Seth got more and more anxious, finally blurting, "If we like each other, does that mean we're—" He tried to find the right words, settling on, "Not casual?"

Logan seemed to have been holding his breath, and he exhaled in a slump of shoulders. "Yeah." He shifted over on the couch and muted the TV with the remote. He spread his hand over Seth's right thigh, and electricity zipped through Seth. "You know how they say 'fake it 'til you make it'?"

"Uh-huh."

"It doesn't feel like we're faking anything now."

Seth slid his arm around Logan's broad shoulders. They were both in jeans and sweaters, and the worn wool of Logan's was soft under Seth's fingers. "You said you want me," Seth whispered.

"Hell yes." Logan squeezed his thigh. "I wanna bust a nut all over you."

Seth had to laugh. "Thank you?"

Logan laughed too, his eyes crinkling beautifully. "I just mean… You get me really hot. I wanna do things with you I never have with a guy." He glanced at the entry to the great room, leaning forward and apparently making sure they were still alone.

Clearing his throat, Logan went on. "What I mean is, I meant it when I said I like you. As more than a friend."

Seth's heart thudded. "And not just for casual sex?"

"No." He frowned. "You don't want that, do you? I got the feeling you're not very good at it." He quickly added, "The casual part! You're excellent at sex."

Now Seth's face was hot, but he said, "Thanks. And yeah. People tell me I should be going on the hookup apps and dating and having fun. But I don't want to hook up with a dozen men. That's not who I am. I want to be with you."

"Yeah?" Logan grinned.

Seth's heart soared. Tracing the shell of Logan's ear with his finger, arm snug around him, he whispered, "I love having sex with you. It's…liberating."

They kissed, moving toward each other in unison, mouths opening and tongues exploring. It was languid and sweet, and Logan rubbed his hand over Seth's thigh lazily. Seth tingled all over but was content to keep it slow and PG-13 for the moment.

"Never kissed a guy," Logan mumbled, nuzzling Seth's cheek. "Turns out it's not so different from kissing a woman." He leaned back. His smile was soft, his eyes vulnerable. "Definitely never fallen for a guy before you."

Seth kissed Logan deeply, tilting his head and wanting to climb right inside his body. With a soft moan, he whispered, "I've fallen for you too, just in case that's not crystal clear."

"Still like hearing it." Logan squeezed Seth's thigh. His face grew serious, and after nuzzling Seth again, he leaned back. "I don't want to fuck this up. I know I rushed into it with Veronica, but I swear it's not my MO. And with her..."

After a few moments of silence, Seth said, "You don't have to talk about it."

"I want to." Logan rubbed his face wearily. "Honestly, I knew it was a mistake. I knew it. She was the one who proposed, and I didn't want to say no. She'd made sure she didn't work as my nurse anymore so there was no unethical shit, but I was still in the hospital. I was fired and none of my friends from the railway had even visited. I felt like garbage, and Veronica was like this angel. And she had insurance, and I was going to be bankrupt from the hospital bills otherwise. We both got swept up in the idea that getting married would fix our problems."

"I understand."

"She was a good woman."

"Of course!"

Logan shook his head, his voice low. "I can't imagine what it was like for him, finding her dead."

Seth couldn't either. Poor, poor Connor. "At least he talked about it. We'll be here to listen and support him."

"I want that. When you two went through the ice—I thought that might be it, that you were both dead and I'd never get the chance to make it right with Connor... Or make it real with you."

Seth could barely breathe as he waited for Logan to finish.

Taking a deep breath, Logan peered at him intently. "The deal was we'd stay until January. Do you—what do you think about that?"

"I think we clearly need a new deal. One involving a lot of very non-casual sex and you and Connor staying here indefinitely. We'll see what happens. We don't need to put any limits or deadlines on it. Except that we'll be partners who don't sleep with anyone else. I know open relationships can be great for some people, but..."

"Hmm." Logan seemed to be pondering it.

The hair on Seth's neck stood up, an icy chill slipping down his spine. Maybe that was a deal breaker for Logan?

"Holy shit, the look on your face!" Laughing, Logan pressed a wet kiss to Seth's cheek. "Sorry. I was just messing with you. I don't want anyone else. I don't do open. Never have."

Seth elbowed him. "Jerk. So I guess we have a new deal?" He removed his right arm from around Logan's shoulders and extended his hand formally. "Boyfriends-slash-partners-slash-whatever we want to call it. Indefinitely. Living together, because why the hell not?"

They were old enough to know what they wanted, and if it was a disaster, so be it. They'd cross that bridge if it ever appeared.

Logan shook his hand firmly. "That's some salty language from you." He waggled his brows. "Makes me want to fuck your brains out."

Seth grinned. "Such a sweet talker."

"Don't pretend you don't like my talk." Lips at Seth's ear, he added, "Later, I'm going to tell you all about how much I want to fuck your tight hole and—"

They both seemed to register the soft thuds on the stairs at the same time, springing apart. They burst out laughing, and Seth felt like a teenager in the best possible way. Connor appeared at the top of the few steps down into the great room.

"What?" he asked warily.

Seth tugged Logan closer on the couch, sliding an arm around him again. "Nothing. Come join us."

"You guys are weird. But yeah, okay." He came and flopped down on the other end of the couch, Logan in the middle. "Hey, can we watch the new season of *Stranger Things*? It just dropped on Netflix. They didn't give any warning."

"Absolutely." Seth nodded at the remote. "It's the button on the top. You'll need to know how to work it since Logan and I have decided you're both staying. Of course, you'll be going back to school in the new year, but we'd love it if you came here on weekends."

"Yeah?" Connor picked up the remote, toying with it. "That's pretty fast. But that's cool." He turned on Netflix and settled back. "Can we order dinner? I'm hungry."

"Are you ever not hungry?" Logan asked, clearly going for teasing.

Connor visibly bristled. "So what?"

"Nothing." Logan lifted his hands calmly. "Sorry. Just trying to joke."

"Okay," Connor mumbled, his pale cheeks going beet red. He fidgeted with the remote, shoulders up around his ears. He blurted, "Mom said I was hungry like it's my job and I'm trying for a raise."

Seth and Logan laughed, and Seth said, "She had your number, huh? Well, don't worry. We'll keep the pantry stocked." Maybe Connor could feel comfortable enough to talk about his mother more.

Connor gave him a little smile. "Cool. Thanks."

Seth knew it would be a long road, but maybe Connor was ready to start healing.

Chapter Nineteen

SINCE IT WAS Christmas Eve and he was at Jenna's kitchen table, Logan should have been concentrating on cutting up the broccoli and cauliflower for the veggie platter.

Not thinking about waking up with Seth that morning. Waking up with Seth naked. Waking up with Seth and making him blush real hard by thinking up new dirty things to say. Morning blow jobs and kissing, and then more kissing.

All the kissing.

"Are you even listening to me?" A big yellow squash in one hand, Jenna turned down the volume on a crappy version of "Jingle Bells" playing through her tablet. Her blond hair was knotted up in a fancy twist, and she wore a Mrs. Claus apron over her velvet blue dress that she complained was too tight but Logan thought was pretty.

He jerked guiltily. "Sorry. What?"

"What's up with you?"

"Nothing," he automatically replied.

She pressed her lips together. "Why did you volunteer to help me instead of going outside to play? What's up? Is it about the job? It was great news that Angela set up that interview for you. Don't tell me your pride is getting in the way."

"No!" Logan sliced into a big hunk of cauliflower. "Trust me, I have zero pride left. I'm grateful for anything I can get." Now Jenna looked sad, and he felt like an asshole. "I don't mean… What I mean is that I'm grateful to Angela. She's really gone out of her way. I'm not looking that gift horse in the mouth, I promise."

"Okay. You deserve good things, you know." There was a burst of distant laughter outside, and she went to the window. "This snowball fight looks pretty epic. You should get out there with Seth and Connor. Although Jun and Ian probably need the help more."

Pop was in his usual spot in the den watching the game show channel with Noah asleep in his playpen. Logan and Jenna were alone, so now was the time to tell her.

Any minute now.

Turning from the window, she fixed Logan in her sights and said way too casually, "That was quite the kiss during musical chairs. Very convincing. I honestly had no idea you were such a good actor. Seth either, since he's the worst liar in the world."

The pressure built in Logan's chest. He'd borrowed a tie from Seth, and he tugged at it, but then he had to laugh. "How do you always know everything?"

Her eyebrows shot up. "Jun said I was being silly. Wait, are you serious?" She glanced at the door that led to the hall down to the den. Pulling out a chair, she leaned forward, voice low. "You and Seth? For real?"

His heart was booming, but he shrugged. "Yeah."

Her jaw dropped. "But you've never…with a guy. Have you?"

"Just sex. In Iraq, and sometimes at the bunkhouse."

She got up and took a bottle of white out of the fridge, pouring them both big glasses. Logan didn't really like the sweet wine, but he drank it nervously as she sat back across from him, gaze distant.

"Say something," he muttered. "Cat doesn't usually have your tongue." He was trying to tell himself this was no big deal, but it was. It was a big damn deal.

"Oh! Sorry. Processing." Jenna reached over the vegetables and grabbed his hand. "You know I love you and support you a hundred percent."

He exhaled. "I figured, but that's still nice to hear." He squeezed her fingers.

"It must be scary."

"Yeah." He swallowed hard. "It's a big change. I'm not gonna wuss out, though. It—he means too much. Maybe some people won't like it, but tough shit. It's not like I have any friends left anyway."

"The people who matter will support you. The end."

"Even Pop?" he whispered.

Jenna winced through her teeth. "I think so? He's kind of weirdly mellowed. He probably won't love it at first, but he'll come around. He wants you to be happy and settled. He worries about you a lot. More than you think."

"Huh." Logan wasn't sure what to make of that.

She sat back and picked up her wine. "You and Seth! It's perfect. You've both been so lonely, whether you want to admit it or not. And it's not just physical?"

"No!" He shifted in his chair, crossing his arms. Talking about this was the worst, especially with his baby sister. "It's different with Seth."

Her smile reminded him of the moony look she got when she watched rom-coms. "You like him."

"Yeah." He grumbled. "A lot, okay?"

"And before it was only physical with men. Never with feelings involved?"

"Right."

"But why?"

"Because!" He grunted, realizing he sounded like Connor. "It's just... I always thought dating and stuff is what you do with women. Getting off with guys once in a while was separate."

"Okay." Jenna sipped her wine. "But you don't think it's wrong, right? Same-sex relationships."

"No," he scoffed. "I just didn't think it was for me. Turns out I was wrong. Seth and I were only pretending at first, but now..." He picked up the knife and cut the stalk off a broccoli spear.

"You're blushing!" Jenna clapped delightedly. "This is the best Christmas present you could give me."

"You're welcome," he said with as much sarcasm as he could.

"So, you're...bisexual?"

It still seemed weird as hell to think of himself as anything but straight after insisting on it for so long. Fooling himself for so long. He cleared his throat. "Yeah. I'm bisexual." He exhaled a long breath, a knot of tightness in his chest releasing.

"I'll drink to that!" Jenna lifted her glass, and he clinked his against it.

"You'll drink to anything," he teased with a grateful laugh.

"Pumped out a ton of milk this morning, so you're damn right I will. It's Christmas." She took a big swallow. "Are you moving in for real? Is that why Connor's in such a good mood?"

"I guess. We're gonna see how it goes, but yeah. Moving in."

"It's going to go wonderfully! I know it."

"That's what I thought about Veronica."

Jenna pursed her lips. "No you didn't. You knew it was a mistake from day one. But now we have Connor. Everything happens for a reason." She grimaced. "Not Veronica's death. I didn't mean it like that."

"I know. I get it." He looked out the window at where Connor was dodging a snowball and laughing as it hit Seth instead. "I wish she was still alive, but I wouldn't want to give him up." He shook his head. "Never thought I'd say that."

"You were thrust into being a single dad overnight, and it's not easy, to say the very least. You're still learning, but you're what Connor needs."

Logan was starting to believe it. "He'll probably drive me nuts soon enough, but we're both trying. We didn't fight at all today. We've been watching that eighties show on Netflix about the kids and monsters. Seth and I hadn't seen it, so Connor said we should start at the beginning. It's been fun watching together."

"That's great! All you can do is try, and keep trying even when he acts like an asshole. Because sometimes kids are the worst, but they're the best." Jenna's eyes filled, and she laughed. "Sorry, you know how emo I get at Christmas. But if there's any time to start fresh, it's now, don't you think?"

"Yeah. Peace and good will and all that shit."

They laughed, and the oven timer dinged. Jenna bolted up. "Need to check the turkey. Maybe you and Pop should talk?"

"What, *now?*"

"Peace and good will and all that shit."

Here went nothing. Logan took a gulp of the sweet wine and headed into the den before he could chicken out. Better to just rip off the Band-Aid.

Noah was still fast asleep in his playpen on the floor by Pop's armchair, his little mouth open, face so innocent that it made Logan want to pick him up and hold him close. Of course that would wake him, and he had to spit out the truth to Pop.

Pop wore a button-down shirt and dress slacks with his ugly old slippers. They'd always dressed up on Christmas Eve for turkey dinner and midnight mass, then spent Christmas Day in their PJs, opening presents and eating leftovers.

Now that Jenna and Jun went to Jun's parents every other year with Pop and the kids, the routine had changed, and they were skipping church to get a good night's sleep before driving in the morning. Logan was looking forward to a day of PJs with Seth and Connor. He wished like hell he was there now, but first things first.

Rip it off!

Sitting on the edge of a couch cushion, Logan looked at the Christmas tree with its golden lights and the old angel on top tilting to the right. He asked, "People giving good answers?" He nodded toward *Family Feud* on the TV.

Pop grunted. "A few."

Do it. Don't be a shit-brick coward. Just fucking say it. "You know how Seth and me have been living together? I'm gonna keep living there in January. We really like each other. We were pretending at first, but now it's real."

Pop's gray, bushy brows met, and he stared at Logan. "What are you sayin'? That you're a fairy?"

Logan's first instinct was to deny it loudly. He forced a breath, his chest tightening. "I dunno. Kinda? I've always liked girls. Still do. But I think I've liked guys too. More than I would admit."

Pop shoved a handful of pretzel mix in his mouth. He chewed noisily, watching a family trying to guess the most popular answer for "favorite way to wake up in the morning."

There was clapping and exclaiming, and blood rushed in Logan's ears, his heartbeat so loud he could barely hear himself think.

He waited.

Then he waited some more, every muscle clenched, his butt barely on the edge of the couch cushion. Was Pop going to tell him to get out? Was he going to say Logan disgusted him? That he was a disgrace to the family and—

"Like the kid on *Schitt's Creek*," Pop said, rooting around in the snack bowl and coming up with an orange peanut M&M.

"What?" Logan could barely get the word out.

"You know, with Eugene Levy. Rich people get stuck in a small town. Funny show. It's like *shit's*, but it's spelled different."

Logan tried to breathe. "Right. Yeah, I get it. I don't—what about it?"

Pop looked at him now. "The kid on the show. He's whaddya call it— bipan-curious or whatever." He shrugged. "I guess it's the popular thing these days, huh? Seems like it's everywhere now. I don't really get it, but no one asks what I think anymore."

Logan's lungs expanded a few more inches. "I'm asking. What you think." He clenched his hands into fists so hard his nails dug into his palms. "About me and Seth."

Frowning, Pop stared at him again. "So you're saying you two are..." He motioned back and forth with a wrinkled hand.

Part of Logan wanted to deny it all, say never mind and run the fuck away. But he didn't. He nodded.

Pop screwed up his face. "I don't get why you'd want to. You're a good-lookin' kid. The girls have always chased you."

"It's not about that. It's not that I can't get a girl and I'm settling or something."

"Huh." He seemed to think about it. "That makes you happy? Bein' with him? Like *that*?"

"I know it must seem weird to you, but yeah. It does."

Pop grunted, and Logan couldn't tell what it meant. Pop said, "You do seem happier. I was sayin' to Jenny before. The kid too. So I guess that's good. And you said you're going to keep living over there?"

"Yeah. We're going to see what happens. Maybe it won't work out, but..."

Pop grunted again, turning back to the TV. "Won't know unless you try. You could do worse." Then he shouted, "Read the newspaper! Doesn't anyone read the newspaper in the morning anymore?"

Her dress swaying, Jenna appeared with a plate of cookies, having clearly been eavesdropping. "You know who reads the newspaper every morning? Seth. He's very old-fashioned that way. He picks one up on his way into the office."

Logan wasn't sure if it was true, but God, he loved his sister. Pop laughed, a wheezing rasp. "Jenny'll be convincing me Seth's the second coming of Jesus soon enough if she has her way." He grabbed three cookies and took a big bite of one. "Only your mother made better chocolate-chip cookies. God rest her soul."

Jenny sat beside Logan on the couch, squeezing his arm and kissing his cheek. He took a cookie. "These really are just like Mom made."

She beamed. "Thanks." Then she whispered, "That went better than I expected!"

"I keep telling you, I'm not fuckin' deaf," Pop grumbled, biting into another cookie. He asked Logan through his mouthful, "Didn't you make your mom's chocolate cake for the big dinner with the boss lady?"

"Yeah," Logan said. "Everyone loved it."

"You should bring some cookies home," Pop said. "Seth and Connor'll miss out if we eat 'em all."

"I might have made an extra batch for you boys this morning." Jenna gave Logan a wink.

Home.

Settling back on the couch, Logan took a bite of sweet, soft cookie. The front door banged open, Noah woke and wailed so loud Logan thought he must be dying, and cold air reached the den.

"Close the damn door!" Pop shouted as Jenna scooped up Noah, a stamping of boots thudding from the foyer.

Jun, Seth, Connor, and Ian joined them in the den, cheeks rosy from being outside. Seth took a cookie and sat next to Logan with a wince. Logan frowned. "You okay?"

"My slacks are damp, but that's what I get for engaging in a snowball fight."

Logan laughed. "Maybe you should take them off." He realized what he'd said, but it was too late.

"Save that for later!" Pop chortled, his belly jiggling as he laughed at his own joke.

Jun had his mouth full of cookie, but mumbled, "Wait, what?"

"Pants off!" Ian shouted, yanking down his little slacks and pulling them free, a sock going with them. In Superman undies and his dress shirt, he raced around the carpet, reaching out to jingle ornaments on the tree as he passed by, gold and silver icicles swaying dangerously.

"Everyone's pants on!" Holding Noah, Jenna gave chase, Ian darting around her and squealing his way toward the kitchen.

Seth was bright red to the tips of his ears, and Connor was laughing his ass off. Logan whispered to Seth, "Christmas at the Derwoods. This is what you're getting into. Don't say I didn't warn you."

Still blushing, Seth only grinned. He nudged Logan's shoulder, and Logan nudged back, not ready to get smoochy in front of his family, especially with Pop there. Seth would probably pass out anyway.

Part of Logan still couldn't believe it. Him and Seth. Him and Seth for *real.* Everyone knowing and not seeming to mind. Maybe it was the peace and good will and all that shit, but whatever it was, he'd take it.

Chapter Twenty

S NOW DRIFTED DOWN on Christmas morning.
Still under the covers, Logan watched fat fluffy flakes fall past the window in Seth's bedroom. The sky was cloudy, but he could tell by how bright it looked that everything below was thick with white. The perfect day for PJs and TV and all the leftovers Jenna had pushed on them.

They'd fallen into Seth's plush bed after sharing a lazy shower, full of turkey and stuffing and chocolate cake. Even though they'd been too tired to do anything, they'd cuddled up, their naked bodies still new and exciting.

He was spooned up behind Seth now, his morning wood prodding Seth's ass. Logan circled Seth's hole, wondering what it felt like to take a cock inside. He'd told Seth that he'd never done it, and that was true. He'd also told him he didn't want to, but that was…less true.

Becoming less damn true every minute.

"Mmm," Seth murmured, yawning.

"Merry Christmas." Logan kissed his shoulder.

Seth tensed. "Right. Christmas." He laughed unsteadily. "You'll think I'm nuts, but it feels naughty to let myself celebrate. This is the first year since I left home that I've done anything at all for Christmas. Let alone so many things. A proper turkey dinner, even."

Fuck Seth's family and him "leaving" home. Fuck their obituary. Fuck them all in their pious, hypocritical ass-faces. "You deserve every single bit of Christmas," he said fiercely.

Seth relaxed back against him, turning his head to kiss Logan softly. "Thank you. I wish I'd bought you more than a new tie."

Logan laughed, letting go of the fury toward the Marstons. They weren't worth hanging onto. Not when he had Seth naked in bed and the door locked. "Um, I might have gotten you socks that Jenna originally bought for Jun. In my defense, it's been really busy."

Grinning, Seth rolled onto his back. "We'll definitely up our gift game next year."

He knew they shouldn't be banking on a year from now, but what the hell. "Deal. At least there's some stuff for Connor."

"Yes, Jenna assured me she chose well and that we could take all the credit."

"She's always been the best at gifts, like our mom. I'll pay her back when—well, if I get that job. If not—"

"Nope. You're getting it. End of story. I have complete confidence in Angela Barker."

Logan laughed. "Fair enough." He dragged his fingers through Seth's chest hair and kissed his throat. "Now what was that about you being naughty? Because I've got a few ideas."

"Mmm. I bet you do." He ran his foot over Logan's calf. "I'm all ears."

"How about you fuck me?"

Seth's eyes went wide. "Oh! I… Are you sure? You don't need to. I mean, not to prove anything to me. Or because you think you have to."

"I want to," Logan insisted. "Maybe I've been curious for a long time, but I squashed it." He fidgeted, his face going hot. "Never even considered doing it for real. It's different with you." He shrugged. "I trust you."

Seth smiled and laughed and almost cried at the exact same time, and Logan had to kiss him until they were panting. Then he got on his hands and knees on the soft bed. This had always been out of bounds, and now he shook with curiosity and lust. Even if he didn't like it, he wanted to *know*.

He wriggled his ass. "Come on. Plow me."

But Seth was apparently in no rush, and he smoothed his long fingers over Logan's thighs, kissing down his spine, murmuring to him and turning him over onto his back.

Logan froze up. He was all *exposed* like this, and he closed his eyes before realizing what he was doing.

"Logan. Look at me. Do you really want to do this? Because you don't have to. I love being…penetrated." Seth scratched the back of his neck, and he was so damn pretty kneeling between Logan's legs. "I'm not good at the words."

"You don't need to be. Just fuck me already."

They both laughed, and Logan breathed easier. Seth pushed at his knees, pressing them back and opening him up, palms against the bottom of his thighs. Logan squirmed, but let Seth look his fill. They were both hard, but Logan knew he was going to droop if he didn't relax.

"Tell me what you want," Seth whispered. "The way you would if you were me."

Logan caught the drift. Seth loved dirty talk but was too shy to say it himself. Now here was Logan being the shy one. He cleared his throat. "Want you to shove your big cock inside me."

Gasping, Seth shuddered. Oh yeah, he clearly liked that.

"You do have a big cock, you know that? You should be proud of it." Logan reached down to run his fingers over the shaft and head. "You're already dripping for me. Gonna feel so good inside. You're so big, you're gonna split me open, and I'll love every second of it. Want you so bad, want you to—*mmph.*"

Logan couldn't talk anymore with Seth's tongue jammed down his throat. They kissed hard and wet, grunting, Seth rutting against him. Logan's legs were still bent back, Seth heavy on him, fingers clutched at Logan's head, tugging his short hair.

He loved unraveling Seth like this, and the earlier nerves faded. They broke apart to breath, spit strung between them. Logan asked, "You want to eat my ass?"

Seth jolted, his face going even more red. Oh yeah, he sure as hell wanted to eat Logan's ass. Logan tried not to grin.

"You want to lick my hole? Stick your tongue in me? Bet you do. Wanna lick me like a dog with a bone. Bury your face in my ass and—" It was Logan's turn to jolt as Seth did exactly that, spreading Logan even wider with his hands and pressing his face into Logan's crack.

His tongue lapped at the sensitive skin, and Logan bit his tongue, his hands grabbing at Seth's shoulders. "Oh fuck, baby. That's so good. I could come just like this. With your tongue inside me."

Seth moaned against his hole, hot and damp and fucking perfect as he opened Logan with his tongue. Logan had done some ass play with women in the past, but this was next level because Seth was so into it.

The words tripped out of Logan's mouth. "Never even thought about letting anyone fuck me, but I want you to pound my ass with your big cock. Want you to fuck me 'til I can't walk."

Moaning, Seth lifted his head. His eyes were dark, his wet lips parted as he breathed hard. He reached blindly for the condom and lube.

"Wish you could come right inside me. Nothing between us." Logan wasn't even thinking about what he was saying now, truths rocketing out of his mouth. "We can after we get tested. You want that? Wanna fuck raw, baby?"

"Yes," Seth groaned hoarsely, kissing Logan again messily. "Oh, *God,* yes."

Logan could taste his own ass, and instead of grossing him out, it just made him even harder. "Come on. Do it." He lifted his hips as Seth pushed lube into him clumsily. "I'm good. Fuck me. Give me your dick."

With jerky motions, Seth lined up and pushed, and Logan bore down. They both gritted their teeth. Seth cried out as he pushed past the rim and rammed all the way inside.

Logan ignored the burning pain, reaching up to slap his hand over Seth's mouth. "Walls. Not that. Thick," he grunted. He kept his hand planted over Seth's mouth as he arched his back, his chest tight. Seth felt way too big to fit, but he was all the way inside, his pubes tickling Logan's ass. Sweat trickled down Seth's face, and Logan felt hot all over, his own skin slick.

"Does it feel good splitting me open?"

Against Logan's hand, Seth nodded hard, his nostrils flaring.

"Move. I can take it. I can take every inch of you." He slid his hand away from Seth's mouth, holding the side of his face.

Panting, his eyes locked on Logan's, Seth eased out and then slammed back in. *Hard.*

"Oh, fuck yeah. Like that. Drill me." Logan had to open his mouth to breathe, trying to keep his moans quiet. "You feel amazing."

Thrusting steadily, Seth flattened his hand on Logan's chest, his fingers moving. At first, Logan thought it was just for leverage, but through the fog of building pleasure, his dick throbbing now between them, Logan realized he was tracing the scars.

His breath stuttered, and for a moment, that old panic exploded. Logan wanted to shove Seth off him and run. He was naked in a way he'd never let anyone see—not even Veronica at their best.

He had Seth's cock deep inside him, and he loved it. He wasn't straight, and he'd never been straight, and fuck, he was going to start bawling if he wasn't careful.

He gripped Seth's head, fingers tangling in his hair, their sweaty bodies rocking. Seth brushed against just the right spot, sending sparks to Logan's tight balls. He was bent almost in half, his hips getting sore.

"Please make me come," he begged. It wasn't dirty talk now. Logan needed it in a way he couldn't explain.

"You're beautiful," Seth whispered as he took Logan in hand, swiping at the fluid leaking from his dick and mixing it with the remnants of lube as he stroked. Leaning on his other hand beside Logan's shoulder, he thrust and stroked. "I love you."

Logan arched, shaking as he came all over himself, his mouth open and gasping. Waves of pleasure crashed through him until he relaxed back, totally empty. Except he wasn't empty. Well, his nuts were, but he was so full of love he didn't know what to do with it.

"Come on," he muttered, squeezing his sore ass around Seth's thick cock. "Let go. I can feel how hard you are. Imagine we're doing it raw, and you can come inside me until your jizz is dripping out."

Seth seized up, and Logan clapped a hand over his open mouth again, muffling his cry as he came, his head back and eyes shut. Logan loved seeing Seth let go—sharing the release with him as if he was coming again.

When Seth collapsed on top of him, Logan grunted. His ass was stinging and his legs were going numb, and Seth was heavy and sweaty.

"Best Christmas ever," Logan muttered.

Seth laughed weakly against his neck. "Ho-ho-ho." He lifted his head, sudden sharpness in his eyes, his hair standing up. "Does it hurt?"

"Yeah, but not in a bad way. Provided you get the fuck off sooner rather than later."

Of course Seth was almost unbearably gentle as he pulled out and lowered Logan's legs to the mattress, pressing kisses to Logan's knees. He got rid of the condom and cleaned them up with a wet cloth, and Logan took his face in his hands. Seth's stubble scratched his palms.

"I love you too."

Adam's apple bobbing, Seth's eyes practically glowed. "You don't have to say it just because I did. I know it's too soon."

"I'm saying it because it's true. I love you."

"Well…heck. I guess we're in love."

"*Heck*, I guess we are."

Seth laughed. "That doesn't sound right coming from you."

"Fuck-a-doodle-do, I guess we're in love. That better?"

"Much." Seth pulled the covers over them.

Logan figured they could stay there all damn day, and he wouldn't complain a bit.

SETH FOUND CONNOR in his PJs by the tree in the great room, looking out at the falling snow. The colored lights glowed, the shiny angel on top beaming down, the world white beyond. "Hey," Seth whispered, because it felt like he should. "Merry Christmas."

Connor turned. "Merry Christmas." His eyes were red, but he'd apparently stopped crying a while before.

Seth wanted so much to hug him, but he wasn't sure about overstepping. "You're up early."

"You guys are kinda noisy."

Oh, merciful lord. "I—I'm so sorry, we—it's—oh my."

Connor laughed. "Don't, like, pass out or anything. It's gross, but whatever." He quickly added, "Not because you're guys! Because you're so…old and stuff."

"We'll keep that in mind." He cast about for any change of topic. "Santa brought some gifts for you."

"Me?" Connor looked at the small pile of wrapped presents under the tree. "Really?"

"Really." Seth had removed the empty boxes Logan had wrapped for Angela's benefit.

Yawning in his boxer briefs and a tee, Logan shuffled in, passing Seth a mug of fresh coffee. "Merry Christmas. We having turkey for breakfast?"

Seth said, "I was thinking bacon and eggs and home fries cooked in the bacon grease. Save the turkey and stuff for dinner."

"Mmm. Sounds good." Logan flicked the collar of Seth's pajama top and winked. To Connor he said, "Yeah?"

Connor was watching them with an unreadable expression. "Yeah. Cool." He looked back at the presents.

Seth knelt by the tree. "Here you are. Come on. Don't be shy."

Hesitantly, Connor knelt by him, and then Logan did too. Seth passed out the presents, seven of the boxes for Connor. He ripped into the paper of one, pulling out some kind of speaker. "Sweet! It's the waterproof Bose. This is awesome!"

"Santa knows his stuff," Seth said. Jenna would definitely be getting a spa day for her help.

Connor was already ripping open another package. "The new *Call of Duty*!" He shrewdly eyed the remaining boxes, picking up a bigger one and tearing it open. "And the latest Xbox!" His face positively *glowed*, and Seth and Logan shared a grin.

"Glad you like it," Logan said.

"I love it! Can we hook it up?"

"Absolutely," Seth said.

Connor tore into his other gifts, a few more games and a pair of Adidas shoes that he declared "sick," which Seth took to be a good thing. Connor was readying the Xbox when he said, "Oh, wait. You guys have to open your stuff."

With wry smiles, Logan and Seth unwrapped their blue tie and black socks, respectively. Connor scowled. "Seriously? That's it."

"We're gonna do better next year," Logan said.

"Shit, I hope so." Connor went back to the cables behind the TV. "But thanks. This stuff is awesome. I… I didn't get you guys anything."

"That's okay," Seth assured him.

Logan said, "How about you not be a little dickhead for the rest of the holidays? We'll take that."

After a pause, Connor burst out laughing. "I'll try my best. Can we make breakfast soon? I'm starving."

Seth chose the Christmas station on the stereo, and jazzy holiday music filled the main floor. He hummed as he got out the eggs and bacon, Logan insisting he and Connor would do the potatoes.

"I think you're supposed to cut them the long way," Logan said.

"Says who?" Connor grumbled.

"I dunno. It looks better like that."

Connor rolled his eyes. "Since when are you an expert in cooking?"

"Since never. Let's Google it."

"Fine. What Google says goes. Deal?"

Logan chuckled. "Deal."

Seth said, "We have a pretty good track record with deals." He grinned at Logan, who gave him a wink while Connor tapped his phone.

As Seth peeled off the strips of bacon, he sipped his coffee and hummed along to Sinatra singing about happy golden days, and all their troubles being miles and miles away.

Epilogue

"HEY!" LOGAN TURNED from the pantry and tried to swat away Seth's hand, but he was too late. "You know you're not supposed to eat raw batter. It can kill you or some shit."

Seth sucked the chocolate cake batter off his index finger with a wet *pop*, making Logan's dick perk up and giving him all sorts of ideas they didn't have time for.

Seth said, "The risk of consuming raw eggs has been greatly overstated. They'll take my cookie dough and cake batter from my cold, dead hands." With a wink, he scooped up more with his finger. "It'll be worth it."

"Okay, but there has to be enough for the cake. And I haven't had any yet."

"Ah, the truth comes out! You're not worried about salmonella—you just want enough left for you to lick the bowl." He sucked his finger clean.

Logan shrugged, trying not to laugh. "Guilty as charged."

Sliding an arm around Logan's waist, warm hand stealing beneath his ratty tee, Seth leaned in. They kissed slowly and deeply, batter still on Seth's tongue. Logan relaxed into him, chasing the sugar.

When they parted, Seth lowered his voice in the cute way he did sometimes when he jokily faked a come-on. "Let me know when you're ready to lick the bowl."

"You know, everyone thinks you're so innocent, but you're really..." Logan tried to find the right word.

"A vixen?" Seth waggled his thick eyebrows. There was a bit of gray coming into the hair at his temples, and it was sexy as fuck.

"Sure. We'll go with that. Because only you would suggest that word. Right, Hercules?" Logan glanced down at their portly tabby cat, who rubbed against their legs, meowing for his snack. Seth had wanted to name him *Hercule* after some detective, and they'd compromised on Hercules.

Logan's phone buzzed where it sat on top of the island. "Might be work," he said as he reached for it. He'd recently been promoted to senior craftsman at Ricci and Sons and was in charge of his own renovation crew. He had to deal with more problems, but it was worth it.

"Oh, it's Connor." He tapped the screen with Connor's picture, a shot from his first day at Harvard several months earlier, exasperation showing in his smile and a few zits still dotting his face. He'd insisted it was no big deal to go to college and there was no reason to take a picture when Logan and Seth dropped him off.

"Hey, Con," Logan said, putting him on speaker. "Where are you?"

"Just past Auburn, but it's snowing." Connor's voice sounded deeper every time Logan heard it. He was taller than Logan and Seth now, but still a beanpole. "People are driving like they've never seen this foreign substance falling from the sky before." Logan could hear him rolling his eyes, and it made him smile.

Seth snorted. "Sounds about right. Take your time. Be safe. Tell Asher to drive carefully."

"*Yes*," Connor said with a sigh and probably another eye-roll. "He will."

Seth asked, "You're sure it's not out of his way to drop you off?"

"Huh? Yeah, I'm sure." Then Connor's voice faded as he talked to someone else—probably his buddy Asher. "I'm coming! Just had to call my dads while I have a good signal. Order me a large fries and a root beer, okay?"

Logan's chest had gone tight, his breathing shallow as he and Seth stared at each other and then back down at the phone on the island.

"Sorry," Connor said, talking directly into the phone again. He paused. "You guys still there?"

"Yes!" Logan answered too loudly. He cleared his throat. "Thanks for calling. Drive safe. Doesn't matter if you're late, okay?"

"Yeah, but it'll suck ass to miss Aunt Jenna's turkey."

"We'll wait for you," Seth said, his voice a little hoarse. "Even if it's midnight."

"'K. But it really shouldn't be past seven. Later!"

Logan jabbed the disconnect button and leaned on the shiny counter, flattening his palms. Seth covered one of Logan's hands with his own and threaded their fingers together.

Logan met his gaze and muttered, "Fuck. Wow."

His *dads*.

"Yeah." Seth blinked rapidly, tears catching on his lashes. "Wow."

With a creak, the front door opened. "Ho, ho, ho!" Jun called from beyond the sitting room. Boots stamped the mat, voices and activity filling the air, a cold blast already finding its way toward the kitchen.

They hadn't even noticed the vehicle pulling up. Logan swallowed the lump in his throat and swiped his thumbs under Seth's eyes before kissing him soundly.

Seth nodded and gave him a shaky smile before going to greet their family with a hearty, "Merry Christmas!"

Logan scooped up his phone and looked at the home screen picture he'd seen a million times—him and Seth in fancy suits in front of the local Unitarian church, friends and the Derwoods surrounding them, Angela Barker and her family too, Connor giving a genuine smile.

The invites to the Marstons had been returned to sender, and Seth had made peace with not trying to contact them again.

Putting the phone in his pocket, Logan said hello as Pop grumbled by, leaning on his walker and making his way toward the great room and the reclining armchair they'd bought specially for him. Seth followed and sat next to Pop, and Logan listened to the rumble of their voices as Seth asked all the right questions to get him talking.

"Coming through!" Jenna carried the big, shiny silver disposable roast pan, foil covering the mound of the turkey. "Trivets!"

Logan quickly slapped down a couple of the big coaster things on the island. "Yes, ma'am."

She plonked the turkey on top. "You and Seth have the potatoes and squash done?"

"Shit, were we supposed to do that?"

She paled. "Tell me you're joking."

"I'm joking, I'm joking."

She kissed Logan's cheek. "You little shit. You'd better go put on some decent clothes." Then she spotted the cake batter. "Are you just baking the cake *now*? It has to cool before you ice it!"

"It'll be fine! It took a little longer than we expected to get the rest of the stuff ready. Chill. Have some wine."

Noah was racing after his older brother, shouting something. Jun told them to cut it out and sighed heavily. "Maybe Ian can drive home later. I need a drink too."

"Six more years until he can be our designated driver," Jenna said, pouring herself a glass of sweet white. "It'll fly by."

Seth came back and shooed Jenna and Jun into the great room to relax. The fresh smell of the pine tree wafted with him, and Logan inhaled deeply as he pulled Seth into a hug.

"Mmm." Seth relaxed against him. "We have got to get that cake in the oven."

"I know. In a minute."

Seth leaned their heads together. "I'm officially going with polka dots, by the way."

"But what colors?"

"Red and green."

Logan chuckled. "You think I got you holiday polka-dot socks?"

Each year, he bought Seth socks, and Seth got him a tie like the shitty gifts of their first Christmas. Betting on the colors and designs had become a tradition too. He'd actually gone with gray and navy stripes, because as much as Seth liked to joke about bright socks, he'd never wear them. At least not to work.

"Maybe you were feeling wild." Seth trailed his fingers down Logan's spine.

"Mmm. We'll get wild later."

After a laughing kiss, they went back to work, and a few hours later, their son's too-deep, grown-up voice called, "I'm home!"

Logan and Seth shared a smile before they went to greet him. They were all home.

The Christmas Leap

BY
KEIRA ANDREWS

Acknowledgments

Many thanks to Leta Blake, Angela O'Connell, Rai, and Samantha for helping make this novel the best it can be. Special thanks also to Scotty Porter for his help with the Scottish lingo and dialogue, and Elaine and Sharna for their Aussie expertise. I appreciate all of you so much!

Chapter One

Michael

THERE WAS AN old saying about best-laid plans. It was probably Shakespeare, and the point was that no matter how carefully you tried to get your ducks in a row, those little jerks had minds of their own.

"I can't break up with him at *Christmas*!" Jared's voice rose incredulously.

Earlier in the day, I'd decided to take the afternoon off work for an early start to two glorious weeks of vacation time over the holidays. After running a few errands, I'd eased open the door of our townhouse to call out to Jared that I'd brought home a surprise—our first Christmas tree together.

But now I strained to listen over the thudding of my heart.

It had to be the TV. Sure, it had sounded exactly like Jared's smooth, slightly nasal voice, but… It couldn't have been. After working my butt off at making this relationship a success, I couldn't have overheard my boyfriend talking about breaking up with me.

Not just my boyfriend—my *partner*. I wasn't a kid anymore. Jared and I were partners. Maybe this was a bad joke. Some kind of terrible, out-of-character prank?

Ho-ho-ho?

Jared muttered, "I know." It sounded like he was in the kitchen at the back of the townhouse. The hardwood floor creaked—which drove Jared nuts even though I thought it added charm. Warm light spilled into the hallway, flickering with his shadow as he moved restlessly. I could picture him pacing by the granite-topped island.

Jared sighed. "There's no good time to tell him. That's true. Still. I have to wait until January. He's so excited about our first Christmas together here. I can't do it." A pause. "I know I'm not a Christmas person, but it's fine. It makes him happy."

I stood there clutching the twine-bound tree, my nose full of pine. The paper shopping bag on the bristly outdoor mat beneath my feet contained an artisanal mulled wine kit and chestnuts for roasting. And wait, Jared didn't *like* Christmas? I knew he wasn't a fan of tacky decorations and cheesy songs, but…

I'd stashed boxes of tasteful gold and silver ornaments that would fit Jared's minimalist style under the bed yesterday. I knew he wouldn't like the idea of dropped needles on the floor, so I'd bought the newest automatic watering system for the tree. The trunk of my Hyundai hatchback was crammed with gifts and rolls of the classiest wrapping paper I could find.

I had planned every detail of our Instagram-worthy Christmas.

Jared exhaled loudly. "I know, Steph. He must see it coming, right? Unless he's in denial. Fuck, I hate this."

Oh, god. I'd thought everything was perfect, and now it was disintegrating in front of my eyes. Well, my ears. Rigid, I waited for him to say more to his sister.

I'd always gotten along with Stephanie, or at least I thought I had? She was only looking out for Jared, and it wasn't about me. That didn't make it hurt less.

And okay, *perfect* was a strong word for my relationship with Jared. But everything was pretty good, wasn't it? I'd been so careful since I moved into the townhouse to keep everything running smoothly. All the experts said compromise was key, and I'd compromised like a champion, hadn't I?

"It's only another couple of weeks. I'll tell him in the new year." A pause. "I know." Another pause. "Steph, I couldn't do it before because we went to Tampa to visit his folks for Thanksgiving. We had plane tickets, and they took us to Universal. And yes, I hate theme parks, but I couldn't back out."

I tasted acid. I'd been so proud to show off Jared to my parents. Proof that I was indeed a responsible adult now, and they didn't have to worry about me or lend me money. They could live their best retired lives.

For too long in my twenties, I'd drifted. Working okay jobs with no future for advancement. Dating okay people while nursing my impossible crush. I had a steady office job now with benefits, and my impossible crush was a hundred percent over.

Gripping the teetering Christmas tree, I braced for thoughts of Will, which were the last thing I needed. Will was straight. He was never going to love me back. I'd had to put distance between us—at least while I got over him. I'd made a plan, grown up, and figured out my life. I was no longer in love with my best friend.

Whether Will *was* still my best friend was another story, but my hands were full with problems at the moment, including being stabbed by pine needles through my thin gloves as I fought to stay quiet while keeping the Christmas tree vertical.

Jared groaned. "I was hoping… I don't know. That it would all magically work out. Of course, I should have ended it months ago."

Months?!

I'd only moved into the townhouse in March. Which meant Jared had decided humiliatingly quickly that he didn't want me to stay. We'd dated for more than a year before living together. I'd been so freaking careful not to jump into anything. Should I have seen this coming? *Had* I? My head spun, and I clung to the tree.

"I just feel so sorry for him."

I jerked violently—then scrambled to keep hold of the tipping tree. Needles clawed my cheek as I tripped backward.

See above, re: *best-laid plans*.

Kicking over the fancy paper bag on my way down, I hit the shoveled stoop, my jeans offering no protection and my peacoat not much more. Glass smashed on the freezing concrete.

The tree pinning me, I sank back in defeat, my head perilously close to the edge of the top step. The jagged granules of rock salt I'd sprinkled over the walkway that morning dug into my skull.

Jared appeared in the open doorway wearing his favorite dress pants and black silk sweater, a furrow between his thin brows before they shot up. "Babe! Are you okay?"

I nodded, struggling to retain a shred of dignity. Jared hauled the tree off me, his handsome face transforming into a familiar smile as he laughed and cracked some joke I couldn't make out over the buzzing in my ears.

My throat swelled painfully, tears burning my eyes. If I hadn't just over-heard him, I wouldn't have had a damn clue anything was wrong. I was so stupid. I'd had no idea he wanted to break up with me. That he didn't love me anymore. God, did he not love me?

Do I love him? Or did I only want *to love him?*

"Mike? Shit, babe. You *are* hurt."

Choking down a scream/shout/sob, I pushed myself up to sitting while Jared wrangled the tree into the narrow foyer. When he turned back, his eyes bugged out.

"Jesus! Are you bleeding?" He lunged out the door in his Italian leather slippers. Dropping to his knees, he groped my left thigh, and I blinked down at the dark stain on my jeans.

"Wine," I croaked. "Careful—you'll get it on your pants."

Jared pressed a hand to his chest, seeming to notice the red-soaked paper bag for the first time. The wine had sloshed all over the stoop, and my hip was wet with it.

He exhaled noisily. "You gave me a heart attack. I don't care about my pants."

"There's broken glass."

He ignored that. "You're sure you're okay? What happened to your face?"

I dodged his hand, squirming away and almost sliding backward down the handful of steps to the tiny front yard where I'd proudly planted a row of petunias that had lived half the summer. I swiped at my smooth cheek—now scratched to hell.

My blond facial hair grew patchy on my pale skin and took forever, so I'd learned to lean into my baby face. Maybe it would scar, and I'd finally look thirty and not like I was still in college. Swipes of blood stained my gray gloves.

Jared reached for me again. "You're hurt. Let me help you."

"What do you care?" I half shouted, cringing at my patheticness. Was that a word? If it wasn't, it should have been.

"Babe, what's—" He blinked, glancing back at the open door. His concern morphed with resignation to form a sad, defeated expression. "How much did you hear?"

I shrugged, ignoring the flare of pain in my shoulder blade. "Enough."

Jared rubbed his face, his stubble scratching audibly before he ran his hands through his gelled brown hair. Somehow, it still looked only artfully out of place. He was rarely messy. It was one of his wonderfully mature qualities I'd been attracted to.

He muttered, "Shit, babe. I didn't want it to be like this. Especially not at Christmas." He carefully stood and stepped back over the broken glass to the beige interior welcome mat, rubbing his slippers on it. "Let's talk inside. It's freezing." He reached out his hand.

I let him haul me up and inside the foyer, where the pine took up almost the whole space. I stopped on the mat, the door still open behind me. Jared shifted from foot to foot, crossing and uncrossing his arms.

"Why?" I asked, the single word scraping my throat.

Deep down, I knew the answer, didn't I?

Jared blinked back tears. "It's not you, I swear. You're great. But it was a mistake to move in together. I should have known better." He held up his palms. "Again, not because of you. Because of me. I love living alone. But like I said, you're great, so I wanted to try." He sighed. "It's not working for me. *We're* not working. We rushed it."

"We didn't! We were together for more than a year. We didn't jump into this without thinking. There was a plan."

"Was there, though? You got evicted by that shitty landlord that sold to a developer, and I thought it was time to stretch my boundaries and get out of my comfort zone." He shook his head. "I'm sorry. I really like you, but..."

"Like. Not love." My mouth flooded with saliva. I was going to hurl all over our scotch pine. Though not *ours* now. There was no more *us* and *we* and *ours*. Just like that.

He dropped his arms to his sides. "I wanted to love you. Honestly."

All I could do was nod. It would be too humiliating to sob.

Evidently having hoarded these words for months, they spilled out of Jared now. "I really do like you! But we don't quite fit. Come on—you have to know that. We don't like the same kind of music or TV shows. I hate that true crime shit you're addicted to."

"So we compromise!" I shouted with a burst of frustration. "Haven't we compromised?"

"Yes!" He stood straighter, fisting his hands. "We compromise on everything. Don't we deserve to get what we really need? What we really want?" He opened and closed his mouth a few times, sputtering before blurting, "I mean, we both like to get fucked! You can't stand there and tell me we've ever really clicked in bed even though we were really attracted to each other at first."

My face was so hot my cheeks had to be bright red. God, did we have to talk about this? "I told you I don't mind topping. It's fine."

And it was! It wasn't like I didn't get off. I'd penetrated plenty of my exes. Giving other people what they needed *did* turn me on. Maybe not quite as much as some other stuff did, but that was okay. It was!

His mouth tugged down, and his voice turned pleading. "You shouldn't be settling for 'fine.' And if it was only about sex, sure, we could talk about options for an open relationship. But it's about everything being 'fine.' As much as I care about you, 'fine' isn't enough. I don't want to settle."

I really was going to puke.

"Haven't I done everything you want?" I cringed at how small I sounded. How young.

Jared exhaled, his face creasing like he was in pain. "Yes. You're so sweet and generous, and you've bent over backwards for me. At first, I thought you were my dream come true. You're the most caring and thoughtful guy I've ever dated."

"Then what did I do wrong?" I was practically begging.

"You didn't do anything wrong. But catering to my whims isn't healthy. I feel like you're walking on eggshells trying to keep me happy. Trying to be this perfect version of yourself. You're too…careful. It makes me feel like shit. Like I can't be real with you. Ba—" He cut himself off. "Mike—"

"I hate being called 'Mike,'" I blurted. He wanted real? There.

He blinked. "What?"

"My name is Michael."

"But everyone calls you Mike." He stared, eyes wide. "Why the hell didn't you *say* something?"

All I could do was shrug. "I'm used to it."

"See, this is the problem! You settle all over the place!" Groaning, Jared shook his head. "Fuck, I hate saying this to you. Which is why I've been putting it off. Also, because it's Christmas, and I know it's a big deal to you to do the cozy, snowy, traditional thing."

"It's not a big deal," I insisted reflexively.

Jared looked down pointedly at the fallen tree at our feet. "Tell me you weren't planning on decorating and taking pics of us in cable-knit sweaters sipping cocoa and pretending we don't have any problems."

"I just thought it would be nice!"

"Because you actually love Christmas or because you want everything to look perfect on Insta?"

I flinched. As much as I wanted to argue, I couldn't.

"We need to face facts," Jared said more firmly. "We can't settle. You're thirty, and I'm thirty-three. We can't coast along in a relationship that's not working. I think we really liked the *idea* of us. The reality? Not so much."

All I could do was nod.

He shivered. "Shut the door. Come on, let's talk this out."

What else was there to say? Broken glass crunched under my boots on the landing and chestnuts rolled down the steps as I escaped, leaving my now ex-boyfriend—ex-*partner*—a nine-foot organic scotch pine, and the life I'd wanted so desperately to be mine in my wake.

"MIKE?"

I would have hit the roof of the hatchback—not hard to do since there were only a few inches of clearance—if I hadn't been wearing my seatbelt.

Cursing myself for spacing out, I focused on Zoe squinting at me from the bungalow's porch. She wore fluffy Ugg boots but no coat, holding her cardigan closed at her throat, the icy wind blowing her dark curls into her eyes.

Zoe's muffled voice came again as she called, "Mike? Is that you?"

The key was still in the ignition, but Zoe was already picking her way down the slick driveway. It sloped just enough to be treacherous in the winter, which I'd learned the hard way more than once back in the day when I'd lived here with Zoe and Will and a few roommates.

Her parents had bought the house as an investment property so she had a safe place to live during college. With prices skyrocketing now, it'd been a smart move.

What was I even *doing* here? In my aimless driving around Albany, trying to process that my hard-earned relationship with Jared was over, my brain's muscle memory had apparently brought me back to my former home. I'd lived in a couple of apartments between this house and moving into Jared's, but it seemed neither had made a lasting impression on my subconscious.

Great. I hadn't seen Zoe in person in a few years, and now I was sitting outside my ex-girlfriend's place like some kind of creep in my extremely recognizable orange car, which glowed like a beacon even in the quickly fading daylight.

Her pretty face creased in understandable confusion, Zoe knocked on the driver-side window, her solitaire diamond engagement ring glinting in the rays of the setting sun. The glass was tinted enough that it was only once I rolled down the window that Zoe saw my scratched face.

She gasped and clapped her hand over her mouth, her cardigan flapping open in the wind. "What happened? Are you okay?"

"I'm fine! It's nothing." Shit, my face must have looked worse than I'd thought. I flipped down the mirror on the back of the visor and grimaced.

Yep, dried blood streaked over my cheek and the scratches had swelled. Was I suddenly allergic to Christmas trees? That would be just my luck after how today had gone.

"Did you get in an accident?" Zoe pressed.

I shook my head. "Christmas tree wrestling. 'Tis the season."

"Right. Okay. So…" She frowned. "Is everything all right with Jared? And work?"

Ignoring the first part, I said, "Work's great! I got a promotion last month."

"Yeah? You're still at that e-commerce company?"

"Yep. Still responding to customer complaints, but now I'm training and monitoring new staff. I've got vacation time until the new year. It's a great company."

"Cool." Her sculpted brows met. "What are you doing here? Did something happen with Jared? I thought everything was going well. Thanksgiving in Tampa looked awesome. You seemed really happy finally."

Could I just drive away? I toyed with the option before dismissing it and confessing, "We broke up."

"Shit. I'm sorry." Zoe tensed and reached through the open window to grab my shoulder. "Did he do that to your face?"

"No. It was the stupid tree. Jared's not like that."

She relaxed and let go of me. "Okay. I thought maybe Will was right."

Blood rushing in my ears, I squeaked, "Will?"

"Our former roommate? Your best friend?" She arched a brow. "Ring any bells? Or did you ghost him right out of your memory?"

"I didn't ghost him!" Hot shame washed over me. Vomiting was definitely back on the table.

"Then why are you being so defensive?"

"I'm not! I've just been busy."

Zoe's dubious expression was sadly familiar from when we dated. "If you say so."

"Why? What…" I swallowed thickly. "What did Will tell you?"

She shrugged as an older woman's commanding voice called out, "Is that Mike?"

"Here we go," Zoe muttered, rolling her eyes. "You're still her favorite after all this time. My parents just arrived for the holidays. We're renovating the bathroom, god help me."

For a stout woman with chronic back pain, Mrs. Schmidt-Wong moved like lightning, appearing at Zoe's side in a parka three sizes too big—likely belonging to Zoe's dad—with her blonde curls flying wild in the wind.

It was her turn to gasp. "Did you get mugged? Or was it a cat? You can't trust cats. Even if you feed them every day their whole lives, they'll eat your corpse without a second thought."

"It was pine needles. Not a cat. No big deal. Christmas tree injury." I tried to smile at Zoe's mom. Torn between formal politeness and reverting to what I'd called her when Zoe and I were a couple, I stupidly said, "It's nice to see you, Mrs....Janice. I was just driving by and..."

Come on. Think of something. Anything. Literally anything.

I had nothing. At least I stopped talking.

The wrinkles around Mrs. Schmidt-Wong's eyes deepened as she gave me a playful smile. "You're here to win Zoe back? Not that I have anything against Peter, but he's not as cute as you."

Zoe smacked her mother's arm, the parka surely taking the brunt. "*Mom.* Peter is extremely cute. Well, he's *handsome.* Distinguished." She glanced at me. "No offense." As a car approached with a rumble, she stood straight, then leaned back down to the window. "Shit, he's home. For real, tell me what's going on?"

"Nothing. I was just...um, around, and I stopped to check a text. I didn't even realize it was your house." Considering I'd previously lived here for several years, it wasn't particularly plausible. I leaned into it anyway. "Texting and driving kills."

"That's true," Mrs. Schmidt-Wong said. "Mike was always very responsible."

Zoe hissed, "*Peter's* responsible! He's a nurse!"

Mrs. Schmidt-Wong conceded, "True, true." To me, she whispered, "He's just a little boring if you ask me. No sparks."

Ignoring her mother, arms wrapped around her middle, Zoe frowned at me. "Seriously, are you okay?"

"Yeah," I lied. "Had a sh—crappy day. Just driving around. It's good to see you." It was—we'd managed to stay kind-of friends after we'd broken up. Before I'd made the worst mistake of my life. Mistakes. Plural. "I've got to get—" I choked on the next word.

It wasn't home. It had always been *Jared's* townhouse, and as much as I'd tried, he didn't want me. I suddenly didn't have a home. Jesus, where was I going to *live?* My heart hammered. I'd been so preoccupied with my failed relationship that I hadn't even considered the immediate issue.

"Are your parents okay?" Zoe asked, still frowning suspiciously.

"Absolutely! Living their best retirement dream." Before she could ask, I added, "My brothers and their families are all great too."

I'd been a surprise baby, a full fourteen years younger than my next oldest brother. My brothers were all miles ahead of me, and I'd thought I'd finally caught up somehow.

"Everything's great!" I cleared my throat. "Merry Christmas!"

As I turned the key and the engine sputtered, Peter—who was definitely handsome if you asked me—joined the party at the window. Good thing this sleepy street didn't get much traffic. I nodded to him, willing the damn engine to catch. It took a minute sometimes.

Zoe introduced me as I stepped hard on the gas, the engine making a sad *whoa-whoa-whoa* whine.

Peter exclaimed, "Oh, the bi guy, right? Hey, man. Great to meet you." He stuck his hand through the open window.

We shook, and I let the engine rest a few seconds since I was about to flood it. "That's me. Good to meet you too."

Squeezing closer to Zoe, Peter apparently caught a better look at the Christmas tree wounds on my face. "You okay? Looks like you were bleeding."

"It's nothing!" The smile hurt my face. My laugh sounded manic.

"Are you coming in for dinner?" Zoe asked—a sort-of invitation that wasn't overly enthusiastic. Completely understandable.

Mrs. Schmidt-Wong said, "There's plenty! Yes, you must join us."

I shook my head. "I can't, but thank you."

Aside from imposing on them and how awkward it would be, my jeans were soaked with red wine. I didn't want to explain why I was such a mess. I turned the key again, willing my rust bucket to just do me this one more favor and get me out of this ridiculous situation I'd put myself in.

The cosmic engine gods were in a benevolent mood. The engine roared to life. More like sputtered, but I'd take it. I jammed down the button to raise the window. "Merry Christmas! Say hi to your dad and the rest of the family."

They stepped back, and I waved as I escaped, turning at the corner and racing out of the neighborhood as fast as I could. I headed out of town, eventually ending up on a lonely two-lane highway in the darkness.

Night came so early this time of year. I'd imagined Jared and I would be decorating the tree with jazzy carols playing, sipping mulled wine and roasting chestnuts in the oven since the sleek, modern fireplace was electric.

In my pocket, my phone buzzed. I'd received at least ten texts since I'd run away from Jared, but I hadn't looked at the screen. Maybe they were just spammers trying to trick me into giving them my bank account information or social security number. Maybe Jared wasn't even worried about me.

I couldn't stand to know.

Where was I even going? Where was I going to stay? I mentally ran through the possibilities of local friends. My closest friends from college aside from Zoe had recently had their first baby, so they were out.

Some people from high school were mutuals on social media, but we hadn't spoken in years. I was only friendly with people at work—not *friends*.

And obviously, I couldn't ask Will.

Ghosted.

Shit, was that what I'd done? I'd needed to take a step back from hanging with Will all the time. I'd needed to finally move on from my hopeless crush. All of our friends were getting engaged, and he'd started dating a girl he was crazy about. I couldn't keep treading water.

But it wasn't like we'd had a fight. We were still friends. I hadn't *ghosted* him. I was waiting until I was sure I was over him to reconnect. Will was fine! He was too busy dating gorgeous women and traveling for work to think about me.

Of course he was. We were older now. This was the way life went. We didn't have time to hang out the way we used to.

"Fuck," I muttered. All my justifications aside, I'd had to stop torturing myself. There was only so long you could secretly love your best friend before self-preservation kicked in. I'd never have gotten over him if I still saw him all the time. And it'd worked! I was very much over him.

I slowed for a curve before accelerating. Everyone was busy with parties and holiday plans. The thought of showing up on anyone's doorstep—let alone Will's—was honestly mortifying after the encounter at Zoe's house.

I'd find a hotel. I'd buy what I needed for the night and deal with returning to the townhouse for my stuff tomorrow. I needed to hole up and lick my wounds.

In silence but for the rough rumble of the engine, I followed the road even deeper into the snowy forest. The pavement was clear with snowbanks rising on either side.

Where even was I? It was time to turn around and find a place to crash. There were chain hotels and motels back in town, and I wasn't picky.

Though there wasn't much traffic, I didn't want to pull a U-turn in the dark on a twisting road. Surely there'd be a driveway or another road soon. I kept going, my mind replaying everything Jared had said yet again.

He was right—I'd been in willful denial. I'd wanted so much for it to work. I'd thought it had all fallen into place with Jared. Granite countertops and a comfortable, functional relationship! Ticking all the grown-up boxes.

Even if it wasn't perfect, I'd decided Jared was the one. Clearly, I was mistaken. If "the one" even existed. What if life was only a series of disappointments and failures, and I never—

I gripped the wheel as the distinct smell of smoke reached my nose. Before I could launch into a full-blown existential crisis, the cosmic engine gods announced they weren't on my side after all.

Chapter Two

Will

A S THE NARRATOR described how the killer slipped into the house through an unlocked patio door, my phone buzzed.

Making a sound I was relieved no one else heard—something which could only be described as a "yelp"—I jabbed the button on the steering wheel and accepted the call, leaving the notorious serial killer poised outside the victims' bedroom with thick shag carpet muffling his deadly steps.

"Hi, Mum."

"Hello, love! Oh, it's so good to hear you. Just what the doctor ordered."

She'd said this, her voice resonant with sincerity, every single time we spoke since my parents moved back to Glasgow when I was in uni.

I smiled in the darkness, warm with affection, and checked my blind spot before changing lanes. The sea of red taillights had thinned and the exits on the freeway became farther apart. The recent storm had dumped a ton of pristine snow on the hilly landscape, but the pavement was clear.

I said, "Haven't missed you at all, actually."

"Bugger off. How was the drive to… Where exactly are you going?"

"I'm still on the road. Just gettin' oot o' the city now." I added, "No much traffic," slipping into Scots now that I was speaking to Mum. "Nae idea where I'm heading, but the address is in the GPS. It'll be a hotel or resort of some kind. Angela always goes all out for these holiday family retreats."

"All bosses should be so generous."

"Aye, but mandatory festivities aren't everyone's cup o' tea."

"Oh, bah humbug! You used tae love Christmas as a wee boy. Mandatory festivities will do you some good, laddie. If you'd come home for once, I'd make your favorite Christmas pudding, you know."

"I was just there in October for three weeks!"

She sighed. "I know, love. Cannae blame me for trying, can you?"

"Not to mention the fact that it was you and Dad who moved us over here when I was too young to have a say and then cruelly abandoned me."

"Wheesht, that's enough of your cheek."

I laughed. "Did I hit a nerve, Mum?"

"Fuck off, ya wee shite. You're no too big to get a skelped arse."

It had been her visiting professorship that had brought us to Buffalo when I was sixteen. I'd gone to uni in Albany and stayed rather than going back to Scotland. I loved visiting, but I had a home here.

Well, at least I'd had one at the time. There'd been a few golden years living with Michael and Zoe and the others, but we'd all moved on.

"William?"

"Aye, I'm here."

I sipped lukewarm coffee and ordered myself not to fall into the endless, cruel loop of wondering why Michael had ghosted me. The simple answer was that he'd fallen in love. I certainly wasn't the first person whose best friend had become distracted by their new partner. It wasn't as though we'd quarreled. It wasn't about me.

Somehow, that didn't make it easier.

"Hello?"

I realized Mum had said something else. "Sorry, the connection's bad. What was that?"

"I hate to think of you alone at the holidays."

"I'll be with Seth and his husband Logan on Christmas Day, remember? Not alone."

"Aye, of course. And I'm glad you've made such good friends at work, but... Are you sure Logan and Seth don't know someone special? Doesn't Logan have a sister?"

"Yes, Mum, he does. Jenna's my colleague. Also a happily married mother of two. Unless you want me to have an affair—"

"Don't be a bloody numpty." She *tsked*, clearly trying not to laugh and failing. "I forgot about that. Oh, love. I just don't want you to get too stuck in your ways as a bachelor. It's time to take a leap."

I rolled my eyes. Mum's philosophy of life was a delicate balance of risk averse and adventurous. "I've taken plenty of leaps. I took one staying here in America."

She grumbled. "Not what I had in mind, as you well know. But yes, I admit that was a leap. So, when's your next one coming? If you get too comfortable, you'll miss out on life."

"I've signed up for sky diving lessons. Plenty of leaps in my future."

"Fuck off. It's not nice to torture your poor old mum."

"You're fifty-seven. Not old yet."

She groaned. "Tell that to my lower back. And honey, you can't coast along being a ladies' man forever. Even George Clooney couldn't."

Gulping my coffee, I tried to ignore the unsettling rush of... I didn't know what. Wrongness, I supposed. Honestly, I wasn't sure how I'd gotten that reputation: *ladies' man.*

Sure, I'd dated my fair share of women since high school, and I'd had a few girlfriends. Those relationships hadn't worked out for various reasons, and a mythology had built up that I didn't want to settle down.

In reality, I'd been happier hanging with Michael. Going to quiz nights at the local bar, watching the Mets, bingeing true crime shows, and playing video games. Until he'd suddenly started doing those things with Jared instead. Presumably. I'd never actually met Jared.

Mum sighed. "I just want you to find the right woman. How's Michael doing? He's coupled up with that lad now, isn't he? Zoe's engaged, and didn't Brittany and Eric have a baby?"

"Mmm." It was best not to engage when she got on this topic. Fortunately, it wasn't often. And I hadn't mentioned that Michael didn't talk to me these days. I'd spoken to Zoe about it once and regretted it. Her sympathy had only made me feel worse somehow.

"I know, your old Mum's nagging. It's just hard not to worry. You've got to put some effort into it. You dinnae want to be left behind while all your pals move on. Have you looked at any flats this month?"

"I was too busy with planning for Seattle. I'll get back to it in the new year. There won't be new condos going on the market over the holidays."

"True enough. You're dragging your feet, though."

"I like my apartment! I'm saving up for a bigger down payment. I don't know why you're so keen on me taking on a mortgage and huge debt."

Mum sighed. "I know, I know—times have changed. We'd just like to see you settled down."

"So you want me to leap into settling down."

"It's bloody rude to point out your mother's logical inconsistencies."

I grinned. "I was also going to mention—"

"No more of your cheek! But yes. Something like that. We only want you to be happy, love. You hardly mention seeing your old pals anymore. It feels like something's missing."

It was unnerving how she could sense that. "It doesn't have anything to do with me being single. I *am* happy. They're busy. We're all busy. Relationships evolve."

"Aye, that's true. I always thought Michael fancied you, but I suppose not. You were two peas in a pod last time we visited."

My laugh brayed out like a strangled goat's. "Me and *Michael?* We're friends, Mum. Nothing more." Were we even friends these days? Barely. "I'm straight, remember?"

"Oh, it's the twenty-first century. It's all much looser now."

I knew she was kidding. After all, she'd called me a "ladies' man" only a moment ago. Mum didn't know. There was no way she could know. *No one* knew. It was fine. 'Course it was.

Knuckles white on the steering wheel and heart thumping, I exited the freeway. Sure, I'd fantasized about men occasionally, but I'd certainly never confessed my curiosity to my *mum*. Or anyone else. There was no need.

I'd been bored and missing Michael one night last year and stumbled down a rabbit hole of male/male videos. So, sometimes now I wanked to videos of anonymous blokes. It wasn't anything to make a fuss over.

It wasn't something I needed to discuss with anyone. I'd never acted on it and didn't plan to. It was fine for Michael to date different genders, and it would surely be fine for me too, but…

I was straight. I'd just said it to Mum, hadn't I? I'd always been straight. If I wasn't, surely I'd have known as a teenager? And honestly, I hadn't been interested in dating anyone lately. It felt like going through the motions.

Aside from my girlfriend in freshman year of uni, Amelia—who I'd been quite keen on—my other relationships had been rather…lukewarm. People thought I was such a player, but more often than not, I'd rather stay home and wank than hook up. Or hang with Michael, but that option had disappeared.

As if he fancied me!

My throat was suddenly dry, and I drained my coffee as Mum said, "Are you there?"

I snapped back to attention. "Sorry, you cut out. What were you saying?"

"Your cousin Fiona is making waves again."

As she regaled me with tales of my cousin's lamentably bad choices, I drove on, my head strangely light and stomach full of butterflies. I didn't think about Michael much nowadays. What was the point? He was in love with Jared, and he had a new life that was too busy for me. Aside from occasional likes on social media, we hadn't interacted in ages.

Our friendship had become a decidedly one-way street, and I'd gotten the hint after what was likely an embarrassingly long time. I supposed Michael outgrew me.

Fancied me? I laughed sharply. No chance.

"Sweetie, don't be unkind. You know Fiona means well."

"You're right, Mum. Sorry. It's, uh, jet lag. I flew back to Albany from Seattle today, and now I'm heading straight out to this retreat. I'm tired." I realized my mistake immediately and cut off what I knew she was about to say. "But not too tired to drive. I'll be there soon."

Honestly, I'd much rather be headed home to my apartment instead of out to this weekend of festivities. Attendance wasn't technically mandatory, but everyone knew it was an excellent way to get face time with the boss.

Angela Barker visited several of her offices in December and hosted these family weekends, cycling through the list every few years. It was our turn in Albany, and I couldn't miss it.

I glanced at the time. "Mum, what are you doing up so late? Must be gone eleven over there."

She grumbled. "Can't sleep with these bloody hot flashes. Your father's out like a light as usual."

Normally I'd tease, but she really did sound tired. Worry tugged, and I reminded myself I'd just seen her a couple of months ago and she was fine. Sometimes I hated the distance as much as she did.

I said, "Sorry. Hope it eases up soon."

"Me too, love. At least I've got Netflix to keep me company."

I chuckled. "You know true crime programs won't help you sleep."

"Did you watch the new four-parter about that awful incident in Kansas? Those poor people never saw it coming."

Of course I'd seen it, and we discussed the case for a few minutes. True crime really was strangely addictive. I listened to spooky podcasts and audiobooks more than music in the car these days.

I wondered if Michael had seen this latest series. Maybe I should send him the link. But what was the sense in bothering him? I'd finally gotten the hint.

Mum said, "All right, I'd better get to bed." She sighed heavily. "And I'm sorry, love. I don't mean to nag. I just worry. Life can pass you by if you're not careful."

"I know. I need to leap—but not out of a plane. Only the right amount of leaping."

"Precisely."

Her philosophy was precise in her own mind, if nowhere else. "Will do, Mum."

"The retreat must be starting soon? You really should get a wiggle on. No speeding, though."

"Wouldn't dream of it." I eased off the gas pedal guiltily.

"Sure, Dario Franchitti. Now don't forget—"

An incoming call beeped, and I glanced at the screen.

I blinked.

Blinked again.

Did it really say *Michael Davis*? Were his ears burning? Was he actually ringing me?

"Mum, I've got another call. Sleep well! Love-you-bye." We always rushed our standard three-word sign-off, the words squished together. As she responded in kind, I jabbed the screen, bracing to hear nothing but the muffled sounds of a pocket dial.

Still, I said, "Hello?" and held my breath.

"Hey. It's me." His tenor voice was incredibly familiar even though I hadn't actually heard it in two years.

"Michael?" I cleared my scratchy throat. "I was just talking about you with Mum." Why the hell did I say *that* of all things? Especially given Mum had put forth her mad theory that Michael fancied me. I shifted uncomfortably and fumbled for the dial to turn down the heat.

After a hesitation, Michael said, "Really?" His voice sounded strange even as familiar as it was. Tense and thin, and there was a loud noise in the background that came and went. A vehicle? It sounded like he was outside.

"She, er, sends her love and says merry Christmas to you and Jared."

His "Thanks" sounded choked. After a moment, he added, "Sorry to bug you. I know it's been a while."

Resentment pinched me sharply. "It has, yeah."

I ordered myself not to fill the awkward silence that followed. Michael was the one who'd ghosted me. I probably should have let him go to voicemail. But Christ, it was wonderful to hear his voice again.

Giving in, I cautiously asked, "What's up?" No sense in getting ahead of myself. Maybe he'd hit my number by accident. I cringed at how happy it made me to hear from him.

He laughed hollowly. "Not having the greatest day. But if you're busy, I don't want to keep you. I'm waiting for roadside assistance to show up, and it's a little freaky out here."

"What? Did you have an accident?" I sat up straighter, looking at the console screen as if it would display an answer. "Where are you?"

"I'm fine. The engine died, and I'm in the middle of nowhere."

My stomach tightened. "It's freezing. What's their ETA?"

"It's a busy day, apparently. Could be three or four hours."

"Fuckin' hell!"

"You sound so much like your parents when you say that. Your accent really comes out."

"Aye, lad. Och awa and beil yer head, ya wee prick." My smile vanished. "Where are you? I'm coming to get you."

"*What?* You can't. I'm at least an hour outside Albany. Probably more. It's my own stupid fault. I just thought if you're not busy, we could talk. Catch up. But I don't want to keep you. I shouldn't have bugged you."

Something rumbled loudly in the background, and I realized it was a passing vehicle. It was dangerous to be stranded on the side of a road. There were stories on the news about people being hit. Not to mention kidnappings and mysterious disappearances.

"Where are you?" I repeated.

"Uh… I was heading south. Toward Hudson, I guess. I'm not on the main road, though."

"Must be fate because I'm on my way to the Berkshires right now. Give me your coordinates."

"*Seriously?*" Michael's voice rose with obvious hope. He sighed. "But you must have plans. I don't want to—"

"Give me the location. I'm coming to get you whether you like it or not."

"But…" He exhaled loudly. "Okay. Thank you so much, man."

It really must have been fate because it turned out Michael was stranded only twenty minutes away. I kept him on the line as I went full Dario Franchitti. I could hear vehicles passing by him occasionally. It was a black night—no moonlight or stars, and I hated to think of anyone stranded out here. As angry as he'd made me, to think of Michael alone in the darkness had me stepping on the gas even harder.

Michael said, "Of course every true crime story that involves car trouble is running through my head."

I tried to make him laugh. "Well, you are a golden-haired ingenue."

He chuckled. "Can I still be an ingenue when I'm thirty?"

"With that baby face? Of course."

"We all can't be as naturally hairy as you."

I rubbed a hand over my cultivated layer of dark stubble. "I really should grow a hipster beard."

"It would only take a week tops. You already have one on your chest."

Here we were talking shite as my dad would say. Like no time had passed. Making him laugh felt more important than demanding an answer as to why he'd ditched me.

"The women love it." Christ, what a lame thing to say.

"That they do." His laugh was thin. "Kara must."

"Kara? I don't see her anymore."

"Oh. You guys seemed so into each other."

"Not for long. It fizzled out. Not enough in common once I got to know her."

"Sorry." He asked, "Who are you seeing these days?"

"No one at the moment." I felt the strange need to come up with an excuse for why I was single. "Busy with work."

"Yeah. I get it. What are you doing in the Berkshires?"

"Going to some kind of hotel. My boss said something about it being glam. One of those eco resorts, perhaps. She's on a green kick these days, making all sorts of environment-friendly changes to the office."

"Cool. That's for the new job?"

"Not new anymore, but yes." I tamped down the flare of resentment at how long it had been since we'd spoken. "It's a holiday weekend retreat. All expenses paid for staff and their partners and kids."

"Whoa. Um, where do you work again?"

"BRK Sync. It used to be Greenware Sync, but it was only a matter of time after Angela bought the company that it transitioned to BRK branding. Took several years."

My GPS, which I'd named Martha, told me to turn right, and I slowed to follow the road, dark forest looming all around. My headlights automatically flipped to the brights.

"Oh, right. Pretty big company."

"We're the northeast hub now in Albany. I just flew back from Seattle earlier today after helping them set up the northwest hub. Did a systems update."

"Is your boss that woman from Texas who's a little…eccentric?"

I chuckled. "Yep. Angela Barker. She's one of a kind. A genius at making money but she gives amazing benefits and prioritizes people and family. She's the most generous CEO in America while being one of the most profitable."

"Are you sure you should be detouring to get me? I can just wait for the tow. Assuming it'll be a tow since the engine made some truly alarming noises. Not to mention the smoke."

"I'm almost there."

"Yeah, but you're going to this retreat."

"I can be late. I already am. Most staff traveled earlier on the buses Angela hired. Oh, I think I see you!" I vibrated with a strange mix of relief and anticipation.

I checked my rear-view mirror to make sure no vehicles were approaching and pulled in front of the hatchback with its hood raised and hazard lights flashing in the darkness. I flipped on my own hazards and climbed out of the SUV.

Backlit by flashing lights, Michael waved. He wore the same dark peacoat I remembered, his silhouette incredibly familiar. I'd known I missed him. 'Course I had. It didn't prepare me for the punch of emotion that made it impossible to breathe.

I couldn't just stand there staring at him, so I forced my feet to move. Salt crunched under my boots, and I tensed as the icy wind whipped. Should I hug him? Why not? We'd hugged plenty of times before. A normal, back-slapping—

"Bloody hell, what happened to your face?" I stopped an arm's length from Michael, squinting in the eerie flashing lights. "I thought you didn't crash?" The car seemed intact, but those were nasty wounds on Michael's smooth cheek.

"No, I got scratched earlier. It looks worse than it is. I think I'm having an allergic reaction or something."

Were those fingernail marks? The hair on the back of my neck stood up. "Did someone hurt you?" I could barely ask through my clenched jaw. "Jared?"

Michael shook his head. "It wasn't Jared." But his gaze flicked away.

He was hiding something. What the hell was he doing out here in the middle of nowhere? A fist squeezed in my belly as a terrible thought occurred. If Jared was abusive, did that explain why Michael had distanced himself? I'd read about how abusers isolated their victims. Was that what had been going on?

Shame at my silly hurt feelings flooded me. I should have tried harder to stay in touch. Had Michael been suffering all this time?

I was trying to think of the right question to ask when he shook his head again. "Seriously, it wasn't Jared." He laughed half-heartedly. "I wrestled a Christmas tree and lost."

"Honestly? Look, I know we—" I cleared my throat. "You can tell me."

Head down, Michael mumbled, "I know. You're always there. *Here.*" He motioned around us. "I don't deserve it." He gave me a sad little smile. "But really, it was a tree. Christmas is dangerous. Hurts like a son of a bitch."

Before I knew what I was doing, I had his face in my hands. I hadn't stopped to put on gloves when I arrived, and his skin was icy beneath my fingers. I peered close at the scratches as if I had a shred of first aid knowledge.

Michael had a slimmer build, but we were both a little over six feet tall, so I didn't have to bend to get a good look at his injuries. I gently examined his cheek. The marks did seem consistent with spiky pine needles.

Michael exhaled in a rush, a cloud pluming between us in the freezing air. He whispered, "God, it's so good to see you."

Our eyes met in the creepy red light, sincerity shining from his. Questions crowded my tongue: *Is it? Then why did you forget about me? Was I just the only person left to call?*

I took a nervous step back, dropping my hands, and joked, "Certainly better than a serial killer showing up."

Looking away, he laughed awkwardly. "Definitely. Um, anyway…" He motioned to the car. "It started smoking and made a bang that sounded like it was about to explode."

"Christ." I joined him by the engine and caught a whiff of smoke still lingering despite the lash of wind. "I can change oil, but this is way above my pay grade. Any word from roadside assistance?"

"Nope. They basically said the truck will show up when it does and not to call in the meantime because it won't make a difference."

"Wonderful." The shoulder of the road was cleared, but claustrophobic and narrower than it would be without the snowbanks. Beyond was only the impenetrable darkness of the forest. "We can't wait here. Come on—I'll take you to wherever you were heading."

"It's okay. I'll be fine. I was freaking out and needed to talk to someone. Thanks for answering. I wouldn't have blamed you if you hadn't. Sorry, I got busy, and…" He trailed off.

Here was the opportunity to clear the air, but I didn't know what to say. That it hurt my feelings? It was stupid for me to make a big deal out of it. It was what it was—we were in our thirties now, and it's not as though we'd be hanging out daily the way we used to. I was probably being a baby. Cutting yer ain nose aff, as my dad would say.

It had also occurred to me more than once that it'd been my pushiness that had caused Michael to stop talking to me. When there was a problem, I wanted to attack it head-on and fix it. Something had been troubling Michael a couple of years ago, and he'd persistently laughed it off when I'd tried to find out what was wrong.

Something sure as hell was troubling him now. This wasn't the time or place to get into it. I shrugged and said, "We've both been busy. Time flies and all that shite."

Before I could say anything else, a large truck approached, speeding as it blinded us with its headlights. I yanked Michael back to the packed snowbank, both of us bracing against the gale of wind as the truck blew past. The hatchback shook.

I shouted uselessly, "Slow down, you reckless prick!" I was still holding Michael's arm, and I felt the tremor that ran through him. I tugged his elbow. "It's not safe here."

"I… Yeah, okay." Michael followed me to the SUV and climbed in.

That was when I noticed the dark stain on his leg. His jeans were a mid-tone, like classic Levi's, and whatever liquid had splattered his thigh was suspiciously red.

"What the fuck happened?" I exclaimed. Everything was off-kilter, from the scratches on his cheek to being out in the middle of nowhere to him actually calling me.

"Oh! It's wine. Probably looks like blood or something, huh?" Michael tried to laugh and failed miserably.

"It does. Why is there wine all over you?" A terrible thought occurred, and I had to ask, "You haven't been drinking, have you?" The Michael I'd known would never drive drunk, and I hadn't smelled alcohol on his breath.

"No!" He shook his head vigorously. "Not a drop. It's all on my jeans. And the stoop of my—well, not mine. The townhouse. Jared's townhouse." He rubbed his face, wincing and jerking his hand away from the scratches on his cheek.

As much as I burned to find out exactly what'd happened so I could fix it, I forced myself not to push. "You know, if you were a stranger, I might think there's a victim in your trunk and *you're* the serial killer. If I didn't know better."

A gleaming smile transformed his face for only a moment, like opening the curtains on a sunny morning. A dimple creased his left cheek. "Maybe I've been killing all these years. Biding my time to lure you into my trap."

"The car works fine, right? Part of the ruse?"

"Yep. My evil plan is all coming together."

"Honestly, you're damn convincing if that's the case. I almost wouldn't begrudge you."

He chuckled. "Almost. Actually, I just watched a doc on a case in Washington State where the killer didn't fit the usual profile at all."

"Oh, with the hitchhiker and the missing red knapsack?"

"Wasn't that wild?"

"I know everyone always says, 'He was so polite and quiet—we never suspected a thing!' But he really put on a bloody convincing show."

"Yeah, that was a good one." Michael grimaced. "I mean, not *good*. What happened was horrible."

"Of course, of course." I had to laugh ruefully. "It's all rather macabre, but I'm still addicted."

"Me too. Jared—" He broke off and inhaled deeply. "Never mind. Maybe it's weird, but at least we're not alone in enjoying it."

"We certainly aren't." I resisted asking one of the many Jared-related questions circling my brain like sharks. "All right, where to?"

"Oh. Really, it's fine. I can just wait here for the truck after all."

I groaned. "Can we just agree that I'm not leaving you out here? Either I wait with you, or I drop you off, or you come with me."

"To your work thing?" He seemed dubious.

"Sure. I don't have to be in a relationship to bring a guest. Angela's big on family, but she actually issued a memo about valuing single people. I guess she caught wind of the rumors that she only promoted married employees."

He frowned. "Isn't that illegal?"

"Depends on the state, but that's irrelevant. It's freezing outside—not to mention dangerous being stuck on that narrow shoulder. I'm on my way to a resort or an inn. It's not far. I'm sure roadside assistance can pick you up there. Do you have any valuables? Shouldn't leave anything in the car."

"There's stuff in the trunk, but I guess I don't need it anymore." He laughed bitterly. "It's just me." He patted his pocket. "I've got my phone. That's all I need."

"We're off, then." I put on a smile and turned on the engine. I had no clue what was going on with Michael, but I'd find out in due time. Step one was getting him somewhere safe and warm.

The narrator's gravelly voice filled the vehicle again. The killer eased open the bedroom door…

"*Poised on the threshold, he watched Shirley and Edward sleeping for long minutes, delighting in their vulnerability.*"

Michael said, "Oh, I haven't heard this one. Is it good? Like, awful-but-good?"

"It is. Fucking creepy. At least it takes place in a city and not the woods."

He peered around uneasily. "Yeah. How is it *this* dark out here? Stupid of me to go so far out of Albany. I didn't think about where I was going."

Hmm. "You were just driving around? No destination?"

"Yeah. I needed to clear my head. Stupid, like I said. We're practically in the Berkshires, I think."

"We are." Pausing the book, I checked the GPS. "Says I'll arrive at my destination in… Oh, only seventeen minutes."

"Really? Cool." He adjusted a vent and rubbed his hands in front of the warm air.

I flipped on his seat warmer before my own. After pressing *play* on the book, we settled into listening, making the odd comment as the narrator described the gruesome scene.

I could almost believe no time had passed and everything was the same as it ever was with Michael.

Almost.

The book paused automatically as the GPS intoned, "*Turn right on Millpond Road.*"

"Thanks, Martha," I said.

"You still talk to the GPS, I see. Why is this one a 'Martha'? At least I know that's not your mother's name."

I had to laugh as I braked for the turn and stopped the audiobook. Books were great on the highway, but I couldn't pay attention once the GPS kept interrupting. "No, I don't have an unhealthy fascination with my mum—or a tortured, too-close relationship. None of the serial killer staples, as you know. She just sounded like a Martha. No idea why."

"Of course that's what you'd say to throw me off the scent… Uh, as you take me deep into the woods to your murder hut?"

I slowed almost to a stop, both of us squinting into the darkness. The snow brightened the forest, but with the moon and stars covered by clouds, the headlights didn't penetrate far.

"*Turn right on Millpond Road,*" Martha repeated.

I asked, "Can you see a sign?" The narrow road was neatly plowed, and the address I'd been given was a seventy-five Millpond Road, so this seemed to be the right place? Aside from the fact that it was the middle of nowhere with no resort, hotel, inn—or anything at all—in sight.

"There—the snowbank's hiding it," Michael said. He squinted. "It says 'Whispering Pines'—nothing about a road."

I pulled up to the tree line so I could see the sign, which was professional-ly made with an evergreen-shaped logo and gentle script. "This must be it."

"*Continue one mile on Millpond Road. Your destination will be on the left,*" Martha told us.

"Well, Martha seems certain," I said. "Guess there's only one way to find out."

"Let's hope those aren't famous last words." Michael frowned. "I don't know if roadside assistance will be able to pick me up here?"

"Oh. Right." Martha seemed to be leading us even farther into the middle of nowhere. "There does seem to be cell service, at least."

The bottom line was that I didn't want Michael to go. To actually see him again—to have him beside me joking around about serial killers like no time had passed—was the greatest Christmas gift I could have imagined.

I had no idea why he hadn't talked to me in two years, but I'd find out. Whatever was wrong, I'd fix it. My bruised feelings didn't matter.

Reluctantly, I asked, "Do you want me to take you to the nearest town instead?"

For a long moment, Michael looked at me. Then he said, "Nah. I'm sure it'll be fine."

Exhaling, I stepped on the gas.

Chapter Three

Michael

HOW DID I end up here?

Not that I knew exactly where *here* was, but it could've been anywhere for all I cared. Siberia. Antarctica. Transylvania. I was with *Will*. He hadn't hesitated to ride in and rescue my dumb ass, though I didn't deserve it even a little.

It was one of the reasons I loved him.

And yeah, fuck me. I still loved him.

Hearing his deep voice again—his Scottish accent that he insisted had faded but still sounded to me like he'd wandered over from the set of *Outlander*—was everything. Hearing my name on his lips made me shiver.

How had I thought I'd be able to get over him? Or that freezing him out would make any difference? What a joke. My careful plan had unraveled spectacularly.

Jared dumped me, and I couldn't even make it more than a few hours without calling Will for help. I'd almost burst into tears and told him everything, but I'd managed to hang onto a shred of dignity.

It was selfish as hell to be crashing Will's work party, but I wasn't strong enough to insist he take me somewhere else. Not when we were warm and safe in his SUV, and I could hear his low, rough voice so close to me that it gave me goosebumps. I'd always loved how he sounded like he'd just woken up or smoked even though he hated cigarettes and didn't do pot.

We wound deeper into the forest, the SUV's headlights passing over hulking evergreens. The road was plowed, reassuring us it wasn't some abandoned trail that would end with us being stranded and stuck in the snow, huddling for warmth—

Nope. Don't go down that *road.*

It had been disgustingly selfish to call him in the first place, but when I was trapped on the side of the two-lane highway in the middle of nowhere, his was the only voice I'd wanted to hear. I thought if he'd just talk to me for a bit while I waited, I could get through it.

I'd woken up beside Jared this morning. Was that right? Yeah, it was still Friday. But he hadn't even been an option when I'd pulled out my phone. Wow, it was epically *over*. How sad. I'd been kidding myself for a pathetically long time. Even bugging poor Zoe again had been a preferable option to Jared, or calling my parents and disrupting their evening swim.

In the end, I'd had to do it. I needed Will, god help me, and I knew he'd answer even though I didn't deserve it. I'd told myself it was only a phone call. It was safe.

Now here we were. Will was back in arm's reach and just as forbidden as ever. Worst—best?—of all, it felt like the two years of distance had evaporated in a blink. He was so familiar and awesome—generous and caring.

I ached for him. Will still owned my heart, and he didn't have a clue. I couldn't choke down a laugh that sounded awfully manic.

Will glanced at me with a leery half-smile. "What?"

His uncertainty reminded me that, actually, two years of distance *hadn't* completely evaporated. As kind and generous as he was, he clearly still didn't quite know what to make of me dropping back into his life without warning, or finding me looking like hell on the side of a road.

"I can't believe I'm here. This is just so weird. In a good way." I poked my injured cheek and winced. "Mostly good." Another laugh bubbled up. What was wrong with me?

The truth was undeniable: I was happy. Joyfully, deliriously *happy*. I wished Will could keep driving all night. I wanted to escape with him and go… Anywhere. Everywhere.

"You're sure you didn't hit your head?"

"I swear."

"Middle finger swear?"

A laugh punched out of me. I couldn't remember why we'd created our own rude version of a pinky swear in college, but it still made me giggle. Solemnly, I gave him the finger and intoned, "Middle finger swear."

With a serious nod, Will lifted his right hand from the steering wheel and gave me the finger too. Then our hands met, and we awkwardly hooked our middle fingers.

His skin was warm, and a smile tugged at his lips. I could have held his finger all night, but I pulled my hand back. He was driving, after all.

Will drummed restlessly on the wheel. After a few moments, he asked, "What happened tonight?"

"Can we talk about it later? It's been a long day."

As if on cue, a text from Zoe popped up on the console screen, and Martha asked if Will wanted her to read it. Gripping the arm rests, I almost shouted, "*No!*" in the most melodramatic way possible.

With his brows drawn close, a cute little furrow where they almost touched, Will said, "That's funny. I haven't talked to her in a while." He reached for the screen.

Before I could say anything, Martha relayed the message in her stilted voice.

"*Hey. How are you doing? I'm good except my folks are here for the holidays, and I wish it was January already. Kind of, LOL. Anyway, have you talked to Mike? He came by the house before, and it was weird. His face was all cut up. He kind of took off, and we're worried about him. I've texted, but no reply.*"

I squirmed at the guilty weight of my phone in my pocket. Both Zoe and Jared had texted, but I hadn't read the messages yet. Martha asked if he wanted to dictate a reply, and Will said no.

Then he said to me, "Something happened with Jared." His jaw was clenched, his blue eyes flashing.

It shouldn't have sent sparks down my spine, but I'd always loved his protectiveness. It made me feel good. Special.

Shit, it was why I'd called him today, wasn't it? Because I knew he'd take care of me, even if I'd honestly only hoped he'd keep me company on the phone while I waited for help. I hadn't dared expect more. Or even that much. More than I deserved.

I said, "Yeah. We broke up." I motioned to my face. "This really was from the Christmas tree and me being a dumbass. He didn't, like, try to scratch my eyes out. I'll tell you the whole story later." Okay, maybe not the *whole* story.

After a tense nod, Will said, "I'm not sure why it's number seventy-five when we've only passed trees." He squinted through the windshield. "I guess addresses don't always make sense."

I exhaled. He wasn't going to push right now. He was so *good*. My chest ached with a ragged swell of affection. How did I ever think I could get by without Will in my life? My plan had been doomed from the start. Even if he'd never love me back the way I wanted, I'd take everything I could get. It would have to be enough.

Realizing I should reply, I said, "Yeah." I checked the console screen. "Martha still thinks we're going the right way." I leaned forward, squinting through the windshield. "Actually, there might be something coming up? I think I see light." A golden glow in the distance grew stronger.

"*You've arrived at your destination,*" Martha announced.

"Is this...a hotel?" I asked.

The trees gave way to a few small buildings, one with a wall of bright windows that looked like a restaurant, and a clearing with a huge bonfire in the middle. Small rectangular structures with rounded roofs fanned out in the distance, set back among the trees. Multicolored Christmas lights were strung around the arched glass-walled front of each little cabin.

Will said, "*Glam.* That's what Angela meant. It's glamping."

Dozens of people congregated by the bonfire, with small fire pits sprinkled around, kids holding sticks in the tamer fires, surely with gooey marshmallows on the ends. The clearing was lined with gold-lit, sparkling Christmas trees.

"Now *this* is Insta-ready," I muttered. Talk about a winter wonderland.

Will parked, and we climbed down from the SUV. Music and laughter carried on the breeze, the wind far less biting here with protective trees all around. Like a little oasis of Christmas cheer and happy families.

The vibe was what I'd imagined for me and Jared and the townhouse—classy and luxurious but festive. Ugh. I cringed as my brain replayed the whole humiliating incident.

Where was I going to go this weekend? There was no way I could stay even one more night at Jared's townhouse. The thought of stepping foot in it again to get my stuff had my stomach churning.

"There you are!" a hot redhead called. She approached with a broad smile for Will. She wore a cute woolen hat, a red coat, and carried a clipboard. "We were—" She noticed me as I came around the vehicle and jolted to a stop. "Oh! Hello."

"Hey!" Shit, this was so awkward crashing Will's work event. The woman stared at me in obvious confusion, and my nervous, embarrassed energy spewed out of my mouth. In words, at least. Not puke. "I'm Michael. Nice to meet you!"

"Uh, hi. I'm Wendy." She smiled and looked between me and Will. "Sorry, I didn't know you were bringing a plus-one."

"Right, this is my—er, Michael," Will said, his words tangling. "It's okay, isn't it?"

"Oh." Her eyebrows shot up. "Oh! Of course! I'll just mark that down." Wendy scrawled on her clipboard with a nervous little laugh. I thought I heard paper rip with the force of her pen. "Okay, super! Welcome to the BRK Sync family, Michael. Terrific to meet you!"

Wendy spun so fast snow flew up around her boots. She didn't even mention my injured face before racing off.

Will said, "That was odd. Usually I can't get rid of her." He grimaced. "That sounds awful. She's a lovely woman. It's just that I've been trying to let her down gently. She knows I'm single, and she's... Very interested."

"Um..." Did he not get what just happened? "Seems like she'll back off now that she thinks we're a couple."

That sure got his attention. "Huh?" Will stared at me.

Honestly, straight guys could be so adorably clueless. "Dude, I'm your plus-one. She clearly thinks we're together. Like, *together*."

Eyes widening, Will practically shouted, "But that's insane!"

It really shouldn't have hurt. It *was* insane. Of course it was! Still...*oof.* I tried to laugh it off, but there was a lump against my windpipe.

Blinking, Will seemed shocked at his own response. He lowered his voice. "What I mean is… I'll clarify with Wendy."

I cleared my throat and joked, "Too late. I'm your boyfriend now. Wendy'll just have to accept you're off the market."

Will smiled weakly, and we made our way out of the parking lot toward the main area of campfires, laughter, and holiday spirit.

Why did I say that?? Being kidnapped by a serial killer might be better than this.

But the thought of being back out there freezing my ass off alone made me shudder. At least I could be safe with Will for a few hours. Surely the tow truck could swing by here and pick me up? Was that a thing? I'd actually never needed roadside assistance before.

I pulled my blood-stained gloves out of my pocket, hoping it was too dark for anyone to notice what a mess I was. The left side of my jeans were stiff from the spilled wine, and I tugged down the hem of my coat.

We approached two men standing by one of the smaller fires roasting marshmallows. Most people were bundled in winter gear, but one of these guys wore a black leather jacket. They were both white and had brown hair, but the one in leather looked as though he'd be more at home on a motorcycle or in the boxing ring.

He was laughing as the other man, who wore dark-framed glasses, tried to feed him a sticky, charred mess. They leaned into each other intimately and were clearly a couple. I watched them and tried to ignore a pang of jealousy.

The guy in glasses noticed us and waved, grimacing at the white goo on his fingers. "There you are!" he called to Will. "We thought perhaps your flight was delayed." He looked to me. "Hello. Goodness, what happened to your face?"

I wished I could wear a sign around my neck that read: *Life and a Christmas tree kicked my ass. I won't be taking questions at this time.*

Will said, "This is my friend Michael. He got scratched by pine needles. Also, his car broke down not too far from here. Michael, this is my colleague Seth and his husband Logan."

I shook with Logan in the leather jacket, and Seth held out his marshmallow-streaked hand before stopping short and waving instead. He pushed up his glasses, then grimaced as he clearly realized he now had marshmallow on his nose. Without a word, Logan swiped at Seth's nose.

"Are you guys hungry? Dinner was delicious. I'm sure they could make something for you." Seth nodded to the restaurant. Through the floor-to-ceiling windows, staff were visible stacking chairs and mopping.

"Thanks, but I can just grab something later," I said before pulling out my phone. Ignoring the texts from Jared and Zoe, I jabbed the new message from my roadside assistance company.

Apparently, the jazzy recording of "Joy to the World" being piped in around the clearing was loud enough that I'd missed my phone dinging. "I don't want to imp—" I broke off as I read.

"What is it?" Will asked.

I scanned the text again. This couldn't be right. Shit. *Shit.*

"Michael?" Will took hold of my shoulder, his gloved hand strong and secure.

"They can't send anyone to get my car until tomorrow."

"That's all right." He squeezed gently. "You can stay here."

Honestly, staying in this winter wonderland with Will sounded like a fever dream come true, but I'd already made him miss dinner, and I was a mess, and—

A breathless, grinning woman appeared. "There you are!" She focused on me and exclaimed, "Whoa! Did a cat attack you?"

I mumbled, "Christmas tree accident." God, was it really that bad? I squirmed, my face burning.

"Ouch." She looked concerned, but then was fighting a smile again. The hair sticking out from under her woolen hat looked freshly dyed blonde.

Logan narrowed his gaze at her. "What's up with you?"

Seth laughed. "Clearly your sister has gossip to share." He lowered his voice. "Is Angela giving our office the new client group from the Boston acquisition?"

"No. Well, maybe—she hasn't said either way. She's still making the rounds and meeting kids. We had our turn, so Jun took the boys on the sleigh ride." She motioned vaguely at the woods, where apparently sleigh rides were happening.

Then she smiled at me. *Beamed* at me. "I'm Jenna. Will and I are on the People Development Committee together."

I wasn't sure I understood what that meant, but it didn't matter. "Nice to meet you. I'm—"

"Will's boyfriend!" She turned her glowing smile on Will. "Congrats! I'm really happy for you. Everyone thought you didn't want to settle down, but clearly, you just hadn't found the right person."

"What?" Will gaped at her before looking at me and dropping his hand from my shoulder like he'd been burned. Which was a perfectly fair response and shouldn't have made me wince internally. He groaned. "You heard that from Wendy already? It's been less than five minutes."

"No, from Matt. Oh, here he is."

Wearing fuzzy red earmuffs over shaggy blond hair, Matt joined us. He slapped Will's shoulder. "Hey, heartbreaker. So you're gay, huh? Awesome."

Will sputtered. "Why do you think that?"

Matt tilted his head, reminding me of a golden retriever. "Oh, are you bi or pan? That's awesome too."

"I…" Will shook his head, even more flustered now. "Michael's bi, but we're only friends. What did Wendy tell you?"

"Actually, Becky heard Michael say he's your boyfriend and that Wendy'll have to deal with it. I think she had plans to make her big move on you this weekend."

Will gaped. "Becky? I didn't see Becky. Was she hiding behind parked cars eavesdropping?" He inhaled deeply, raising his gloved hands. "It doesn't matter. What matters is that it wasn't—it was a *joke*. Wendy jumped to conclusions, and Michael joked about it."

Great. Me and my stupid joke. How much more could I mess up today? I'd probably get Will fired in a minute.

Seth and Logan shared a glance, and Seth asked, "Why would Wendy think you're a couple if you're not?"

Will explained about the plus-one, and I added, "I'm only here because my car broke down, and Will came to get me."

"Where were you heading?" the woman—Jenna?—asked. Yes, her name was Jenna. She was Logan's sister, and she worked with Will and Seth, who was Logan's husband. And Logan wore the leather jacket. There were so many new people and names flying at me, and if I didn't repeat info to myself, I'd go blank and not remember anyone's names.

Jenna added, "There's not much around here."

Everyone was looking at me, including Will, and I could practically hear his unanswered questions about Jared filling his head again. I hoped the firelight was orangey enough that they all couldn't tell how hard I was blushing.

I fidgeted and motioned vaguely with my hand. "I was going to a thing. But anyway, I shouldn't even be here. I'm sure I can call a cab." I pulled out my phone. "Uber probably isn't out this far, but…"

Seth said, "I'm not sure there are any taxi companies in this area. Perhaps if we were in the Berkshires proper, but this is a bit of a no-man's land."

"You're not going anywhere tonight." Will's tone was firm and final, but not sharp or pissed off even though I deserved it. He was reassuring and in control, and I could breathe again, my racing heart calming.

I nodded. "Okay. Sorry to cause all this confusion. I can explain to everyone that it was a joke."

Matt said to Will, "Bro, you should just roll with it. Angela *loves* promoting LGBTQ-plus people. I mean, not like you don't also have to be good at your job, but she has a hard-on for disproving Texas-related assumptions about her being bigoted. It'll make you stand out."

Scoffing, Will said, "I'm not going to tell Angela of all people and lie to everyone."

Matt winced. "What if I guarantee she already knows? I mean, Becky told me because I'm her fiancé. But Christopher was nearby, and you know he's pals with Dale, Angela's assistant. I swear Christopher's her inside man for intel on our branch. Anyway, you know people wonder how a guy as hot as you is single. Our jobs are boring. We need something to gossip about."

My head spun as Matt rattled on. Hadn't it only been *minutes* since we'd arrived?

I refocused when he frowned at me. "Dude, what happened to your face?"

Ignoring the question, Will said, "Becky needs to tell Christopher or Dale or Angela herself if necessary that she was mistaken."

Jenna said, "You know, pretending to be boyfriends worked out for these two." She shot Seth and Logan a grin.

Hold on—they were pretending? Weren't they married? This was getting weirder and weirder. I had so many questions, and my face really did hurt, and my relationship was over, and where was I going to live? God, I'd have to call my parents in Florida and make them worry about me right before Christmas…

Will stared at Logan and Seth. "But you're married."

Seth smiled sheepishly and raised his hands. "Now, yes. But at the beginning, we were strangers. Angela's track record on promoting single people has improved, but she does seem to feel that staff with families are more reliable, even if it's subconscious. Anyway, it's a long story."

Will had just gotten the job at BRK when I'd had my epiphany about needing to grow up and get over him, so this was all new to me. Apparently this aspect was new to Will too.

"Give me the short version," Will whispered.

Logan shoved his hands in his leather jacket pockets and shared a guilty glance with Seth. Seth cleared his throat, keeping his voice low. "Logan and I pretended to be dating when we met to give me a better chance at a promotion I really deserved."

"Which you got!" Jenna added. "You're welcome. Also, you and my brother fell in love, so again I say *you're welcome*." She winked at them.

"Caper, caper, caper!" Matt chanted under his breath and raised his palm to Jenna for a high five.

Seth rolled his eyes. "Yes, it was Jenna's impulsive idea, and Matt was our enabler. It was completely harebrained." He gazed at Logan with a tenderness that brought another lump to my throat before saying, "But it changed my life."

"Yeah, now you're stuck with me and Connor," Logan joked, but he leaned into Seth, their fingers brushing. I had the feeling that they would kiss right now if we weren't all standing here. I assumed Connor was their kid? I was never going to keep all these names straight.

Jealously and longing filled me like a balloon about to burst.

Matt said, "Awww. And you *did* get that promotion." He gave Will a pointed look. "You should consider it."

"I'm not going to appropriate an identity that isn't mine," Will said.

"Fair enough," Jenna agreed.

"But everyone's a little bi, right?" Matt elbowed Will. "Come on, it's been way too long since we had a caper. Don't you think, like, Chris Hemsworth is hot?"

Crossing his arms, Will laughed awkwardly. Was he blushing? He shrugged. "Who doesn't? I do have eyes. That doesn't prove anything."

"See?" Matt held up his fists triumphantly. "Be bi for the weekend. It'll be fun! Plus, it'll keep Wendy off the scent. She's been stuck crushing on you for way too long." He put on an announcer voice. *"Operation Fake Boyfriend Two: The Reboyfriending."*

Will being bi like me *and* my boyfriend would be my greatest Christmas wish come true, and obviously it was never happening, even if it was only pretend.

"Shh!" Jenna hissed at Matt, putting a finger to her lips before motioning with her head to a group of people approaching.

A petite white woman with aggressively blonde hair curling out from under a pink woolen pom-pom hat and wearing a pink ski outfit—including snow pants—marched toward us. She was with a slim, brown-skinned man with designer glasses wearing a sleek black ski outfit that also looked very expensive.

Judging by the way everyone watched her with a mix of awe, respect, and a dash of fear, I assumed this was Angela Barker. Seth and Logan were closest when we widened our circle for her, and to my surprise, she pulled them both into fierce, familiar hugs.

"How *are* you?" she demanded more than asked in a nasal tone mixed with a warm Texas drawl. "Nice glasses, Seth."

"Thank you. The joys of aging."

Angela swatted his arm in his puffy parka. "You're still a spring chicken, trust me. Speaking of which, where's Connor?"

"Finishing up a late exam before he comes home next week for Christmas," Seth said. "He's sorry to miss you."

She clucked her tongue. "Well, I suppose I'll forgive him. Gettin' good grades at Harvard is important. Is he still studying economics? I have a pal opening a company in Boston. I was thinking Connor would be perfect for a summer internship. Fully paid, of course."

Logan smiled. "That's so generous of you. Actually, Connor's switched to pre-med."

She gasped in delight. "That's wonderful! Hmm." Her gaze went distant for a moment, and she seemed to be running through a list in her head. "Lemme know where's he's thinking of applying for med school. I have some connections."

Logan and Seth thanked her again, and Angela waved them off. Was she wearing rings on the *outside* of her leather gloves? "It's my absolute pleasure. And you know I can't resist being nosy. Does Connor have a girlfriend yet?"

Logan shrugged. "Not that he's told us. Too busy studying. He's working damn hard."

"I'm sure you're both so proud. Logan, how's work going for you? Must be tons of contracting jobs these days. Albany's really spreading. Lots of new buildings. My friend Susan was thrilled with the work you did on her new office."

I could almost see Logan puff up with pride. "Thank you for recommending us. Yeah, things are great. I hired three new full-time workers for my crew."

Okay, I could *definitely* see how Angela Barker was a valuable person to know. Especially if you caught her attention and were in her good books.

Angela said, "You know I don't recommend anyone I don't fully believe in." She turned her laser focus on Will with a grin. "Now, Will, I haven't seen you since your interview. I hear you were out in Seattle this week helping them get off to a strong start. I've loved team players since my daddy took me to my first Rangers game. Great work. And I hear you've got a new boyfriend!"

She shifted her gaze to me, and of course this was the part when Will and I would explain the misunderstanding and—

"Sugar!" Angela gasped. "What in heavens happened to your pretty face?"

"Oh, I'm fine! I was carrying a Christmas tree, and I fell, and—"

She grasped my wrist and tugged with surprising strength. "Let's get you cleaned up. Dale, where's the first aid?"

"Really, I'm okay!" I had no choice as Angela marched me over to an outbuilding, Dale somehow walking even faster across the clearing and leading the way. Will scrambled after us, mouthing, "*Sorry!*"

We climbed the few steps to the little one-room building, which sat at the edge of the clearing closest to the restaurant. Inside, there were pallets of water bottles and piles of boxes—probably corporate gifts judging by the words written in black marker on the cardboard: *T-shirts, hats, blankets, mousepads.*

A table and four chairs sat in the middle, and Dale hefted a large plastic container marked with a red cross onto the table.

Angela had me in a chair prodding my cheek in record time. "Sugar, are you allergic? These scratches sure puffed up. Was it a pine tree?"

"I don't know. Maybe? I mean, yes, the tree was scotch pine. I didn't think I was allergic? But I guess I might be."

I glanced at Will, who hovered nearby looking worried and also devastatingly handsome. I'd muted him on my socials, aside from the few times I'd broken down and looked at his posts. It wasn't like I'd forgotten how gorgeous he was, but that furrowed brow of concern over blue eyes made me feel weak.

I added, "This isn't blood," motioning to my stained jeans before she noticed and had me on the way to the ER before I could get a word in.

Hands on hips, Angela whistled as she shook her head. "Well, I'm sure glad to hear that! I have some over-the-counter antihistamines in my purse if you want. Never leave home without 'em." I nodded, and she added, "And it's wonderful to meet you. Is it Mike?"

"Michael," I said. "But you can call me Mike if you want. It's fine." I weirdly wanted to make her happy. "Most people call me Mike. Except Will and my parents."

Angela's very smooth forehead didn't move as she smiled. "If Michael's what you prefer, that's what I'll call you. And if you'd rather be they/them, that's okay too. More than okay! It's great. I'm she/her, just so you know."

"Oh, thank you. I use he/him." I had the feeling Angela was new to the concept of different pronouns, but she was making the effort. "And really, I'm fine. You must have more people to greet."

She looked to Dale, who nodded. She said, "That I do. Will, do you know how to clean him up? My girls are beyond the scraped-knee phase of life now, but I got lots of practice. First, you dab on the antiseptic." She pulled out a bottle from the first aid kit and gave Will a quick rundown. "All right, I'll leave you two lovebirds to it."

Will said, "Oh, well—"

"I hope you know how very, very welcome you are here." Angela took hold of both our arms, peering up at Will and then down at me in the chair with such sweet sincerity. "Bisexual, trisexual, transgender, asexual, and plain ol' gay—or just queer as a three-dollar bill. Whatever your identity, you are welcome and part of the family. Okay? Okay. Oh, and Will, I'd love a debrief on Seattle. You know, I think you might be just the right person to help me with an exciting new secret project. But no more shop talk this weekend! We're just here to have fun. Get patched up now, you hear? Bye-bye!"

Before either of us could reply, Angela Barker whirled away like a pink, supportive hurricane with Dale on her heels.

"Angela, wait!" Will called. He ran a hand over his thick hair, messing it up.

Was his hair still soft? I obviously hadn't had many opportunities to touch it, but once after an unfortunate incident at a party in junior year, I'd slowly picked gum from the soft waves. I'd been on the couch, and Will had sat on the floor between my legs, his eyes closed, leaning back into my touch. He'd been hungover, though. It hadn't meant anything.

"Michael?"

"Huh?" I jerked back to the present. "Yep. Um, that was a little nuts."

"A little? What just happened?" He dropped his hands to his sides. "I'm sorry. I'll talk to Angela in the morning."

"It's fine. I mean…" I shrugged, my heart skipping as a wild idea crashed into my brain and right out of my mouth. "You heard what she just said about a special project. This could help your career. I don't mind being your boyfriend." *What am I saying?* "Pretending on this retreat, I mean. But I get it if you don't want to be bi for the weekend."

Picking up the antiseptic bottle, Will unscrewed the cap with jerky motions. "I…" He read the label, then screwed the cap back on. Then he twisted it back off before digging through the first aid kit. "Of course it wouldn't bother me, but… You don't feel like I'm appropriating your identity?"

I had to laugh. "No. Sexuality is fluid. I thought I was straight until I wasn't. It doesn't bother me at all." *In fact, it's my deepest fantasy that you'll realize you're not actually straight.* "The truth is, I could use a place to crash this weekend. If it's okay with you, I could stay?"

Will did look at me then, his blue eyes shining with concern. "Yeah. They can tow your car tomorrow. You're staying here with me."

A shiver ran down my spine at his no-arguments tone. Mouth dry, I nodded.

He smiled tentatively. "Maybe a caper is just the distraction you need?"

"Can't hurt, right?" *Don't answer that.*

Will dabbed a cotton ball with antiseptic and sat on the edge of the table, leaning down to take my chin with his fingers. His breath tickled my cheek, his dry fingertips gentle but firm. Desire curled lazily through my belly. I closed my eyes, imagining a brush of his lips on my hot skin…

He murmured, "This is going to sting."

He wasn't wrong. In fact, this would hurt a hell of a lot more than that. Pretending to be Will's boyfriend would break my heart all over again.

Chapter Four

Will

Hadn't Mum nagged me about taking a leap?

Bi for the weekend.

Well, this was certainly a leap. It wasn't hurting anyone, was it? Not that it felt good to lie to Angela or Wendy or other colleagues. And I was sure this wasn't at all what Mum had had in mind, but…

Is it really a lie? Does wanking to blokes qualify me?

Leaning over Michael, I held his chin with my fingers and dabbed at the cuts on his cheek. He didn't move a muscle even though it had to hurt. Clearly it did since his hands were clenched into tight fists, his shallow breath ragged.

"Sorry. My mum used to let me squeeze her," I said with a smile.

"Huh?" Michael stared up at me, his body so tense he might snap in two.

"Here." I took his right hand, urging his fingers wide over my knee where I perched on the side of the table. "Go on and squeeze."

Adam's apple bobbing, Michael dug his fingers into the flesh around my knee, his palm warm through my jeans.

"There you go," I murmured as I dabbed another cut. "Helps, doesn't it?" Michael was of course stronger than a child, but I didn't mind the bruising pressure. I liked the idea that I was absorbing some of his pain.

He was still my best friend. That remained true without a doubt. It wasn't that I was over him ghosting me with no hard feelings. But I hadn't been prepared for how wonderful it was to see him again. I was going to find out what happened with Jared and get to the bottom of Michael's distance. I wasn't a violent man, but if Jared had laid a finger on Michael…

Patience was key. Tonight, Michael needed bandaging up, food in his belly, and a good night's sleep. I eyed his stained jeans, the fabric clinging to his lean thigh. It was probably sticky as hell.

"Want to take a shower?"

Michael blinked up at me, his hand ready to crush my knee. "Yeah. I'm such a mess. I assume there are real bathrooms and not just outhouses?"

"If there are bloody outhouses, this is *not* fucking glamping."

"I promise there are no outhouses!" a chipper young woman with a dark pixie cut said as she entered. "Hi!"

Michael whipped his hand back to his lap. "Hi," he croaked.

"I'm Abby. I heard we had latecomers and that you might need first aid?" She was short, chubby, and wore a Whispering Pines jacket with a pinned nametag reading: *Abigail Lee.*

"Hello." I stood and nodded to Michael. "Christmas tree mishap earlier."

"A danger of the season!" Abby winced. "Ouch. I'm afraid there's not much to do for it other than the antiseptic and applying a bandage."

"Any chance of a shower?" I asked.

Abby said, "Of course. Every pod has a complete en suite. We provide wash-and-fold laundry service as well."

"This really is glam," I said. "How about a late supper?"

"I'm afraid the kitchen's closed, but we have delicious gourmet sandwiches and snacks available at all hours." Abby pulled out a packet of waterproof bandages. "We'll make up a picnic basket for you."

"You don't have to go to any trouble," I said, but Abby insisted. I got out of the way as she expertly finished with the first aid and led us outside.

"Any food allergies?" She dutifully tapped out a note on her mini tablet that I was allergic to kiwi. "Where's your luggage? The system says you haven't checked into your pod yet."

"Right. My suitcase is in the car, and—bugger. Michael, er… There was a bit of a mix-up, and he doesn't have his things."

A quizzical smile touched Abby's lips for only a moment. "No problem at all." She typed rapidly on her tablet.

Before I knew it, Abby had the keys to my SUV, and she and her team leapt into action. While they handled the luggage, we checked into our pod, which was one of the farthest from the clearing. The little snow-dusted buildings reminded me of Yule logs and were roofed with thick, bark-like brown shingles.

Thick evergreens grew between each pod, and the rows were angled in such a way that each had privacy through the arched, glassed-wall front. The colored Christmas lights strung around the window cast a warm glow as Abby led us inside and turned on the overhead recessed lighting with a remote control.

"We have a small seating area just to the right." She motioned to two chairs with a slim table between them at the foot of the bed. "Along the left wall is shelving for clothing and a small kitchenette with bar fridge and coffee station. The en suite bathroom is beyond the sliding barn door at the back. Of course, most of the space is taken by the bed, as you can see."

"Indeed," I said. The queen-sized bed against the right curving wall was neatly made with pristine linens and looked soft and inviting.

And it was only the one bed.

Which made perfect sense, but still somehow surprised me. Not that it *mattered.* It was perfectly fine.

Michael said, "Yep, that's a bed!" and laughed slightly hysterically. He really must have been tired.

As Abby went on about the Scandinavian-farmhouse design inspiration, featuring pale pine wood and white granite accents on the counter over the bar fridge and into the bathroom, I couldn't stop staring at the bed for some reason.

"You're probably wondering why we didn't go for a folding bed design, but we decided comfort was king." Abby patted the end of the snow-white duvet. "Firm yet soft. It's amazing, honestly."

Well, if there was only going to be one bed, at least it was an amazing one.

"And though you have privacy with the design and spacing of the pods and pathways, there's a custom-shaped blind that can be lowered." She picked up the shiny remote control from the counter and pressed the button. The cream-colored blind lowered with a soft *whir.* "Of course, it must be raised to use the front door," she added, pressing another button and sending the blind back up.

Another staff member arrived with my small suitcase, SUV keys, and a Whispering Pines sweatsuit and pouch of toiletries for Michael. Abby assured us food was on its way, gave us the Wi-Fi password, and left.

"Do you want to go first?" Michael asked, nodding toward the bathroom.

"No, go ahead."

"Cool, thanks." Michael hung up his coat on one of the hooks positioned on the wall by the door just under the curve of the roof. In the middle of the pod, the ceiling was a few feet over us, but the headroom decreased on the sides.

I hung up my coat as well, and why was there suddenly a strained silence? Distant carols were barely audible, and I could hear the thud of my own heart. Michael and I had undressed in front of each other a thousand unthinking times.

The only difference was we'd never pretended to be dating before. That and the fact that we had barely spoken in two years.

Still, there was no reason for nervousness. This was *Michael.*

"I missed you," I blurted.

Michael jerked up straight from where he'd bent to put his boots on the tucked-away mat—and bashed his head on the low curve of the ceiling. "Ow, fuck!" He rubbed the crown of his head.

"Are you okay?" In a stride, I reached him.

He gritted his teeth. "Uh-huh. Yep. Come on, this is the part where you make fun of me for being a dumbass."

Historically, that was true, but it didn't feel right to rib him right now. All I did was take his head in my hands. "Let me see." Whatever had happened today, he'd been battered enough.

Michael lowered his head, and I gently probed to make sure he hadn't done any damage. "I'm fine," he murmured.

The red, green, pink, yellow, and blue lights from outside reflected in his golden hair, which was fine beneath my fingers. He raised his head, and I dropped my hands. His unbandaged cheek was flushed pink.

I forced a careless tone. "Might have a bump in the morning, dumbass." I slugged his arm like we were back in uni at a frat party. It was like squeezing my feet into shoes I'd long outgrown.

Michael slugged me back, though not hard. "That's me. Remember that time I got wasted and jumped off the roof into the pool at that party?"

"Christ, you were lucky it was deep." The memory of watching his reckless leap made my gut twist. I shook my head. "That feels like another lifetime."

"Yeah. I guess we really did grow up. Or I tried, at least. Now…" He ran a hand through his hair, wincing.

"Now?" I prompted after the silence went on.

Not meeting my gaze, he said, "Now I really need to get out of these jeans. I'll just…" He hooked a thumb toward the barn door and disappeared inside the bathroom.

I blew out a long breath. This morning, I'd woken alone in a hotel room in Seattle. Tonight, I was sharing a bed with my MIA best friend in a cabin in the woods. Scratch that, a *pod* in the woods.

Oh, and I was bisexual for the weekend, and said MIA—or *formerly MIA*—best friend was my boyfriend. Not a problem! This wasn't real. It didn't mean anything.

I gulped down a bottle of water from the mini fridge. Maybe a mad caper was the distraction we *both* needed. Why not have fun with it? Put everything else aside and take the weekend to reconnect and relax. It was Christmas, after all.

The shower turned on, and the soothing sound filled the pod. I took a deep breath through my nose and exhaled.

Right, here we go. Relaxation time. Caper time. Fun time.

Easier said than done. There wasn't much room to pace, yet I managed quite a few narrow laps before opening my suitcase and rooting around for my toiletries and the baggy shorts and tee I lounged in before bed. I didn't typically wear anything to sleep, but I would tonight.

I found myself staring at the bed again. Why was I so… I didn't even know. What was this jumbled mix of emotions? Mum would call it a "tizzy."

It was wonderful to finally see Michael again in person, yet questions nagged, and hurt lingered, along with anger that popped up without warning.

The knock at the glass was barely a tap, yet I jumped a mile. An apologetic staff member delivered the basket of food and asked for the laundry he'd been told to collect. I tapped lightly on the barn door and told Michael I needed his clothes.

The water turned off, and as I was about to say I could just grab them, wet feet slapped on the tile. With a white towel snug around his waist, Michael slid back the door and held out a bundle. Steam wafted out, and Michael's pale chest was faintly pink from the hot shower. Water clung to his red nipples.

I snatched the clothing, dropping Michael's black boxer briefs. Laughing nervously, I bent and grabbed the soft cotton. "Here you go!" I said far too loudly and merrily to the young man waiting.

He opened a black tote marked *Laundry* in white. I'd noticed *Coffee* and *Sugar* on the counter. What was with this farmhouse trend of labeling everything as though we'd struggle to identify basic household items otherwise? At least Whispering Pines was too posh for reminders to *Live, laugh, love.*

"Anything else I can do for you this evening?" the boy asked. His gaze slid to Michael and back to me. There was no judgment evident—his polite smile didn't falter. But I was very aware that he surely thought Michael and I were lovers.

A strange sensation rippled through me, and I practically yelped, "No, thank you!" before closing the door after him. What was that reaction? It wasn't embarrassment or shame. I supposed it was a bit of a thrill. This was the first time I'd been perceived as anything but straight.

"What's so funny?" Michael asked. He picked up the sweatsuit from the bed and unfolded it.

"Hmm?" I blinked at him.

"You're smiling."

"Oh!" I grabbed the food basket and brought it to the counter. "I'm hungry. Let's hope there's something good." From the corner of my eye, I could see Michael retreat into the bathroom. The sliding door was still open, and I spotted the white movement of his towel.

Channeling all my focus on the covered basket, I opened it and announced, "Turkey and Havarti on multigrain, corned beef on rye, club on white—you'll want that. Mmm, these cookies are still warm." I took out the peanut butter for Michael.

"I'm done with the bathroom if you want it. Oh, are those peanut butter?"

I handed him the two cookies half-wrapped in white paper, and he bit into one eagerly and mumbled, "Oh my god."

Along with the other peanut butter cookie, I put the club sandwich on a plate for him. The picnic basket also included utensils and cloth napkins.

"I'm going to clean up, but don't wait for me." I handed him the plate. "Crack on."

A smile tugged at his lips. "I love how you say that but you insist you hardly sound Scottish anymore."

"Trust me, I don't."

"Sure, I believe you. Cheerio, guv'nor?"

"Oi! I'm not *English.*" I grabbed his wet towel from the floor and snapped it at him as he laughed and dodged.

In the compact bathroom, the tile floor was so warm under my bare feet that it had to be heated. After traveling all day, I really did need a wash. Michael had left the towel bathmat in front of the glass-walled shower. There was just enough room for a toilet and sink on either side of the barn door.

There was still plenty of hot water, and though I'd only planned on a quick rinse, I stayed in the shower's cocoon for a good ten minutes. Afterward, standing on the damp bathmat and toweling off, I listened to Michael putter around. Still had to pinch myself that he was here with me.

And everyone thinks we're boyfriends.

Almost everyone, at least. They were going to look at me the way the kid who collected the laundry did. Not that he did anything but smile. Shaking my head, I swiped at the condensation on the mirror above the sink. I was being daft. It wasn't a big deal. Who cared what anyone thought—whether they fancied me a "ladies' man" or not. No skin off my nose.

"Hey, um… Did you want to go back out and socialize?" Michael's voice came from just on the other side of the barn door, which should have seemed thicker somehow.

I rubbed the towel over my hair. "Frankly, no. It's getting late anyway."

"Yeah, I can't hear the music anymore."

"I'll socialize plenty tomorrow."

After pulling on my shorts and tee over damp skin, I slid open the door. Michael glanced up from where he crouched in front of the mini fridge, then sprang to his feet. Belatedly, he winced and put his hand up as if he was about to bonk his head again.

"You're good this time," I said, squeezing past him to grab my phone from the white bedspread. "I should reply to Zoe. Not right to leave her worrying."

Michael's shoulders slumped. "Shit, yeah."

"I'll just tell her you're with me and you're safe."

"Thanks. I'm sorry to be such a pain in the ass." He rubbed his face, apparently forgetting about the bandage. "Ow! Shit."

"Don't be sorry. You're helping me potentially advance my career, so it all works out."

"Never been a beard before."

"Not with that peach fuzz."

"I'd throw this cookie at you, but it's too good."

Chuckling, I texted a quick response to Zoe. At the same time, Michael looked at his phone and groaned. "Fuck me," he muttered. "Jared must have talked to my mom."

"Okay," I said cautiously.

Michael's parents were a bit strange. He'd been a surprise baby and his siblings were substantially older. Honestly, I'd always felt like his parents were rather over the job by the time he came along. Not that they didn't love him, but he used to stress about handling everything himself and not asking them for help unless he absolutely had to.

"Why would he—" Michael scrubbed a hand through his damp hair. "Fuck. I guess he really was worried when I didn't reply."

Michael's thumbs flew over the screen of his phone, and then he groaned again. "I texted Jared, but I have to call my mom for a minute. Is that okay? She'll worry too much. Sorry."

"Of course. I can…" I glanced around. This pod was definitely not designed for privacy.

"No, you stay here." Michael shoved his feet into his boots and ducked outside, the phone to his ear.

Fat snowflakes had begun to drift down, and they caught in his hair and landed on his shoulders, white on the navy sweatshirt. He faced the trees. I wanted to tell him to put on a hat so he didn't catch cold.

His voice was muffled, but I could still make out most of what he was saying. I should have popped in my earbuds or run the tap, but I listened to snatches of Michael's half of the conversation.

"*I'm sorry he worried you. I'm fine.*"

"*Yes, of course.*"

"*No! I'm not in trouble! Honestly.*"

"*Mom, we just had a fight. Jared's being a drama queen.*"

So they didn't break up? Hmm. I wasn't sure I believed that. I also wasn't sure why I was so disappointed to hear it. I'd never even met fucking Jared.

There was that resentment ballooning up. I should've been glad if he and Jared had only had a fight. Except it had been around the time he got together with Jared that he'd ghosted me, so maybe it was okay that I didn't jump for joy if they were going to patch it up.

Outside, Michael had one arm wrapped around his middle, and he shifted from foot to foot. It was too cold to be standing out there, but before I could bring him his coat, he hung up and hurried back inside, stamping his boots on the mat.

"Everything okay?" I asked.

"Yeah. Thanks. Brr." He shook like a dog.

I poked at the coffee machine. "Want a hot drink? Or there's wine and beer in the fridge." I examined a bar selection on the counter. "They have those little bottled cocktails as well. How about a Manhattan?"

"Sure, I'm not picky. Thanks. I'll pay for it."

I scoffed. "Angela's paying for it, remember? I'm sure she won't mind, *sugar*." I poured the cocktail for Michael into a glass over ice since I'd never known him not to want booze on the rocks.

We adjusted the chairs and low, narrow table so they were right in front of the glass. I fiddled with the remote and turned off the lights overhead. With the colored outdoor lights reflecting off the snowy evergreens, it was bright enough to see.

"Weird to have a hotel room without a TV," Michael said. "It's kind of nice though."

I glanced around. "I hadn't thought about it. I fell asleep watching terrible crime shows on cable in my room in Seattle this week."

That it was somehow still the same day that I'd left Seattle was surreal. Here I was in the middle of the woods with Michael of all people? Pretending he was my boyfriend? I took a long swallow of Merlot.

"Oh, what did you watch? The ones with the cheesy narration?"

"You'll have to narrow down that field by a large margin."

"True. There's a series all about murders in Orange County. Crappy narration, but the crimes were interesting. They were all solved too."

We chatted about true crime, movies, and the Mets off-season trades. It was all so blissfully normal, as if the past two years of near silence hadn't happened at all.

Then it was time for bed.

Why was it so awkward to crash together? We'd slept where we fell plenty of times back in the day, including in the same bed. Now, we hemmed and hawed. I asked, "Which side do you fancy? I don't mind."

Michael fiddled with the bandage on his cheek. "Jared likes the left side, so I'm used to the right."

I hesitated. "But which side do *you* prefer?" Was Jared some kind of control freak? A million questions flooded onto my tongue, but I held it. Michael didn't need an interrogation tonight.

"The left if it's cool?"

Putting on an exaggeratedly flat American accent, I said, "It's cool AF, bro."

He chuckled and crawled across the mattress since the left side of the bed was under the pod's curving roof. "Thanks, *Brett*. You going to that kegger later?"

"Fuckin'-A."

We laughed. I hadn't thought about "Brett Yankface," my frat boy alter ego, in ages. I couldn't remember how we'd dreamed up the character, but it had become a running joke between us.

I'd lowered the shade, but the Christmas lights shone through faintly.

"Should I switch off the outside lights?"

"Nah. Unless they bug you? It's nice for a change. I don't need pitch black to sleep."

Presumably, Jared did? I reminded myself that it wasn't a character flaw to prefer a dark room for sleeping as I slipped under the fluffy duvet and adjusted my pillows. With the shade down, it was much darker than it had been, and the string of colored lights was faint.

"It is nice," I murmured.

"Mmm."

My body didn't have a clue what time it was, and despite the awkwardness earlier, I found myself relaxing into the very soft—yet firm—mattress. As I drifted off, the lyrics of one of the holiday songs that had been playing in the clearing echoed through my head.

It came upon a midnight clear
That glorious song of old...

Chapter Five

Michael

WHY WAS IT light?

Stretched out on my back, I tried to make sense of the pale glow through a cream-colored blind over a huge window and the pillowy mattress under me. In a rush, everything flooded back, and I sucked in a breath, fully awake in a thump of my heart.

"'Morning," Will rasped beside me, his blue eyes watching me. "It's all right," he murmured. "You're with me."

Perhaps he thought I'd jolted with fear. "Yeah. Thanks."

Oh my god, here I was. Safe with Will. Waking up next to Will. Here *we* were, the duvet rumpled, Will yawning and arching his back as he stretched his arms overhead.

I tried not to stare at the dark thatch of hair in his armpit and failed epically. His white undershirt was also thin enough to see the circles of his nipples and his chest hair.

As I forced myself to look at the ceiling, I became extremely aware of how close our legs might be under the duvet. I inched my right foot over, wondering how near I could get because I guess I liked torturing myself? The brush of my skin against his would only make me want to press him back into the soft mattress more.

Also, bless whoever had picked out the extra-thick duvet, because my dick was embarrassingly hard. I could laugh it off as morning wood, but I'd rather not have to. The heat of Will's body was so close, and his unique scent filled my nose, along with Head and Shoulders, the shampoo he'd always used though I don't think he'd ever had dandruff. Maybe that was *because* of the Head and Shoulders?

"Michael?"

"Uh-huh?" I lay rigid as I focused on Will's frown.

"Did Jared hurt you?"

I wanted to roll over and face the low, curving wall of the pod, go back to sleep, and not have to think about Jared or where I was going to live. But

Will had been patient, and I recognized the determination in that brow furrow.

"Yes." As Will inhaled sharply, I shook my head. "Not like that. I swear."

Will shifted onto his left side, propping up his head with his hand. Raising an eyebrow, he gave me the finger. I had to laugh as I wrapped my middle finger around his.

Also, I was right about the effect of skin-on-skin.

I let go of his finger and tugged the duvet up around my neck, burrowing underneath. My bandaged cheek was itchy, but I tucked my hands in the pockets of the borrowed sweatpants. Oh wait, too close to my dick. I clasped my hands over my stomach. As I fidgeted, Will waited patiently.

Why was this bandage so itchy? Squirming, I snaked out a hand and peeled a corner loose.

"Oi. Should you be doing that?"

"It's driving me nuts."

"Here." He batted my hand away and sat up.

I held my breath as Will leaned over and took my face in his hands. His thumbs were warm and a little dry, and as he angled my chin, I remembered that moment on the side of the road when he'd first noticed the wounds and had touched me similarly. I'd wanted to throw myself into his arms and never let go.

Wait, had I done that? We'd hugged but I couldn't remember who'd moved first. My memory was a mess of fantasy and reality. Now I was in bed with Will, and if this was a dream, I'd happily sleep forever.

His exhalation tickled my nose. My heart hammered. Will slowly, slowly peeled off the bandage and tape. He brushed the scratches with his fingertip.

"How is it?" I whispered. There was no reason to be whispering, but in the slowly brightening dawn and the silence of the pod surrounded by the snowy forest, it felt necessary.

"Better. I think the antihistamines helped a lot. Not all red and puffy now."

"Cool. Thanks."

Will relaxed back under the duvet. "No problem."

Pull off the other Band-Aid already.

"So, it turns out Jared has wanted to break up with me for months. It all came out yesterday."

"That prick. Right before Christmas?"

I squirmed, humiliation washing through me. "He was going to wait until January, but I overheard him on the phone. The Christmas tree I was bringing home attacked me. I fell and broke a bottle of wine." And surely had a massive bruise on my ass. The left side ached dully, but the pain was manageable and hadn't kept me awake. I added, "I ran away. And you know the rest."

"Mmm. You went to Zoe's?" He asked it carefully, weird tension in his voice.

"Oh, right. It wasn't on purpose. I was driving around, and I ended up there. She spotted me and came outside." I groaned. "And her mom was there, and then her fiancé came home. It was a whole thing."

Will chuckled. "I can imagine." He rolled onto his back and was quiet a few moments before saying, "I didn't think you were seeing Zoe much these days."

"I'm not!" Ugh, that sounded way too defensive. But I knew he was pissed about the way I'd basically disappeared. Understandably! I cleared my throat. "I know I kind of dropped off the map for a while."

Basically. Kind of. I cringed at my own…what? Weakness? Lack of accountability? I needed to take responsibility for ghosting my best friend. Will deserved a real explanation and apology.

Before I could say more, Will was out of bed and about to slide the bathroom door shut. He said, "Don't worry about it. You want to piss before I shower?"

Now he didn't seem to want to hear it? At least not at the moment. "Nah, I'm good," I lied, ordering my full bladder to simmer down. Not to mention my erection. At least the guilt was taking care of that.

"LAST CHANCE TO back out," Will said as we tugged on our boots.

I straightened to button my coat. "I'm good. Unless *you* want to back out?"

He fiddled with his laces. "I don't like lying. At the same time, it would be so bloody awkward now to say, 'Just kidding! We're only mates.'"

"It seriously would. And will Angela still consider you for that project she mentioned? I wouldn't if I were her."

"Nor would I." Will zipped his coat and pulled down a woolen hat over his head. "This is quite a ridiculous situation we've gotten ourselves into."

"It is. But, I mean, it's two days. It's not a big deal. I need to pay my way, after all."

He scoffed. "You don't. It's good to have you here."

This was why I loved him. One of the reasons, at least. If only I could tell him how amazing he really was… I ran a hand through my still-damp hair, my fingers brushing the tender spot where I'd bonked my head.

I stiffened as it occurred to me that when he'd said he missed me I might not have said it back? Did I? All I could remember was his sweet concern and big, warm hands on my head.

"Michael?" There was that concern again as Will's brows met.

"I missed you too. In case I didn't say that before. It's so good to see you again."

Will looked away to pull on his gloves. Was he blushing? "Cheers. We'd better get to breakfast."

"Okay." I added, "Honey."

Will laughed. "That's right, we need to sell this. What shall I call you? Dearest? Darling? Pookie?"

Giggling, I led the way out of the pod. "Does anyone actually call their significant other 'pookie'?"

"I once dated a woman who called me 'snuggle-wuggle-puss.' It was the first and very much the last time."

"Oof. And I thought 'cupcake' was bad."

Snow crunched under our boots as we made our way to the clearing past cozy pods. We kept our voices low, though no one was close by. Kids shouted distantly, and there was a general buzz of activity coming from the main area.

Will asked, "Is that what he called you?"

"Jared? Hell no. He kept to the standard 'babe' kind of thing."

"Mmm."

I'd put on a gray BRK Sync beanie Will had from a previous event, but the ends of my damp hair were already crispy in the cold. "Pookie-wookie?" I joked, not wanting to think of Jared.

"Maybe we should keep it simple. Shall I call you 'sweetheart'?"

God, the way my heart soared high into the brilliant blue sky at those words. I nodded and said, "Sure" instead of "*I'm begging you to call me that and only that forever and ever.*"

Breakfast in the glass-fronted restaurant was a buffet that smelled overwhelmingly of bacon in the best way possible. The delicious scent distracted me for a few seconds as I stamped my boots on the mat. Then I realized everyone—and I meant *everyone*—was staring at me and Will. The chatter had died down too.

The restaurant was half-full, but I didn't see Angela. Clearly, the gossip that Will had a boyfriend had made the rounds since almost everyone but a group of kids playing cornhole stopped to watch us.

At a big round table for eight by the farthest window, Jenna stood and waved us over. I tugged at my scarf as we made our way, my skin itching with all the attention. At least my cheek looked less like I'd been mauled by a pissed-off cat.

Jenna introduced me to her husband, Jun, and pointed out their two kids amid the loud group of children devouring pancakes. Seth and Logan were there too, and Matt and his fiancée, Becky—who had overheard us in the parking lot—arrived right after us.

"How'd you two lovebirds sleep?" Becky asked with a wink.

"It was a great night," I answered honestly. I realized how that sounded as soon as the words were out of my mouth. "I just mean that bed is really comfy."

There were a few smirks, and Will was smiling tightly. Even if he was down with pretending I was his boyfriend, he probably didn't want me acting like we'd had some amazing night of sex.

Oh, nope! That train of thought is not happening. No thank you.

Matt winked broadly. "Sure, sure, we believe you. Mmm, that bacon smells incredible."

I stood in front of Will in the buffet line, and when I offered to put a croissant on his plate because I was already holding the tongs, I swore to god I heard an actual *"Awww"* from someone. It was a little creepy how excited Will's coworkers seemed to be about him having a boyfriend.

Back at the table, I dug into my scrambled eggs, bacon, and sausage. I admit, I was really curious about Seth and Logan. As they ate their breakfast, I listened to Seth chatting with Jenna and Jun about family Christmas plans.

Jenna said, "You know Pop won't want anything but the same turkey and stuffing we always have. I'm not saying game hens wouldn't be delicious, but we have to do the usual stuff as well."

As they debated it, Seth speared one of the sausages on his plate and wordlessly dropped it onto Logan's, where only eggs remained. Logan ate the sausage eagerly.

So, they had pretended to be boyfriends too? And had ended up getting married for real? If only I could be that lucky.

"Ready for your big performance?" Seth asked me and Will quietly.

Will nodded, and I said, "Yep." Little did they know I'd had years of practice. This time, I'd just have to override my usual pretending-not-to-be-desperately-in-love-with-my-best-friend routine and turn on my pretending-my-best-friend-is-desperately-in-love-with-me charms. Piece of cake.

"Our very own throwback Adam Sandler movie for the holidays," Matt joked.

Logan frowned. "*Happy Gilmore*?"

Becky said, "No, the one where he pretends to be gay for the health insurance benefits or something like that. I think he was a firefighter."

"Oh, right," Jun said. "That was a terrible movie. I'm sure the performances today will be far superior."

I chuckled. "I haven't seen that movie, but I'll take your word for it. Also, I'm not straight. I'm bi."

"Like Logan." Seth gave Logan's muscled forearm an affectionate squeeze.

"Cool." I smiled.

Logan took another bite of toast. He brushed crumbs from his chin and mumbled, "What?" at Seth's pointed look. Logan added, "Mike and I can do the secret handshake later."

"Michael," Will corrected.

I waved a hand. "It's fine."

"It's not, though." Will sliced through a pancake, giving me a quizzical smile. "Why do you do that?"

"I don't want to make people feel bad."

"But what about *your* feelings? It's *your* name."

Everyone was watching us, and I laughed awkwardly. "It's not that big a deal."

"Wow, you guys are really good at playing a couple," Becky whispered.

Laughter rippled around the table, and I elbowed Will. "Stop nagging, pookie-wookie."

This got a real laugh out of Will—and everyone else. I wasn't sure why Will was so on edge. Yeah, having so much attention from his coworkers probably made him feel weird. But was it so bad to pretend he wasn't straight? Maybe it was the *me* part.

"Okay, time to spill everything about Will that he doesn't want us to know," Becky said with a wicked grin before sipping her fresh-squeezed OJ.

"I'm technically his supervisor," Seth said. "I'm not sure I should be hearing this."

Jenna scoffed. "You're my actual supervisor and you know way too much about me."

"Yes, it's a cautionary tale," Seth replied.

Everyone was looking at me, and Will seemed...curious about what I'd say? I shrugged. "We met in college and eventually became roommates off-campus."

"Aww, that's nice," Becky said. "And you've been BFF ever since?"

Guilt joined the party, but I managed to nod as I chewed a mouthful of extremely sweet and sticky pancake. Would Will mention that I hadn't talked to him in two years before calling him out of the blue for a roadside rescue?

He didn't, because of course he didn't. He was too generous for that, and it would have been awkward and weird for everyone else.

"He must have been beating off girls with a stick in college," Jenna said. "That face, that accent, that—" She seemed to remember this was a work event. "Personality," she finished.

"As if," Will muttered, shaking his head with a smile.

I said, "Oh yeah. He was extremely popular. There was a new girl all the time."

The table laughed and teased Will. His jaw clenched as he smiled, a vein beating on his temple. "Come on, mate. That's not true."

I swirled the black coffee in my mug. "Um, it is. You dated a new girl almost every week back then. They just didn't usually stick around long."

"Love 'em and leave 'em, huh?" Jun said.

Now Will really was bristling. "*No.*"

"I didn't mean it like that!" I insisted. "Will's not a jerk. Not at all. He's amazing. He's sweet and generous and loyal and—" I broke off. "What I mean is he's not a player."

"Of course not," Seth said, the others murmuring agreement.

"Sorry," Jun added sheepishly, pushing up his round glasses.

Will laughed. It was *almost* genuine, but I wasn't sure the others could tell the difference. "It's all right." He glanced around and kept his voice low. "I have this reputation, but the truth of it is I just haven't met the right person yet."

"But you *have*." Becky winked. "It was your best friend right under your nose all along. Swoooooon."

A.K.A. my dream come true. I laughed along. Ha, ha, *ha*.

Fortunately, Seth changed the subject. "Matt, do you know anything about the video game that's really popular these days?" He asked Logan, "What's it called?"

Logan mumbled the name through a bite of food and added, "Trying to come up with a surprise for Connor. Little shit guesses everything." He smiled fondly.

Seth said to him, "Well, we could always surprise him with that motorcycle he's been saving up for."

Logan glared. "No goddamned way."

Honestly, I'd have expected Logan to be the one who was pro-motorcycle given his leather jacket and rougher vibe.

Seth raised his hands. "You know I don't like it either, but… Video game it is. We'll have to think of a few more gifts too."

I was so curious about Logan and Seth's son and how he played into the fact that they'd initially been pretending to be in a relationship. But it seemed rude to ask. I stayed quiet as Matt practically bounced in his chair and talked a mile a minute about the video game.

My phone chimed with a text, and I read the message with a sigh. At Will's raised eyebrow, I said, "They towed my car to the garage. The mechanic said it'll be after Christmas until he can even look at it."

"Don't worry." He lowered his voice, leaning closer and making my heart skip. "You'll be with me."

I wanted to argue that he didn't need to be my chauffeur, but…I only nodded and whispered, "Thank you." Letting Will take charge was comforting in ways I didn't need to examine right this second.

Soon enough, breakfast was over and it was time to…do whatever people did at corporate retreats. Honestly, I wasn't sure, especially since this was a family event. Wendy, the woman from the parking lot, called out instructions as we were herded from the restaurant. She looked away as we approached.

Grinning, Matt leaned close as we got outside and asked, "Ready for Operation Fake Boyfriend Two: Bigger, Badder, and—" He paused. "Something I still need to come up with?"

Will laughed while I stupidly said, "How hard can it be?"

Chapter Six

Will

I'D NEVER BEEN much of an actor. Aside from my stirring turn as a kitchen rat in the Cinderella Christmas panto when I was eleven, I'd never had any need to perform. Well, I supposed we all performed in some ways at the office or in our lives, but this was no time to get philosophical.

Because Michael was holding my hand.

And I was holding his hand. We were mutually grasping hands, which was something couples did.

We were bundled up and crossing the clearing under cloudy skies, and a minute earlier, Michael had tugged my wrist and whispered, "Should we hold hands or whatever?" He'd leaned in, his breath tickling my ear.

Right, this was what couples did. "Absolutely." I clumsily entwined our gloved fingers, the leather squeaking.

Michael squeezed my palm. "Um, is this good?"

"Totally. Isn't it?" Was this how people held hands? Surely it was. There was no special queer way to hold hands.

Why was I being a numpty and overthinking this? Yes, this was a perfectly acceptable manner in which to hold hands. With a man. With Michael.

Fresh snow crunched under our boots as we followed Seth and Logan to a hut where people queued for cross-country skis. They were also holding hands.

Logan had to be freezing in his leather jacket, but he seemed perfectly comfortable as they walked along, talking and laughing about something.

I'd been to their house for a summer barbecue, and it was warm and welcoming and very much a *home*. I'd never suspected for a moment that their relationship started as a fake arrangement.

"You sure you're okay?" Michael murmured.

"What? Yes. Why?"

"You just seem really quiet."

"Just thinking."

"Ahh." He nodded seriously. "I thought I smelled smoke."

Laughing, I nudged his shoulder with mine. "Bugger off."

Michael nudged me back. "But are you sure you're okay with this?" He squeezed my palm. "Because it's not like we have to be all cozy or whatever. Some couples aren't into PDA. You don't need to prove anything."

This was my chance to let go of Michael's hand, but it wasn't as though it was a hardship, was it? "Nah, it's fine. If I'm only going to be bi for the weekend, I should go all in."

"Right." He nodded, looking down at his boots. "Uh-huh."

"Okay, no. I'm not skiing," Seth said to Logan. "I'm going to fall."

We'd reached the ski shack and benches where families strapped into equipment. The trail with two grooves carved into the snow with some kind of machine disappeared into the forest.

"I'll catch you," Logan said simply.

Seth rolled his eyes. "With poles in your hands? That'll be a great trick."

As Seth and Logan went back and forth, I eyed the people on skis dubiously. Some were clearly experienced, striding off confidently on the trail with smooth motions, their limbs working in concert.

Michael and I shared a look. "Maybe we should try something else," Michael said. "I have enough bruises."

"Yes!" Seth agreed. "Because this is clearly a bad idea. Why are all winter activities so darn risky?"

"Darlin', you read my mind!" a familiar voice exclaimed.

We turned to find Angela in her pink snowsuit. "Seth, these Northerners are real daredevils, ain't they? Now, there is one activity here that's smack dab in my wheelhouse. You fellas want to try it with me?"

Naturally, the four of us agreed and followed Angela down another trail. Seth asked hopefully, "Is it sitting in a lodge drinking hot cocoa by a fire?"

I could only laugh as we rounded a bend and the stable and horses came into view. Logan said, "Hold your fucking horses."

"That's the idea!" Angela chirped.

"How is this less risky than skiing?" Logan demanded and rightfully so. He didn't seem to have any compunction about swearing in front of Angela and spoke to her in a way that made it clear they had familiarity. She seemed to like it.

"Oh, horseback riding!" Seth said. "I did it all the time at bible camp as a kid. It's easy."

As Logan and Seth bickered, I asked Michael, "Are you up for riding? I haven't done it in years, but they don't look like wild stallions."

Michael eyed the horses. "Um, yeah. Why not? I rode a camel at the zoo once."

This prompted Angela to sing a song about a camel named Alice, and some of the nearby children joined in.

As we waited to saddle up, Michael whispered, "This is all extremely wholesome."

"It really is."

Also, we were still holding hands, and I was in no rush to let go. It had been a while since I'd dated anyone long enough to indulge in PDA. Joanne from marketing passed by on horseback and gave us a wave and an encouraging thumbs-up, which was quite unnecessary but sweet all the same.

Again, this was the first time—to my knowledge—I'd been perceived as anything but straight. It was… What? I felt oddly giddy, so I supposed it was a bit of fun? A laugh to be pulling the wool over my coworkers' eyes?

My stomach twisted. No, that wasn't it. I didn't enjoy lying. Even as a boy, I'd never been one for telling tales. It was just a relief to not have people asking why I didn't have a girlfriend and when was I going to settle down, etc.

While there were certainly plenty of coworkers that didn't seem to care, it was amazing how often people I didn't know well felt welcome to comment on my relationship status.

On cue, Joel from accounting clapped my shoulder. "Hey, Will!" A fuzzy blue hat covered his balding head. He introduced us to his wife who wore a matching hat and ski jacket. They looked to Michael expectantly, and I realized it was my turn.

"This is my…Michael. Boyfriend." Wow, smoothly done.

"Hi!" Michael shook their hands with a smile.

"Great to meet you, Mike. It all makes sense now!" Joel gave me a quizzical smile before I could correct him on Michael's name. "Should've just told us you were gay!"

As Joel's wife elbowed him and glared, I replied automatically, "I'm not." Since I wasn't. "What I mean is, I'm…" All I had to say was, *I'm bisexual.* Yet my gut tightened, which didn't make sense. If I enjoyed being perceived as bi, why shouldn't I be able to say it?

"We're not sure about labels," Michael said. That wasn't true in his case, and he'd said it for my benefit. He squeezed my hand reassuringly, and I took a deep breath.

"Oh!" Joel slapped his forehead. "Right, okay. Sorry." His face reddened.

Now I'd made Joel feel bad when the deception was all my doing. I shook my head. "No need to be sorry! I'm just—er, this is all new to me." That was certainly the truth.

Joel's wife gave an encouraging smile. "I'm sure you'll figure it all out in due time. All that matters is you're happy! Everyone can see you two are crazy about each other."

A few more colleagues appeared, eager to get in a word. Dana from communications exclaimed, "I never would have guessed!"

I smiled and nodded, and Angela was saying something about horses, and Michael was gripping my hand, and I guess I was a better actor than I thought if "everyone" was buying into the idea Michael and I were together? It was the whole point of having a fake boyfriend, so I wasn't sure why it threw me.

Maybe I really should just come clean to Angela and everyone. But Michael was holding my hand, and we were so deep into it now. If being bi for the weekend could potentially help my career with Angela, confessing it had all been pretend would undermine her confidence in me as a person and damage my reputation with my colleagues. How would they trust anything I said?

It was too late. I was all in, and I had to accept it.

"Will?"

I focused on Michael. "Sorry, I was miles away."

He tugged on my hand. "It's my turn. You have to let go."

"Right!" Laughing awkwardly, I released him. He buckled on a helmet and followed the young woman's instructions on pulling himself up and over the saddle.

From my vantage point, I could see the faint red stain that remained on the left side of his jeans, although the laundry department had made a commendable effort. The denim clung to his lean thigh, his coat riding up to his hips as he got settled—and turned pale.

"Michael?" I stepped closer. "Are you all right? Is your arse sore?" How had it not even occurred to me? He'd had that fall last night—horseback riding was a terrible idea.

He flushed pink and glanced around, and I realized too late the implication of my words if we were meant to be lovers.

I had to clear my dry throat before adding loudly—possibly too loudly?—"Is your arse sore from that fall you took?"

Michael shrugged tightly. "A little, but it's fine as long as we're not, like, galloping." He clutched the reins and sucked in a sharp breath when the horse fidgeted.

"Come on, now. Something's wrong."

"I'm fine!" He nodded too vigorously.

I sighed and raised my eyebrows.

He relented and mumbled, "It feels higher up here than I expected."

"But you've jumped off two-story roofs."

"One time! And I was very young and drunk!" He gripped the leather reins. "It's fine. I know it's weird, but I've developed this little vertigo thing. I don't even like being on stepladders these days."

"What?" I reached for his knee. "Why didn't you say so? We don't have to ride! Come on, I'll help you down."

That Michael apparently had a new condition I didn't know about was very unsettling. I'd known everything about him before. Or thought I had.

"Sir? It's your turn."

"Oh, we're not riding after all," I told the woman.

"We are! I'm up here already!" Michael patted my hand where it rested on his knee. "I'm fine. Honestly. Saddle up." He slapped my shoulder playfully.

Reluctantly, I stepped back and put on my helmet. Boot in the stirrup, I mounted my own horse, a mare named Stella. She barely moved a muscle as I got comfortable in the saddle. The leather was cold under me, but it would surely warm up soon.

As we were led out of the stable at a sedate pace, Stella swaying easily beneath me, I watched Michael's straight back in front of me. Beyond him, Logan was complaining, and Seth was laughing and telling him how brave he was. The way they teased each other reminded me of my parents, and I could imagine Mum praising Logan for taking a leap.

Michael glanced behind, and I asked, "Okay?" He gave me a real, crinkling smile and nodded.

The horses obediently followed the trail, our group riding single file behind the guide. The air was cold and crisp, the snow-muffled forest quiet around us.

Even Logan seemed to be enjoying the peacefulness—until, with a rumble, a horse suddenly galloped up from behind us and charged past with a cheering preteen boy on its back.

Amid the shouts for him to stop, another rider passed us, and then another—perhaps one of the parents—brushing too close. Snorting, Stella sidestepped and the low branches of a bare oak or maple scratched my cheek. I jerked away, overcorrecting far too much.

It wasn't that Stella threw me or anything that dramatic. No, I simply leaned past the point of no return and plopped off into the cushion of snow with a *whomp*. Staring up at the gray sky, all I could do was laugh.

There were shouts of concern—quite a cacophony, really—and before I could stop laughing enough to assure everyone I was all right, Michael appeared in my field of vision.

"Guess it was my turn to take a tumble," I said.

Eyes wide, Michael peered at me seriously. "Are you hurt?"

"No, not at all. Don't worry yourself."

But Michael still leaned over me, biting his lip as he peeled off a glove and tenderly touched my cheek. I winced. My skin felt too hot. "Ah, guess I'm cut. We have matching wounds."

Logan was saying, "You see? That could be you, Seth!"

Sitting up, I laughed. "Didn't even knock the wind out of me." Michael knelt in the snow, now gripping my arm with his bare hand. I gave him a smile. "Really, I'm fine." I passed him his glove. "Hey, you got down pretty fast. No vertigo?"

"Oh. Uh, nope! I told you it was nothing." Michael looked around, seeming to realize the rest of our group was staring at us from up on their horses and tugged the leather glove back on his hand.

Angela said, "He's just worried, sugar. You sure you're good?"

The guide was speaking on a walkie-talkie before hopping down and hurrying over with the reins of her horse in hand. "I'm so sorry about that. The medical team is en route."

"Oh, I don't need it!" I pushed to my feet. "Just my pride that's bruised. Did they fetch that kid?"

The guide nodded, seeming to barely resist rolling her eyes. "There's always one."

"At least it wasn't Connor," Seth said wryly.

Angela laughed. "Oh, he's too old for shenanigans now, I'm sure."

Logan snorted. "We'd like to think so, but..."

Michael stood beside me, hovering as if he thought I might faint at any moment. I took his hand and squeezed. "It was way worse when you jumped off the roof into the pool."

"Oh, *this* we have to hear!" Angela said.

Michael obliged and told the story while we waited for two staff with first aid training to ride up and give me a mandatory once-over. I only realized once they arrived that Michael and I were still holding hands. Apparently we were better actors than I'd imagined.

MICHAEL'S CHEST ROSE and fell rhythmically in the soft, distant glow of the Christmas lights through the blind. I'd fallen into a sort of trance counting his breaths.

After a day of riding—and falling—skating on a frozen trail through the forest, a massive buffet dinner, and carol singing around a bonfire, I was beat.

Not to mention a day of introducing Michael as my boyfriend, holding his hand, and even feeding him a sweet, gooey marshmallow at Angela's insistence that it was "romantic."

I'd washed my hands hours ago, but somehow, I could still feel the brush of Michael's lips on my fingertips as he'd taken the marshmallow into his mouth. It had been silly and awkward, and I didn't know why I was still thinking about it when I should have been fast asleep.

I shifted inch by inch, rolling onto my back and trying not to disturb Michael where he stretched out beside me. If I were alone, I'd wank to release any lingering thoughts from the day and slip into dreamland.

I'd always loved wanking. Granted, most people did—at least as far as I could tell. But sometimes I wondered if there was something wrong with me. I didn't think many would choose wanking over a date with a flesh and blood person they had the opportunity to sleep with.

Speaking of sleeping with another person, Michael was snoring very softly, dead to the world and completely unaware he was in bed with a pervert. What the hell was I doing thinking about wanking? I'd be getting hard in a second if I didn't stop.

Shifting again as quietly and gently as possible, I curled on my side away from him. Perhaps I should have showered and taken care of it earlier. My cock throbbed at the idea. I supposed it had been too long. Normally, I wanked every day or two.

Now that I thought back, I couldn't think of many times I'd have been keen to fuck a woman rather than get myself off. There was Amelia in freshman year, of course. Christ, I'd been wild about her.

She'd been my first real love, but she'd called it off right after the start of sophomore year. We'd been long distance over the summer while I'd been in Scotland, and Amelia's heart had not grown fonder. Mine had broken rather dramatically.

I'd been miserable at school and had considered dropping out and going back to Scotland after all. Then I'd met Michael, and Zoe and the whole gang at the house. So it had worked out for the best.

Even when Michael and Zoe were together, he'd always made time for me. I'd gotten over Amelia eventually, but Mum would say I hadn't taken any more leaps after that, and I should have.

But I'd had Michael. Until I suddenly hadn't.

Making a little whimper, Michael kicked and fidgeted in his sleep. In the faint watercolor light, I could see his eyes moving beneath his lids in a dream.

The scratches on his smooth cheek were still visible, though he'd assured me they didn't hurt. My own face was fine, the scratch from the branch much ado about nothing.

The extra-large T-shirt hung low under his collarbones. Fidgeting again, he murmured, and I watched his Adam's apple bob as he swallowed. He snored lightly—a hollow sort of rasp. Was he too hot under the duvet? He kicked at it again, so I eased the fabric down to his waist.

The sweatpants rode low on his hips. The T-shirt was bunched up and askew, exposing his soft, pale skin and the surprisingly dark hair leading down from his belly button.

I fought to breathe. Why was lust tearing through me so powerfully my veins could have been on fire? Clearly it *had* been too long since I'd wanked. Christ almighty, Michael was going to wake up and wonder what the hell I thought I was doing.

After ducking into the bathroom, I inched the barn door closed. There was no window, so I flipped on the light and leaned over the sink, resting my forehead on the cool glass of the mirror. My dick was so hard it was almost painful.

I almost laughed. What a drama queen I was being! Christ, I'd gone a few days without wanking plenty of times. Yet I vibrated with pent-up energy. I'd wake Michael if I wasn't careful—he was right there, only a few feet away in the compact pod.

Spreading my legs and bracing, I pulled my cock out of my shorts. I didn't need lube—I was leaking already. It was a little rough, but oh, that made my toes curl on the lovely warm floor. My cock was full and thrummed in my grasp as I stroked.

I bit my lip, gasping shallowly through my mouth. When I wasn't watching porn as I wanked, there were fantasies I relied on. Images, really. Curved buttocks, breasts, hard cocks. Bodies driving into each other, spread open, surrendering. Kissing, swallowing, moaning.

I'd never sucked a cock, but I imagined what it might be like as I rubbed and tugged my shaft, my balls aching and heavy.

On my knees, lips stretched, spit on my chin, my mouth perfectly full. Licking and tasting, barely breathing, pulse thundering, wet sounds echoing. A hand cupping my head, fingers gentle in my hair, his voice a moan: "Oh, Will."

My back arched as I came, shuddering silently, my body on fire. I jerked as I imagined swallowing his cum. He was no one in particular—an outline. Only a shadow even though—

I focused on the cum as I milked myself, shaking with aftershocks. I reckoned it would be salty and warm in my mouth. Splattered on my face. I'd lick up every drop.

Bending over the sink, I washed up and splashed my cheeks with cool water. When I straightened to face myself in the mirror, my skin was blotchy and red all the way down my neck. My throat was parched, and I filled one of the small glasses, gulping it down and refilling.

Well.

I'd always insisted I had no plans whatsoever to act on my attraction to men. And I hadn't! Yet the excitement and release still buzzing through my body was new. That had been…next-level wanking, and I'd thought myself rather accomplished in the field.

"Will?"

I almost hit the ceiling, spinning around guiltily. "Yes?"

"You okay?" Michael's voice was sleepy and soft.

Not really! Couldn't say that. He'd only worry. So, I checked myself in the mirror, turned off the light, and edged open the door. In the faint colored glow of the Christmas lights, Michael sat up on my side of the bed, the duvet twisted around his waist.

"Sorry I woke you," I murmured. "Go back to sleep." His hair stood up, and my fingers twitched with the need to smooth it down. "Everything's fine."

"You sure, man? Are you sick?"

"Nah, just had to piss. Shove over."

Michael crawled back to his side under the curved roof. He yawned widely as he snuggled back under the duvet. "Okay." Then his voice sharpened. "I wasn't snoring, was I? That can happen after I've been drinking."

I almost lied and said he'd been quiet as a mouse. But I didn't want to lie to Michael. "Only a little. It doesn't bother me at all."

"Okay." He curled on his side away from me, tensed. "Sorry, though."

"I told you—it doesn't bother me." I reached out to squeeze his shoulder, but stopped in midair, pulling my hand back and tucking it under the duvet. "Honestly," I added. "Go back to sleep."

It was true—it didn't bother me. I could sleep through a hurricane. I was being a hundred percent honest. About that much, at least. As for the rest of it… What even was *it*?

I rubbed my damp face. I was being daft, as Mum would tell me—not that I was going to discuss this with her. I could sort it all out in the new year. A fake boyfriend was enough of a leap for now, thank you very much.

Chapter Seven

Michael

WITH OUR ARMS snug around each other's shoulders, Will and I stood hip-to-hip, the sides of our bodies flush as his left ankle was bound to my right. In other circumstances—minus the hundreds of people around and wearing snowshoes—this might have been the beginning of a very satisfying wet dream.

That it was Wendy, the woman who'd apparently had a crush on Will, tying us together only made it more awkward. She'd given us a brittle smile before crouching down. I couldn't see her face now under her beret.

"Cool hat," I said, because I felt like I needed to say something to her. That was the best my brain could do, apparently.

Wendy glanced up, adjusting the beret. "I know it's not very fashionable these days."

"No, I like it!" Had it sounded like I was making fun of her? Shit. As someone with a years-long crush on Will, I hardcore related to this woman.

"Me too," Will said.

"You don't have to say that." She knotted the rope, yanking at it almost desperately. I recognized my own humiliation at unrequited love in her, and I wanted to hug her and say it was okay.

Will seemed genuinely puzzled. "It's a great hat. Wendy, just so you know—"

"No, please!" She sprang to her feet, gripping a spare rope to tie up the next contestants. "You don't have to say anything. I'm very happy for you. All right, bye!" If the snow hadn't been so deep, I think she would have run for it instead of clomping over to Matt and Becky to tie their ankles.

Will sighed. "I just wanted to apologize."

"For not liking her back?" I shuddered. "Don't do that. She's embarrassed enough already. Just act normal with her."

"But she has nothing to be embarrassed about." His brow furrowed under his woolen hat.

"Dude, she's humiliated. Your pity does not help." My skin prickled at the thought of Will finding out that I'd been in love with him for years. Jared's words echoed in my head.

"*I just feel so sorry for him.*"

Will's pity would be *so* much worse. At least with Jared, it was over. But there was no way I could stop seeing Will. Being with him again now made me realize just how lonely and crappy those two years of not talking to him had been. I needed him in my life. He was my best friend no matter what.

Even if I wanted to move my head a few inches, press my face to the strip of stubbly neck where his scarf had slipped, and breathe forever, I'd just have to make do with Will's arm around me, the weight of it perfectly secure.

Our heat of the three-legged snowshoe race also contained Matt and Becky, and Angela and Dale. If it was weird for Dale to be tied up to his boss, he didn't show even a flicker of discomfort. The snowshoes on our outside feet were the big old-fashioned ones that were handmade from wood and…twine? I wasn't sure, but they were large and in charge.

I leaned into Will, soaking up his heat. Sunday had dawned brilliantly sunny but frigid. There would be a morning of activities followed by lunch, and then heading home to Albany. Only a few hours left to be Will's boyfriend.

Home. My gut tightened at the thought. I'd have to get my stuff from the townhouse. I'd have to talk to Jared. Be a grownup and deal with sorting through any shared possessions and bills and all the little things that came with living with someone.

"Okay?" Will asked.

"Yeah. We should come up with a strategy."

"For this race? Isn't it just not to fall down? And go fast?"

"Right." I laughed. "I guess it's not that complicated."

At the starting line, the young man and woman on my left introduced themselves to me, and since Will was talking to Dale on his other side, I said, "I'm Michael. Will's boyfriend."

It was actually the first time I'd said those words since Will had introduced me previously. At the stables, he'd called me "*My Michael,*" with that beautiful Scottish lilt that made my heart sing. I'd be his for every minute I could.

It turned out that three-legged snowshoe racing was exactly as difficult as it looked. Bumping and stumbling, Will and I jerked forward, our boots sinking in the snow on our bound legs while the cumbersome snowshoes didn't sink as far, which was the whole point of snowshoes.

"Left! Left!" Will chanted like he was trying to do some military march.

"But that is *your* left!" I protested.

We pitched forward, sprawling in the snow. I was practically doing the splits with my left leg, the snowshoe clearly having a mind of its own. We were laughing so hard our breath huffed out in cloudy bursts. The assembled crowd howled along with us.

Will and I were practically crawling now, and as the crowd roared, I looked up to see Angela and Dale crossing the finish line. Angela was so small that Dale was practically just carrying her, hitched up against his side.

"The PA/boss relationship in a nutshell," Will said. "Okay, we need to stand up. Ready?"

"Yep."

We pushed to our feet—and took one step before Will tripped and we lurched forward on our bellies, our chins in the snow. I could only wheeze through my laughter. My peacoat and jeans were going to be soaked by the time we got out of this ridiculous situation.

Matt and Becky were having the same issues we were, as well as the other couple I'd spoken to. It felt like Will and I were wrestling even though we were on the same team, one of us pushing or pulling or stumbling at exactly the wrong time.

"How is this so hard?" Will demanded through another grin. "Lean on me. Stop fighting and let me lift you."

Putting more weight on Will to my right, I tried to stay still as Will shoved to his feet with a grunt. I had my arm around his shoulder, and he lowered his to my waist.

"That's it. Keep leaning on me. Okay, I'm walking."

At the finish line, Angela cheered loudly. "Come on! Everyone can finish this race! Teamwork!"

As Will hauled me forward, I had this bananas fantasy of him sweeping me up in his arms like a princess in a fairy tale. Which he couldn't do because our legs were tied—and he wouldn't do anyway because *why would he?*—but just leaning against him made me feel safe and warm and special.

This is going to be over in a few hours. Don't get used to it!

I'd woken that morning and watched Will sleep on his belly, one knee drawn up and his lips parted, drooling a bit on the pillow he'd clutched. His knee had been so close under the duvet. Even though I'd had to piss, I'd remained frozen, knowing it was the last time I'd get to wake up with Will.

Now, we raced forward. I followed Will's rhythm, and we found our groove. I wasn't just leaning on him and letting him haul me across the line. My muscles strained as we ran, the crowd cheering us on. Our boots sank into a divot, and we stumbled.

Sprawling face first into the snow, we sputtered, the snowshoes on our outside legs making it even more awkward and hilarious, judging by the audience's reaction. Matt and Becky motored past us as we tried to get up.

We were on our knees with the snowshoes sticking up into the air. Will's whole face was dusted in white. "Here," I said, brushing at his stubble. "I think victory's off the table." My gloves weren't helping, so I peeled off one and said, "Close your eyes."

He did, and I lightly brushed the snow from his facial hair and eyebrows. The way he closed his eyes and let me sent a rush of emotion swelling through me.

My fingertips touched his lips, and I murmured, "Sorry. You're good now."

Will opened his eyes, and I swear, my heart just about stopped. A fat, fluffy snowflake sat on the end of his nose, and I caught it with my middle finger. "Make a wish."

"Like an eyelash? I didn't know people did that with snowflakes."

"Sure, why not?" I shrugged. "My mom always did it. You have to wish before it melts."

Will watched me with a little smile playing on his lips, the creases beside his mouth deepening. He closed his eyes purposefully, then opened them. "Okay. Wish made."

"Just under the wire," I said, and we watched the snowflake dissolve on my pink skin.

"You guys okay?" someone asked. "You need the medics?"

"Not again," Will grumbled. He shouted, "We're fine!"

We made our way to our feet. I realized everyone was watching us, and I imagined from their point of view we must have looked...what? Close? Maybe like a real couple? Maybe...

Nope. Stop that train of thought.

Getting carried away wouldn't do me or Will any favors.

Later, I found myself with Seth as Logan and Will took part in a massive snowball fight. I asked, "So, you and Logan pretended to be together too?"

Seth laughed ruefully. "We did. It was quite a 'caper,' as Matt likes to say. Or chant, to be more accurate. Logan and I were thrust into it like you and Will were, but I can't imagine where I'd be if we hadn't. *Who* I'd be." He gazed at Logan dodging a snowball from the kids. A little smile lifted his lips.

"And it was for Angela's benefit?"

"Yes. I realize that sounds absolutely demented. She had just taken over our company, and there were all these rumors about her only promoting married staff. It's turned out to not be true, although I have to admit she does get very excited about supporting queer couples and families. She's done so much for us, both knowingly and not. Honestly, she gave me my family. Not that she knew it."

Will was packing snowballs with a little girl, shielding her with his body. Meanwhile, one of Jenna's kids shrieked with joy as Logan hefted him over his shoulder. Seth tensed, though I couldn't figure out why.

I asked, "You okay?"

He exhaled in a puff of white air and took off his glasses, cleaning the lenses with his scarf with tight movements. "I'm fine. Logan was injured some years ago, and he should be more careful." He shook his head with a laugh. "I can be a worrywart. Or an 'overthinker' as Connor would put it."

"But you're the one who wants to get him a motorcycle?"

Seth chuckled ruefully. "Not at all, believe me. But I don't like it when he and Logan butt heads. And he's worked so hard at summer jobs saving money, insisting on paying his dorm fees in Boston. It would be such a wonderful surprise for him on Christmas morning, and he's going to get a motorcycle one way or the other."

"I hear you. So your son's at Harvard in pre-med?"

Seth's face lit up. "Yes. It's hard to believe how far he's come. He was Logan's stepson when we met. His mother had recently died, and Connor was really struggling. As was Logan. As was I. We were all…alone."

"Then the caper saved the day?"

He grinned. "It really did." After a few moments, he added, "Who knows? Maybe it'll lead you and Will down an unexpected road too."

I'd been watching Will and the little girl again. Whipping my head back to Seth, my voice raised several octaves. "*Us?*" I cleared my throat. "Oh, no. I'm bi, but Will's straight. And we're just friends! We can't—we're not—it wouldn't—" I'd never be that lucky. It wasn't possible.

Seth raised his gloved hands. "Of course. I was only joking."

Oh. "Right. Yeah!" I tried to laugh. God, was I about to *cry?* What was the matter with me? I'd been scraped raw the past couple of days, and suddenly my eyes burned with tears.

"My goodness." Seth peered at me with concern. "I'm so sorry to upset you."

"I'm not upset!" I practically shouted in an extremely convincing way. Heart racing, I lowered my voice. "I'm not. It's fine. Even if I wanted it, Will doesn't—he'll never feel that for me."

Wait. What did I just say?

Before I could organize my chaotic brain, Seth squeezed my shoulder and said softly, "It's all right. I understand."

"No, wait! I'm not saying *I* feel that for Will either." My pulse raced, and the mascarpone-stuffed French toast I'd had for breakfast threatened to make a dramatic return all over the pristine snow. "That's not what I'm saying. I didn't say that." I wasn't sure now what I *had* said.

Seth patted my shoulder. "Of course not."

The more I protested, the worse I made it, so I forced myself to shut the fuck up and watch the snowball fight. Guilt flooded me as my gaze found Will. He was now piggybacking the little girl while she hurled the snowballs. I was supposed to be helping my best friend, not making this more complicated than it already was.

In our pod a little while later, I stood by the front window, my eyes locked on a snow-dusted pine tree as Will changed into a spare pair of pants after getting his jeans soaked playing with the kids. Mine were still a bit damp from the three-legged race, but I'd live.

Fabric *shushed*, and Will had just started talking about how the little girl had received an expensive new medical treatment that Angela had paid for when Angela herself suddenly appeared outside. She gave me a wave, a bright grin lighting up her face as she approached the pod.

"Dude, she's here." I turned to find Will buttoning a plaid shirt over his slacks, his chest hair exposed. "Katie?" He looked past me. "Oh!" After hurriedly tucking in the ends of his shirt, he did the last buttons as I opened the door.

"G'day, mate!" Angela exclaimed.

I blinked at her. "Uh, okay? I mean hi." Maybe doing a terrible Australian accent was one of her things? I looked to Will, who seemed just as perplexed.

"Hi, Angela. It's…yes, a good day."

She laughed. "I bet you're wondering why I sound like Crocodile Dundee."

I vaguely recalled that was some old movie my parents liked. I closed the door behind her as Will said, "I suppose we are, yes."

Angela grinned. "I know I said no work talk this weekend, but the retreat's almost over and I have a proposition for you. It's about that special project I mentioned."

"Oh!" Will nodded. "Yes, I'd love to discuss it."

"I'll head out to lunch and leave you to it." I grabbed my coat from the hook.

"This might involve you too," Angela said. "If you want it to."

"Uh, okay?" I glanced at Will.

"Do y'all have plans for the holidays?" Angela asked.

Will and I shared another glance. "Nothing in particular."

"No family plans?" she asked. "Because I don't want to get in the way of family time at the holidays. It's sacred."

Will said, "No, I saw my parents when I went to Scotland recently. And Michael visited his parents in Florida for Thanksgiving."

Ugh, of course that made me think of Jared and how he'd been pretending the entire time, and nope, I needed to focus on now and whatever Angela was building up to.

Angela tilted her head. "You didn't want to spend Thanksgiving together? Not that it's any of my beeswax!"

Shit. Right, we were supposed to be a couple. Will was blinking and clearly had nothing, so I blurted, "My work schedule! We couldn't get vacation at the same time to go to both Scotland and Florida. But we're definitely spending Christmas together. I'm off for the next two weeks, actually."

Angela beamed. "Then how do you boys feel about a trip down under?"

Chapter Eight

Will

MUM WOULD HAVE admonished me to close my mouth because I was catching flies. Staring at Angela, I tried to make sense of what she'd said. Australia? She wanted us to go to *Australia*? Beside me, Michael appeared equally dumbfounded.

Angela laughed. "I know, you're wondering what in tarnation I'm going on about. Sit down. Let me explain." She motioned to the two chairs even though this wasn't her pod.

We shifted them around to face her and sat while Angela perched on the end of the bed in her pink snowsuit and earmuffs. I was glad I'd haphazardly pulled up the duvet earlier. It still felt oddly intimate for Angela to be here in our room.

She asked, "What do you know about Australia?"

My mind raced. Australia? The company didn't do any work there to my knowledge. "Uh, there are kangaroos and koala bears?"

"And crocodiles," Michael added.

"Correct!" Angela grinned. "Now, I'm sure you've heard of Sydney and Melbourne. Plenty of companies in our field doing business there. But I've discovered there's an untapped market in Western Australia."

"Oh, Perth?" I asked.

"Yessiree Bob. That whole side of the country seems to get overlooked, and I think there's huge potential for the company. I've scheduled a few exploratory meetings, and Will, I think you're just the person to come with. You've done a dynamite job coordinating the new hubs in North America. My family will be tagging along, and of course, I'd love it if Michael joined us. The holidays are about family even if we're on the other side of the world throwing shrimp on the barbie or whatever the heck it is they do at Christmas."

"Uh…" I struggled to corral my thoughts. A trip to Australia? Yes, please. Trip to Australia with *Michael*? Yes, yes, *yes*. He was at loose ends with the breakup, so perhaps this was perfect timing? Was there a downside?

"I know!" Angela held up her hands. "I sprang this on you. I was going to go alone, but I got to thinking about how nice it would be to have a partner in crime to talk things over with. Dale usually has to listen to me, but he's off for the holidays. Like I said, no pressure."

I glanced at Michael, who watched me for cues. I said to him, "A trip to Australia sounds like a fun way to spend the holidays?"

He smiled tentatively. "Totally."

Angela added, "And of course, it's all expenses paid. There'll be some meetings for Will and me, but there'll be plenty of time for relaxing too."

I nodded. "Right. It sounds great. I don't think I see a downside?"

She grinned. "That's because there isn't one, unless you lovebirds don't like fun in the sun."

Ah. There it was. Michael and I would have to keep pretending to be a couple. A weekend was one thing—could we keep it up for two weeks? Would Michael want to?

Angela tapped her earmuffs. "I'm ready to trade in this winter gear for sundresses and sandals. Whaddya say, Mike? Sorry—Michael."

"Uh, that does sound great. We just need to…"

Springing up, Angela said, "Say no more. You two hash it out. No hard feelings if it's too last-minute. Did I mention we'd be leaving Tuesday morning? So, you have to have your passports already in order and all that. Regardless, I'm sure there'll be another opportunity before long, Will. Don't let me pressure you. I'm just jazzed up. I think we'd have a lot of fun and hopefully lay the groundwork for an exciting new chapter at BRK Sync. Talk it out and let me know. Bye!"

Before we could say a word, she was gone, only leaving a puddle on the floor where snow had melted off the bottom of her boots.

"What just happened?" Michael asked.

I blew out a breath, puffing my cheeks as I stood and paced. "Bloody hell." My mind raced with the possibilities. Travel overseas and the potential for a promotion. Doing a job I enjoyed for a company and a boss I liked and respected. Excellent for my career.

Yet all that was overshadowed by the opportunity to spend two more weeks with Michael. Sharing a room. Reconnecting. My heart raced. My belly somersaulted like Tom Daley flipping off the diving board.

"There's no way you can pretend to be into me for two weeks," Michael said. His face was flushed pink, and he fidgeted in his chair. "You must hate that idea. Two days was one thing—two weeks would be…"

Exhilarating.

As I struggled to land on an emotion, that was the one that bubbled to the top. After not seeing Michael at all for too long, this seemed too good to be true. "I don't hate it," I said, my voice sounding oddly distant.

Michael smiled hesitantly. "You're not sick of me yet?"

Frustration and hurt elbowed their way past the excitement, and I stepped in the puddle, my sock soaking instantly. "I'm not the one who didn't talk to you for two years."

Michael's face fell, and he dropped his head. "I know. I'm sorry."

Awkward tension stretched between us. Here was my opportunity to get to the bottom of what had happened, yet I found myself saying, "Don't worry about it."

I hated the slump of his shoulders and the discomfort in the room. I wanted the excitement back. I had to let go of the past. What did it matter now anyway?

Ignoring the voice insisting it *did* actually matter because I deserved an explanation, I cracked on. "Think of the fun we'll have. I could do with some sunshine."

"Yeah?" Michael peered up at me hopefully. "Me too. It would be amazing to get away." His smile faded. "Although I really should be apartment hunting over the holidays."

"You know you can stay at mine as long as you need."

"You're not sick of my snoring?"

I chuckled. "You'll have my guest room anyway."

"Right. Of course. Makes no sense to sleep together at your place."

Looking away from him, I peeled off my wet socks and said, "Exactly. Suppose we might have to in Perth, but it's fine. Right?"

"Right! Totally." He shrugged and lifted his hands in a shaky gesture. "Doesn't matter to me one way or the other. I'll do whatever you want."

Hmm. He'd clearly meant that as a positive, but I shifted uncomfortably, pulling off the other sock too and flexing my toes on the wooden floor. "That's not—I don't want you to do anything you're not into." Did that sound like I was talking about sex? My heart thudded. "What I mean is…" Christ, I had no idea.

"I get it." Michael stood and smiled softly. "I'm saying that if you want to go, I'm all in. It'll be an adventure. We can hold hands and say we're a couple. It's easy. No big deal."

"Right." I nodded. "No big deal." It was true, wasn't it? "Holding hands and whatever. Maybe we should practice kissing just in case."

As Michael's eyes grew so wide they were in danger of popping out of his head and dropping onto the heated floor, I cursed myself. Why on Earth had I said that? What had gotten hold of me?

I watched Michael's throat work, my heart about to hammer free of my chest.

"Just kidding!" I practically shouted.

"Oh!" He laughed, and it sounded too loud in the pod as well. "Good one."

We stood there laughing until I forced myself to turn away. My head was so hot I was afraid it might explode like we were in a sci-fi movie. Practice kissing. I'd actually said that aloud.

After casting about for something—anything—to say, I landed on, "Is your passport up to date?"

"Yep." Michael pulled the clothing he'd been given out of the Whispering Pines tote bag and refolded the T-shirt and sweatpants. "I'll just have to get it from… Uh, from Jared's place." He sighed. "And my stuff. I don't have any furniture or anything, at least."

"Nothing?" That seemed odd.

He shrugged as he refolded the T-shirt for the third time. "Jared's stuff was way nicer, so I got rid of mine. Do you mind taking me over tomorrow? He should be at work."

"'Course not. I'm sure Angela will give me the day off to prepare if we're flying out so soon. That is… If we are? Are we really doing this?"

Michael stuffed the T-shirt and sweatpants back into the tote, making a mess of the careful folding. "I mean, I'm up for it if you are." He frowned, watching me. "You're the one with everything to lose. I get a free trip to Australia with my best friend for Christmas. But are you comfortable pretending to be my boyfriend for that long? It was only supposed to be for a couple of days. And then in the new year, you could invent a dramatic break-up story."

Why did the thought of breaking up with Michael make my stomach roil? This wasn't a real relationship. Except it was, and at the end of the day, Michael had been the one to break up with me two years ago. Even if we'd only been friends, it had been a break-up nonetheless, and I still didn't know why.

A panicked thought invaded my mind. What if I went to Australia alone and didn't see Michael again for another two years? What if this weekend had been a blip—right place, right time—and then Michael would find a new place and go back to his life? His life without me.

"I'm up for it," I said confidently, sticking out my hand. "Boyfriends for Christmas?"

Michael took my hand, his palm warm against mine as we shook. A smile lifted his lips. "Boyfriends for Christmas."

"WILL!"

I turned at Seth's call and waved as he jogged up to me in the parking lot. "Hey. Glad you caught me. I need to speak with you about Christmas."

He wore a quizzical smile. "Are you about to tell me you're going to Australia with Angela?"

I had to laugh. "That rumor mill really never stops, does it?"

"You've been providing it with some juicy grist this weekend." Seth grimaced. "That sounds indecent."

"It really does." I knew Seth had grown up in a very religious household, and he was charmingly prim and proper, especially in comparison to Logan's blunt, rough-around-the-edges approach. They'd always seemed to have a wonderful yin/yang connection.

But I was suddenly wondering what it was like between them in the bedroom and whether strait-laced Seth had occasion to get, well, *indecent.* Which was absolutely none of my business! What on earth had gotten into me?

"Are you all right?" Seth asked with a frown.

"Couldn't be better. I'm well chuffed."

Seth chuckled. "You tend to sound even more Scottish when you're nervous."

"Do I?" My cheeks were warm. "No, just excited. We've never been to Australia, and it seems like a wonderful opportunity career-wise."

"Absolutely." Seth hesitated. "So, Michael's going with you?"

"Yes, Angela insisted. Should be lots of fun."

"Right! Although…" He glanced around to make sure we were alone amid the parked vehicles. "It's one thing for you and Michael to pretend to be a couple for a weekend. Are you sure it's a good idea to do it for two weeks?"

"It'll be fine," I insisted, forcing a smile. It would be, wouldn't it? It had to be, because the thought of leaving Michael behind was… No. I didn't like that idea one bit. We'd only just reconnected. I needed more time with him.

Seth nodded. "I'm sure it will be. I'm just wondering about whether it's wise to pretend to be someone you're not for that long."

"I—I" Why was I sputtering? Why did those words punch my sternum like a fist?

Someone you're not.

"It'll be grand. Besides, everyone at the office already thinks I'm queer now." My breath caught, and I cleared my throat. "We're best friends. And Michael's bi. It's not a big deal."

"Right. Of course not. I just wanted to make sure it wouldn't be too difficult for either of you." He smiled ruefully. "Logan and I know firsthand that pretending can be…intense. Surprisingly so. But of course, we were strangers and both queer. Not that Logan was out. Not even to himself."

Curiosity got the better of me, and after all, Seth had brought it up. "He didn't realize he was bi?" I shifted from foot to foot, glancing around the lot. Janet from HR and her partner were climbing into their SUV but were definitely out of earshot.

Seth shrugged with a smile. "Nope. Even though he'd had sex with men on multiple occasions."

My laugh was an awkward little guffaw. "Wait, what?" My stomach fluttered.

Seth still smiled. "I know, it sounds impossible. And Logan would tell you this himself—it's not a secret. Not that he posts about it on Facebook. To be fair, he refuses to get a Facebook. What I mean is, friends know, and we consider you a friend." He seemed to want to say something else as he frowned and grasped my shoulder. "I just don't want you to get hurt."

"I won't! There's nothing to worry about. I'm sorry I won't be spending Christmas with you. Do you think you could talk Angela into bringing you and Logan along?"

He laughed. "Perhaps, but no. Connor will be home for Christmas with his friend Asher. We'll let you and Michael take the reins on Angela-related capers."

"Fair enough." I found I had to ask, "Back to Logan for a moment— he... Why didn't he...?"

"It's not as uncommon as you might think. Men who have sex with men but still identify as straight. For Logan, there'd been no emotional component." Seth smiled shyly, ducking his head and fiddling with his glasses. "Until he met me, which feels extremely egotistical to say."

I smiled. "True, though. That sounds quite special. And you seem very happy together."

"We are. I never would have imagined it the day Logan and I met. To say we were opposites is an understatement. We still are in some ways, but it works."

My body hummed with a confusing mix of emotions I couldn't quite identify. Was that envy for Seth and Logan's relationship? Yes, it seemed to be. Sure, I'd been jealous of couples before. Everyone was once in a blue moon.

"I never would have guessed that the start of your relationship was caper-related."

He laughed. "I'm not sure how convincing we were to start. But..." He cleared his throat. "You know, I'd think you and Michael were madly in love." He quickly added, "If I didn't know better, that is."

Laughing and waving a hand, I exclaimed, "Oh! It's because we're mates. For ages. That's all."

"Must be," Seth agreed.

"It'll stand us in good stead for our trip to Australia. I should finish packing up! See you in the new year."

We hugged and said our goodbyes, and I stowed my suitcase in the back of the vehicle, which was the extent of the "packing up" I had to do. More people were leaving, and I waved and nodded and wished happy holidays to all while waiting for Michael. He must have gotten hung up talking to someone.

Pacing, I replayed the conversation with Seth over and over. Had I said the right things? Why was I even concerned? What was that nagging sensation I couldn't quite catch, like a buzzing mosquito out of reach?

My mind returned to what Seth had said: That there had been "no emotional component" to Logan's previous interactions with men. That felt…what? Oddly familiar, I supposed. After all, I wanked to gay porn sometimes. Yet I'd assured myself I didn't want to do those things myself.

But…why? There was nothing wrong with it. Why was I so…*what*? Hesitant? I didn't know. I climbed in the SUV and turned on the engine.

Drumming my fingers on the wheel, I checked the mirrors for Michael's approach. I adjusted the vents and tried to think of anything else.

"Bloody hell," I muttered. "Right. What's the problem?" I had the mad urge to call Mum and talk it through with her. I was a grown man. I could deal with this. Still, I found talking to myself could help, so I kept going.

"Right. I've been 'bi for the weekend,' and I liked being perceived that way. I'm attracted to men and women, even though most of the time I'm happier at home wanking than actually fucking. With some notable exceptions. Just not nearly as many as people think."

I shook my head. Was I getting off track? Was I even on the right train? Was I headed for a collision? Was I torturing this weak metaphor?

"Why can't I be bisexual for real?"

As the question swirled in the heated air blasting from the vents, the passenger door opened, and I jumped a mile.

Michael froze with one boot in. "Sorry! Did I scare you?"

I forced a laugh. "Just gave me a start, yeah. All good."

"I had to run back to the pod to make sure I didn't forget anything." He shut the door and buckled his seatbelt. "Sorry. I get paranoid. Last year, I forgot my jacket hanging in the closet of a hotel and we had to drive back an hour."

We meant Michael and Jared, I presumed. Where had they gone? Had they had fun? Had Jared been a pill about going back for the jacket? "All good," I repeated. "Should we crack on?"

He laughed. "Tally ho? Or something? Oh, were you saying something just now when I opened the door?"

"Why can't I be bisexual for real?"

"Nope! Let's tally ho." I shifted into drive. Figuring out what was real could wait.

Chapter Nine

Will

"A RE YOU SURE I should come in?" I hesitated on the threshold of the townhouse. Though the sun was high in the sky, the townhouse was dark and hushed, the gray blinds drawn.

"Yeah, it's fine. He should be at work." Michael tugged off his boots and left them on the mat. He tossed his gloves on a narrow hall table but didn't remove his coat.

I did the same and followed him into the living room. The fireplace was one of those sleek, modern rectangles in the wall with crystals that might not have been real fire. A huge flat-screen TV hung above it. The white couch was low and straight-backed and curved in a cool shape like a…bean?

"I'd be afraid to sit on that," I said. "How do you keep it so clean?"

"No food or drinks." Michael had bent to unplug a phone charger from the outlet by the couch. He grimaced as he stood. "I know. What's the point of a couch?"

"Remember the one at Zoe's? There must be a happy medium between a massive, stained beanbag in zebra print and this."

Michael chuckled. "I'd like to think."

"Is it always so…dim in here?"

"Yeah. Sunlight fades the furniture and the floors. And the art." He motioned to an abstract painting that was mostly white. I reminded myself there was nothing wrong with being neat, and it was practical to keep out the sun. It was Jared's home, and fair play to him.

I supposed that was the problem—there were no signs of Michael at all.

He led the way through the dining room past a shiny round table and gleaming wooden chairs and into the kitchen. He stood by the island, looking around pensively.

I ran my hand over the flecked gray counter. "Nice. Quartz?"

"Granite." He huffed out a bitter laugh. "I thought it was so grown-up."

"'Tis. Bloody expensive, I imagine."

"Yup." He stuffed his hands in his pockets, gazing around. "I don't think there's anything in here that's really mine. You thirsty?"

"I'll have a glass of water. Thanks."

I waited while Michael opened the fridge and poured two small glasses from a Brita jug. Like the living and dining room, the kitchen was sparse and sleek and neat as a pin, as Mum would say. I could believe it was one of those model homes you toured in a new subdivision.

We drank quickly, and Michael turned to the sink, washing the glasses and flipping them over to dry on a semicircle rack even though there was a dishwasher in the island. He seemed about to speak when he was distracted by something through the small window over the sink. Leaning in, he exhaled sharply.

"What?" I joined him, holding up my hand and squinting, the sun glaring on the fresh snow in the postage-stamp yard.

A Christmas tree bound in twine lay outside to the left. I realized there had to be a sliding door in the dining room behind the drawn blind. The tree was askew, partly covered in snow and half resting on what was likely covered patio furniture. As though it had been tossed outside carelessly.

Michael stared at the tree before he swallowed thickly and reached up and rubbed his healing cheek. Then he shook his head and strode from the kitchen.

I trailed him to the foot of the—of course—gleaming hardwood stairs, then hesitated. Perhaps it would be best if I let him do this alone.

What the *fuck* was wrong with Jared that he didn't want Michael? How could he not appreciate Michael or the tree Michael had bought for Christmas? And maybe there was an explanation, but it was his loss. The prick.

If we weren't jetting off to Australia—a plan that was still surreal—I'd haul that tree out of the yard and take it back to mine. We could go to Target for decorations and when we got back, we'd turn the radio to the Christmas music station and the TV to that channel that showed nothing but cheerfully burning logs in a fireplace for the month of December. We'd flop on the couch and eat and drink and be fucking merry, *Jared.*

To hell with him. I liked that idea for me and Michael. Why not be roommates again in the new year? I wanted to buy a condo with a guest room anyway, so two bedrooms was already in the plans. Or we could just stay in my current place. No rush on moving.

Assuming Michael would be keen to live with me. He'd agreed to come to Australia, and it'd been so much fun spending time with him again. Now that *Jared* was out of the picture, surely *my* Michael was back. He wouldn't ghost me again.

I still stood at the foot of the stairs. Michael was surely packing, but it seemed awfully quiet. I crept up, my socked feet silent on the wood flooring. I stopped on the second-floor landing, listening. Footsteps thudded softly on the third floor.

Feeling like an intruder, I tiptoed up the other flight of stairs, then followed the sound of rustling, stopping in the open door of the master bedroom. Michael was tossing clothing into a pile at his feet. An open suitcase on the floor in front held toiletries, a laptop, and I wasn't sure what else.

"All right?" I whispered. Why was I whispering? We weren't breaking and entering. This had been Michael's home. Though again, the monochromatic bedroom looked barely lived in. The blinds were down in this room too, and Michael had switched on the light in the adjoining bathroom.

"Yep," he said tightly. He yanked a shirt from a hanger, and the end of it bounced off the closet's back wall with a bang. "Can you grab a few garbage bags from under the sink downstairs for my clothes?"

"Sure." My gaze slid over the neat corners of the duvet. I turned away. The sight of the bed they'd shared while Michael hadn't even spoken to me filled me with… It didn't matter. I gritted my teeth against the unpleasant sensation and hurried downstairs. The sooner we left, the better.

Black bin bags in hand, I froze by the kitchen island as a key turned in the front-door lock. I had a perfectly unobstructed view of Jared bustling into the townhouse with cloth grocery bags he deposited on the floor.

Bloody buggery hell.

He kicked the door shut behind him as he straightened and saw me.

I raised my free hand. "Hi. It's all right. I'm here with Michael."

The alarm on his face gave way to suspicion—then a flare of…derision? He snorted. "The famous Will Stewart in the flesh."

All I could do was stare. "I'm sorry?"

He lined up his boots on the mat, unzipped his jacket, and hung it in the hall closet. "You're Will, aren't you?"

"Er… I'm Will, yes." I wasn't too sure about the "famous" bit.

Jared picked up the groceries and marched into the kitchen, brushing past me by the island. "Nice accent. You're even hotter in person. The pics on Mike's phone don't do you justice."

"I…"

Sighing noisily, Jared shook his head and opened the fridge. "Never mind. Sorry. I'm being a dick. That's got nothing to do with anything." Holding a jar of kimchi, he met my gaze. "How's he doing?"

"Fine. As well as can be expected."

Jared's face pinched, and he rolled up the sleeves of his thin black sweater before plugging the sink and turning on the tap. "I feel terrible about how it went down. He's such a sweet guy. We're just not right for each other. I should have told him that a long time ago. Although he already knew it—he had to. Though the denial runs deep with that one. I'm sure you know."

Before I say anything, Michael appeared in the kitchen entry. "Right, I should have gotten the hint when you happily came to my folks' place for Thanksgiving and promised my mom you'd take good care of me. Stupid me," he spat.

Jared faced him. "You're right. That was on me." He winced. "Those scratches are worse than I thought."

Michael shrugged. "No biggie."

Jared unpacked the groceries, stacking cans and boxes in the pantry before filling the fridge with sharp movements.

As much as I didn't want to leave Michael alone, I said, "I should go so you two can talk."

"I don't think we have much to say," Michael muttered.

After tossing leeks into the water filling the sink, Jared said, "It's up to you. But there are a few things we should discuss. The internet's on your account."

Michael rubbed a hand over his hair. "Yeah, okay. Let's talk." He turned to me. "Do you mind going up and packing the clothes on the floor?"

"Sure." I was still gripping the black plastic bags, and I forced myself to head upstairs. Michael had assured me Jared wasn't abusive. It was fine. Everything was fine.

In the bedroom, I shoved clothing into the bags. Why was I "famous"? What had Michael said about me? *Why* had he said much at all when he'd stopped actually speaking *to* me?

Raised voices echoed from downstairs. Crouching on the wood floor, I didn't move a muscle. I couldn't make out what they were saying from two floors up, and I didn't allow myself to creep out to the stairs to eavesdrop.

What if Jared is abusive? What if Michael needs me? What if he gets hurt?

I crammed more clothes in the first bag and knotted it shut as I told myself I was letting my imagination run away from me. There were more clothes to bundle, but I found myself pacing restlessly.

How strange to be in Jared and Michael's bedroom. The closed suitcase sat on the bed. I imagined Michael on the right side and Jared on the left.

And I tried not to imagine anything else, banishing memories of gay wank material I'd watched online. Christ, that was the last thing I wanted to think about. Not Michael with *him*.

I paced again. Why was I thinking about any of this? It was none of my business! I was here to support Michael. It didn't matter what their relationship had been like. Especially not in *bed*. Hell, I wanted to be anywhere else.

Yet I couldn't look away from the mattress and its smooth gray coverlet. Jared had been bloody lucky to wake up with Michael every morning. He hadn't even appreciated it. I'd only shared a bed with Michael for a weekend, but I'd felt strangely bereft this morning to wake alone, even though I was home. Even though I'd known Michael was in the guest room next door.

Footsteps sounded on the stairs, and I hurriedly stuffed the rest of the clothes in the other bin bag. Michael returned. His face was flushed, but his eyes were dry. He grabbed his suitcase. "Thanks. Let's go."

"Are you all right?" I hefted the bags.

He nodded a little too vigorously and led the way downstairs. Jared was mercifully nowhere to be seen. In my SUV, I barely resisted gunning the engine and peeling away from the curb. Michael didn't look back at his former home as we left.

"Is it cool if he forwards my mail to your place? Just until I find an apartment." He fiddled with the air vents.

"Of course. You know you can stay at mine after we get back." From the corner of my eye, I could see Michael unclip his seatbelt, loosen it, and snap it closed again, silencing the alarm that beeped. He was silent, and perhaps he didn't actually know? Had I not made it clear?

Before I could ask, he said, "You've already done too much for me. I'm sure I can find a motel."

Frustration flared. "Fuck off—you're not staying in a bloody motel." I wasn't sure why I was so bothered. We were quiet as I braked for a red light, the air thick with tension. I forced a laugh. "You're doing me a massive favor, remember?"

He scoffed. "An all-expenses paid trip to Australia?" He tried to joke. "Gee, such a hardship!"

I smiled more genuinely this time. "Good point." Relaxing my grip on the wheel, I adjusted the rear mirror even though it hadn't moved. "But really, it's not a bother at all for you to stay at mine. You can do the dishes and clean if it makes you feel better."

"Um, you do remember living with me before, right? Cleaning isn't exactly my best event."

"The townhouse was spotless."

He shrugged tightly. "That's the way Jared likes it." He quickly added, "Obviously I won't be messy at your place either."

"It's not a worry. You can be yourself."

After a long moment, Michael cleared his throat. "Cool. Thanks. I guess we need to pack when we get back. The flight's tonight."

"No, it's actually tomorrow after all. Tuesday."

"Uh, Tuesday at zero-twenty-five. That's twenty-five minutes after midnight. That's tonight."

"Bloody hell!" I gaped as my mind did the calculations. "I had it all wrong in my head. Good thing you're here or I would've stood up Angela. So much for advancing my career."

"Glad to be of service. You don't need to speed, though. We have all day."

I eased my foot off the gas pedal. Mum would be pleased there was someone else to keep an eye on the speedometer. The frustration and tension disappeared. If I wasn't driving, I might have hugged Michael and told him again how much I'd missed him.

"You need to give me a primer on anything I should know before we meet up with Angela again."

"Right." Guilt nagged. Lying didn't sit right for so many reasons. "The trip down under is great, but are you sure about the rest of it? Being my boyfriend. Pretending to be my boyfriend, I mean."

Eyes on the road, Michael nodded. "It's just what I need, actually. A chance to be someone else for a while, even if it's only for Christmas. Real life will be waiting in January, but for the next couple of weeks, we don't have to be ourselves."

I shifted uncomfortably. I was already uneasy with deceiving Angela and my colleagues. I still wanted to be *myself*.

Whoever the hell that was.

A few days ago, I'd had it all under control. Now, I wasn't sure if I was coming or going.

Michael met my gaze, giving me a crooked smile. "It'll be fun." He imitated Matt, punching his fist and chanting, "Caper, caper, caper."

No need to overthink it, was there? Why not enjoy the holidays together in the sunshine and possibly further my career? "Suppose we all need a good caper sometimes, don't we?"

I thought of Mum and her leaps. Grinning at Michael, I stood on the edge. All I could do was dive in headfirst.

Chapter Ten

Michael

A S AN APPARENTLY endless stream of people filed past us to the economy section of the plane, I sipped the free glass of champagne and stretched out my legs. "I've never been in first class before," I murmured to Will, who was sitting next to me by the window.

"This is actually premium economy," he said. "I bet the bastards in first have beds."

In the window seat ahead of us, Angela turned around. "They do. But I didn't get where I am by spending company money on beds in the sky." Grinning, she sipped her champagne. "Good thing they had these empty spots or you'd be stuck back there."

Will grinned. "Definitely not complaining! Thanks again."

It really did seem luxurious to have two wider seats by the window instead of the usual three. There were only six rows of premium, and when I glanced back at the rest of the plane, it looked like a *lot* of people were crammed in.

Will was tapping on his phone, and Angela went back to hers, soon making a call and firing off orders in the friendliest way possible. Her family was flying from Texas and joining us in Perth in…two days?

We'd flown a quick hop from Albany to JFK, and now we were going to Hong Kong and then onto Perth after a layover. I was pretty sure that because we were crossing the dateline it would take us two days.

Not that it really mattered. It could take a week, and I'd be happy to spend it with Will. Not just *with* him, but as his boyfriend. My two days of fantasy had morphed into two weeks, and it was the greatest Christmas present ever.

Will snorted and showed me his phone screen. It was a text from Seth:
By the way, Angela is very big on mistletoe, so be prepared.
My mouth went dry, and I tried to think of a good joke. I leaned over and whispered right in Will's ear given Angela was so close, though she was still talking on the phone. My lips brushed his skin.

"Maybe we should practice kissing after all."

Oh, my *GOD*. I'd really just said that. Like, out loud. To Will. Of all the jokes, *that* was what my asshole brain coughed up? Awesome.

Will laughed and fiddled with his phone, not looking at me. I gulped the rest of my champagne in one mouthful and wondered if it was bad manners to ask for more. Maybe once we were up in the air. I scrolled through my phone restlessly, crossing my ankle over one knee and then the other. Then back again.

Shit, the plane hadn't even left the ground, and we had almost sixteen hours to go. I needed to calm down. Everything was fine. Will had joked about practicing kissing, and I'd only been bringing up *his* joke.

My phone buzzed in my hand, and I eagerly read the text, desperate for a distraction. Zoe had written:

Glad you're okay. You kind of freaked me out. So you and Jared are done?

I choked down my bitterness and hurt. Oh yeah, Jared and I were done. It had been so freaking weird to be back in the townhouse to get my stuff. "The townhouse" that had been "home" for months. How had I ever believed I belonged there? That Jared and I belonged together?

I hadn't expected him to get off work early, and I definitely hadn't expected him to narrow his eyes and grit his teeth about Will being there with me. Like, what? He was *jealous*? He didn't want me in the first place! And there was obviously nothing between me and Will. It was all pretend, and Jared didn't even know about that.

Now Jared was free to sit on his pristine couch and joylessly celebrate the holidays without any food or drinks or inconvenient Christmas trees messing up his plans. The sight of my tree tossed outside and forgotten, almost completely snowed over, really summed up the whole thing.

I wrote back to Zoe, tapping out:

Definitely done. We should never have been together.

Fidgeting, I crossed and uncrossed my legs. It was honestly humiliating that I'd moved in with a man who was such a terrible fit. I reminded myself he wasn't a bad person, even if I felt bitter at the moment.

"Okay?" Will's warm breath tickled my cheek as he leaned close and put his hand on my knee.

Aside from fighting an instant, massive boner, I was swell. "Uh-huh!"

He arched an eyebrow. "You're jiggling your knee so much they can probably feel the vibrations in coach."

"Oh!" That explained his big hand resting on my knee. "Sorry. Just, you know." I tried to think of an excuse. "Nervous to fly," I blurted even though I'd always been fine on planes.

"Are you?" Both his thick eyebrows shot up. "I didn't realize. I guess we've never flown anywhere together before. Don't worry. You're far more likely to be…" He waved his free hand. "Trampled by elephants than die in a plane crash."

"Am I though? How about if I never go to Africa."

"Hmm." Will seemed to ponder it, and while he did, he stroked my knee with his thumb. Did he realize he was doing that? Angela was still on the phone and not paying any attention. Will said, "There could be a stampede at the zoo."

I tried to breathe and act normal. His hand felt so heavy and huge on my knee, and I could barely look away from him. I was legit going to be visibly hard if I didn't get a grip. "Seems unlikely, though. And it's easy to avoid zoos."

"What if they escaped from the circus?"

"Do circuses still have elephants?"

Will made a face. "I'm not sure. They really shouldn't."

"Honestly, I think I'm safe from the threat of rampaging elephants."

He squeezed my knee gently. "You're safe here too. The odds are very much in our favor."

Even though I wasn't afraid to fly, I still felt soothed and safer—as if Will could protect me from a plane crash. I believed he'd try, and that felt better than it had any right to. This was exactly why I'd called him from the side of the road.

This was exactly why I was in love with him.

"Welcome aboard," a smooth voice said over the speakers. "Please remove your headphones and turn your attention to the safety demonstration."

Will's hand slipped from my knee, and he sat up straighter, dutifully watching the flight attendant a few rows up as she pointed out the exits. Honestly, it wouldn't have surprised me if he examined the laminated safety info in the seat pocket as requested.

He glanced at me and whispered, "What?"

"Huh?" I hadn't said anything.

"What are you smiling at?"

"Oh! Nothing. Just, um, thinking about elephants. They're so—" *Think of a word! Any word.* "Cute," I managed.

Will chuckled. "Probably not so much if they're trampling you to death, but yeah. They are."

My ears burned as I forced my attention back to my phone. There was another text from Zoe.

Sorry it didn't work out. Glad you're hanging with Will again.

We had to put our electronics in airplane mode for takeoff, so I didn't have time to over-analyze why exactly Zoe was glad I was with Will. I quickly tapped out:

Yeah, it's great. We're on our way to Australia for Christmas for his work. Long story—I'll fill you in later. Sorry I freaked you out, and say hi to your parents. Especially your mom.

I ended the text with the little heart/winking/blowing a kiss emoji and switched off my phone.

We'd been in the air an hour or so when the flight attendants served more drinks and directed us to the printed menu in our seat pockets. I whistled under my breath. "Nice. This food actually sounds good. Short ribs? Although it's weird having dinner at, like, two o'clock in the morning or whatever."

"Totally," Will agreed. "I've never flown this far. I guess we eat dinner, then try to sleep." He tapped his screen on the back of Angela's chair. "Plenty to watch, at least."

I could see that Angela had her headphones on and was watching what looked to be old episodes of *Sex and the City*, which felt very on-brand.

Soon, dinner was served, and the short ribs were delicious. I sipped my glass—actual glass, not plastic!—of Australian Shiraz. "Not that the egg salad sandwich and Coke I had on Delta weren't great, but this is next level."

Will swallowed a bite of roasted root vegetables. "But have you had United's ham and Swiss and 7-Up? Not to be missed."

"A fine vintage, I'm sure."

"Only the best."

I had to admit this all did feel wonderfully grown-up even though I knew it was more about having the money for premium. Still, sitting up front on a business trip with my partner gave me a rush.

I scooped up garlic mashed potatoes on my fork and internally rolled my eyes. Will wasn't even my actual boyfriend, and now I was thinking of him as my partner? *Dial it down there, my guy.*

We idly scrolled the entertainment options, swiping our screens. Will asked, "Have you watched this doc? A wild murder story, that one." He pointed to a movie thumbnail on his screen.

I shook my head. "What's it about? I mean aside from murder."

"I don't want to spoil it. Can't say too much."

"Okay, I'm intrigued. Thanks." I took another sip of wine. "By the way, are you sure I don't need a suit?"

"Positive. I'm bringing one for meetings if I need it, but it'll probably be business casual anyway."

"Yeah." Still, it was cringey I didn't own a suit that actually fit me anymore. "I should have one though. For weddings and funerals if nothing else."

"Not a bad idea. We can go shopping for one when we get home."

Boy, did I like the sound of that word. "*Home.*" Not "shopping." Shopping was fine and all, but the thought of *home* with Will—and making plans together for the new year—made me want to jump up and dance down the aisles as we flew over the North Pole.

Watching the flight path on the screen, I said, "I had no idea flights went up this way. I always pictured everything going left and right."

"Me too! It's wild, isn't it? Wouldn't want to crash in Siberia. Or anywhere, for the record."

"Not so much, no." I grimaced. "My mother's worst fear would come true."

"That you'd die in a plane crash?"

"Me or any of her kids. She's always been paranoid about flying."

"Makes sense it would rub off on you. You're feeling all right, though?"

Ugh, I didn't want to continue the lie. "I'm good. It's more just before the plane takes off. Then I'm totally fine."

Will peeled the lid off a small container of chocolate ice cream that had been frozen very solid and was now thawing in time for us to eat it. He said, "Not so for your mum?"

"Nope. She hates it with a passion."

"Even though it's far more dangerous to drive?"

"Yep. No logic works." I peeled the lid from my ice cream tub.

"I get it. We all have those fears."

"I guess. At least this time there was no need for me to tell my mom I'm flying. I'll let them know when we arrive, but no sense in making her worry in the meantime."

"Mum would skin me alive if I pulled that."

I laughed. "Yeah, but you and your mom are tight." After swallowing a creamy, sweet, and impressively cold mouthful of ice cream, I asked, "What did you tell her about me?"

Will frowned and looked pointedly toward Angela, who still wore her headphones as she ate dinner and watched TV. Oh, right. I leaned close and whispered in Will's ear, "My bad."

He mouthed, "*It's okay.*" Then he murmured in my ear, "We need to be careful, though. We should really try to pretend all the time if we can. Except for when we're truly alone."

Nodding, I tried not to let my imagination take off running.

We finished dinner, and the cabin lights dimmed. Both Will and I picked a movie to watch and tried to get comfortable to sleep.

While I was tempted to watch the true crime doc Will had recommended, for the moment I went with *Almost Famous*, which had been one of my favorites as a kid. I knew it practically by heart, so I could close my eyes and doze and still know what was happening. It was weirdly comforting.

If only I could get *comfortable*. I shifted every few minutes even though the seat and legroom weren't bad at all. The guy sitting beside Angela had his seat back a few inches, and I followed suit, adjusting the pitch of the screen.

Will reclined the same amount—and slipped his arm around my shoulders, urging me wordlessly to lean on his shoulder as my heart thumped. Right—we were a couple. This was what couples did.

I adjusted my headphones and found the right angle to relax against Will without jamming my headphones against him. He squeezed my arm in a way that said this was a good spot.

At least, I was pretty sure that's what the squeeze meant. Asking would mean moving, and he'd nudge me if he wasn't comfortable. I closed my eyes, listening to the movie as I drifted off, Will's warmth and the weight of his arm just as comforting as the familiar songs on the soundtrack.

Chapter Eleven

Will

"**A**RE YOU TOGETHER?"

I blinked at the airport worker waiting expectantly. It took a moment to realize she was asking if Michael and I were a couple. "Oh! Er, yes."

"Step up to number three and wait at the line." She announced this emotionlessly, and I wasn't sure why I was bracing for judgment.

Michael and I shuffled forward to the assigned customs booth to wait. It hadn't occurred to me that couples typically went through customs together, and I shifted nervously. Which was ridiculous—it wasn't as if the customs agent would grill us on our relationship and declare us a fraud.

Michael groaned softly, stretching his arms overhead. He wore sweatpants, and his hoodie and T-shirt rode up, exposing a few inches of pale skin at his belly.

He said, "God, it's been a long day. Days? I'm ready for bed. And another shower."

We'd been fortunate that Angela had sprung for one of the lounges at the Hong Kong airport for our ten-hour layover. We'd been able to shower and change and enjoy the constantly replenished buffet.

Still, the flight to Perth had been another seven hours, and now it was just past eleven p.m. local time.

"Did you sleep at all?" Michael asked.

"Hmm? Here and there," I lied. Well, I had slept a bit on the first flight, though eventually my arm had gone numb where Michael had leaned into me. I hadn't the heart to wake him, so I'd flexed my fingers as unobtrusively as possible and watched the latest fast cars action movie with Vin Diesel.

I knew he was asking about the second flight. He'd dozed after the first meal around four p.m., but I'd hit overtired. Hopefully I'd be out like a light once we reached the hotel.

The customs agent waved us up to the booth. Taking our passports with a serious expression, she scanned them and asked, "What's the purpose of your visit?"

I cleared my throat. "I'm here on business with my boss."

She eyed Michael. "And you?"

"Um, I'm just coming along. With my boyfriend."

"Any alcohol or tobacco?"

We shook our heads and answered a few more questions before being released. We'd officially entered Australia as a couple. Impulsively, I took Michael's hand as we fetched our luggage and waited for Angela and her family.

Michael laced his fingers with mine and smiled absently before saying, "Oh, I see your blue hardshell."

For a few moments, I could hardly breathe. It all felt so natural and normal. Like Michael and I really *were* a couple. Again, I was being perceived as something other than straight—by the customs agent and airport employee—and it felt…ordinary in the best, most thrilling way.

Michael tugged my hand, giving me a quizzical smile. "We should probably grab that suitcase."

"Right!" I let go to circle the carousel and fetch the suitcase before it did another loop. I really did need some sleep.

Angela, her husband Paul, and their two daughters approached. Even Angela appeared exhausted, only giving us a wan smile. She said to Paul, "Honey, I'm gonna use the little girls' room."

Her teenaged daughters, Olivia and Makayla, followed her. Paul yawned widely. "Hoo boy, is it good to have solid feet under my ground again." He shook his head. "What the heck did I just say? Y'all know what I meant."

Michael said, "Yeah, we get it. That was a long trip."

Paul ran a hand over his shiny, bald head. He was white, stocky, and wearing a purple golf polo, Levi's, and actual cowboy boots. We'd all had lunch in Hong Kong, but Angela had done most of the talking about the business opportunity in Perth. Paul had seemed content to listen while the girls had been busy with their phones.

He pointed to the carousel. "Oh, there's one of Rosie's suitcases." He squeezed through the growing crowd to snatch the massive pink hardshell.

"Rosie?" Michael asked. "Sorry, I thought it was Olivia and Makayla?" He bit his lip. "Did I get that wrong?"

"No, no! Angela and I met in Rosebud, Texas. Rosie's my little pet name for her."

I smiled. "That's sweet."

"Where'd you two meet?"

"Albany," Michael said. To me he added, "You can call me Al."

"Like the song!" Paul chuckled. "Good one."

Michael and I frowned at each other, not getting the reference, but we didn't ask.

Just as we picked up the last suitcases, Angela and the girls returned. Olivia was nineteen and in her freshman year at Columbia, while Makayla was fourteen. They were both Asian and slim with long dark hair, while Olivia was almost my height and Makayla smaller than even Angela. Makayla also had braces that she sadly seemed self-conscious of given how often she covered her mouth when she spoke.

The terminal was small, and it was easy to spot a driver holding a sign bearing Angela's name amid the groups of people hugging and kissing.

I'd always enjoyed airport reunions. I watched an older couple run to an adult woman who was probably their daughter, and I missed Mum and Dad with a fierce pang.

The driver called, "Merry Christmas!" as we approached. He checked his watch. "In about twenty minutes, that is."

"Wait, is it?" Michael asked.

"Too right," the driver replied. "It's Christmas Eve right now. Santa's on his way for biccies and milk. Though he'd probably prefer a fry-up and a tinny."

Outside, we all exclaimed at the warm summer night air. After the frigid damp of Albany, it felt luxurious. Pulling his small suitcase, duffel slung over his shoulder, Michael spun around in a circle, his eyes closed and bliss written all over his beautiful face.

His…wait… What had I thought? I laughed to myself. I was really getting into character, apparently.

The driver led us to a black minivan. Olivia sighed loudly. "Couldn't you get a limo, Mom?"

"No, I couldn't. We're not too good for a van, young lady."

Paul said, "It's a Mercedes-Benz, Liv. You'll manage."

We climbed in, Michael and I volunteering to take the back seat. The streets were deserted and tree-lined, and I wished I could open the back window and breathe in the blossoms. Being dropped into summer was magical.

"This is an amazing Christmas present," Michael murmured to me. "Thank you."

"Hey, this is Angela's gift, really," I said.

Paul nodded. "Indeed! Let's all thank her for organizing this wonderful Christmas vacation."

"That she's going to work during," Olivia muttered. At her dad's glare, she looked abashed. "But yeah, it's awesome. Thanks, Mom."

"It's my pleasure, y'all. Besides, Dale gets all the organizing credit."

"That goes without saying," Makayla added. "Dale is a saint. Why couldn't he come along?"

"He had family plans," Angela said. "But Will's gonna be my partner in crime. Did I tell y'all about the terrific job he did in Seattle last week?"

"No more work talk until after Christmas, Rosie," Paul said gently.

"You're right!" Angela dramatically mimed zipping her lips.

We drove on through the empty residential streets past dark houses, everyone apparently tucked away snugly with dreams of sugarplums in their heads.

Michael muttered to me, "Dude, I'm so tired." He rubbed his face.

"Bro, tell me about it," I drawled with my Brett Yankface flat accent. "That kegger really wiped me out."

Makayla giggled while Olivia shot us a dubious glance. Angela clapped delightedly. "You sound very convincing."

I laughed. "Thanks. It's an old joke with Michael. I know I don't usually sound so American."

Not looking up from her screen, Olivia asked, "Since when do you sound American even a little bit?"

Michael said, "I've been telling him that for years, but he swears his accent has, and I quote, 'dulled significantly.' He's in serious denial."

"I am not! My family all sound much more Scottish than me."

"Oh, aye…captain?" Michael said in a truly terrible brogue.

"Oi!" I pinched Michael's side, and he squirmed away.

"Don't! You know I'm ticklish."

"*Really?*" I wiggled my fingers lightly over his ribs. "Had no idea. Is this bothering you?"

Everyone laughed—even grumpy Olivia. She said, "You guys are disgustingly cute."

And that shouldn't have made me smile so hard, but it did. In the glow of streetlights as we stopped at an intersection, it looked like Michael was blushing. Without thinking, I reached up and brushed his heated cheek with my knuckles before pulling my hand back and looking out the window. His eyes had widened just for a heartbeat before I'd turned away.

It was fine. I was the one who'd suggested we lean into our fake relationship, and clearly it was all going right to plan.

Chapter Twelve

Michael

BEYOND THE STEADY hum of the ceiling fan, cheerful voices drifted on the air. The sun was up, so it was clearly time to open my eyes. I knew where I was—if this was Jared's townhouse in Albany, there'd be no fan or distant laughter through an open window.

It was amazing to open my eyes and see an incredibly blue sky through the big window in our hotel room. To see Will standing on the balcony looking out over the marina and hear birds—seagulls, maybe?—calling.

Dressed in a green polo and a pair of cream linen pants that hugged his round ass and thick thighs spectacularly, Will fit right in with the tropical vibe of the blue room. Wait, was Perth tropical? I thought I'd seen palm trees the night before, but it had been dark.

There was definitely a beachy vibe, and Will matched it. God, he was gorgeous. Inside and out. How did I get so lucky? Here we were on the complete other side of the world, and I got to share a bed with him and hold his hand and—

And it's all pretend.

Right. Sleeping in the same king-sized bed wasn't a big deal. It wasn't like we were fucking. No kissing or touching or cuddling or blow jobs or—

I rocked up to sit on the side of the bed before my morning wood got any bright ideas. The mattress squeaked, and Will turned. He smiled broadly, teeth gleaming, with his gold aviator sunglasses propped on his head.

"Merry Christmas."

"Oh, right! Yeah, merry Christmas. That's so weird that it's the twenty-fifth now. Although we were on a plane forever, so I guess it makes sense."

Will smiled. "It's discombobulating to be sure. Did you sleep well?"

"Yeah, I guess I did." I'd gone to sleep in a fresh pair of boxers and noth-ing else because I'd been too tired after a quick shower to paw through my suitcase for a tee.

I spotted a small box on the round breakfast table in front of the window. The box was wrapped in red, green, and gold with a glittery bow on top.

"What's that?"

"Merry Christmas." Will passed the box to me.

"Huh? When did you get this?" I held the perfectly wrapped box in my hands, guilt washing through me.

"There's a little gift shop downstairs in the lobby. I was surprised it was open today. Apparently, they do a steady business on Christmas Day for the blokes who forgot to get something for their wives."

"You've been downstairs? What time is it? How long did I sleep?" I grabbed for my phone on the wooden side table, relieved that it was only showing just past ten a.m.

"You're good. I woke up around six and couldn't get back to sleep. Jet lag, I suppose, although I've no clue what time it is in Albany." He motioned to the gift, which was very light. "It's just a little something that made me think of you."

"I didn't get you anything."

"Sure you did. You're here, aren't you?"

"Yeah, it's a real hardship. However will I survive all this luxury?" I peered around Will. "Wow, that balcony looks huge."

His face pinched. "Oh, wait. Does it bother you? The vertigo thing you mentioned? Granted, I was the one who fell off my horse, not you. But if this is too high, I'm sure we can move."

"No, I'm good on balconies as long as I'm not right near the edge. It's weird, I know. A ladder or horse shouldn't be scarier, but... Besides, this room is amazing. How did Angela get this at the last minute at Christmas?"

"Dale's nothing if not a miracle worker."

Sitting on the side of the bed in my boxers with the duvet tangled around my waist, I unwrapped the box. "It's so neat. I feel bad wrecking it."

"I can take zero credit for the wrapping job." He shifted from one bare foot to the other and back again. "As I said, it's just a wee something."

Inside the box, surrounded by tissue paper, sat a koala Christmas tree ornament. On the end of a gold string, the koala wore sunglasses, a red and white Santa hat, and stood on a surfboard. Grinning, I held it up. "Oh my god."

"I know you'd bought that Christmas tree, and it all went wrong, so I thought if you get one next year, you might like a new ornament. It's tacky, I know."

"I *love* it. It's fun." I laughed. "Jared would hate this so much. It's perfect. Thank you."

Hands shoved in his pockets, Will shrugged. "You're welcome. It's just a little bauble. They had some lovely classy ornaments as well, but I tried to imagine which one you'd pick for yourself. I was torn between this and a kangaroo holding a beer."

"That sounds amazing." I hopped up and pulled him into a hug. "Seriously, thank you. I love that you know I'm not classy."

Will hugged me and rubbed my bare back. "I knew you'd want something fun."

"Classy's overrated." I leaned against him, yawning widely "Merry Christmas."

"I'm glad you're here." Will ran his hand up and down, up and down. "I'm glad *we're* here."

It honestly took me a minute to realize we'd been hugging way longer than normal, especially considering I was only wearing underwear and Will's hand seemed glued to my back.

What were we doing? This was all very non-hetero even though we didn't have an audience. We'd never hugged like this in the past. Definitely not. I could have closed my eyes and snuggled closer, pressing my face into Will's stubbly neck to kiss him softly…

Would he let me?

Would he…like it?

Whoa. That morning wood was about to roar back to life, so I gave Will's back a bro-y slap and wriggled away toward the bathroom. I paused to hang the ornament from the lamp sitting on the desk in the corner of the spacious room. The sparkly koala grinned against the smooth cream of the lampshade.

I said, "I should get in the shower. Do we have plans?"

"Not for an hour. Take your time."

I scrubbed under the water in the glass stall shower, setting the jets to cool to wake myself up and get a grip. Will was straight. Of course he wouldn't like it if I kissed his neck.

That had just been a hug. A long, weirdly intimate hug. I couldn't get carried away. It was the jet lag. I was imagining things.

But seriously—since when did Will tenderly stroke my back? My shirtless back at that.

I twisted the knob on the shower and ran the water as cold as it would go. Which wasn't very cold given how hot Perth was. Tepid would have to do.

After my shower, I stood on the plush bathmat in front of the sink with a towel around my hips and leaned close to the mirror, inspecting a zit growing on my chin. I guess I shouldn't have been surprised given we'd just spent two days traveling.

Still, I wished I had some stubble to cover it up. On my pasty face, it stood out like a…really red thing. Oh well.

I squeezed styling cream into my hair and fiddled with it. Even though I'd just slept more than eight hours, my brain was definitely still in a previous time zone.

When Will knocked softly on the door, I told him to come in. He asked,

"Can I brush my teeth? Forgot to do it earlier somehow."

"Jet lag is how." I moved over at the sink and pulled out my toothpaste from the big Ziploc bag I'd thrown my toiletries into. I passed it to Will even though he'd probably brought his own.

My morning breath was probably hellacious, so I pulled out my toothbrush. Will squeezed the paste over his and passed it back. Side by side, we cleaned our teeth, pausing to spit into the sink now and then.

Toothpaste dribbled from the side of Will's mouth, and he mumbled as he bent over and spit, turning on the tap to wet his brush. He muttered, "All I need is to spill toothpaste on my clean shirt." Looking in the mirror, he carefully wiped his mouth.

I laughed and immediately drooled frothy toothpaste onto my right pec. Because of course I did. It just made me laugh more, and around my toothbrush, I mumbled, "Like this?"

Will grinned. "Can't take you anywhere. Good thing you're not dressed yet."

Then, he lifted his hand and swiped up the toothpaste with his finger.

From my bare chest.

With his *finger*.

Also, he brushed my nipple in the process.

Will froze with his finger hovering in midair, the toothpaste drool on his skin. He blinked, looking at his finger and seeming to belatedly realize what he'd done.

We were only inches apart. My dick was hard. My skin tingled. My heart was about to pound right out of my chest. This casual intimacy was going to kill me.

Will's laugh was loud, echoing off the white tiles. "Jet lag!" He bent and scrubbed his hands in the sink while I stood rooted to the spot. Were his ears turning red?

He blurted, "Coffee?"

I'd gone back to brushing even though there was hardly any toothpaste left in my mouth. I spit in the sink and said cheerfully, "Yeah, thanks!"

"I'll figure out the machine. It looks fancy, so it should be pretty good."

"I'm not picky about coffee. Not like—" I needed to stop talking about Jared. Or thinking about him. "I'm not picky," I repeated.

"Great, I'll…" Will jerked his thumb over his shoulder and disappeared into the main area.

Puffing out my cheeks with a big exhale, I looked in the mirror. *Ugh, that zit.* But what I really had to focus on was that it had taken all my self-control to keep from kissing Will.

Not just *kissing* him but shoving him against the pristine white wall and devouring him.

This was all supposed to be pretend, and yeah, I'd known I was still in love with him, but I swear he was acting differently too. What was up with that hug? It wasn't possible that Will could... For me?

Nope. Don't even go there.

I'd been so tired the night before that I'd barely registered sleeping in the same bed with Will again. At least I hadn't been tormented by how close-but-far he'd been.

I had a feeling tonight would be a different story.

"MERRY CHRISTMAS, Y'ALL!" Angela held up her mimosa, and we all clinked our champagne flutes.

Including Makayla, who said, "Happy birthday, Jesus," before gulping.

Paul gave her a pointed look. "Mimosas are a privilege, not a right. And you're only getting one, so I'd sip."

Makayla giggled while Olivia rolled her eyes. We sat at a round table on the huge balcony attached to the Barkers' suite on the top floor of the hotel. The balcony wall was glass, and there was an amazing view of the marina and incredibly blue ocean, with lighter shades closer to shore.

The sun beamed down above a roof of wooden slats with pale fabric woven through. A ceiling fan kept us cool, which was good, because holy shit, it was *hot.*

But I'd put on sunscreen, and I wasn't complaining after the cold, gray December in Albany. "I've never seen a fan on a balcony before," I said. My mimosa tasted a little funny thanks to the toothpaste, but it still went down smoothly.

"Such a good idea, isn't it?" Angela said. To the young blond man serving us, who was already mixing another pitcher of mimosas, she added, "Your hotel is just lovely."

He nodded. "Thank you."

"It's not like he owns it," Olivia muttered. She asked me, "Haven't you ever been to Mexico or the Caribbean?"

She played with a pink pearl necklace. All the Barkers were dressed in summery pastels, and Will fit right in with them. I wore long khaki shorts and a short-sleeved button-up shirt in red and blue plaid. It was my only dressy summer shirt, and it probably needed ironing even though I'd carefully rolled it in my suitcase.

"No, actually," I answered. "My parents live in Florida, though." I cringed. What did that have to do with it? "But it's, uh, cool. The fan."

"Quite literally!" Angela grinned. "Now, tell us all about your family. Are they supportive of you and Will?"

"Um, yeah. They think Will's great." I finished my mimosa and smiled at

Will beside me.

It wasn't a lie—my parents had no issues with Will and Zoe and my other friends from college. I mean, they weren't super interested in my friends, but they liked them all fine. They'd said they enjoyed meeting Jared at Thanksgiving. Not that it mattered now.

The Barkers seemed to be waiting for me to say more. I almost wished the girls were allowed to have their phones at the table. Why did I feel like Olivia in particular would spot any inconsistency and roast me? Not that I had any reason to lie about my family. Only my boyfriend.

I was still jittery as I gave them the rundown on my parents and siblings. Another mimosa went down like water, so it was a good thing the food started coming in waves.

It was a pretty fancy brunch, with eggs Benedict and a seafood frittata, amazing warm sourdough bread, grilled prawns—which I discovered were shrimp—and waffles with the best fresh fruit I'd possibly ever tasted. They were all small courses, but soon I was getting full.

Angela may not have sprung for first class on planes, but she didn't seem to rough it when it came to hotels and food. Dishes kept coming, and there were juicy grilled sausages that the server called "snags." I groaned as I took a bite.

Chewing, Will nodded and gave a thumbs-up.

"Ain't this all to die for?" Angela said. "Such a nice change from turkey and stuffing, though I do love those traditions." She asked the server, whose name we'd learned was Lachlan, "Is this a typical Australian Christmas brunch?"

While working off the wire on another bottle of sparkling wine, he said, "It all depends, really. My nan would do a glazed ham and a turkey and all that stuff. But my parents are more into salads and prawn cocktails. Skewers on the barbecue and that sort of thing." He popped the lid on the bottle. "And sparkling shiraz."

Another server—they came in and out with more food, all wearing crisp white shirts and khaki shorts that were embarrassingly similar to mine—gave us clean flutes. I'd never had sparkling red wine, though I didn't say that.

Angela took a sip and declared, "Delicious! Now, I've had my fair share of rosé—no comments from the peanut gallery," she added to Paul with an affectionate wink, "But I've never had a bubbly red. Have y'all?" she asked Will and me.

I was relieved when Will said no. It wasn't just me being uncultured.

Makayla asked Lachlan, "Do you have to work all day on Christmas?"

He smiled. "Nah, I'm off in a couple of hours. I'm meeting my folks at the beach. That's an Aussie Christmas tradition for sure."

"Oh yes, there's a famous beach right near here, isn't there?" Angela asked.

Lachlan grinned. "Yep. Barking Beach. It's been called the best beach in Oz. You've got to head down to Barkers once this lot's digested."

"They named the beach after us!" Angela exclaimed.

"Oh my god, we totally have to go!" Makayla grinned.

Olivia said to Lachlan, "Barker's our last name. Well, my sister and I are Barker-Robertson."

"Sweet," Lachlan said. "It's only five or ten minutes on the boardwalk. It'll be hectic today since it's Christmas, though it's hectic most days in the summer. Just be careful and swim between the flags. Mind the lifeguards."

Olivia perked up. "Lifeguards? Yeah, we should go down this afternoon."

"Sounds good," Will said. He glanced to me. "If you're up for a swim?"

"Totally. I might need a nap first though." I shifted in my chair. "This was a lot of food."

"Mmm. A nap," Paul said contentedly, sipping his shiraz.

The sparkling red really was refreshing, and my head buzzed pleasantly. I wasn't close to drunk, but my cheeks felt warmly flushed. A nap sounded awesome.

Angela held up her glass. "Merry Christmas. I know no one wants to say grace these days, but I'm so grateful to be happy and healthy and here with y'all." She beamed at Paul and then the girls. "With my beautiful family." She turned her smile to me and Will. "And new friends. Such a beautiful couple. Love is love. I believe that so firmly. I remember once when my daddy—"

"*Mom*, please don't tell that story!" Olivia exclaimed. "You're so extra, oh my god."

"I know, I know." Angela shrugged with a smile, not seeming bothered. To me and Will, she said, "If you boys have kids one day, be prepared for them to find you very embarrassing. Do you want to have kids?"

"Don't grill them!" Olivia shook her head and muttered something under her breath.

I took another swig of bubbly wine as Will said, "It's okay. We haven't gotten that far yet. But I'm sure my mum and dad would be thrilled."

"Family really is life's greatest joy," Angela said solemnly. "Everyone should get to experience it."

"I think Mom's getting drunk," Makayla whispered, though she didn't seem bothered.

Olivia muttered something again that I couldn't make out and swatted at a buzzing fly.

Angela only laughed. Her cheeks were pink, and she very well might have been buzzed. She leaned over and took Olivia's chin to kiss her cheek. Olivia let her.

Angela said, "You're in college now, baby. You're too old to be embarrassed by your parents."

Olivia raised a sleek eyebrow. "I didn't say anything about Dad."

We all laughed as Paul reached up a hand and mimed patting himself on the back.

Unfazed, Angela said, "Christmas is a time for family and traditions, and even though we're here in the sunshine on the other side of the world and we can't have a tree, that's okay." She winked at me. "Trees can be dangerous anyway." Reaching into her pocket, she pulled out a green plastic sprig with white berries and held it over her head.

As Paul leaned over to plant a kiss on her, the girls cried with laughter, Olivia repeating how embarrassing it was. Angela tossed her the mistletoe, and Olivia batted it toward Makayla, and somehow, we were suddenly playing a game of hot potato.

It was probably a combination of jet lag and wine, but we couldn't stop laughing as we tossed the plastic sprig around the table. Then Lachlan appeared and snatched it out of the air before holding it over his golden head. He waggled his eyebrows at another server who'd arrived pushing a cart of desserts.

The older woman, who had to be nearing retirement, sighed wearily, trying not to smile. It was silly and *fun*, and we clapped as she pressed a kiss to Lachlan's cheek in what was probably an HR violation, but no one seemed to mind.

Then the mistletoe flew wildly in my direction, and I reached up to grab it before it sailed too far and went over the side of the balcony. "Got it!" There was more applause, and I kept my arm raised triumphantly.

And Will leaned toward me.

And Will kissed me.

We were both smiling, and our lips only met for a moment. An endless, perfect Christmas moment under plastic mistletoe on a warm Australian balcony with people we hardly knew, who hooted and laughed and clapped joyfully.

Will *kissed* me, and I wanted to pause that moment like it was a movie and take a screencap I could keep on my camera roll.

But life wasn't a movie, and it was over in a few thudding beats of my heart. Our eyes met as Will leaned away, and all I could do was grin, giddy laughter bubbling up. I'd never loved anyone as much as I loved Will, and I couldn't imagine how I ever would.

Will would never be mine, but I'd always have our kiss under plastic mistletoe in the sunshine.

Chapter Thirteen

Will

I HADN'T MEANT to kiss Michael.

Not that it was a *problem* or anything of the sort. I simply hadn't planned it. It wasn't choreographed for Angela's benefit. He'd lifted the mistletoe, and we were all laughing, and kissing him had felt like the most natural thing in the world.

Now, we left the elevator and strolled back to our room for a snooze before we met up with the Barkers again in a few hours to visit the beach. Correction: I attempted to "stroll," which proved a challenge given I was having an out-of-body experience.

I'd kissed Michael, and I had to do it again.

Did he feel the same? It'd likely been nothing to him. A Christmas kiss between friends at a boozy brunch. It had only been a peck. Not a deep, sexy, tender, rough, wet, dirty—

Stumbling, I caught myself on the door frame outside our room. I forced a laugh. "Oops. I'm cut off." In reality, I could drink a fair sight more before I got stocious, as they said back home.

Michael chuckled, resting his hand on my shoulder. "Okay?"

Christ, no. I'm not okay.

I managed to nod and fit the key card into the slot. We'd left the Do Not Disturb sign on the door, so the bed was still a rumpled tangle of sheets. How had I slept beside Michael without having him? I'd die if I didn't have him.

Before I could do anything profoundly unwise, I escaped into the loo to splash my face. Leaning over the sink, I breathed deeply as water dripped from my chin. A splodge of toothpaste stained the side of the basin, and I shivered thinking of touching Michael's chest.

It truly hadn't been intentional. Again, it had simply felt…natural. I'd missed him so much the past two years when he'd cut me off—*no, don't think about that!*—but it hadn't been like this. My curiosity about men and new wanking material hadn't been about Michael.

Fuck me. *Had* it been about Michael?

Lifting my head, I gave myself a good hard look in the mirror. It didn't matter. What mattered was that now, in a hotel room on the far side of the world, I wanted Michael desperately.

Heart hammering, I flung open the door. Michael turned from the sliding balcony door, a little crease between his eyebrows. Before he could ask, I blurted, "Can I kiss you again?"

His blue eyes widened. His mouth opened and closed—Christ, his *mouth*—and he glanced around with a tentative smile, as if he thought I'd made a joke and was waiting for the punchline.

He said, "Sure?"

"Oh, thank god," I muttered as I strode to him and claimed his mouth, gripping his face as I kissed him properly. Not a sweet wee peck, but like I meant it this time, pressing our lips together powerfully.

Michael startled against me before pressing back, whimpering and grasping at my sides with his hands. There was still a hint of sweet meringue from the Pavlova on his lips, and I wanted to lick inside his mouth. I wanted to suck his tongue and tear off his clothes. I wanted to—

His palm flat against my chest, Michael stepped back. He regarded me warily and whispered, "What are you doing?"

I was panting already, my cock swollen in my linen trousers. "Er… I don't know." What *was* I doing? I'd kissed women before. Was I crap at kissing a man?

"You don't know?" Michael's brows met. Something flickered in his eyes. Hurt? He dropped his hand.

I laughed, sounding unhinged. "I'm drunk." I backed away, panic taking over.

"You're drunk?" Michael peered at me dubiously.

That he apparently still knew me well enough to know I wasn't drunk made my belly flip. Which was ludicrous because I was being dramatic. It had only been a couple of years—of course he could still tell. Yet it made me happier than it had any right to.

"I'm not drunk," I confessed. "I'm… I was kissing you." Not that there was actually any doubt. Michael's lips were shiny with spit. I looked between his eyes and his lips, caught in a helpless loop.

"Why? For…practice?" Michael watched me warily.

Here was the perfect excuse. Well, it was remotely plausible at least. But I couldn't look into his eyes and lie. "No," I rasped. I cleared my throat. Sweat prickled my palms, and the hair on the back of my neck stood. "No," I repeated. "Not for practice. Just…for us."

Michael's lips parted. "Us?" he whispered.

"If you want? I'm—I'm…curious."

"Curious?"

"Are you just going to repeat everything I say?" I tried to laugh.

"Sorry." Michael's cheeks flushed red, and he still watched me uncertainly.

My mouth was dry. My heart pounded. I was hard. I tore my gaze up to his eyes—which were dark with desire. His chest rose and fell, his harsh little breaths filling the sleepy, sunny quiet of the room.

"I want to know what it's like to be with a man," I said, my voice rough. "I've wondered for a long time."

Michael's eyes widened at that, his fingers twitching.

Before he could reply, I blurted, "Not just any man. That's not why I—" I ran a hand through my hair, laughing rather hysterically. "I'm making a right mess of this, aren't I? What I'm trying to say is that, yes, I've wondered what it would be like with a bloke, but I haven't done anything about it because I didn't want to until now. And now, I really, really want to know what it's like. With you."

"With me," he repeated slowly.

"Will you show me?"

There was no time to dangle on the end of the hook waiting for his answer since Michael didn't so much kiss me as leap against my mouth. With Michael in my arms, we crashed back against the bed so forcefully we were lucky the whole thing didn't collapse.

There was no more hesitation or confusion. This wasn't a sweet, curious, gentle kiss. This wasn't indecision and tentative exploration. This was tongues and teeth and spit, and I was gasping for every touch.

He was hard in his shorts on top of me, and I thrust up, desperate for friction, full stomach be damned. Michael pulled back suddenly, his teeth almost bringing my lower lip along.

Before I could worry he was having second thoughts, he tore at his shirt, struggling with the buttons, and I went to work on mine, my fingers clumsy. Between us, we got our shirts off, and Michael straddled me, which had every right to be strange yet wasn't.

He laughed—in delight, I hoped—those gorgeous dimples creasing his cheeks. I had to kiss him again, taking his face in my hands, both of us smiling as we'd been on the balcony under the mistletoe.

He slid his palms over my stomach and up to my chest, his rough fingers teasing my nipples. Electricity shot straight to my dick—still achingly hard in my linen trousers—and I groaned.

It was like Michael drank in my noises. He kissed me deeply, touching me and rocking our hips together. I strangely remembered being tossed about in the ocean in Mexico on holiday once—that feeling of the tide and the sea's power, of being helpless to do anything but ride the sensations until I landed on the sand.

My spinning head managed to focus on the sensation of Michael's tongue sweeping through my mouth. I didn't want to be carried along in the tide. I was finally getting my chance to be with a man. With *Michael*. Christ, *had* I wanted this all along?

All I knew was that I needed to grab this opportunity with both hands.

Or at least one.

Michael moaned as I fumbled for him. Suddenly all I cared about was feeling him all over, skin to skin. Knowing this was real. I managed to get his shorts open and shoved my hand inside and—

"Oh, *fuck*," I groaned. "You're hard." *For me.*

My best friend was hard for me. I could feel the proof right there, hot against my palm. I wrapped my fingers around Michael's thick, curving shaft, teasing and gripping the way I'd do to myself, albeit with a different angle.

I'd imagined this countless times. Not with Michael, but various random men, typically faceless. Now, there was a real cock throbbing in my hand, and I wanted every inch of it. I wanted everything.

He tasted like the meringue and berries and sweet cream, but with a perfectly sharp edge of the cappuccino he'd had with dessert. I moaned into his kisses, squeezing his shaft. It should have been bizarre to get off with my best friend, but it felt like puzzle pieces slotting into place.

Coarse hair tickled my fingers, and I explored his heavy balls. It was different than sex with a woman in obvious ways, but I supposed it was all the same principle at the end of the day: touching and rubbing and delighting.

When Michael cried out through parted lips, his eyes wild, my own balls drew up. That I was giving him pleasure—that I could make him happy— filled me with a rush of joy and purpose.

Michael was hard for me, and I was going to make him come.

He braced a hand on my chest, digging his blunt nails into my flesh as I stroked him with more confidence. He whimpered, his face flushed and eyes wide. I'd always loved knowing my partner was genuinely getting off, and feeling his excitement build against my hand was everything.

"*Will*," he moaned helplessly.

"It's all right," I told him, thumbing drops of precum from the head of his hot cock.

I wanted to roll him under me and sink down to swallow his cock whole. Make him come and take every drop. I wanted to spread his legs and drive into his body and come inside him until neither of us could walk.

He was supposed to be showing me how it all worked, but I wanted to take care of him. He shook and gasped, clearly right at the edge, and even though he was on top of me, I felt totally in control.

"It's all right," I repeated. "I'm going to make you come."

With another gasp, Michael rutted into my hand, his spine arching. His face and neck were flushed red down to the middle of his chest, his mouth open and eyes closed as he sprayed cum over my stomach. He curled over me, trembling with a few final drops.

Dazed, I whispered, "Mission accomplished."

Michael shook again. Was he cold? Our skin was slick with sweat, and the sun was beaming through the window. I wrapped my arms around him, his breath hot on my neck, and I realized he was laughing.

Then I was too, but I was so hard it turned into whimpers as I rubbed myself through my trousers. I hadn't come in my pants in years, but I was dangerously close to it now.

"It's okay, baby. I've got you."

My best friend just called me *baby*, and somehow it was exactly what I wanted to hear. Michael tugged my trousers and white boxer briefs down mid-thigh, and nestled between my legs in a blink, my cock in his mouth.

I'd been sucked plenty of times but this was different. Even though Michael barely had any facial hair, I could feel the faintest tickle of it against my balls, and though his golden waves were soft under my fingers, there was a hardness to his jaw. A maleness I'd never experienced and that I'd wondered about for too long.

And of all men, it was *Michael*. I'd missed him so fucking much. Much more than I'd let myself acknowledge. But he was here now, and he was bringing me off with fingers against my taint and the sweetest suction on my cock.

I let go, the pleasure crashing over me, that wild ocean ride returning. I could only gasp as Michael swallowed around me. I watched him milk me, and there were white splashes on his rosy lips as he pulled off. All I could do was take his face in my trembling hands and kiss him, tasting myself, a thrill rippling through me.

When I could talk—but likely shouldn't have—I said, "So, it's like that? Being with a man, I mean."

Michael's eyes searched my face, the crease returning between his brows. He was heavy on me, but I liked it. He murmured, "Not always. But, um, yeah."

I didn't know what to say, so I went with, "Thank you," because I was a bloody idiot.

But Michael smiled, that dimple appearing. "You're welcome." He pressed his face into the side of my neck, kissing my damp skin. I tugged the sheets over us even though we were sticky and half-dressed. I wasn't about to let go of him yet.

Chapter Fourteen

Michael

U H, YEAH, IT was *never* like that.

At least not for a long time. I'd had good sex with Zoe and a few other people, but it hadn't been like that with anyone. Maybe the sex with Jared had been so unsatisfying that getting a hand job from Will blew my entire mind in comparison?

Or maybe love was the difference. Laying tangled with Will—on top of him, hiding my face against his neck—I loved him so much that tears burned my eyes. I was afraid to look up. Was this real or some fucked-up dream fueled by jet lag and years of wanting him?

Will traced my spine with his fingertips. His warm breath tickled my shoulder. I could taste his cum and sweat. If this was a dream, it was pretty realistic.

This was the greatest Christmas ever. I'd gone from cherishing one laughing, public mistletoe kiss to *all that*.

What was this though? Aside from sex, did this mean Will…liked me back? I cringed at what a kid I sounded like. But I felt young and stupid and unsure. I'd been in love with Will for so long that even thinking he might feel anything close to the same left me shaking and sweating.

"Michael?" His low voice rumbled beneath me.

He probably wanted me off him. I rolled onto my back beside him and stared at the smooth white ceiling. "Yeah?" My voice came humiliatingly close to cracking.

Nope, I could not start crying. It would freak out Will, and I couldn't do that to him. This wasn't about me. If he was really bi-curious—and, uh, yeah, apparently he was!—I had to be there for him and not make this any weirder than it might already be.

I kept rolling, pushing to my feet and ducking into the bathroom. I ran a washcloth under warm water and tensed to stop my knees from trembling.

"Michael?"

I turned my head to finally look at Will again. He sat up, his dick still hanging out of his open pants, hair sticking up, and was that my jizz stuck in his chest hair? He was *gorgeous.*

"Yeah?" I realized I was smiling.

He smiled back, tilting his head. "Are you… Is it…?" He frowned toward the sink.

Oh shit, had I been standing here too long? I said, "Water took a while to heat up," and squeezed out the cloth. My dick was hanging out too, and I figured I should clean myself while I was standing there.

Will watched.

My skin tingled, goosebumps spreading over my arms that I couldn't blame on the A/C. Will and I just had sex. We gave each other orgasms. We'd *kissed.* I'd wanted this for so long, and now I didn't know what the hell to do with any of it. Was he okay? Had he liked it?

I touched my swollen lips. Anyone would come from being sucked. It didn't really mean anything that he'd shot down my throat. I couldn't get ahead of myself. I'd screwed up our friendship already, and I had to get this right.

Whatever *this* was. I couldn't just hit him with all my bottled-up feelings. He'd had his first bi-curious orgasm. I couldn't spew my *I've-been-in-love-with-you-forever-please-love-me-back* bullshit all over him.

I rinsed the cloth and brought it to him. "Here." He took it, and our fingers brushed. I was standing there with my wet dick still hanging out of my shorts. Will looked away, and I looked away. I had no clue what to say.

To stop myself from saying all the wrong things, I busied myself stripping off my shorts and tugging on the boxers I'd slept in the night before.

"Are you okay?" Will asked.

I turned to face him. He sat on the side of the bed, his boxer briefs and linen pants balled up in his lap. His legs were sprinkled with dark hair, and I wanted to drop to my knees and just rub my cheek against his thigh.

I nodded. "What about you?"

He nodded too, smiling tentatively.

"Cool," I said. "So…" We were adults, and we needed to talk about this. I sat beside him on the bed. Our knees brushed, and more goosebumps spread over my leg. "How long have you been into guys? You never said anything. Which is okay! I'm just kind of confused."

Will laughed under his breath. "You could say I've been confused too. It's been fairly recent. You weren't around."

"Oh." Guilt gurgled in my belly. "I'm sorry."

Will shrugged tightly, not looking at me. That didn't put my mind at ease. Also, I'd pushed him away—no, I'd *run* away like a coward—because I'd had to get over him for my own sanity. It hadn't worked even a little, and now we'd messed around together, and I thought Will had liked it, and maybe we…

I was dizzy. There were a shit-ton of maybes.

Will asked quietly, "Can we get under the covers?"

"Totally." The wet cloth sat on top of Will's bundle of clothes, and I stood and grabbed it before hesitating. "You missed a spot." Leaning in, I dragged the cloth over Will's chest, the rough fabric rasping over his hairy skin. I rubbed at the flecks of dried jizz.

He let me, his eyes on me, but it wasn't sexy this time. He suddenly seemed vulnerable in a way I wasn't used to. Will had always been strong and capable and in control, and now I was about to tuck him in and kiss his forehead.

I took his clothes from his lap, dropping them in the corner with mine. We'd deal with laundry or whatever later. Will curled under the top sheet, and I slipped into bed so we faced each other on our sides.

We weren't touching, the king mattress big enough that there were several inches between us. I wanted to pull him into my arms and tell him everything would be okay, but was that for my own benefit?

I wanted to ask him what he needed, and I would have in the past. You know, when we hadn't just had sex. It was hard to say the right thing, and now it was like we were speaking a brand-new language.

I went with, "Do you want to nap?"

He shook his head, his forehead creased, tension radiating from him.

"Okay." I had to get this right, but all I could do was blurt, "Are you freaking out?"

A laugh punched from him, and his frown relaxed. "A little. You?"

"Yeah. It's… We can just talk, right? It doesn't have to be weird."

"Right." Will folded his hands under his head on the pillow. The sheet slipped down, and I pulled it back up to his shoulder. He said, "So… What did you want to talk about?"

His deadpan delivery cracked me up, and we both laughed. I pretended to think about it. "Hmm. Anything new going on? How about this weather? I've never had a tropical Christmas before."

"Me either. It's nice, though. Shit, don't let me forget to ring my parents later. I need to check the time difference again. I looked it up last night, and now I've forgotten completely."

"Were you distracted by something?"

He tapped his chin thoughtfully. "No. It's all been business as usual."

"Same old, same old." God, I itched to reach out and play with his chest hair.

"You know, I'm not sure exactly when I started fancying men as well as women."

Okay, we were doing this talking thing. I made a soft listening sound and gave him an encouraging nod.

"I've never done anything about it. Aside from wanking to gay videos."

Now there was a mental image that threatened to make my dick hard again *really* fast. "That's okay. You don't have to do anything with anyone."

Knowing I really was the first man he'd been with made my head spin. I wanted to beg him, "*Why me?*" but this was about Will.

His forehead furrowed again. "It's odd. There have been a few exceptions—Amelia, especially—but most of the time I find I'd rather just get off with porn or a fantasy."

I'd never met Amelia, but I'd wondered if she regretted letting Will go all those years ago. I couldn't imagine what she'd been thinking. But wait—did that make me an exception?

I tried to focus. "There's nothing wrong with just pleasing yourself. We all jerk off. Or most of us do. I guess some people don't?"

"Yeah, but most of the time I prefer it. I don't think that's the norm."

Most of the time but not today? Was it only curiosity? I cleared my throat. "It's not *abnormal* or anything. Like, some ace people really like masturbating, I think. It all depends on the person."

Will seemed to be considering this. "I do love sex, though. I think about it a lot. And I loved—" He waved a hand over the mattress between us. "What we did."

God, do you love me too?

Okay, no. I could not even hint at that. If Will said it, awesome, but he was clearly confused and working through his stuff.

Still, I had to ask, "You enjoyed it?"

He burst out laughing as he propped up on his elbow. "Was that not abundantly clear?"

Relief flowed through me. "I don't want to assume! This is all new. I mean, obviously I've fucked guys before, but you haven't. And we're—we've never—" My face went hot, and I know I was turning red. "I want to make sure everything's cool." I barely resisted pulling the pillow over my head.

Will smiled sweetly, and my stomach flipped. "It's cool." He hesitated. "I'd like to…explore. We're not really boyfriends, but we are friends."

My joy balloon was punctured with a sad little *hiss*. Right. Okay, not boyfriends. That was fair. I could handle that. Scratch that. I *had* to handle it. There was no other option. I'd ghosted Will once, and I'd never do it again. I'd love him as much as he'd let me, and if all he could give me was friendship, it had to be enough.

I said, "Friends with benefits? It's definitely good practice for being Angela's bisexual wingman."

"I suppose it is. So… While we're here we can have fun? Be bisexual for the holidays?" He quickly added, "You always are, of course. And I'm…"

"You're figuring it out. It's cool. There's nothing wrong with having fun. It's Christmas, after all."

"Yes, Christmas is famous for sexual exploration."

"It's in all the best carols. You know 'We Three Kings' is about a hot poly hookup."

Will laughed, his shoulders shaking. I loved seeing him like this—the tension that had been coming and going vanishing. At least for now.

He said, "'O Come All Ye Faithful' is about a Bethlehem orgy."

"Have you ever noticed how many Christmas songs have an 'O' in the title? I'm just saying."

Still smiling, Will bit his lip. His gaze grew darker, flicking between my face and…my nipple? Slowly, watching me carefully, he reached out and brushed up over my nipple with his knuckle the way he had when I'd drooled toothpaste. Lust tugged low in my belly, my balls tingling.

"You're up for it? Playing?" He'd inched his hand back, and it hovered in the air as he waited for my answer.

Kicking off the sheets and my underwear, I licked my palm and stroked my swelling dick because I was a sucker for puns. "I'm up for it."

Will made a sound that might have been a growl as he rolled half on top of me and latched his mouth onto my nipple. Moaning, I clutched his head—and were my nipples directly connected to my balls? It sure felt like it.

Had he wanted to do this earlier during the Toothpaste Incident? I bet he had, which made my dick even harder.

My nipples were wet and ready to cut glass by the time he was finished with them. Breathing hard, he propped himself up with one hand on the mattress, half hovering over me, his eyes locking on my cock.

His lips were shiny with spit, and *fuck*, I could imagine them closing around my dick with a slurp.

I had the feeling Will was imagining the same thing—but he hesitated. I ran a hand over his deliciously hairy chest as it rose and fell.

"It's okay," I murmured. "No rush."

He seemed embarrassed, nodding but not meeting my eyes. He started to say something else but stopped.

"What?" I smoothed my palm back and forth over his furry pecs. "You can ask me anything."

He seemed to consider this. "Can I look at you?"

"Um, yeah. You already are." I laughed, trying not to fidget. "Go to town. Not much to look at," I joked.

"That's not true." Will met my gaze sharply, his voice firm. "I hate it when you do that. Put yourself down."

"Oh. It's fine! I'm just not—I don't work out as much as you do. I try, but…" Jared loved the gym, and I'd gotten a personal trainer but was still on the skinny side.

"You look great just the way you are."

Will said it so confidently, his gaze dropping down to my chest. I barely stopped myself from sucking in my tummy and puffing up my pecs. Instead,

I concentrated on breathing as Will examined me.

This is about him.

I watched him watch me, butterflies flapping all over the place in my stomach. I wanted to make another joke. His gaze might as well have been his fingers or lips or tongue. My whole body tingled, and my dick leaked.

Being on display for Will excited me in a way I hadn't expected. I didn't think numbers went high enough to count the times I'd fantasized about touching Will and kissing him and being fucked by him. But I hadn't pictured this.

Somehow, I said, "Do you want me to jerk off for you?"

Eyes practically bugging out of his head, Will did that growly thing again. "Yes."

I spread my legs wide, and he shifted to sit back on his heels, his big hand like a brand on the inside of my left thigh. Honestly, I wasn't sure why I'd said it. But as I worked myself, spitting into my palm and liking the roughness, my dick getting sore from being jerked again so soon without lube, my instinct was proven right.

Will panted as he watched me, his fingers digging into my thigh. His gaze roamed from my dick to my face to my chest to my dick to my face and back again. Sweat shone in the hollow of his throat, and his cock leaked even though he didn't touch it and we'd come recently.

I'd never been like this with anyone else. A, a—what was the word? Exhibitionist? But knowing he was so turned on by watching me was the greatest rush. I'd fucked up so many things with Will, but I could give him this. I could make him happy and turn him on.

I reached down with my other hand to play with my balls, knowing that would get me there.

The orgasm ripped out of me, and I shouted as I shook with deep, burning pleasure. Gasping as if it was him coming, Will watched me milk my cock. God, I wanted to lift my legs and beg him to fuck me. But we had to take this slow. I laughed on the edge of hysteria. As if this was "taking it slow."

Adam's apple bobbing, Will watched me, probably confused about why I was laughing like that.

I said, "It's okay," and sat up to kiss him. Like before, it only took a few long pulls of my mouth on his cock for him to come. I swallowed as he tangled his fingers in my hair, his jizz dripping from my lips since I was bent over.

We flopped back on the mattress to catch our breath. "Holy shit," I mumbled. Again, the salty, bitter aftertaste of Will in my mouth was proof that, yep, we'd actually just done that.

I wasn't usually a… I tried to think of the right word. Displayer? No. Show-off? That didn't quite fit. Whatever, the point was that I'd jerked off for Will shamelessly, and it felt like he was really *seeing* me.

Aside from being literally naked, it had been like showing him how much I wanted him. It'd been raw and real.

Seemed it was easier to be brave here on the other side of the world. Like we were in a magic bubble or something. Though as I caught my breath, my bravery started to fade, and worry slithered back in. Was it about to get awkward again?

I turned my head to the left. Beside me, Will panted softly, a dazed expression on his flushed face as he stared at the ceiling. Then he looked at me, lighting up with a bright, beautiful smile.

"Promise this won't get weird?" I blurted, even though *I* was the one in love with him and he'd only talked about friends with benefits.

Grinning, Will gave me the finger, and I hooked my middle finger around his before we got lost in slow, lazy kisses. No mistletoe required.

Chapter Fifteen

Will

"Y'ALL HAVE A good nap?" Angela asked as we greeted her in the garland-festooned lobby by a gold, silver, and red-themed Christmas tree towering over several couches. One of the classic carols played overhead, though I wasn't sure if it was one of the ones with an "O" in the title.

Adrenaline shot through me as flashes of what Michael and I had done—no napping involved—cartwheeled though my mind. Desire sizzled through my veins, heat flushing my face as I attempted to formulate a response that involved a recognizable word and not solely the giddy noises eager to burst forth.

Fortunately, Michael apparently recognized my struggle and replied, "Yeah, it was really relaxing." He squeezed my hand, threading our fingers together.

"Nothing like a Christmas Day nap," Paul agreed, patting his stomach under a bright Hawaiian shirt. "Now if only we had football on TV."

"Going to the beach is way better than stupid football," Makayla said, adjusting the brim of her wide woven hat.

"The beach and football are both awesome," Olivia said. "Dad, did you check the score? What time is it at home? I'm all f—messed up."

Bugger, I really had to call my parents. I'd declined a video chat from Mum when Michael and I had just gotten out of the shower. Where we'd made out like teenagers under the spray of hot water. Even if I'd pulled on a robe and sat on the balcony to talk to Mum and Dad, I was sure they'd have known something was up.

Gripping Michael's hand now, I glanced around the lobby. Did we look different? Could everyone *tell*? Christ, I was a grown man, but I felt like a teenager. The rush I'd felt at the glamping retreat at being perceived by people as bisexual, or at least not straight, was amplified by a thousand. By ten thousand. A hundred, a—

"You okay?" Michael whispered.

I nodded. "Just…happy. Thrilled. Delighted."

He laughed softly. "Ecstatic?"

"Yep." I bit my lip to stop myself from grinning madly. I could have danced a jig around the Christmas tree.

After a hotel employee brought us an insulated picnic basket that I offered to carry, we made our way along the crowded boardwalk. Even with sunglasses, I blinked against the glare of the afternoon sun. Our palms quickly became damp where we held hands, but I wouldn't have let go of Michael for anything.

We'd held hands in public several times in the past…week? Must have been a week by now, or almost. Time had lost meaning with the travel and being in our bubble under the sun so far from home.

I'd become comfortable holding Michael's hand more quickly than I would've expected, but now? Oh, now it was magical.

The warm pressure of his fingers made me think of the sensation of those fingers on my body. I thought of watching him wank and the way he used his hands to tease and touch himself. It was all new and thrilling. I'd lost my virginity more than a decade ago, but I hadn't been bisexual then. Well, perhaps I had been if I was now.

Which I certainly seemed to be, didn't I?

Another giddy rush of happiness bubbled through me like champagne, and I nudged Michael's shoulder before pecking his cheek. That brief brush of my lips on his cheek would have to do for now when I'd have loved to drop the basket and haul him into my arms for a proper snog.

Michael laughed, whispering, "How long do we have to stay at the beach? Also, are there any drug stores open today?"

It took me a moment to understand he was talking about buying lube. And likely condoms. A shudder of lust gripped me, nervousness quick on its heels. I wanted to do everything with Michael, but it was daunting at the same time.

Perhaps it would be good if we couldn't buy supplies until Boxing Day. Because waiting until the twenty-sixth would be *plenty* of time, right?

The beach was absolutely chock-a-block with people, as promised. Santa hats and bikinis were the order of the day, and it was a noisy, merry scene. We made our way through the throng to find an empty spot, sand hot and fine between our toes.

The Indian Ocean was spectacular, the water crystal clear as it washed over the pale sand. Even with the crowd, I could see why this was such a popular spot.

We laid down blankets provided by the hotel and got settled next to a family playing Mariah Carey's Christmas album on Wi-Fi speakers.

Angela immediately started speaking with the parents, cooing over a gurgling baby in a holly-and-ivy onesie. Paul cracked open a bottle of sparkling water and settled in while Makayla tried to convince Olivia to swim with her.

The beach was only about a thousand yards or so long, and there had to be thousands of revelers squeezed onto the sand. I hoped this was the busiest day of the year, because I couldn't imagine many more people could fit.

Michael looked around. "Wow. This place is packed."

The woman chatting with Angela bounced her baby on her lap and said, "This is the busiest time of year. School holidays and all that. Be sure to swim between the flags." She pointed to her right and the north end of the beach. "There's a bad rip up there. Stay away from the Croc. It'll drag you out in a blink."

Olivia looked up from her phone sharply. "There are crocodiles here?"

The woman chuckled. "It's just what we call that rip. A dangerous current. Swim between the flags and mind the lifeguards and you'll be right."

I tugged Michael's hand lightly, and he knelt beside me on the blanket. "Okay?" I asked.

He nodded. "It's just a *lot* of people."

"Do you want to go back?" I murmured, sliding my hand behind his neck. I rubbed softly with my thumb. "We don't have to stay." And if we returned to our room…

Makayla had apparently heard my question—and to be fair, quarters were close—and she pleaded, "Please go swimming with me first? Olivia doesn't want to get wet. *At the beach.*" Her sister ignored her, and Makayla added, "My parents don't like swimming unless it's in a shallow pool."

I said to Michael, "Do you want to head back, and I'll be along in forty-five minutes or an hour?"

He gave me a sweet smile. "Nah. Let's go swimming." He pulled up the hem of his Old Navy tee. "Strap on your sunglasses, Makayla. You're about to be blinded."

She giggled as Michael stripped off his shirt, her eyes widening. I followed her gaze and choked as I realized Michael's pale white chest had red beard burns and marks I'd left.

Olivia gave me a thumbs-up, and my face burned with a combination of embarrassment and silly pride. Fortunately, Angela and Paul were now deep in conversation with our neighbors. I didn't need my boss to have that much info about my sex life.

My sex life. With a man. With Michael.

I found myself laughing. Practically *giggling*. I hadn't felt this excited or *young* in years. It was a sort of euphoria, as though I was drunk or high. I likely should have been more embarrassed than I was at the girls seeing the evidence, but Christ, the thrill at marking Michael for my own!

Only meant to be friends with benefits, remember?

Michael smiled quizzically and passed me a bottle of fifty SPF sunscreen. "Can you?" He motioned to his back.

Hell yes. I eagerly squeezed the white cream into my palm, kneeling behind Michael. I smoothed the lotion over his back while he spread it on his chest and arms. I swooped and dipped my hands, following the planes of his slim, firm torso, my fingers sliding around his ribs. Down his spine, across the top of his board shorts, skimming just under the waistband to be sure to get every inch of pale, vulnerable skin…

Michael cleared his throat. "I think you got it."

Blinking, I dragged my hands up to his shoulders. "You sure?"

He looked back at me with a laugh and hissed, "Dude, this is a family show."

Right. Yes. Excellent point.

I stripped down to my swimsuit, and we quickly spread the sunscreen over my bare skin as we tried not to snicker like kids. After promising Angela and Paul we'd stick with Makayla, the three of us made our way through the maze of towels, blankets, drunken pyramids of people, and sun worshippers.

We neared a buggy with two lifeguards, one standing up in the back and the other behind the wheel, both surveying the water closely. They wore blue long-sleeved uniform shirts and long black shorts.

Makayla elbowed me, nodding to the blond lifeguard standing over the buggy's roof. "That guy looks just like Chris Hemsworth! You know, Thor?"

Just how old did she think we were? "He does," I agreed with a smile.

"Maybe he'll have to rescue me." She grinned.

"No, let's not need rescuing today. Cheers."

Michael said, "I mean, I wouldn't mind either, tbh," and gave Makayla a grin.

An acidy, unpleasant sensation stabbed me. I glanced back at the lifeguard as we passed, taking his measure. Was tanned, muscled, and strong-jawed Michael's type? I imagined how I'd compare next to this Hemsworth doppelganger, and—

Why was I *jealous*? How absolutely ridiculous. Even if Michael and I were… He wasn't about to go hook up with a lifeguard. Surely not.

"Will?"

I'd slowed to a crawl, glancing back at the lifeguard in question, who'd pulled out binoculars as he surveyed the water. I looked guiltily to Michael, who frowned back at me.

"Coming!"

The stretch of water between the red and yellow flags planted in the sand teemed with shrieking children and people of all ages rolling about in the surprisingly strong surf. We quickly discovered we needed to time our splashing run into the water properly or risk being flattened by the incoming waves.

Sputtering and wiping salt water from my face, I retreated a few feet, letting another wave crash around my knees. Makayla tumbled onto her butt, but she was laughing as Michael and I pulled her up. She was so small that we almost yanked her right off her feet.

Gulls cried, and the sun bore down as I inhaled the briny air deeply. It had been too long since I'd been to the seaside. Not a typical Christmas, but it was joyous in its own way, especially with Michael at my side.

"We have to get past the break!" Makayla shouted with authority. She straightened the straps of her cute polka-dot two-piece and eyed the incoming waves with steely determination. "I'll tell you when!"

Like runners on the starting line, we waited, letting another wave crash and swirl around our legs. On Makayla's command, we raced forward.

How was running in water so bloody hard? I lifted my feet sideways, eyeing the waves barreling our way. I stumbled, and Michael and Makayla surged ahead.

"Oh shit!" Michael lunged forward into the water, stroking with his arms and riding over the top of the wave just before it broke.

Makayla dove under, and I froze with indecision. Dive? Turn and ride it? Or—

No time! Planting my feet in the sand, I closed my eyes and braced with all my might, fists clenched. The wave scoffed at my attempt to withstand it, tossing me backward arse over teakettle as Mum would say—a perfect back somersault.

I slammed onto the sand on my backside, coughing and sputtering as the wave carried me to shore. Another wave crashed into my face, and I shoved to my feet, stumbling to shore along with a few other people who'd mistimed their entry.

It was already tough to find Michael and Makayla amid the sea of heads, but I spotted them bobbing over another swell. Coughing, I waved and motioned with flat palms, hoping Michael would know I meant to stay there. I wasn't about to be defeated.

This time, I sucked in a huge breath and dove under the incoming wave, water bubbling over me. I came up the other side and narrowly avoided smacking into an old man with his granddaughter. Michael called out, and I paddled over.

"Okay?" he asked, reaching for me and sliding his arm around my back securely. "You can stand here. We found a sand bar."

"Yeah, I'm fine." A swell of water lifted us, but it was mild compared to where the waves broke near the shore. As we found the sandbar again with our feet, I kissed Michael and slipped my arm around his shoulders. "Missed you."

He blinked at me, smiling quizzically but looking pleased. "It was, like, three minutes, tops."

I shrugged as we surged up and down with another passing wave. "I still missed you."

Makayla cooed, "I missed you *tooooo*."

"Sorry, we're being one of those annoying couples," I said, Michael jerking against my side before we surged up on a stronger wave.

"God, they really weren't joking about how crowded this beach gets," he said.

It really was just a sea of people in the water and on the narrow stretch of sand. A low concrete wall ran across the back of the beach area separating it from the boardwalk and a grassed park with tall evergreen trees beyond. A windowed lifeguard tower sat in the middle of the beach. I couldn't imagine how the lifeguards could spot anyone drowning in this chaos.

As we dropped down the back of another big swell, the sandbar no longer under us, a guy chasing an inflatable ball suddenly appeared. Makayla dodged him, sputtering with a face full of water as he kicked and almost hit her head.

Michael and I shouted, "Hey!" in unison, but it was an older woman around sixty in a bright green one-piece who got the guy's attention.

"Oi!" she snapped. "Rack off, you bogans! I told you it's too crowded to be roughhousing like that."

The guy grumbled but took his ball and swam back to a group of people in their early twenties. I took hold of Makayla's arm gently and made sure she was all right. I wasn't sure what a "bogan" was, but it didn't sound complimentary. We thanked the woman, but she waved us off.

"Just keep an eye out. Some people don't give a stuff about anyone else's enjoyment, especially when they're on the grog. Sometimes I wish Barking had never been named the best beach in Oz. It was never this busy when I was younger." She snorted. "Then again, when I was younger, the Earth was flat, and we thought the sun revolved around us."

Michael laughed. "Sorry, you must hate tourists like us."

"Nah. As long as you can actually swim and you mind the lifeguards, you're good in my books. It's idiots that don't follow the rules that do my head in."

"Why would anyone go in if they can't swim?" Makayla asked, treading water as another big swell lifted us up and down.

"That's the question, isn't it?" the woman laughed. "But they do, in droves. The lifeguards have their work cut out for them, especially today when the drunk backpackers are causing mischief. But I've had a swim in the arvo here on Christmas Day every year since I could walk, and they're not driving me away."

Under the water, as we circled our arms on the surface to stay afloat, I rubbed my foot against Michael's, the need to touch him simmering through me constantly. He shot me a smile and rubbed back, and our fingers entwined as we bobbed up and down on the swells.

I tuned back into the conversation as Makayla said to the woman, "One of the lifeguards looks like Thor with short hair."

The woman laughed heartily. "Ah, that's probably Liam Fox. He was a star footballer. Now he's famous for being gay. It was a big drama. His partner Cody's in the service as well. Good blokes."

"That's so cool!" Makayla grinned at us.

Before I could answer, someone shouted on a megaphone from shore. Michael's grip on my hand tightened and he asked, "Is there a shark?" as he glanced around.

The woman laughed. "Nah, they're moving the flags. There's a siren for shark sightings."

That there were enough regular sightings to necessitate a siren somehow wasn't reassuring. "Why are they moving the flags?" I asked.

"Currents and conditions change," the woman said as she began stroking confidently, heading south. "Come on or get back to shore. Merry Christmas!"

The wind had whipped up, seemingly in a blink. "Let's go back in," I said. The conditions were getting too rough for my liking.

Michael and Makayla agreed, and I let go of Michael's hand so we could swim. On the crowded shore, lifeguards motioned to their left, shouting on megaphones for us to shift down the beach.

We kicked and stroked with our arms, glancing behind to keep an eye on the waves that never stopped coming.

"Why are we going the wrong way?" Makayla asked, her voice rising.

My stomach sank like a stone. She was right—though we'd been swimming toward shore, it looked farther away. I kicked harder, but the sickening sensation of being dragged backward toward the open sea was unmistakable.

"It's all right!" I shouted even though it felt like invisible tentacles were ensnaring me. It had to be a rip current. I looked to Michael, who kicked vigorously, his eyes wide. I had to stay calm. He needed me. Makayla needed me. Everything was fine.

Except for the fact that we were undeniably being dragged away from safety. Waves swallowed us, our hair plastered to our heads. Makayla pushed her hair from her face, grimacing as she kicked and struggled. In the growing swells of water as we bobbed up and down, the shore appeared and disappeared.

I realized with a start that Michael was out of reach. I opened my mouth to shout for him and choked on saltwater crashing overhead. My heart hammered as I kicked to the surface and coughed.

We'd been happily bobbing along a minute ago! I kicked hard, swimming madly toward Michael and Makayla.

Though the sun was still high in the cloudless sky, I shivered, the current's vicious pull like icy fingers. My head buzzed, pulse racing and my limbs suddenly like lead as I fought to keep my head above water and get back to Michael and land.

Michael and Makayla bobbed in and out of sight. Michael was saying something to me, but I couldn't hear him over the buzzing. We initially hadn't been that far out, but now the beach looked terrifyingly distant.

I'm going to die!

The lifeguard appeared as if from thin air, grabbing my arm and hauling me over the front of his longboard as he sat up and straddled it, his legs in the water. "You right, mate?" He kept an iron grip on my upper arm.

I took a proper breath for the first time in what seemed like hours. It was Thor—no, what had that woman called him? Liam? He said, "I've got ya. No worries."

The few seconds of relief I'd enjoyed evaporated. "Michael!" I squirmed and struggled to sit up and find Michael and Makayla.

Liam's grip didn't waver, but he angled the board and pointed. "Your mates are fine."

The sweet relief flooded back—so strongly this time tears pricked my eyes. "He's my boyfriend," I rasped, even though there was no need to pretend with a lifeguard.

"That's *my* boyfriend picking him up." Liam squeezed my arm reassuringly. "He's safe."

Makayla and Michael hung onto the sides of a female lifeguard's board, and I watched as Liam's boyfriend—Cody?—powered over a swell and sat up, grabbing Michael and transferring him onto his board. Cody was fair, compact, and wiry.

Liam manhandled me the same way—pulling me onto my stomach on his board and settling between my legs to paddle us side-on to the beach before pointing the nose toward shore. He expertly navigated the waves, and I couldn't hold in a whoop as the water surged beneath us and carried us all the way into the shallows.

We rolled off, and Liam tugged me to my feet as I wiped more water from my face. My throat was dry, and I coughed, ignoring it as I reached for Michael. He hugged me tightly, face pinched in concern.

Makayla laughed as she splashed to shore. "That was *awesome!*"

Liam, Cody, and the female lifeguard—a beautiful young Asian woman—laughed too, but as I coughed again, Liam insisted I sit down on the sand just beyond the water's reach.

"Did you swallow much water?" Liam asked.

I shook my head, squirming at all the attention, my skin crawling with all the eyes of the little crowd that had gathered around us.

Kneeling beside me, Michael rubbed my back and said to the lifeguards, "Everything was fine and then it was pulling us out."

"Flash rip," Cody said. "Permanent rips like the Croc happen in the same place, but flash rips can spring up anywhere. That's why we moved the flags. It's getting hectic out there." His accent sounded strangely North American.

"Most important thing is not to panic."

A voice on a radio in the nearby buggy crackled to life and said, "Got another head out the back—fourth ramp."

The woman picked up her board and sprinted back out, paddling so fast my head spun. I felt like I'd swallowed concrete. I blinked at the crashing waves, distantly listening as Cody spoke on the radio. Michael's hand sweeping up and down my back was the only thing that felt real.

Crouching on my other side, Michael still anchored to my right, Liam said, "You're sure you didn't swallow much water?"

I almost joked, "*Just concrete*," but Liam was too busy for that. I croaked, "No. Just a mouthful."

Nodding, Liam stood and shared a glance with Cody, communicating silently. There was quite a size difference between them, and Cody looked a fair bit younger too. I'd have to look up their story online, assuming Liam was as famous as that woman said.

Liam nodded at Cody, apparently signaling the end of their silent conversation, and said to me, "If you start to feel crook, see a doctor right away. The problem is that you might have gotten water in your lungs without realizing it. But I think you should be okay."

I nodded. "I just feel like I ran a marathon."

"Panic does that to you," Cody said. "Sucks all your energy. But you'll be right. Happens to the best of us, believe me."

Shame slammed through me like another wave. I'd panicked. I'd made everything worse. Since when did I panic? I kept a level head in crises. I told other people what to do when they started flapping. Angela wouldn't have brought me on this trip if I was someone who *panicked*.

I wiped my mouth. My lips tingled from the salt, and my head was so hot it was in danger of exploding.

Michael stood and shook the lifeguards' hands. "Thank you so much." Makayla thanked them profusely too.

Cody smiled. "No worries. That's why we're here. You did great."

"More heads out the back—the Croc's waking up!" Liam called to Cody from the buggy. "Fifth gate."

Cody had their boards on the buggy's side rack in a blink before hopping in, Liam leaning on the horn as they sped north along the wet strip of sand at the water's edge, weaving around people to save more lives.

"Wow," Makayla sighed. "That was so hot." She clapped her hand over her mouth adorably, and Michael shook with laughter beside me. He still rubbed my back steadily.

I had to laugh, but it didn't dispel the shame that I'd failed so miserably. *What must he think of me?*

"Come on, we have to tell Mom and Dad!" She tugged at my hand.

I groaned. "Can't wait to tell Angela and Paul that I almost drowned their daughter. Merry Christmas!"

"Huh?" Hands on narrow hips, Makayla looked down at me. "It's not your fault there was a—what did they call it? A flash rip?"

I shrugged, knocking Michael's hand away unintentionally. "Still, I was supposed to be watching you."

"I'm fine!" She shook her head. "It's not your fault. It's, like, the whole reason they have lifeguards."

Michael's hand felt cool on the back of my flushed neck. "Makayla's fine. We all are."

"No thanks to me," I muttered. What if the current hadn't pulled me away from them? Would I have been one of those people who drowns their companions in a blind panic in these situations?

"Are you sure you're okay?" Michael squeezed my neck, leaning around to peer into my face with obvious concern. "Is it hard to breathe? We can call an ambulance."

Wonderful, now I was being a drama queen and worrying him on top of my failure in the water. "No, no. I'm fine." And I *was*. I could sleep for days, but there was nothing wrong with my limbs as I forced myself to stand and walk and smile.

Chapter Sixteen

Michael

"HAPPY BOXING DAY, Mum. Is Dad there too? Sorry we didn't get a chance to speak properly yesterday."

I'd been half-awake for a while, drifting in and out of sleep as I listened to Will putter. It was a surprise when I opened my eyes now to find that he was on the balcony with the sliding door shut. It sounded like he was sitting beside me. I guessed that it made sense in such a warm place to only have single-glazed glass.

"Yes, it was a lovely Christmas at the beach. We're having a grand time."

Curled on my side, I could see the back of Will's head through the window. He wore a pale blue shirt with cuffed short sleeves that probably had buttons down the front, and most likely his plaid shorts. The sky was a cloudless blue again, and I'd probably slept too late even though we'd crashed early.

"Aye, the weather's gorgeous."

I had to smile. Will's accent really did immediately get thicker as soon as he was talking to his parents. But *were* we having a grand time?

We *had* been—uh, understatement of the year considering all the orgasms we'd shared yesterday. Merry Christmas to me and god bless us everyone and all that stuff.

But Will had withdrawn after we went to the beach. Had our near-death experience made him realize he didn't want me after all? That he wasn't bi, and this experiment was over, and we were going back to being strictly fake boyfriends?

The glittery surfing koala ornament watched me from where it hung against the cream lampshade. "Hey, uh…mate," I whispered. Because now I was talking to Christmas tree ornaments. "What do you think?" The koala didn't answer for obvious reasons.

Rolling onto my back, I stared at the ceiling. I'd slept naked, and so had Will, but we'd barely touched. I'd been ready for round…four? Five? Whatever number it was, I'd been ready.

But Will had been quiet the rest of the day after we were rescued. I'd waited for him to kiss me, but he'd turned off the lights and gone to sleep.

I'd looked up the symptoms of what was often called dry drowning, but he'd insisted he was fine. Maybe it really had only been jet lag, but if something was wrong, I wished he'd just tell me.

That's rich coming from you, mate.

Great. Now a sparkly surfing koala bear was dunking on me in my head. "Shut up…" I pulled a name out of the air. "Kevin. Kevin the koala doesn't get a vote."

Will was making listening noises, and he held the phone to his ear, so there was no risk of me tiptoeing by in the background of a video call. I slipped into the bathroom and had a shower. When I stepped out, I rubbed my head with a towel and wrapped it around my waist.

"Michael?"

I almost groaned out loud hearing Will's low voice. He'd never once called me "Mike," and my name on his tongue was sweet and sexy. I swiped my palm over the steamy mirror and made sure my voice was worry-free. "Come in! Good morning. Afternoon? I'm not sure." Normally, I'd look at my phone before I was out of bed, but who cared what time it was here?

Behind me, Will tentatively opened the door as I winced and poked the bruise on my shoulder where I'd smacked the lifeguard's board. His eyes widened.

"Are you hurt?" He strode forward and examined the top of my shoulder.

I watched his serious intensity in the mirror, my belly flip-flopping. "It's just a bump." His fingers were warm on my wet skin. "Yesterday was scary, huh?" I said quietly. We'd been so tired last night that we hadn't really talked about it. "Did you tell your parents?"

In the mirror, I saw him…clench up and make a face. He dropped his hands and walked back into the bedroom. "No. They'd only fret."

I caught his wrist by the bed, needing to touch him. "What's wrong? And before you say 'nothing,' I know it's something." If anyone should know when someone was trying to hide their feelings, it was me. "Even Kevin can tell something's wrong."

Will's brow creased. "Kevin?"

I motioned to the lamp. "Kevin the koala. He's wise."

Will snorted, then smiled softly. "What's gotten into you?"

"What? I always talk to Christmas tree ornaments. It's totally normal." I wasn't actually sure what was up with me. What I did know was that yesterday was the most amazing, magical day of my life—until Will got quiet and distracted. Maybe what we'd shared had only been a limited-time Christmas miracle.

The thought almost buckled my knees.

Sitting on the end of the bed, I tugged Will down beside me and took a deep breath. If he wanted to go back to only being friends, I had to know. Even if it killed me. Because it might.

In one day, I'd fallen so much deeper in love with Will. It had felt so *right* kissing and touching and coming.

I was still gripping his wrist. I let go and clasped my hands in my lap. "Do you want to stop?" I motioned between us, forcing myself to look at his face. "Having sex, I mean. It's okay if you want to stop. I know it's new, and maybe you decided you're not into it."

"*No.*" Will said that one word with so much conviction and low baritone power that my dick got hard instantly. He squeezed my knee, then hesitated. "Unless you want to stop?"

I shook my head so violently I probably gave myself a concussion. "Nope. I'm good."

A smile tugged at Will's full lips. "Then we're in agreement to keep…experimenting."

"Uh-huh." I pulled his face close and kissed him. We opened our mouths, our tongues meeting.

He hadn't shaved, and I loved the rasp of his stubble as we kissed and kissed. If this really was only an experiment that was going to end after the holidays, my heart was going to shatter into too many pieces to find.

That's future Michael's problem, Kevin said, and that glittery koala was right. After all, we could die tomorrow, so fuck it.

I had Will stretched out on his back and his shirt unbuttoned, and I was about to open the fly of his plaid shorts when I stopped. I'd straddled his hips, and he ran his hands up and down my thighs under the towel, which was barely hanging on.

I'd bitten my tongue so many times with Jared. I'd said nothing to Will when I probably should have told him everything—even though the idea of confessing how much I loved him still made me want to throw up. I had to swallow hard and push away the fear. This wasn't about me.

"Michael?" He frowned up at me.

"So, if it wasn't about what we're doing together, what's wrong?" My heart thudded. Was I going to mess everything up by not letting this drop? Maybe I should have just kept my stupid mouth shut, because Will looked away, his grip on my thighs loosening.

But he didn't let go.

Slowly, I ran my hands over his chest. We were both hard, but that didn't matter right now. I wanted to soothe him and make whatever was wrong okay again.

"Baby, please tell me." I'd never called anyone "baby" before, but it felt right. "Are you upset about what happened at the beach?" It seemed logical since he'd been acting differently after. "It was really scary."

He puffed out his cheeks, still not looking at me, and laughed hollowly.

"Yeah, but you and Makayla didn't panic. I made everything worse."

"Wait, what?" I honestly couldn't believe my ears. "Are you shitting me? Dude, I was totally freaking out."

Will looked at me, his gaze narrowed. "Come on. Cody said you and Makayla did great. *I'm* the one who panicked and almost drowned."

"Did he?" I tried to play back the conversation on the beach with the lifeguards. "I don't even know what he said. I was so relieved we were all okay. It would have really impacted your promotion prospects if we lost Angela's daughter on day one."

A laugh burst out of Will, and I swore I could sense a bit of tension easing. He said, "We should really wait a week at least."

"Exactly." I rubbed my thumb over his collarbone. "Believe me, I panicked. But I guess I realized it wouldn't help, so I stopped fighting. I could see the lifeguards coming. Honestly, Makayla was a superstar. She just treaded water and held her breath when waves came. I might have freaked out more if I'd been alone." I shuddered. "One second you were beside me, and then you weren't."

Will nodded, spreading his fingers over my thighs. "I couldn't reach you. I didn't know the lifeguards were coming." His throat seized, and his fingers dug into my flesh. "I couldn't think."

"It's okay, baby. It's not your fault."

He sighed noisily, shaking his head. "It shouldn't happen to me! I'm stable. Reliable. I shouldn't be bloody panicking."

I smiled, affection for Will filling me to the bursting point. "You're still stable and reliable, I promise. That's why I called you that night on the road. I knew you'd answer. You're just like those lifeguards, swooping in to make the rescue."

"Hardly." He scoffed, but I could tell he liked to hear it. Why shouldn't he? It was true.

"It's okay that you panicked. It's over now. It doesn't change who you are, I promise."

Will took a deep breath and lifted his hand—middle finger up. "Swear?"

I wrapped our fingers together. Leaning in, I pressed a kiss to his fingertip before licking across the top. A shudder ran through him that I felt where I straddled him. I sucked our fingers into my mouth, and Will grabbed my hips, thrusting up against me.

Who knew middle fingers could be so sexy?

Chapter Seventeen

Will

MICHAEL PULLED HIS hand free to work on my shorts, keeping my finger firmly between his lips as he sucked. I groaned, thrusting up helplessly as he took out my straining cock. When my finger dripped with saliva, he pulled off with a filthy *pop* that tightened my balls.

The towel's knot had finally given out, and he tossed it aside and said, "We still need to go to the drug store, but that should be enough. For your finger, I mean."

I was apparently supposed to respond to this, which was a challenge given I was already close to the edge. "I… Okay?"

He leaned down to kiss me messily, his breath hot on my mouth. "Will you just, you know. Play with my hole?"

Gulping, I nodded. "I don't really know what I'm doing, though." My laugh sounded erratic and high-pitched. I'd felt so guilty about the incident at the beach, and Michael had soothed those worries away. But now I was all knees and elbows when I should have been able to easily give him what he wanted.

Michael slid off me onto his side, urging me to face him. He gently pushed his leg between mine and slipped his hand under my open shirt to lightly trace my ribs. I held onto his waist, wishing I was better at this.

I said, "You must think I'm…"

He watched me patiently, finally prompting softly, "What?"

"I dunno." I closed my eyes. "I have this ridiculous reputation for being a player, when the truth is, I've never even done…you know."

"Butt stuff?"

Laughing, I opened my eyes. "I suppose that's one way to put it. But no, I haven't really. I realize it's not solely something between men, but…"

"Yeah, women can definitely be into butt stuff. Nonbinary people too, obviously. Butt stuff is for everyone. Only if they're into it."

"I know." I ran my hand up and down his side. "Honestly, even though I've been curious about men, I never thought I'd actually do it. Didn't ever imagine…experimenting.”

His gaze dropped. “Right. I totally get it.”

“It’s embarrassing, really.” I wanted to roll away and cover up, but Michael’s leg was lodged between mine, our skin hot and getting sweaty in a way I surprisingly enjoyed.

“What is?” He watched me closely.

“That I’m supposed to be a, a—lothario when most of the time I had straightforward sex that was enjoyable enough but nothing to write home about.” Not since Amelia, and that was a decade ago now.

“Ohh, ‘lothario,’ huh? That’s a twenty-five-cent word.”

I laughed. “More like a dollar at least with inflation these days. A pound-fifty in the UK.”

Michael laughed too as he stroked my back and torso before scratching his nails through my wiry chest hair. “It’s because you’re so gorgeous. Everyone assumes you’re getting laid every five minutes.”

My heart stuttered. “Gorgeous?”

He rolled his eyes with a smile. “Come on, you know you’re extremely good-looking.”

I supposed I did know I’d been blessed in the genetics department, but the idea that *Michael* thought I was gorgeous was very pleasing. I squeezed his thigh between mine.

My cock was hanging out of my open shorts. I needed everything off, and I tugged and yanked until I was naked too. I murmured, “There. That’s better,” and kissed him softly.

“Mmm. It is.” With his leg between mine again, he rolled our hips together.

Perhaps it was because we’d known each other for years, but I couldn’t recall being this comfortable hanging about naked with someone. Even Amelia, though we’d been young and still settling into our adult bodies.

“You said you usually like jerking off, right?” Michael asked. “Will you show me?”

How was I expected to *breathe* let alone wank? It had been such a turn-on to watch Michael yesterday—was that right? Was it only yesterday? Yes, it had to be.

Christmas Day was yesterday, and that was the first time we’d kissed, and then the first time we’d done all those other wonderful things…

I corralled my disarrayed thoughts. Michael wanted me to show him. I swallowed hard, trying not to overthink it as I took myself in hand. Michael inched back, giving me an encouraging smile, his gaze avid.

“Do you need lube?” He asked. “God, I hope drug stores are open today.”

I cupped my right hand and spit a few times. “S’all right. I’m a wanking expert. Years of experience.”

He laughed and grabbed my wrist. "Here." Michael leaned over my right palm and spit. He slowly licked across my fingers before spitting again.

The soft, wet sounds were beautifully intimate. Sunlight poured through the windows, and on our tangle of white sheets, we could have been in the clouds. Just the two of us in our world.

Michael lifted his head. "Is that good?"

I groaned and stroked myself. "*Yes.* You did a very good job." I'd meant it as a joke, but his eyes widened briefly, his breath catching. Mmm, so he liked that kind of praise, it seemed. I'd have to remember that—when I wasn't working myself with long, hard strokes.

Honestly, I'd have been embarrassed by how quickly I was on the verge of coming, but Michael was so rapt with the show that I was strangely proud. Panting softly, I squeezed the base of my cock.

Michael ran his thumb over the leaking head. "Seeing this is so hot." He lifted his thumb to his mouth and licked up the drops. "I love cum."

I shuddered. "*Fuck.*"

He grinned and stroked my shaft slowly with his fingertips. "It's like when you slip your fingers inside a girl, and her pussy's wet for you. I love that."

Nodding, I groaned. My whole body pulsed with heat.

Michael tangled his fingers in my hair and kissed me hard. I could faintly taste my own precum, and it had no right to be as hot as it was. Because *Christ*, I was about to explode.

Stroking me again, Michael whispered urgently, "I love feeling how much you want me. Tasting it."

I nodded. "I want to suck you." I wouldn't likely be much good, but I was dying to try. "It feels so good when you do it to me."

Before I could blink, he shimmied down the mattress and swallowed me almost to the root.

"Jesus!" I shouted, arching my back.

Sucking forcefully, Michael pulled off with a loud, wonderfully filthy slurp. "Will you fuck my mouth? Hard. I want to choke on your dick. I want you to come down my throat."

All I could do was nod and make a strangled noise of assent as we scrambled into a new position, both of us almost frantic in our need. I straddled his chest—no, his *neck*, which felt so very kinky and forbidden to me.

I'd never done anything like this before, but Michael was gripping my arse and urging me into his mouth, opening wide and moaning as I filled him.

Bracing my hands on the headboard, I did what he'd asked. I fucked his mouth, pulling back when he choked and coughed, pushing inside when he dug his fingers into my flesh. My cock was slick with his spit, and he gasped around me.

"*Michael*," I moaned. "You feel so good. I'm going to…" Sweat dampened my forehead, and I rocked into Michael's perfect mouth, my balls so tight they were about to—

I shot down his throat, pulling out as he coughed and tried to swallow. The next spurts landed on his red, swollen lips and his flushed cheeks, dripping down his chin. My whole body shook with white-hot pleasure, and I made a sound I barely recognized.

"That's it. Everything," Michael muttered.

I could barely breathe, but I didn't stop to regroup before crawling backward and pushing Michael's thighs wide. As I took his throbbing dick in hand, he moaned, "Oh god, yes. *Baby*."

Hearing him call me that gave me a thrill. Taking his hard cock in my mouth, I sucked the head, boggling at the thought of swallowing the whole thing the way some people could. The way Michael could.

It was earthy and hot and raw, and part of me couldn't believe I was actually sucking a man's cock.

Michael's, which made it all the better. I wanted to bring him off and please him—which I seemed to be accomplishing given his cries and fingers tangling in my hair. He caressed my head as I licked around his shaft, slurping noisily.

Sucking him a little deeper, I swallowed, spit dribbling from between my stretched lips. To feel Michael's desire hot and hard in my mouth gave me a heady burst of confidence. I fumbled for his balls, and it was only a few moments before he flooded my tongue with salty jizz as I swallowed desperately.

Cum dripping out of my mouth, I panted and groaned, muttering unintelligibly. I had no idea what I was trying to say. Michael tugged at my shoulders, and I returned to him, licking my own splatters from his face before kissing him deeply.

Sweaty and sticky, we kissed, moaning into each other's mouths. The rush I'd felt when I'd first pretended to be bi at the work retreat returned, spinning me around joyfully.

Safe to say *pretending* to be bi wasn't necessary and never had been. This was me.

I kissed Michael through a giddy grin. "Thank you," I whispered, holding his face in my hands.

Red-faced, he laughed. "Anytime."

There was so much else to thank him for, wasn't there? The ghosting had cut me to the quick—and I had to breathe through a bolt of hurt—but I was so grateful he was here with me in Australia. In this bed. In my arms.

I couldn't hope to make sense of the whirlwind in my mind, so I kissed him, and kissed him, and kissed him.

Chapter Eighteen

Michael

EET SINKING INTO the wet sand, I waded through the shallows along Barking Beach. Will had gone to meet Angela for a meeting about the meeting they were having tomorrow with one of the companies Angela wanted to partner with.

I chuckled to myself. A meeting about a meeting. Why was that funny to me? Probably because I felt drunk without having anything stronger than coffee.

I turned my face up to the sun under the brim of my Mets cap, breathing the ocean air deeply. I'd slathered any exposed skin with sunscreen and wore a loose T-shirt over my shorts.

Carrying my flip-flops, I walked the length of the beach again, dodging splashing kids and surfers returning to shore at the north end. Grinning to myself, I could have held my arms out and twirled the length of the beach like whatshername at the beginning of *The Sound of Music*. Except on the sand and not in the Alps.

That was my mom's favorite movie, and I found myself humming the song about favorite things, my mind jumping around like pop rocks were fizzing in my head. Will was one of my favorite things. No, my absolute favorite thing. My *favoritist* thing, even though that wasn't a word.

Gulls fought loudly, squawking in outrage over what was left of an ice cream cone. I dodged a frisbee as the next wave washed by, swirling around my ankles. The surf was calmer than it was yesterday. Despite the crowd, it was paradise, except not because Will wasn't with me.

"Dude, it's been, like, two hours. Calm down," I muttered to myself.

A small bodyboard bumped my calf, and I scooped it up to return it to a little girl who'd tumbled off but seemed totally unfazed. I was happy to stay on land today, though the swirling waves were refreshing as they washed by and retreated.

Besides, I'd promised Will I wouldn't swim without him. Because he said he'd "fret" about me all through the meeting.

The hills are alivvvvvve!

Fuck, I was being such a weirdo, but I didn't care. It was hard to believe that everything Will and I had done had actually happened and wasn't just one of my fever-dream fantasies. Thinking now about him sucking my cock was—

Dangerous. This was a family show here at the beach. No thinking about cock sucking or kissing or the amazing feeling of being held down by Will's weight as he'd fucked my mouth…

Nope! Think of the singing nun again!

I dug my toes into the sand, my feet disappearing. Maybe it was a good idea to call my parents. That would definitely get my mind off sex and Will and how even though we'd agreed this was a friends-with-benefits situation… This was way more, right?

That wasn't all in my head. It couldn't be. The connection between us was stronger than it had ever been. I'd loved him for years, and I'd been right all along. He was the one. We fit together. I wasn't imagining it or forcing it the way I had with Jared. I was being myself, and Will wanted me.

Before I actually started doing cartwheels or something, I hit my parents' number on my phone. I'd texted them yesterday on Christmas, but it would be good to talk. They'd been disappointed about the breakup with Jared, but now I had good news.

Oh shit, what time was it in Florida? And wait, I couldn't tell my folks I was screwing Will. I couldn't say a word until we were actually a couple, and I had to stop assuming we would be. It had only been twenty-four hours since we'd first kissed, even though that seemed impossible.

The phone was ringing, so I couldn't hang up, but seriously, what time was it back home? I was trying to do the math when my father gruffly said hello.

"Hey, Dad. Sorry, did I wake you?" Ugh. Great way to start the conversation.

He grunted. "What's wrong?"

"Nothing! I just wanted to say merry Christmas. I guess Christmas Day is over."

"It's…four-thirty."

Shit, so it was definitely way too early. "Sorry. Go back to bed." It had to be thirteen hours behind in Florida.

He said, "I'm up now. Hold on." He mumbled something, and I realized he was talking to my mom—probably telling her everything was fine and to go back to sleep. There was a soft slapping sound that had to be his flip-flops, which had become his slippers of choice in Florida.

The long, low metallic noise of the patio door sliding open followed. I said, "It's warm enough to sit outside so early?"

"I've got my robe. Besides, we're having a winter heat wave. The humidity is ridiculous. At least I can sit by the pool thanks to global warming."

I could imagine him on the flagstone patio in a Costco deck chair in the darkness with his legs crossed and the small in-ground pool lit from under the water. There was a remote control that could change the colors of the lights—red, blue, green, purple—but Dad always kept it on plain white.

He asked, "What's the weather like there?" His voice was familiar and sharp. His questions usually sounded like a cross-examination even when I knew he didn't mean it that way.

"Hot and sunny." I smiled as a wave surged up to my knees as I walked along the shore. "Perfect beach weather. It's beautiful here. The Indian Ocean is incredible. Have you ever seen it?" I took in the endless blue again, breathing the sea air deeply.

"No, I don't think so. You'll have to send us some pictures."

"Sure! I will." I held the phone closer to my ear as I passed a group of teenagers playing hip-hop on wireless speakers.

"You talk to Jared?"

For a second, I thought I heard him wrong. "Um, no. We broke up, remember?"

He sighed. "Well, you argued. Surely you're not giving up on your relationship so easily. The holidays can bring people back together."

"Jared's not into Christmas." I thought of the tree abandoned in the yard. "Besides, I'm all the way over here. I'm not—Jared and I aren't getting back together anyway. We're not right for each other."

"Pity. We liked him. How's Zoe?"

"Good. Engaged to a nurse."

His voice rose in surprise. "A nurse? I didn't realize Zoe liked girls."

"His name's Peter. Men can be nurses too."

Dad laughed. "I suppose they can. Well, that's good for Zoe, then."

"Yeah, I'm not getting back together with her either."

"Of course not. Where are you going to live when you get back?"

"I don't know yet."

He sighed again. "You'd better figure it out soon."

I laughed half-heartedly. "Yeah, I will. It's Christmas. It's fine."

"What's the vacancy rate in Albany now?"

"I don't know."

As my dad talked about leases and how renting long-term was throwing money away, I reached the end of the beach. I turned back, but now the sun on the water glared too much, even with my sunglasses and cap. Kids shrieked, and the number of people around suddenly got to me. I headed up to the closest exit.

The sand was burning in the late-afternoon sun, and I hurried to the grassy area beyond the boardwalk, trying not to yelp. Still holding my flip-flops, I dragged my feet over the shorn grass to dry them as I swatted at a persistent fly. Considering how dry Perth was, their grass was surprisingly green even if it was a strange, spongy texture.

I said, "Yeah, I definitely want to buy something at some point."

"That really would be wise. When we were your age, we had a house and car and two kids already."

"I have a car." Sure, it was a beater that was in the shop after breaking down on the side of a deserted country road, but Dad didn't have to know that. It was fine. And, yeah, Will had to rescue me, but it had all worked out.

Still, I shifted uncomfortably and started pacing. I should have been able to buy a newer car. I added, "Things are different now than when you and Mom were my age."

"True. Young people don't want to work anymore."

I inhaled, pressing my lips together to stop from blurting something defensive. "It's not that people don't want to work. It's that wages are below the poverty line, and so many people have student loans they can never pay off, and—"

"You don't have loans."

"I know. I'm really lucky you guys paid my tuition. I'm just saying in general, it's not easy these days. It took me a long time to find a steady job where I could at least make a decent living." I could admit I hadn't tried as hard as I could have out of college. I'd felt…lost.

But now I had a good job, and maybe Will and I could actually make it work. I exhaled, remembering his kisses.

"Are you paying rent?"

Blinking, I focused on my dad's voice. "Sorry, can you say that again?"

"Are you paying Will rent while you stay with him?"

"Oh. I… I hadn't thought about it. I was only there one night before we got on a plane."

"Yes, well, you need to think about it, Michael. No one likes a freeload-er."

I paced near one of the tall pines, its long, strange needles—leaves?—looking like dried snakes under my feet. "His boss is paying for this trip. I'm his plus-one."

He sounded dubious. "Pretty generous boss to bring along her employ-ee's pal."

"Yeah. She's really generous." Of course Dad didn't have to know she'd brought me along because she thought Will and I were a couple.

But maybe we are now? Maybe it's not a lie.

The buzz of happiness at the thought of Will being my boyfriend—my *partner*—for real evaporated as my dad said, "We don't want to see you floundering again. You were finally settled with Jared. You know, your brother—"

"Dad, I've got to go. It's getting close to dinner time. I should get changed." I didn't even know what we were doing for dinner. It didn't matter. "Tell Mom merry Christmas. Enjoy the heat wave. Or not since global warming sucks." Sweat dampened my forehead under the brim of my cap.

"Merry Christmas to you and Will. Just think about what I said, son. Take care."

We hung up, and my dad would be delighted to know I fucking couldn't think about anything else.

Will had said I could stay with him, but it was probably a bad idea, wasn't it? I'd rushed and forced it with Jared. I couldn't risk messing this up with Will. Whatever *this* actually was. God, maybe I was kidding myself. Was I reading too much into it?

I had to laugh thinking of the things we'd done in the past how-ever-many hours since yesterday. It was a blur of nakedness and coming more times than should be legal. But we'd made an agreement. He was curious, and I was helping him figure out if he liked fucking guys.

The results seemed pretty conclusive, but I had to remember that didn't mean he felt the same way about me. How could he? It hadn't been long enough, right? Orgasms didn't mean he'd ever love me back.

"I just feel so sorry for him."

Jared's voice filled my head as I circled the park, walking blindly, and for a horrible moment, I thought I'd puke all over the grass. Will wasn't Jared. But even though Jared and I hadn't been right for each other at all, the humiliating truth was that I hadn't realized Jared had been wanting to dump me for *months*.

Even if I'd known deep down we didn't fit, I'd been clueless. I'd still been trying so pathetically hard.

My skin prickled, sweat dripping down my spine as I relived standing in the doorway clutching that stupidly huge Christmas tree and hearing Jared complain about having to wait to break up with me.

"Will isn't Jared," I whispered under my breath. Holy shit, I was going to start crying in a second.

"You right, mate?" a woman asked, peering up at me from her yoga mat and shielding her eyes from the sun. She sat cross-legged with her flexed feet up on her knees.

"Uh-huh!" It was funny how Australians seemed to leave out the "all" in "all right." I tried to smile. "I'm good. Thanks." I probably looked sick and desperate and like I was about to star in a true crime story.

I had to get my shit together. Phone gripped in one hand and flip-flops in the other, I escaped her concerned squint and found a spot on the low concrete wall running along the boardwalk.

Facing the ocean, I let my feet dangle above the sand not far below, trying to recapture the joyous peace I'd felt before the phone call.

Okay. I had to be proactive. I could do this. I was not going to fuck up my friendship with Will. I had to do something productive. The question was, what? Sitting around feeling sorry for myself was definitely not productive.

Feet jiggling, I ran through possibilities before settling on apartment hunting. There! That was productive. Will had said I could stay with him, but moving in with Jared too soon had been a huge mistake. Will wasn't Jared, but it still made sense to find my own place. The last thing I wanted to be was a freeloader.

I hooked my sunglasses on the neck of my tee and scrolled the rental listings in Albany. It was weird to be doing it in the sunshine on the other side of the world. Reality had burst in and demanded a seat at the table. That's what I got for calling my parents.

"Hey, you," a familiar voice said right in my ear—and I jerked so violently I almost fell off the wall.

"Jesus!" I shouted as Will wrapped a strong arm around my chest and pulled me back. I found my feet on the boardwalk, and we both laughed.

"What are you so engrossed in?" Will asked. He propped his sunglasses on his head. He'd rolled the sleeves of his navy button-up shirt to his elbows and wore long shorts and loafers without socks. Business casual in eighty-five-degree temps.

"Just looking at apartments back home. How was the meeting with Angela?"

Will blinked, opening and closing his mouth. "It was fine."

"Are you sure?" Another knot of worry tightened in my stomach. "Is there a problem with the pitch or something?"

He shook his head. "No, it went to plan. We have our first meeting tomorrow morning. What was that about apartments?"

"I'm just looking to see if there's anything decent open for January."

"You're staying at mine, though. Unless…you don't want to?"

"It's not that. I just don't want to be a freeloader, you know? Although I'll pay rent, obviously. I should have said that before."

His brows met. "I'm not concerned about money. What's this about?" Rocking back on his heels, he shoved his hands in his pockets, his shoulders hunching.

"Nothing." I put my phone away. "Don't worry about it. What are we doing for dinner? I'm not sure if we're meeting up with the Barkers, or…?"

A family brushed past us on the boardwalk, an inflatable penguin almost smacking Will in the head. But he didn't crack a smile like he usually would. "Did something happen this afternoon? I thought we were…" He motioned between us. "Are you cross with me?"

I laughed genuinely, affection warming my chest. "No, I'm not 'cross.' Or any other cute words." I held out my hand. "Come on, let's go back."

But Will didn't take my hand. "Are you going to ghost me again?"

Dropping my arm, I struggled to inhale. I had to swallow hard. "Of course not!" As soon as I said it, guilt slammed me. I had no right to act like it was something I'd never done.

We stood on the boardwalk staring at each other as sunburned beachgoers shuffled by, the crowd starting to thin. The hurt shining in Will's eyes might as well have been a flashing neon billboard.

I'd owed him an explanation that first weekend at the glamping retreat—not to mention that I should never have ghosted him.

Because that's what I did even if I hadn't wanted to admit it. "I'm sorry," I said hoarsely. "I did ghost you. I didn't mean to, but—" Raising my hands, I shook my head. "No. It doesn't matter what I meant to do. The bottom line is that I stopped talking to you. I tried to pretend you didn't exist most of the time. Then I'd break down and look at your Facebook or Insta." I shook my head again, trying to find the right words.

"You didn't want me to exist?" Will asked. I could barely hear him, the words sounded like they were being dragged across a desert.

"No!" I reached for him, but he stepped back. I dropped my hands. "I'm doing this all wrong. What else is new?" Closing my eyes, I took a deep breath—maybe the deepest breath ever. Down to my soul. I opened my eyes and finally said it out loud.

"I loved you." *Loved, loves, will love.*

Will stared at me for the longest few seconds of my life. Then his brows met. "I loved you too. You're my best friend."

Oh, wow. He didn't get what I was saying. Okay. Another deep, soul-fortifying breath. In and out. My voice sounded far away. "I was *in* love with you. I still am. I love you. Like, right now. I'm in love with you."

Was it making sense? Will was still staring at me, his lips parted and his body completely frozen. So I kept talking.

"I've been in love with you for years. Since I was still with Zoe, honestly. But I knew it was never going to happen. At least, that's what I thought. And I just—I had to get over you. I was…wallowing. I think that's the right word?"

Will still stared like a statue, his eyes wide. I added, "You'd started seeing Kara, and I couldn't just keep wanting you uselessly."

"*Kara?* We barely dated a month. It was great to start, but it went downhill after a week. I would have ended it then, but I felt guilty and limped along for a while more. But even if I'd been mad about her, you got together with Jared and I was, what? Out of sight, out of mind?"

"*Never.* Jesus, I thought about you all the time. I ordered myself to face reality. It was like a mantra: I had to grow the fuck up and move on. I met Jared, and I thought if I kept my distance from you, I could get over you, and then we could go back to being best friends."

"Get over me," Will whispered.

God, was I making this all worse? I had no fucking clue. "Yeah, but I couldn't. I really tried, and then weeks went by, and then months, and I kept telling myself I just needed a little more time. Another week, and then we could hang out and watch a game or binge the latest murder show, and I'd be fine. I was going to make it work with Jared, and I'd stop loving you."

"You never said a word." He looked dazed. An ice cream vendor rode by with a freezer on the front of her bike, dinging her bell. Will didn't even blink.

"I couldn't." I shook my head, tears burning behind my eyes. "I was afraid you wouldn't want to be friends anymore."

He jolted like I'd slapped him. His voice rose. "Instead, you stopped being friends with me? How was that better?"

"It wasn't." I grabbed my Mets cap off my head and squeezed the brim down, needing something to break even if it would only bend. "I was a coward. And it got harder and harder to face that as time passed. To face you."

I raised my head to meet his eyes. "I missed you so fucking much. I told myself you were better off without me. I never thought in a million, billion years that you could ever want me the same way. You never said…"

"Because I didn't know!" Will practically shouted. His chest rose and fell, his breath shallow. He was definitely unfrozen now. "I didn't know that I'm…" His voice broke, and I reached for him again, but he raised his hands. I fell back.

After clearing his throat, Will asked, "Do you remember how my mum has a philosophy about taking leaps in life? Taking chances." At my nod, he added, "I think I've wanted to take this leap for ages, but I didn't know how." He squared his shoulders. "I'm bisexual. It's not just pretend, or for the weekend, or only the holidays. It's not a lark. It's who I am."

Not able to stop a smile, I wanted to twirl again—full *Sound of Music* vibes. "Thank you for telling me." I wanted to throw my arms around him, but I managed to stay put. I nodded encouragingly.

"I'd never fancied a bloke before. And when I started to, it wasn't anyone in particular. It was…just for me. Getting off alone. Fantasizing. But when you rang that night, and I picked you up on the road…"

I could barely breathe. My heart was going to actually explode this time. Or my head. Maybe both.

"Hey!" Olivia approached with a wave as she glanced up from her phone, and yep—my head exploded.

Chapter Nineteen

Will

OLIVIA ASKED, "ARE you guys going swimming? I want to get in quickly before the lifeguards go home. My hair's shit today anyway. Can you watch my stuff? Makayla's too sunburned from yesterday. I *told* her to put on more sunscreen after she got out of the water. She never listens to me."

Michael and I only stared at her, both of us apparently at a loss for words. My mind was a complete tangle.

She blinked, straightening her tote bag on her shoulder. "Shit, sorry. I'm interrupting."

"It's fine," I lied, managing to access my reserves of politeness.

Olivia lifted her hands. "You're obviously fighting."

Was that what we were doing? I honestly didn't know at this point.

With every ounce of strength, I tapped into that politeness. Mum and Dad would have been proud. "Don't be silly. We're happy to watch your things while you have a swim." I glanced at Michael, and he nodded. It wasn't Olivia's fault we were…

Confessing love to each other? Well, Michael had confessed. He'd said he was in love with me.

Michael was *in love with me.*

As we made our way through the thinning crowd, my loafers filled with sand until I had to stop and carry them. I fought to comprehend exactly what was happening.

My heart skipped erratically. A seismic shift was occurring, yet I felt as though I was hovering over the ground, watching cracks and fissures fan out from the epicenter.

Michael was in love with me.

Michael had been in love with me for years? *Years?* Was I completely daft? Mum had even said she'd suspected it! I'd laughed it off. I'd only thought about my own burgeoning curiosity about men and my secret wanking material. Michael had ghosted me, and I'd only considered my own pain, not his.

We had to sort this out, but for the moment, Olivia was there. Perhaps it was fortuitous timing, and Michael and I both needed to gather our thoughts.

Michael, who was in love with me.

Olivia was saying something I'd missed. Michael laughed weakly, not looking at me. She said, "Just don't break up—Mom'll be heartbroken. She totally ships you guys."

I tried to smile. I had to say something, and I couldn't talk about Michael and breaking up—those two words made me feel nauseous. So I said, "Angela does seem to get quite invested in queer relationships."

Olivia smiled ruefully and tucked her long hair—which looked smooth and lovely and not shit at all to my eyes—behind her ears. "She can be so cringe, I know. But she means well. My uncle was gay, and it was a massive family drama back in the day. He died before I was born."

"Oh. I'm sorry to hear that," I said. In all the office chatter about Angela, I'd never heard this mentioned.

"It's okay." Olivia pulled a face. "Not that it wasn't sad, obviously. He had AIDS. It was horrible. It was way different in the nineties, you know? Tons of people died."

Michael and I nodded.

"My grandpa sucked. He kicked out Uncle Andrew when Mom was just a kid. She always felt bad that she'd never said anything to defend him, but she was, like, eight. Years later, Uncle Andrew was sick, and he asked for help. Grandpa actually said no. Can you imagine?" She stopped on an empty area of sand near one of the red and yellow flags and unfurled her towel. "Here's good. You want to sit on my towel?"

We sat, and I asked, "What about your grandmother?"

Olivia took off her sunglasses and rolled her eyes. "One of those stereotypical white Southern ladies who never said shit to her husband. That house was a patriarchy, that's for sure. But Mom was like, fuck this. She moved out and worked two jobs while she looked after Uncle Andrew. Dad moved in to help as well. They were still teenagers and not married yet, which was a huge scandal. So ridiculous."

"Wow," Michael said. "She inherited the company, though?"

Olivia tugged her striped sundress over her head and rolled it neatly before straightening the straps on her bikini. "Yeah. Grandpa disowned her when she left, but he eventually put her back in the will. I think it was after Mom and Dad adopted me from Korea. I guess Grandma and Grandpa couldn't resist the lure of a baby."

She shrugged. "They sucked in a lot of ways, but they had good sides too. Aside from being insanely rich, I mean. I dunno. I couldn't totally write them off. Mom couldn't either."

"I get it," Michael said quietly. "It's hard not to love your family."

"They did eventually say they were wrong about Uncle Andrew. I mean, he was dead, so it didn't do him a lot of good. At least Grandpa gave a shit-ton of money to LGBTQ-plus charities and stuff. Mom does too. It wasn't her fault that they turned their backs on him, but she really tries to make up for it now."

"She's very generous," I agreed.

"Anyway, I'm going in. You guys are cool here?"

We nodded, barely looking at each other. I watched Olivia navigate the shore break. There were still a fair number of people in the water, but her bright orange and red bikini made her easy to spot.

Michael and I sat watching, our shoulders only inches apart. I hugged my knees to my chest. I hadn't expected any of what Olivia had divulged about Angela and her brother. For long minutes, we were silent.

"Imagine your parents throwing you out like that," Michael finally said quietly. "Not even helping when you were dying. My folks can be really frustrating and distant, but I'm lucky to have them. I'm so glad Andrew had Angela."

"Me too."

We fell silent again. There was so much to say, but it seemed we both needed to catch our breath. Perhaps it should have been awkward, but... It wasn't. We'd known each other too many years.

The sun was lower in the sky, feeling close overhead as it began its slow descent to the horizon. There were still distant sounds of laughter and the steady heartbeat of the tide. A lifeguard slowly patrolled the shore, announcing on a megaphone that the tower would be closing soon.

"I'm sorry I left you alone," Michael whispered. The sun's caramel light reflected in his glistening eyes.

The air punched out of my lungs as I took his face in my hands. "I forgive you." I swiped his tears with my thumbs.

A sob escaped him, and he threw his arms around me, almost vaulting into my lap. I held him close, my throat too thick to speak.

Michael was in love with me—and I was in love with him.

"How was I so blind?" I eventually murmured, stroking a hand over Michael's hair. His breath was warm on my tear-damp neck.

He raised his head, sniffing loudly. "I guess I hid it well."

"My mum figured it out, so not that well. How did I not see it? How did I not realize I felt the same? What a bloody numpty I am."

Adam's apple bobbing, Michael sat back a few inches. Our knees bumped on the towel where we faced each other with legs bent to the side, and I ran my palm over his calf, needing to touch him.

Michael said solemnly, "You don't have to say that. Not that I don't—obviously I want you to love me. To be in love with me." He sniffed again and cleared his throat. "But we only kissed and stuff for the first time yesterday. Which is unreal. It's like Christmas had more than twenty-four hours. It seems like we've been hooking up for way longer."

"It does. Maybe it's the time change. We had Christmas Day here in the sun, and then had it all over again back in Eastern Time. In our hearts. That makes absolutely no sense whatsoever."

I loved to see the dimple in Michael's flushed cheek. His eyes were red-rimmed from crying, and he sniffed noisily, swiping his hand across his nose, and I'd never been so in love before. Not ever.

"I love you," I said with complete confidence. "It's not too soon. I'm not experimenting. I want you, and I'm in love with you. All those years, I was a fool."

"You weren't." Michael leaned in and caught my mouth in a sweet kiss. "You just didn't have all the information yet."

I chuckled. "I suppose not. I was rather slow on the uptake." I ran my thumb back and forth over the swell of his warm calf. "I always hated how people perceived me as such a player. It had been wonderful with Amelia, and I kept trying to recapture that. But none of the women I dated compared to her—or you. You were with Zoe, and maybe that's why I never thought of you that way? I'm not sure. All I knew was that you were my favorite person. Then you disappeared with no warning, no explanation—nothing. You were my best friend, and we spoke almost every day, at least in texts, and then there was *nothing*. Which is what I felt like."

Michael made a plaintive sound of distress, his eyes shining with emotion. "I'm so sorry. It was all about me. I was selfish. I told myself you were happy with Kara. I couldn't tell my straight best friend I was in love with him. I imagined how horribly nice you'd have been about it. No, not nice—*kind*. You'd have been so understanding and felt sorry for me. It was torture. It hurt too much to be near you. Then it killed me to be away from you. But I convinced myself we were both better off."

"Meanwhile, I discovered gay porn and was desperately wanking to men and pretending it wasn't about you."

He exhaled sharply, his gaze flicking between my eyes and my mouth. He licked his lips. "I guess we make a good pair, huh?" He cupped my cheek, his fingers gentle against my rough stubble.

"We do. And we are, yes? A couple? Officially?"

Michael grinned before kissing me soundly. "We are," he mumbled against my lips before kissing me again and pulling back. I followed, nuzzling his jaw, leaning against him, trying to ease him back onto the towel.

Laughing softly, he stopped me with a firm palm on my chest. "This is a family show, remember?"

Blinking, I gazed around at the groups of people on the beach of all ages, some strolling the shore as the sun sank, others watching the sky blaze orange from their picnic blankets, still others splashing and playing as the lifeguards pulled up the flags, gathering their equipment and packing it away.

We disentangled ourselves, laughing as we straightened any clothing that had become askew. I lifted my hand over my eyes, searching for Olivia and finding her chatting with a young man in waist-deep water just beyond the shore break. The surf was calmer than it had been the day before.

With our arms around each other's backs, Michael and I watched the sunset. Michael played idly with the ends of my hair, rubbing the fuzzy, shorn area on the back of my neck and sending flickers down my spine.

"Why did you ring me that night?" I asked. "I suppose it was breaking up with Jared. Otherwise, you'd have called him."

Michael shuddered. "God, I'm so glad he dumped me. I was in so much denial." He rubbed my neck slowly. "I knew I could rely on you even though you couldn't rely on me. I honestly didn't expect you to pick me up, but I knew you'd understand why I was freaking out on the side of the road replaying every true crime story that took place in the woods. Even though I ghosted you, I knew when I needed help, you'd answer. At least, I'd prayed you would. I didn't deserve it, but you answered."

"I thought it had to be a pocket dial." I squeezed his shoulders. "It was so bloody good to hear your voice again." He opened his mouth, and I lifted my other hand to his lips. "I know you're sorry, and I forgive you. I've buggered up plenty of times in my life. Let's leave it all in the past."

He blew out a shaky breath. "Deal."

After kissing him softly, I nodded to the golden-orange sky, the sun reflecting on the water as it sank. "Time to leap into the future. Mum will be proud."

His hand was a comforting warm weight on my neck. "You're going to tell your parents? About being bi? About us?"

"Of course. Mum will be chuffed to bits that she was right."

"Glad to hear it." A fly buzzed around us, and he swatted it.

I swatted at it as well. "That's one thing about an Aussie Christmas I could do without—all the wee beasties."

Michael laughed. "The what?"

"Beasties. Insects. Not to mention the sharks, snakes, and crocodiles. And spiders! Kangaroos can be quite dangerous too, I understand. Everything's out to get you in Australia."

"Mmm." Michael's gaze dropped slowly over my body and back up. I could almost feel his gaze like a caress. "I can't blame them for being out to get you."

He ran his hand slowly down my back. I gasped softly as he slipped his fingers under the hem of my shirt, teasing the sensitive skin below my waistband.

Michael circled the dimple at the top of my arse and nuzzled under my ear, whispering, "We beasties can't resist you."

"Naw. You're too bonnie to be a beastie, lad," I said, thickening my accent.

He laughed, shaking lightly against me. "God, you're sexy when you go ultra Scottish. Not that you're not sexy all the time." He inched back, biting his lip. "'Bonnie' means pretty, right?"

"Aye." I traced his mouth with my finger. "You're beautiful."

He scoffed. "I mean, I wouldn't go that far. I'm no supermodel, but thank you."

"I mean it. It's not about being a supermodel—though you sell yourself short. There are a million attractive people in the world. Millions. But I don't want to actually be with them. I need to really care about the person."

Michael nodded. "I get it. I think there's a term for that on the asexual spectrum."

I frowned. "I like sex, though. I mean, Christ, if wanking was an Olympic sport…"

He laughed. "That's why it's a whole spectrum. I think it's demisexual when you really only want sex with other people if you're in love with them. Like with Amelia. Although I'm sure there's not just one way people experience being demi or anything else. There are a bunch of labels on the ace spectrum."

"Do I have to choose one?" My mind already felt as though it had run a marathon.

Michael smiled. "Nope. You don't have to do anything. There's no right or wrong way."

I exhaled in relief. "Okay. I'm bisexual. That's all I need for now." Saying it aloud gave me a thrill. "I'm bisexual," I repeated.

"You are." He grinned. "So am I. Just a couple of bi guys watching the sunset."

The horizon was now painted a deep orange-tinged pink as the sun disappeared. "You know, it really was different with Amelia than any other woman I dated. I wanted her all the time."

Michael licked his lips. "And with me?"

"Yes." The word rasped from my throat without hesitation. "All the bloody time. From the moment I saw you again on the side of that road. It was the same on one hand—familiar and easy the way it always had been. But something had changed. I wanted you. I think it was you I'd been wanting all along. It was you I'd been missing like a limb, so I watched men fucking, and I touched myself, wishing I was with you."

Michael gulped as he swept his fingertips back and forth across my lower back under my shorts. "If I'd known, I would have begged you to fuck me over the hood of my crappy car."

I laughed as my face blushed hot. "Naughty!"

With a sly smile, he dipped his fingers lower, barely touching me and still north of my arse crack but lighting my nerves on fire, my cock swelling. I glanced about guiltily, but there was no one nearby, and the sunset seemed to have everyone else's attention.

"Do you want me to fuck you like that?" I whispered. "Not over the hood of your car, but…"

He sucked in a shallow breath. "Yes."

"Have you thought about it?" My throat was dry. We were in public, but I couldn't stop myself from asking.

"Your cock in my ass? Oh, yeah." His hand was pressed flat on my lower back now, our skin damp. "I've thought about it a million times. Jerked off imagining you holding me down."

Lust flared red hot. "Christ," I muttered, the thought of Michael taking me, begging me for more was almost too much.

"I know you'll take care of me. I won't have to worry."

"You won't," I agreed, stroking his hair.

"I want you on top of me, inside me, giving it to me hard—"

We kissed, moaning into each other's mouths, our tongues meeting and—

"*Ahem.*" Olivia said, "Glad to see you guys made up, but can I have my towel?"

Chapter Twenty

Michael

IT WAS ONLY ten minutes back to the hotel, but it was an *eternity*. Olivia told us about the cute guy she'd met and given her number to while we smiled and nodded and tried not to say "fuck it!" and get arrested for public indecency.

Because we were going to get extremely indecent.

Will was bi, and most importantly, he *loved me back*. It was twilight, but it felt like the sun was lighting me up from the inside. Full-on twirling in my heart. These hills were *alive*.

We passed the huge Christmas tree in the lobby, where a jazzy version of "Joy to the World" played. I was about to start dancing to instrumental jazz if we didn't get back to our room.

Olivia was still talking as we rode the elevator. I watched the numbers tick up. It was only a small boutique hotel, and the doors slid open mercifully soon.

"So what do you guys think?" Olivia asked.

We'd already rushed out into the hallway, and I had nothing. Will looked at me with a hint of panic before saying, "Uh…"

She smirked. "Bless your hearts. I'll tell Mom and Dad you're doing your own thing for dinner. Bye!"

Safely behind our locked door with the privacy tag hanging on the knob, I laughed as Will flipped on the lamp beside the bed. Night had settled in beyond the windows. We stared at each other. Now that we could tear each other's clothes off, we weirdly hesitated.

Will said, "I found an open chemist after my meeting."

Was my brain fried? "Huh?"

"A drugstore."

"Oh! Oh. That's good."

He took off his loafers and tucked them under a chair where a paper bag sat. He dumped the contents onto the smooth bedspread: a bottle of lube, box of condoms, and a pack of mint gum.

Will picked up the gum. "That's for the plane ride home. I hate it when my ears pop."

"Me too."

Fiddling with the gum, he asked, "Do we need condoms? I haven't been with anyone in quite a while. I've been tested since at my physical."

"I've been tested too, and I never actually had sex with Jared without a condom. He doesn't like jizz."

"Oh. Right." Will nodded.

"Which is fine! To each their own, blah, blah, blah. I mean, we've been swallowing each other's cum, but the risk profile for oral is different. I'm good either way with condoms."

Will seemed to contemplate it, turning the thin gum package over and over. "So, you'd be open to having sex without them?"

"Wide open." I raised an eyebrow, and Will laughed, ducking his head. Was he blushing? I loved everything about this. "Seriously, though—I know you're new to this. We can totally use condoms, or we can keep doing other things. Don't need to rush."

He nodded. "But if I wanted to?"

"Um, hell yeah." I hesitated. "It can get messy. Just to make sure we're on the same page, do you want to fuck me without a condom?"

"Yes," he said in that low burr that made me hot all over.

Every available drop of blood flooded south to my dick. "You want to come inside me?"

"Oh, good Christ," he muttered as we lunged at each other.

Through laughter and kisses, it took longer than I wanted to get naked, but finally we made it. I shoved the covers down to the foot of the bed and stretched out on my back. With Will's dark eyes locked on me, I spread my legs and jerked my erection. He knelt between my knees with his knuckles white on the bottle of lube.

"You still down with this?" I asked, stroking myself slowly. "I want it to be good for you."

He smiled tenderly and pressed a kiss to my raised knee, his stubble scratchy. "Anything with you is good."

"Anything, huh?" I rubbed his hard dick with my foot. "What if I had a foot fetish?"

He laughed. "You can suck my toes to your heart's content, darling."

My chest swelled. "Or you could just call me sweet names. Maybe *that's* my kink."

"As opposed to?" Will lifted his brows. "Is there something you're not telling me, sweetheart?"

"Oh god, that sounds good."

He grinned. "You like it, my precious? Wait, that sounds like Gollum."

I sputtered, "Gollum is definitely not my kink!"

"So, is there something else that is?"

Despite myself, I could feel heat creeping up my face. "Just this." Why was I hesitating? Liking a rough pounding wasn't exactly an extreme kink, and Will definitely seemed into it.

"I'm going to have to start guessing outside the box." He frowned. "Do you want me to piss on you or something?"

Laughing, I shook my head. "No golden showers. Not my thing."

"All right. Do I need to google? Because I admit, I don't have much out-of-the-box experience."

"So to speak."

We burst out laughing, and I sat up, the need to touch my dick satisfied for the moment. We had all night, and I loved being like this with him. Naked and smiling and easy.

"No, not much experience outside the—what was that stupid name for it? *Vajayjay.*"

"My mom still says 'hoo-haw,' I think."

"I'm sure my mum still says 'fanny,' but it hasn't come up in conversation for some time. When I was a kid, my mates would say 'snatch' and 'muff.' 'Penis flytrap' was a personal favorite."

"Oh my god! That's amazing."

Somehow, we spent the next who-knew-how-long sitting together on the bed and listing off the most ridiculous names for genitalia. My sides hurt from laughing as Will rhymed off UK slang for a cock, beginning with "knob" and finishing with "tadger."

As we caught our breath, I ran my fingers through his chest hair. "Honestly, American imagination pales in comparison to the UK."

"Oh, I don't know." He ran his fingertip down my shaft from the head and back up again. "You said you imagined me while you got off."

I shivered. "Uh-huh."

"And you imagined me fucking you? Hard?" He watched me intensely, still lightly tracing the length of my dick.

"Yeah, I guess my biggest fantasy has always been bottoming. It's been a few years. Jared didn't like topping, and I do, so it was fine that way."

"'Fine' isn't exactly a ringing endorsement, honeybun."

I smiled. "I know. Honestly, though—I'm good with whatever. We can experiment."

"But what you'd like right now is to be fucked hard?"

I couldn't hold in a little moan. "I love hearing you say that. And yeah. Like, rough and overpowered, but not anything extreme. Vanilla dom/sub stuff if that makes sense?"

"Mmm." Will dragged his finger up my belly, making it quiver. "It makes perfect sense."

Without warning, he shoved me flat on my back and pressed me into the mattress, heavy and muscled and *god*. He watched me carefully. "Do you like this, sugarplum?"

My throat was way too dry to talk or laugh at the silly name. I nodded.

He ran his hands down my arms and took my wrists, holding them over my head. "Maybe something like this?"

Another nod. My dick throbbed against Will's stomach.

Still holding down my wrists, he pushed his knee between my legs, and I eagerly spread them wide. He was hard too, and I was in danger of coming before he got anywhere near my ass.

Will asked, "Is it roughness or being held down?"

"Yes!" I gasped hoarsely.

A light brightened his beautiful face. "Both, then? All right. Like this? Or on your hands and knees? Or bent over something like the desk?"

All I could moan was, "*Yes*," and we laughed.

"Keep your hands there," he ordered before sliding back to kneel between my legs again. He picked up the lube and squeezed a glob onto his palm before looking at me. "Haven't moved. Good boy."

I moaned, keeping my hands high over my head. "Use your middle finger first." I rounded my back, giving him better access to my ass. "Just stick it in."

Will laughed. "Such sweet talk from my lover. Patience, pumpkin." He circled my hole with his slick fingertip, using his long middle finger as I suggested. "If it's been a few years, you'll be tight, won't you?"

My breath caught. "Yes. But I can take it. Please."

He pushed past my rim, the lube doing its job as his finger stretched me. I bore down eagerly, squeezing as his whole finger filled me. Will watched where it disappeared inside me, his chest rising and falling faster as he explored.

"Crook your finger. No, the other way, like—" Gasping, I arched my back and clutched at the sheets, keeping my hands in place. "Right there. You got it."

I wasn't sure if I'd ever talked so much during sex aside from the standard encouragement. I'd always enjoyed all kinds of sex with all kinds of people, but I couldn't remember ever feeling this free.

As Will rubbed my gland, I took my cock in hand and stroked, my other fingers circling my nipple. I didn't even think about the fact that I'd lowered my hands before Will pulled out his finger and jerked my wrists over my head again.

"Oh, god, *yes*." I bucked my hips up as we kissed desperately. "Fuck me, Will," I groaned into his mouth.

He pulled back, spit wet on his lips. "Pardon?"

"I said, *fuck me, Will*. Get your cock in me." We were closer to the end of the bed, and I grasped for one of the pillows above me with my outstretched hands. I squeezed the feathers tightly, my arms locked over my head. "I'll be good. I promise."

"I know, baby." Will kissed me, our tongues pushing and sliding. He held himself over me, one hand pushing back my sweaty hair. "We should have done this years ago. Why did I ever think I was straight?"

"I wish I knew."

We laughed and kissed until we could hardly breathe, and as Will finally slicked his cock and pushed into me, moments of joy and laughter switched back and forth with grunts and demands.

My legs were as wide as they could go, but I wanted more. Gripping the pillow above me, I hitched my knees higher, lifting my ass. Will groaned, buried all the way inside me, his pubes tickling me. Mouth open, he sucked on my neck.

He muttered, "You feel so good," against my skin. "*You're* so good, sweetheart."

Part of me could have stayed like that all day, or night or whatever time it was, with Will filling me, heavy and *real* on top of me. This wasn't a dream or my imagination. Will was inside, stretching me to the point that it was tough to take without wincing.

But it wasn't enough. I wanted everything. I wanted it to hurt. My muscles were already trembling, and I wanted more.

"Please fuck me," I moaned.

Will lifted his head and took my mouth in a rough kiss. "Tell me if it's too much, love."

The fact that he'd called me that so simply—"*love*"—had tears pricking my eyes. I blinked them back, groaning as he took both my wrists in one hand, squeezing them with his fingers.

He was really holding me down now as he pulled back and thrust deeply, his other hand powerful on my hip to keep me in place. All I could do was gasp and cry out, our skin slapping and the headboard thumping as he fucked me the way I needed.

"*Yes, god, yes,*" I chanted, fighting the urge to throw my head back and close my eyes, letting sensations carry me away. No, I had to watch him.

Sweat dampened his forehead, his face flushed and veins sticking out on his neck. His muscles bunched and strained, and he never tore his eyes from my face. I was spread open and stripped totally bare, the rough sensation of his raw cock pounding me hotter than I'd ever dreamed.

Since I didn't have to think about keeping my hands in place, his fingers like iron around my wrists, I could let go totally and wallow in being helpless.

I knew I wasn't—Will would stop in a heartbeat. But stopping was the last thing I wanted. Will would protect me.

I didn't have to think, or worry, or do anything but take him as he brought me to the edge. As much as I didn't want to stop, my balls were tight, and I needed to come. Pinned by Will, I couldn't touch my cock, and I could only whimper.

That and beg Will. "I need to come. Please." I squeezed my ass around his dick.

Panting, Will looked down at me in the golden light of the bedside lamp. "Are you sure I should let you?"

All I could do now was moan. He was amazing at this already. "Please."

He rocked into me, his movements smoother but still powerful. He dragged his hand from my hip up the side of my thigh. My legs were sweaty behind my bent knees. I squirmed, squeezing around his cock again.

Will sucked in a breath. "Naughty."

"God, please touch me."

He relented—of course he did—and it only took a few strokes of his hand for the pressure to blow, pleasure sweeping through me as I shot onto my stomach. Will was still in me, and I squeezed even harder, jerking with aftershocks.

Gasping my name, he thrust one last time and came deep inside me. Knowing there was nothing between us as he shuddered and emptied brought fresh tears to my eyes. I trusted him, and he trusted me, and I couldn't believe this was real.

Perfectly heavy on top of me, Will nuzzled my hair and eased my arms down. I closed my eyes as he pressed gentle kisses to the insides of my wrists. His cock was still partly inside my tender hole, and I had to clean up, but I couldn't move yet.

Will whispered something I couldn't make out across my cheek—before he inhaled sharply and went rigid. I opened my eyes.

His face pinched in concern as he wiped the tears that had leaked from my eyes. "Did I hurt you?"

"God, no. *No.*" I ran my hands over his shoulders to touch his face. "I promise. It was incredible, baby. It was exactly what I wanted. And more. Thank you." I paused. "Did you like it?"

He grinned. "Did I ever. I'll bugger you senseless morning, noon, and night as long as I'm not truly hurting you."

"You didn't. It was perfect."

"You're sure?" He kissed me softly.

"Positive. Ask Kevin. He'll tell you."

Will went still again. "Who?"

I nodded to the koala ornament hanging from the lamp beside us. "How could you forget our surfing Christmas koala already?"

Laughing, Will flopped onto me, his voice muffled in my neck. "Right, Kevin. Bloody hell. I thought I'd fucked you into insensibility."

"That does sound good though, doesn't it? Give me a few minutes and we can try it."

Will kissed me, a long, slow, deep sweep of his tongue. "Don't you think poor Kevin's seen enough tonight?"

"Good point. Also, I don't think you can get it up again after that."

"Oi!" Will seemed about to say something else but smiled ruefully. "Yeah, no chance in hell. But there's always tomorrow."

"Tomorrow and tomorrow and tomorrow." I punctuated each word with kisses.

"Are you quoting Shakespeare to me?"

"Huh. I don't know. Am I?"

"I think it's *MacBeth*."

"Shouldn't you know? I mean, you're Scottish, FYI."

"Ah dinnae ken."

I groaned. "If you start talking cute Scottish words, you'll definitely have to fuck me again."

"We can coorie doon in the meantime."

I had no clue what it meant, but we laughed and kissed, and I couldn't wait to find out.

Chapter Twenty-One

Will

"ACE! FOUR CARDS."

As I closed the door to our room behind me, I swallowed a flare of disappointment that we weren't alone. Through the screen door to the balcony, Michael, Makayla—who had apparently just laid down an ace—and Olivia sat around the small round table. I'd just have to wait a bit longer to be alone with Michael.

Granted, I'd buggered him over the end of the bed before I'd left in the morning, but I woke each day gagging for him. It hadn't even been a full week yet since we'd first touched, and this feverish, constant need for each other would surely wane.

Not today, though.

"Hiya," I called, tucking my work satchel away beside the desk. I hung my suit jacket in the closet and tugged on my tie as I joined them on the balcony. "What's the game?" I kissed Michael on the head before running my hands across his shoulders. This was innocent enough.

"Strip poker," Makayla said, straightening a stack of cards.

"Er, interesting choice?" I raised an eyebrow dramatically, but they were all still fully dressed, the girls in floral sundresses over their bikinis and Michael in his board shorts and a T-shirt. And obviously Michael wouldn't be playing that game with teenagers.

They'd clearly been swimming, their hair frizzy from having dried in the sun. The table was littered with empty plates, crumpled napkins, and dark brown bottles of Bundaberg ginger beer, which was the best ginger ale I'd ever tasted.

Michael sputtered. "Strip Jack Naked!"

Makayla waved a dismissive hand, her nails glittering with new art that looked to be little lemons. "Same difference."

"Still sounds questionable," I said, giving Michael's shoulders a playful squeeze.

"It's what my grandfather called it! He was really old, okay?" Michael flipped over a card. "Ha! King."

Olivia muttered, "Son of a…" and laid down three cards on top of the king.

I watched them play, idly rubbing Michael's neck. Makayla had the biggest stack of cards, and sure enough, she soon had them all and declared victory.

I quickly said, "We should get ready for dinner!" before anyone could suggest another round.

Makayla picked up her phone. "Wait, I have to show you the pic I got with that lifeguard! You know, the Thor guy."

Olivia sighed. "You have zero chill."

"Great shot!" I said, looking at the picture of Makayla beaming beside Liam Fox, who towered over her and gave a thumbs-up to the camera with a handsome smile.

"Thanks! He was *so* nice. He's gay like you guys—remember that lady at the beach told us? Isn't that cool?"

"Zero. Chill," Olivia muttered as she tapped her phone.

I shared a glance with Michael, and he smiled encouragingly. It was nonsense that my pulse suddenly spiked, but it did as I said, "Actually, I'm bisexual. We're both bi." I nodded to Michael.

Makayla looked stricken and exclaimed, "Oh, sorry!"

"Nothing to be sorry for," I assured her.

I glanced at Olivia, and why was I nervous as to what she might say? I supposed because this was the first time I'd told anyone else. I'd been perceived by colleagues as bi at the retreat, but now it was real—well, it had always been real, but I'd been in deep denial.

Now I was announcing it officially. Which felt damn good.

Olivia thumbed off her phone, declared, "Hot," and added, "See you at dinner," before leading out Makayla.

Exhaling, I kissed Michael as he stood and asked, "Okay?"

"I'm grand."

"How'd the last meeting go?"

"Terrific. We're already discussing remote integration of BRK Sync systems so there'd be no need for a satellite office or anything. You should see Angela in action. She's a force of nature."

"I'm familiar. I'm here in Australia after all. With my best friend turned fake boyfriend but now real boyfriend. Also, I'm really glad she has a thing for mistletoe, or who knows if you would've had the guts to kiss me."

I chuckled, then gave Michael what I hoped was a seductive look. "I wouldn't have been able to wait much longer. Trust me."

"Mmm." He pulled me close, running his hands down over my arse. "Speaking of waiting, it's been a long day without you. I should get in the shower, though. Are you sure I don't need a tie for dinner?"

"Positive. It's 'smart casual.'" You'll be grand in your slacks and button-up shirt. And I'll join you in the shower. I need one."

Michael raised a dubious eyebrow. "You look exactly the same as you did when you left. All businessy and well-ironed." He nuzzled my neck, inhaling forcefully. "You smell good too."

"I'm filthy." I held his hips tightly against mine.

His warm breath tickled my ear. "Sure you don't want to shower with me so you can put your tongue in my ass?"

Lust gripped me. "Well, I did just say I'm filthy."

He bit my earlobe, scraping it with his teeth slowly. "Or maybe you want *my* tongue in your ass?"

"Do I have to choose?"

"Nope. Now let's get in there before we get carried away out here and there actually is stripping."

Under the rainfall shower in the blissfully huge shower stall, I braced a hand on the steamy tile as I stroked myself and pushed back against Michael's face.

I'd watched rimming in porn and had always gotten off on it, and I'd discovered the combination of wanking while Michael licked into me was a quick way to come.

He spread my arse cheeks wide with his hands, licking around my hole with rhythmic movements, pushing right into me every so often as I moaned.

"Christ, your mouth," I mumbled. I could feel him smile, and that was what tipped me over the edge.

Still on his knees, Michael suckled my twitching balls until I squirmed away from too much sensation. I eased him to his feet and pushed our tongues together in a lazy kiss before murmuring, "Your turn."

Michael spread his legs and braced with both hands as I knelt behind and licked and kissed his hole. It was shockingly intimate in a way that even cocksucking wasn't quite—at least to me.

"Wish I had time to fuck you," I muttered against his flesh.

He moaned. "We can just do New Year's Eve tomorrow, right? We'll stay in and fuck and then celebrate in twelve hours when it's midnight at home."

"Tempting, but Angela's surely paid for dinner and the concert already." I turned Michael, urging him to lean back against the tile.

He jolted. "Tiles are still cold." Smiling down at me, he ran his fingers over my wet hair. Water streamed down his body, which was marked with my love bites.

I slowly licked the length of his rigid cock, and he tightened his grip, tugging my hair just slightly.

"Get me off. Please," he full-on whined.

I chuckled. "Perhaps I should make you wait until next year."

Michael's eyes widened, his breath hitching and his hips jerking. Oh, he liked that idea. He liked that idea very much.

I stood and snapped off the water as I said, "We're out of time. I'm afraid you'll just have to wait all night to come, my darling."

A laugh punched out of him as he groaned. "This is cruel and unusual punishment!"

"And you fucking love it."

He grinned. "And I fucking love it."

I kissed him hard. "And I fucking love you." I slapped his bare, wet arse. "Now let's get moving."

DINNER IN THE hotel restaurant, which was still fully decked out in gold, red, and silver Christmas decorations, was fantastic. Between each of the seven courses on the tasting menu, I ran my palm across Michael's thigh beside me under the white tablecloth, inching toward his cock but then retreating while he bit his lip or sighed long-sufferingly.

As usual, Angela did most of the talking, Paul gazing at her affectionately and the girls chiming in from time to time.

As we ate a perfectly marshmallowy Pavlova for dessert, Angela exclaimed, "Don't you just love New Year's? A fresh start for all of us. Say, what does the song actually mean?" she asked me.

I knew she meant "Auld Lang Syne" and tried to think of the best way to summarize it. "It's about reconnecting with old friends. That the people who matter most should never be forgotten, and we should see them again if we can. That's my take at any rate."

Under the table, Michael took my hand and squeezed.

A concert started around ten in the park by Barking Beach, and we had VIP seats near the front in lawn chairs with drink holders. It was a perfect summer night, warm and close but with a cool sea breeze and a blanket of stars visible even with the fairy lights strung around the trees and lampposts. The couple next to us pointed out the stars of the Southern Cross and Seven Sisters.

I didn't recognize the Australian band, but their music was upbeat and fun, and they played plenty of covers of Elton John and the like. We all sang along to "Tiny Dancer," and even Olivia and Makayla somehow knew the words.

Beside me, Michael sipped his beer and idly ran his finger down my bare arm under the short sleeve of my linen shirt. As the band started a new song I didn't recognize, I took his hand and pressed a kiss to his palm.

"'Tis a perfect Hogmanay," I half shouted over the music. "I don't think my new beginnings have ever been quite this new before."

He smiled. "Me either. This is the fresh start to end all fresh starts." He checked his phone. "Only ten minutes to go."

I sat up straighter. "You know, I need to do something to make this a proper fresh start. I'll be back before midnight." I kissed him quickly.

"You'd better be. You're already making me wait—I expect a real kiss!"

I darted out, leaping over the Barkers' feet, glad we were near the end of the row. The boardwalk and beach were crowded with revelers, some people ignoring the extra signs warning that lifeguards weren't on duty at night.

Plugging one ear, I held my phone up to the other and paced a little section of the boardwalk as it rang.

Then Mum's voice echoed down the line. "Happy Hogmanay!" she exclaimed before calling, "It's Will!" to my dad.

"It's almost midnight, I said loudly. I can barely hear you, but I have to tell you something before the new year begins."

"You've about six or seven hours left here, I think," Dad said, their phone now switched to the speaker.

"But I'm here, so I need to make it quick."

"All right, love." Mum chuckled. "What is it? Have the meetings gone well?"

"Aye, but it's no about work."

"Right. We're all ears," Dad said.

I was strangely calm. "I took a leap, Mum. The thing is, you were right—Michael does fancy me. He's in love with me, actually."

After a beat of silence, they exclaimed, "Oh!" in unison.

"And it turns out I'm in love with him. I'm bisexual."

The silence stretched out this time. I lifted the phone from my ear to check that we were still connected. My heart skipped. "Er, hello?"

"We're here, honey," Mum said. "Well, this is quite a leap indeed! You and Michael. How lovely!"

I hadn't expected any other reaction, but it was still a relief. "You think so?"

"Of course," Dad said. "As long as you're happy, we're happy."

"I should've known," Mum mused. "I was right, though, wasn't I? It was time for a leap."

I couldn't stop grinning. "Aye. It was."

With a minute to spare, I squeezed through the growing crowd on the boardwalk, showed my VIP badge to the security guards, and tripped into my chair. "Mum and Dad send their love," I told Michael.

"Yeah?" He raised his eyebrows in question. "Like..." He motioned between us.

"Aye."

He took my hand, threading our fingers together tightly.

On the screen behind the band, a countdown clock appeared, and as we all stood, Angela shouted to me, "Here's your song!"

Hundreds of people counted down with the clock: "Ten! Nine! Eight!"

When the clock struck midnight, Michael and I wrapped our arms around each other as our lips met in a long, sweet kiss. Then we sang my song—*our* song—at the top of our lungs, laughing and hugging the Barkers and wishing everyone nearby a happy new year.

Soon enough, we'd slip away to our bed, and I'd reward Michael's patience handsomely—a prize for us both, of course.

Until then, we sang and swayed in the warm night under bright constellations we'd never seen before, charting our future.

Epilogue

Michael

WITH STRAY NEEDLES way too close to my face, I shifted my grip on the tree and kicked the heavy condo door open again with my right foot.

Because I was cursed, I kicked it too hard, and the door rebounded off the entry foyer wall and smacked back into me and the tree. I hit the hall closet on the left.

The hall closet with the mirrored, sliding door that I'd left open.

On my ass, fully in the closet, sitting on shoes and what had to be the handle of Will's tennis racket at an *interesting* angle, I was now in danger of being suffocated by the twine-bound tree on top of me.

"What on earth!"

I heard Will before I could see him thanks to the tree. His face appeared as he heaved the Douglas fir off me. He grunted, struggling to shift it enough to let the front door close as he asked, "Are you hurt, love?"

"Only my pride, I think?" I crawled out of the closet instead of trying to stand up under all our coats. I took the other side of the tree and kicked off my boots. "Mistakes were made."

Will laughed. "It's a little big, isn't it?"

"I might have gotten slightly carried away. Hey, we only have our first Christmas tree in our new home once."

He chuckled. "We did have a tree last year in the apartment, but fair enough."

We wrangled it into the corner of the living room and into the stand I'd set up earlier. The wall of glass to the right of the tree overlooked our balcony and the nature preserve beyond.

Up on the ninth floor, we weren't too low or too high. I couldn't wait to sit out on the balcony in the mornings to sip our coffee when it wasn't below freezing and snowing.

I'd assured Will the vertigo honestly didn't bother me here. It was only when I felt unstable, and with Will there, I'd almost be ready for rock climbing. Almost.

"It's gorgeous," Will said, drawing me in for a kiss. He caressed my face. "I love you with rosy cheeks."

I knew he meant from the cold, but of course my brain jumped farther south. "People will be here soon. Don't tease."

"Naughty!" He slapped my ass lightly and returned to the kitchen as a timer beeped. His dress shirt sleeves were rolled to his elbows and a red apron was knotted behind his waist.

The apron had been a gag gift from me last Christmas and said: *THIS GUY RUBS HIS OWN MEAT* with an arrow pointing up.

If we'd had more time, I would have dropped to my knees and sucked him under that apron.

Our condo was an open-plan living area, and we'd lucked out with an older building with character. We were still unpacking—the guest room was a maze of boxes—but we had the new couch, TV, side tables, and dining table and chairs ready. We'd gone with beachy neutrals. I couldn't wait to put up the gallery wall of photos in the dining area.

Will had blown up a few from Australia, including one of us and the Barkers smiling and sun-kissed on our last visit to Barking Beach, the beautiful turquoise blue of the Indian Ocean behind us. Our last visit for now. Will and I had already discussed Australia and New Zealand for our honeymoon.

Sure, we had to get married first, but we would.

"Rockin' Around the Christmas Tree" came on the holiday playlist we'd made, and I hummed as I quickly buttoned a nicer shirt over my jeans in the main bedroom.

We still had boxes to unpack, and most of our clothes were hanging in their garment bags in the closet, but we'd both taken time off over the holidays next week.

Still humming while Will put his cheese and crab dip in the oven, I carefully snipped the twine from the tree and fluffed the needles before winding the multicolored lights around the branches.

Snowflakes drifted down outside, but the roads had been okay. I checked the flight arrival info on my phone and smiled. On time.

"That all smells amazing," I said. "Can I help?"

"I think we're good. Cheese plate and first round of nibbles are ready to go. Are the decorations set?"

"Yep." I motioned to the boxes I'd laid out. "Actually, if you have a sec before everyone gets here…" I unwrapped the tissue paper from our most important ornament. The star went on last, and Kevin went on first.

Wiping his hands on a dishcloth before slinging it over his shoulder—how was that so damn sexy?—Will joined me in front of the tree.

He slipped his arm around my waist and said, "Cheers, Kevin. Where should we put you?"

"How about front and center." I waited for Will's nod, and because we were stupidly superstitious now apparently, we placed Kevin together, tugging his string over a branch by a pink light. He'd lost a bit of glitter, but still sparkled as he hung ten or whatever surfers did.

"Perfect," Will murmured just before our buzzer on the wall by the front door sounded. He quickly took off his apron while I tried unsuccessfully to bribe him into keeping it on.

Seth and Logan were first to arrive, with Matt and Becky right after. Matt insisted on referring to all of us as "Team Caper," and I supposed there were worse things to be called.

Seth raised his glass of Prosecco. "Congrats to you both on your promotions."

Will and I clinked our glasses with everyone. I said, "Thank you. Mine isn't such a big deal, but Angela's going to make Will vice-president of the whole company if she has her way."

"I'm goddamned shocked she hasn't convinced you to work for her too," Logan said.

I laughed. "Never say never." It had been extremely tempting given how generous the benefits were, but I didn't think it was a good idea at the moment. Maybe in a few years, but for now, I wanted my job to be independent from Will's even if we would have been in different departments.

While Will drifted to the kitchen with Becky and Matt, I asked Logan and Seth, "How's Connor doing in med school? Columbia, right? This is his first year?"

Seth answered, "It is. He's working very hard. It's a lot of stress."

"I bet. I can't even imagine."

"Had to practically beg him to come home for Christmas," Logan grumbled. "He stayed in New York for Thanksgiving and went to some fancy party with his buddy."

Seth absently rubbed Logan's back. "He *is* coming home for Christmas, though. We'll have to get used to him being too busy to visit as much as we'd like. Not to mention that we'll have to get used to him being a full-fledged adult. With a motorcycle."

Logan grudgingly agreed before ducking into the bathroom. Seth sighed heavily and polished his glasses on his buttoned shirt.

I said, "Sorry to bring up a sensitive subject."

Seth shook his head. "Not at all. We're just worried. It feels like there's something weighing on Connor, but he insists everything's well. Logan gets frustrated, and then they argue." He seemed to give himself a mental shake and forced a smile. "At least we don't have to worry about him being alone in New York—he's living with Angela's daughter Olivia."

"Oh! Are they a couple?"

Seth chuckled. "I don't think so, much to Angela's dismay. But she's paying for the apartment and charging Connor very reasonable rent for his room."

Sipping a festive cranberry and vodka cocktail, Becky joined us as Logan returned. She said, "But knowing Angela, I'm sure she'll be thrilled Connor's dating Reid Cabot."

I could have sworn an actual shockwave reverberated through the air. Logan and Seth stared at Becky for so long without saying anything that she laughed nervously.

"Um… At least, that's what I heard from my cousin in Manhattan? They were together at a party or something."

Logan demanded, "What the fuck are you talking about?"

That got Matt and Will's attention, and they approached warily. Matt slipped his arm around Becky's shoulders. "What's up?"

Seth raised one hand, his other on Logan's arm. "Everything's fine. It's a misunderstanding. Connor's best friend is Asher Cabot. Reid's his older brother." He frowned. "Connor isn't *dating* him. He isn't dating anyone. He's always been too busy with school."

Becky said, "I'm sure my cousin's wrong. She's an even bigger gossip than I am." She laughed weakly. "If you can believe it. I didn't mean to upset you."

Logan scrubbed a hand over his short hair. "Sorry I talked to you like that. I didn't expect to hear—" He turned to Seth. "That can't be true, right? Why the hell wouldn't he tell us? Asher's *brother*? Is this what he's been hiding?" He shook his head, muttering something I couldn't hear.

"I'm sure it's a misunderstanding," Seth soothed, taking Logan's hand. "Let's take a minute." He eased Logan away, and Will pointed them toward our bedroom.

When the door closed softly behind them, Will smiled awkwardly. "Brie bite, anyone?"

Keeping her voice low, Becky said, "I really am sorry! I didn't think it was a secret."

Matt hissed, "So, wait—Connor's really dating some older guy? His best friend's brother?"

Becky raised her eyebrows. "Well, you know Marcia *is* even more of a bigmouth than me, but… She's rarely wrong. That's all I'm saying."

"'Tis the season for drama-rama." Matt raised his glass, and we all ruefully cheered to that.

Jenna, Jun, and their boys arrived next, followed by Zoe and her husband Peter, and our other old friends from college who'd just had another baby.

Seth and Logan reappeared, and Seth was definitely better at pretending nothing was wrong, although Logan was clearly trying.

Soon, I could barely hear the music over the laughter and talking. It was perfect.

We ate and drank and slowly decorated the tree, everyone taking turns hanging ornaments while the youngest kids threw the shiny silver icicles everywhere but on the actual tree.

It was still perfect.

I gave Will a break in the kitchen, wincing at the waft of hot air as I pulled out a tray of cheese pastries. Zoe came around the island and opened the fridge, saying, "I'll just help myself."

"You always do."

We laughed as she topped her glass almost to the brim. "Whoops." She shrugged and took a gulp. "My mom says hi, by the way. She wants to see pics of the condo once you're finished decorating."

"She should just friend me on Insta."

Zoe groaned. "Don't encourage her, Mike." She took a sip and added, "Sorry. Michael. This place is great, by the way."

"Thanks. How's the bathroom reno going?'

"Well, my dad's not doing it, so better already. How are your folks?"

"The same. Maybe a little happier now I've co-purchased a condo and I'm an official grown-up by their standards."

She smiled. "Who would have thought back in the day that I'd still be living in that house and you'd be shacked up with Will?"

"Who even says 'shacked up' anymore?"

"Me, apparently. And hey, put a ring on it and I won't have to say it again. It's a win-win."

"Cute hair, by the way."

Zoe patted her sleek bob. "Thanks." She gazed around. "This place really is gorgeous. I really am so happy for you and Will. You know that, right?"

I grabbed the spatula from the pale quartz counter. "I know. You're not getting sentimental already, are you?"

"Oh god, I am." She held up her wine glass. "I'm such a lightweight these days."

My phone dinged, and I read the text with a grin and handed Zoe the spatula. "Can you put these on the platter for me? I've got to let someone else in." I hurried to the buzzer, opening the lobby door as quickly as I could.

Will somehow still heard the buzz and appeared in the short hallway. "I thought everyone was here?"

"Just about." I tried to hide my grin and failed miserably.

His brow furrowed. "Who's coming?"

I opened the door to Will's parents, and his jaw dropped. Judy yanked him into a fierce hug, Robert not far behind. Will stared at them, and then at me. He sputtered.

"You all planned this?"

"No, you numpty, it's a big coincidence," Judy said, giving Will another hug. "Merry Christmas, love. Now where's your guest room?" She nodded to the suitcases they'd squeezed into the hall behind them. "We need to unpack."

Will turned to me in horror. "But there's no bed yet!"

I said, "It's okay—they're cool with sleeping on the floor."

"Anything to be close to you, William," Robert said solemnly, his accent adorably thick.

As Will blinked and tried to smile, Judy and I couldn't stop from laughing. I assured him, "I booked the guest suite downstairs."

Shaking his head, Will laughed. "There's a guest suite downstairs?"

"Yep." I couldn't stop smiling. "You kept talking about wanting to see your parents, so I texted Judy."

"My partner in crime," Judy said, pulling me into a warm hug. "It's so good to see you again." She pulled away with a grimace, "But Christ, I must stink. We need to clean up before we join the party."

"You're not too tired from the flight?" I asked.

"Pour us a drink and we'll be up in no time," Robert said before hugging me too.

Will and I took his parents and their suitcases downstairs. I felt stupidly proud to lead the way to the guest suite we were able to rent from the building. In the elevator on the way back up, Will was quiet.

My happy, bubbly high burst as I looked at his serious expression. Shit. Had I totally screwed up? "It's a good surprise, right?"

His lips tugged up into a smile, and he hugged me close. "It's the best gift I could imagine, sweetheart. Thank you."

Our condo buzzed with laughter and music when we returned, the old U2 version of "Christmas (Baby Please Come Home)" playing. Matt, Zoe, and Seth of all people were singing along loudly as they hung some of the final ornaments. Logan handed Seth a glittery candy cane, looking at him with such bare affection that my throat tightened.

I slipped my hand into Will's, and we paused on the threshold of our new home, watching our friends and their families talking and smiling and singing while snow floated down to blanket the world outside.

Lips brushing my ear, Will whispered, "There's only one thing you forgot."

I shivered. "What's that?"

"Mistletoe."

"It's in the bedroom. You'll have to wait to kiss me."

"Is that right?" Will took my face in his hands, and I melted into him as our lips met.

We'd waited long enough.

The Christmas Veto

BY
KEIRA ANDREWS

Acknowledgments

Huge thanks to Anita, Leslie, Leta, and Rai for their help in bringing Connor and Reid's romance to life.

Chapter One

Reid

Thanksgiving

FINDING A FAKE boyfriend on short notice was proving a challenge.

I glumly gazed around the exclusive upstairs lounge at the Utopia Grand as guests trickled in for my grandmother's annual charity event. Fresh fir boughs lined the cream wainscoting along with wreaths each tastefully decorated with a single red bow. The lights of New York City glowed through floor-to-ceiling windows.

Beside me from our position in the corner practically hiding behind the enormous gold-decorated Christmas tree, Addison nodded to Richard Wolverhampton. Excuse me—Richard Wolverhampton the Third. He was scowling at his phone from one of the cream settees and combing his thin hair forward with his fingers as if that would hide his already-receding hairline.

I nearly spit out my Manhattan and sputtered, "Veto!"

Addison frowned and tucked a dark, glossy curl behind her ear. "Why not? He might agree for the right price. You know he's probably checking the latest bad trade he's made. Rumor has it his parents are cutting him off soon."

"He's a homophobic prick. We both went to Rencliffe, remember? In tenth grade, he made Edward Linney's life hell. Eddie wasn't even queer, I don't think."

Addison stirred her cranberry holiday mojito with a cinnamon stick. "Maybe Richard's grown as a person."

After a beat, we burst out laughing too loudly, garnering glares from a few of the old society ladies who'd arrived early and now sipped sauvignon blanc while gossiping in whispers. Nostalgia washed over me with memories of our teenage years when Addison and I were perpetually skulking in the corner of these events.

"Do you want me to call my matchmaker auntie in Mumbai? I'm sure she has some hot tips."

"I'm not looking for a *match*. That's what I'm trying to avoid."

"Mm." Addison fingered her silver necklace, the encrusted diamonds gleaming against her brown skin. "Okay, unless you want to rethink one of the Masterson cousins—" She paused for my response.

The fake-boyfriend selection pool was truly grim. "Veto, veto, and veto."

She raised an eyebrow. "You're really channeling Bitsy."

"What? Oh, I guess I am." My grandmother was famous—make that *infamous*—for her one-word dismissal of any ideas she didn't care for. "Look, it has to be believable."

"Fair, but pickings are slim, and everyone will be arriving soon. You need to consider a fake girlfriend instead."

Sighing, I muttered, "I guess so."

"What does it matter? You're bi—as long as you have a significant other for the holidays, your grandmother should lay off her matchmaking scheme. Or, you could remind her you're twenty-nine years old and are a big boy now."

Addison took another sip of her cocktail before adding, "You know, it would be easier just to—hear me out—actually date someone. You've been hooking up with guys on the downlow since Rencliffe. If you're set on finding a man to thwart Bitsy's matchmaking dreams, there must be someone you know who's boyfriend material."

"Definitely no one from high school. Also, I never told you I hooked up with guys back then."

Addison rolled her eyes. "As if I couldn't always sniff out your chaotic bisexual energy."

I had to laugh, affection swelling in my chest. "Did it smell anything like Tom Ford Soleil Brûlant?"

"You wish. Axe Body Spray was more like it."

"Ouch. And I know it would be easier to have a partner for real. But after Gwen, I'm just not in the mood for anything serious."

She sighed. "I hear you. Gwen was a heartbreaker."

"She didn't *break my heart*," I insisted. "I'll give you bruised."

Addison didn't argue, which was why she was my best friend. She simply said, "May I point you back in the direction of telling your grandmother once and for all to butt the eff out?"

"You know my grandmother. Nodding and smiling and agreeing with everything she declares is the only way to go. I'm the oldest. Asher can do whatever he wants. Meanwhile, it's my responsibility to carry on the Cabot family legacy."

Addison dramatically put a hand to her chest, covering the V-neck of her sleek, green cocktail dress. "If only the world could understand the suffering of this rich white man in his custom Armani suit."

I chuckled. "Fair. Though I didn't say I was *suffering*. I just don't want to deal with my grandmother's meddling. If I'd known Cecilia was back from

France, I'd have skipped dinner tonight."

"And miss Bitsy's traditional Thanksgiving charity event? You wouldn't dare."

After a burning gulp of my drink, I muttered, "I wish she'd actually do the place up for Thanksgiving. I'm sick of Christmas already, and it's still November."

"Like what, pilgrim hats and paper-mache turkeys? I'm sure the tables will feature decorative gourds."

"Grandmother does love a decorative gourd."

"Who doesn't? Also, why is she so stuck on marrying you off to Cecilia Weston?"

I snorted. "Money and status, why else? It's her world—we just live in it. And to be clear, her world might as well be Jane Austen's Victorian England."

"Pretty sure Austen was the Regency period."

"Whichever." I desperately gave the lounge another scan. A string quartet played carols, and arriving guests made small talk in clusters. Before I could bite my tongue, I blurted, "I'd rather find a fake boyfriend because Grandmother doesn't believe bisexuality exists."

Addison's plucked eyebrows disappeared under her fashionable bangs. "In you specifically, or in the world at large?"

"Both."

Addison smiled sharply. "Does Bitsy believe in lesbians, or am I your imaginary friend?"

"I think she'd much rather everyone be cis and hetero, but being gay is a binary she can accept. You're also extremely rich."

Addison was part of the Rupani family, who'd made their fortune in India in telecoms. We'd met in an Upper East Side preschool and had an instant affinity for each other based on our shared love for all things SpongeBob.

Addison frowned. "You said your family was cool when you came out this summer."

I shrugged, going for careless and likely missing the mark. "My mom and stepdad and Asher were cool. Aunts and uncles and various cousins. Grandmother's in denial."

She reached for my hand and gave it a squeeze. "I'm sorry."

"It's fine!" I squeezed back before shoving my hand in my pocket.

"Okay, let's find you a man." Addison slurped the rest of the mojito. Her gaze narrowed. "There. Your brother's hot friend. They just walked in."

Confused, I searched the growing crowd. I found Asher, but it took a second to place his companion. "*Connor?* No. Veto. *Veee*-to. He's a kid."

Or he *had* been.

Addison's eyebrows met. "Are we talking about the same guy? White and a bit pasty—doesn't look like he gets a lot of sun. About six feet tall. Dirty blond hair definitely has some product involved in making him look so carelessly sexy. Hot black leather jacket and that tight ass in those Levis?"

Seeing through Addison's eyes, I tilted my head and watched Connor and Asher laugh about something.

Bright, sweet smile that dimples his cheeks.

Huh. When had Connor Lisowski grown up? So *well?* He and Asher were twenty-three now, and I hadn't seen Connor since they were undergrads.

"Ohhh, nice dimples," Addison noted.

Regaining my sanity, I scoffed. "I've known him since he was an angry, pimply teenager." Well, "known" was a strong word. Connor had been Asher's sullen shadow.

"He sure isn't now. I direct you again to exhibit D: *dat ass.* But even if you're not into his wannabe James Dean vibe, it's not like you have to hook up with him. The whole idea is a *fake* boyfriend."

"I know, but…"

"He's less of a risk since no one here knows him. Besides, you're out of vetoes and time, my friend."

On cue, my grandmother strolled into the lounge, chatting with—of course—Abigail Weston and Abigail's only child, Cecilia. It wasn't that I had anything against Cecilia, who was a golden-haired high society ingenue straight out of central casting.

The few times we'd been forced into small talk, she'd been perfectly pleasant. But I'd just come to terms with being bi, and I wasn't looking for anything but a good time.

As Grandmother surveyed the room as the Terminator might, I practically lunged behind the Christmas tree, narrowly avoiding the fragrant pine needles.

I was well and truly out of options. "*Fine.*"

"You think he'll go for it?"

"I think Asher said he's gay, so maybe? Guess there's only one way to find out. Can you wave them over?"

After a few aborted attempts, Addison grumbled and strode across the lounge, deftly grabbing a champagne flute and skirting a massive poinsettia. She returned with Asher and Connor, and we crowded in the space between the tree and the window.

"What's up?" Asher asked suspiciously. He leaned to the left, peering around the tree. "Ah. Bitsy's back on her bullshit. I'm sorry to inform you that you can't hide here all night. No doubt Gamma's got you sitting with Cecilia so you can bond over turkey and stuffing and get married and have perfect heirs." He gulped from his flute. "You remember Connor, right?"

"We sure do," Addison said, though they'd probably never met. "Actually, Reid's in need of your services, Connor."

His forehead creased. "My…huh?" He scanned up and down my body, which gave me a strange little tingle. "Are you sick or something? I'm only in med school. I'm not a doctor yet."

"Oh, not those services," I said. "Look, time is of the essence, so here goes: I need a boyfriend for the holidays to thwart my matchmaking grandmother. In the new year, she'll go south to the Caymans, and I'll be off the hook until spring."

Connor stared at me. Up close, I could see he had stubble. "You… What?"

Addison said, "You wouldn't have to *really* date. Just come to a few more of these stuffy parties in December. Maybe a few PDAs to sell it."

Connor's brown eyes widened, and I asked, "You're queer too, right? I thought Asher said—" I spotted the flash of alarm in my brother's eyes, but of course it was too late.

Connor jerked his gaze to Asher. "Why the hell would you say that?"

"I didn't!" Asher lifted his palms. "My idiot brother's confused."

"Apologies. I must've gotten you mixed up with someone else." I thought Asher had mentioned it back when he and Connor were in high school, but perhaps I'd misremembered. I tried not to feel defensive. "You don't have to sound so outraged. There's nothing wrong with it."

Connor scoffed. "I know. I have two dads." He drained his champagne.

That rang a faint bell. "Right, right." Connor had been a scholarship kid at Rencliffe when he and Asher met. I vaguely recalled his mother had died, and he'd been classified as "troubled" before settling down. I thought there was something about his stepfather raising him?

It didn't matter—we could only hide behind the Scotch pine for so long.

"Look," I said. "You'd be doing me a huge favor."

Eyes on his empty glass, Connor fiddled with the zipper of his leather jacket, which most certainly did not fit my grandmother's dress code.

Asher added, "There's always free food and booze at these events. It'll be fun." We both wore our dark brown hair short, though his bangs flopped over one eyebrow as he waggled them.

Connor glowered at him. "Why would it be fun pretending to be, um, Reid's—" He motioned at me as if he couldn't bring himself to say the word *boyfriend.*

Asher grinned. "I love my grandmother, but messing with Bitsy's always a good time."

"We've been spotted," Addison hissed.

"I'll make it worth your while," I added.

Connor met my gaze, clearly still dubious. Not to mention *handsome.* Seriously, when had this happened? I didn't remember his voice being this low.

He asked, "How?"

"However you want."

He shifted in his Doc Martens. "You really need help?"

A server in black and white appeared and asked Connor, "Sir, may I take your coat? It will be uncomfortably warm for you at dinner." The guy had likely been dispatched by Grandmother.

Asher said, "Dude, I promise they won't lose it." To the server, he added, "You won't lose it, right?"

"Never," the man replied seriously.

"*Fine*," Connor muttered as he shrugged out of the jacket. The leather squeaked and seemed new.

Under it, he wore a white dress shirt and gray striped tie, which was at least semi-formal. His Levis—which really did hug his long, lean legs—and Doc Martens were less so, but it didn't matter. It wasn't as if my grandmother would approve of him in any outfit.

Besides, she just had to believe we were a couple long enough to back off, and—

"Incoming," Asher whispered, and as the server left with Connor's jacket, we all turned to face Elizabeth "Bitsy" Cabot as she marched toward us, her glossy black pumps striking the marble floor in staccato annoyance.

Her skin was creamy white—never tanned nor too pale—and her hair was decidedly silver rather than gray, styled in a sleek bob. She wore a long-sleeved cocktail dress in an orangey-red that was likely called "burnt sienna" or something else appropriately autumnal for Thanksgiving.

"Gamma!" Asher opened his arms wide, and she hugged him, allowing the childhood nickname that was a relic from the time when Asher couldn't pronounce "Grandmother." Also allowing the hug itself, which was rare, especially in public.

She turned to me, saying, "Reid," and leaned slightly toward me so I could kiss her cheek while our hands briefly met. Her manicured fingers were cool and moisturized.

She gave Addison an air kiss on each cheek and said, "My dear, I'm so glad you're not caught up in that terrible violence in Pakistan."

"Me too," Addison replied with a sweet smile. "I've lived here my whole life, and my family's from Mumbai. India."

"Of course," Grandmother said, already moving on to Connor, who she regarded with the slightest tension at the corners of her red lips. She didn't extend hand nor cheek. "How lovely to see you here with Asher."

Connor's gaze flicked to me. "Uh, actually…"

Was he in? We looked at each other, and after an endless moment of deliberation, he lifted his eyebrows, waiting.

He was in.

Chapter Two

Connor

MY HEART WAS about to rupture and burst through my ribcage. Reid. Was. Touching. Me.

His arm was around my shoulders. Any second, the costal cartilage in my chest would go *bam*, and…

Reid was saying something while old lady Cabot stared at me like I was gum she'd peeled off the bottom of her shoe. Not that she'd pick gum off her own shoes—she had staff to do that.

Focus for fuck's sake!

"We've been dating a while now," Reid said. The way his grandmother didn't blink was alarming. I monitored her for signs of a stroke as Reid squeezed my shoulders and said, "It's going great, isn't it, Connor?"

I realized I was standing frozen like a cadaver on an exam table with my arms straight at my sides. "Um, yep." I reached around Reid's toned, firm waist. The right side of my body was at risk of igniting where it pressed against his side. We were both tall, but Reid was a couple of inches above me. He felt big and comforting.

And hot. Did I mention hot?

Back in the day, he'd inspired way too many wet dreams to count. Not that I'd ever, *ever* admitted that to anyone. Seriously, *why* had Asher told Reid I was queer?! No one knew that. Not even my dads, because…

It just wasn't the right time. It was fine—it wasn't like I was seeing anyone. I was a loser virgin, and—

And now, I *was* suddenly seeing someone? Maybe this was the answer to my prayers. Not that I prayed since god was bullshit. If there was actually a god up there who let my mom die, he/she/they could go to hell. If only it existed.

As far as heaven went, touching Reid Cabot qualified. Reid with his thick, dark brown hair, his deep brown eyes, and perfectly even, white smile that made me lightheaded.

Mrs. Cabot still hadn't blinked. "Darling, you didn't breathe a word of this at the board meeting a few days ago."

"Oh, there wasn't an opportunity," Reid said smoothly, still a wall of warmth pressed against my side. "We had so many motions to vote on." He motioned broadly to the buzzing lounge with his free arm. "I'm sure Filling Bellies and Minds will be thrilled with the proceeds from tonight's event."

Reid's friend—Madison? Addison? That was it. *Addison* said, "You've both done such wonderful work on the board. Transformed the charity in the best way. I know they're so grateful for your patronage. How many years have you been hosting this Thanksgiving dinner now, Mrs. Cabot? You must be responsible for millions and millions raised for worthy causes over the years."

Mrs. Cabot was forced to answer, smiling tightly at Addison as she talked about tradition and giving back. Meanwhile, Reid and I stood there like an actual couple. It was a good thing I took off my jacket—sweat dampened the back of my neck. My pits would probably reek soon.

Reid casually brushed his fingers back and forth on my upper arm. If I were in a tank top, I'd be able to feel it on my skin… Good thing I was in a dress shirt, because popping a boner wasn't going to make his grandma like me. Not that anything could probably make her like me. Not that it mattered since this was all pretend.

Jesus, was *I* having a stroke?

As Addison and Asher asked Mrs. Cabot more questions she was clearly annoyed to answer, red flashed in my peripheral vision. Good news: It wasn't a stroke symptom. Bad news: It was Olivia in her new cocktail dress approaching on Dylan van Arsdale's arm.

Shiiiiiiit.

I met her gaze and shook my head as much as I could without drawing attention. She was already frowning, staring at me with Reid. Olivia's mind was usually five steps ahead of me as we often joked. Yet she seemed stumped by me and Reid with our arms around each other.

Which was fair since this was absolutely bananas as my dad Seth would have said because he didn't swear.

Olivia's long, dark hair was curled perfectly, and her strapless red dress was a knockout. People often wondered aloud how I could live with her and not be fucking her. The answer was pretty simple.

Apparently, Asher had figured it out, but he was my best friend. Did other people suspect? Did they know somehow? They were sure as shit going to now that I was pretending to be Reid's boyfriend.

I thought back to Asher telling me around the Fourth of July that Reid was bi. He'd acted a bit too casually. We'd been on the roof of my apartment building, which Olivia and I had turned into our secret little patio by wedging gum into the door lock.

Asher and I were up there drinking beer at the little table, sitting in folding chairs and sweating in the thick, humid night air. We listened to sirens and fireworks and watched the displays shining from skyscraper windows. He'd kept his gaze on the view as he'd mentioned that Reid had come out, and my heart had thumped.

I'd waited for him to say something about me, or demand the truth, or at least ask. He hadn't. Hours later, when I'd been almost passed out in bed, I'd jerked off furiously thinking about Reid. Just like I had dozens of times before. *Hundreds.* I'd always had it so bad for him.

Olivia and Dylan were too close now to avoid. Sweat dripped down my spine. Just ten minutes ago, I'd walked into this party looking forward to an open bar and fancy dinner, and now—

I had to say, "Um, hey," to Olivia and Dylan.

"Hey," they replied in unison. Dylan opened his mouth to speak, his forehead furrowed, but Olivia cut him off. "Mrs. Cabot, what a lovely event this is. My mother's sorry she can't be here in person."

Still barely blinking—maybe it was just her thing—Mrs. Cabot gave Olivia and Dylan a smooth smile. "Your mother?"

Her own practiced smile in place, Olivia said, "Angela Barker. One of Filling Bellies and Minds' biggest donors."

"Oh, of course." Mrs. Cabot's smile widened fractionally. "You're her adopted daughter. From China?"

"My sister and I were both adopted from Korea. We're Angela's only children." Olivia was smiling fakely too, and god, rich people were exhausting.

I was used to it after going to Rencliffe and Harvard and tagging along with Asher to these parties, but I should have just gone home for Thanksgiving with Logan and Seth, and my Aunt Jenna, Uncle Jun, and Pop and the kids.

I'd been too stressed by my upcoming finals to make the short trip to Albany. If I were there, right about now we'd be watching football, talking about how stuffed we felt, and having a belching contest while Seth and Jenna complained about how gross we were.

Asher said, "Oh, Gamma, Mom asked if you want to go to the Belvedere dinner since she won't be in town for it."

"Veto, darling. My calendar is full to the brim," Mrs. Cabot said briskly. "I must attend to my duties." Her gaze swept over us all, and if I could read minds hers would probably say, "*Look at this bullshit I have to deal with. Remember when everyone was white and straight and had respectably old money?*"

What she actually said was, "Enjoy the evening. Reid, let's regroup tomorrow, yes?"

It was apparently a rhetorical question since she swept away with head high. She should have considered wearing a cape or cloak to amplify the effect.

We all seemed to exhale in unison. Olivia sipped her champagne and muttered, "Always a pleasure, Bitsy."

"Babe, ignore that old bat," Dylan said, rubbing her arm. He glanced at Asher and Reid. "Uh, sorry. I know she's your grandma, but… How's it going? Asher, you still working for the Allard Group?" He extended his hand, and there was a round of shakes and chat, all while Olivia's piercing gaze bore into me.

She held out her hand to Reid. "I don't think we've met. I'm Olivia Barker-Robertson. Connor's roommate."

"Reid Cabot."

"He's Asher's brother," I said quickly, as if that would answer why Reid and I were still standing close with our arms around each other.

"Uh-huh," Olivia said, nodding. "*And?*"

"Um…" I was really sweating now, the back of my hair damp with it. I was seriously going to reek. "Right, we actually, we're—"

"Dating," Reid finished, giving my temple a kiss. "It's okay. Don't be nervous, *mon amour.*"

"Uh-huh!" was all I could manage, and it was more of a squeak. The warm, slightly wet sensation on my skin from his lips, and the French words—my love?—were too much. Also, why French? Rich people were so weird.

Head tilted, Olivia exclaimed, "What a fascinating development!" She said to Dylan, "Don't you think so?"

Dylan, who wasn't the shiniest coin in the collection plate as my mom used to say, said, "Yeah! Cool. Congrats, guys." He wasn't a homophobe, at least. For a rich white guy who worked for his daddy's company and was extremely privileged, he was okay. He was wild about Olivia, so he had good taste.

"It's wonderful news," Addison agreed, finishing her drink. I needed another one, stat. The empty glass was damp in my free hand.

To Reid, Olivia said, "Like I mentioned, I'm Connor's roommate." She grimaced dramatically. "New money, which I know is cringe. But I'm sure you know all about me. Since you and Connor are dating."

"I'm sorry about my grandmother," Reid said smoothly. "And yes, it's wonderful to finally meet you."

"Isn't it?" Olivia grinned. "Hey, Asher, what's up?"

"Hey." He gave Olivia a lazy salute. "Oh, I think it's time for dinner."

Reid kept his arm firmly around my shoulders as we filed toward the banquet hall or whatever they called it at the Utopia Grand, one of the fanciest hotels in Manhattan. Reid and I were definitely garnering attention from other guests, and my face was hot with the weight of their stares.

Whispers sliced through the air like knives. My asshole brain imagined: "*See? Being raised by those two men led to this. It's their fault.*"

Which was ridiculous because these people didn't know me or my parents. I was glad for the grounding weight of Reid's arm. I realized I was clutching his waist too tight and relaxed my fingers.

"Sorry," I mumbled, almost dropping my glass while putting it on a tray held by an impassive server.

"It's okay," Reid replied, his breath warm on my cheek. "I've got you."

Operation: No Boners was going to take every ounce of my will power.

"Thanks for doing this," he added in that smooth tenor that went right to my dick as though it was injected in my veins. Was this really happening? My head was spinning, and *Jesus*, he smelled amazing—like a forest. Not just pine trees, but rich and earthy soil.

Did I just think that he smelled like dirt? What was my damage? And since when was I attracted to dirt? Whatever it was, I wanted to lean closer and breathe deeply.

Reid added, "I really owe you one."

The reminder of what I'd be asking from Reid Cabot later in exchange for my fake boyfriend services worked like a bucket of ice water dumped on my head. He'd probably say no, but I had to try. Considering I was completely screwed otherwise, I had nothing to lose.

"Are you sure about this?" Reid murmured in my ear.

Not even a little bit.

One thing was guaranteed: The holidays just got a hell of a lot more interesting.

Chapter Three

Reid

I FINALLY HAD a boyfriend.

Next to me, Connor picked up and put down his dessert spoon. He knew we didn't use *that* spoon until the end, right? That the soup spoon was on the outside?

I needed to get over myself. This wasn't *Pretty Woman*.

"You okay?" I murmured.

"Everyone's staring," he whispered.

I wanted to argue, but it was true. Maybe not *everyone*, but we'd garnered our fair share of attention. Forget the soup—gossip was the favored first course of this crowd. Not to mention the main *and* dessert.

At least Grandmother was seated at a head table with the charity's top executives and not at our round table of eight with Asher, Addison, and a few of the younger Lawrence cousins. Not to mention the conspicuously empty seat designated for my plus-one since Connor was Asher's and Addison had her own invite.

My collar felt tight, and I loosened my tie half an inch, careful not to mess up my Windsor knot. Naturally people were gossiping—I'd known academically it would happen when I'd assessed the risk of this last-minute plan.

As a rule, I wasn't a fan of doing anything last-minute, but the panic of having to play nice with Cecilia Weston had felt far more threatening.

I supposed at the root of this scheme was my hurt and anger at Grandmother's denial of who I'd told her I was. Who I was whether she believed it or not.

Not that I wouldn't date a woman—I had, and I surely would again. But Grandmother needed to see me with a man. Here in front of God, New York society, and the Utopia waitstaff.

"Gamma's laser beams are getting a workout," Asher muttered from Connor's left side as the butternut squash and roasted red pepper soup arrived around our table at the exact same moment with pinpoint accuracy from the servers.

I refused to meet her gaze, smiling broadly as if I didn't have a care in the world. "Good. Let her look." Let her *see*.

"Can you guess what she's thinking?" Connor whispered.

Beside me—leaving the extra seat on her other side—Addison said, "Hon, better to never ask that question."

I smirked. "She's probably thinking, 'If he has to suck cock, can't it be a *wealthy* one?'"

Choking on his spoonful of soup—using the correct spoon, for the record—Connor grabbed his water glass and gulped it down before coughing into his elbow.

"You okay?" I stopped myself before I could thump his back, since that was probably not actually helpful for choking victims. I laid my palm gently between his shoulder blades.

Face pink, he nodded. "Went down the wrong way." A server refilled his water, and Connor drank it with muffled thanks.

Leaning closer, I whispered, "Sorry to make you uncomfortable."

He shook his head. "You're not. Between Olivia and your grandma, I feel like I'm being dissected. With dull instruments."

I chuckled. "I assume you're going to have to tell Olivia the truth."

"Oh, yeah." Connor laughed, the nervous edge softening into fondness. "No way she'll be letting this go. Understandably, since this morning I didn't have a boyfriend. I wasn't even—" He stammered. "Um, well, you know."

"I get it. Do you two go to school together?"

He scooped his spoon back and forth through the rich orange-red soup. "No. We do both go to Columbia, but I'm in med school. One of my dads and my aunt work for Olivia's mom. Olivia wanted out of the dorm, and her mom rented an apartment for us. No way I should be able to afford it, but Angela's really generous. Understatement."

Addison and Asher were doing their part to make conversation with the rest of the table, so Connor and I were able to chat quietly. I asked, "Where are you guys living?"

"It's an apartment at Tenth and Forty-eighth. Five-story walk-up. Not fancy, but obviously *way* nicer than anything I could afford. And I get my own room as opposed to a saggy futon in a studio shared with, like, three people."

"I've heard Angela Barker's quite a character."

Connor's smile took on a soft fondness. Not dimple material, but sweet. "Small, brassy Texan who's like a tornado. She's done so much for me and my dads."

"That's wonderful."

"Yeah. Actually, it's kind of funny." He leaned in closer, his eyes lighting up. His lashes were thick, and there were a few freckles dusted across the tops of his cheeks. "Logan and Seth didn't even know each other when they met Angela, but they pretended to be engaged. For reasons. It probably sounds nuts."

"I couldn't possibly relate." I brushed back his hair and leaned in flirtily for the benefit of Grandmother and the curious onlookers. "I'd never get caught up in something so weird," I whispered in Connor's ear.

He swallowed thickly, Adam's apple bobbing. "Good thing I have experience in this arena."

I laughed. "Carrying on a family tradition."

A dimple appeared briefly in his right cheek. "Apparently. Logan and Seth ended up falling in love for real, though. Different situation."

I leaned back. "Totally." Sure, Connor was adorable, but falling in love? No chance.

After a spoonful of creamy soup with a perfect note of sweetness, I asked, "Logan was originally your mother's partner, right?" Our table mates were still wrapped up in their own conversations, so it felt safe enough ask a few questions of my brand-new boyfriend.

My heart performed a silly little somersault at those two words—"my" and "boyfriend"—in close proximity. I'd had girlfriends, but this was a first. Even if it wasn't true, to be sitting in the Utopia on Thanksgiving in front of everyone with a man gave me a deep thrill.

I really needed to get out more.

"Yeah, they were married," Connor said, circling his spoon through his half-full bowl. "It was really rushed and stupid." He shook his head and started eating his soup again hesitantly, as if he was afraid to spill it.

I finished mine as I tried to remember what Asher had said about Connor's mother. I knew she'd died suddenly and quite young. Some kind of unexpected heart attack, perhaps? Along those lines. Understandable that he didn't want to talk about it.

He did add, "So, Logan was my stepfather, and I guess Seth's my step-stepfather. I only knew Logan a year or so longer, though." He paused. "I guess it's been about ten years since we moved in with Seth."

"And that was part of the…" I waved my hand.

"Yeah." He smirked and whispered, "Operation Fake Boyfriend."

I lifted my wine glass. "Here's to family legacies."

We clinked our glasses and drank. Still watching me, Connor swallowed. He really had grown up to be quite handsome. I'm not sure I would have recognized him as my little brother's pimply, perpetually scowling friend.

"Asher said your mom's staying in Europe for the holidays?" Connor asked.

"Yes, she's enjoying the sunshine with her new husband. You'll be in Albany with your dads and the rest of the family?"

"Yeah." That fond smile was back. "It's been months. I can't wait to chill out."

"What about your biological father? He's in…Florida, I think?"

Smile vanishing, Connor's shoulders practically hit his ears as he reached for the bread basket, sending a piece of sourdough tumbling onto the white linen.

He said, "Dunno. I mean, yeah, he's in Florida as far as I know. I've never had Christmas down there. He's not—I just have his name. I wish I didn't."

Okay, that was a sore subject. I quickly asked, "How's school?"

Connor's shoulders un-hunched a fraction. "Pretty good. Hard." His cheeks flushed. "I mean, obviously. It's medical school. It's hard."

I chuckled. "I've heard rumors. What drew you to medicine?"

We were interrupted as the servers brought the main course. I couldn't imagine how many turkeys had been sacrificed since we all had white and dark meat on our plates, along with perfectly golden roast potatoes, slightly charred brussels sprouts, and a gourmet twist on green bean casserole that most definitely did not involve a can of Campbell's soup.

I sipped the buttery Chardonnay and nodded my thanks to the server who'd filled my glass.

Connor inhaled deeply, mumbling, "Oh my god, this smells amazing."

Asher grinned. "The Utopia's gravy is the best."

Our table settled into eating, the clink of silverware louder around the room before the din of conversation increased again. Addison, Asher, and the others at our table returned to debating something boring about football. I'd never been much of a sports guy.

After a few bites of the rich, creamy beans, I prompted Connor. "Well? Why med school?"

"I dunno."

"Sure you do. Clearly your grades were high enough, but it's too big of a commitment for that to be the only reason."

He ate a potato and finally mumbled, "I want to help people feel better."

I had to smile. "That's nothing to be embarrassed about. As someone who works for a family business that primarily helps itself, I'm glad there are people like you who want to do some good."

He scoffed. "Sure, but it's the most cliché answer. It's facile. 'I want to help people.' What does that even mean?"

"Hmm. Okay. Well, what *does* it mean? To you?"

Connor fiddled with his fork, eyes lowered. Had he always had those freckles? "I'm not sure. I still need to figure it out."

"That's what school's for, isn't it?"

"I guess. But most of my classmates know exactly which specialty they want to do already. I have ideas, but I'm not *sure.* It was the same at Rencliffe and Harvard. Everyone had a plan, and I was just scraping along."

"I'd hardly call Harvard and Columbia 'scraping along.' But you have the freedom to do anything. Isn't that empowering?" I couldn't stop a surge of envy. "I'm the oldest Cabot son, so I have zero choice. Our dad's dead, so it'll be me taking over the company. The end."

Connor frowned. "I mean, old—uh, your grandmother can't *make* you."

My laugh was too bitter. "Oh, you'd be surprised." I shook my head. "But yes, you're right. And I have absolutely nothing to complain about. I couldn't be more privileged if I tried."

"You're in hotels, right? Like this one?" He motioned around us and almost lost his fork before putting it down carefully on the table. "I never really paid attention. Everyone else at Rencliffe except the scholarship kids were loaded one way or another."

"Hotels, yes. The Utopia brand is our biggest."

"Oh, cool. Are they all as fancy?"

"Most, but this is the flagship."

"Must be a good business. Do you like it?"

Had anyone ever asked me that before? I wasn't sure. I refolded my napkin on my lap. "It's fine. The brand's steady. Can't ask for much more."

Connor seemed about to reply but glanced at his phone when it pinged, then rolled his eyes. I couldn't resist being nosy. "What prompted that face?"

"Just Logan telling me not to drink too much if Asher and I go out later. He's always telling me stuff like that. 'Don't drink too much.' 'Stay away from the edge of the subway platform.' 'Don't speed' and 'wear your helmet'—as if I'd go out on my motorcycle without a helmet."

"*Motorcycle?*" My pulse increased just thinking about it. "Isn't that dangerous?"

He groaned softly. "Not you too. Yes, there's higher risk associated with riding a motorcycle, but that risk can be mitigated. I took driving courses. My engine is less than five hundred CCs. I always wear a helmet and safety gear. I drive like everyone else on the road is trying to kill me."

I held up my hands. "Sorry. I can see you've had this conversation before."

"You could say that. And I get it—I do. It's risky. But it can be incredible too." His gaze went distant. "My mom always wanted one. She'd been saving up for years. Then…" After a moment, Connor dropped his head and scooped up a mouthful of beans.

Ah. That helped explain it. Without thinking, I rubbed his shoulder. Connor swallowed and looked at me, and I remembered the angry, scared boy I'd first met years ago.

I couldn't recall where—likely at an alumni day at Rencliffe, or maybe Asher had brought Connor home for a weekend. He'd been a bundle of contradictions then, and apparently that hadn't changed much. He still had jittery, rough edges.

I jumped as Addison cleared her throat loudly enough to wake the dead. I blinked at her, biting back an impatient "*What?*" and going with, "Pardon?" The whole table was watching me and Connor.

"Sorry to interrupt your *tête-à-tête*," Addison said smoothly. "Morgan asked if you're attending the tree lighting next weekend."

I blinked at Morgan Lawrence. "Of course! It's the event of the season." Or, it was a bore and a half, but I was obligated to make an appearance.

Morgan, a banker who sat with his pregnant wife, Louise, nodded to Connor. "I hope we'll see you both?"

Okay, Morgan wasn't so bad. I had to smile at my fake boyfriend being included. Hopefully, one day if I was serious with a guy, it wouldn't be an issue.

"Uh…" Connor looked at me before nodding. "Sounds great. Thanks."

Morgan glanced at the head table—as if afraid Grandmother could hear him—before adding, "Good for you, man. Haven't seen you look happy in a long time."

Before I could respond, the charity president tapped a microphone, and it was time for the back-patting and congratulations. I listened and clapped on cue while chewing over Morgan's comment.

Had I looked *unhappy* before? It wasn't as though I was miserable.

Sure, perhaps I wouldn't describe myself as "happy," but…I could admit that coming out hadn't been quite the liberating, joyous event I'd secretly dreamed of for years. Still. I'd have to work harder.

While I wasn't a gambler, I thought my poker face was better than that.

Chapter Four

Connor

TIME TO TELL Reid. Even though it had tasted like a sweet, spicy cloud, the pumpkin pie soufflé was sitting in my gut like Pop's old bowling ball.

Icy wind whipped on Fifty-ninth Street, and I wished I could do up my jacket. But I'd have to let go of Reid's hand, and his warm fingers were laced with mine, and I tingled all over. I was holding hands with a man. With *Reid.*

Reid Cabot holding my hand would have filled my spank bank to the brim in high school. Hell, Reid Cabot *looking* at me with a nod and distracted, "*Hey*" when I visited Asher's house had been enough. And the few times he'd smiled at me? Epic.

Where were we walking? Central Park unfurled on our right with Columbus Circle ahead. We'd left the hotel at the same time as a lot of other people who'd been at dinner, so I supposed we should keep up the act while we were still in the vicinity.

Damn, I'd have to keep holding Reid Cabot's hand while pretending this was just something we did because we were a couple. What a hardship. Though I did need to address our arrangement.

Couldn't I just enjoy holding his hand for another minute?

Spit it out already.

Instead, I said, "They really need to change that."

Reid's long-legged stride faltered. "Sorry, who should change what?"

"Oh, I guess that only made sense if you could read my mind. Quick, what am I thinking?"

He stopped to peer at me intently as he dramatically put his finger to his temple. A family of tourists eating pretzels brushed by, and I shivered under Reid's gaze. He wore a long charcoal coat that hugged his lean frame. A burgundy scarf hung around his neck. It looked soft. What would his cheek feel like? His face was smooth, but would I feel the hint of stubble?

"You're thinking…" He glanced back toward Fifth Avenue, then ahead of us. "That there must be Italian-Americans to celebrate who weren't colonizers."

"Yes!" It pleased me more than it should have that he'd guessed correctly. We walked on toward Columbus Circle and the tall monument and pedestrian area in the middle with traffic flowing around it. I said, "I read that it was made a landmark so it can't be removed."

"Grandmother was probably on the committee," he muttered before inhaling deeply. "I'm stuffed, but damn those street nuts smell amazing."

I inhaled the honey-salt scent deeply as we passed the cart. "Jesus, they do. You know, I don't think I've ever had them."

Reid gasped. "And you call yourself a New Yorker?"

"Do I? I don't think Albany counts, and I was in Boston for four years. I've only lived in Manhattan a few months."

"It's a state of mind. Wait, am I about to break into Billy Joel?"

"I don't know, are you?" In the distance, "Jingle Bell Rock" echoed from the ice rink in Central Park. "Dunno if you can fight the rising tide of Christmas music."

"Challenge accepted. My dad *loved* Billy Joel." Reid cleared his throat and launched into a song I'd never heard before that was apparently by someone named Billy Joel. Reid had a rich, smooth voice, and the fact that he could sing was sexy AF. Could he speak French or another language fluently? I was afraid to ask in case I just came on the spot.

"Not bad," I said when he finished the chorus.

"All those years I was forced into the choir at Rencliffe."

"Oh yeah, Asher was too. Lucky for me, I can't carry a tune to save my life."

"Come on." He tugged my hand lightly. "I bet you're better than you think."

"Trust me. I am not." The day I let Reid hear my screeching would be right about never.

He smiled. "Okay, I'll let you off the hook. For the singing—the nuts are non-negotiable. If you're going to be my boyfriend, you have to eat the nuts."

After a pause, we burst out laughing. "That should be your new Grindr bio," I said.

"Maybe I'd have more luck with it."

"Uh… How are *you* not having luck on Grindr?"

Reid scoffed. "So many guys, but… Just call me Goldilocks. You know what it's like."

"I've never seen it!" I said too quickly and too emphatically.

Just call me a liar with a side of cowardly.

"Oh, right!" He waved his free hand. "Sorry. Anyway, you're not missing anything. Which apps do you use? I met my last girlfriend on Love or Bust. It wasn't love, but… Well, maybe I thought it was for a little while, but it was only a summer thing. You should try the app. Once the holidays are over and we're both 'single' again."

"Right. Uh-huh. I will—thanks for the rec."

"Anytime. And tomorrow, we pop your cherry."

My heart lurched into my throat, and I suddenly sounded like a soprano. "What?"

"Street nuts. What other New York institutions haven't you tried?"

I managed to catch my breath. "Probably a lot of things. School's intense."

"There's the food category, and then museums and galleries. Shopping at certain stores. We should make a list."

"Okay." I couldn't hold in my grin. "That would be fun. Are you sure? You've probably done them all already."

"Most. There might be a few obligatory experiences I'm missing. Besides, you're doing me a massive favor."

The little bubble of happiness went splat. "You said you'd do something in return, right? I mean, besides nuts and stuff."

Thanksgiving dinner suddenly threatened to come back up. I hated this so much, but if Reid could help me, Logan and Seth would never have to know how much I'd fucked up.

"Absolutely. Yes, we should talk terms and conditions." He dropped my hand and took his phone from his pocket, suddenly all business. "Happy to put it in writing if you prefer?"

"No, that's okay. Not for my sake, I mean. Unless you want to, which you probably will. Um, you said anything, right?"

Reid chuckled, then gave me an intense look and raised his eyebrow. "Why? What's your price?"

My dick swelled in my jeans like I was a dumb, horny kid. Which I still felt like I was too much of the time. I reminded myself I was in med school. Soon enough, I'd be an actual doctor. An adult. Maybe I'd even find the balls to get over myself and finally get laid.

Okay, that wasn't a helpful train of thought. Reid was waiting, and I had no time to come up with a graceful way to put it.

"Ten grand," I blurted.

Reid's teasing smirk flattened into confusion. "Dollars?"

"Yeah." I kept my chin up. "You've got a lot of money, right?"

"You want me to pay you ten thousand dollars to be my boyfriend for the holidays?"

"No!" My cheeks flushed hot. "*Fake* boyfriend, and I'll pay back all of it. With interest. It would be a loan."

Reid seemed to take this in, his dark gaze assessing me. I willed my dick to behave. He actually stroked his chin. He'd always been clean-shaven since I'd known him, and I'd often wondered what he'd look like with scruff. Not that I was complaining about his amazing face.

Focus.

"Why do you need ten thousand dollars?"

I shifted and crossed my arms, trying to breathe through the flood of shame and rage and pain as I ducked out of the way of a group of teenagers. "Does it matter?"

Reid's thick brows met, and he joined me at the edge of the sidewalk on the park's border. "It does if it's illegal."

"Huh? No way! Nothing like that." At least I wasn't *that* stupid.

Reid was still contemplating me, and despite the humiliation, my hot skin tingled. "Gambling?"

I snorted. "I'd achieve the same outcome from setting my fucking money on fire and watching it burn."

He arched a brow, and I wanted to run my finger over it. "Wise words."

"Seth always says that when Pop wants to go to the casino to play the slots. That's my grandpa. Sort of. Logan's dad." I shook my head, trying to stop rambling. "Anyway, I don't gamble."

"Except on surprise propositions from your best friend's brother."

Some of the tension evaporated, and we shared a smile. There was that tingle again, traveling down my spine.

"Um, right. But seriously, it's not gambling. It's..." The icy-hot shame washed back through me, and I shoved my hands in my jacket pockets. "It's nothing illegal, I promise. It's just..." I struggled to land on the right word. "Embarrassing. I can't cover it, and I can't ask my dads."

He nodded. "Okay. I can transfer it now."

"For real?"

Reid said, "Yeah, no problem," so easily that it was hard not to resent him just a little even as gratitude and sweet, *sweet* relief filled me.

"Thank you. I'll pay you back, I swear. With interest."

"Sure. I know. Interest isn't necessary." He tapped his phone, not really seeming to care if I did or not. But I would—every single red cent, and I'd never, ever be such a moron again. I should have known better. I hated myself for being so gullible.

At least this way, Logan and Seth never had to know. If I asked, they'd give me the money. I knew they would. They'd drain their savings for me, but I'd rather eat glass than disappoint them like that. They'd never really been obligated to do anything for me, yet they'd done *everything*.

Logan had barely been married to my mom before she died, and yet he'd taken me on like I was his. Then Seth had too. No, I had to deal with my stupidity on my own.

"Text me your details," Reid said.

I scrolled my contacts. "I don't think I have you, actually."

"Me either." Reid gave me a wide, gorgeous grin. "Guess we should rectify that, *boyfriend.*"

Miraculously, I managed to give him my number without stuttering or forgetting a number as my heart thumped. I should have just AirDropped him.

Boyfriend.

It wasn't real, but that word on those wide, sexy lips was music to my ears.

THE JINGLE OF keys from the hallway made me jump even though I was on the couch waiting with my anatomy textbook open on my lap. Not that I'd read any of it in the darkness. Too bad I couldn't learn the info by osmosis.

The muted TV flickered blue over the long space that included the couch, a small dining table, and the kitchen. Our bedrooms and shared bathroom opened off the living room.

As Olivia entered, she was backlit by the bright hallway. She dropped her keys on the little shelf attached to the wall, a shadow sweeping over her as the door closed.

"Well, if it isn't Reid Cabot's new boyfriend pretending to study."

I didn't bother to insist that I could see fine by the light of the TV since it was an obvious lie. The open textbook was more of a weird security blanket. I tugged at the neck of my ratty old Lake Placid T-shirt and said, "Look, I can explain."

"Oh, you will." She grinned as she kicked off her heels. "This should be good."

"It's not what you think." Olivia and I had hit it off right away, and she was alarmingly good already at calling me on my shit.

She hung her coat in the closet and headed for the bottle of red on the kitchen counter. I closed my eyes, still slouched on the sofa, listening as she poured herself a healthy glass with a familiar *glug-glug*.

She asked, "Why? What do I think?"

I shrugged, keeping my eyes closed and head back. The sofa dipped as she settled on the other end. Then she got up, muttering about her tights before settling again. She poked my arm with her now-bare toe.

"Spill."

I laid out what happened when Asher and I arrived at the event, my eyes still closed even though I couldn't have slept if you'd paid me. Speaking of which, I shifted uneasily and kept *that* part of the arrangement with Reid to myself.

I could have asked Olivia's mom for the money, but it made me queasy to even consider it. Angela was a little…out there, but she'd done a ton for me and the family. I couldn't ask for more from her. Much better to have the deal with Reid. Quid pro quo and all that.

"Dylan said there was a lot of gossip when Reid came out as bi. To be expected from that crowd."

I opened my eyes. "How's Dylan? You looked happy together tonight. Did you talk to him about the text thing?"

Olivia gave me a shrewd look over her wine glass. "Uh-uh. You're not distracting me. Dylan also said Mrs. Cabot told his mom that Reid was 'rebelling' and it was a 'phase,' because she's ridiculous. I mean, he's thirty or something."

"Twenty-nine."

"He's your boyfriend, so you would know."

I closed my textbook and thudded it onto the wooden coffee table. I'd been trying to focus on any other sound than the thumping of my heart, which echoed in my ears as though I had increased intercranial pressure.

"He's obviously *not* my boyfriend. I'll go to a few stuffy holiday events. The end."

Olivia sipped her wine. "You guys looked good together."

I hoped it was too dim for her to spot the blush as my cheeks went hot. "Please," I scoffed.

"You seemed wrapped up with each other at dinner."

"Huh? We were talking. Small talk. That's it."

"Hmm. If you say so." She took another sip of her wine while raising an eyebrow.

I'd grabbed a beer when I got home, and I tipped up the bottle, only getting a few warm drops and remembering belatedly I'd finished it. "Dude, I'm not gay."

"Okay." Olivia ran her finger around the rim of her wine glass, making a low vibration. "I mean, you know it's totally okay if you're gay or bi or…questioning or whatever?"

"Obviously! I have two dads. I mean, kind of. Stepdads."

She frowned. "They are a hundred percent your dads. No qualifiers necessary."

"Yeah. I know."

It had taken years to get used to even thinking of Logan and Seth as my dads. Even longer before I could describe them that way. I'd always called them by their first names and still did.

Actually, I'd probably called Logan "asshole" more than his name the first couple of years. I'd hated him when he and Mom married after he had a serious accident and she was his nurse.

Nothing changes if nothing changes," Mom had said. That philosophy had led to a few great choices—and some epically bad ones, including the snap marriage to Logan. Then Mom was gone, and—

I inhaled sharply, shoving away those memories. That image I'd never,

ever get out of my head.

"Hey." Olivia squeezed my arm gently with her soft hand. "It's okay. Whatever you're feeling, it's okay."

Shaking her off, I strode to the kitchen, the tile there cold under my bare feet. "I'm not *feeling* anything!" I popped the top off another beer and chugged. "Just worried about my exams."

"Okay." She sipped her wine. "Which one's first?"

That was the great thing about Olivia. She could be persistent—similar to her mom even though she'd deny that fiercely—but she knew when to back off. I rejoined her on the couch, and we talked about my exams for a while.

Eventually, Olivia yawned widely. "I'd better get my contacts out. Hey, you want to decorate this weekend? We need to glitter up this joint. I bought a fake mini tree. Speaking of buying things, what are you getting your dads for Christmas? I need to find something for Mom. Want to go shopping?"

"If I have to."

She laughed. "I guess you really aren't gay or you'd be a much better shopping partner." She gave my thigh an affectionate bump with her foot before disappearing into the bathroom.

I swallowed down the flood of nausea with a *gulp*. She'd only been joking. It was a lame stereotype that gay men liked shopping, and I knew Olivia didn't really believe it. She'd been trying to make me feel better since I'd reacted so strongly earlier.

"Fuck me," I muttered. Not that anyone had, which was all on me. I was gay. I could download a dozen apps and find a hookup in Hell's Kitchen in five minutes. "Fuck," I muttered again, finishing the rest of the beer even though it wouldn't settle my nerves.

Most people wouldn't care that I was gay. My dads and the family would accept me. Marrying Logan might have been a massive mistake on Mom's part—boy, had the shiny glow dulled on that relationship quickly—but in the end, he'd been the best change to my life she ever made. Even if it took me years to realize.

My friends would support me too. Olivia, the med school crowd I was still getting to know. Asher apparently already knew? A reminder that made me squirm and leap off the couch to start pacing.

I'd considered saying those two little words—*I'm gay*—a million times. Most people would think it was insane that I had two fathers and was afraid to come out. It probably was, but that didn't change the cold fist of fear that still had a grip on me.

What was I even afraid of? Not being believed—like people would think it couldn't be true that I could have two dads and coincidentally be queer too.

Most of all, I was terrified people would think it *wasn't* a coincidence. That Logan and Seth had turned me gay or some bullshit.

Olivia's phone chimed as she came out of the bathroom, and she muttered, "Good thing I'm still up," before swiping the screen. "Hey, Mom! How's Japan? What time is it? It's late here."

"I know it is, but since when are you hitting the pillow before two a.m.?"

"She has a point," I said.

Olivia rolled her eyes and faced the phone toward me. On screen, Angela called out, "Hiya, sugar! How are your exams going?" She wore a fuchsia suit, and her blonde hair was still almost bigger than she was.

"Good, thanks."

"I was just gabbing with Seth the other day. He and Logan are so proud of you. You'll be a doctor in no time."

That still felt a million years away, but I thanked her. I knew Seth and Logan were proud of me, but it was sad how happy it made me to have it independently confirmed.

Would they still be proud if they knew how stupid I'd been?

My stomach clenched as I nodded and smiled to whatever Angela was saying about the best sushi she'd ever had. It was better for everyone if I dealt with it myself. And I had—Reid was lending me the money, and that would be that.

"Connor, will you please tell my daughter she's being a silly goose?"

I refocused. "Um…"

Olivia sighed. "Mom, I'm not qualified for this board."

"How so?" Angela asked. "This is a charity to help teenagers. You were recently a teenager. They want young people to have a voice instead of a bunch of old fogies like me. And it ties in perfectly with your studies."

I said, "Totally. You want to work in the nonprofit sector. This is an awesome opportunity."

"Stop with the imposer syndrome," Angela said.

Olivia laughed. "*Imposter* syndrome, Mother. And fine, you're right."

Angela whooped. "Connor, you're my witness! Olivia Barker-Robertson said I'm right."

"Duly noted."

I waved bye to Angela and took my textbook to my room as she and Olivia started bickering about Olivia needing to give her little sister more attention. I flopped onto my bed, not bothering to open the textbook. There was no way I could focus.

Especially not when I'd held hands with Reid Cabot.

It'd been bizarre to hang with Reid without Asher there. Reid had always seemed so grown-up and sophisticated to me. He'd barely paid me any attention before, but now we somehow felt like equals.

I was apparently someone he could pretend to date and people didn't laugh their asses off at the concept. Teenage me was amazed.

And horny.

God, the way he'd had his arm around me. He'd smelled like a forest in the best way, and his suit had been perfectly tailored to his long, lean body. I'd had a million daydreams about what being Reid Cabot's boyfriend would be like.

I'd once seen him kiss a girl at a party Asher and I had only been able to attend because it was Asher's house too and I was spending the weekend. Reid and his college girlfriend were drinking with their friends before heading out to a club.

"Attend" was a strong word. Asher and I had lurked in the background, gulping any booze we could get our hands on from red Solo cups. Even rich kids in Manhattan weren't above Solo cups.

The memory of Reid kissing his girlfriend was vivid yet fuzzy. I only had a vague recollection of her being…girl-shaped. It had been all Reid. His expensive jeans clinging to his ass. The way he'd smiled at her like she was the only one in the room even though hip-hop was blasting and some obnoxious guy was bumping into everyone as he "danced" around the living room.

Reid had whispered to her and kissed her like she was something fragile before enclosing her in his arms. I'd watched from behind a tall potted plant in which someone had left a crushed can of beer, aching for it to be me with Reid.

Now it was.

"As if," I muttered aloud before putting on my noise-canceling head-phones to block out Angela's nasal Texas twang that could wake the dead.

Reid would never look at me like he had that girl. This was a temporary arrangement. The only place Reid Cabot would actually be my boyfriend was in my wildest dreams.

Chapter Five

Reid

HOLDING MY BREATH, I strode from my office as quietly as I could while still appearing confident and not as if I were a teenager sneaking out past curfew.

"Reid."

I jolted at the quiet command and painted a pleasant, neutral expression on my face as I turned to Grandmother's glass-fronted office. She was typically only in twice a week given all her social commitments, and I'd avoided her until now.

The door was ajar, and I stepped inside. "I didn't realize you were here today," I lied.

Grandmother peered at me over the top of her sleek reading glasses. "I'm still president of this company."

"Of course. I just know how busy the holiday season is for you."

"Mm. I presume you're leaving early to attend the Lawrences' tree lighting."

I resisted reminding her that six-thirteen p.m. wasn't "early" to leave work. She wasn't going to change after all these years. "Yes."

Her eyes on a stack of paperwork, she asked, "And are you going alone?"

Here we go.

"I'm going with Connor." It had been a week since I'd dropped the bombshell, and I was surprised it had taken this long for Grandmother to address it. "My boyfriend," I added.

Still not looking at me, she said, "Are you sure it's…suitable?"

"Am I sure *what* is suitable?"

Even as I reminded myself I was an adult and there was nothing she could do to prevent me from dating whomever I wanted, my heart raced. I wanted to loosen my tie. It had been so much easier before I'd come out. Safer.

I scoffed at myself for being melodramatic. I was a wealthy, cis white man. I was quite safe even if my grandmother found my bisexuality distasteful and inconvenient. Besides, pretending to date Connor had been my choice.

She faced me squarely now, still sitting behind the oak desk that had been her father's. The rest of the office was modern and monochrome compared to the scuffed wood with drink rings staining the right-hand surface. Whether from coffee or whiskey, we'd never truly know.

"This young man is, well, *young.*"

"Connor's twenty-three. I'm only six years older. He's an adult like Asher."

For a moment, I thought she might actually snort before she said, "Your brother might be nominally an adult, but we both know he's not quite there yet."

"Maybe he would be if he had more responsibility. He could go to the Lawrences' party instead of me."

"Veto. You know how important these events are to maintaining and elevating our position. Which is why I think it's best you attend alone. Cecilia will be there."

"Who?"

She glared. "Cecilia Weston, as you well know. I don't understand why you refuse to take her for dinner. The club has a wonderful holiday menu."

"Because I have a boyfriend."

Grandmother exhaled noisily. "If you insist."

"I do! Connor's my boyfriend. He's smart and sweet and has the cutest dimple when he's happy."

"How can I argue with a dimple?" She raised her hands in surrender before flipping a page from the file on her desk. "I'm sure the Lawrences will be impressed."

Gritting my teeth, I said, "You're welcome to attend instead."

Friday night with Connor would be far better spent starting on the New Yorker activity list I'd made. We could go down to the Meatpacking District and get dinner from one of the vendors at Chelsea Market.

There was a pop-up art exhibit involving household objects crafted out of candy canes. To me, a random modern art pop-up was quintessential New York.

"You know we receive far too many invitations not to divide and conquer. Did you work on the proposal this week?"

I blinked at the abrupt shift of topics. For a foolish, ridiculous moment, I thought she meant my secret project—which was nonsensical since it was *secret.* I automatically answered, "Of course," which was my stock response when my mind had drifted and I wasn't sure what was being discussed.

That happened far more often than I liked to admit.

"This island is an emerging market. We don't want to let Marriott get there before us."

Right. *That* proposal. "Yes, it's all I've been working on. It's not quite ready yet. It'll be next week."

"Mm. All right, darling." She flipped another page, her gaze lowering.

I'd have to work extra hours to get it done, but I would. We'd opened plenty of resorts, and this one wouldn't be much different. She didn't have to know I'd spent the week researching the list of activities for Connor. I was the Senior Vice President under our CEO, who answered to Grandmother yet performed the majority of the practical duties.

Once upon a time, I'd been highly invested in my role and the company. Now, I was damn lucky the CEO was Type A and happy to do most tasks herself.

It was reassuring Grandmother had called me "darling," as pathetic as that was. Even when my father had been alive, Grandmother had been the authority figure I'd most wanted to please for as long as I could remember.

"And you'll arrive early at our holiday breakfast at the community center?"

"As always." It was weeks away, so I wasn't sure why she was asking now.

I attended her Christmas Day event annually. It was sponsored by Utopia and featured hot food as well as baskets of nonperishables and giftwrapped toys. Asher hadn't been since before college, but I supposed I couldn't blame him for not wanting to be up early on Christmas morning for Grandmother's photo ops, no matter how worthy the cause.

I asked, "You'll be ready to dish out the apple-cinnamon oatmeal?"

"With ladle in hand."

"Your annual use of a kitchen utensil."

Grandmother laughed genuinely, her eyes crinkling as she looked up. "Yes, darling. As I've told you since you were a boy, it's better to leave the cooking to the experts."

I returned her smile. "Remember when Asher and I snuck downstairs at midnight on Christmas Eve to bake cookies for Santa?"

"How could I forget the fire department's visit?" She shook her head ruefully. "The co-op board was not pleased. You were ten. You should have known better."

My smile grew brittle. "Yes, well, I haven't tried baking since."

While I had fond memories of attempting to bake cookies without a recipe with my little brother on a step stool beside me, the aftermath had been decidedly un-festive.

"I have to meet Connor," I said. "See you next week."

She flipped another page so forcefully I heard it rip. "I'll be here over the weekend making sure everything's in order for the general meeting in the new year."

I groaned internally at the implication that I should also be working through the weekend. "Sounds good," I said noncommittally. "Have a lovely evening."

As I pulled the door half-closed, Grandmother murmured, "All this will be yours sooner rather than later."

I turned back warily. "Why do you say that?" Was she sick? She didn't look it—granted she'd had some work done, but she could pass for fifteen years younger than she was.

"Because it's true." She examined me over her glasses. "I won't live forever despite my best efforts."

My stomach tightened. "Are you—"

"I'm perfectly fine. No need to be dramatic. I just want to make sure you remember your priorities." She ran a palm over the oak. "I'd always imagined your father sitting here by now." She swallowed thickly, and for a terrifying moment, I thought she might cry.

I'd never seen her express the emotions she *must* keep buried deep down. Dad had been her only child, and I know she'd loved and mourned him. Now I was the one to shoulder her expectations.

"Grandmother…"

She snapped back to business, flipping another page. "This desk still has plenty of wear in it. You'll look just right sitting here."

All I could think to say was, "Thank you."

"Give my best to the Lawrences."

With that dismissal, I nodded and escaped.

In the elevator, I ordered a ride to the Upper East Side. As I watched the app find a driver, a text from Connor appeared at the top of the screen. I quickly tapped it.

Hey. I'm on my way. Meet you outside? They might not let me in otherwise.

Chuckling, I replied:

You must be wearing the leather jacket again. If you bring the motorcycle, they might mistake you for a gang member. You know, if gangs looked like they did in movies from the fifties.

I watched the three dots appear, flickering as he typed.

You're saying I should leave my switchblade at home? Fine.

In the lobby, the security guard said, "Wow, you look happy for once, Mr. Cabot." He hastily added, "Must be because it's Friday!"

I realized I was grinning. "You got it, Drew. TGIF."

In the car, I went back to the New Yorker list and texted Asher a question. A few minutes later, he replied:

Huh? Why?

Grumbling under my breath, I muttered, "Just answer." What did it matter to him? Before I could respond to my brother, my phone buzzed with an incoming video call. The ride share driver was engrossed in his own conversation through his Bluetooth headset, so I swiped to accept.

Asher's face filled my screen with a frown, his white kitchen cabinets behind him. "Why do you care what Connor likes to do?"

I'd simply asked Asher if Connor would prefer walking the High Line or across the Brooklyn Bridge. I'd received wildly conflicting advice from several friends for my top New Yorker activities, so I was going with my gut.

"Just curious," I said dismissively.

What was the harm in tailoring the list to Connor's preferences? I'd do the same for anyone. Not that the list was part of the deal we'd made, but I'd enjoyed planning the options. I'd found myself looking forward to seeing Connor's reactions to the items on the list and wondering which ones he'd be most excited for…

"That's a really weird thing to be curious about."

"It's nothing. Forget it." Why was he making a big deal out of nothing?

He exhaled with a huff through his nose. "I'm not sure this is such a good idea."

"You were all for it on Thanksgiving." It was too late now. The idea of calling it off made me strangely antsy.

"I thought it might be good for him. Loosen a few of his screws. Why are you asking about the High Line? Gamma sure as hell won't be there. So why would you be taking Connor there? Or across the Brooklyn Bridge, where Gamma *definitely* won't be. The only way she leaves Manhattan is by air."

I really didn't feel like explaining the list to my brother. It wasn't a big deal. The driver laid on the horn at the perfect time, and I shrugged and motioned to my ear as if I hadn't heard the question.

Apparently he didn't feel like repeating it since now he asked, "Is Connor going to the Lawrences' party tonight?"

"Yeah, I'm meeting him there now."

Asher screwed up his face. "I hope people there won't be weird about it. You and him. Not that it's real, but…"

"I'm sure it'll be fine." I fidgeted and readjusted the seatbelt, which threatened to strangle me. "Morgan and his wife seemed very welcoming."

"I guess. Will Gamma be there?"

"No, she has another party. You'd know this if you did your part."

"Hey, I show up to Gamma's events. Well, most. You can handle the rest."

Not that I had a choice. It had always been on me, particularly after our father died, but before then too. I'd dutifully attended the endless events and smiled and made small talk and schmoozed even when I was a kid.

Addison's voice echoed in my mind: "*How will the rich white man ever survive these hardships?*" I was being ridiculous to complain.

Asher blurted, "I don't want Connor to get hurt."

I blinked. "What? Why would he get hurt?"

After hesitating, Asher said, "He's been through a lot. He's finally settled, and now he's in med school. I don't want this to mess him up."

"Why would it mess him up? We have an agreement. An arrangement. It's…business."

Asher made a dubious sound and mumbled something I couldn't make out. I braced myself on the back of the passenger seat as the car swerved around a double-parked delivery van.

"Has Connor mentioned needing money to you?" I asked.

Asher's eyebrows flew up. "No. Why?"

"Nothing," I said dismissively. All right, so this debt wasn't the source of Asher's disquiet. "Hey, did I imagine that you told me Connor's queer? I could have sworn you mentioned it when you guys were at Rencliffe."

"Thanks for spilling that, by the way. Connor's barely answered my texts this week."

"He told me he's studying for a big anatomy exam. I'm sure he's just busy."

"Glad he's talking to *you*."

I shot him a grin. "I'm irresistible."

Asher looked like he was going to say more, but eventually rolled his eyes. "Apparently."

"So… Do you think he really is queer?" It didn't matter, but I'd chewed over the question all week.

"Maybe. I think so." Asher shrugged. "He says no, and he's the one who gets to decide. I dunno. I've been waiting for him to come out for years. I could be wrong."

"Wouldn't be the first time."

He held up his middle finger. "Hilarious."

"What makes you think he's not straight?"

"The way he stared at Greg McBride's ass at Rencliffe, for starters. Not to mention—" Asher broke off and looked away.

"What?"

He seemed to ponder it, about to say something but cutting himself off again. "It's a vibe, I guess. He's always been tightly wound. He's never seemed interested in girls. Which doesn't mean anything. It's little things that added up, I guess. What do I know? I just don't want things to get weird."

"Don't worry about it." Asher was being dramatic. As the car pulled up outside the building, I added, "Gotta go!"

Waiting on the sidewalk under the glow of a streetlight, I added a tip for the driver in the app and peered up and down the dark street. No sign of him, but I was early.

I opened my notes app and surveyed the list, deciding to keep both the High Line and the bridge. There was no reason I had to limit the New Yorker activities to ten.

As Connor rounded the corner in his leather jacket, he saw me and lifted his hand in a wave. I waved back, and as his cheek dimpled, a flare of excitement sparked through me. What would he think of the list?

His cheeks looked flushed with the cold. "Hey. Am I late?" The deepness of his voice still surprised me.

"Right on time. No motorcycle?"

"Nah, I took the subway here. My bike's in Albany. Costs way too much to park it in Manhattan. Can't wait to ride at Christmas."

I shuddered. "I still think it's way too risky."

"You and my dads will get along great." Was he blushing now? He quickly added, "Not that you'll meet them. This isn't—whatever."

"Right." Was it odd that I *did* want to meet Connor's parents? "Ready?" I held out my hand.

For a long moment, Connor only stared at my gloved hand, and I was about to awkwardly retract it when he said, "Right. Boyfriends," and took it with a firm grip. Our leather gloves squeaked.

My stomach flip-flopped.

We made our way past the massive, draped tree in the foyer, and Connor gave his coat to a staff member with very slightly less reluctance than he had at Thanksgiving. He wore dark jeans that hugged his lean hips and a form-fitting sweater.

"Nice," I said, running my hand down his arm. "Cashmere?"

"Uh-huh," he rasped, then cleared this throat. "It was a gift from Angela Barker. Olivia picked it out." He leaned closer. "Speaking of Olivia, I told her the truth." He fidgeted suddenly. "Most of it. Not about the…loan."

"Right. No problem. Everything's taken care of?"

"Yep. You got the payback schedule I sent?"

I smiled. "Yes. But as I said, there's no rush. I'm not worried about it."

Connor jammed his hands in his pockets. "That's nice of you, but I am. I don't like owing anyone."

Morgan approached as we entered the living room, where guests chatted under a high ceiling by beige furniture. The holiday decorations were rich, velvety green and red, and servers with trays of hors d'oeuvres circulated.

As we chatted with Morgan and others, I was aware once again of garnering more attention than usual. Everyone was friendly, and I was relieved as I chewed over what Asher had said. He was protective of his best friend, which was admirable and to be expected.

If Connor really was queer like me, maybe this would be a way for him to… Give it a test drive. Find his sea legs? Whichever metaphor fit the bill.

As I made small talk with Paul and Brittany Matheson, I monitored Connor. He nodded and made the right listening noises but gave off a jittery vibe. I laid my hand on the small of his back.

"Want a break?"

Connor nodded, and I guided him into the adjoining dining room. The table was laden with more finger foods, and we helped ourselves to a few bites. This seemed like a good time to bring up the list. My belly swooped, which was very strange since this wasn't *important*.

If he wasn't into the activities, it was no problem. I'd gotten carried away, but it had been a welcome distraction. Nothing more. Would he even remember we'd talked about it?

I popped a walnut and gouda tartlet into my mouth. "About the nuts…"

Connor swallowed a plump shrimp, dropping the tail into his napkin. "Nuts?"

"The street nuts. Sorry, I wasn't clear. I…" There was a drop of red cocktail sauce at the corner of his mouth, and I couldn't look away. "You've got…"

"Oh!" His tongue darted out just before he wiped with his napkin. "Gone?"

I was still staring at Connor's mouth. "Yes."

"So, what about the nuts? I haven't had any yet."

Right. Focus on nuts. I laughed, since my mind immediately zoomed down all sorts of different avenues.

"That's good," I said. "That you haven't had them. We'll have them together. I mean, if you want to. I thought it would be fun."

The dimple appeared in his cheek. "Totally."

"I made a New Yorker activity list. We talked about it briefly last week."

"Right, yeah." He smiled.

I wrapped my hand around my phone in my pocket. Why did I feel like I was about to give a presentation to the board at work? Connor was just my little brother's best friend. I'd known him for years—even if he was different now.

"Reid?"

"Yes." I pulled out my phone and opened the notes app. "I've created a list of what I believe are quintessential New Yorker experiences. For me, at least. Because every New Yorker will have their own top ten, and some could be wildly different. And you can veto any of these options for any reason."

"*Okaay.* This sounds weirdly official."

I laughed. "Sorry, 'veto' is Grandmother's favorite word, and it rubbed off on me."

"All right, cool. I accept the terms and conditions."

"Are you sure? I might have sneaky clauses in there."

"I'll exercise my veto power in that case. Besides, I trust you."

The rush of pleasure those three words—*I trust you*—gave me was a surprise. I nodded and gulped my glass of bubbly. We both took a spring roll from a passing server, and I swallowed it too quickly in my eagerness, which made me cough.

"Okay?" Connor asked, leaning closer.

"Yep! No need for first aid." After another sip of my drink, I added, "These are in no particular order, and like I said, you can veto." I hadn't looked at the note on my phone since I'd memorized the list, but now I was questioning my choices.

Connor's brows lowered in a cute little quizzical expression. "I'm sure I'll like them all."

"Of course. It's not a big deal." And wait—*cute?* I needed to slow down on the champagne. I was practically lightheaded. "Number one—but not in any order of importance."

He nodded seriously. "Understood."

"Visit an underground club or bar in the Village. I have one in mind."

His eyes widened, which was also cute. "Oh! That sounds awesome. I'm down."

Off to an excellent start, but I hesitated. I did look at the list then. Even though I'd said no particular order, it would be better to present the options in an optimal way.

"*Annnd* number two is eat street nuts?" Connor asked.

"Yes. Sorry. I'm not quite satisfied with the list. Why don't we start with those, and I'll keep refining."

Actually, rethinking it now, surprising Connor with the list items as we went would be far more fun. Excitement bubbled up. Gifts were always more fun when you didn't know what was under the tree. Not that I'd had anything under the tree in years. Or a tree, for that matter.

"Sure." That quizzical expression was back, and it was still cute.

What was happening to me?

"Everyone, if we can gather in the foyer for the unveiling?" Morgan called as servers ushered us through.

Though the Lawrences' foyer was massive, it was still crowded with the guests and a ten-person choir in red and gold robes gathered around the base of the tree. The lights were dimmed, and we all *ohhed* and *ahhed* on cue as the curtain draping the dark tree was dropped. Even before the lights were on, it was impressive.

The soprano-led choir launched into "Angels We Have Heard on High" as children hung the final ceremonial ornaments on the tree, using the grand curving staircase to reach the higher branches.

As the song ramped up and the soprano earned her paycheck with a multi-syllable "*Gloria*" that sent chills down my spine, someone flipped an unseen switch.

Even though I knew it was coming—we were standing there in the foyer for a tree-lighting after all—I blinked in surprise as the glittering multi-colored lights blazed to life with a golden star on top. The whole tree seemed to shimmer as if it was alive somehow.

We clapped and exclaimed on cue. I leaned down and whispered to Connor, "They really outdid themselves this year."

He didn't immediately answer, his gaze locked on the tree. "I wish Seth could see it. He loves Christmas. Are we allowed to take a pic?"

"Allowed? The Lawrences would love nothing more than for their tree to trend on social media."

Connor diligently took several pictures of the tree from different angles, then tapped out a message, presumably to Seth.

"You're a good son," I said.

He shook his head dismissively, but bit his lip as if trying to hide a smile. I really wanted to see that dimple again.

The party went on, and I had to make dull small talk when I wanted to hear more about what Connor was studying, even though when I'd asked, he'd demurred and said it was "boring." After doing my duty and schmoozing with everyone I felt Grandmother would prioritize, I managed to corral Connor into one of the hallways off the foyer.

"You ready to go?" I asked in a low voice.

"If you are?"

"Definitely. Let's get our coats and make an early exit."

"Sorry to interrupt," Morgan said as he appeared.

"You're not!" Connor and I exclaimed in perfect guilty unison. Laughing, I asked, "What can I do for you?"

"My mom just wants a picture by the tree. You too, Connor."

"It's okay," Connor quickly said. "I'm not photogenic at all."

I said, "What? That's not true." I'd scrolled back through his Insta once or twice this week, and he had great pics there. Some selfies with his med school friends and a bunch with Asher over the years. It was fascinating to chart his growth from the Rencliffe days as he'd filled out into a man.

There was one photo of Connor straddling his motorcycle in the leather jacket that did make riding it seem more appealing. I still thought it was too risky, but he'd looked so satisfied and in control.

Connor waved us off. "I'll see you after."

I followed Morgan, who was talking about New Year's Eve plans, and looked back to watch Connor tapping at his phone. His pants clung to his long, lean thighs, and I imagined riding behind him on the bike, my legs hugging his hips—

Then the floor somehow disappeared, and there was nothing I could do to fight gravity as I flew.

Chapter Six

Connor

AS SOMETHING HEAVY *crashed* and glass *smashed*, voices rose in alarm. I spun around to find Reid…gone. But Morgan Lawrence, his wife, Louise, and a few other people were staring down with wide eyes. I raced to the top of the three steps leading into the foyer.

Reid sprawled at the bottom on his left side. He laughed tightly. "Who put those stairs there?"

"Oh my god, are you okay?" Morgan exclaimed, still rooted to the spot staring down at Reid.

I crouched at Reid's side before anyone even moved. "It's okay," I said, channeling the confidence my clinical skills professor reminded us was key. *Fake it until you make it.* "Stay very still, okay?"

"I'm fine!" Reid pushed himself up to sitting with his left hand, wincing.

"I'm calling an ambulance," Louise said.

"No!" Reid tried to jump to his feet, but I gripped his shoulder, keeping him sitting. If he hit his head, I didn't want him to stand and pass out.

Reid said, "I just tripped." His cheeks flushed, and he glanced around at the gathering crowd. "I'm clumsy, that's all. Thanks for the concern."

Cataloging his potential injuries, I gently took his right hand, where he'd been holding the shattered wine glass. He'd definitely cut himself, and Louise handed me a cloth napkin I quickly pressed into Reid's palm after making sure there was no glass remaining.

"I'm getting up!" he hissed to me.

I could imagine how embarrassed he was, although of course he had no reason to be. His dark brown eyes implored me, and I relented, holding his right arm as he stood.

"My boyfriend's a doctor," he said loudly. "He'll take good care of me. Thanks for your concern."

Morgan and Louise led us into a small bathroom, and pulled out a first aid kit from under the sink before Reid waved them away with a smile and closed the door.

"*Fuck.*" He leaned back against the door. "Please let no one have caught that on their phone."

Staying close to him in case he got dizzy, I said, "Don't worry. Everyone falls and stuff."

He groaned, closing his eyes. His face was red, and in the bathroom's bright light, I could spot the very faint five o'clock shadow coming in on his chin and cheeks. And on his neck when I leaned a little closer...

Nope. Continue assessment of the patient. Examine his injuries, not his stubble. Or his Adam's apple, or the hollow of his throat.

"I can't believe I just did that," he muttered, eyes still closed.

"What happened? Were you looking at your phone or something?"

He opened his eyes, immediately dropping his gaze to the white tile floor. "Yep. Wasn't looking where I was going."

"Happens to all of us. Now look at me."

He did.

Holy shit, we were standing *really* close in the tiny bathroom. One of those... What did people call them? Powder rooms. "Um..." Assess the patient! "Are you dizzy?"

"No. Just from humiliation."

"Did you hit your head?"

"No." His mouth pinched. "I'm sure I didn't."

"You don't sound sure."

"No, I'm sure. I didn't hit my head."

"Let me see."

Gently, I took his face in my hands and ran my fingertips over the curves of his head, naming the bones in my head to stay focused on my job and not the softness of his thick hair. I was going to be humiliatingly hard in a second.

"Don't feel any swelling," I murmured.

Not on Reid's skull, anyway.

"I'm telling you I didn't hit my head." His breath was warm on my face.

"Okay." Ugh, my voice came out all fluttery. I dropped my hands. "I'll just do the concussion protocol."

Reid groaned, and the sound did *not* help my efforts to stay professional. "I'm fine! Aside from injuring my pride, I cut my hand. That's it." He pushed away from the door, but I didn't budge.

Which meant that now we were practically kissing we were so close.

Somehow, I managed to speak. "If you didn't hit your head, you'll pass no prob."

"Come on. I should get back out there. Can you put a Band-Aid on my hand?"

"Do I have to go ask if someone *does* have video of it?"

Reid sighed. "I surrender."

We were *so close.* The heat from his body seemed to radiate.

"Are you going to do something?" he asked, his gaze dropping. Not to the floor this time, but I swear to my mouth.

Did *I* hit my head? There was no way Reid Cabot was looking at my mouth like he wanted to kiss it.

No. Way.

I blurted, "What day is it?"

"Friday."

I nodded. "Date?" I could do this. Clinical. Professional.

Reid rattled off the full date, adding, "the new millennium."

"I'm going to say a few words, and I want you to remember them and repeat back to me. Okay?"

Reid put his finger to his temple. "Should I try to read your mind?"

I had to laugh. "Not this time. Okay, here we go."

"Okay, here we go," Reid repeated.

"Not yet."

"Not yet," he said.

"You're giving big older brother energy right now." Somehow it was still sexy but now wasn't the time to examine that. He was the patient, and I was the not-actually-a-doctor-yet. "I'm starting now." As Reid opened his mouth, I pressed my finger to his lips.

A slight puff of warm air met my finger as our eyes met. My mouth went dry. How many fantasies had I had over the years about being this close to Reid?

Fantasies about Reid looking down at me with his eyes dark and intense...

Jesus, maybe his pupils were dilating because of the concussion—which I was supposed to be ruling out!

Dropping my hand, I dictated a little too loudly, "Cat. Horse. Meadow. Bus. Cafeteria."

Reid's lips quirked. "Are the cat and horse friends? Did they take the bus to the cafeteria, or are they still in the meadow?"

I had to laugh again even as I gave him what I hoped was a stern, authoritative expression. "You're being a terrible patient."

"Yes, doctor. Apologies."

I took a deep breath and exhaled. "Can you remember the words?"

"Cat. Horse. Meadow. Bus. Cafeteria." Reid's voice was low and confident.

"Very good."

"Thank you, doctor."

Lust wasn't just sparking—it was erupting.

This isn't real. He's joking around. Not. Real.

"Anything else?" Reid asked softly, his eyes locked on me.

We were only a few inches apart, and I wanted to lean into the heat of his body… Jesus, Reid could have a concussion, and I was being incredibly unprofessional. I might not have been a doctor yet, but I had to act like it.

"Please name the twelve months backward."

"Ohh. A challenge. December." He paused. "Rebmeced."

It was a struggle to concentrate as it was, and it took me an embarrassing beat to get it. "Very good. You can just recite the twelve months from December back to January."

"Where's the challenge in that?"

By the time Reid finished saying each month itself backward with "Yraunaj," we were laughing.

I said, "Congrats—you passed the standardized assessment of concussion test."

He bowed slightly. "Thank you, doctor."

My pulse fluttered, and I cast around for what to say next, landing on, "Hand!" I cleared my throat. "Um, let me see your hand."

I maneuvered him to sit on the closed toilet seat and bent over his wound in the light of the vanity. In the cramped space, I had to stand around his leg, his knee between mine. With tweezers from the first aid kit, I made sure I hadn't missed any glass slivers before I disinfected the two small cuts on Reid's palm.

"Ouch."

Chuckling, I applied a large Band-Aid, pressing the adhesive to his skin. "All set."

"Aren't you going to kiss it better?"

Boom.

My heart and dick came to life as I met Reid's dark gaze. He was only joking—*obviously* he was joking! A wry smile played on his full lips, and this was the part where I laughed and made some joke or did *anything* except stare at him with all my blood rushing south.

Reid's smile faded. We stared at each other with his injured hand still cradled in mine. I couldn't breathe. I could be in his lap in a heartbeat and—

"Is everything okay?" Morgan asked as he knocked loudly.

I jolted back, almost falling myself and only saved by the wall. "Yep!" I shouted, opening the door.

We left after assuring the hosts Reid didn't need an ambulance, and my mind raced as the car Reid had ordered drove through the park to the west side. Reid groaned, and I snapped to attention.

"Headache?" I asked.

"Yeah." He pinched the bridge of his nose. "I can't believe I did that. Grandmother will not be happy."

"When did this headache start?"

He groaned again. "I passed the concussion test! This is just a schmoozing headache. It's exhausting having to be my best self with so many people. I'm fine. Unless you want to stay over and wake me up every hour to ask me who the president is."

"That's not necessary."

"Right, because I didn't hit my head, and I don't have a concussion. Glad you agree."

"No, because that's been debunked. There's no need to stop a concussed person from sleeping in the vast majority of cases. They need sleep. If you can carry on a conversation, walk without difficulty, and your pupils aren't dilated, sleep is indicated."

"Great. Then I can go to bed and try to forget this."

"Let me see your pupils again."

"Isn't it a little dark?" He laughed. "Okay, why don't you stay at my place tonight? You can check my pupils and put me to bed. I mean, if you'll be worried otherwise."

"Right. Yeah. Okay." What was I doing? This would be torture!

"I have a guest room. All above board. Not that you would think I'd…" He waved his left hand.

"Of course not."

We both laughed awkwardly. Because while I'd always thought Reid was smooth and sophisticated and cool, it turned out he was a little awkward like me. Well, I was a *lot* awkward, but still.

Reid lived in one of those amazing prewar apartment buildings on the Upper West Side. The doorman ushered us in, and there was a concierge as well. I half-expected a guy waiting in the elevator to push the button, but Reid did it himself.

The wallpapered hallway was bright, yet the light was golden and the light fixtures gleaming. Reid's front door led into a small foyer with closet. As I toed off my dress shoes, I gaped at the huge windows in the living room. The ambient light from the city cast a warm glow.

"Wow. This place is amazing," I said. Reid's style seemed a little monotone, but the space was incredible. I couldn't begin to imagine what it cost.

"Thanks." Reid seemed uncomfortable as he motioned to doors on either side of the living room, which held a leather sectional, massive wall-mounted TV, and a full dining table and smooth-edged chairs. "My bedroom's on that side, and the guest room is next to the kitchen."

"Cool. No Christmas tree yet?"

Reid seemed taken aback. It was admittedly a dumb question since there was clearly no Christmas tree. I could imagine exactly where it would go by the window beyond the dining table. Seth would have a field day decorating in here.

"I've never had one."

"You did as a kid, though. Right?" Asher and I had never spent the holidays together, and thinking about it now, I supposed he hadn't said much about his family traditions.

"Sure." Reid shrugged and flipped on a lamp. "When I was young. By the time I was in high school, we'd outgrown it. We didn't have Christmas morning with presents under the tree—too busy going to events. Grandmother's charity breakfasts."

"Oh." That sounded like torture. "I guess you think it's weird my dads still put up a tree even though I'm not a kid."

"Of course not. I'm sure Christmas at your house is very…cozy. Let me show you the guest room. Oh, you'll need pajamas."

"It's fine. I can just sleep in my underwear."

Reid nodded and cleared his throat but still brought me a Knicks T-shirt after he showed me the brown and beige guest room. It had its own bathroom that was stocked with packages of toothbrushes and everything I could need.

We watched TV for a while, Reid flipping channels until landing on *Scrooged*. We watched the rest of it with the commercials even though we probably could have found it on one of the streaming services.

"How's your headache?" I asked as the credits rolled. I'd been surreptitiously monitoring him, and he seemed fine. He'd relaxed into the couch beside me, and we'd had more wine.

Reid smiled. "Much better. Thank you, doctor."

Shit, the way he said that made me hot all over. "Let me look at your eyes again," I said in a weirdly gravelly voice.

Reid swallowed a sip of red wine, and it stained his lips for a moment. He nodded.

Since Reid had his feet up on the leather ottoman that was also a sort of coffee table, I couldn't stand in front of him. Instead, I just kneeled next to him on the couch with my feet tucked under me. Leaning close, I examined his pupils.

His lashes were thick, and there was one sitting just under his eye. I gently grasped it and held it up on my fingertip the way my mom had years ago. "Your pupils are good. And you get to make a wish."

"A wish," Reid repeated, his eyes locked with mine.

Ugh, he probably thought I was a dumb kid. "I guess you already have everything you want." I started to move, but he grasped my wrist.

"I still get my wish."

Reid closed his eyes, and I was frozen in place, his fingers warm on my skin. Then he opened his eyes and blew a puff of air to send the eyelash flying.

"I guess you can't tell me what you wished for or it-it won't come true," I stammered. God, he was gorgeous. How many times had I daydreamed about being this close to Reid Cabot, and now here I was…

"Those are the rules, doctor."

"Yep!" I bolted back, almost tumbling off the couch as I found my feet. "We should go to bed," I said.

And I said it *out loud.*

I swear, Reid's eyes darkened, his lips parting as his gaze dropped down my body.

Whoa. No. I was clearly imagining it. There was no way Reid would actually be into me. He thought I was straight, and I was an awkward kid he'd known forever. No way in hell.

I jerked a thumb toward the guest room. "'Night! If you feel sick, wake me up, okay?"

"I will." His full lips curved up. "Thanks again, doctor."

I escaped without blowing my load right then and there, so I counted it as a win.

MY PHONE BUZZED around five as I scrolled mindlessly after barely sleeping. I blinked in surprise at Logan's name and jabbed the screen.

"Hello?" I whispered, throwing off the covers in the very soft, very comfortable bed in the guest room. "What's wrong?" I curled my toes into the thick carpet.

"Nothing. What the hell are you doing awake? Don't tell me—you haven't been to bed yet."

He was mostly right since I'd been too wound up to relax, but I said, "Up early studying."

"Whatever floats your boat. I was just going to leave a message."

I rolled my eyes. "You know you could text me."

An engine rumbled, and I figured Logan was in his truck. He said, "And you know I hate all that stuff. Since when do you get up early? You're usually dead to the world with your ringer off until noon."

"I guess I'm growing up. I've had early classes all semester, FYI."

"No shit. I guess you are. Have any exams yet?"

"One. I probably bombed it."

Logan barked out a laugh. "You always say that, and you always do amazing."

I paced on the plush area rug. "I dunno. It's not like I'm the smartest one in the room anymore. I wasn't at Harvard either."

"You're still damn smart. Don't sell yourself short."

I had to smile at how emphatic Logan's tone was. "Yeah. Okay. Seth's all right?"

"He's good. Going Christmas shopping, so you'd better get your list to him pronto if you want anything. That's what I was calling to say."

Part of me thought I should argue I was too old for that, but I only said, "Okay. Where are you going?"

"Working Saturdays to finish up a job before Christmas. Why are you being so quiet?" He paused. "Got company?"

My heart skipped as I imagined Reid sleeping. On his back, or was he a side or stomach sleeper? Maybe his lips were parted and chest hair sticking up from the low neck of his tank top…

"No!" I protested far too strongly with a strangled laugh. "I mean, yeah. Olivia. Don't want to wake her up."

"Right." Did he sound disappointed? Before I could overthink it, he added, "Oh, I almost forgot. If you and Olivia are free next weekend, Will and Michael invited you to their holiday party. Michael's secretly flying in Will's parents from Scotland, and we're decorating the tree or some shit."

"Awesome. Seth'll love it."

Logan's voice went soft, and I could picture the goofy smile on his face as he said, "Yep."

"And wait, they invited me and…Olivia?" I huffed. "You guys know we're just friends, right? Jesus, you're worse than Angela."

"Nah, it's not that. Will and Michael went to Australia with Angela and her family at Christmas a few years ago, remember? They hung out with Olivia. I'm sure you both have better things to do, but in case you want to come home for the weekend to hang with the lame adults, you're invited."

"Uh, I think we'll pass."

He laughed. "Can't blame ya. You'll be home the weekend before Christmas though, right? For a week at least?"

"*Yes.* But I'm coming back here for New Year's Eve."

"To watch the apple drop?"

"Actual New Yorkers don't go to Times Square on New Year's Eve. That's for tourists."

"Well, la-di-da. So, you're an actual New Yorker now?"

"That remains to be seen." I grinned thinking about Reid's list. "I'm taking an exam on that soon."

"Huh?"

"Nothing. It's a dumb joke."

"Okay, get back to studying for your real exams. You're going to ace them."

I shrugged even though he couldn't see me. "Thanks."

"Hey, one more thing. Have you, uh, heard from Mike?"

The bottom of my stomach dropped, dread crashing through me. I almost asked, "*Who?*" but Michael of Will and Michael always went by his full name.

There was only one Mike we ever talked about, and it had been a long,

long time. And "talked about" was an exaggeration.

My lungs constricted, I managed to get out, "No. Why?" It was kind of the truth.

"There was a weird call for you from Florida. The man on the phone gave another name, but I think it was Mike. He's still down there?"

"Dunno. I guess." Before I could stop the stupid words from bursting out, I snapped, "Why? What do you care?"

"I don't." He inhaled audibly, and I could imagine Seth's imaginary voice in Logan's ear telling him not to get mad.

"Okay, whatever." Jesus, why was I acting thirteen again? Logan hated my father, and why shouldn't he?

Why couldn't I?

I forced a deep breath. "Sorry."

"S'okay. I'm glad you haven't talked to him. I know I'm not supposed to say that."

I had to laugh. "It's fine. Anyway, I have to study. Later."

Acid bubbled in my stomach, and I crept into the kitchen to gulp water and poke around in Reid's fridge. Huh. There were actually vegetables and raw meat, like he was going to cook them. I'd assumed he lived on takeout like me and Asher and Olivia. Like most people I knew.

I opened the cupboards one by one, of course opening every plate, bowl, glass, and mug storage place before finding the food. I should have realized the long cupboard was the pantry, though in my defense, everything in the kitchen including the fridge had identical doors and it was impossible to tell anything apart.

It made me smile that Reid had a bag of goldfish crackers, and I hoped he wouldn't mind if I munched on a few. I wandered to the window in my bare feet and realized the wooden floor was heated. I could see the treetops of Central Park a few avenues over, and lights coming on in other pre-war apartment buildings, including one with actual gargoyles on the roof.

The days were so short in December. The sun wouldn't be up for two hours. I should have probably gone back to bed and tried to sleep, but I stayed by the wide window, sitting sideways on the ledge, eating cheesy goldfish and watching a woman stories below walk a gigantic dog.

The city was so peaceful right now. I wasn't sure I'd ever been up this early to see it when I wasn't rushing to shower and get somewhere. Usually, I rolled out of bed with just enough time to make my first lecture of the day. In undergrad, I'd often missed early classes, but med school was different.

For a moment, I thought I heard something coming from Reid's bedroom. I stayed very still, listening, but there was nothing. I was tempted to peek in on him again, but it would be intrusive. I reminded myself he'd passed all the protocols and needed his sleep.

"So do you," I mumbled to myself, but I stayed on the windowsill. If Reid needed me, I'd be close at hand.

Chapter Seven

Reid

I MAY NOT have had a concussion—I truly didn't hit my head, so definitely not—but the embarrassment was enough to keep my headache lingering.

It was bad enough that my *splat* had been witnessed by so many acquaintances. What was keeping me tossing and turning was that Connor had been there. At least he hadn't seen me go down. I should know since I'd been watching him instead of where I was going.

He'd been at my side before I could really register what had happened. So confident and capable—he'd make an excellent doctor. It was even reassuring to know he was in the guest room on the other side of the apartment.

Good lord, that didn't make any sense. I had a couple of scrapes. I didn't need a doctor—or a med student. There was no reason I should be comforted by Connor staying over.

No reason to look forward to cooking him breakfast or ask him more about how concussion protocols had changed nowadays. Not because I had one, but because I enjoyed listening to him.

It was still early, but after waking before five, my brain refused to quiet. The duvet felt too hot, so I kicked it off and strode naked to the window to crack it open and peek through the blinds.

In the building across from mine, most windows were dark. Others glowed with the blue light of TVs. Still others had the curtains open and lights on. I smiled to see the old man on the tenth floor sitting at his kitchen table doing what I assumed was his regular crossword.

I'd refused to buy binoculars and be the creepy neighbor, as tempting as it could be when insomnia struck and I found myself in the darkness at the window.

Could anyone see me? I didn't think so since my lights were off, but maybe one of my neighbors was watching, wondering why that naked guy didn't sleep better.

Determined, I stole back under the covers. I'd sleep another hour before getting up to make Connor breakfast. Was there bacon? I could always run out to the bodega if not.

Oh! There was another item for the list: befriending a bodega cat. The cat at my local store was named Bran Muffin, and she always let me pet her.

I rolled to my other side. Then back again. Onto my stomach with one leg pulled up.

"Oh, for..."

With Herculean effort, I resisted grabbing my phone to check the time. Because if there were any notifications, I'd open them. Even if there weren't, I'd be doomscrolling before you could say *blue light doesn't help insomnia.*

Flopping over on my back, I sighed loudly. Addison was right—I needed to get laid. Release the pressure valve. But I obviously wasn't having a booty call with Connor in the guest room.

My mind helpfully filled with images of Connor—his cheek dimpling. His surprised laugh when he let down his guard a fraction. His calm, competent concern when he'd done the concussion tests on me. The way he'd gazed intently, his brown eyes close to mine...

"None of this is real," I repeated in the still of my bedroom.

The swoop of Connor's adorable James Dean hair, the pink of his lips, *dat ass.*

"*Fuck*," I gritted out, reaching for my cock.

My fully erect cock.

I lunged for the lube in the bedside table. Keeping my lips pressed tight to hold back my moans, I bent my knees and stroked myself. The Band-Aid on my palm added delicious friction even though it was already sliding off.

Honestly, I did try—briefly—to stop thinking about Connor.

It was hopeless.

As I toyed with my nipples with one hand, I thrust up into my fist and imagined Connor was with me.

Kissing me with those pretty pink lips. Those lips stretched around my cock as he sucks me deep. His soft, blond hair under my hand as I caress him and tell him how beautiful he is...

Shit, I was going to come already. My whole body strained as I squeezed the base of my shaft and took a few breaths. I was desperate to give in, but I didn't want this fantasy to be over yet.

Connor spreading his long legs for me. Wide. Vulnerable and eager, looking up at me as I fuck him. Filling his tight ass with my cock, rocking into him as he cries out. Or Connor on his hands and knees taking me, our skin slapping together as we grunt and groan. Connor fucking me hard, his cock so deep in me I think I might break. On my knees sucking him and swallowing his cum. Connor swallowing mine—my cum dripping out of his mouth, splashed on his ruddy skin where I can lick it up and feed it to him in a filthy kiss...

My balls were tight, my nostrils flaring as I choked down my moans.

Because Connor *was* here. He was in the guest room, and there were only two doors between us. What would happen if he heard me and thought I was having a seizure or another kind of medical emergency? Would he burst through the unlocked door to my bedroom and find me like this?

Gasping, I spurted everywhere, my vision whiting out as I shook through the orgasm. "*Ohh,*" I whined, milking myself. My legs flopped down to the mattress. My chest heaved.

I hadn't jerked off like that in ages. It was usually a sleepy wakeup in the shower—not this frantic, desperate drive.

Well. I'd let my mind—and cock—get away from me. It was the insomnia. It had been entirely inappropriate, but it was over. Connor would never know. Clearly I was pent up, so I'd swipe right on a few cool profiles online and reset. Connor was probably hooking up left, right, and center.

Never mind that the thought of Connor hooking up with anyone made my blood pressure rise instantly. I unclenched my fists and rocketed off the bed to wash up in the bathroom. I scrubbed my hands, getting out my nail brush for good measure.

It didn't matter since this relationship was *not real,* but… *Was* Connor queer? Asher had initially seemed so certain, though he'd changed his tune. He couldn't know for sure. Connor said he wasn't, which was all that mattered.

I enjoyed the steady hum of the water but switched off the tap with my forearm as I continued scrubbing. Until several months ago, I would have told anyone who'd asked I was straight. I just hadn't been ready to come out as bi.

It didn't help that Grandmother didn't seem to believe me. Or that other people thought bisexuality wasn't quite queer enough.

I'd had sex with men, women, one nonbinary person—I wasn't making it up to be rebellious or edgy. I was genuinely queer.

I was also scrubbing my fingernails raw. Wincing at the line of blood under my index finger, I turned on the tap and rinsed. My heart thudded, and any release from jerking off had evaporated.

Not looking in the mirror, I returned to the bedroom and pulled on my flannel PJ bottoms. I stripped the sheets and remade the bed in the faint light coming through the blinds.

It was still dark outside. Through the cracked window, a distant siren wailed. There was no way I could sleep now, so I shuffled out into the living room and jumped a mile when I saw Connor sitting by the window.

"Sorry." Connor held out his hands and spoke softly even though there was no one else in the apartment to wake up. He was still wearing his dark boxer briefs and my old Knicks tee. His James Dean hair was messy, and I had the absurd urge to smooth it down.

A fresh burst of desire gripped me—swiftly followed by guilt at what I'd just done. He was my little brother's best friend! He was a guest in my home. I should never have let myself get caught up in fantasies.

"Reid?" He was moving toward me. "Do you feel okay?" He'd snapped into doctor mode with that calm, concerned, capable manner.

He could seem so young and unsure at times, but when he was worried about someone's wellbeing, he was immediately reassuring in a way I never would have expected. A way I found incredibly attractive.

I managed to laugh, though it was strangled. "Yes—I'm great. You're up early." Cold sweat prickled my skin. "I didn't wake you, did I?" Wait, I'd just come out of my room. "I was, er, working out."

"In your…PJ bottoms?"

"Yes. It was an ab routine. And squats. Body weight conditioning that doesn't need any equipment."

"Cool. You start early. I've been out here a while." His gaze dropped to my chest. "Are you sure you're okay?"

Did I miss some cum? "Yes! I'm great."

Connor frowned. "You didn't cut yourself anywhere else, did you?"

I had no choice but to look down. I'd scratched my own chest while jerking off—not breaking the skin, but enough to leave red marks. "Oh! No. That's a, er, allergic reaction. Very mild cheese allergy."

"Just cheese? Not all dairy?"

"Only gouda, if you can believe it." Which he surely couldn't because it was a ridiculous lie. I hurried back into my room and tugged on the first T-shirt I pulled out of the drawer.

When I returned to the living room, Connor grinned. "Didn't peg you for a *Phantom of the Opera* fan."

Naturally, *that* was the shirt I grabbed. "Gag gift from last Christmas courtesy of Addison. But I have to admit it's really soft."

"I believe you," he deadpanned. "Totally."

"Look, I'm not cool. It's best that you understand that now."

He scoffed. "Of course you are."

"Please allow me to direct you again to the *Phantom* T-shirt I'm currently wearing. Hey, are you hungry?"

"Yeah. I had some goldfish crackers. Hope that's okay."

"Of course, but I can do better than that. We'll start with coffee, yes?"

He groaned. "*Yes.*"

I ordered my cock to behave and led the way into the kitchen, using the dimmer to keep the lights soft. As I turned on the coffee maker and gathered omelette ingredients—I did indeed have thick-cut bacon—Connor sat at one of the stools on the island.

"It's cool that you cook and everything," he said.

I shrugged. "I'm not a gourmand by any stretch."

"You're cool whether you like it or not. I mean, look at this place. And you practically run a worldwide hotel chain. That's pretty awesome."

As I cracked the eggs into a bowl, I made a noncommittal noise. "Grandmother and the CEO are running things. I mostly do as I'm told."

"You don't like it?"

"It doesn't matter. It's my job." I motioned with the whisk. "I can't complain. I'm extremely fortunate."

"Yeah, but…I assumed you liked it. Asher definitely doesn't have any interest in the family business."

"Don't I know it," I grumbled. "It is what it is. I can't complain," I repeated.

"That's bullshit. Sure you can. I went to Rencliffe with Asher and all the other rich kids. They complained all the time."

I chuckled. "True."

Connor played with the tiny tongs that accompanied the bowl of sugar cubes I'd put out for him. "So, what would you rather be doing?"

"It doesn't matter. I have a great job." I chopped the green onions with quick movements.

"It still matters."

Glancing at Connor, I could see he wasn't going to let it go. He waited patiently, with that calm, concerned aura. "You have a great bedside manner," I said. "Maybe you should be a shrink."

He blinked in surprise. "Me? Thanks. But I want to be more hands-on."

"I meant to ask you what specialty you're considering. You said you had an idea of what to choose."

"I'll tell you when you tell me what you really want to do."

Groaning, I shredded the aged cheddar, grateful I hadn't had gouda in the fridge. "Fine. You're going to laugh."

"I won't," he said, and I could tell he meant it. Sitting in my kitchen as gray light slowly brightened the apartment, the smell of rich coffee filling the peaceful air, it felt safe to tell him.

"You know how we run luxury hotels and resorts?"

"Uh-huh."

"I've been working on a proposal for diversifying the company and building low-cost, sustainable housing. Utilizing solar energy, recycled materials, creating urban green spaces and community hubs." Before Connor could reply, I poured the coffee and said, "I know. It's ridiculous."

Connor took his mug from me, his forehead creasing. "Dude, we need housing people can actually afford. Why would that be ridiculous?"

"Because I'm the heir to a luxury hotel chain. Look at where I live. What do I know about sustainability or affordable anything?" I paced restlessly to the fridge and opened it blindly before going to the fruit bowl on the counter. I unpeeled a banana and offered Connor half, which he took with a smile.

"Okay, yeah. But I assume you've researched."

"Yes. For the record, none of my ideas are original—many people who know a lot more than me are spearheading similar projects."

"Right. There are only so many ways to reinvent the wheel. But you feel passionate about it?"

My heart was racing. "Yes. I know I should be proud of Utopia, but... I don't care about building more extravagant hotels. We do all this charity work—Grandmother is always fundraising. Which is wonderful! But I want to do more than donate and show up to charity events. I spend my days going through the motions at a company that's chugging along and hasn't innovated in decades. Making a product I don't care about." I took a breath. "I know. Poor little rich boy. Man. Whatever."

Connor said, "No, I get it. Just because you're rich doesn't mean you're not allowed to have feelings. You must be bored as hell."

Relief flooded me. "I *am*."

I'd never had the guts to say any of this out loud, even to Addison. Maybe it was easier with Connor because he wasn't wealthy. Or maybe it was easier with Connor because he just had this straightforward, nonjudgmental bedside manner.

"When I was fresh out of my MBA, I had so many ideas for how we could innovate at Utopia. Grandmother and the board shot down every one. After a while, I stopped trying. There's no way they'd ever invest in this. The company is incredibly profitable. Why change anything?"

"I guess one day you'll be in charge though, right? Then you can do what you want with Utopia."

"I hate the thought of waiting for Grandmother to die, though. Like I'm in a royal family trapped by birth."

Connor smirked. "You need to pull a Prince Harry and run away."

"Tempting."

Connor stirred three cubes of sugar into his coffee. "Couldn't you start your own company?" He laughed. "Not that I know anything about that. Or get a job somewhere else?"

"I can't actually *leave*. I have to take over eventually like you said."

He frowned. "Do you, though?"

For a moment, I was speechless. "Of course. I've been groomed for it my whole life. Especially since my dad died."

"Right." His shoulders hunched a fraction, and I knew he could relate. "You're the heir and not the spare."

I grimaced. "Exactly."

"Okay, so if you don't want to actually leave Utopia—or you don't feel like you can—what would you do if your grandmother didn't... What's that word? Veto?"

"I'd ideally like to start a new division. A pilot project to expand the company. I'd need capital from Utopia to fund the division, but in the long term, it would diversify our income streams and make the company stronger while providing much-needed housing."

"Sounds amazing."

"Except Grandmother doesn't like change. The question is whether I can get enough support from the CEO and board members, and I'm not optimistic. It's foolish to even be wasting my time with this, but I feel like… How many luxury hotels and resorts can we build? There's a huge market for quality affordable housing, and the profit margin is still favorable if not spectacular. Alongside the hotels, we'd still be making plenty."

Connor seemed to ponder that, his hands wrapped around his coffee mug. "Couldn't you ask one of your business buddies to read the proposal? Get some feedback?"

"Sure. If I wasn't a coward."

He didn't laugh. "We all have fears. What's the worst that can happen if you float the idea? It's not like you'll be out on the street, right?"

"No." I flushed. That was the most foolish part—acting as though I didn't have a privileged safety net. "You're right. I haven't because I'm afraid of what they'll say. That it's not feasible. Unrealistic. Laughable."

"Dude, I hope your friends wouldn't laugh at you."

"I'm sure they wouldn't. It's my own insecurity."

Connor shook his head. "It blows my mind that *you'd* be insecure about anything."

"Thank you?"

"Sorry—I didn't mean it as an insult. You've always seemed so together and cool and—" Connor stopped abruptly and gulped his coffee. "Stuff," he added.

I flushed with pleasure although I wasn't exactly sure why. Which was bullshit—I knew exactly why it pleased me that Connor apparently admired me.

"You know, I could ask Angela Barker to look at your proposal," he said.

"Really?" It wasn't a bad idea. She was incredibly successful and smart from what I knew of her.

"Totally. Even if it's not her field, she knows a lot about, well, every-thing. She's kind of like my wacky aunt even though we're not related. Well, wacky aunt crossed with a business tycoon."

"Really? It wouldn't be too much of an ask?"

"Nah, it's cool. Angela always wants to help."

"I really appreciate it. That would be great if you can approach her." Excitement sang through my veins like a gulp of champagne.

"No prob. Just remember, nothing changes if nothing changes," Connor said.

My chest felt strangely light, and I smiled. "Wise words."

"My mom used to say that." His gaze went distant. "Sometimes, she made huge changes that freaked me out. Like marrying Logan. If she'd lived, that never would have worked out."

I'd turned on the burner under the frying pan, and the bacon sizzled. "I'm sorry you lost her."

Connor stirred his coffee, the spoon clinking on the mug. "It's weird to think about. If she'd—if I'd—" He broke off. "She and Logan were already breaking up, so that would have been that. I'd have lost touch with Logan's sister Jenna and her husband Jun. Their kids. Pop. I would never have met Seth at all. *Logan* probably wouldn't have met him. I wouldn't know Angela Barker or Olivia either. It's trippy to think about how people can come into your life. Or how they might not."

"It's true. Imagine if you hadn't come to the Thanksgiving dinner with Asher. We wouldn't be here together right now."

That thought kicked me in the gut far harder than it had any right to given that dinner had been barely more than a week ago.

Connor met my gaze. "Guess you'd have another fake boyfriend."

That thought made me grimace in distaste. I quickly said, "Or I'd be stuck fending off Cecilia Weston."

"We wouldn't want that."

"To be fair, I doubt Cecilia has any more interest in me than I do in her. But once Grandmother gets an idea in her head…"

"She'll just have to get used to me." He laughed. "I mean, for December." He inhaled deeply. "That smells amazing, by the way."

I took the bread out, and we transitioned into talking about breakfast food as I cooked. "Tapioca pudding has got to be down at the bottom," I said.

"Is that actually a breakfast food?"

"To my dad it was. Not that he cooked a day in his life." I laughed fondly. "He had many strengths, but I doubt he could boil an egg."

"Why did you learn?" Connor sipped his coffee with a cute little satisfied sigh. "You can afford to order in everything."

"I enjoy cooking. Helps me relax. It's something that's just…mine. Low risk."

"You don't cook for other people? Aside from right now, I mean. No fancy dinner parties?"

"I have to attend far too many. Now, have you ever tried black pudding? It's a UK thing."

Connor screwed up his face, and it was cute too. God help me, it really was. He said, "Doesn't sound good."

"You'd be surprised. I—" My phone buzzed, and I frowned at the screen. "It's my grandmother. Not her PA—she's calling me herself."

"Her ears were burning. Shit, does she have your place bugged?"

I laughed weakly at Connor's joke and swiped to answer. "Hello? Are you all right?"

"Good morning, darling. Do you have plans for this evening?" she asked, ignoring my question.

"I do," I said immediately. She wasn't asking out of idle curiosity. "Connor and I are going to a jazz club." I shrugged at him as if I'd just made it up. "Actually, we're just having breakfast together," I added because it would make her uncomfortable. She had to get used to this. Not me and Connor per se, but me and men.

And why not Connor? Why does this arrangement have to stay pretend?

Muffling that internal voice, I smiled as Connor loudly said, "'Morning, Mrs. Cabot!"

Grandmother cleared her throat delicately. "Yes, well. What time is this jazz performance?"

"Seven," I lied.

"Reid, I might be a woman of advanced years, but I do recall through the distant sands of time that live music establishments rarely opened so early."

"It's, uh…"

"I'm not feeling well. I need you to go to dinner with the Seyfrieds. It won't go late, so you'll have plenty of time for your jazz."

Guilt washed over me. "Are you okay?" For her to cancel, it was more than a sniffle. She sounded normal, though.

"Upset tummy," she said. "I think the caterer at last night's event will be blacklisted as I'm not the only sufferer."

Yikes. "What about Asher? Doesn't he know the Seyfried son? Whatshisname? Or is it the daughter? Whichever."

She sighed. "Darling, you know what a responsibility these events are. How important they are to the company and our family. Asher's too…inconsistent."

"He's not a kid anymore. He's working at a brokerage."

"Yes, but you're the future of Utopia."

The bacon was about to burn, and I hurriedly transferred it onto a paper towel-lined plate. "What time should Connor and I be there?" I eyed him, and he nodded.

"Darling, I'm sure Connor would be bored stiff. I was attending on my own, so there's only one seat at the table."

I almost growled in frustration. "We're a couple, Grandmother. I'm not going without him." Maybe I could get out of this after all.

But she gave in, and soon I had a text from the Seyfrieds' assistant confirming.

"You don't have to go," I told Connor.

"No, it's cool. I'm sure the food will be good. This was the arrangement, right? Be your boyfriend for these parties until the new year. Speaking of food, can I have a piece of bacon?"

"Of course. You can have everything." I quickly put the bread into the toaster and plated the omelet after separating it into two halves with the spatula.

Connor took a bite of bacon. "Mmm. Perfect."

I sat next to him at the island. "You're sure you don't mind me roping you into extra events?"

"Nope." He seemed about to say something, but then stopped himself. After a gulp of coffee, he added, "Besides, you loaned me the money. The least I owe you is being your date at dinner."

"Is everything…okay with that?" I was dying to know why he'd needed it, but it was an invasion of privacy to ask.

"Yep." He took a big mouthful of eggs and moaned. "Dude, you are such a good cook."

The compliment made me happier than it had any right to, and we went back to debating breakfast foods. Somehow, it didn't feel strange at all to be hanging out in my kitchen with Connor still in his underwear.

Not that I was *looking* at him in his underwear. I strictly kept my gaze up. It had been incredibly inappropriate to get lost in fantasies earlier. It wouldn't happen again. But we were free to hang out and become friends.

I could get used to this, I thought, hoping the holidays went by very, very slowly.

Chapter Eight

Connor

"YOU'RE SURE I shouldn't wear another jacket?" I asked as Reid and I walked from my apartment toward Ninth Avenue. I'd gone home to study for a few hours after we ordered in Chinese food for lunch and watched *Christmas Vacation*, and Reid had insisted on meeting me outside my building and walking together through the park to dinner.

But this isn't a date. This. Is. Not. A. Date.

"A hundred percent," Reid said. "The leather looks good on you."

Even as I reminded myself Reid's compliments didn't mean anything more than him being kind, my heart skipped.

I'd changed into my dressiest pants and another sweater that Reid insisted was fine. My other jacket option was a ratty ski parka, so the black leather did seem the better choice.

We turned uptown, chatting as we walked. Reid seemed to be interested in my explanation of the pathologic processes of inflammation, repair, and neoplasia for my exam.

After seeing him that morning in his *Phantom of the Opera* tee, he was back in his form-fitting designer clothes, including a long tan winter coat and burgundy scarf that brought out the rich depth in his brown eyes.

"Connor?"

"Uh-huh! Sorry, I got distracted by..." I glanced around as we crossed Fifty-seventh Street, remembering our conversation that first night. "Nuts. We should eat some, right?"

That was apparently the right thing to say since Reid's face spread into a grin. "You really want to?"

"Of course. It's on the list, right? How else will I become a real New Yorker?"

The sidewalk thronged with people rushing by as we found a cart. I inhaled the sweet, salty scent deeply. Reid insisted on paying and ordered two bags of the mixed nuts.

We ducked into the doorway of a closed bookstore decorated with a red-bowed wreath strung with fairy lights. The store window display was a mother mouse reading *A Christmas Carol* to little stuffed mice.

As I breathed through a pang of longing, Reid turned to peer into the window. "Cute." He looked to me again. "You okay?"

"Yeah. Just…" I waved my hand. "Never mind. Time for nuts."

"What is it?" He watched me with concern.

"Nothing bad. My mom loved mice. Weird, I know. Not, like, *real* mice."

"Fictional mice only. Wise."

I smiled. "Indeed. When I was little, my father took me to the mall and gave me money to get her a present. I tried to buy a mouse from the pet store to put in her stocking, but the clerk thought that would be a bad idea for both my mom and the poor mouse."

"Your father didn't think it was a bad idea?"

"He was in the bar at the TGI Fridays."

Reid's eyes widened. "How old did you say you were?"

I shrugged. "Too young." Why had I brought up my father? He was the last person I wanted to think about. "So, how about your nuts?" I shook my head. "I mean—you know what I mean."

Instead of laughing at how awkward I was, Reid arched a dark eyebrow. "Well, they're a delicacy. Or so I'm told."

He seemed completely serious and…flirty? My heart thumped.

Then Reid burst out laughing. Not just laughing—he *snorted.*

And it was the sexiest thing ever.

I laughed along, still amazed that smooth, sophisticated Reid Cabot was actually a bit of a dork like me under that polished veneer.

"Okay, we need to focus," Reid said. "Disclaimer. Many New Yorkers would probably disagree with this choice, but for me, eating nuts on the street at Christmas was quintessential New York as a kid. I hated it when we spent the holidays in the Caymans."

"Yeah, that must have been rough," I deadpanned.

Laughing, Reid elbowed me. We were standing close in the alcove, and the multicolored lights stringing the wreath and store window cast a warm, cozy glow over Reid's face. It was the most incredible, amazing torture being this close to him. After shoving my gloves in my pocket, I held the warm bag in my hands.

Reid bumped his bag against mine. "Cheers."

I popped a cluster of cashews and peanuts into my mouth, the honey flavor mixing perfectly with the salt and crunch. "Oh my god," I mumbled. "These are delicious."

They really were, but I'd have lied about it all night to see the way Reid beamed at me. "No veto?" he asked.

"No way. What's next?"

Reid checked the time on his phone. "We might just make it."

"Right now? Don't we have a dinner?"

"It's on the way."

I followed Reid north, and he wouldn't tell me where we were going. Anticipation buzzed through me. We ate the rest of our nuts as we walked and dodged other pedestrians. We were close to the Utopia, where we'd had Thanksgiving dinner and agreed to pretend.

When I'd said yes, I hadn't imagined it would be anything like this. I wasn't sure what I *did* imagine, but it hadn't been this playful vibe. Even though Reid had loaned me ten grand, he hadn't asked about it or nagged me for an explanation even though it would have been a reasonable request.

"Thank you again," I said. "For lending the money. And not grilling me. You're really…cool." I cringed internally. I sounded like a kid with a crush. I *felt* like a kid with a crush.

He smiled. "You're cool too." As we headed into the park, he said, "And if you need help with whatever's going on—whatever you needed the money for—I'll help you."

I was warm all over even though an icy gust of wind whistled through the park. "It's over, but thank you. And I'll make the next payment on Monday. I know the amounts are on the small side right now—"

"Any amount is okay." He gently grasped my shoulder. "I know you're good for it. And now I know where you live."

We laughed, and I was surprised as we bypassed Wollman Rink, which was crowded with skaters, Kelly Clarkson belting about a Christmas tree through the speakers.

"Hmm. Not skating?"

Reid shook his head. "Nope. Not that I'm opposed to it, but for my list, there's another attraction."

"Penguins at the zoo."

"Try again."

"That castle. Belvedere?"

"Nope."

I'd been to Central Park several times, and I racked my brain for what other activities I might have walked past. "There's no way we're renting a row boat on the lake in December."

Reid laughed. "Definitely a summer activity. Actually, I'll add that to the summer list. It's a good one. We can go when falling in won't be as life threatening."

Butterflies *whooshed* through my stomach. We were making summer plans? "What else will be on the summer list?" I tried for casual and probably sounded like I was in cardiac distress.

"Spoiler alert! The rest will be a surprise." He squinted up the path and increased his pace. "They're closing any minute."

I followed his gaze to a sort-of round brick building. Tinny, old-fashioned music echoed, and I realized it was the enclosure for the carousel.

"Oh!" I exclaimed. "I forgot this was here."

"Veto?" Reid asked.

"No way! Let's do it."

"Come on." He took my bare hand with his—we hadn't put on our gloves since we'd been eating the nuts—and we jogged up to the ticket window.

The woman peered at us over the rims of her glasses. "Closing time," she said.

"One more?" Reid asked. "Please? I promised my boyfriend. He's never ridden the carousel before."

"A virgin, huh?" The woman tapped her screen with an exaggerated sigh. "I guess young love deserves one last ride."

As my face flamed, Reid paid for the tickets. A few families rushed up behind us, and soon we were all clambering onto the platform. There were plenty of horses to pick from, and Reid and I climbed a black pair with saddles painted in bright blue, red, and silver.

A woman stood by one of the stationary horses, her young daughter in the saddle squealing in delight as the carousel began to spin. Her enthusiasm was infectious, and I grinned. The classic instrumental carnival music played, and even though it wasn't explicitly Christmassy, it was merry as hell.

"This is awesome!" I said as we spun, my horse bobbing up and down in opposition to Reid's beside me. The carousel gathered surprising speed, and I gripped the pole, the cold wind messing up my hair. I wanted to reach across and hold his hand again, but that would probably be weird.

Reid grinned. "Never too old to ride the Central Park carousel! I haven't done it in years. I've been missing out."

Even if it was childish, it was *fun*. I felt like we were flying. "Makes me miss my bike!"

"*What?* These two things are not similar!"

"They are, I swear. I think you'd be surprised how much you'd enjoy riding a motorcycle."

"Veto." Reid shook his head, laughing. "The wooden horsies are the limit of my risk tolerance."

The ride slowed and eventually came to a stop, and Reid swung his leg over and hopped down, straightening his long woolen coat. We both had long legs, so it should have been just as easy for me to get down gracefully.

"Should" being the operative word.

Because my foot got caught on the stirrup, and I hopped and made a sound that could only be described as a "squeak."

Reid was suddenly behind me, his arms around me and his breath in my ear. "Steady. Hold on."

I tugged my foot, and my leather shoe went flying as I staggered against Reid. I barely moved since he was holding me up so strongly.

"Thanks." I tried to laugh, my head spinning and body tingling. God, he smelled amazing—that earthy pine scent.

My black sock was half off, and I tried in vain to tug it up as Reid deftly pivoted us so he could crouch. At my feet, he held up the leather Oxford and said, "I believe you lost a glass slipper, *mon amour?*"

We laughed, and his fingers tickled my bare ankle as he pulled up my sock and guided my foot back into my shoe.

I shivered, sounding weirdly breathy as I said, "I guess the laces were loose. This is what I get for not wearing my Docs. Trying to be respectable."

Reid looked up with a little smile. "Good thing I was here to lend a hand." He tied my shoe with neat, firm movements that turned me on because I was so *weird.* Or maybe it wasn't the shoe-tying but the whole kneeling-at-my-feet thing.

"To be fair, I wouldn't have been riding the carousel if you weren't here."

"True. But you could have tripped. I'll check the other one too." He retied those laces, then stood. "Who knows what catastrophe has been averted? We're both klutzes, it seems."

"Hmm. Good point." We were standing so close between the wooden horses that the tips of our shoes touched. "I could have—"

"I hate to break up…whatever this is," said the woman from the ticket booth loudly by the gate, wearing her coat and hat with her purse on her shoulder. "But we'd like to go home."

We jerked apart and hurried off the now-empty carousel, apologizing profusely and practically running.

"I can't wait to see what else is on the list!" I exclaimed, and when Reid winked, I came very close to tripping even though my shoelaces were both knotted tightly.

We walked north through the park past trees and posts strung with holiday lights. Flurries of snow danced in the breeze.

"I should bring my dads here to see the lights. The city's amazing at Christmas. Seth would love it, and Logan will do whatever Seth loves. And secretly he'll think it's cool."

Reid glanced around. "Huh. I guess it is beautiful. I don't usually pay attention. Christmas drags on for so long. There are so many events and parties I have to go to." He raised his hands. "I know, I know. Call me Scrooge."

"I get it. After my mom, I didn't think I'd ever care about Christmas again. But Logan and Seth and Aunt Jenna put so much work into it every year. She makes the best turkey. There was one time—" I broke off. "Sorry, this is so boring."

"Not at all," Reid said, but of course he'd say that. He was polite. I wasn't sure exactly what he did in the office, but being polite and looking interested in boring stories was probably his job.

"Anyway—oh, isn't that your friend?"

As we exited the park on Fifth Avenue, a woman across the street waved. It was Madison—no, Addison—and we joined her for the last few blocks.

"Connor, you really are a saint to be coming to this dinner," she said. "It's going to be intensely boring. I can't believe Bitsy bailed. Uptight dinners are her favorite thing ever."

"She must genuinely be sick," Reid said. He nudged my arm. "But seriously, thank you."

"It's okay. We have a deal." I wasn't sure if Addison knew about the money, so I kept my mouth shut.

She said, "Hopefully we can escape early. Want to come over to Paul's? Colette is back from Paris. Should be chill."

Reid shook his head. "Actually, we have plans." He shot me a grin. "An underground jazz club in the Village, assuming Connor has no objections."

"Wait, for real?" Excitement fizzed through me. "I thought you made that up for your grandmother. I'm definitely in."

His grin widened. "You'll love it. And even if you don't, it's a New York experience."

"Great!" Addison smiled at Reid, her head tilted. "So, you two are basically spending the whole weekend together."

Reid laughed. "Well… I suppose so. We didn't plan it this way."

"No, of course not," Addison agreed, still smiling at Reid.

My phone buzzed, and as I glanced at the screen to check the incoming call, I froze.

Dad

Mike had been listed in my contacts as that one word for as long as I'd had a smartphone. Even though it was a lie—he had never been my *dad*. Logan and Seth were my dads.

But I'd never changed the listing. It would have been weird to list him as, what? Father? Mike? The latter, probably, but when I'd opened my contacts to edit, it had seemed so…final.

God, I was pathetic. Why did I care? I wished so fucking much that I didn't.

"Okay?" Reid asked.

"Uh-huh!" I jammed my phone in my pocket. I wasn't answering. What the fuck could he say at this point? Nothing. I had to grow up and block him, but this wasn't the time or place. I was here for Reid.

We arrived at one of the very fancy apartment buildings with a view of the park, and I felt like if I was separated from Reid and Addison, the doorman would toss me out by the scruff of my neck like I was in an old movie.

The dinner was indeed stuffy and boring, and I nodded and smiled and let Reid do the talking. After dinner, we were ushered into a massive living room dominated by a Christmas tree decorated in silver, white, and gold. Rich people didn't seem to go for the multicolored bulbs or—heaven forbid—anything flashing.

A string quartet played old carols that Seth would know the words to since he'd grown up going to church. Reid and I stood at the edge of the room, ready to slip out.

"Grandmother's best friend is staring at us," Reid murmured. "Don't look."

"Why are you telling me if I'm not supposed to look?" I kept my gaze on the musicians.

Reid chuckled, a warm, low sound that I could listen to all day. "Touché."

"If you mean the old lady at four o'clock, yeah, she apparently thinks we're an exhibit at the zoo."

"That's her. Bunny Epstein."

"Bunny and Bitsy. Good combo."

Reid sipped his wine. I loved the way the red liquid painted his lips for a moment. His tongue was likely stained too…

"Can I kiss you?" he asked under his breath.

As I tried to tear my eyes away from his lips, my brain screamed, *YES!!* Meanwhile, my eloquent mouth spat out, "Huh?"

"Is that crossing a boundary?" He raised a hand. "You're under no obligation. I just know Bunny will be reporting back, and I'm so tired of Grandmother's attitude."

"I get it," I croaked before gulping the rest of my wine. "I'm down."

Reid examined me silently. "Are you sure? I know you said you're straight. I don't want to pressure you or overstep. This isn't a requirement of our arrangement."

"No, you're good." If I believed in spontaneous combustion, I'd be afraid I was about to explode and all that would be left of me would be a pile of ashes in my shoes. "Go for it. It's only a kiss."

"Smile like I said something wonderful."

No acting was necessary since, duh, Reid Cabot just said he wanted to kiss me. Even if it was all pretend, I grinned. Reid smiled back, then leaned down and did it.

He actually kissed me.

His free hand slid around to my lower back, and his lips brushed mine, feather-light and moist. I inhaled his woodsy scent and pressed closer to him as our mouths hovered together. It was sweet and soft, and our lips were open just enough that it wasn't like we were mashing our faces together. I tasted a hint of wine.

It was *everything*.

God, it was almost impossible not to grab him and keep kissing. As we parted, I had to stop myself from touching my lips with my fingertips. *Only a kiss*, I'd told him.

I hadn't mentioned it was my very first.

But Reid didn't need to know that aside from being a virgin, I'd never even kissed anyone during spin the bottle or whatever. Unless he'd figured it out because I had no idea what I was doing. I met his warm, brown eyes and braced for his reaction. It was fine if he laughed, or—

My heart swelled as a tender little smile lifted his extremely kissable lips, and he looked down at me like I was something precious as he brushed his thumb across my bottom lip.

I shivered, and the insane thought popped into my head that I wanted to take his thumb in my mouth and suck it.

As the string quartet launched into "Joy to the World," Reid whispered, "Thanks for playing along," and I managed to nod.

My first kiss was in the books, and the only way it could have been more perfect was if it'd been for real.

Chapter Nine

Connor

THE BUZZER ECHOED through the apartment, and I jerked awake on my bed, knocking a stack of notes onto the floor in a flutter of paper. "Fuck," I muttered as I rubbed my eyes. I could hear Olivia talking to whoever was outside on the old intercom, followed by the long *beeeep* that meant she'd unlocked the lobby door.

I fumbled for my phone to check the time. Where the fuck was my phone? Wait, what day was it? Sunday. Right. It was Sunday morning, and I'd been up studying most of the night until I'd crashed. I reached around the mattress and under the tangled covers.

It had been a week since I'd seen Reid, though he'd texted me encouragement and checked in quite a few times. As I lifted my phone, I fantasized that maybe he'd come over with coffee and bagels to surprise me...

I bolted to my feet as I scanned the texts from Seth. "Wait. What the fuck?" I blurted out loud.

Sure enough, I could hear Olivia welcoming Seth and Logan inside our apartment. They were here? What the hell? I stumbled out into the living room, almost knocking our mini Christmas tree from its perch on the low storage unit under the TV. I caught it, silver tinsel now sticking to my flannel boxers.

"What's wrong?" I demanded.

"Hello to you too." Seth chuckled as he unwound his scarf. "Didn't you get my messages?" His glasses had fogged up, and he waved them through the air before putting them back on. For a second, I thought there were snowflakes in his dark brown hair, but I realized it was just grayer at the temples.

"Just now. I fell asleep." It was somehow almost eleven. Shit. I still had so much studying to do. At least after tomorrow, I could take a break. I still had two exams after, but they were easier. I could definitely go out with Reid a few times.

Thinking of him still made me giddy and fidgety, and I had to focus.

What was going on with my dads?

Seth said, "We're picking up a sink for Logan's client, and we thought we'd pop in. Nothing's wrong." He hung his coat in the closet, reaching out a hand for Logan's leather jacket.

But Logan was tense. He unzipped his jacket and didn't say anything, which wasn't completely out of the ordinary, but I recognized the set of his shoulders and the vein sticking out near his temple under his clipped hair. It wasn't as buzzed as it would have been when he was a Marine, but he still went for a no-nonsense style that was very…him.

His pale skin was ruddy, and I wasn't sure if it was from the cold or if he was worked up about something. They were here for a reason. There was a vibe. I tried to think of what I'd done to piss them off but came up blank.

Unless… No. There was no way they could know about the money. I shifted from foot to foot, my stomach lurching. I'd dealt with it, and there was no way Reid would tell them. He didn't even know what the money had been for. Even if he did, he wouldn't.

"Sorry I missed your texts." I shook tinsel off my hand, trying to act normally. "I've been studying all week. My biggest exam is Monday, so this weekend has been intense."

Olivia motioned to my boxers and ratty Harvard tee. "He's been wearing that all week too. I'm hoping he remembers to shower again one of these days." She checked her watch. "I'm meeting Dylan for brunch, so I'll leave you to it. I hope everything's good in Albany?"

Seth nodded. "Yes. We were at Will and Michael's last night for their holiday party. We decorated the tree, and Will's parents arrived from Scotland. Michael had arranged the surprise."

Olivia grinned. "That's awesome! I'm sorry I couldn't make it. Will and Michael are the cutest. Sounds like a great party."

"It was." Seth smiled, but… Shit. He was tense too. He was way better at hiding it than Logan, but something was definitely up.

After Olivia left, the three of us stood there looking at each other. "What's going on?" I asked.

"Nothing," Seth said. "We were nearby. The place looks great, by the way." He waved a hand at the glittery garlands Olivia and I had hung to go with our tree.

"Thanks. Nothing compared to your tree, but it's nice. Olivia's going home to Texas, and she said you wouldn't believe how many trees and stuff Angela puts up, but you probably would since you know she's big on Christmas." I was rambling while my brain tried to figure out why they were here—and then a terrible thought hit me. "Are you sick?"

Seth and Logan blinked at me and looked taken aback. "Huh?" Logan said.

"Is that why you're here? Is one of you sick or something? And you didn't want to tell me over the phone?" My stomach twisted into an acidy knot as my brain helpfully supplied a list of diseases they might have and I examined them for signs and symptoms.

"No!" Seth held up his hands. "We're not sick. We're fine, and everyone at home's fine."

I eyed them suspiciously. "Even Pop?"

Logan nodded. "My old man's trucking along like usual. I swear."

"Okay." I exhaled in a rush.

Seth said, "We won't stay long—we know you're studying, and we have to get back to Albany by late afternoon. Jenna's having us over for dinner so she can practice a new scalloped-yet-roasted potato recipe for Christmas. Can't we stop in and say hi?"

"No—yes, of course." I rubbed my face and shuffled to the kitchen. "I need coffee." Okay, if they knew about the money, they'd just yell at me, right? Get it over with? After a moment, I asked, "Um, do you guys want some?" It was weird playing host to my dads.

"Sure," Seth answered. "That would be great. Right?" He gave Logan a look.

"Yeah," Logan said. He went to my bedroom door and peered in. "No one else here?"

"Just me, my textbooks, and my notes." Even though I took notes on my laptop, I printed them out to study to give my eyes a break. "Why? You just saw Olivia leave." I really needed caffeine. "Who else would be here?"

Logan stuffed his hands in his jeans pockets and shrugged.

I got the coffee machine going while Seth talked about the antique sink they'd picked up for one of Logan's clients. They didn't seem mad, and they'd promised they weren't sick, so maybe everything was fine and they really had just stopped in because they were in the city.

"The sink sounds cool," I said, yawning widely. "Sorry. I went out too much last weekend, so this week has been all studying."

"What were you doing last weekend?" Seth asked casually. But maybe *too* casually?

I crossed my arms. "What's going on? You're being weird."

"Because you're not telling the truth!" Logan's nostrils flared. "Why wouldn't you just tell us?"

My heart dropped, and I tasted bile. They *did* know about how incredibly stupid I'd been. That the debt might fuck up my credit rating for years, and even if I became a doctor, what if I'd screwed myself forever? How had they found out? Fuck, fuck, *fuck*.

Seth raised his hands. "Let's all take a breath. Everything's okay. We're just…puzzled, Connor. We didn't expect to hear it from someone else."

Jesus, had my father told them? No. Why the hell would Mike do that? Panic clawed at me, and I felt like I was back at Rencliffe and the headmaster had hauled my dads into her office to tell them what a fuck-up I was.

But I was supposed to be an adult now. I tried to keep my voice steady. *Fake it until you make it.* "What exactly did you hear?"

"That you're dating Asher's older brother," Seth answered.

I stared at them, playing Seth's words over in my head to make sure I hadn't misheard. "Oh!" I almost laughed in relief. "I…"

But wait—this wasn't great either. Fuck. I wasn't ready for the me-dating-men conversation. Blood rushed in my ears, and I was sweaty and light-headed. I automatically ran though a symptom checklist before trying to focus.

"We're not angry," Seth said.

I scoffed in Logan's direction. "Did you get that memo?"

A reluctant smile tugged his lips, and he snorted. "I'm not *mad.*" He blew out a long breath. "I'm worried. I just don't get it. What's going on with this *Reid*? How old is he?"

"Twenty-nine. Look, it's not what you think. But also, I'm twenty-three. I'm not a kid." Sure, I was a virgin who'd never even been kissed before a week ago, but that wasn't the point.

"So, you and Reid Cabot are in a relationship?" Seth asked gently as the coffee machine finished pouring out a mug.

I handed it to Seth before busying myself with another pod. My face was hot, and I knew I was blushing. "No, we're not," I said truthfully. I didn't want to lie to them. Yes, the money was a lie of omission, but this was different. They were right here in my kitchen.

They'd never asked me much at all about my love life—or lack thereof. Aside from safe sex talks, they'd never pressured me. I'd told them I was too busy with school to date, and they'd always accepted that.

"You're not?" Seth asked. "This was a misunderstanding?"

"Actually, we're following your example," I said, facing them as I flipped the empty coffee pod from hand to hand. "I'm Reid's fake boyfriend for the holidays."

They shared a surprised glance. Logan said, "You're pretending? Does he work for Angela or something?"

I laughed, relaxing a fraction. "No, but his uptight grandmother won't accept that he's bi and keeps trying to fix him up with heiresses like it's the olden days. So, I'm going with him to a few parties as his boyfriend. That's it."

"He's not…taking advantage of you?" Logan asked.

"What? No!" I rolled my eyes. "Oh my god, I'm not twelve!"

"I know, but…" Logan's shoulders finally relaxed. "Okay. Good."

Seth sipped his coffee. "You're carrying on the family legacy."

"That's what I said!" I grinned. "Except you guys really did end up to-gether." And as much as I wanted Reid, it was out of the question.

At least, I thought so? Sure, I'd been obsessing over that kiss all week, and I was dying to see him again to do another item on the New Yorker list. He'd been texting me hints, and he was meeting me at school right after my exam.

Almost like he missed me too.

"Will and Michael went from fake dating to living together," Seth said. "So, you never know. Maybe you and Reid… If you might want that? With Reid, or with another guy." He quickly added, "Or girl. Person. Or not. You don't need to date. Plenty of people don't. It's up to you. We support you in whoever you want to date or not date."

I gripped the empty pod, glad when the next cup finished and I could hand Logan that mug. He and Seth seemed to be waiting for me to say something, doing that patient dad thing they were so good at.

This was it. I could just tell them. I could finally say it. I'd always imagined it would be an eloquent speech I'd prepared for the right moment, but now in my kitchen, exhausted and sleep-sweaty, was this the moment?

My heart pounded. "Um, I've never, like… I don't think…" I tried to find the right words and failed miserably. So much for my perfect speech.

Seth nodded. "Okay. Hey, we never got a hug." He opened his arms, and I gratefully stepped forward.

He murmured, "You know you can tell us anything, right?"

"Everything," Logan said. "Whenever you want."

I hugged him next, and Logan patted my back the way he always did. As I grabbed my coffee, I had to blink my burning eyes hard. I opened the fridge to get the cream, giving myself a minute.

I really could tell them.

Being queer, about the money—everything, like Logan said. But I'd paid the debt. Why upset them for no reason? I couldn't disappoint them now. The thought of it made me queasy again. And shouldn't I wait until I'd actually been with a guy before I came out?

"Con?" Logan's deep voice was tinged with concern.

I splashed the cream into my coffee—and all over the counter. At the sink, I wet the environmental bamboo cloth Olivia had bought and wiped up the mess. Forget the money—that was done and there was no reason to upset them.

But for the rest… I thought of the conversation Olivia and Angela had had. *Imposter syndrome* wasn't something I'd ever thought about applying to myself, but it fit, didn't it?

"Hey." Seth's warm hand clasped my shoulder. "I think you got it."

"Right." I laughed shakily and rinsed the cloth, still not looking at them. I could feel their concern like snow falling all around me in a blanket. "I mean, if I *was* gay—"

Fuck. I'd said it.

I forced myself to turn from the sink and face them. They were both right there waiting like always.

"If you're gay, then that's wonderful," Seth said. His eyes glistened, which was totally going to make me cry too. "We love you just the way you are." Beside him, Logan nodded.

"I *think* so. But I've never…" It was hard to breathe, and I was a hundred percent going to cry. "I am, though. I'm gay."

Then Seth was hugging me again, and Logan had his arms around us, and I wasn't just crying. I was *sobbing*. How had I ever thought even for a second that my dads would react in any other way but this?

"You're okay," Seth whispered. "We've got you."

"And you know it's not your fault, right?"

Seth eased back to look at me, a furrow between his brows, Logan wearing a matching expression. Seth asked, "What do you mean?"

"That I'm not gay because of anything you guys did."

Seth's dark eyebrows shot up, and Logan exclaimed, "Why the hell would we think that?"

"You wouldn't," I quickly said. "I just know how ignorant some people can be."

"I know very well, but those people aren't a concern of ours," Seth said firmly. "They can go to the devil. You hear me?"

Those were strong words from Seth, and I nodded and swiped at my snotty face. "Okay. So, um, now you know. Man, I didn't expect this to happen today."

"Guess we ambushed you," Logan said. "But when we heard you were dating Asher's brother, we were just confused as hell."

I shook my head. "Who told you?"

As they explained, I blew my nose on a paper towel.

I just came out.

Part of me thought I was going to wake up with my textbook jammed into my hip and find out this was all a dream. But it was real, and even though I was sniffling from crying, I felt like I could breathe more easily. I'd done it, and it hadn't been as scary as I'd imagined.

"Did you know?" I asked. "That I'm queer too?"

They shared one of those looks where they had a whole conversation. Logan shrugged. "It crossed our minds. Jenna said you pinged her gaydar."

The reminder of the rest of the family had me tensing again. "Are you going to tell her? And everyone else?"

"It's up to you," Seth said. "There's no rush."

"Yeah. Okay, cool. Can we just wait a bit?"

Logan nodded. "Whatever you want. You know it took me a while to wrap my thick head around being bi, right?"

"Yeah," I said. "I remember." If it wasn't for falling in love with Seth, I wasn't sure Logan would have had that reckoning.

Logan rubbed his stubbly face. "I'm just glad you're okay and I don't have to kick Reid Cabot's ass."

"Again, I'm twenty-three actual years old," I said, but I had to laugh. "Reid's a perfect gentleman. He's pretty cool, actually."

"Oh?" Seth sipped his coffee. "Glad to hear it. Should we get brunch?"

"When in Manhattan," Logan said. "I think it's the law."

I had a quick shower, still wired with excitement from telling my dads. It wasn't what I'd expected from the morning, but I really did feel relieved.

We managed to snag a table at the Galaxy Diner, my favorite greasy spoon in Hell's Kitchen. I told Logan and Seth about the jazz club Reid had taken me to over bacon and eggs and another coffee.

"It was amazing. They were playing Christmas songs, and the whole place was velvety and cool. We brought our own bottle of vodka, and they gave us glasses and mixer and ice."

Logan's lip curled as he sliced into a massive stack of pancakes. "Couldn't they just get a liquor license and be a regular bar?"

I laughed. "Well, yeah. But then it wouldn't be *underground*. It makes no sense, but it's cool." I didn't mention that it was so crowded we had to sit shoulder-to-shoulder, and that our knees touched under the little round table with a tealight candle on it.

My phone buzzed, and I grinned as I looked at the text from Reid that appeared on the screen. "He just sent me another clue about the next thing we're doing."

"The next thing?" Seth asked before taking a bite of his Western omelet.

"Oh, Reid made a list of genuine New Yorker experiences for me."

"That sounds fun." Seth smiled quizzically. "But I thought you were only pretending to be a couple in front of his grandmother?"

I tore my gaze away from the text, which I was rereading again. "Oh, right. We are! This isn't—this is extra. We're friends, I guess. We met before, but it was years ago." Reid and I were friends now, right? It seemed like it. "Here's the clue for the next activity: 'Don't go low.' Hmm."

Seth loved puzzles. He pondered it. "Obviously, the opposite of low is high."

"He wants to get you high?" Logan tore his attention from the pancakes and glowered.

I rolled my eyes. "You're not even listening. "Hmm. Something high… The High Line! It's this cool elevated park. I've been there once, but I was pretty wasted."

"Do tell," Seth said dryly.

"Hey, I'm old enough to get wasted. It's not like before when Asher and I skimmed off the bottles in the liquor cabinet and made ourselves puke."

Logan laughed as Seth grimaced and said, "Thank goodness." He shook his head. "It's still hard to believe you're old enough to be in medical school, let alone drinking."

I shrugged. "I guess." I started typing out a response to Reid, but then deleted. Should I tell him I'd guessed? I didn't want to ruin his surprise. Although I might have been wrong.

"Earth to Connor." Logan raised an eyebrow. "No phone at the table."

"I know, I know," I mumbled.

"You're old enough for med school, but some things never change," Logan said.

"Well, you'd know way more about being old than I would." I gave him a shit-eating grin.

"All right, you two," Seth said, though he was smiling.

I ate another piece of bacon, and it hit me that I'd come out and everything with my dads was the same. I'd been afraid of telling them for so long, but it was fine. More than fine. It was pretty great. They were still the same dads.

"We're so proud of you," Seth said—like he was reading my mind. How did he do that?

I joked, "Wait until I get my grades, and then we'll see."

Seth chuckled. "You always say that, and you always do wonderfully."

"Seriously, that was one of the first things your mom told me about you," Logan said. "That you're a goddamned genius, and you're full of shit when it comes to predicting your grades."

"I assume you're paraphrasing," Seth said.

I smiled through the pang of affection and pain and longing. "Nah, that sounds like her. Did she ever tell you how she tried to prank me when I got into Rencliffe?" I asked Logan.

"I don't think so."

"I'd been going on for weeks about how I failed the admission test, and I'd never get the scholarship. The day the letter came, I was too nervous to open it, so she did. She kept a totally straight face as she read it, and I was like, Oh my god, I actually blew it. She looked so serious, but when she tried to talk, she couldn't keep it up and started crying and screaming about how I got in."

Logan smiled. "Sounds like Veronica. A total softie."

My throat was suddenly thick, and I croaked, "Yeah," and gulped my coffee.

"She'd be damn proud of you," Logan said gruffly.

I nodded and asked, "Did you, um, see the Knicks game?" before I started crying for the second time that day.

As Logan and I talked basketball and Seth listened patiently, I thought of wearing Reid's Knicks T-shirt when I'd stayed over at his place. One more day of cramming for this exam, and then I'd see him again.

I knew I shouldn't have been so excited. Like I'd told Logan and Seth, I *wasn't* in a relationship with Reid. I'd obsessed over our kiss in every moment I hadn't been studying, but that made sense. It was my first, and it had been with the guy I'd crushed on for years.

It didn't mean anything.

"Connor?" Seth asked. "Are you listening?"

I blinked back to attention. "Sorry. My brain's in overdrive. Studying, and then…" I paused. "I was so nervous to tell you guys. For *years*. Now we're sitting here hardening our arteries like nothing happened."

Logan mumbled through a mouthful, "That's a good thing, right?"

"Yes." I laughed, and it might have been a bit manic. "It's good. It's the best. You know, Asher had apparently told Reid I was queer. I guess he always knew. I should tell him he was right. He's safe to tell. He won't think anything weird."

"Who's gonna think anything weird?" Logan asked. "And if they do, they can get fucked."

"Right in the ear," Seth added.

Logan and I looked at each other and burst out laughing. Logan slid his arm around Seth's slim shoulders and kissed his cheek. "Those are fighting words from you."

Seth's face reddened. "I'll leave the profanity to you two." He shook his head and smiled. "You can tell Reid too that you came out," he said to me.

"Right. I guess I can." I gulped my coffee and waved to the passing server for a refill. Logan suggested pie and ice cream for dessert, and I agreed even though I was full. I half listened to Seth tell us about Angela's latest expansion of her company.

The nerves returned full force as I thought about telling Reid. It'd only been a couple of weeks since Thanksgiving when I'd forcefully insisted I was straight. He was going to think I was flaky at best and a liar at worst. Or maybe…

I couldn't stop thinking about that kiss. Even if it had been part of the act… Maybe it didn't have to be? I could tell Reid that I wanted him for real.

What was stopping me?

Gee, aside from the fact that he might laugh his ass off at the idea of actually dating? That was too cruel for Reid, actually. He wouldn't laugh, but he'd be unbearably kind in turning me down. That would possibly be worse.

Nothing changes if nothing changes.

My mom's voice echoed in my mind. I'd been in the closet for years, and I'd finally changed that. It had been, like, an hour, but I vibrated with jittery energy and the need to make it more official, if that made any sense. I'd told my dads I didn't want to tell anyone else right away, but it turned out I did?

If I confided in Reid, could something monumental change between us? Or was I just fooling myself?

Only one way to find out.

Chapter Ten

Reid

As Connor left the subway station and strode across the street in his Doc Martens in the fading gray light, I knew I had a serious problem.

The klaxon was blaring. The risk profile was intolerably high. I needed to veto. I had to make my escape before he spotted me on the crowded sidewalk amid the falling snow.

But I didn't move. I only watched him approach, his face lighting up like a proverbial Christmas tree as he spotted me and waved.

I wanted to kiss him again.

It was unacceptable yet undeniable. I'd sleepwalked through meetings all week and thought of little else but how I wanted to kiss Connor again. *More* than kiss him. A frisson of excitement rippled through me at all the things I wanted to do with Connor.

All the things I *couldn't* do with him since he was only pretending to be my boyfriend.

Only pretending to be queer—although I did wonder about that. I sincerely doubted he was straight, but the only thing that mattered was what Connor thought and felt.

I waved as he approached, and *god*, how had I missed him so much this week? It was ludicrous! He wore his usual ensemble of boots, jeans, and that leather jacket. Snow dusted his head, and his hands were bare. Why didn't he at least have gloves?

"Hey!" I said as we met. Then I was opening my arms, and we were hugging each other, Connor's lean body tight against mine.

Apparently, we hugged now when we saw each other? Connor held onto me tightly, and we only separated because we were blocking the sidewalk and the people rushing past threw elbows.

We laughed awkwardly, and Connor said, "Um, hey." His pale cheeks were pink, and a snowflake melted on his nose.

"How did it go?"

He groaned. "I dunno. I want to say it was a disaster, but Asher and my dads would roll their eyes and tell you I always say that. Which is true.”

“I have complete confidence it wasn’t a disaster. Sorry I couldn’t meet you right after.”

“Nah, it made no sense for you to go back uptown after your meeting. Besides, the High Line is right here.”

I grinned. “You figured out the next item on the list.”

“You gave me a huge clue.”

“Or it’s that big brain of yours. Still up for it?” I lifted my chin and peered at the heavy white blocking out some of the buildings. “We seem to have picked the first big snowfall of the season to go for a walk.”

“I’m game. Didn’t you say you had to go to a holiday thing first?”

All other thoughts but Connor had evacuated my mind as soon as I saw him. “Shit, yes.” I checked my watch. “It’s only a happy hour at a bar, but it’s a major client and my grandmother will be there. I have to make an appearance. We’ll just have one and duck out.”

“It’s cool. I could use a drink after that exam.” He yawned as we started walking.

“Up late again studying?”

Connor nodded. “I get paranoid that I haven’t studied enough, and I’ll miss something obvious.”

“I thought Asher said at Rencliffe you got straight As.”

“Yeah, once I got my shit together. I was almost expelled.”

I motioned for us to turn at the next light. “Wow. I didn’t realize.”

“I wasn’t working to my potential.” He grimaced. “It was after my mom died, and things were shitty with Logan. Then he got roped into pretending to be Seth’s fiancé, and everything turned around. Honestly, I was such an asshole that I’m not sure why Logan didn’t drive me out to the woods and leave me there.”

I barked out a surprised laugh. “Good thing he didn’t. Although maybe you would have been adopted by wolves or something.”

“I think you have to be a baby for a Tarzan scenario to work. But anyway, this is medical school. I can’t take anything for granted. I’m on a scholarship thanks to my grades, and I need to keep them up.”

I squeezed his arm. “I’m sure you did great.” Tilting my head, I checked the sign as we approached a bar with its window decorated in pine boughs and gold fairy lights. “Here we are.”

“Right. Boyfriend mode activated.” He gave me a smile and seemed to almost say something else. Before I could ask what, he slipped his arm around my waist. I settled my arm on his shoulders, letting myself enjoy the feeling of him pressed close. Though “enjoyed” was too mild a word. Reveled was more like it.

As we walked into the welcome wave of heat, I scanned the long room. People spoke in clusters along the bar and at high-top tables creating a din of sound that was accompanied by jazzy Christmas music. I thought I recognized Ella Fitzgerald crooning about Frosty, the debonair snowman.

I spotted Grandmother right away, raising a hand to her and smiling with my other arm firmly around Connor. Her smile in return was thin, and she immediately returned to her conversation with one of the VPs from the client's company, her bejeweled fingers wrapped around a glass of white.

Not wanting to stay long enough to check our coats—and knowing Connor was still leery of losing his jacket—we just slung them over our arms and grabbed two glasses of bubbly from a server. Another had a tray of delicate spring rolls, but Connor declined.

"Not hungry?" I asked as I waved the server away too.

He shrugged and mumbled something. He seemed nervous for some reason, and I stroked my hand up and down his back slowly. I could feel him shiver, and I moved us farther away from the door.

I made small talk with a few VIPs while Connor nodded and smiled when necessary. I kept my hand securely on his lower back.

When we were alone for a moment by the bar, we hung our coats over a stool. I murmured, "Are you sure you're okay? You seem jumpy?"

"Do I?" He seemed alarmed, but laughed it off. "Post-exam nerves, I guess."

I hesitated. "You're sure you're still okay with…this?" Raising an eyebrow, I hoped he'd understand my meaning.

Connor nodded immediately. "Yep. All good." He finished his champagne in a gulp.

"As long as you're sure." Something was off. I spoke quietly. "We can stop. You've already done your part."

His brows met. "It's only the twelfth. I still have a week before I go home. I don't want to stop."

Perhaps this was about the loan? I hadn't pressed him about why he'd needed the money, but could that reason be the source of his nerves? "I don't want to stop either," I said truthfully. "As long as you're sure."

"I'm sure." His eyes glittered, and he opened his mouth to say something before closing it. Then he leaned closer to whisper, "You can kiss me again." He watched me intently before adding, "If you want to, I mean. For…this."

Was it dishonest to kiss him now? It probably had been last weekend, but I hadn't been able to resist asking. Now Connor was offering, and desire unfurled in my belly. The responsible thing to do would be to refuse and put distance between us. I'd always been responsible. As the elder brother and heir, I'd had to be.

Would it be so bad to be irresponsible for a minute?

The heat from Connor's body felt like a crackling fire, and I inched closer as I cupped his flushed cheek with my hand. His lips parted, and he met me halfway with a press of our mouths. It lasted several thumps of my heart before we eased apart and met each other's eyes.

Then we kissed again.

With more power this time, our heads tilting as our arms slid around each other. I remembered we were in public just before our tongues met. I pulled away with a breathless smile.

"That should do it, *mon amour*," I whispered, and Connor grinned.

We laughed and busied ourselves with fresh glasses of wine. When I glanced around to see if Grandmother was shooting daggers, I jolted in surprise to find Asher in the doorway.

"Hey!" I said far too loudly.

Asher watched us warily. "Hey." Then his expression brightened, and he waved to Grandmother before taking off his wool coat, which was covered in snow. He grimaced and apologized to the server who took it away to the coat cubby.

"What are you doing here?" I asked.

"I'm taking Gamma for our holiday dinner. This is the only night she has free. Well, after this." He slugged Connor's arm. "Hey, man. How did the exam go? I texted you back last night."

"Yeah, sorry," Connor said. "I had to concentrate."

"Cool. You said there was something you had to tell me?" Asher snagged a glass of white from a server. "What's up?"

"Oh, nothing!" Connor flailed, and half his wine sloshed out of the glass onto his sweater. "Whoops. I'll be back in a sec." He squeezed past a few people and disappeared in the direction of the bathroom.

Asher glanced around before jabbing me in the side with his finger and hissing, "What's the deal? Is the thing Connor wants to tell me that you two are fucking?"

I hissed back, "Shh! And no. Don't be ridiculous."

"Dude, I just saw you two kiss like you were about to get busy on the bar in front of Gamma, god, and the staff of whatever company is throwing this shindig."

"If you paid the slightest bit of attention to Utopia, you'd know whose party this is."

Asher boggled. "As if *that's* the important part? Spill it. I was right, wasn't I?" He winced. "No, don't tell me. Connor gets to do that."

"Look, I don't know what he wants to tell you, but we're not having sex." My face burned. This was not the place for this discussion.

"Okay. I believe you." He winked broadly. "Tell Con I'll talk to him tomorrow. I'd better say hi to Gamma."

"Tell her I have to leave early." I shrugged on my coat and grabbed Connor's as he made his way back.

"Tell her yourself!" Asher insisted. "I don't want to get in the middle."

"Too bad." I ushered Connor out the door. I'd shown up and done my duty, and that would have to be good enough for Grandmother.

Naturally, doubt and guilt hit me immediately. Connor and I ducked our heads as a gust of snow swirled around us and we did up our coats.

Would Grandmother be disappointed I hadn't stayed longer? Was I shirking my responsibility to Utopia? Was I endangering the chances of convincing her to invest in my housing project?

"Do you still want to go?" Connor asked. There was already fresh snow in his hair, and his cheeks were flushed and eyes bright.

All my worries melted away. "Absolutely," I said. "Here." I pulled out the beanie from my pocket and smoothed it over his head.

"What about you?" he protested.

"I'll take it back in a bit."

We climbed the stairs up to the park that had been built on an old elevated railway line and snaked through Chelsea. Sirens echoed and horns honked from below as Monday rush hour traffic clogged the streets.

"It's amazing how far away it feels up here," Connor said as we started along the boardwalk, which was covered in a few inches of snow. "I've been meaning to come down, but I never got around to it."

I was glad I'd worn my boots, and I handed Connor one of my gloves. "Did you forget yours?"

After a moment, he took the leather and slipped it on his left hand, putting his right hand in his jacket pocket. "Thanks. Yeah, I'm happy I remembered to wear pants, honestly."

The thought of Connor *sans* pants warmed me, and I laughed as we passed an art nouveau sculpture of a tree slowly being covered in thick, perfect snow. It muffled everything, including our steps. While other people passed by in both directions, the incoming storm seemed to have driven most indoors.

Dried grasses poked up, and thick snow balanced on the husks of dormant flowers. "I've never been up here in winter," I said. "Actually, I haven't been up here in years. That's one of the great things about our list. I take too much in New York for granted, and I need to make an effort to take advantage of what's right on my doorstep."

Connor peered around. Darkness had swiftly fallen along with the snow. "The lights are amazing. We're right in the city, but we're apart from it. In a bubble. Central Park has the same vibe."

"It does," I agreed, watching him watch the skyline. A little smile curved his lips, and I remembered how they'd felt soft yet firm under mine, and how he'd made a tiny sound—a sweet sigh that—

"Buddy!" a man shouted as our shoulders collided. Connor had tugged me aside at the last second, his cold hand gripping mine, or I'd have crashed straight into the guy.

"Watch where the fuck you're going!" the man added before continuing in the other direction.

"Whoops." I tried to laugh it off.

"You okay?" Connor was squeezing my hand and peering up at me with concern that made my heart swell.

"Yep! No concussion, I promise. The only thing injured was my pride. Maybe a shred of dignity. And I might have a bruised shoulder tomorrow. I swear I'm not normally this clumsy."

Only when I'm watching you instead of where I'm walking.

Connor smiled as he let go of my hand to gently prod my shoulder. "You always seemed so cool when I was a kid. So sophisticated."

"Uh-oh. My secret's out. I'm none of the above despite my designer suits." I rotated my shoulder. "It's fine. Really." I took his hand again, our bare skin meeting. "Cold," I said, further proving I was neither cool, sophisticated, suave, or any other synonym.

We stood face to face in the falling snow by the railing, out of the path of the few people hurrying by. Connor threaded our fingers together even though there was no one we knew here to see us and report back to Grandmother.

He blinked up at me, his lips parting as he sucked in a breath and blurted, "I want to tell you something. Ask you something, I guess." The words came out rapid fire.

It took me a moment to process. "All right."

Connor hesitated, biting his lip in the cutest, sexiest way.

I squeezed his fingers gently. "You can tell me."

"What if I'm not straight?"

In my mind, Handel's "Hallelujah Chorus" burst forth. "Then I'd want to kiss you again," I managed to say. "But we should probably talk about—"

With his gloved hand tangling in my hair and pulling down my head, Connor kissed me. He pressed his mouth to mine in a rush, a shudder going through him as we clung to each other, tasting until we had to gasp for air.

His eyes were dark with lust, his lips shiny as he blinked up at me. "Sorry. I interrupted you."

"You're good. This is good." Breathing hard, I held him close, my hand slipping around his lower back. I wanted to push him against the railing or find the closest tree so I could grind our cocks together, but I resisted. Barely.

He was hard against me, and after a glance around—bless Mother Nature for the increasingly heavy, thick snow—I gripped his denim-clad ass and rubbed against him.

Connor gasped softly. "I'm not wrong? You really want to…with me? I know this is supposed to be pretend and everything, but…"

"I want to kiss you all night." I trailed my lips along his jaw to his ear. "I want to do a hell of a lot more than kiss." Connor stiffened, his breath catching. Was that excitement or something else? I lifted my head. "Veto?"

He shook his head, snowflakes catching on his nose and eyelashes. "No veto. Can we kiss again first?"

In response, I captured his mouth, sliding my tongue inside. I waited to see if he tensed again, but he melted against me, moaning. I stroked our tongues together, and Connor made little whimpering sounds. He seemed happy to let me take the lead, so I explored his mouth.

He tasted of champagne, and I could have devoured him—would have if we weren't in danger of being snowed in on the High Line.

Reluctantly, I broke away. "My place. Cab." Connor nodded vigorously.

Our bare hands entwined, we practically ran down the nearest stairs, almost colliding with a parks employee who was shoveling. After apologizing, we made it to the street and groaned in unison at the standstill traffic.

"Subway's faster," I said, and we found the nearest station.

If we'd been in a cab, we could have kissed a bit more. At least hugged and snuggled. On the C train at rush hour? Not so much.

"I missed you this week," I murmured as we held onto the overhead pole, our bodies crushed together thanks to the aforementioned rush hour. I ached to be even closer. I wanted him skin on skin.

"Me too," Connor said. His face was flushed, eyes bright, and his hair mussed as he took off my hat and gave it back to me.

Had I *ever* wanted to kiss someone this badly? If I had, I couldn't remember.

"I'm so glad you said yes on Thanksgiving. I never expected this." I laughed. "Understatement of the year."

"Me either." Connor's laugh was giddy. He glanced around, then lowered his voice. "I used to dream about this."

My heart skipped. "About me?"

He nodded.

I leaned close to his ear and whispered, "How did you imagine me?"

Connor's face went beet red as he stammered.

"It's okay," I murmured, resting my hand on his hip under the hem of his leather jacket. "You can show me."

"You make me feel like I'm having a myocardial infarction."

I laughed. "The feeling's mutual. I think."

Connor smiled up at me, and there was that dimple. Why was the subway moving so slowly? We crawled along before picking up speed again. I reminded myself this was still faster than a cab uptown in the snow and traffic.

We squeezed together as passengers pushed past us to exit at Forty-second Street. Even in the crush of people and the stench of someone eating a hot dog with sauerkraut, Connor's shampoo filled my nose. It was clean and simple and perfect for him.

Not that he was *simple*, but…innocent, maybe?"

"What are you thinking about?" he asked suddenly.

"You," I answered truthfully. "And why the damn subway isn't going faster."

Finally, we made it to my stop at Seventy-second. Bare hands grasped, we passed riots of holiday lights amid the falling snow. An old carol—the one about angels singing—played in my lobby. I waved to Gus at the desk and jabbed the close button on the wood-paneled elevator, not able to wait to kiss Connor again.

We gasped and laughed into each other's mouths, kissing messily. I wanted to taste every inch of him, then start again at the beginning. I could have drowned in him, my whole body buzzing with lust and euphoria. He was just so sweet and wonderful, and I wanted to climb into his skin.

"You're gorgeous," I muttered as we stumbled from the elevator still half-entwined—and right into the path of my neighbor. "Mrs. Trent!" I exclaimed, wiping a trail of spit from my mouth with the back of my hand.

With wide eyes, the older woman stared, her mouth agape. Her gaze swept over us, her small black and white sheepadoodle barking at her feet and wagging its tail so hard it was in danger of snapping off.

"Hi, Pepper. Who's a good boy?" I crooned, bending to pet him before tugging Connor forward. "Merry Christmas, Mrs. Trent."

"And to you," she replied, laughter in her voice.

"Oh my god," Connor mumbled. "Is she going to tell everyone in your building?"

I fumbled with my keys, finally getting the deadbolt unlocked. "She's more than welcome to tell them I was sucking face with my gorgeous, sexy-as-fuck boyfriend in the elevator."

Connor smiled, but tension rippled through him, the air going thick as my words registered. Well, one word in particular.

I shut the door behind us. "What I meant was…" That. That had been exactly what I'd meant. Part of me wanted to sweep it under the rug with both hands so I could get back to touching Connor, but I forced myself to stop, think, and address it. "I know you're not really my boyfriend. Not yet? But maybe? If you even want that?"

"Um…" Connor swallowed hard. "I guess we should talk about all that?"

"Yes. It doesn't have to be right now, does it? We can agree that right now, we'd very much like to have sex with each other."

He groaned, stripping off my glove before moving to the zipper of his jacket. "Yep. Sex now. We're on the same page." His fingers twitched.

"Excellent." I abandoned my glove, coat, and boots.

The lights were off and the switch was too far away. I'd left the blinds in the living room open, and golden light from the snowy city cast a warm glow. For the first time, I wished I did have a Christmas tree to make it even cozier.

Since when did I care about coziness? As much as I wanted to rip off

Connor's clothes and fuck him until we passed out, I had to stop and take his face in my hands to kiss him softly.

We stood kissing until I blindly took a few steps backward, hoping to hit the couch. I backed into a wall instead, but that would do. Our kisses turned demanding, and I moaned at the sensation of Connor's cold hands on my stomach under my sweater.

Breathing hard, he dropped to his knees and held onto my thighs with tense fingers. Looking up at me under his thick lashes, he asked, "Is this good?"

The sight of Connor kneeling at my feet was *extremely* good, and my cock swelled against the fly of my trousers. "Yes. Did you want something in particular down there?" I teased.

Instead of answering coyly or filthily, Connor looked down. "Um…"

Frowning, I ran my hand over his soft hair, now damp with melting snow. "You don't have to do anything you don't want to," I said.

"I'm tired of being chickenshit." Connor gulped, and if he wasn't out of college, his voice probably would have cracked as he blurted, "I want to suck dick."

"Mine specifically, I hope? Well, to be fair it's the only one in the room. Unless you're *very* flexible."

He blinked, breathing harshly, and I could see him start to fold in on himself, withering in the face of my joking that had clearly missed the mark. I tilted up his chin and gave him what I hoped was a reassuring smile.

"Hey, it's okay. You can do whatever you want. Or we can stop. There's no reason to be nervous."

Connor blinked up at me again, and *wow*, he really was beautiful. Those huge brown eyes were so vulnerable, even as his tone grew forceful. "I don't want to stop. I want you."

He unzipped my pants and freed my cock, peering at it intently and touching the head with his fingers. Shivers tripped down my spine.

"You're cut. I always wondered. I figured because Asher is, you would be too. Sorry, I shouldn't bring up your brother right now."

"It's okay." I traced the shell of his ear.

He licked his lips. "I want you in my mouth."

I nodded, my balls heavy with desire. "I'm all yours."

With a deep breath, Connor practically lunged at my cock, taking me almost to the root before choking. He sucked hard, and his mouth felt amazing wrapped around me—hot and wet and eager.

A little *too* eager—he coughed and gasped for breath, mumbling, "Sorry."

"Hey, hey. Slow down. We have all night."

Shaking his head, he muttered, "Why can't I get anything right?"

"Whoa." I tilted up his chin. "Is this your first time giving head?" It stood to reason since before tonight he'd insisted he was straight. Although

I'd certainly sucked a lot of cock before coming out.

Looking anywhere but at me, he nodded, his cheeks flushed. He shrugged—a twitch bordering on violent. He'd dislocate a shoulder if he wasn't careful.

Connor mumbled, "I've never really done anything."

The rhythmic blaring of my mental alarm system erupted. "You mean with another man?"

Another painful-looking shrug. "Not with anyone."

"Nothing at Harvard?"

Head down, he mumbled, "I had to work hard to keep my scholarship. My parents can't afford things like yours can."

Right, but surely in four years at college there'd been a spare moment to hook up? He could have gone to a party once in a while and—

Why was I trying to problem-solve? It didn't matter why Connor hadn't hooked up in college. Nothing else mattered but being here with him now.

"It's okay." I caressed his hair, but he was so tense I wasn't sure if he wanted me to touch him.

"Sorry." He dropped his hands from my legs, and I realized how tightly he'd been squeezing my thighs. "I know this isn't what you signed up for."

This was going all wrong. "Come up here. Please?" He stood with his head low, and I caressed his cheek, encouraging him to meet my eyes, though he didn't. "Don't be sorry. You didn't do anything wrong."

Crossing his arms tightly, Connor bit out, "I know it's pathetic to still be a virgin. It's okay. You can laugh."

Stunned, I blinked. "*No.*" I held his cheek, then pressed my lips to the hot skin. "Baby, I'm not laughing." I kissed his other cheek, his forehead, and the tip of his nose where snowflakes had melted earlier. I stroked his back and sides gently. His eyes swam with unshed tears, and I could barely breathe through the urge to kiss this beautiful boy.

In a *whoosh* of breath, he relaxed into my arms, and I gave a silent prayer of thanks. Now I just had to figure out the right thing to say.

"It's all right," was all I could murmur, my neck damp with his breath where he'd pressed his face into my skin.

Connor swallowed with a *click*. The warmth of his whisper brushed my skin. "I was too chickenshit before," he repeated. "I just want…"

Fuck, I could imagine all too well what he wanted, because it simmered through my veins. "Tell me," I coaxed, rubbing his hip, which felt intimate without grabbing his ass and being too pushy.

"I'm sick of being afraid."

"Good. There's nothing to be afraid of here. Not with me."

Connor lifted his head. His red face was tear-stained. "I know. After you kissed me at that party, it was like this big mysterious, huge thing was suddenly real." He pressed his hands over my chest, making my nipples tingle through my sweater. "Like we could touch, and even though I'm probably a shit kisser because I have zero practice, it wasn't up on a pedestal anymore. I'm probably not making any sense."

"Are you saying that was your first kiss?"

"Like I told you, I'm pathetic." He couldn't look at me.

I had to kiss him then, capturing his mouth gently but firmly. Connor sighed into me, and we kissed slow and deep. I held him in my arms, and I simultaneously wanted to keep him safe and innocent and protected—while my body hummed with lust and the need to be naked and coming with him.

Breathing through my nose, I imagined the smooth female voice from the latest meditation app I was trying.

"Breathe in Peace. Hold it in your heart center. Don't let it go yet. And now exhale slowly, keeping that peace within you, guiding you even as you breathe out."

Except my cock was still rock hard, my pulse pounded, and sweat dampened my hairline. This was why meditation was BS. Connor moaned into my mouth as our tongues explored.

Once I'd kissed him breathless, if he wanted to get on his knees for me again, I'd push between his swollen lips and teach him how to lick and touch and suck without pushing too far the first time...

It hit me that the best way was to show him. He was hard against me, and I slid my hand against his cock before breaking our kiss and asking, "Is this okay?"

Connor nodded, thrusting against my hand.

"You need to come, don't you?"

He could only whimper in response.

"I've got you, baby. I'm going to take care of you, okay?" I squeezed him before letting go and reversing our positions. Before dropping to my knees, I asked, "Do you want me to suck you?"

"Fuck." He knocked his head against the wall. "Yes."

"Careful. Can't have the doctor getting a concussion." With a wink, I kneeled and slowly opened his jeans. His cock strained against the white fabric of his boxer briefs. Slowly, I kissed him through the cotton, licking at the damp spot where he'd leaked.

"Oh, fuck," he muttered, hands fisted at his sides and body rigid.

"It's okay. You're not going to come yet." I tugged down his jeans and underwear to his knees. His cock sprang out and nearly hit me in the eye, which would have been *real* smooth considering I was supposed to be the expert.

"You can touch me," I said. "Put your hands on my head." I leaned into his fingers. "Like that. Perfect."

I nosed at his groin, wiry hair tickling my nose. Then I nuzzled at his hip while tracing circles on his thighs with my fingers. Light hair dusted his legs, and his muscles quivered. The temptation to touch myself shocked me in its intensity.

I didn't even have him in my mouth yet—I wasn't supposed to be the horny, pent-up one here. I couldn't remember the last time I'd needed to come this badly.

"*Reid.*"

I chuckled. "Did you want something?"

His fingers tightened in my hair. "Please."

Slowly, I licked his balls, then along his thin shaft from the base to the tip, easing down his foreskin. Sitting back on my heels, my own cock still out, I looked up at him while I gave in and stroked myself.

"Can you say it? What you want me to do?"

Connor's dark eyes were locked on me. In the snow's glow, his face was pale and beautiful. "I want you to suck my dick," he whispered.

I bit back a moan, stroking myself harder. "Good boy." I let go of my cock and took hold of his hips, stilling the quaver in his body. Leaning close, I licked at his shiny tip, savoring the bitter drops of precum. "I love how you taste."

He jerked, his cock pulsing. Gazing up at him, I wrapped my lips around the head and sucked. Not as hard as I wanted to, remembering to go easy.

"Fuck, Reid! I can't believe this is happening." His hands shook on my head. "I dreamed of this so many times."

A thrill raced down my spine, and I pulled off with a slick *pop* to grin up at him. "You really did?"

He nodded. "I had the biggest crush on you."

How had I missed that? It didn't matter—we were here now. I licked at his cock, stroking around the base with my hand. "When you imagined us together, was it like this?" My heart pounded, excitement sparking on my skin.

Connor nodded again. "Like this. Like…doing everything."

Without warning, I sucked him deeply before pulling off. *Everything* sounded amazing to me. "Did you imagine coming in my mouth?"

Gasping, he shuddered, his cock straining by my lips as if desperate to get back inside. "*Yes.*"

"I want to swallow your cum, baby. Will you give it to me?"

At Connor's hoarse assent, I swallowed him again, swirling my tongue around the head of his cock and reaching down to tease his balls. I was ready to blow too, and it only took seconds for Connor to stiffen, his fingers tight in my hair as he spilled in my mouth.

I swallowed convulsively, milking him until I saw stars, my nostrils flaring. He repeated my name like a prayer, staring down at me in wonder as I came with a few strokes, the musk of him lingering on my tongue.

Knowing I was the first to kiss him—let alone suck him off—was an undeniable thrill. Was it tacky for me to get off on being his first? Probably. Did I care?

As I stood and Connor tugged me close for a breathless kiss, his hands still tangled in my hair, the only thing I cared about was giving him more.

Giving him *everything*.

Chapter Eleven

Connor

THAT WAS MY cum I could taste on Reid's tongue. I was practically panting into his mouth, but he kissed me slowly, patiently, so gently. Tears pricked my eyes. He was being so *kind*.

Of course, my asshole brain had to hiss: *He's being nice because you're pitiful.*

I broke free and blurted, "Sorry. I know that was—I'm—" I shook my head. "Sorry."

"Hey, hey." He brushed back my hair and examined my face, which was probably red and blotchy as shit. "Why are you apologizing?"

"Because you're—and I'm—" I rolled my eyes. "You know."

"I don't, actually. You're so damn sexy."

Me. Reid Cabot was saying that to me. After blowing me. *Me.* I tried to think of something to say that wasn't totally cringe. I went with, "You too," which was definitely cringey, but whatever.

He gave me that gleaming red carpet smile. "Hungry? We could order in."

"Okay."

"What do you feel like? Maybe pizza?"

"Okay."

"Or we could do Chinese."

"Okay."

Reid laughed, a low rumble in his chest that made my stomach somersault. "Are you so blissed out you'll agree to anything right now?"

"Yeah." I was grateful to the wall behind me and Reid's big hands rubbing up and down my sides. Jesus, I wanted his hands on my bare skin. We were wearing way too many clothes still.

He laughed again. "How about keto protein bars?"

I smiled. "Okay."

"Day-old tuna sandwiches from a vending machine?"

"Okay."

Reid kissed me, slipping his tongue into my mouth, and another thrill shot through me. He murmured, "Let's order for real. There must be something you're craving."

"Um… Empanada Mama's always good. It's in Hell's Kitchen."

"I don't think I've had it."

"And you call yourself a New Yorker?"

He grinned. "Showing me up. Classic New York move." He kissed me again, then fished his phone from his coat pocket. "Tell me what to order."

It took me a second to recover from the way he'd just kissed me so casually, and how it had felt so normal. How was kissing Reid Cabot *normal*?

"Connor?"

"Right. Uh…" My mind was blank. Jesus, I wasn't a *food* virgin, and I'd ordered from this place a zillion times—I could recommend the best dishes. I was about to ask him for his phone to refresh my memory when I blurted, "Viagra!"

He blinked. "Pardon?"

I had to laugh. "It's a seafood empanada."

"Oh!" Reid tapped his phone. "Okay, got it. Wheat or corn?"

I rattled off suggestions as he tapped and nodded. There. Not a food virgin. Go, me. "And the chicharrónes are amazing."

I pondered whether or not I was still an actual virgin. I mean, I knew it was a bullshit construct of our society, but it was something I'd built up in my head for so long that it was hard to shake it off.

"Connor?"

"Uh-huh?" I still leaned against the wall with my dick out. I debated whether putting it away would be more awkward than not drawing attention to it. Though Reid didn't seem bothered or anything.

"Dessert? Or are you sweet enough?" He waggled his eyebrows.

How was a guy with custom Armani suits such a *dork*? And how was I? Because that cheesy line made me grin like an idiot. "They've got a coconut dulce de leche cake to die for."

"*Oh.*" He tapped the screen. "Yes. Sold. Okay, order's in."

He stripped off his sweater, and I stared at his bare, hairy chest in the bright snowy glow from outside. *Then* he kicked off his pants and underwear and was naked, so nope, didn't seem like Reid minded that my dick was hanging out.

He took a few steps and extended his hand. "Come on. Let's get comfy."

I took his warm hand even though mine was sweaty and probably gross. "I'm not sure it's possible for you to put on anything more comfortable." I was trying to mimic that cheesy old line people said in movies, but it probably sounded weird.

Reid only smiled as he led me into his bedroom. "Naked is comfy, it's true." He opened a drawer and pulled out flannels and T-shirts. "I'm not a big naked eater, though."

"Good point. That can be…messy."

He let go of my hand to peel off my clothes, undressing me like I was a little kid but in a sweet, cool way and not a weird one. "Want the Knicks again?" He held up the worn tee I'd used before. At my nod, he handed it over.

We were both temporarily naked, and outside of a locker room, I'd never experienced that. We both looked at each other, not trying to hide it because there was no reason not to look. For a second, I wanted to turn and cover up, but it was also exhilarating. The way Reid's gaze roamed over my skin made me hot all over.

He seemed to like what he saw.

His body was toned and hairy in all the right places. As I bent to pull on boxers, I stared at his dick. It was still wet, and part of that was from *my* mouth. Fuck, I'd loved the feeling of him warm and straining and filling me so completely I'd choked.

Reid was thick, and his balls were bigger than mine. Hairier than mine too, but I could tell he trimmed his pubes. He was rich, so he probably went to a salon or some shit. I was ready to drop to my knees and suck him again as he strolled to the en suite bathroom and ran a washcloth under the tap.

I pulled up the boxers and put on the tee and watched him clean his junk. He knew I was watching—I mean, I was openly staring—and a little smile tugged at his insanely kissable mouth. A mouth I'd kissed. A mouth I'd had my own dick inside. A mouth I was going to kiss again ASAP.

"C'mere."

Mouth dry, I joined him in the bathroom, where he kissed me softly, a finger under my chin. My belly fluttered. If this was a dream, I never wanted to wake up, please and thank you.

We drank beer while we waited for dinner and found the end of *Die Hard* playing. On the couch with our feet up on the coffee table, I leaned into Reid, his arm snug around my shoulders. There was no other word for it—we were cuddling.

The Stella Artois bottle was cold in my hand, and my feet could have used socks, but the rest of me was hot and tingling—and honestly a little crampy from staying still. I could feel the steady rise and fall of Reid's breathing, my arm jammed in between his ribs and mine. I cautiously sipped my beer.

"You can move, you know." Reid squeezed my shoulder.

I stiffened. "Why would I want to move?"

"Because you feel so tense, I'm afraid you're going to snap in half." He chuckled. "It's okay if you're not a cuddler."

"No, I am!" I exhaled forcefully. "I guess I'm not sure if I am? I'm not used to being this close to someone for an extended period of time. Or any time."

"That's fair." He stroked my arm, his fingers dancing over my bare skin beneath the old T-shirt. "Relax. Breathe. Drink your beer. And we can sit apart if it's more comfortable."

"Okay. This is good, though. I like this." Tentatively, I slid my palm over his thigh and rested it there. "At least until the food comes."

"Sounds like a plan."

Once it came, we watched *Home Alone* while we ate. Empanada Mama's was delicious as always. I was pleased that Reid made appreciative moans—moans that also pleased my dick—and praised the food. He had a blob of guacamole in the corner of his mouth, and before I could over-think it—or even think about it at all—I was swiping it away with my thumb.

Plantain chip in hand, Reid's lips curved into a smile, and he sucked my still-hovering thumb into his mouth before releasing it slowly. "Too good to waste," he said with a wink. I made a sound that was a cross between a bleating goat and I don't even know what.

Kevin McAllister had just given the Wet Bandits their seventeenth injury that should have killed them sixteen injuries ago when I realized Reid was asleep. We'd slouched close together after eating, and his hand sat heavy on my thigh with his fingers touching my inner thigh.

His lips had parted, and his breathing was deeper, his eyes moving in REM sleep. His dark, thick eyelashes fanned over his skin, and I wanted to kiss each one. How was he so beautiful and smart and funny and kind—and somehow into *me*?

Was it weird that I almost wanted to call my dads and tell them I'd hooked up? Answer: *Yes*, that was incredibly weird, dude. But after so long in the closet, I wanted to shout it from the rooftops. I'd told my dads I didn't want to broadcast that I was gay yet, but now I wasn't so sure.

Reid mumbled something and shifted, and I held my breath, hoping he'd keep his hand on my thigh. He did, moving it a few inches and sending sparks straight to my balls. Just being touched like that—so intimately— made me want to do cartwheels.

It would probably also be weird to tell Asher since Reid was his brother. Worry tugged at me. Would Asher be cool with us? Not to get ahead of myself or anything.

The loud beep of my phone made me jump, and I cursed as I raced into Reid's bedroom to grab it from my jeans. Reid had shifted and murmured, and hopefully I hadn't wrecked his nap. I answered the call as I processed the name on the screen.

"Can I speak to Connor Lisowski?" a woman asked. "This is CVS calling about the job application you submitted."

"Oh, hi!" I cleared my throat. "Yes. This is Connor."

"It says on your application you're a student?"

"Yes, I'm in med school at Columbia. I just need to make some cash."

She was silent a moment. "You know this position is overnight restocking? It's not in the pharmacy."

"Right, I know. I have classes and studying, so overnight's great."

The woman rattled off more questions, and we made an appointment for an in-person interview that sounded like a formality to make sure I wasn't serial killer material. She said, "One to three shifts a week starting in January works for you?"

"Perfect."

I'd left the bedroom door ajar, and I knew Reid was awake as soon as I tiptoed out into the living room after hanging up. He waved from the couch. "Hey."

"Um, hey. Sorry to wake you. It was a job thing."

"Aren't you a little busy with school for a job?"

I stood halfway between the couch and bedroom, weirdly frozen on the spot. "It's just part time. It's cool. I need to pay you back and stuff."

Reid waved a dismissive hand, something like annoyance flashing over his face. "Don't worry about that. I don't want you burning out. Forget the money."

Whoa. "Um, yeah, I'm not going to forget that I owe you ten grand. No way." I crossed my arms. "Even if we—if we're—no way. I'm paying you back all of it."

He raised his hands. "Okay. Just know you can take as long as you need."

"Yeah. Thanks."

Fuck. Now we were suddenly awkward. I wasn't sure what to do. Rejoin him on the couch for more cuddling? Or was I overstaying my welcome? He didn't seem to want me to leave, but I also shouldn't have taken it for granted he wanted me to stay, right?

"Sorry I fell asleep. Amazing sex followed by beer and great food is a surefire way to knock me out."

I couldn't suppress a grin, the tension releasing. "Was it really amazing?"

"What do you think?" He stood and slowly approached, reminding me of a jungle cat on the prowl. His boxers hung low on his hips, and he peeled off his white tee, letting it drop from his fingers.

"It was amazing. I also don't have a frame of reference for comparison."

He laughed, low and sexy. "So you're saying I might be terrible in bed?"

"Excuse you, I am *not* saying that."

He prowled close and slipped his hands under the Knicks T-shirt, making me shiver, goosebumps spreading over my skin. "How about we go to bed and explore this issue further?" he whispered in my ear before nuzzling my neck.

"Uh-huh. More investigation needed."

Being naked with Reid on his bed, the covers pushed down to our feet, felt incredibly grown-up. Here I was in New York City in bed with my…what? Crush? Hookup? Potential boyfriend?

"This good?" he asked.

"Uh-huh."

We faced each other on our sides and kissed. It only took a minute before we were hard and groping each other. Spit shone on Reid's lips as he broke our kiss with a gasp.

"What do you want to do?"

"I don't know."

He traced my lips with his finger, smiling. "What are you curious about? Anything in particular?"

"Like… Do you do butt stuff?"

"I do." He answered so easily. "Should I elaborate?"

"Yep." My dick throbbed, and I rolled my hips against his looking for friction.

"I've had cocks and dildos inside me. One of my ex-girlfriends loved pegging me with a strap-on."

I swallowed hard. "Wow." Even though I wasn't into girls, that mental image was *hot*. Reid getting fucked? Jesus.

He ran his hand over the swell of his ass. "If you have questions, ask away."

"Did you—were you, like, on your hands and knees for that?"

"Yes. Not just for her. For men too. On my hands and knees. On my back. Riding their cocks. There are all kinds of ways to do it."

My throat was so dry I could only croak. "And you've fucked people in the butt?" We were rubbing our dicks together as we talked, and Reid's fingers were skimming along the crack of my ass.

"I have." His fingers brushed my hole. "Have you experimented here by yourself?"

How was I supposed to make words happen? Ugh, especially *these* words. I managed, "Not really."

"That's okay," he said smoothly, like he meant it.

I cringed anyway. "Aren't you going to ask why not?" I demanded. A mix of embarrassment and weird anger burst up. Not directed at Reid, but myself for being a chickenshit. I felt like a kid, defaulting to defensive aggression in a way I hadn't in a long time.

He stopped his caresses, and I was grateful he didn't remove his hand and roll away from me. He watched me carefully. "You can veto talking if you want. We can—actually, no."

"No?" I was rigid, my heart pounding. I'd fucked this up. The warm weight of his hand on my hip was the only thing anchoring me from breaking into a million brittle pieces.

"We have to talk. I need to know what's going on in there."

"Everything's fine! I'm sorry. Just keep going." I was ready to beg. I was supposed to be an adult. How would I be a doctor if I felt like a stupid kid? Reid was still watching me. Waiting.

I blurted, "I was too scared. To finger myself." Oh my god, how pathetic. "It's okay, you can laugh."

He didn't even smile, his expression calmly serious. "You're safe here. I'm not laughing at you. You can tell me anything."

I had to kiss him for that, sighing with relief as he kissed me back and wrapped me in his strong arms. The temporary spike of anger faded, soothed away by Reid's patient, sweet touches.

When we caught our breath, he said, "Do you want me to show you something?" His rich, deep voice made my toes curl. I nodded desperately. Reid rolled away for a second, and I was already grabbing at him to bring him back.

He laughed then, lube in his hand. "I'm right here, I promise."

"Cold without you," I said, which was partly true.

"Do you want to get under the covers?" He paused. "Turn off the light?"

It was honestly tempting, but I shook my head. "I want to see you."

Reid kissed me hard, his tongue deep in my mouth. We moaned together, and I could have rubbed off against him easily. But no, there was more he was offering, and I wanted every bit of it.

I was on my left side facing him. He coated my right middle finger in lube before urging my hand behind me. "Veto any time. Yes?"

"Yes."

There was no way in hell I was vetoing a single thing.

"You have to push past the rim." He nodded, coaxing me. "That's it."

It was bizarre to be fingering myself in the first place, but especially with Reid watching. But at the same time, it wasn't?

As I tentatively wriggled my middle finger inside, he encouraged me with the confidence I'd always admired when I'd watched him from the corner at teenage parties, crushing on him. Fantasizing, but never imagining in a million years Reid would turn out to be bi and into guys.

Into *me*.

Because he clearly seemed to be, evidenced by the fact that he was watching me finger myself, and his dick was rock hard against my thigh. It burned as I pushed inside deeper, but I liked it. *Loved* it.

"Crook your finger. A little more." He guided me, my right leg hooked over his hip. His hand stole between my legs, and he rubbed my taint, which made me shiver.

"Not sure if you can really reach it from that angle. Can I try?" he asked.

At my nod, he lubed his own finger and reached between my legs. I moaned as his finger replaced mine, and then he touched what my scientific brain knew was the prostate gland and what my sex brain decided was the greatest piece of flesh in history.

"Fuck!" I almost shouted.

"There you go. Feel that?"

"Jesus, yes, fuck, oh my god! Fuck, I need—" The sensations were almost too much as he touched that perfect spot. I winced.

Immediately, Reid eased out his finger, and I full-on *whined* even though it had been intense.

"It's okay, baby." He urged me onto my back. "You want me to finish you off?"

I nodded eagerly. "You can fuck me."

Reid hesitated as he pushed my legs open, his hands warm on my thighs. "Is it okay if we wait until another night?"

Part of me wanted to whine again and say no. "You want another night with me? Not just now?"

"You bet your tight ass I do." He bent and kissed me, biting at my lip. "I want it all. But right now, I want to suck you again while I finger fuck you."

"Yeah, that sounds pretty good." Understatement of the damn year. I opened my legs all the way, and he pushed up my knees, exposing me.

"You're beautiful," he murmured, his hands roaming over my legs and butt. Crap, I hoped I didn't have any pimples down there.

He leaned down and kissed my ass cheeks. His five o'clock shadow was the perfect amount of rough on my flushed skin.

Especially as he lapped at my balls, licking and sucking as he pushed his finger past my rim again. It burned again to have him inside me, and—

"Oh god! Yes. *Reid.*" The prostate really was a gift I should have been exploring years ago.

My dick leaked, and he didn't even get to suck me again before I came all over myself. I was bent in half, shaking and saying his name. He called me beautiful again and licked the cum off my belly while still stroking inside me. I spurted out a few more drops.

"How do you want me to come?" Reid asked breathlessly, and instead of being awkward, it was incredibly sexy how he kept asking me stuff.

I almost said, "*On me,*" but he'd jerked himself to finish earlier. "I want to make you come this time."

He groaned, "Please," and seemed to be waiting for me to decide exactly how.

It wasn't original, but what the hell. "On your back the way you just did it for me?"

Reid eagerly flopped over and opened himself for me, holding his legs. He nodded to the lube, and I squeezed more onto my finger with shaky hands.

It really did help that he'd shown me how to finger myself. I pushed into his hole, and even though the angle was different, the basics were the same. I found the right spot as he cried out. It took some doing to get his dick in my mouth so I could suck him while I rubbed inside him, but he only encouraged me.

"So good, Connor. You're a natural."

That word—*natural*—elated me. I moaned around his shaft, which throbbed in my mouth, bitter drops leaking onto my tongue. Fuck, I loved sucking cock. I knew I wasn't very good at it, but I stretched my lips around him, taking him as far as I could.

"Baby, I'm gonna—" Reid tensed, his hand suddenly on my head as if to urge me off.

No, this time I wanted it all. I wanted Reid to come in my mouth, and I was going to swallow everything—

I choked and sputtered, his jizz dripping down my chin as I kept going and swallowed as much as I could. His fingers had clenched in my hair, and the tug of pain tightened my empty balls. It was the perfect mix of sensations, especially when Reid loosened his grip and caressed my head.

I didn't want to let go of his cock, but I knew from experience—hey, I had some now!—that it would get oversensitive. I released him from my mouth and eased my finger from inside him as he softened. Breathing hard, we stared at each other, me sitting up between his legs.

"Wow," I said. "Butt stuff is incredible."

Reid grinned. "And there's more where that came from."

More! I grinned back. "With no vetoes in sight."

He pulled me down on top of him for a kiss, and we were sticky and gross, but amazing. It felt right. *Natural.* That word echoed in my head. I'd worried for so long that people wouldn't believe my feelings were real, and maybe some would still be dubious and blame my dads. But there was no way anyone could *influence* me into feeling at home in Reid's arms. This was right.

In the bathroom, we cleaned up, and Reid brushed his teeth before offering me the brush. The thought of sharing anyone else's toothbrush would be gross, but my heart fluttered at the casual way Reid held it out. It felt easy and right as I spit into the sink and he smoothed on moisturizer from a small container that probably cost a ton.

He didn't seem to want me to leave. It would have been a punch in the nuts if he had. But no, he went through what I assumed was his nightly routine and asked questions about school. We were still naked, and the bathroom floor was warm under our feet.

Reid said, "Before you know it, you'll be Dr. Lisowski." He frowned. "What's that face for?"

"Huh?" I looked up from reading the side of the moisturizer.

"When I said 'Dr. Lisowski' you made—there. That face. A wince crossed with a grimace."

I laughed uneasily. "A grince? A wimace?"

"Yeah. What's that about?"

"Nothing. It just feels like a million years away." I hadn't realized I'd made a face. Twice, apparently.

Leaning his hip on the marble counter, Reid examined me. "I'm going to have to veto that explanation."

"Is that how vetoing works?"

"Irrelevant, and you're changing the subject. Shouldn't hearing 'Dr. Lisowski' excite you?"

I wanted to turn away from his intense gaze. Suddenly, I was very aware of my nakedness. I shrugged and straightened the towel hanging by the sink. "It's not the doctor part. It's my crappy name."

"What's wrong with your name?"

"Nothing technically. It's not the name itself. It's that I got it from my father."

"Ah." Reid smoothed his palm down my back. "I have the impression that's about all he gave you?"

"Yeah, something like that." I hadn't realized how lucky I'd been as a kid when he'd ghosted me for months or sometimes years at a time. Then he'd reappeared in the summer. Now he'd left me with a lot more than his name. Yay, thanks for the crippling debt. At least I'd have this new job. I could handle a couple of midnight shifts.

"You're not close to any of your other family on that side?"

"Nah. Mike burned a lot of bridges."

"That's too bad. You ever think about reaching out to them?"

I blinked. "Actually, no. I haven't thought about them in years. I have my dads, and their whole family. Logan's family. Seth's are terrible. They totally cut him off when they found out he's gay."

I'd picked up scraps of info over the years, and I knew it had hurt Seth deeply. I also knew Logan would have loved to tell them exactly what he thought, which would probably involve a lot of profanity.

"That's terrible," Reid said quietly. He dropped his hand from my back and screwed the lid back on the toothpaste. "I'm lucky my family is accepting."

"Yeah, but you 'grinced' when you said that."

He laughed ruefully. "I'm sure you can guess that's about my grandmother. It's fine. It's not as though she disinherited me."

I slid my arm around his back. "Yeah, but it's like when people talk about tolerance. It's not the same thing at all as acceptance."

Reid blinked down at me before cupping my cheek. "That's exactly what it is. Thank you for putting it into words."

"Um, you're welcome."

He stroked my cheek with his thumb. "Does your family know?"

I smiled, remembering Logan and Seth's visit. "My dads actually just found out. They were awesome about it, obviously. I dunno why I was so nervous about telling them. They believed me right away. That I'm gay."

Reid's eyes tightened at the corners. "Why wouldn't they have believed you?"

"It's stupid." I fidgeted and crossed my arms. "I tied myself up into knots for years for nothing."

"It's okay. It's in the past now." He pressed our lips together before hugging me. "Let's go to bed."

We cuddled naked under the covers with Reid's arm around me, urging me to rest my head on his chest. He brushed his fingers through my hair, making my scalp and neck tingle.

Listening to the steady *thump* of his heart, hair tickling my cheek and the sensation of his nipple against my jaw, how was I not supposed to fall in love?

Chapter Twelve

Connor

"WOW, EITHER YOU crushed that exam or you got laid." I froze in the middle of unzipping my leather jacket. Asher was grinning up at me from the booth in the back of the pub, dressed in a gray suit for work. I stupidly glanced around to see if anyone had heard and had the ridiculous urge to find a mirror. Did I look different?

Asher's eyebrows shot up. "Holy shit, you did!"

"Shh!" I glanced around again, but the long table of office people laughing over their lunch and doing a noisy gift exchange weren't paying attention. I managed to toss my jacket into the corner of the stained red fabric booth and slide in across from him. "Yeah, exam went great."

He poured me a pint from the pitcher. "*And?*"

"What?" I gulped the cool lager gratefully and realized I hadn't taken off my gloves. Asher was watching me with a shit-eating grin as I stuffed the gloves in my jacket pocket.

We'd never discussed that I was still a virgin. At Rencliffe, I'd gone along with him and the guys in talking about tits and hot chicks, but at a certain point, Asher had stopped asking me about girls when it was just the two of us.

He'd told me all about losing his virginity in way too much detail, but my sex life—or the lack thereof—had become an unspoken topic.

He sipped his beer. "When you walked in, I could tell you'd loosened a few screws."

He'd always teased me about being uptight. "Yeah, like I said. Exam went great." I ran my fingers through the condensation on the glass. Fuck I hoped it had gone great. What if—

"A-ha! There it is. You're worrying about that exam. Something else loosened you up."

"How much beer have you had? You have to go back to work. You're cut off." My cheeks burned, and I took another gulp.

Asher's grin faltered. "You know you can tell me about stuff, right? Like, if you hooked up with someone. Or if you didn't, or whatever."

That old panic flapped its wings, and I was about to scoff and change the subject but stopped. In the now-awkward silence, we stared at each other.

Asher knew. I knew he knew—hell, he'd apparently told Reid in the past that I was queer. Why was this still so hard? It wasn't only because the guy I'd hooked up with was Asher's brother.

Okay. One step at a time. "Um, yeah. I guess I did. Get laid."

Asher lit up like the Christmas tree near our table. "I knew it!" He raised his hand for a high five, which I automatically gave. "Tell me about…them."

"It's um…" Another gulp of beer, my pint already drained. "A guy."

Asher nodded eagerly. "Cool, man. That's awesome."

Affection swelled in me. He was trying so hard to be supportive. He didn't narrow his eyes and look skeptical, or ask *why* I was queer and whether Logan and Seth had made me that way. *Of course* he didn't. And I hadn't really suspected he would. Not Asher. Yet I'd stayed silent with everyone.

"I'm stupid for not telling you years ago," I said. My chest tightened. "I'm gay. Which you know, obviously." My lungs expanded, relief flowing through me. Saying those words was getting easier.

Asher gently kicked my boot with his under the table. "I'm glad you told me now." His concerned expression morphed into a devilish grin. "Now spill. Have you been banging dudes all along?"

I laughed. "Nope. Last night was my first time," I mumbled.

Asher's eyes widened. "Whoa. Bro, you have a lot of catching up to do. I'm almost jealous. Sex has gotten *so* much better over the years. My first time…" He winced—*grinced*, which made me smile to myself. "Oof. We had no clue what we were doing. It was fun, but…short."

"I bet." I nodded to the server as she took our usual food order of burgers and fries.

Asher refilled my glass. "We're older now, though. Did this guy have experience? Judging by how loose your screws were when you walked in, I bet he banged you good."

Oh god. This was the part when I had to tell him that the guy who'd screwed me was his brother. Which he clearly didn't suspect somehow? Before I could say anything, Asher screwed up his face at his phone and typed with his thumbs.

I asked, "What?"

"Reid wants me to go to some charity event for the company this week-end. No way. I have plans."

At the mention of Reid's name, my pulse leapt, my balls tingled, and I fought irritation. Had Asher always been this unfair to his brother? Probably. Even though I'd always crushed on Reid, it had never occurred to me that he'd had unfair pressure piled on him after their dad died. Reid did *so* much for the family.

I sipped my beer. "Can't you just go to one thing for him?"

Asher blinked at me. "What's up with you?"

Okay, I'd done a piss-poor job of keeping my tone casual. "Nothing. It just doesn't seem like a big deal."

"I have plans. This is Reid's thing. I don't work at the company. I do enough of Gamma's events."

I almost blurted that maybe Reid didn't *want* to work at the company but managed to bite my tongue.

"Besides, I thought you were fake dating him and the whole point was to show up at these events on his arm so Gamma would cut the shit with trying to fix him up with whatshername."

"Yeah, but we've done a few already. I'm pretty sure your grandmother believes it."

"Hmm. Yeah, true. She didn't say a word about you two at dinner last night. If she was suspicious, she would have grilled me in a polite, roundabout way that would somehow be more effective than demanding answers."

Why did it make me happy that Mrs. Cabot believed it? Maybe she could accept us? If Reid and I were a real couple—

Nope. Beep, beep, beep. Back that up. One step at a time.

Asher said, "Anyway, back to this guy you hooked up with. Are you seeing him again? Is it going to bug him that you and my brother are acting all lovey-dovey in public? You guys put on a good show."

"Um…"

His jaw dropped. "Holy fuck, dude. Wait, wait, wait. It wasn't an act, was it? I thought maybe, but—no way. You and Reid? *Reid's* the guy you banged last night? Holy *shit*. He is. I can tell by that dopey look on your face. Wow. I guess some teenage dreams do come true."

"What?" I sputtered. "What are you talking about?"

Asher snorted. "Dude. You had a massive boner for my brother all through Rencliffe. And college."

"You knew?" I groaned and dropped my face into my hands. "Tell me you never mentioned it to Reid."

"Duh, obviously not."

Our lunches arrived, and we took turns with the ketchup bottle. Asher dipped his fries in a side of mayo and then ketchup on his plate. On cue, I screwed up my face, "Ew, mayo."

And on cue, Asher put on a super strong French accent. "Peasant, you know nothing of cuisine. If you'd been to Europe as I have, I would have no need to explain."

Then we laughed the way we always, always did, and I wanted to pull Asher to his feet and hug him tightly.

He said, "Man, I had this funny feeling yesterday, but I told myself I was imagining it. On Thanksgiving, I encouraged you to do the whole fake-boyfriends thing because I thought it would be fun for you since you'd always had a crush."

I took the pickle off the side of my plate and put it on Asher's. "Did you think it might help me come out or whatever?"

"Yeah, maybe? It happened so fast. Mostly I just thought it would give you fresh spank-bank material. So, spill. I mean, not about my brother dicking you." He quickly added, "Not because it's gay. If it was anyone else, you could tell me anything."

"It's cool. I get it." Another surge of affection warmed my chest. "I dunno. We've spent a lot of time together the past few weeks."

Asher swallowed a bite of his burger. "Right, going to boring holiday parties."

"Yeah, also Reid came up with a list of quintessential New York things to do."

"What do you mean?" He swiped at a blob of mayo/ketchup on his tie and cursed under his breath.

"Quintessential means—"

"Ha ha, asshole. I got fifteen hundred on my SATs too. Wait, was that why he asked me if you'd like the High Line or the Brooklyn Bridge?"

He'd asked Asher about what I liked? "I guess so." I remembered last night on the High Line in the snow, the city right there but seeming far away, me and Reid in our own world...

Asher laughed. "Dude. You are *swooning* right now. It means—"

"Shut up!" I kicked him, and for a minute, our feet tussled under the scarred wooden table.

We stopped when the server came by to ask how we were doing, both of us trying not to giggle. We hadn't had a foot fight in ages.

"*Anyway*," I said. "We've been doing these other things on the list."

"Like what?"

I told him, finishing with, "I'm not sure what's next. He's been keeping it as a surprise."

"Shit, I had no idea my brother was such a romantic."

My face burned, and I fought a smile. It *was* romantic, wasn't it? "It's fun. Not a big deal."

Asher's smile faded. "Right. Are you guys... Are you still going to see each other after the holidays?"

Yes, or I'll die.

The thought of not seeing Reid again after Christmas knocked the air out of me. I forced a shrug. "Guess we'll see."

"Right," he repeated, worry creasing his brow despite him adding, "just have fun. Get your freak on. Don't stress."

"Totally. No stress. We're just having fun for the holidays. It's a Christmas miracle that I finally came out and got laid."

And fell in love.

Asher lifted his glass. "I'll drink to that."

We clinked, and I ordered myself to stop thinking about being in love. It was only because I'd crushed on Reid for so long that I was being swept away in big emotions. Add in the virgin factor, and of course I felt like I was in love. I needed to keep my head on straight and enjoy my time with Reid. I was heading home in less than a week now.

While the thought of Christmas at home usually filled me with anticipation and counting down the days, now I hoped time would crawl and limp or maybe slip into a nice long coma.

As the bill came, Asher gave the server his card and said, "It's on me."

"But it's my turn."

"Nah, it's Christmas." He glanced away, and I tensed. There was something cagey in that avoidance of my gaze. I'd been at Rencliffe on a scholarship, and Asher had always been generous in buying me stuff. Once I'd gotten summer jobs, I'd insisted we go half and half.

I scowled. "Dude. Spit it out." He'd never been a very good liar.

Asher sighed. "Reid said something about you needing money."

My heart dropped like a rock. For the most part, I'd been successfully compartmentalizing the fact that I owed Reid ten grand. I'd also thought it was our secret, and a stab of hurt knifed through me.

"Did he…tell you?" I asked.

Asher's brows met. "I don't think so? He asked something about it a couple of weeks ago."

"What did he say exactly?"

"Dude, I dunno. I think he asked whether you needed money." He still frowned. "Do you? You know you can ask me, right?"

"I know." I would have had to if not for the deal with Reid. Okay, so Reid hadn't told him. It was fair that he'd asked Asher if he knew anything. I couldn't get mad at him for being curious when I wasn't giving him any hints.

"But do you?" Asher asked.

"No. I'm good. Thanks, though."

"Okay." He checked his phone. "Shit, I have to get back. More spreadsheets to toil over."

"Thoughts and prayers."

He flipped me the finger, and we headed out. As I rode the subway north, I chewed over admitting the truth to Reid. I knew I should just rip off the Band-Aid. But everything was so perfect right now. My ass was a tiny bit tender, and I squeezed my inner muscles, loving the reminder.

I imagined I could still taste him and smell his peppery cologne with the sweet hint of…lily? Lilacs? Jasmine? As if I could identify any floral scents aside from rose. I had no clue.

Sure, when I inhaled now, my nose filled with the gross subway smells of BO, greasy food, and lingering cigarette stench from the guy standing a few inches away as we leaned to the side, bracing for the next station.

But in my head, I could smell Reid and taste his mouth instead of beer and burger. I shivered in anticipation of seeing him again tonight. I still had to study, but the worst exams were over. All I wanted was to be with Reid and touch him. It was like a drug, or what I imagined that kind of craving might be like.

I pushed through the crowd at Times Square, weaving through tourists and scammers and people handing out flyers for comedy shows. It had been the easiest route to get off there and walk a few avenues over to my neighborhood. Hell's Kitchen was still busy with people, but it was always a relief to get past Eighth Avenue and leave most of the tourists behind.

The afternoon was heavy and gray, and the Christmas lights and glittery wreaths and garlands brightened the concrete and brown buildings. Not that I needed the holiday glitz—to me, the sun was beaming down, birds were chirping, and I could have been home in Albany bent over my motorcycle with the wind in my face.

The thought of telling Reid how painfully, pathetically gullible I'd been made me want to puke into the gutter. Everything with Reid was brand new, gleaming and sparkling like a Christmas tree ornament. I couldn't stand thinking of saying those words out loud. The virgin thing had been bad enough, and Reid had been amazing.

Amazing.

My heart swelled to think of how patient and sweet and wonderful he'd been last night. He wouldn't judge me for how stupid I'd been with the money. I was almost positive, reminding myself there were no guarantees in life.

I ducked into Amy's Bread to see if they had any cupcakes left. I wasn't sure if Reid would prefer red velvet or devil's food, so I got both for later, along with a few snickerdoodles.

I'd tell Reid after the holidays. I was going home so soon, and then I wouldn't see him until New Year's. At least, I hoped I would. Anxiety bubbled up, but I tamped it down as I crossed Tenth Ave and neared my place. I was due to take the train home Saturday. That gave me four more days with Reid, and I still had to study and write two exams, and he had to work.

It was barely any time, and I wasn't going to ruin it. I didn't want to talk about money or Mike or any of it. These days were mine and Reid's. I'd finally come out, and all I wanted to do was laugh and kiss and fuck and pull the covers over our heads.

Chapter Thirteen

Reid

"SO, YOU'RE DICKING my best friend."

I blinked up at Asher in the doorway of my glass-fronted office still wearing his coat and woolen hat. "Close the door," I hissed, relieved the hallway seemed empty.

He came in and flopped into my guest chair, crossing his arms.

"Shouldn't you be at work?" I asked.

"It's six."

Jerking, I squinted at the time in the corner of my computer. I'd been researching classic New York restaurants. Sardi's often came up, and I thought a Broadway night with Connor would be great for our list. I was meeting him soon for one last holiday party, this one in the restaurant of a hotel that was our chief rival, which would make Grandmother more brittle than usual.

"Also, what's the deal with dicking my best friend?"

"Shh!" I knew from experience the glass wasn't very thick.

"You're pretending to date him. Why be quiet about it? I guess you *are* dating him now?" Asher glared. "Right?"

"Are you asking my intentions?"

"Yeah. Because you'd better not break Connor's heart."

My own heart skipped. Hurting Connor was the last thing I wanted. *Were* we dating for real now? "It's been five minutes. Take a breath."

Asher sighed. "Okay, but just be careful."

"Always." I closed a few tabs and asked casually, "What did he say about me?"

"Oh no. No, no, *no*." Asher jumped to his feet. "I'm not playing this game. I just dropped by to make sure you're not messing with my boy. You two can figure out your shit without me in the middle. That's a hard veto."

"Message received." I gave him a mock salute.

Asher paused at the door. "I will say that he couldn't go more than five seconds at lunch without looking like he was about to doodle your name in a heart in the margins of the menu." He pointed at me. "And making that same goofy face you're making right now. So don't blow it."

"Hey, does Connor like musicals?"

"I dunno. If you're taking him, he'll like it. Also, aren't you glad I encouraged him to be your fake boyfriend? Addison and I get producer credits on this relationship. Assuming you don't screw it up."

Asher left as quickly as he'd appeared, and I spent another ten minutes searching Broadway ticket sites before hurrying to the Grand Hyperion. Connor wasn't outside, though he'd texted that he'd arrived. Inside, a host took my coat and ushered me toward the restaurant.

Voices murmured, a pianist played "The First Noel," which I'd had to sing in the Rencliffe choir, and servers in black and white passed around elegant hors d'oeuvres. I had no interest in a bacon-wrapped asparagus bite with a walnut-orange confit. Not when I spotted Connor.

He wore a red sweater that hugged his tight, lean body, his skinny black jeans painted on his thighs. I grinned to see he was in his Doc Martens, remembering the shoe incident on the carousel.

God, I wanted to fuck him so badly.

As I crossed the room, nodding and smiling to faceless people who greeted me, my eyes were locked on Connor. It was only after I drew him close for a long kiss, inhaling him gratefully, that I realized he was standing with Addison and Olivia.

I broke my gaze away from Connor's dreamy smile and settled my arm on his shoulders. "Well… Hello, ladies." *Say something else.* "Merry Christmas."

Addison wore a too-delighted smile and a shimmery gold blouse. "And to *you.* God bless us, everyone. I didn't realize you'd joined the Actors Studio." She turned to Olivia and—what was his name? Dylan. Addison said, "Aren't you impressed with this performance?"

Dylan seemed a little puzzled. "Um, sure?"

But Olivia nodded and slow clapped. "This is Oscar-worthy stuff."

Connor hissed, "Shh. No one's supposed to know."

Addison and Olivia looked at each other and laughed. "Don't worry your pretty little head," Addison said. "No one will suspect your relationship is anything but the real deal."

Tense under my arm, Connor met my gaze. I shot Addison a death glare. Even if she and Olivia suspected Connor and I were hooking up, that didn't mean Connor wanted to come out. His face was red, and his knuckles were white on his cocktail glass.

Addison and Olivia's shit-eating grins vanished. Olivia quickly said to Connor, "Hey, how did the exam go? I meant to ask earlier."

But the abrupt change of subject didn't loosen Connor's shoulders. "Good, I think. Maybe."

"You always do amazing," Olivia assured him.

I rubbed his back before realizing that might not be helping. I dropped my arm. On one hand, we were supposed to be publicly a couple, but now that we were *privately* a couple and our friends had clearly figured it out, there was pressure on Connor since he'd only come out to his parents.

My head spun, and I had to jam my hands in my pants pockets to keep from touching Connor, who was now frowning at me. Something caught his gaze beyond me.

"Incoming," he whispered, leaning into my side and slipping his arm around me. I couldn't have stopped myself from doing the same to him even if I tried. The need to touch was irresistible. He felt so good pressed into my side, like he'd always belonged there.

I smiled at Grandmother, who nodded back coolly and veered away from us, going to talk to one of her society ladies instead. On one hand, it was a relief, yet it still stung. Connor must have sensed that and squeezed my waist gently. I kissed his temple, and he smiled up at me softly.

"Wait, are you guys really together?" Dylan asked, Olivia immediately nudging him with her elbow. Hard.

The pianist began "Jingle Bells" as our group looked at each other in silence. Then Connor laughed softly, his shoulders hitching under my arm.

"Yeah," Connor said. "I don't know why I'm being so weird about it. I'm gay, by the way."

"Welcome to the party," Addison said, raising her glass with a wide smile.

Dylan said to Addison, "Wait, you too?"

Olivia groaned softly. "Babe, try to keep up." She beamed at Connor and kissed his cheek. "I'm proud of you," she whispered.

I was too, and I kissed him again. Then one more time. And one more time after that until the girls told us to get a room. We all laughed. From the corner of my eye, I spotted Grandmother watching, a looming specter.

I kissed Connor again, hoping she was getting an eyeful. Hoping it would sink in that I really was bi. Then, before I could stop and assess the risk, I was leading Connor by the hand and stepping in front of Grandmother as she tried to escape.

"Grandmother!" I exclaimed too loudly. "How are you?" I leaned in and kissed her cheeks. "You remember Connor? My boyfriend?" I was practically shouting, and Grandmother blinked at me.

When I'd introduced them on Thanksgiving, Connor had been a near stranger. No longer the surly kid in the background, but only a business partner. Had that only been less than a month ago? Now, Connor was so much more.

He was rapidly becoming everything.

Squeezing my hand gently, Connor cleared his throat. "Hello, Mrs. Cabot. Lovely to see you again."

She smiled coolly. "Yes. Hello, Mr… What is your surname?"

"Lisowski," Connor replied, and I imagined a ripple of tension in him, remembering what he'd told me about not liking his name because of the association with his biological father.

"Ah," Grandmother said.

We waited for her to say more, but no. Apparently that was all.

He added, "Please just call me Connor."

Grandmother nodded and most certainly did not tell Connor to call her anything but Mrs. Cabot. Frustration and resentment boiled up from a simmer, and it was all I could do not to keep shouting. I wasn't even sure what I'd say. I just wanted to *shout*.

In the silence, Connor asked Grandmother, "What do you have planned for Christmas?"

"My traditional breakfast event for the less fortunate. Reid will be there with me." That sounded like an order.

"Cool," Connor said.

I let go of Connor's hand to rest my palm on the back of his neck. "You should come one year. We serve breakfast to hundreds of people, and there's a Santa and gifts." To Grandmother, I said, "We always need more volunteers, right?"

Her lips briefly arched into an expression that could generously be considered a smile. "Of course."

I fought not to clench my fists. Before, Connor had only been my fake boyfriend, and I'd been frustrated with Grandmother. Connor was so real now, and why couldn't she look past gender to see what a wonderful, kind, funny, fun, loving person he was? Couldn't she see how much I cared about him? It had to be emanating from me like a flashing neon sign.

She made an excuse about needing to talk to someone across the room and was gone before I could formulate my roiling thoughts into words. Likely for the best since I'd have a better chance of success the more articulate I was.

"Okay?" Connor murmured, rubbing my back.

"Let's get out of here. Yes?" I pushed Grandmother out of my mind.

He grinned. "No veto here."

IN THE DOORWAY of my apartment an interminable time later, we stumbled back, laughing and kissing and stripping off our coats.

"Hi," Connor said breathlessly.

"Hi." God, when was the last time I'd felt this giddy?

Possibly never.

"Are you thirsty?" I asked, trying to focus on being a good host instead of just standing there staring at Connor's wet mouth.

"Uh-huh."

Before I could ask what he wanted to drink, Connor was back in my arms, his tongue exploring my mouth. I ran my hands down his back, then up under his sweater to spread my fingers over his bare skin. His hands were cold on my neck and face, but everywhere else was fire.

My phone dinged, and we broke our kiss. Connor bent to take off his boots as I read the message from a ticket broker. I yanked off my own boots and socks and asked, "You're free the night before you leave for another item on the New Yorker list?"

"Yep."

"Okay. But you're going to laugh."

"I won't." Connor straightened and peered at me with such seriousness, his hand moving to rest on my waist. "I promise."

It was just a musical—if he wasn't into it, no problem. It wasn't as though I was a huge theater nerd or anything. Yet I wanted his approval. I wanted it more than I'd wanted anything in a long, long time.

"Reid?" He squeezed my hip gently. "You didn't laugh at me. Why do you think I'll laugh at you?"

I blurted, "You'll be a great doctor."

"Huh?" He laughed, clearly confused.

"You have really good bedside manner."

Connor glanced down at his hand on my hip. "Uh, this isn't appropriate for patients."

I laughed too. "I meant the way you listen. Not *that*. Although I'm not complaining about it."

"No complaints?" Connor stroked over the swell of my ass.

"Nope."

"So, what's your idea?" He gazed at me again with that patient, steady interest, and I led him to the couch. We sat side by side, the leather squeaking as we settled close together.

"How do you feel about singing werewolves? I believe they also rap."

Connor blinked. "Uh… Oh! That new musical everyone's talking about?"

"*Full Moon.* You've heard of it?"

"Yeah, Olivia said it did for werewolves what *Hamilton* did for the dead white men on our money."

"I can get tickets. Unless you want to veto?"

He grinned. "No veto. It sounds bananas. The only show I've seen is when Rencliffe took us to *Hamilton*. This seems like a perfect follow-up."

"If rapping werewolves aren't authentically New York, I don't know what is."

"Totally. Also, are we done talking?" he asked.

"Absolutely."

Connor's lips parted under mine, and I kissed him deeply, sliding my tongue against his as I cupped his face. He made that sweet, glorious little sound—a sigh that might evolve into a moan at any moment. I could have kissed him forever.

With a jolt, I pulled back. Since when was I contemplating *forever?*

Connor's lips were shiny and pink, and I was powerless to resist kissing him again. This time, I took his face in both my hands, deepening the kiss even more. Connor gripped my thigh, leaning into me.

He leaned so far that the next thing I knew, he straddled my lap with a moan that went straight to my cock along with what had to be most of my body's blood supply. We laughed and kissed messily.

Connor was on the same page, and he rocked against me with his erection. He broke the kiss with a gasp and unbuttoned the top few buttons of my shirt after yanking off my tie. Pressing his lips to my neck, he inhaled and murmured, "You make me so hard."

I ran my hands down his back and squeezed his ass. "The feeling is entirely mutual."

"Can we get off?"

"I don't know. Can we?"

Connor lifted his head and stared at me. "Are you seriously bringing annoying big brother energy to our sex life?"

I laughed. "Apologies." *Our sex life.* Those words probably should have sent alarm bells blaring, but instead gave me a thrill I felt deep in my balls. "How ever can I make it up to you?"

"I want to ride you." His beautiful face flushed red, and he dropped his eyes.

The speed of the answer and his blush made me think this was something that wasn't spur of the moment. "Why is that embarrassing?"

"It's not," he mumbled. His fingers dug into my shoulders as he fidgeted.

"Then why can't you look at me?"

After a big exhalation, Connor met my gaze. I caressed his back in slow, gentle sweeps.

"Tell me, baby," I whispered.

His breath caught, and he bit his lip. "You'll think it's weird."

"I won't." I kept my voice steady and serious, emulating his bedside manner. "I promise." I had a suspicion, and I asked, "Have you fantasized about that?"

He nodded. "It was one of the big ones. When I was younger and I had a raging crush on you."

"Adorable."

He groaned and dropped his forehead onto my shoulder. "I was the most awkward kid ever."

"You're all grown up now, though." I groped his ass, and lust simmered in my veins. "Tell me your fantasies. What were the other big ones?" I rounded my spine and tilted up my hips as I lifted a brow. "Aside from *this*."

A laugh burst out of Connor, and I could feel some of the tension in his body ebbing away. I kissed him softly and nuzzled his nose.

"Do I have to tell you right now?"

I drew back. "Of course not. Do you want to stop?"

He gripped my shoulders as his thighs tightened on my hips. "*No.*"

"Okay. We won't stop. I need to come too. You need to come, baby?"

Connor moaned, rocking against me again. "Yeah."

"You want to ride me? That was the fantasy?"

He nodded. "But we need stuff, and it's all the way in the other room."

We were rutting against each other, in serious danger of spilling in our pants. "God, I know."

I hadn't been this desperate for someone in a long time. I tore at my belt and our flies, and Connor lifted up enough so I could pull our cocks free. We groaned as I grasped our shafts in my hand, using our precum as lube. I was still wearing a suit that had cost way too much to ruin, but I couldn't stop.

"Tell me about riding me," I said.

Panting, Connor gaped at me. "Like…"

"Tell me what you've imagined. Was it like this? Sitting on me?"

"Uh-huh. But naked."

I stroked us, fighting to keep my voice even. It came out hoarse as I asked, "On a couch like this?"

"In bed." Connor licked his lips, his chest rising and falling.

I wanted to tear off his shirt and suck his nipples, but I couldn't have let go of our cocks until we came if armed gunmen had burst in. "You want me inside you?"

He nodded desperately as he rocked with the motion of my hand.

"But you want to have your way with me? Ride me and take me just the way you want?"

Connor nodded again, sweet little sounds of pleasure escaping his throat.

"Do you want me to touch you?"

"*Yes.*"

"Like this?" I jerked us harder. It was rough without lube, but that added to the pleasure. Sweat dampened my temples, and my whole body strained, my bare toes clenched on the floor. "How hard do you think you'll come with my cock buried in your ass and—"

With a cry, Connor shook and shot his load on my shirt, the rest dripping down over my hand. His back arched, his head tipped back, eyes closed as he rode the wave. I licked his throat and tasted his salty sweat, and he tangled his hands in my hair.

"*Fuck*," he whimpered.

I was still aching, but I let go of our shafts to suck my fingers. Connor stared at me with wide, lust-blown eyes. "*Double fuck*," he groaned.

Our eyes locked as I ran my tongue up my index finger, tasting him. Wordlessly, I offered him another finger, and he sucked it into his mouth.

We both moaned.

My balls threatened to explode, and before I could finish myself off with my messy hand, Connor lifted up, pushed my thighs apart, and dropped to his knees. He only had to take my eager, leaking cock into his mouth for a few pulls before I flooded him.

Pulling him back onto my lap, I kissed him, tasting both of us. It was dirty and wonderful, and I whispered, "Next time you ride my cock."

He nodded vigorously, and I made a mental note to find out what Connor's other fantasies were and make every single one of them come true.

We were sticky and needed to clean up, yet we stayed sprawled on the couch. I leaned back, my dick still out and my legs spread. Connor curled beside me with his legs flung over my lap. I could get used to this.

I could *really* get used to this.

My phone buzzed on the coffee table. I said, "I'll pass on an unknown number from Texas, thanks." I was mostly talking to myself.

Connor sat up straight, his legs still draped over my lap. "It could be Angela. She said she was going to look at the proposal this week."

I snatched up the phone and answered. A nasal twang greeted me, "Hiya, sugar. This is Angela Barker."

"Hello, Mrs. Barker." I lifted Connor's legs and started pacing by the windows, juggling the phone while I tucked myself back into my pants. She couldn't see me, but it felt disrespectful.

"I'm not fancy—it's Angela. Now, I'm intrigued as heck by your business plan. You've clearly done your homework. I'm very interested in exploring how BRK can help and wanna discuss it further with y'all."

My mouth was dry. "Oh, it's just me. My grandmother and Utopia aren't involved at the moment."

Angela snorted. "You don't say. I'd be surprised if she was on board for this—even though it makes dynamite business sense. The 'y'all' wasn't literal, don't worry."

"Oh! Right. Okay."

Connor watched avidly from the couch. He'd straightened his clothes and sat up straight.

"I have a few suggestions if you're open to it. I'm waiting for my flight and thought I'd give you a buzz and take your temperature."

"Right. Thank you! I'm hot." *Wait. What?*

"That's what my daughter says."

"No! I meant—" I rubbed my face. Why were words so hard right now? "I'm interested in pursuing this...um..." Thing?

"Just teasin'. All righty, I'll be in touch soon with more."

"Thank you so much. I swear I'm usually more articulate."

"I believe you, sugar. Besides, any friend of Connor's is a friend of mine. He said he went to school with your brother?"

"Yes." I faced Connor, who was smiling. "Recently we've gotten to know each other better."

"Isn't he a doll? Smart as a whip, and he's grown up into such a terrific young man. I'm so proud of him."

Connor rolled his eyes at the praise, which he could clearly hear since Angela's penetrating voice was surely echoing through my apartment. Still, he fidgeted in a way that I suspected meant he was secretly pleased by said praise.

Whoa. How did I know that? But every instinct told me I was right.

I said, "He's actually here now. He says hi."

"Is he? Put him on the horn."

While Connor answered questions that seemed to be about holiday plans and his family, I looked out at the lights of the city. Beyond snow-dusted rooftops, I could see the dark swath of Central Park. The spired roof of the Utopia was just visible to the south. My heart thumped.

It had been months—no, *years* now since I'd first started researching and developing my business plan. Honestly, I'd figured Angela Barker would perhaps make perfunctory comments as a favor to Connor.

I hadn't expected this. I hadn't expected anything to actually *happen*. And nothing had happened yet, but it might. I'd never shown Grandmother or the board my idea because I knew they'd never fund it. Not in a million years. *Veto.*

And I'd slink back to my office and continue phoning it in as VP for a company that might be my heritage but didn't excite me or challenge me. Every day was the same, and I knew exactly what to expect.

I looked back at Connor as he hung up with Angela, and my thudding heart felt like it might burst out of my chest.

Connor half smiled. "What?"

He had been entirely unexpected, and I'd never been more excited.

"Nothing," I said. "Thank you for getting me in with Angela."

He joined me at the window. "Of course. It was no problem." He nodded with his chin. "Is that your hotel over there?"

"It is." I gazed out. "One of many."

"What got you interested in sustainable housing? I don't think you said."

I grimaced. "You're going to laugh."

Connor slid his arm around my waist. "Again, I'm not laughing at you."

"Even though we're having this conversation in my luxury Upper West Side apartment? In view of the luxury hotel my family owns?"

"People with money have the resources to actually get things done. We need more rich people to give a shit beyond charity dinners." He quickly added, "Not that your grandmother doesn't raise a lot of money for good causes."

"It's okay." I put my arm around his shoulders.

How did it feel so *right* with him? Like I could say anything, and he truly wouldn't laugh at me.

I said, "I know what you mean, and you're right. Okay. It was a random YouTube video. The housing crisis, rents out of control, that kind of thing. I fell down a rabbit hole of videos, and I couldn't concentrate at work the next day. Who cares about fancy hotels that serve a fraction of the population when we could build sustainable, affordable housing?"

"I'm still not laughing," Connor said seriously, his arm locked around my waist.

I had to kiss him. There was simply nothing else I could do or say before tasting him again and holding him close. As tempting as it was to take him to bed, his stomach rumbled. We chuckled.

"How about we tick another experience off the list?" I asked. "The best slice of pizza in New York."

"I've had it already—Joe's in the Village."

I mock gasped. "Sacrilege! It's Patsy's on Seventy-fourth. We can walk over."

"Okay, but we need to do a taste test. Patsy's today, Joe's tomorrow." Connor groaned. "But I have to study." He checked his phone. "I should head back to my place."

"After Patsy's. You need brain food. I'm not letting you study on an empty stomach. And we can do Joe's next week if you're busy studying."

He bit his lip. "I won't be here. I'll be in Albany for Christmas."

"Right, of course." I put on a bright smile. "First step: Patsy's. A.k.a. the best pizza in New York."

"We'll see about that. But no way am I vetoing. Too hungry."

We headed out, and I'm not sure which one of us reached for the other's gloved hand first. It was so natural to entwine our fingers as we fell into step together.

I tried not to think about how unbearably lonely it was to think of Christmas next week without Connor.

Chapter Fourteen

Connor

T HE NOTE FROM Olivia stuck to the bathroom mirror said:

Spending the night with Dylan. Hope the exam went well!

Yawning, I peeled the sticky paper off the glass and crumpled it into the trash can. It was sweet how Olivia would leave notes like that instead of just texting me. She said her mom had always left notes in the bathroom where they were sure to be seen because "everyone needed to tinkle," to quote Angela.

I pissed—excuse me, *tinkled*—and had a hot shower while I tried to relax and not second guess every answer I'd picked on the multiple choice exam. It was done now, and obsessing wouldn't change my grade.

With a towel around my hips, I wandered past the glittering Christmas tree to the kitchen and stared at the decidedly un-festive contents of the fridge—a head of iceberg lettuce, a carton of eggs, leftover kung pao chicken, and an apple. Along with ketchup, mayo, and a few other condiments.

Sighing, I closed the door and glumly pulled a box of Ritz from the cupboard. It was almost empty, so I polished off the buttery crackers. I missed always having dinner on the table. Logan had become a surprisingly good cook when he wanted to be, and Seth was always trying new recipes.

Would Seth offer a new dessert at Christmas, or go with one of the amazing cakes he'd made before? I should ask him to do the eggnog tres leches again. Or maybe the sticky toffee pudding from his phase of trying British classics after binging *Downton Abbey*.

The pang of homesickness had my eyes prickling. "Get a grip," I mumbled as I tore open the cracker box and squeezed it into the recycling bin under the sink. Sure, I missed home sometimes, but I'd lived away for years now. Why was I so emo and lonely tonight?

Fine, yes. It bummed me out that Reid was busy. Especially since he'd been vague about why, exactly. He had to work late, which I totally understood. When I'd asked what he was working on, he hadn't really answered.

I was leaving in two days. *Fine*, yes, I wasn't blasting off to the moon, and I'd be back on the thirty-first. But didn't he want to spend every second together that we could? Was he getting sick of me already?

I groaned aloud and muttered, "Jesus, way to be a stage-five clinger." I might have had a crush on Reid since high school, but I was a grown-ass man now. I couldn't expect to spend every night together now that we were hooking up.

A thrill shivered through me to even think those words. But they were true! Not just in my horny imagination but real life. I still wasn't sure what Reid saw in me, but he seemed just as into it as I was. God, the way he'd held me so tight and kissed me with that hot little moan…

I ran a hand over my damp chest and played with my nipples. I could go jerk off, which would definitely help in the relaxation department. My exams were over, and the holidays had officially begun. Ho-ho-ho, right? I should treat myself.

Was it weird that I wanted to save it for Reid, though? I laughed out loud. Since when did I have a problem getting it up? It wasn't like I wouldn't be horny for him tomorrow if I got off tonight.

Still, I wanted to wait. I wanted Reid's expensive, sweet-yet-peppery cologne in my nose and his taste on my tongue. I wanted his cock inside me finally and—

I would *definitely* have to jerk off if I kept up this train of thought.

Even more than that, I wanted to make Reid smile and find out how his day went. Talk to him about my exam and my constant worry that I didn't study enough even though I had the textbooks memorized.

Encourage him to quit the job that made him miserable even if it was his family legacy or some shit. I wanted to have dinner and talk about everything. And also nothing. Like, talk about that hilarious new viral vid with the baby and the pug puppy.

The thought of dinner made my stomach growl—and gave me a neon-bright idea as my mom would have said. I breathed through the familiar pang of affection and grief.

I knew she'd be thrilled for me. That if she was alive, she'd accept me and Reid—or me and whichever guy since I couldn't get ahead of myself—wholeheartedly.

The problem was that I was already ahead of myself. I'd revved the engine and zoomed off on my bike with Reid on the back, his arms locked around me, his thighs tight on my hips.

Okay, one step at a time. If Reid was working late, I could make him dinner and invite him over, right? I was done studying, so I didn't care if it was late. We could just eat and go to sleep if he was too tired for sex.

What could I make? Iceberg lettuce wouldn't add much, but I could throw together some kind of omelet with—was there cheese?

With a burst of energy, I opened the fridge and did a victory dance when I found the block of sharp cheddar and wedge of Parmesan in the crisper drawer. Olivia kept fruit and vegetables on the fridge shelves instead of the crisper so we wouldn't forget to eat them. It was occasionally successful.

I hurried to grab my phone from the pocket of my jeans, which I'd left in a ball on the bathroom floor. Shit. How was I supposed to ask him to come over later? Casually? It wasn't a big deal, right? Why was I making a bigger deal out of making him a crappy omelet?

After tapping a quick text—*fine*, I rewrote it seven times—asking if he wanted to come by for a late dinner, I slapped on moisturizer and debated shaving before deciding against it. It would be just my luck to nick myself or worse. An open wound wasn't sexy.

When I opened my bedroom door after checking for a reply again, I jerked to a stop and almost full-on screamed. My phone flew out of my hand and thankfully landed on the bed and not the hardwood floor.

Reid was also on the bed.

On his back, sprawled out, one knee bent, lazily stroking himself. With condoms and lube beside him on the mattress.

Naked. Did I mention naked?

"W—what?" I sputtered, grabbing my towel as it came loose.

"Good evening." With his free hand, he held up his phone. "You know, I *am* free for a late dinner. That sounds perfect, thank you. Should we work up an appetite first? You mentioned wanting to take a ride." He looked down at himself as he slowly stroked himself to full hardness. "Surprise. I thought you deserved a reward after your exam."

My eyes were caught in a loop between Reid's gorgeous face and his gorgeous, flushed cock. It grew as I watched, and all I could do was stand and stare.

"Uh…" After the stress of the exam, I had very few brain cells left.

Suddenly, Reid's easy, sexy vibe vanished. He propped himself on his elbows and asked, "Veto?"

"God, no!" I dropped the towel and practically jumped between his legs. "Merry Christmas to me!"

We bounced on the mattress, and he laughed as he drew me down for a long, dirty kiss with lots of tongue. I kneeled over him, painfully hard already. I could have happily collapsed and humped him, but I had to be patient.

"I thought you'd never open the door," he groaned. "I was about to give up and tell you to get your sweet ass in here."

"Sorry!" I laughed and kissed him again.

"You didn't think it was strange that your door was shut?"

"Nope. It's usually shut because, as you can see, my room is a mess." I motioned to the piles of textbooks and notes and clothes in a heap.

"Olivia did warn me." Reid tugged my head down and sucked hard on the side of my neck. "I don't care," he mumbled against my skin.

Sitting back on my heels, I drank him in. The dark curls of chest hair, his shit-eating grin, the trail of hair leading down to his amazing cock. His toned thighs, long fingers, the jagged scar on his shoulder he'd said was from falling off a jungle gym and landing on a broken bottle. The—

"Connor?"

Blinking, I met his gaze. "Uh-huh?"

"You can touch too, you know. You don't have to only look." He was gentle as he said it. Not making fun of me.

"Right." I'd touched him before, but somehow it was intimidating AF to have Reid in *my* bed. Where I'd only ever jacked off and fantasized. "Teenage me would never, ever believe this was real." I hadn't meant to say it out loud, and my face went hot.

Again, Reid didn't laugh at me. He only smiled and took my hand, placing it on his chest. "To be fair, I'd never have imagined this would happen either. But you're all grown up, and I want you so badly I'm about to beg for you to please touch me."

I caressed his chest, gratified when teasing his nipples earned a moan. Leaning down, I kissed them and sucked, and Reid's big hand rested on my head.

"Mmm-hmm," he murmured. "That feels good."

I experimented with more touches and kisses, and Reid encouraged me. It was still nerve racking to be the one in charge. He was sweet and patient as I fumbled around, and I ran through different scenarios in my head.

Should I just grab a condom and climb on his dick? That was what we'd talked about, and we were both hard. But it felt like he wanted more first. Like he was offering himself to me even though I didn't have a clue what the fuck I was doing.

"Hey." He lifted my face and rubbed my temple slowly with his thumb. "Why are you so tense? Are you sure you don't want to veto?"

"I'm so sure. I just—" I hesitated, and Reid nodded, silently urging me to spit it out. "I don't know what to do."

His eyebrows shot up. "I beg to differ. That was you who climbed on my lap the other night and turned me on so much I almost came in my pants, yes?"

"Yes, but..." I shrugged, looking away.

"It's okay. Do you want a suggestion?"

I nodded.

Reid leaned up on his elbow as he urged my face down. His lips brushed my ears. "Before you ride me, will you fuck my mouth, baby?"

I honest-to-shit *gasped*, and all I could do was nod and crawl up his body. He tossed the pillow away and opened his mouth for me—for *me*!—and it was wet and tight and incredible.

Reid ran his hands up and down my thighs and around my hips as he took my cock as far as he could. Having him under me like that made me hot all over, and with a surge of confidence, I found a rhythm. That he trusted me to do this when I was on top of him, pinning him down, had my head spinning in the best way.

He slurped and groaned, and I don't even know what sounds I was making. My room was filled with heat and body noises, and it was everything I could have imagined from my dirty dreams.

Almost.

I pulled out and squeezed the base of my dick, forcing back the orgasm that I didn't want yet. I awkwardly backed away from Reid's face until I was straddling his waist. His lips were red and glossy, and he grinned as he reached for a condom.

"Ready, cowboy?" he asked.

Was I *ever*.

After lubing myself with shaking fingers, I took Reid inside me inch by inch as he kept hold of my hips. Not pushing or directing me—only there with me every step.

"You're so big," I gasped before bursting out laughing. "I sound like a porno."

He laughed too. "As long as it feels good, that's all that matters. I'd apologize for my *clearly* above-average cock, but… Sorry not sorry."

Jesus, he did feel big. I wouldn't have stopped for a nuclear bomb, though. Not a chance. I took a deep breath and fully seated myself. My breath stuttered. I'd never felt so *full*. Everywhere, not only in my ass.

My chest was tight as if my heart had swelled. I tried to swallow past the knot in my throat. After all the years of being too chickenshit, I was *doing it*. I had a dick inside me.

"Baby?" Reid brushed his thumb over my cheek, and I realized a tear had slipped out. "Does it hurt?"

"No. Yes. A little. It's not—" I forced a long, deep breath. "I was starting to think I'd never get the nerve to do this. And now I'm doing it. With you." I blinked away more tears, a wild laugh bubbling up. "You really are big. Feels amazing." I squeezed around him experimentally.

Reid groaned. "If this was a porno, I'd say, 'You're so tight,' and tell you that you're going to make me come. For the record, even though this isn't a porno, you are so tight and you're going to make me come so fucking hard."

We laughed again, and I wiped away the lingering tears before squeezing around him again. It was tender inside, but the pain was part of the pleasure. I slowly rose up a few inches and then back down, experimenting with the sensations. The feeling of fullness made my head spin.

There was so much going on at once. Reid's cock inside me, stretching me. Our skin sweaty everywhere we touched. Reid rubbing my thighs and hips, more heat with each stroke of his commanding hands.

"That's it," he murmured. "You feel amazing, baby."

Reid couldn't seem to stop touching me. He ran his hands hungrily everywhere he could reach, telling me how good I was doing. I arched my back as I started to really ride him, finding a steady cadence and rubbing my prostate in a way that made my dick pulse with precum.

My thighs trembled as I worked myself on Reid's cock, and I couldn't believe he'd been waiting naked in my bed to surprise me while I'd been showering and moping with crackers.

"Thank you," I said, or gasped or moaned or some other sound I couldn't name.

"No thanks necessary." He inhaled sharply and bit his lip, his fingers tightening on my thighs. Sweat glistened on his forehead. "I was about to say I could do this all day, but that would be a lie since I'm going to come soon." His breath hitched. "Very, very soon."

His cock was curved, and I rolled my hips to find the perfect angle, leaning on his chest. "Me too," was all I could manage.

"Can I touch you?"

"*Please*," I groaned, and as Reid took my dick in his slick hand, it only took a moment before I stuttered and shot all over him.

I clamped down on his cock, jerking and seeing stars as pleasure crashed through me. Reid clutched my hips and thrust up, gasping and moaning my name.

My name.

Reid Cabot was coming inside me with only a thin layer of latex between us. I slumped over him, and we shook and mumbled nonsense as Reid wrapped his arms around me. Our skin was sticky like we'd just run five miles.

"Okay?" Reid eased me onto the mattress beside him.

"Uh…" How was I supposed to form words right now?

"Judging by your dopey smile, I'll take that as a yes." Chuckling, Reid ran a damp cloth—he really had been prepared—over my junk and then gently wiped it between my ass cheeks. "Sore?" He prodded tentatively.

"I'm good." My ass was tender, but I tried to hide it.

"I saw that. That was a grince."

I laughed. "Just a little. I mean it—I'm good. Great."

"Marvelous? Splendid?"

"One might even say spectacular."

"Sublime?" Reid offered.

"Mmm. Wondrous."

We smiled through sweet little kisses. We were both such nerds some-times, and somehow it made Reid even hotter.

"I feel like I just took an epic ride on my bike for hours. Sore muscles, but exhilarated."

"Riding me is far safer than that motorcycle." He nuzzled my cheek before rolling away.

"No, stay here." I reached for him as he tucked the covers around me.

"I'll be right back. Need to get rid of the condom." He glanced down at his chest. "And scrub your load out of my chest hair."

"We should have a shower together. I've always wondered what that would be like."

He cocked an eyebrow. "Did you fantasize about it? You and me under the water? *Soaping* each other?" He said it slowly, suggestively.

"Yeah. Pretty much every time I jerked off in the shower in high school." Maybe I should have been embarrassed to admit that, but the words flowed so easily.

A slow grin lifted Reid's gorgeous mouth. "I'll keep that in mind."

As much as I wanted to get in the shower with him now, my limbs were heavy, and I couldn't stifle a yawn. Reid kissed me and straightened the pillow under my head before ducking out. He was back in a minute.

Snuggled under the covers, I ran my fingers through his damp chest hair. "I wish you didn't have to stay here for Christmas," I said, too sleepy to stop myself.

He sighed heavily in the darkness. "Me too. But I can't miss Grandmoth-er's Christmas fundraiser. She's annoyed enough with me—I can't risk really making her angry."

"Why not?" Screw her. I knew that was easier said than done, though. I'd never even cut my father out of my life, and I should have years ago.

Reid tensed. "Asher and I are all she has. Our dad was her only child. I've disappointed her enough already."

"By being bi?" Frustration and anger broke through my sleepy haze. "That's so unfair. And it's *her* problem. Not yours."

"I know," he whispered. He could go from confident and in control to vulnerable so quickly.

"Risks aren't always bad." I kissed his neck softly. "Sometimes, taking a leap ends up being the most incredible decision." To lighten the mood, I added, "One might say astonishing. Remarkable. Heart-stopping." I punctuated the words with little kisses to his cheek, neck, and shoulder.

"Breathtaking?"

"Mmm, definitely." I leaned up and pressed our lips together. We sighed into the kiss before settling again, this time Reid spooning me and nuzzling the back of my neck. I yawned and said, "I was going to cook you a terrible omelet, but I'm too tired."

His warm breath tickled my skin as he chuckled. "Let's order. Empanada Mama again? I'm hooked."

"Sure." I was pleased he'd liked it so much. "Hold on, my phone's somewhere under here."

"I've got it." The warmth of his body shifted as he picked up his own phone.

"No, you ordered the other night." I sat up and rooted around in the covers. I'd be lucky if we hadn't crushed it.

Reid was already tapping. "Don't worry. I've got it."

Something bristled in me. "No. This is my place, so I pay. You paid at your place. I already owe you enough."

He sighed noisily. "Let's just write it off. Forget about it. I have money."

"*Ten grand?* No." I wanted to grab the phone away, but I choked down that impulse. Through gritted teeth, I asked, "Reid, will you please stop ordering?"

He opened his mouth as if to argue before closing it and putting down his phone on the side table. "Sorry."

"Thank you." I'd gone from drowsy to zipping with anger, and I took a deep breath. "I'm not hand-waving ten thousand dollars. I'm paying back that money."

"Okay." He nodded. "I get it. I just hate to think of you working nights at CVS when I have more money than I could ever need."

"Give it to charity."

"I do! Believe me, I do."

I did believe him. "Okay, but I'm not a charity case. I was an idiot, and I have to pay off that debt, and I will."

"What happened?" he asked softly.

Ugh, that was the last thing I wanted to talk about in the afterglow of my first time being fucked. To be fair, I'd brought it up, but no. That had to wait.

"I don't want to talk about it right now." I rubbed my face. "Can we just go back to happy cuddling, please?"

He reached for my hand, and I squeezed his fingers. He said, "Absolutely. Let's find your phone."

It was wedged between the mattress and the bottom of the headboard, but unharmed. I tapped out our order and said, "I pay at my place. You can pay at yours. Deal?"

"Deal. Now we have some cuddling to do before the food arrives." He lifted the covers and we got comfy again. Tracing the shell of my ear with his fingers, Reid asked, "Still feeling marvelous?"

I snuggled against him, letting myself relax. "Yep. Stupendous, even."

"Mmm. Phenomenal."

I thought of another word: *fantastical.* Although that could mean quirky or odd or bizarre, it was definitely wild that I was in Reid Cabot's arms.

And it was *real* between us. We were in my bed. This wasn't fake. No matter what happened, Reid wanted me tonight. I ordered myself not to think about the possible outcomes for our relationship in the long run, or about the money I owed him.

Those conversations would come. I'd be going home for Christmas without him too soon. Whatever tomorrow and tomorrow and the days after that brought, tonight was ours.

Chapter Fifteen

Connor

"HOW'S YOUR FAKE boyfriend?" Seth asked as we buckled into his SUV. "I suppose your task is complete? I think you said it was only leading up to Christmas."

The question hit me harder than I expected. For a second, I thought I might burst into tears, which would have totally freaked out Seth.

"Uh, yeah. It was all good. Totally fine." Geez, why was every muscle in my body clenched? Reid and I hadn't broken up or anything. We hadn't talked about that at all.

"Are you sure?" Seth braked for a yellow light. "I know Logan was being quite…overprotective, but Asher's brother is an honorable man, isn't he?"

"A hundred percent! Yeah, he's great." I'd almost said "wonderful," and now I was in danger of gushing. I fought to even my tone, but my boot tapped restlessly. "He's a cool guy. I'm glad I could help him out."

All true.

There was nothing stopping me from telling Seth that Reid and I had hooked up for real—minus the details, because no, I actually did not want to discuss getting busy with my dads.

But it was still so new and…delicate. I had to find out where Reid and I stood in the new year before I told my family. That was reasonable, wasn't it?

"Okay. Are you sure your exams went all right? Are you feeling a bit dysregulated?"

I laughed softly. "Haven't heard that word in a long time."

Back when I was a teenager and Logan and I were still fighting too much—even though we were better than when Seth met us—Seth had read a bunch of psychology books to try and find coping strategies. He'd calmly mediate while I snarled and swore.

I said, "It's weird to think about how angry I was back then. How…on the brink. I don't know how you guys put up with my mood swings. And yes, my exams went well. I hope. I guess I'll find out in January."

"Okay, you sound remarkably calm about that." He checked his blind spot and exited onto the highway, and we passed malls and a blur of outlet stores.

"Super regulated over here."

Seth squeezed my arm. "Glad to hear it. Now that your pretend relationship is over, are you thinking about dating?"

"Sure, I guess." My foot jiggled again, and I shifted in my heated seat.

"I'm sure you know all about which apps are popular these days, and how to be careful."

I groaned. "*Yes.* Stop right there, I'm begging you."

"All right." He chuckled.

"And you guys haven't told Jenna and everyone, right? I do not want to spend Christmas with people trying to hook me up with so-and-so's cousin or coworker because they know one other queer person."

"We haven't said a word. Though you know that whenever you're ready, the rest of the family will be delighted. To say nothing of Angela."

I had to laugh. "She does love to roll out the rainbow carpet."

I almost told him about Angela helping Reid, but I wanted to keep the Reid talk to a minimum. Also, nothing might come of it. I really hoped it would, though. Reid needed to take a risk instead of being buried under family obligations, even if those obligations involved being rich.

I scrolled through Seth's playlists, grinning as I found the *Full Moon* soundtrack. "I saw this last night! It was awesome."

"How did you get tickets? It's been impossible. Since when are you interested in musicals?"

"I am gay now," I joked. "I think it's in the job description."

"Har, har."

Reid and I had laughed and clapped and had an amazing night on Broadway. He'd scored incredible seats—I didn't want to think about how much they'd cost—and we'd had dinner at the Italian restaurant with all the caricatures of famous people on the walls.

I said, "I got lucky with the lottery. Besides, I'm a New Yorker. I have to see the hot new Broadway show."

"In your job description," Seth agreed. "Tell me all about it!"

I did, without giving away any spoilers he might not have known just by listening to the soundtrack. As he talked about his favorite song, my mind wandered to Reid. We'd had a few drinks, and sitting in the fifth row with Reid's knee pressed against mine, I'd felt loose and happy and…

In love.

That was an issue for another time, and I refocused on Seth, agreeing with him about the song's crescendo. Reid and I had had our own crescendo back at his place at the end of the night, with me riding him again with more confidence.

There were so many positions I wanted to try, and I already missed Reid more than I thought would be possible.

Obviously, I missed my mom a huge amount. But this longing was entirely different. Electric and immediate, an ache of anticipation. I was home for a week, and it seemed like an *eternity*.

The afternoon was darkening already, and I watched the Christmas lights twinkle to life as we headed into Aunt Jenna's neighborhood of small, neat houses with little yards.

Jenna and Jun's place was ablaze with gold lights along the gutters and around the windows. I couldn't wait to see our house—Seth and Logan always went all out.

The driveway was full of cars, so Seth parked his SUV on the street. I asked, "Is Jenna having a party, or is it just us?"

"A party, but there won't be too many people."

Inside, there was a flurry of greetings. Logan gave me his patented back-slapping hug. Jenna pulled me close, smelling of Victoria's Secret vanilla perfume, and predictably said I was taller, which I was not. Jun waved from the kitchen and asked Jenna if the dipping sauce was supposed to be boiling.

It was not.

The other guests were Seth and Jenna's friends from work—Will and his partner, Michael, and Matt and his fiancée, Becky. Will's parents were visiting from Scotland, and I shook hands with them and immediately forgot their names. They went to the kitchen, insisting on helping with the food.

Matt had always seemed fun to me as a kid with his shaggy blond hair and jokey attitude, but now as he asked me casually, "Anyone come home with you for Christmas?" alarm bells rang.

Too many avid expressions waited for my answer. "Nope," I said. "Just me."

Becky said, "My cousin saw you at a dinner in New York with Reid Cabot."

I appreciated that she didn't beat around the bush at least. "Oh yeah, we're friends. I went to school with his little brother."

Maybe it would be easier to just come out and tell everyone the truth. Call for attention and announce that I was gay and fucking Reid and wasn't taking questions at this time. But I tensed, my heart thumping. No. Not yet.

"Leave the lad alone," Will chided in his extremely sexy Scottish accent. He had dark stubble and blue eyes, and I hoped it wasn't disloyal to Reid to admit that Will was hot.

Will only had eyes for Michael, who was blond and cute and currently shaking his head at Matt. Michael said, "You two are shameless."

"Who, us?" Matt put a hand to his chest. "I'm mortally wounded by your accuracy."

I should have taken the out and gone over to Seth and Logan, who were probably talking about me too. Instead, I couldn't resist asking Will and

Michael, "Is it true you guys pretended to be a couple before you got together?"

They shared a sweet smile that would have made me so jealous in the past, and Michael slipped his arm around Will's waist. Michael said, "Yep. I'd been in love with him for years, and he had no idea. Then we ended up pretending to be boyfriends because… Well, it sounds ludicrous."

"Situation normal around these parts," Matt said. "We love a caper. Just look at Connor's dads."

"Yeah, it worked out pretty well," I agreed. I smiled at Will and Michael. "Glad it did for you too."

"Best thing that ever happened to me," Will said before kissing Michael's cheek. "Of course, I had to remove my head from my arse first."

If Reid and I ended up together, we'd be three for three on fake couples becoming real.

Don't get ahead of yourself!

Still, it was hard not to daydream….

Jenna and Jun's sons, Ian and Noah, were playing a video game in the lounge, where Logan and Jenna's father, Pop, sat in his chair in corduroy pants and a green sweater, his swollen feet up and clad in extra-large slippers.

Cross-legged on the carpet, the kids tore their attention away from the screen for a second to call, "Hey!" and I waved back as they jabbed their controllers.

In the past, I'd have been right there with them, but I realized I didn't even recognize the game they were playing. Jesus, I was getting old. Or maybe just insanely busy.

Tell me you're in med school without telling me you're in med school.

The Christmas tree across from Pop's chair beside the TV glowed with gold lights and shiny silver tinsel. The ornaments were a mix of school macaroni projects and sparkling balls and teardrops from the store. Wrapped presents spilled out around the base.

"Hey, Pop." I squeezed his hand and perched on the arm of the couch. Pretty much everyone called him "Pop," so I did too.

He grunted and squeezed back, his gaze on the screen even though I wasn't sure he understood the fast-moving game. The edema from his congestive heart failure had worsened, and I bit back the urge to ask him about his prescriptions and investigate whether they needed to be tweaked.

"How are you feeling?" I asked, shifting my fingers to his wrist for his resting heart rate.

Pop shook me off. "Acting like a doc already. I'm fine, boy." He wheezed softly as he breathed, and his white hair had gone even more wispy. He wasn't frail, though. That grit remained.

I had to laugh. "Okay. Glad to hear it." I leaned over, trying to get a look at his legs. "Are you wearing your compression stockings?"

His response was a grumble that I recognized as a no, and I knew it was a subject he'd argued with Aunt Jenna and Logan about. I said, "You know it'll help even if it's a pain getting them on and off."

He grunted. "How're you doing? Knockin' 'em dead at school? Breaking girls' hearts?"

I let the stockings go—for the moment. "Trying not to kill anyone. It's a bad look for med students. And nah. No girls. No hearts breaking." I hoped mine wouldn't be shattering soon.

"Boys, then."

Pop still stared at the TV. Ian and Noah shouted over each other, the game making a ton of noises from beeping to explosions. I had to take a deep breath and blow it out, sawdust in my mouth as I stared at Pop. How did he know?

"Um… Yeah, actually," I said. "There's one in particular." I wasn't sure why I was spilling this when I'd only reaffirmed minutes ago that I wasn't ready to come out to everyone tonight.

This had been so easy, though—no announcement necessary. Another one down.

"That's good. Wanna grab me another beer?"

Part of me wanted to advise him on the risks of alcohol at his age with his conditions, but I only squeezed his arm and said, "Sure, Pop."

Returning from the lively chaos in the kitchen, where Jenna and Jun bickered over mini quiches and bao buns filled with crispy pork belly, I flopped on the couch beside Pop's recliner. We both drank Pabst from the bottle and watched the boys play their game.

As a teenager, I'd spent countless hours on this end of the couch near Pop, watching football, NASCAR, game shows, and even soap operas. We'd rarely spoken, but the silence had been a comforting warm blanket while I'd still been finding my feet and navigating my prickly relationship with Logan. Silence had suited me just fine.

Occasionally, over a commercial, he'd said things like: "*My boy can be a dumbass, but he'd give you the shirt off his back.*" Or "*It's okay to miss your momma. But she won't mind a bit if you're happy. She's happy in heaven.*" Then he wouldn't say anything for hours.

While I didn't believe in heaven, I remember being amazed Pop had known that as I'd settled into the family, my guilt for being happy had worsened. He had a way of saying things that resonated more than what my therapist had said, even if the messages were the same.

I realized I didn't know how the conversation had gone when Logan had told Pop he was bi and in a relationship with Seth. Maybe something like this?

"Thanks," I said, my throat thick.

"For what?"

"You know."

He grunted, and I smiled to myself. Pop had always made his words count.

AS THE VIDEO call made a low beeping, I lunged for my phone beside me on the mattress, sending Hercules, my dads' tabby cat, leaping off the bottom of the mattress where he'd been curled by my feet.

I sat up and swiped. Reid's face appeared on screen, and we said, "Hey!" in perfect unison. We were both shirtless.

"I miss you," I blurted before I could hope to gather a tiny shred of chill. My calm, cool, and collected well was bone dry. Reid had gone with me to Penn to catch the train that morning—it had only been hours.

But he didn't laugh at me. He only said, "Me too," and normally, I'd have gone through a checklist to make sure my erratic heart rate wasn't a symptom of a bigger issue.

Also, the fact that he'd gotten up early with me still made my heart skip. I'd insisted I could just order a ride and go myself since there was no point in him going with me when he'd just have to get a car back uptown. Penn Station was a mess of people and smells and *ugh*, but Reid had held my hand right to the crowded train platform.

"Are you in your room from when you were a kid?" he asked.

"Teenager, yeah."

"What's that behind you? And why are you grincing?"

"Because it's a poster of Ricky Tortuga. Yes, the race car driver. I went through a NASCAR phase, okay?"

Reid laughed. "And Ricky was the object of your affections?"

"Oh, yeah. Along with you."

He smirked. "I was in esteemed company."

"Indeed. Teenage me would die to know I'd one day be in this bed talking to you."

"Well, we could do more than talk." He gave me a suggestive smile.

I honest-to-god *squeaked.* "Like, phone sex? I can't! My dads are right down the hall."

"Mmm. You might get caught." His voice was still low and seductive.

"You're supposed to be risk-averse!" I hissed. "Veto!"

"All right, all right. We'll save phone sex for another time."

"It's not that I'm opposed to the idea in general, for the record. I don't want you to think I'm a prude."

"You've had your finger in my ass and my cock in your mouth. Not to mention *my* cock in *your* ass. 'Prude' is not a word that springs to mind."

Heat washed through me, my dick twitching in the old boxers I wore to bed. "You're not making this easier."

Reid raised a hand. "Apologies. I surrender."

"Besides, Hercules is in here. I can't do *that* with the cat watching." I turned my phone and cooed to Hercules. "Say hi to Reid."

Hercules only scratched at the door, so I got up to let him out. "He'll probably want back inside in, like, two minutes."

"Sounds about right for a cat. So, you haven't redecorated since high school? Let me see the rest. I only got a flash."

I groaned. "It's way too embarrassing."

Reid quirked an eyebrow, and I wanted to reach through the screen and lick it. Was licking eyebrows normal?

He said, "I'm waiting."

Sighing noisily, I turned my phone and panned it around my small room. The jeans and hoodie I'd worn today were thrown over the desk chair. The desktop was cluttered with old notebooks and Harvard textbooks that didn't fit on my overstuffed bookcase. Also an old deodorant stick, a pile of expired bus passes, and I didn't even know what.

"It's messy, I know." He'd seen my room in New York, so that surely wasn't a surprise. The more embarrassing part was the poster of a Victoria's Secret model with angel wings from one of those fashion shows. "My attempt to be straight," I said.

Reid chuckled. "Adorable." He squinted. "What's that painting over the dresser?"

"I don't know, actually." The framed print was so familiar to me that I almost didn't notice it. I focused on the golden strokes of wheat in a field and low-hanging clouds tinged with the orange glow of sunrise—or sunset? Unclear. "My mom got it at a garage sale when I was little. We moved a lot, but this print always came with us."

"It's beautiful."

"Thanks." I cleared my throat, which had become uncomfortably thick.

"You must miss her," Reid said quietly.

I climbed back into bed and curled on my side under the blankets, holding my phone and leaning it on the end of my pillow to keep my face in frame. He was in bed, and he did the same. I could almost imagine we were together, our knees bumping and feet sliding together.

"I do," I said. "It never goes away. It changes shapes, but it's still there. You know what I mean?"

Reid nodded and leaned his head on his hand. "I miss my dad, but it's not the same as it was initially."

"If he was still here, do you think you'd be stuck working at Utopia?" As soon as the question escaped my mouth, I regretted it. "I'm sorry. That's a dick question."

"It's okay. Probably. Or maybe I'd be working somewhere else before ending up at Utopia eventually to keep it in the family. It's my legacy, et cetera, et cetera."

"But not Asher's."

"It's ridiculous, I know. If this was the olden days in England, I'd inherit the title, and he'd get scraps. I'd love for him to take the title now, but he doesn't want it." Reid shrugged, his bare shoulder appearing into frame briefly. "Did you always want to be a doctor? I don't think we've talked about this."

My gut clenched, and my gaze flicked to my mom's painting. "When I was little, I wanted to be—"

"Wait, let me guess. A race car driver?"

"Nope. And I never considered it during my NASCAR phase either."

"Hmm." Reid tapped his chin exaggeratedly. There was a tiny divot in his chin—not a cleft, but a minuscule scar. I wanted to lick that, too. He asked, "Pilot?"

"No!" I shuddered. "Flying's scary."

"What? But you ride a *motorcycle!*"

"Only in good conditions, and I'm in control. It's different."

Reid scoffed. "You know the statistics on plane crashes versus motorcycles have to favor air travel by a massive margin. The risk of flying is incredibly low. It does increase depending on the airline—there are certain airlines in various countries that I'd never use since their safety regulations aren't up to par. But overall, it's the safest way to travel by a landslide."

"I know intellectually that this is all true," I conceded.

"Okay, okay, lecture over. I get it. Hmm. Did you want to be a firefighter? Cop?" He kept guessing as I shook my head. "Teacher? Astronaut—no, too risky." He tapped his chin again. "Musician?"

"Yes!" I was pleased he'd guessed. "A percussionist. My mom took me to the symphony once because she said I had to get 'cultured.' I loved the drums and especially the cymbals."

"Sounds about right for a kid."

I laughed. "I think she regretted it immediately but wanted to support my dreams."

"When did you start dreaming of medicine?"

I knew he was going to ask that, and I'd tried to prepare myself to answer steadily without reliving it. Huge fail, as usual. I tensed, the vision of her bare feet with pink-painted toenails filling my head. They'd been the first thing I'd seen when I opened her bedroom door.

My voice was hoarse. "When my mom died."

Reid's eyes widened. "Was it… Was she ill?"

"You don't know the story? Asher never told you?"

"I don't think so. I'm sorry—you don't have to talk about it."

Strangely, I wanted to. Even as I fought for breath, I wanted to tell Reid. I wanted to download my memories into his brain and climb into his skin and have him know *everything*.

I swallowed thickly. "My mom died of a brain aneurysm. It happened in the night, and I found her in the morning when it was too late."

Reid sucked in a breath. "Oh, baby. I'm so sorry."

Shit. My eyes burned, and I blinked rapidly. I'd told this story multiple times and had managed to keep it together, but the tenderness in Reid's deep brown eyes was undoing me. Rigid, I breathed through my nose.

He murmured, "You can cry."

I'm sure he wasn't the first person to tell me that—Logan and Seth surely had—but it was different somehow. Reid had been *inside* me. And even if that didn't mean much to other people, it meant a ton to me. I'd never felt as naked as I did with Reid—even though I was wearing my boxers at the moment.

So, I did. I cried.

I didn't try to stop the tears, my face wet and blotchy as I sniffed loudly. I told him about finding her on the floor, gray and waxy, and knowing she was dead deep down. Calling 911 and doing CPR, her ribs cracking even though I only had bony, weak arms.

I swiped my hand over my nose. "I wondered if I could have saved her if I'd been there when she collapsed. The doctors said it wouldn't have made a difference, but I still thought about it constantly. I decided if I couldn't help her, I'd help other people." I shrugged. "That's the story."

Reid blew out a long breath, his eyes gleaming. "Thank you for telling me."

"It's not a secret or anything." Still, this time when I told it, I didn't feel the residual anger I usually did. I'd never be at peace with losing her, but the rage that had taken over my life really was in the past.

"No, but I can see it takes a lot out of you. I wish I could kiss you right now."

"Me too."

"I'm so glad you came to that Thanksgiving dinner."

My heart skipped. "Me too," I repeated. I wanted to tell him I was falling in love—that I'd fallen already, and I was still falling and falling. Would he catch me?

"Guess it's time for bed," Reid said. "Get some sleep."

"Yeah." It was jumping the gun for love declarations, so I went with, "I wish you were here." I hesitated. "I mean—obviously that would be weird, right? It's too soon to meet my parents. And I know you have to be in New York for Christmas. Anyway, I meant to ask if you're coming to Asher's party on New Year's Eve? That's when I'm coming back. I know you wouldn't normally go. You have your own friends and stuff."

I was babbling, and I forced myself to stop. I'd wanted to ask him before I left, but everything had been so perfect that I hadn't wanted to think about the future in case he said no. Even if it was only a week and a bit away. At Penn, we'd only said we'd see each other soon.

Reid smiled. "I wouldn't miss it."

I let my grin say it all.

Chapter Sixteen

Reid

HAD MY APARTMENT always been so…plain? Boring? Why didn't I have holiday decorations? Sipping coffee in my bathrobe, I wandered into the living room. It was still dark—one of those winter mornings where it could have been the middle of the night instead of seven.

I should have gone to the gym, but I'd hit snooze. Three times. Or five. I hadn't slept, though. I'd been up half the night, tossing and turning and wishing Connor was beside me.

In the light from the kitchen, I imagined a tree by the window gleaming with a rainbow of colors and sparkling decorations. Presents piled underneath with big bows on top.

I snorted. Presents for who? Connor was in Albany. I'd never exchanged gifts with my family as an adult. The fun parts of Christmas were for kids, and all we were left with was social and business and charitable obligations. And the hard truth was that the charity work was intrinsically tied to Utopia and our reputation. It was all business.

If Connor were here, how would he decorate? He and Olivia had fun garlands and a wonky little tree that reminded me of Charlie Brown in the best way.

I let myself imagine Connor stringing lights on our tree—would we get real or fake? The smell of a real tree would be hard to beat…

"I'm losing it," I said out loud to the empty room. Through the window, the lights of the briefly quiet city seemed to agree.

Connor was only in Albany a few hours upstate, and I was acting as though he were on the other side of the world. How did I miss him this much? We'd talked, we'd texted, we'd talked more. But I ached to be with him.

I didn't know what his mom had looked like, but I was haunted by images of Connor finding her. My dad's death had been sudden—a heart attack likely brought on by drinking and smoking—and it had been unbearable at first. But I couldn't begin to fathom the trauma Connor had experienced.

All I wanted was to hold him and make sure he was never, ever hurt again.

"What is wrong with me?" I muttered. I couldn't be in love already. I'd never been in love before, so I couldn't compare these feelings to anything else, but…

If this wasn't love, I had to have acquired a tropical disease. And there was a distinct dearth of mosquitoes in New York City in December. It wasn't malaria, no matter how feverish and restless I was.

From the kitchen, my phone pinged with a reminder, and I groaned. I had obligations to fulfill. Reports to finish at the office, another charity lunch, blah, blah, *blah*. Had I ever enjoyed these things? Had I ever enjoyed *anything* before Connor?

"That's absurd," I told myself sternly. "Get a grip."

The problem was that I didn't want to. I wanted to recklessly plunge forward the way I had on Thanksgiving. Asking Connor to pretend to be my boyfriend had been wild and ridiculous—and potentially the greatest decision I'd ever made.

I needed to step back and assess the risk. Take this time away from Connor to breathe and figure out if this was only infatuation or if we could really have a future together.

My phone rang, and I crossed to the kitchen island in what might have been called a run. Bordering on flying. It was only as I swiped to answer that I realized it was Grandmother's assistant, Sonia.

"Hi, Reid. Sorry to call so early. You need to clear your schedule for lunch."

"Brett couldn't share my calendar?" Typically, my assistant would handle this sort of thing. I'd always been informal with Sonia and Brett and insisted they call me by my first name—much to Grandmother's distaste.

"He said lunch was blocked off, but he didn't know why. This is urgent, so I decided to call myself. I apologize for the inconvenience."

"It's fine. Let me just…" My brain was so full of Connor that I'd barely been thinking of anything else. I put her on speaker and tapped my phone, skimming my calendar. "Oh. I can't." I had a follow-up call with Angela Barker, who was being incredibly generous with her time and energy. "I have…" I tried to think of anything that could plausibly pre-empt a demand from Grandmother and came up blank. "I can't."

Sonia paused before saying quietly, "I don't believe Mrs. Cabot will accept any response except for meeting her and the other parties at Le Gabriel at noon. Sharp."

"Fine." I softened my tone. "Thank you, Sonia. I hope you and your family have a wonderful holiday if I don't see you before then."

"Thank you. You'll be at Mrs. Cabot's breakfast event on Christmas Day, I presume? I hope you have something else fun planned as well."

"Yes, definitely. Thanks."

If missing Connor and questioning all my life choices except for him was "fun," then sure. Christmas would be a *blast*.

AFTER TIPPING THE driver and closing the ride app, I checked my messages again. Still no reply from Grandmother to my call and two texts asking for more details about lunch. I was in front of the restaurant, so at least I'd find out soon.

Angela had been gracious and understanding of the last-minute cancellation, and we'd rescheduled the call for after the holidays since she was "going dark" for family time in Texas. Connor had mentioned Olivia was flying home.

Beside the restaurant, I stepped into the doorway of a bar that was currently dark to get out of the miserably cold drizzle. The snow had melted, the city was dreary and wet. With Connor, it had felt like Christmas magic was in the air, and now it had vanished.

I'd tried to choke down the disappointment at not speaking with Angela today, but I needed a minute before I put on my happy Utopia business face. I could have had Angela's suggestions to work on over Christmas since I'd only be killing time until Connor was back. Now, the days stretched out even more dismally.

How could I miss someone so much when we'd only been dating for a few weeks? And half the time we'd been pretending?

Sighing glumly—and admittedly feeling extremely sorry for myself, which I had to shake off—I stepped back into the drizzle and ducked into Le Gabriel with its crisp white linens, hushed piano carols, and appropriately measured murmur of conversations muffled by the spotless cream fabric wall coverings. Everything at Le Gabriel was exquisitely curated from the wine cellar to the foie gras to the clientele.

Clientele that included Cecilia Weston, her golden hair settling in soft curls around her shoulders, complimenting her cranberry dress perfectly.

I froze as I handed my coat to the hostess, my gaze locking on Cecilia across the dining room in a plush corner booth. She looked as lovely and polished as ever, smiling at something her companions said. They sat in padded chairs with their backs to me, but I would know Grandmother's perfect posture, pink skirt suit, and sleek silver hair anywhere.

"Mr. Cabot? This way, please."

I blinked at the hostess. I could ask for my coat back and make a run for it. I'd text Grandmother with an excuse, and she'd have to deal with it. Or I—

Cecilia waved, her smile widening. Grandmother and the man beside her—Stephen Weston, Cecilia's plastic-surgeon father—turned in their chairs, and there was no escape now. Marshalling my strength and patience, I joined them, sliding in beside Cecilia on the banquette since that was the only option. I didn't stop first to kiss Grandmother's cheeks, which was a petty rebellion.

After a round of pleasantries and champagne cocktails, we ordered lunch, and I said, "What brings us here today?" with gritted teeth I couldn't quite hide. Cecilia's smile faltered, and she glanced at her father. I added, "Though I appreciate the opportunity to catch up."

Cecilia said, "It's been years, hasn't it? I think we were in college the last time we actually spoke."

Grandmother's expression was placid enough to fool most people, but I detected the twitch of tension in her eye as she said, "Did you know Cecilia is working with her father now? Expanding his business."

That didn't answer my question, but I made interested noises, and Cecilia said, "I opened a spa hotel in the Hamptons focused on medical tourism."

"Medical tourism," I echoed. "Plastic surgery?"

"Yes, but only simple, low-risk procedures."

"Ah. Face lifts and liposuction for the rich and famous?"

Cecilia lifted her glass in a mock toast. "Precisely. It's a lucrative business, and we think there are certain other world markets where we could combine a luxury hotel experience with wellness and appropriate procedures."

Servers arrived with our lunches, and I poked at my duck and pork cassoulet, dread building in me. This was why Grandmother had been so eager to set up me and Cecilia? So Utopia could open new properties for plastic surgery tourism? Cecilia and I didn't need to be a couple to go into business together. Perhaps Grandmother had simply decided Cecilia was the most eligible young woman in town.

Emphasis on *woman*.

My tie felt like it was choking me. I loosened it, garnering pursed lips from Grandmother. I was tempted to order another drink as Stephen detailed a new procedure involving neck fat. I wondered what Connor would think. Had Dr. Weston gone into medicine as an idealistic youth hoping to help people, or had he always preyed on people's insecurities?

I ate a bite of rich duck and white beans with dill. I was probably being unfair. I asked Stephen, "Do you ever treat patients with disfigurements or people who've been in accidents?"

"Occasionally, but my focus is on cosmetics. Don't worry, we won't be bringing desperate cases to your hotel."

There it was. I smiled thinly, swirling my glass of Bordeaux. "My hotel?"

"That's what we need to discuss," Grandmother said smoothly.

"You know, I'd actually like to discuss affordable housing," I blurted.

Three sets of eyes stared blankly. I gulped my wine and ordered myself to stop talking.

Cecilia asked, "Affordable housing? Yes, I imagine there's a need for it." Her sculpted brows met. "But you don't need to worry about that."

"No, I don't need to. None of us do." I motioned around the table. "We should, though. We should worry about a lot of things we ignore."

"Darling, I appreciate your passion, but let's stay on topic," Grandmother said.

"You don't, though." What was I doing? Why wasn't I nodding and smiling like usual? "My passion doesn't lie in luxury hotels. You know that, but you ignore it."

Grandmother's nostrils flared. She'd spilled a drop of coq au vin on her crisp white blouse. "We're here to celebrate the season and discuss an excellent business opportunity with the Westons. You and I can speak later about…other topics."

As Grandmother and I stared daggers at each other, Cecilia said, "Er, uh, what are your plans for Christmas? My parents are leaving tomorrow for a South American cruise that looks incredible. Doesn't it, Daddy?"

"Oh yes, we'll be hitting all the highlights. Machu Picchu, that huge waterfall in Argentina. I think it's Argentina?"

"You'll soon find out," Grandmother said.

"I suppose you'll both be at Elizabeth's annual Christmas breakfast," Stephen said.

"Yes," I replied. "I'd much rather be with my boyfriend, but I don't get a choice." I cringed as soon as the childish words were out. I didn't regret mentioning Connor at all—to hell with what Grandmother thought—but petulance wasn't a good look.

Grandmother's face had flushed pink and her mouth pressed into a grim line. In the silence, Cecilia said, "It… Well, it is a good cause."

Shame rushed through me. "Yes, of course. A wonderful cause." I shook my head. "Forgive me. I'm just missing Connor." That probably wouldn't improve my grandmother's mood, but it was the truth.

Cecilia's face brightened. "Understandable. You two looked very much in love when I spotted you last week." She leaned closer and whispered conspiratorially, "He's very cute. I hear he's in med school?"

So, it seemed Cecilia had no interest in me, which was a relief. I answered, "Yes, at Columbia. He's going to be a wonderful doctor."

"If he decides to get into plastics, let me know," Stephen said through a bite of his steak.

"Will do," I said, belatedly tapping my reserves of politeness. "Thank you."

Grandmother delicately cleared her throat. "Yes, well. Cecilia, dear, why haven't you been snapped up?"

Cecilia waved a dismissive hand. "Oh, I'm not looking to settle down anytime soon."

For a moment, Grandmother was stunned into silence.

I said, "Your parents haven't tried to fix you up?"

"Oh, they've tried." She winked at her father, who shrugged nonchalantly. "They even suggested one of the Masterson boys."

I grimaced—*grinced.* "Veto."

"Indeed," Cecilia agreed. "Why isn't Connor coming with you to the breakfast on Christmas?"

"He's visiting his family in Albany." What was he doing now? God, I wished I was there.

She asked, "How did you two meet?"

Before I could answer, Grandmother coughed and pretended to nearly choke, which was an excellent distraction. Honestly, I wanted to sit back with my arms crossed until she was done, but I managed to make the required sympathetic noises.

"Goodness, what a fuss," Grandmother said after drinking water. "I'm quite all right. Cecilia, we'd love to hear more about your wellness venture. I think Utopia could be an excellent fit for your vision."

"I think so too, Mrs. Cabot." Cecilia glanced at me with an apologetic smile before launching into her spiel.

I listened and nodded and said all the right things. Grandmother relaxed by degrees, and by the time she paid the huge bill, you'd never have known I'd upset her.

When I walked her out to the waiting town car, holding her umbrella aloft, she gripped my arm with surprising strength, her tone ice cold. "Darling, I simply can't imagine what got into you."

"We need to talk." I opened the car door for her. It was time to say everything on my mind. Show her my proposal—everything. What was I waiting for? "If you're free now—"

Without meeting my gaze, she simply said, "Veto," and slid into the back seat. "I'll see you Christmas morning, bright and early."

Chapter Seventeen

Connor

EIGHT DAYS. *EIGHT days*. As much as I loved Christmas, how could I be expected to be apart from Reid for *eight* more days?

Tomorrow was Christmas Eve, and even in my room at midnight, the house smelled like the gingerbread cookies Seth had baked hours before. It was comforting and cozy, and I was tucked in my bed with snow falling beyond my window, the sky glowing white.

And I was horny as fuck.

I'd gone years without sex, but now that the seal was broken—so to speak—I was ravenous. How was I supposed to go *eight* more days?

It wasn't only sex. I wanted to hug Reid and smell his pepper-lilac-or-maybe-lily cologne. Hold him and feel his arms around me and the rumble of his laughter against my chest. Talk to him for hours about anything. About everything.

And, yes, I wanted to fuck him every way known to man. If the aliens had any ideas, I was all ears.

I flipped from one side to the other, sighing so loudly I half-expected Logan and Seth to shout for me to pipe down. I hadn't heard from him in the afternoon, but then he'd texted that he was out for dinner with Addison and some friends, which was great. Great! This was the part when I was supposed to go to sleep and talk to him in the morning.

I kicked at the blankets and flopped onto my stomach. My boxers were bunched, and I felt hot. I restlessly stripped off my T-shirt. Then goosebumps spread over my chest and I pulled it back on.

Obviously, I could jack off. I'd done it a million times, and I could get the release I needed. But it would be hollow without Reid. I wanted *him*. I wasn't just normal horny. This was next-level horny. I'd thought I'd known just how horny a person could get, but nope.

NOPE.

My phone buzzed with a video call, and I flicked on the lamp, eagerly swiping to reveal Reid's gorgeous face. He said, "Hey, baby," and I could have melted into a puddle of goo. He was *beaming* at me, and god, I wanted to lick his whole face. That couldn't be normal.

I sat up against the Ricky Tortuga poster. "Hey, yourself."

Reid asked, "Were you sleeping?" His brow furrowed, and I imagined tracing the creases with my tongue. "You have bed head."

"Oh!" I squinted at my image in the corner of the screen and tamped down my hair.

"It's adorable. Don't change a thing. I just don't want to keep you up if you're tired."

"I wasn't sleeping," I said honestly. "How was dinner? How was your day?"

"Dinner was great. Addison says hi."

"Cool. Did you talk to Angela earlier? I think that was today?"

His expression tightened. "I had to reschedule. It'll be after the holidays since she's busy with her family."

"Shit. I'm sorry. Waiting sucks. Did something come up at work?"

Reid did this shrug-nod that was definitely tense. He still wore a suit, so he must have just gotten in. "Yeah, there was a thing. No big deal."

"Are you sure? It kind of looks like it was a big deal."

He smiled, but he was clearly upset. Along with the frustration I'd seen in him before was tiredness. More than that—sadness.

Reid said, "Don't worry about it. What's happening in Albany? Did you get snow? That weather system stayed north of the city. Don't think we're getting a white Christmas here."

"I want to worry about it. What's wrong?"

He rubbed his face, and the camera jostled, the camera sweeping over Reid's living room before he propped his tablet on the coffee table and slumped on the couch. His charcoal suit jacket was undone, and he loosened the knot on his purple tie before slipping it free and dropping it to the cushion beside him. The camera looked up at him—and his crotch, but I focused on his weary, beautiful face.

"I think I'm having a midlife crisis. At twenty-nine." He snorted. "I'm almost thirty, and what have I accomplished? I could leave Utopia tomorrow, and it wouldn't make even a tiny bit of difference. The company and Grandmother would keep going without missing a beat."

"Then what's keeping you there? Other than guilt?"

"Great question." He shook his head. "Do I have to answer that right now?"

"Nope. You don't have to do anything right now. We can hang. Relax."

His smile was undeniably fond this time. "That sounds good." He shrugged out of his jacket and popped open the top three buttons on his white dress shirt. I could see a smattering of dark hair below his throat. Predictably, I wanted to lick that triangle of tender flesh.

Memories of grinding in his lap resurfaced. I swallowed hard. "There's a way we could relieve stress."

"Mm?" He yawned. "Night time yoga? What do you prescribe?"

"I was thinking orgasms."

That perked him up, but his grin was quickly replaced by a frown. "You vetoed phone sex."

"I can change my mind, right?"

"Yes, as long as it's not to cheer me up. You have to want it too."

"Trust me, I want it. I'm inspired by the view. Jesus, do you know how good you look in that suit? So hot."

He grinned. "I try. You look hot too."

I snorted. "In my Harvard crew T-shirt with Ricky Tortuga behind me?"

"Take it off if you don't like it."

Lust zapped me like a lightning strike. "Right. I could do that." I shifted, holding up my phone and tugging at my tee collar with my free hand. Did I have a fever? Blood rushed in my ears.

"You don't have to. I'm very capable of jerking off and thinking about you. My spank bank has had recent deposits."

I burst out laughing. "You're such a nerd. I never would have dreamed in a million years I'd hear Reid Cabot say 'spank bank.'"

"I'm all class. How could you possibly resist me?"

"I can't. The thing is, I need you." I glanced at my door. I hadn't heard a peep from my dads since they'd gone to bed around ten. "Like, *that.*"

Reid licked his lips, and boy, was that a smirk and a half. "Tell me what you need."

I sighed noisily. "I'm horny as hell, okay?"

"Me too." He spread his legs wide and palmed the bulge of his cock through the smooth, tailored pants. "You wanna do this?" he asked, his low voice sending shivers down my spine.

"Hell, yeah."

"Yeah?" He watched me intently, pausing to give me another out.

"Yes."

"Take it off."

I glanced at the door. "Hold on." I leapt up and turned on the pedestal fan in the corner for the noise, pointing it away from the bed before locking the door. I stripped off the tee and my boxers before clambering back on the bed and grabbing my phone. I reached for the lamp.

"I want to see you," Reid said. "Unless you want to switch to audio only?"

"But then I can't see you. Fuck it. Let's do it." Holy shit, was I actually having phone sex? On camera? *Here?*

"Are you naked yet? I can't tell from this angle." Reid had unbuttoned his own shirt completely and left it hanging open. He toyed with his nipples.

"Yeah," I whispered. "I'm naked. We have to be quiet."

He rubbed his dick. "Mmm. I'll try."

I turned down the volume on my phone, Reid's breathing still sounding loud even with the fan. I leaned back against Ricky's feet, checking my image in the bottom corner to make sure it was okay and I wasn't showing Reid up my nose or something.

With my fingers hooked around the pop socket on the back of my phone, I propped my left wrist on my bent knee.

Reid whispered, "Doctor, I have a painful condition. I've tried everything."

My heart *boomed.* Phone sex *and* role play? Teenage me really would never fucking believe this, though I also wanted to tell Reid not to jinx it. I wasn't a doctor yet. What if I'd bombed my exams? They might take away my scholarship. Then I'd be working at CVS every night…

"Veto?" Reid asked in his normal voice.

"No!" I croaked out, "What seems to be the problem? This is your, uh, doctor here." I reached blindly for the lube in my beside table drawer, my eyes locked on my phone.

With the low angle of Reid's camera, his cock looked *huge* as he pulled it out. "I'm so hard." His eyes twinkled, and I couldn't bite back a laugh.

I put on a serious doctor voice. "We'll have to run some tests. I've never seen anything quite so large and…tumescent."

Reid snorted, and we both giggled. Like, actually *giggled.* Reid put on a serious face, and I did too. "Doctor, it hurts. I can't stop myself from touching it."

"Take off your pants and stroke it. Let me see."

He did, stripping off his trousers and briefs, leaving only the open dress shirt. A flush spread up his chest as he worked himself. I breathed quickly, shallow little gasps as I jerked off. In the bottom of my screen, I could see my face was pink, my lips parted.

"Do you like watching me, Doctor?" Reid whispered.

I could only nod. Not being able to smell him or feel him or taste the salt of his sweat or lingering coffee on his tongue made watching him even more intense than usual.

I'd looked at him a million times and admired his hotness, but watching now, I zeroed in on the hair around his left nipple, the cords of muscle in his neck as he stroked himself, the flex of his wide thighs.

"It's helping. I feel better already." He moaned, thumbing the drops of precum from the tip of his shaft. If we'd been in the same room, I would have dropped to my knees to swallow him. I wanted to choke on his dick. Biting my lip, I swallowed a moan.

"Let me see you," Reid murmured.

I held my phone farther away, trying to get the right angle. I probably should have been embarrassed, but it was Reid. I wanted to give him whatever he needed. I wanted to give him everything.

"Doctor, I need to watch you come. It's the only cure."

I gasped, and I would have slapped a hand over my mouth if I'd had one free. Bent legs wide, I dug my heels into the mattress and jerked faster, arching up into my hand, straining, trying to keep the camera on my dick, my arm shaking, balls tightening—

I sprayed my load on my stomach while Reid moaned and encouraged me. "Baby, that's so good. Fuck, you're beautiful."

Bringing my phone screen back up, I focused on him. I was still breathing hard, slumping back against Ricky. Reid's arm worked, his back arched. His balls were flushed and heavy, and I wanted to suck them and feel his wiry hair on my tongue.

"That's it," I whispered. "You're such a good patient. Show me your hole." I had no clue where these words were coming from, but I didn't try to stop them from spilling out.

Reid eagerly spread his hairy legs even more, putting his feet on the coffee table and shifting his ass to the edge of the couch. It was hard to actually see, but then Reid pushed his middle finger inside, his gaze locked on me. I shook through an aftershock as I teased my spent dick.

"You're going to make me hard again." I moaned softly.

That sent Reid over the edge, and I couldn't have looked away for a million dollars as he came all over his stomach and chest while he finger fucked himself.

"Jesus," I whispered.

Panting, Reid nodded. "I'm cured."

"Same."

"What's that old saying? 'Physician, cure thyself?' Achievement un-locked."

We laughed, and Reid swiped at the mess on his skin with his fingers. He was boneless against the couch, clearly in no rush to go clean up.

"Oh my god," I mumbled. "How are you this hot?" *And how do you want me?* "I would have shit twice and died if I'd seen you do this when I was in high school."

"Glad to be of service now. And thank you," Reid murmured. He'd dragged a velvet throw blanket over him and yawned widely.

Soon, I'd have to creep out to the bathroom to scrub the drying jizz off me, but in the meantime, I pulled the covers up.

"It was my pleasure. As you saw." Another thrill shivered through me. Being with Reid was better than my wildest dreams, and I'd had some…inventive fantasies. "Hey, did we get to everything on your New Yorker list?"

"Not quite. I keep expanding it. We can tackle more in the new year."

My heart leapt. "Cool. Any hints?"

"Hmm. Maybe. Pick a number."

"Twelve."

Reid curled on his side, his head pillowed on the arm of the couch. "Why twelve?"

"It was my mom's favorite number."

"Favorite? Not lucky?"

"No. It was just the number she always picked."

"Example?"

I held up my phone and shimmied down so my head was on my pillow. "If we were trying a new Chinese place for takeout, she'd go with entree number twelve, no matter what it was. When she bought lottery tickets, twelve was always her first number. Stuff like that. I guess she hoped it would be good luck." It certainly hadn't worked.

Reid dug his phone out of his pants pocket and tapped the screen. "Well, number twelve is possibly the most authentic New York experience there is: step on a rat."

Laughing, I cried, "Veto!" before remembering my dads were sleeping close by. I put my finger to my lips and shushed as if Reid was the one who'd shouted.

"I don't make the rules. New York does." His shoulders shook with laughter under the blanket.

"You're a weirdo."

"I love that I can be a weirdo with you."

My breath caught. *Love.* We stared at each other, both of us falling silent.

I whispered, "I can imagine Bitsy doesn't enjoy weird."

"Not in the slightest." He reached for something on the floor, picking up the discarded purple tie. "I feel like I've been wearing a disguise for as long as I can remember."

"You came out, though. You've been peeling it away."

He seemed to ponder this, stroking the smooth, shiny material. "I suppose so." His gaze locked on me. "But you're the first person to really see me. To listen to me. To *hear* me."

"I…" My mouth was bone dry. "I'm glad." It wasn't enough of a response, but it was all I could come up with. I'd undoubtedly think of a million eloquent thoughts tomorrow.

"We should sleep. Thank you again. For trusting me with that."

"Of course. It's the next best thing until I see you again."

"Eight more days," Reid said.

That he was counting too was the greatest Christmas present ever.

Chapter Eighteen

Reid

ASHER GROANED AS he mumbled, "Hello?"

"Hey, it's me." Fiddling with the belt of my robe, I paced the length of my apartment, the hardwood creaking in places under my bare feet. It was still dark and also foggy, a low haze hanging over the city and dampening the familiar lights. "Did I wake you?"

"Dude, it's seven in the morning on Christmas Eve. *Duh.*"

"Sorry. Look, I need a—" I was about to say "favor," but I stopped myself. "I need you to do something for me. For our family."

"Huh? What's going on? Are you okay?"

I bit back my usual answer, which would be that I was fine. Peering out at the shrouded buildings, I said, "No, actually."

Asher's voice sharpened, the sleepy slur disappearing. "What happened? Did you get in an accident?"

"No, nothing like that. I'm not injured. But I need you to go to Grandmother's breakfast event tomorrow."

After a beat of silence, Asher said, "Wait, what? Dude, why are you being so dramatic? And no way—I'm going skiing at Stowe."

"I really need you to step in for me." To step *up*.

"That's always been your deal. You're Gamma's golden grandchild."

I sputtered. "As if you aren't her favorite?"

"Me? Are you on drugs? Gamma loves me, sure, but you two have your whole Utopia thing."

"Yeah, well, I don't want it." I jammed the phone against my ear.

"What? Since when?"

"I don't know. A few years now."

Asher was silent a moment. "But...*what*? Hold up. Are you talking about tomorrow specifically, or in general?"

"In general."

"But it's always been your thing. Even when Dad was alive, we all knew you were going to take over the company one day."

"It's all yours."

"No, no, no. I don't want it. I'm going to be a broker. I know it's not very original, but I like it, and I'm good at it. The family business is all you and Gamma."

"I don't want to spend my life servicing the one percent when I could be helping people."

"You do a ton of charity stuff."

"Yeah, and that's great, but it's not my *job*. It could be, though. Why not? Why should I be Grandmother's golden boy? I'm already not the straight, perfect grandson she wanted. Why stop there?"

"I mean… Yeah. If you're not happy, you should do something about it."

I inhaled and exhaled deeply, excitement zipping through my veins. "I should. I *need* to do something about it. Starting with Christmas."

"Okay, why can't you do Gamma's event tomorrow?"

"I want to spend Christmas with Connor. I've spent every Christmas for a decade in public representing Utopia and our family. The breakfast and toys go to deserving people, which is great. But I want a Christmas that's for me for once. Maybe that's awful and selfish, but I miss Connor. I'm tired of following Grandmother's orders."

Asher sighed heavily. "I get it. Also, it is seriously weird that you're, what—falling for my best friend?"

"Maybe. I don't know. Actually, yes. Yes. I've fallen for Connor. Hard."

"That was quite a journey." He groaned. "*Fine.* I'll drive up to Stowe tomorrow afternoon instead of today."

Relief *whooshed* through me. "Thanks, man. I owe you. Actually, no. I don't. You need to pull your weight with Grandmother."

"Took me on another journey there. Yeah, okay. That's fair."

"It is? I mean, yes. It is." I felt light enough to float away. Instead of pacing, I spun in a silly little dance move. What was that saying? Dance like no one was watching? I could have done a cartwheel if I hadn't been holding my phone.

"It means that much to you not to have to do this breakfast tomorrow? Since when do you give a shit about Christmas?"

"It's not just one event. It's symbolic. And yeah, I've never really cared about Christmas. There are so many social obligations. But this is the first season when I've actually had fun. I want to decorate. I want to buy presents and roast chestnuts. I keep humming Mariah Carey Christmas songs."

"Holy shit, you *are* in love."

I waited for a bolt of fear or denial.

Nothing.

All I wanted to do was that cartwheel. I laughed—a fizzy bubble of joy. "I am."

"Huh. You sound…happy. I didn't realize how tense you normally are.

Wow."

"I'm in love. I need to call Connor. I need to tell him."

"On the phone? No. Veto. If you're going to tell my boy you love him, you are doing that in person. Go buy him gifts as soon as the stores open, then dust off your Audi from the underground parking lot and surprise him in Albany."

My pulse galloped. Was I actually doing this? "I can't surprise him on Christmas Eve! He's with his family."

"They're cool, trust me. This will be the greatest Christmas present ever."

"But they have plans. They aren't expecting me. Connor might not want me to come."

Asher laughed. Loudly. "Bro, he wants you to come. Trust. Hold on. Let me just…"

After the silence stretched out, I asked, "Let you what?"

"There. I just texted Con and asked if I can visit for Christmas."

"And I'm supposed to tag along and impose? No way!"

He sighed heavily. "*I'm* not going. *You're* going. But this way, they know someone's crashing and it won't be a surprise."

"This is a terrible idea. They might say no."

"Logan and Seth love me. They won't say no. They're going to say, 'the more the merrier.' Like, those exact words will come out of Seth's mouth, I guarantee it."

"But they don't even know me."

"What better time to meet the man who's railing their baby boy?"

I groaned. "This is not helping."

"A-ha! Conner just replied: *Of course. Is everything okay?* There. It's done. They're officially expecting a guest, and you can climb down Connor's chimney. God bless us, everyone."

My head spun, and despite my persistent doubts, the urge to cartwheel returned. "Make sure you tell him you're okay. Don't make him worry."

"Yes, *Mom.* Oh, speaking of whom, did she send you pics from that sailboat? Maybe we should spend Christmas with her next year."

After we hung up, I started searching for gift ideas online. I needed something perfect for Connor, and what about his dads? And his extended family gathered on Christmas Eve, I thought he'd said. I needed to get organized.

Before I did, I put down my phone and performed a wobbly cartwheel that culminated in me sprawled on my back by the couch laughing at the ceiling.

All I wanted for Christmas was Connor—and I was going to get my man.

"YOU HAVEN'T SHAVED."

Grandmother stared at me in the foyer of her two-story apartment. She must have heard me speaking to the housekeeper who'd let me in—and who now quickly disappeared down a hallway past framed prints of Utopia ads from decades past. One headline beckoned:

Escape to a world where the sea meets the sky.

What did that even mean? The sea met the sky everywhere there was an ocean on the planet.

"Darling? What's wrong?"

It was Christmas Eve and she wasn't in the office, but Grandmother looked like she was. Navy pantsuit and Hermès scarf knotted at her throat, pearl earrings and matching bracelet on her wrist. The only indication that she wasn't expecting company was that her reading glasses hung from a gold chain around her neck. She never wore them in public.

In stark contrast, I'd tugged on jeans and a sweater. I'd unbuttoned my coat in the sweltering cab on the way over, and no—I hadn't shaved for the first day in…possibly forever?

"Are you ill?" she asked, her sharp gaze intense.

"No," I croaked. I cleared my throat and thrust out the binder I'd been gripping in my sweaty hands. "Please read this. I've been working on it for months. I want to diversify our business. Invest in affordable, sustainable housing. We can easily fund a pilot project while maintaining our current hotels and resorts if we pause any further hotel expansion temporarily."

She peered at the simple black binder uncomprehendingly. "Is this what you were talking about at lunch with the Westons?"

"Yes." I still held out the binder, willing my hand not to shake. She might not have been actual royalty, but in my world, she may as well have been. I felt like I should curtsey. "Will you please read it?"

Lips pursed, she took the binder, then leveled me with a piercing gaze. "Is that all? You'll shave tomorrow morning before the event."

"Actually, I won't be there."

Eyes wide, her mouth gaped. I couldn't remember if I'd ever seen Grandmother look so discombobulated—not even when I announced Connor was my boyfriend on Thanksgiving.

I plowed on since she was apparently stunned silent. "Asher's going to be there, though. Don't worry—the family will be represented."

Grandmother's nostrils flared. "Asher isn't the future president of Utopia. That's wonderful that he's volunteered, but you know how important this event is to our brand. You're always there to give generously to those in need. You are required to be there."

I shrugged. I actually *shrugged*, which felt as huge as if I'd given her the finger. "The brand will have to survive without me."

"What does that mean?" she asked sharply.

"I'm not sure. For now, it means I won't be at the event tomorrow, and that you and Utopia will be just fine."

She clutched the binder. "Where exactly will you be?"

"In Albany with Connor for Christmas."

The *crack* of the binder spine hitting the marble floor could have been a gunshot. From the corner of my eye, I spotted the housekeeper hurrying toward us—then just as quickly backing away.

Grandmother clenched her fists. "Enough with this nonsense! That boy is not suitable."

"He's not a boy. And why not?"

"You know precisely why."

"His gender or that he was on scholarship at Rencliffe?"

"Enough." She turned on her heel, the binder still flung open and abandoned on the floor.

"No! Tell me why Connor isn't good enough. Because he has two dads?"

Her nose wrinkled as she faced me. "Good god. They've clearly corrupted that boy."

"Jesus Christ, don't be ridiculous."

"I will not stand here in my own home and be spoken to in this manner. What has gotten into you? What would your father say?"

"I have no idea. I barely remember him. He's like a shadow."

"I remember every minute."

Guilt and grief punched. *Hard.* "I'm sorry. I wish I did remember him more."

"You were twelve when he passed. You must remember."

"Not much. He was always working, and I was away at Rencliffe. I've been alive longer without him."

Her brow furrowed, and she was silent as if counting the years and thinking it couldn't possibly be true.

"He's been more present in his absence and the pressure that put on me than he was when he was alive." At her flinch, I added, "I wish that wasn't the case. And I know you don't want me to be bisexual—"

"Enough." She raised her palm, schooling her expression back into stone. "This ridiculous rebellion needs to end. You and Cecilia aren't a match, that much is clear. But—"

"This isn't rebellion. This is who. I. Am. I'm bisexual, and I'm in love with a man." I motioned to the binder. "And I want to help make the world a better place. I want to use my privilege to make a practical, sustainable difference. At least try to. Not open new hotels for facelifts and collagen injections."

Grandmother pinched the bridge of her nose. "I might have expected this idealistic claptrap when you were in college. I suppose I have *Connor* to thank."

"This has been building for a long time. And yes, Connor helped me see more clearly. I'm spending Christmas with him. If you'll read my proposal over the holidays, we can discuss it in January. Angela Barker's very interested in it."

Grandmother exhaled in disgust. "That tacky woman."

I gritted my teeth. "She's gone out of her way to help me."

"How wonderful." Sarcasm dripped from Grandmother's tongue.

I couldn't leave my proposal abandoned on the floor, so I placed it on the small round console table beside a wing-backed chair no one ever sat in.

"I have to get on the road. They're calling for a major snowstorm upstate. Merry Christmas."

Striding to the private elevator, I jabbed the button. I didn't let myself look back in the silence as the old door slid open slowly, though I sensed she was still there.

"Darling."

My heart clenched. I shouldn't care what she thought of me or my relationship with Connor, but I did. I wanted her to love me in all my bisexual glory. I wanted to still be her darling. I turned, extending my arm behind me to keep the elevator open.

"Drive carefully."

With that, she gracefully walked out of the foyer, head high, her heels tapping the marble. My proposal still sat on the table, but at least it wasn't on the floor.

Two hours later on the highway as snow fell more and more thickly and traffic slowed in a sea of red taillights, I paused the podcast I hadn't heard a word of and tapped the navigation screen to see if Connor had replied to my texts and the system somehow hadn't notified me. No red dot on his name. I dialed his number with a tap. It rang out, and I didn't leave another message.

I'd decided once I was on the road that surprising him—and his parents—was a terrible idea no matter what my little brother thought. Did the silence in response to my messages mean that I wasn't welcome? Surely if it was a problem, Connor would have simply told me that.

It was still early afternoon, but it could have been sunset. Visibility was decreasing, and we crawled past a car that had spun into the ditch, the flashing lights of a state trooper casting an eerie glow in the gloom. Every mile farther from the city had me questioning if it was time to turn around.

"Where is he?" I said out loud.

Had he been in an accident? Was he breaking up with me—he'd lived up to his fake boyfriend obligations, and perhaps he'd rethought continuing our relationship? Had I done something or said something? I replayed the last conversation we'd had—the incredibly hot phone sex and afterglow.

Naturally, remembering that made my cock swell, and I shifted restlessly. The windshield wipers thumped back and forth, the thick, wet snow sticky. I deeply regretted not buying winter tires for my car, but I drove it so infrequently and usually only in the city. At least I could stay slow and steady in the right-hand lane while more daring drivers passed on the left.

"Where is Connor?"

Chapter Nineteen

Connor

"RESOURCE CARD, PLEASE," I said, extending my hand to Seth. He grumbled and passed one over. He wasn't very competitive generally speaking, but Catan brought it out in him.

"I can build a road now," I said. "Sweet."

Across from me at the dining table, Logan rolled the dice. He leaned back to read the number, and I finally asked, "When was the last time you had your eyes checked?"

Logan practically growled, but there was no heat to it. "My eyes are fine."

"You need reading glasses," Seth and I said in unison.

"I was a goddamn Marine," Logan muttered as he played a Year of Plenty card.

"I'm afraid that doesn't exempt you from the ravages of aging, my dear." Seth squeezed Logan's arm and kissed his cheek.

The ornamental clock ticked on the wall below green garland boughs decorated with white berries and red ribbons. I squinted out the window. "I hope the roads are okay. I should check if Asher's texted."

"Nice try," Logan said. "No phones during game time."

"What if he gets in an accident?"

Logan and Seth shared a glance, and as usual, they had a whole conversation in a blink. Seth said, "Yes, I think this is an exception."

I practically ran to where our phones sat on the kitchen island, hoping there'd be messages from Reid too. God, I missed him so much. But when I looked at the screen, there were no messages from anyone. No notifications.

"Shit!" No Wi-Fi signal, and the cell coverage was terrible out where we lived, the one bar not giving me anything. "Wi-Fi's out!" I called to Logan and Seth.

Seth joined me in the kitchen. "I'll reboot it and see if that makes a difference. Hope we don't lose power."

I peered out the window. The snow was piling up, but at least it wasn't too windy. Visibility would hopefully be okay. "I hope Asher gets here soon. I hate not having a way to contact him." Or Reid.

"Ahem," Seth said pointedly, followed by a low buzzing sound.

I turned and found him holding out the old land line phone that sat in the corner of the counter in all its beige, plastic glory.

"Oh, right."

"This is exactly why we still have it," Seth said with an arched eyebrow.

"Okay, okay." I'd teased them about it and how it wasn't even a cordless. Apparently, cordless phones didn't work without power, but the ancient ones just plugged into the wall did. It was strange to hear a dial tone as I punched in Asher's numbers on the buttons. A number I had to look up in my contacts since I knew zero phone numbers off by heart except my own.

"No answer," I said after getting Asher's voicemail. I left a quick message and considered calling Reid, but Seth was still in the kitchen checking on a recipe for later. I'd barely put the phone back in its holder when it rang again.

I picked it up. "Where are you, jackass?"

"I'm at home freaking out over the weather report," Aunt Jenna said. "Though I'd appreciate not being called a jackass."

Laughing, I clapped a hand over my mouth. "My bad. I thought you were Asher. This phone doesn't even have call display."

"At least it's working. I've been texting and calling Seth and Logan, but I assume they aren't going through."

"Yeah, sorry. Here you go."

I handed the phone to Seth and opened the fridge, poking around and idly peeling the wrapper off a cheese slice. My dads always had processed cheese in the fridge when I visited since I loved grilled cheese. Actual cheese was good too, but there was something weirdly comforting about the processed slices.

"Mm," Seth was saying. "I agree. You don't want to take the risk. You only see Jun's parents a couple of times a year. It's best to get on the road now. Let me get Logan."

I ate another cheese slice and leaned against the island while Logan talked to Jenna and Seth waited with slumped shoulders.

Logan said, "You sure you want to take Pop with you? He can stay with us. I know he can't do the stairs, but we could bring down a mattress or something." After a silence, he said, "Okay."

When Logan hung up after telling her to drive safely and call when they arrived, I asked, "They're not coming tonight?"

Logan sighed heavily. "The snow we're getting now is moving west overnight and gaining momentum. They're going to get hit with a huge storm tomorrow. The highways might close."

"Shit," I said. "Yeah, I guess it's better if they go now." It had become tradition to celebrate together on Christmas Eve with turkey and all the fixings before having a more chill Christmas Day. Usually, Aunt Jenna and

Uncle Jun went to his family or had them visit for Christmas Day. "Even if that means we don't get Aunt Jenna's turkey," I added in a tone dangerously close to a whine.

Seth was already looking in the freezer. "We have steaks. We can shovel off the back porch and fire up the grill."

"Sure," Logan said distantly, staring at his feet, arms crossed and leaning against the counter.

"It sucks that we can't all have Christmas Eve together like usual," I said.

"Yeah," Logan agreed, still clearly preoccupied.

Seth left the meat on the counter and joined Logan. He didn't say any-thing—just waited until Logan spit out whatever it was on his mind.

After a minute, Logan said, "This medicine Pop has to take for the swell-ing in his legs—Jenna has to keep nagging him to take it." He looked at me. "Is there something else he can take instead? He hates it."

"I'm not sure, but from what I know, I doubt it. Is the reason he doesn't want to take it because he has to urinate too frequently? Which means getting up more often? It's likely a mobility issue."

"Right." Logan seemed to think about it. "That's probably it. He just wants to sit in that chair even more than he used to."

Seth asked, "Why does the congestive heart failure cause the swelling? I'm not clear on the reason."

He was asking me, and Logan looked to me as well. I explained the corre-lation between his heart condition and the edema as they nodded, answering a few more questions that came up.

"Talking like a doc already," Logan said with a big smile, and I flushed with pride.

"I still have a ton to learn," I insisted.

"And you'll learn it," Logan said firmly. "You were always so good at learning. Do you remember the first time I met you? Most kids would be playing video games, but you were memorizing the periodic table with those cards. There's a name for them..."

I fiddled with Seth's recipe for butternut squash casserole sitting on the island counter, spinning the paper under my finger. "Flash cards."

"Right, right." Logan had that distant look again. "Veronica was so damn proud of you."

My throat was too thick to speak. I shrugged and opened the fridge, thinking of the night she died and how I *had* been playing video games. I knew I shouldn't let myself spiral down this hole, but my asshole brain was off and running.

If I hadn't been wearing headphones, would I have heard her call for help? Even if she hadn't been able to call out, I might have heard her hit the bedroom floor...

Instead, she'd lain there all night. Alone. Until I'd finally gone looking for her in the morning, annoyed that she wasn't making me breakfast because I was a selfish little—

"You okay?" Logan asked. I could sense he and Seth close behind me. I stared into the fridge, blinking back tears.

"Yeah," I rasped, grabbing the water pitcher and closing the fridge too hard. I poured a glass, splashing water all over the counter and over Seth's recipe. "Shit! Sorry."

"It's okay," Seth murmured, squeezing my shoulder and shaking the paper.

Sometimes, the memory of finding her there that morning punched so hard that it eclipsed everything else in the world. I breathed through it, knowing it would pass, and I would go on. I'd be happy again, and that was allowed.

God, I wished Reid was with me. As much as I loved my dads, I ached for Reid's comfort. It was probably only infatuation, I knew that. Everything was shiny and new, and I couldn't let myself get too invested.

I laughed harshly. Too fucking late for that.

"Hey." Logan nudged my arm. "What's up?"

"Sorry. I'm in my head. I'm fine."

Maybe keeping Reid to myself was a mistake. As much as I wanted to keep this amazing new thing to myself until I knew for sure it was real and not going to disappear tomorrow, the urge to let it all spill out in an excited rush was strong.

Asher would be here soon, and I could talk to him. I managed a genuine smile for my dads, pulling the door on my mom memories ajar. I'd never close that door entirely, but I'd learned over time how to function with it in the background.

I said, "Really. I guess we should defrost the steaks and stuff."

Seth chuckled. "Who's 'we'? Since when do you help out in the kitchen?"

"I help!"

"Please provide evidence of past 'helping,'" Seth said.

"I grated the Parmesan when we had that walnut pesto pasta."

"That was last year!"

The phone rang again, and Logan picked it up while I tried to think of a more recent example. I said, "Um… Oh! I totally made sangria this summer for the barbecue on Uncle Jun's birthday."

Seth submerged the bagged steaks in water in the sink. "I'll give you that one. Barely."

Logan growled, "No. Connor doesn't live here anymore. No idea where he is," and hung up the phone with a bang.

Seth frowned. "Who was that?"

Grim-faced, Logan turned to me. My stomach clenched. "What?"

Seth raised his hands. "All right. Whatever's going on, let's all take a deep breath and talk about it calmly.”

“That was a fucking collection agency,” Logan gritted out.

No. No, no, *no*. I shook my head and sputtered, “I—I paid it! Last month.”

Fuck me. *Fuck.* This wasn't supposed to happen. I borrowed that money from Reid, and I paid the whole stupid debt. It was done, and my dads were never supposed to know. It was Christmas Eve, and this wasn't right.

“If you've gotten into trouble with money, tell us what happened,” Seth said steadily.

“No!” I protested—not sure what I was actually saying and cringing at how childish I sounded. “I mean, I'm not. It's fine!”

Logan's mouth was a thin line, and he paced on the other side of the island. “Why would they call?”

“I don't know,” I heard myself say. “You hung up on them, or I could have asked.”

He scoffed. “You never answer a collections call or tell them they have the right number. Trust me.” His nostrils flared. “Just tell us.”

The doorbell rang, and relief rushed through me. Asher was here, and hopefully he could be the distraction we needed to at least table this conversation—more like a confrontation—until after Christmas. I needed time to figure out how to explain.

Logan stalked out of the kitchen and into the front room, disappearing into the little foyer as Hercules scampered off upstairs. I was about to follow Logan to the door when his terse question rang out.

“Who the hell are you?”

Chapter Twenty

Reid

BRUSHING FLUFFY SNOW from my hair in the falling darkness, I waited on the doorstep of the lovely little house and tried to calm my racing heart. Connor still hadn't been answering his phone, and now I was showing up unannounced—which wasn't how I wanted to meet his dads. I checked my screen one more time, but I didn't have a signal anymore.

They'd surely notice the car in the driveway eventually, and I couldn't stand on their stoop all night. I rang the doorbell, which chimed pleasantly. My suitcase and bag of gifts were still in the trunk since I already felt uncomfortable appearing on the doorstep.

"This was a terrible idea," I muttered under my breath, cursing my brother. I glanced around. I'd parked on the left side of the long driveway, and the car was already almost covered in snow. Connor's dads lived outside Albany, and though I could see the blue and gold and red holiday lights of neighbors beyond stands of bare trees, it was private and felt very much like being in the country. To me at least.

I was so used to the noise of Manhattan, and it was almost eerie in the complete stillness, my breath clouding on every exhale. What a perfect place to celebrate Christmas. Footsteps approached, and I squared my shoulders. The house was lit with rainbow bulbs, warm golden light shining from inside. I could imagine how cozy and peaceful—

The merry wreath made of bright ornaments jingled violently as the door was wrenched open and a thunderous man glared. "Who the hell are you?"

"Uh…" Okay, Connor definitely hadn't gotten my messages. "I'm Reid Cabot."

The muscled man—Logan, based on Connor's descriptions—blinked at me in obvious confusion before barking, "What do you want? Asher's not here yet."

"I know. He's actually not coming."

Logan's scowl softened. "Is he okay?"

"Oh, yes! He's fine. Nothing to worry about. Is, uh, Connor home?"

Good lord, I sounded and felt sixteen years old.

Relief flooded me as Connor's voice neared, saying, "Since when do you ring the bell?" As he appeared behind Logan, his jaw dropped and eyes widened.

And wow. I was in love with Connor.

Any doubt evaporated. I'd missed him more than I'd thought it was possible to miss another human. It was actually *painful* not to leap into his arms. I needed to touch him and taste him and breathe him into every cell in my body.

First, I needed to speak. "Hey. I know I'm here unannounced—uninvited, actually. I had to see you."

Connor reached for me immediately. "Are you okay? Did something happen?" He had hold of my hand, and I realized I'd left my gloves in the car.

"Yes. No. I'm fine, and so is Asher. You didn't get my messages? Clearly you didn't. I'm so sorry to show up like this. I can get a hotel."

"What?" Connor tugged me inside, elbowing Logan out of the way. "Don't be ridiculous."

I stepped into the warmth, stamping my boots on the mat. I smiled tentatively at the other man who appeared. "Hi. I'm Reid."

"Hi. I'm Seth, and this is my husband, Logan." Seth's gaze dropped to where—oops, Connor and I were holding hands. "It seems we have something to chat about."

"First things first," Logan muttered, closing the door.

Connor squirmed, letting go of my hand and crossing his arms. "I told you, it's nothing."

I stooped to take off my leather ankle boots and tried to make sense of the tension that seemed to only partially involve me. Seth took a hanger from the hall closet and was clearly waiting to hang up my coat. I smiled awkwardly as I passed it over.

I thanked him and said, "I'm interrupting. Do you want me to…?" I wasn't sure what to offer.

"No," Connor said, rubbing his face. "You need to hear it too." He took my hand again, then seemed to realize what he was doing. He glanced at his dads, shrugged, and led me through the neat house past pale gray walls and a stainless-steel kitchen with pale blue subway tile backsplash, gray quartz countertops, and white cabinets.

We stepped down into a lovely den at the back of the house with a vaulted white beam ceiling. I inhaled pine from the fresh Christmas tree with multicolored lights and a mishmash of ornaments with no discernable theme as opposed to the orderly trees my family had up even when I was little.

There was a sectional leather couch and well-padded recliner across from a wall-mounted TV. A gas fireplace stove flickered in the corner by sliding glass doors. Beyond, snow blanketed a patio.

Connor motioned for me to sit on the couch, perching beside me, his foot tapping the hardwood floor. He let go of my hand, fidgeting. Logan prowled back and forth, Seth sitting on the other end of the couch.

Not how I imagined this going.

Seth asked Connor, "How did you get into debt?"

Oh. Not what I'd expected either. I couldn't pretend I wasn't eager to find out.

Connor cracked his knuckles rhythmically and said, "It doesn't matter. It's paid off now."

Presumably, that was the ten grand. Was there more? I murmured, "If you need more money—"

"*No.*" Connor didn't look at me. "I paid off the rest with the money you loaned me. I don't want more. That's not why—" He motioned between us. "It's not for your money."

I honestly hadn't considered that for a moment, and the idea was like a slap in the face. "I know," I said evenly. "It was a loan, and it has nothing to do with us. With the us we've become."

Connor squeezed his eyes shut. "I know. I'm sorry." He looked at me beseechingly. "I don't know why I said that."

He was clearly on the defensive. "I get it." I took his hand gently, giving him a chance to pull away. My breath caught when he gripped my fingers.

"Why did you feed us some bullshit about being fake boyfriends?" Logan asked sharply. "I don't get it."

"It wasn't bullshit when I told you," Connor snapped back.

Seth held up his hands, his expression pinched in concern. "Time out. We're upset because we're worried. Remember that we're all on the same team." He looked to me. "Including Reid, it seems."

"Definitely," I agreed.

After rubbing his face, his stubble scratching, Logan nodded, pacing again. "Okay. Let's leave this Reid thing for later. Collections agency first. Spill it. Why didn't you tell us you were in debt?"

When Connor didn't answer after a few moments, Seth said, "I imagine it's because he knew we'd be upset and concerned. So, we're all going to breathe, and *sit down*, and talk about it. Without yelling. Right?" He gave Logan a pointed look.

Logan nodded as he sat on the edge of the recliner. "I—" He took another deep breath, rubbing his chest with his knuckles.

"Okay?" Seth stood and perched on the arm of Logan's chair. As Logan leaned slightly forward, Seth ran his palm over Logan's back in slow circles.

"I'm sorry," Connor whispered miserably, his shoulders hunched. He still gripped my hand, and I squeezed back.

Seth leaned over Logan, and they murmured to each other. Logan squeezed Seth's knee, and I watched with a swell of longing. Their years of loving were apparent not only in the big moments, but in the smallest.

Logan exhaled noisily, and when he spoke, his voice was much calmer. "I know what it's like to have those fuckers hunting you. I never wanted that for you. I don't understand what happened. You have a full ride for tuition, you've worked summers, and we help with your rent and food. You saved up for years for that goddamn motorcycle. How do you have collections on your ass?"

"Mike," Connor whispered.

"That motherfucking piece of—" Logan's nostrils flared, his face red. If he was a cartoon character, steam would be coming out of his ears. But he didn't say anything else.

"Okay," Seth said, still on the arm of Logan's chair, his hand on Logan's shoulder. "Did he get you to lend him money?"

"No." Connor sighed. "He texted to see how I was doing. He asked for my address, and I thought…" He *grinced*. "It's pathetic, I know. I thought maybe he wanted to send me a birthday card or something. That maybe he wanted to keep in touch better. I've never even visited him in Florida once despite all his promises. But what he wanted was to take out credit cards in my name."

The awful betrayal of that punched my gut. As absent as my parents were, they'd never have hurt me like that. "It's not your fault," I said softly.

Connor's smile was brittle. "It is. I should have known better. I didn't get bills in the mail since it was all digital. But eventually a collections notice came. Connor Lisowski had accounts in arrears."

I asked, "Did you tell them what happened?"

"Yeah. They told me they were putting out an alert or whatever. That he wouldn't be able to open any more accounts in my name. I guess that didn't work."

"We'll call and get some answers after Christmas," Seth assured. "Maybe he'd opened it before and it slipped through."

"This shouldn't be on you," Logan said. "We should be able to clear your name. It's not your debt."

I'd never seen Connor so dejected, and I ached to hold him. He said, "They told me I had to file a police report. I just…" He shrugged, an almost violent motion. "I couldn't do it. I know I'm supposed to hate him, but…"

"No, sweetheart," Seth said, coming to Connor's other side.

"It's my job to hate that selfish piece of shit," Logan snarled. "Not yours."

Connor nodded. "You must hate him more than anyone. If he'd been a half—*quarter*—decent father, you wouldn't have been stuck with me."

"*Stuck*," Logan repeated like he'd swallowed something rancid. "Is that what you think after all these years? After, after…" He motioned with his arm. "All this?" He blinked, jerking as though he'd been slapped.

I wished I could take the words back for Connor, but all I could do was watch as his eyes widened in horror and he shook his head. "No," he rasped. "No! I don't. I'm sorry. I know that's not true. I just—"

Connor dropped his face into his hands, releasing mine. "You've both done so much for me, and you didn't have to, and I want to make you proud. I'm supposed to be a grown-up. A doctor soon! I didn't want you to know how stupid I'd been."

"We *are* proud," Seth said, his Adam's apple bobbing and voice thick.

Logan stood. "We couldn't be prouder."

"I know," Connor mumbled. He lifted his head, blinking back tears. "I thought being an adult would be easier."

His dads shared a glance and laughed. Logan said, "Welcome to adulthood, where everyone's just trying to get and keep their shit together."

Connor shook his head. "I paid off five grand with the rest of my savings from summer jobs, and then I borrowed ten from Reid to end it. I *thought* I had my shit together."

I snorted. "Join the club."

He peered at me. "What about Bitsy's event tomorrow? You're bailing?"

"Asher's taking my place. Grandmother and I had it out, and I wanted to be with you for Christmas." I laughed nervously. "It was Asher's idea to say he was coming and for me to surprise you instead. A truly terrible idea, and for the record, I've been calling and texting to warn you I was coming. I can still go to a hotel."

Connor's face transformed, that perfect dimple appearing. "It's the best surprise. I missed you so much this week."

"Me too." I couldn't wait to be alone so I could kiss him senseless.

"Anyone who puts that smile on our kid's face can stay for Christmas," Logan said. He extended his hand. "Logan Derwood. We didn't meet the right way."

I jumped up and shook his hand. "It's wonderful to meet you." I shook Seth's hand as well. "Both of you."

Seth said, "And you loaned Connor money for this debt?"

I nodded. Connor stood too and said, "I'm paying him back the ten grand. I got a job at CVS starting in January."

Seth and Logan exclaimed in unison, talking over each other about how school had to come first, and they'd give him the money. Connor held up his hands with a smile.

"Thank you. We can talk about it later, right? It's Christmas Eve. Can we just open some wine and make dinner and open a few presents?" His eyes widened on me. "I don't have anything for you."

"You've given me more than enough." I brushed back his hair, needing to touch him.

"All right, all right, keep it PG," Logan said without heat.

Connor playfully huffed. "I'm not thirteen anymore."

"Good thing," Logan said. "You were a real pain in the ass back then."

I automatically opened my mouth to defend him, but Connor laughed. "I really was."

Seth said, "You were both pains in the rear end. Luckily, you met me." He kissed Logan lightly. "Now, let's open that wine and hear how our son and his new boyfriend got together—and why we're just hearing about it now."

Around the kitchen island, we drank and talked, Seth preparing a steak marinade while Connor and Logan chopped vegetables. I was given the job of peeling potatoes in the sink, and I didn't admit I'd never done it before in my life. I rolled up my sleeves and got to work.

Connor told his dads our story, and I interjected here and there. Christmas carols played in the background while outside the windows, snow nestled the world in a beautiful, peaceful blanket. Holiday lights shone in the darkness.

My face was flushed from wine and laughter, and as "Silent Night" played, the lyrics "all is calm, all is bright" had never felt more true.

I turned to Connor as he explained about the New Yorker activities and blurted, "The lights are brighter with you."

Three sets of eyes stared. Connor asked, "Which lights?"

"All of them. Like in the city—I've been sleepwalking. Not paying attention to how amazing the world around me is. When I look out my window now, I see it through your eyes. Everything's brighter." I forced a laugh. "I'm not saying this properly. It's the wine."

Connor watched me, biting his lip. "You're saying it just right."

We smiled at each other, and he was so beautiful and sweet and kind and smart and—

Logan coughed loudly and nodded to Seth. "Let's shovel off the barbecue."

Maybe it should have been strange that Connor's dads were leaving us alone to kiss, but the only thing that mattered was Connor back in my arms and his sigh against my lips.

Chapter Twenty-One

Connor

"IT SUCKS THAT we couldn't see everyone and have Aunt Jenna's turkey, but these steaks are awesome," I said.

"Mm." Across the dining table, Reid swallowed his bite. "Compliments to the chef."

At the end of the reclaimed wood table with a fresh pine and ribbon wreath on the wall behind him, Seth smiled. "Steak may not be traditional holiday fare, but I admit it's delicious."

"I haven't had a Christmas celebration at home since I was a little boy," Reid said. "Whether it's turkey or steak or tofurkey, I'm happy."

To my left at the other end of the table, Logan shuddered. "No tofu for Christmas."

"You know we need to start trying more plant-based protein," Seth said, spearing a roasted potato. "Though perhaps not on Christmas Eve." He frowned at Reid. "Your family doesn't celebrate?"

"Not like this. My grandmother has a charity breakfast event Christmas morning. It's a wonderful cause, but..." He glanced at me. "It's refreshing to have a quiet Christmas."

I couldn't believe Reid was actually here across the table from me. I was still shellshocked from having to admit what had happened with my father—and I had a phone call to make that was long overdue. First, I could have dinner with my dads and my for-real actual boyfriend.

"Thank you again for including me," Reid said. "Not that I gave you much choice."

I watched Logan and Seth's smiles, looking for cracks under the surface. But they seemed to like Reid—or they were faking it really well, and Logan was the worst at pretending he liked someone when he didn't.

Please let them like Reid. Maybe even love him one day.

I shouldn't have been thinking about love, but it filled me like a helium balloon trying to rise, bouncing around inside me. I loved Reid. I loved my dads. I loved Christmas, and wine, and grilled meat.

Did I mention I loved Reid?

There was only that one black shadow looming in the corner. As Reid told Logan and Seth about his housing project ideas, I psyched myself up the way I would for an exam. Maybe I'd been studying for this one my whole life.

When we were stuffed, I helped bring the plates to the kitchen before telling Reid I'd be back. Upstairs in my room, I shut the door. I had just enough of a signal now. The phone rang. And rang, my nervous energy faltering.

Don't tell me he's not going to answer.

I wanted to get this over with. Done. I *needed* to get this *done.*

"Hey, kiddo," Mike drawled in his raspy smoker's voice. "Calling to say merry Christmas to your old man? Can't remember the last time."

I gripped the phone, ordering myself to stay calm and keep focused. "No," I said.

"No?" He laughed awkwardly. "Well, okay. Actually, I could use you. I've got this pain in my stomach."

"Where?" I asked, cursing myself.

"On the left side. Comes and goes, but it hurts like a son of a bitch."

"Lower left quadrant? Or upper?" Why wasn't I just telling him to go to hell?

"Lower." He described a few more symptoms.

"Go to the doctor. I bet you need a colonoscopy. It sounds like diverticulitis, which is when you have diverticulosis in your colon and it's inflamed."

"Colonoscopy? Is that where they stick a camera up your butt? No fuckin' way."

I gritted my teeth. "It's a medical procedure." *It doesn't make you queer, you homophobic idiot.* I knew what he was thinking. I could read his small, pathetic mind.

I was so *done.*

"I know what you did. I know about the credit cards you took out in my name."

There wasn't even a pause before he launched into a strident defense. "What're you talking about? I didn't do that!"

"You did. I know it, and you know it."

"I didn't do anything. Why are you accusing me? What about those two—"

"Don't! Don't you dare say that word."

I could practically hear him roll his eyes. "So sensitive. I always said they'd be a bad influence, didn't I?"

He had. My father had been saying that for years. From the time he'd learned Logan and Seth were in a relationship, he'd sneered and spouted insults. More than that—*hate.*

He seized on the opportunity to deflect attention away from what he'd done. Listening to him now launch into a familiar rant about how Logan and Seth had made me soft, and that they shouldn't be allowed to have children, I couldn't breathe.

My pulse thundered in my ears, and I shook all over. My chest was so tight I couldn't move from the pain.

But I didn't need to assess myself for signs of a heart attack. After years of trying to ignore him without alienating him because I'd still somehow wanted my father's approval, this was over.

It wasn't only his approval I'd longed for, but signs that he cared about me even a tiny bit. Maybe I'd put up with his hatred because if he was angry about Logan and Seth that meant he had to care about me.

He didn't.

My father didn't care about anyone but himself. I didn't owe him anything, and I never wanted a single thing from him again.

"Shut. Up." I gritted out the words. "Shut your hateful fucking mouth."

Silence.

Then, "What did you just say to me?"

"You heard me." It was the first time in my whole life that I'd stood up to him. Even if I was shaking, I wasn't backing down. Not now. Not ever again.

"Boy, you don't talk to me like that. I'm your father—"

"No!" I screamed. My throat was raw from the force of that single word. I had to pull in a few shuddering breaths before I could go on.

"*No.* You were nothing more than a sperm donor. You've never been a real father. My mom raised me on her own, and then Logan and Seth took over. They've done everything for me. So much more than I deserved. Even when I was an ungrateful little asshole, they were so good to me. They're my dads. The only fathers that have ever mattered. You're *nothing.*"

I could imagine his lip curling in disgust. "Those queers—"

"Yeah, they are! You think it's an insult, but it's not. Fuck you. And you know what? I'm queer too. And it's not because of Logan and Seth. They didn't brainwash me, or 'groom' me or any that other ignorant, hateful bullshit you've been spouting at me for years. I'm proud of who I am and who they are."

I pressed the phone to my ear so hard it hurt. As Mike swore and shouted, I took a deep, cleansing breath and exhaled slowly. I wasn't afraid anymore.

Over his tirade, I calmly said, "I'm telling the police what you did. Never talk to me again. You're the one who needs to be ashamed."

I hung up.

My knees trembled on the way downstairs. Reid, Logan, and Seth stood near the foot of the stairs, waiting with worried expressions that filled my soul with even more love, the helium back. I could have floated.

I managed a smile. "So, that went well. But I'm okay. I am. Is it time for dessert?" I was babbling, but I really *was* okay. "I was afraid of proving him right. I knew it was irrational, but every time I came close to telling you guys or Asher or anyone that I'm gay, I got too scared. I could hear him in my head saying terrible things."

Before any of them could reply, I added, "Not you, Reid. I wasn't going to tell you. Mostly because I had such a giant crush on you and we didn't really *talk*." A laugh bubbled up on that awesome helium. "I promise I'm not having a breakdown."

The three of them exchanged worried looks, and I hugged them in turn, letting myself linger for a few extra seconds to inhale Reid's now-familiar scent. I couldn't wait to get him alone and—

Wait. I stepped away. "So, we don't have a guest room." I looked to my dads. "It's cool if Reid sleeps with me, right?" *Awkwarrrd.*

Seth said, "You're both adults. And we trust you to be respectful."

"Of course." Reid nodded seriously. "I should get my things from the car."

"Oh, let me show you my bike!" I practically bounced. "It's in the garage."

"All right. Even though I think it's far too risky."

Logan exclaimed, "Thank you! Glad your boyfriend has a good head on his shoulders."

"Yeah, yeah," I muttered, not able to hide my grin. *My boyfriend.*

I shrugged into my leather jacket and clomped outside, not bothering to lace my boots or grab a hat and gloves. Snow fell thickly around us as we hurried to Reid's car and then into the cold, concrete garage. He left his suitcase and a large Nordstrom's bag by the entrance.

Reid followed me deeper into the garage, slipping between Seth's SUV and Logan's pickup. The lightbulb overhead didn't do much in the shadows, but I still made a flourish with my hands.

"Here she is. My pride and joy." I rubbed my palm over the leather seat.

"Very nice. Looks sturdy."

I swung my leg over the cold seat. "Extremely sturdy." I motioned to my helmet, which sat on the cluttered workbench nearby. "And safety is a priority, I promise."

"Uh-huh." Reid watched me, licking his lips.

With a wicked grin, I leaned forward, showing off my ass. "You're re-thinking your veto, aren't you? Imagine wrapping yourself around me from behind. The powerful engine between our legs, the wind on our faces, the road unfurling before us. Did I mention how close you'll be pressed against me?"

"I admit it has…appeal."

"Promise you'll think about a ride? No pressure."

"Oh, I'll think about it. Especially the way your ass looks when you're sitting on that bike."

"C'mere." I crooked my finger.

It was going to be too weird getting off in my room later with my dads right down the hall. I stumbled off the bike and tugged at Reid's fly as he devoured my mouth.

We had our dicks out in record time, Reid's big hand wrapped around both as we kissed and panted. I licked Reid's cheek and chin. "Love the stubble."

"Mmm. Maybe I'll keep it. By the way, I have a present for you."

"I know," I moaned, thrusting my hips into his grasp, our shafts rubbing roughly.

We laughed at how cheesy I was, and then all we could do was gasp into each other's mouths as we came.

Good thing Reid had an extra pair of socks in his suitcase that we used to clean up. I eyed the Nordstrom's bag. "Is my present in there?"

"No peeking. Although I will tell you I bought your dads a Le Creuset casserole dish. Do you think they'll like that? There are some chocolate truffles as well, and—"

I kissed him soundly. "It's all perfect. Thank you."

"You're okay? After that talk with your…Mike?"

"I am. I really am. And before you say it, I'm paying you back. I can do a couple of shifts a week at CVS. Whether you or my dads like it or not."

"*Or*—and hear me out—we defer the loan until you're a working doctor."

My jaw tightened. "Reid. We agreed."

"Yes, but it's insane for you to work nights for minimum wage at CVS when you should be resting and studying."

"I need to get used to sleep deprivation."

He sighed. "Aren't there summer jobs at hospitals or clinics or research labs med students can get that will pay better?"

"Well, yeah. And I will! But that's not for months."

"Baby, that's fine. You know I don't need the money. And I know that you'll pay me back. Please don't burn out working a crappy night job." He cupped my face, stroking gently with his thumb. "I'll worry about you. Wouldn't you if our positions were reversed?"

I wanted to argue, but he had me there. "But I don't know what other debt there might be. Although I am going to report him to the police, so maybe I'll be off the hook for it. Clear my record."

"Yes! See? Let's get that ball rolling right after Christmas. And in the meantime, you can focus on studying. Not to mention spending time with me. I'm selfish. I want you all to myself at night. CVS can butt out."

I had to admit I wasn't looking forward to stocking shelves and getting no sleep, and relief flowed through me, mingling with the euphoria from finally telling Mike where to go.

"Okay," I said. "It's settled. Thank you. Now will you kiss me again even though it's freezing out here?"

Reid grinned. "Damn right I will."

Later, we sprawled on the sectional with my dads watching *Die Hard* because it never got old. Reid and I held hands, and so did Logan and Seth. It was really honestly so fucking sweet I could barely stand it.

As Hans Gruber ordered his henchman to *Shoot. The. Glass*, I said, "I don't want his name. Lisowski. It's the only thing I'm stuck with from him, and I don't want it."

Logan and Seth shared a glance before nodding. Seth said, "How can we help?"

Reid stroked my knuckles as I swallowed a lump of emotion. "You already have. So much. I know when you got married, Seth changed his name to Derwood."

Seth nodded. "Marston is the name of a family who want nothing to do with me. I don't miss it at all."

"Would it be cool if I changed my name to Derwood too?"

Logan was beside me, and he exhaled forcefully. "Are you kidding? Of course. I'd love it. We'd all love it."

It was the answer I'd expected, but it was still a relief. "My mom wouldn't mind, right? She'd had Mike's name, and then changed it to yours. She always said that being a foster kid, she'd never been attached to her old name."

Logan nodded. "I think Veronica would like for you to have our name."

"She would, right?" My eyes burned.

Logan was the only one who'd known her. As disastrous as their short marriage had turned out, he'd loved her once. And I was so, so lucky that he loved me.

"Damn right," Logan croaked, his eyes glittering. He swiped at them. "Connor Derwood. Has a nice ring to it."

"That'll be *Dr.* Connor Derwood," Seth said thickly. "And it's music to my ears."

"Yeah." Joy bubbled up, and I laughed as I swiped my eyes. "Me too." Beside me, still holding my hand, Reid grinned.

"Come on, enough of this sappy stuff," Logan said. "Let's open a few presents. It's Christmas."

He and Seth loved the blue casserole dish from Reid, and I was pleased that they'd wrapped a box of Lindt chocolates for him while we'd been outside. I ripped the shiny paper off the slim box Reid gave me and lifted the lid.

"Whoa." I gingerly lifted one of the buttery black leather gloves and pulled it over my hand.

"The clerk said they're perfect for motorcycle riding. Should be flexible and form-fitting," Reid said. "But with reinforced material that will protect your hands."

"They're perfect. Thank you." I put on the other and flexed my fingers. I drew Reid close for a kiss before remembering my dads were sitting right there.

They only smiled and passed me another gift.

Chapter Twenty-Two

Reid

GRANDMOTHER'S POISED PROFILE picture appeared on my phone screen the next morning, and I bolted up in Connor's bed, going from a drowse to wide awake. Not her assistant, but her. I straightened the collar of my T-shirt even though she couldn't see me.

Sitting up in bed beside me in sweats, Connor put down his tablet and watched me as I put the phone to my ear and answered.

"Reid, it's your grandmother."

"Yes. Hello. Uh, how did the breakfast go?"

Asher had texted that everything was good, but Grandmother might have a different perspective. He'd also said that he'd "had a little talk" with her, though wouldn't go into details.

She said, "It went smoothly as always. We didn't even miss you."

Beside me, Connor could clearly hear her because his eyes bugged. I wasn't sure whether to be offended or relieved. "I'm glad it went smoothly."

"I misspoke. What I mean to say is that Asher stepped in without a hitch. You were right. You don't have to be there every Christmas. I'm glad you can take some time off with your…friend."

Even as relief flowed, I had to say, "Boyfriend. Connor's my boyfriend."

"Yes." She cleared her throat delicately. "I…acknowledge that."

Wow. Apparently, Asher's "little talk" was bearing fruit? Part of me wanted to roll my eyes at her acknowledgment and say, "*Big whoop,*" but I found myself grinning. "Thank you."

"I took a look at your proposal this morning. It's well reasoned and intriguing."

My pulse thudded, and Connor rubbed my thigh. "It is? What I mean to say is, yes. Thank you. I really think it's an opportunity to grow our business and do good in the world."

"Mm. Prepare to present it to the board at the next meeting in January. I'll postpone my trip south so I can be there in person."

"So you can veto?" I asked before stopping myself.

Her voice stayed clipped, all business. "No, darling."

Darling. That word of approval meant more to me than I wanted to admit. "Thank you. I'll see you in the new year. I'm taking these days off work."

"Evidently," she said, and I could picture her back in the office behind that old desk. Before I could say anything else, the line went dead.

"I guess that went well?" Connor asked.

"Amazingly."

"That's dark."

I had to laugh. "It's a low bar."

"I guess Asher's come-to-Jesus with her worked."

"Hold on. You know details? Spill. What did he say?" I wasn't sure whether to laugh in delight or cry that my little brother had stood up for me.

Connor raised his hands. "You'll have to ask him. But I'm glad she's coming around." He nuzzled my face, rubbing against my stubble.

We kissed, and I chased the rich coffee flavor in Connor's mouth. I'd woken earlier to find him gone, the murmur of voices coming from downstairs along with the scent of fresh brewing dark roast. It had been so comforting that I'd fallen back asleep.

"You're sure your dads are gone?" I asked.

Connor nodded. "They're hiking the trail to the river. Won't be back for hours."

"How about a shower?"

"Sure. It's just next door, remember? Do you need a fresh towel?" He got up.

I caught his wrist. "I mean together."

"Oh!" Connor's face flushed that adorable pink. "Right." An adorable smile lifted his lips. "Sounds good."

The shower was a standard bathtub with shower curtain setup. The water pressure was nice and strong, and we took turns shampooing and shuffling around to get under the nozzle.

I had to laugh. "I confess I'm used to a roomier shower."

Connor grinned. "Is showering together one of those things that looks sexy in the movies but is awkward and annoying in real life?"

"Well, yes. But all is not lost."

I lathered my hand with shower gel and slipped my fingers between Connor's ass cheeks, urging him close for a kiss. Our semi-hard cocks rubbed together. I circled the rim of his hole.

"Mmm." Connor gave me a lazy smile. "It's getting better already."

I whispered in his ear, "Just wait," and sank to my knees.

He jumped at the first touch of my tongue to his hole, but I steadied him with my hands firm on his hips. The next swipe of the flat of my tongue was long and slow, up and down his crack, my thumbs spreading his cheeks.

"Jesus, Reid!" Connor's knees trembled already.

"Are you cold?" I huffed a hot breath on his hole.

"What?" He leaned against the wall at the end of the tub, his arms folded on the tile. "I'm shaking because you're licking my ass and it feels incredible."

"I meant is the tile cold." The hot water fell on my back where I kneeled.

"Oh. Yeah, but who could give a shit about that when *you're licking my ass*?"

Laughing, I stood and turned off the water. "You said hours, right? Think we can risk going back to your room?"

Connor didn't bother answering—he practically tripped out of the tub, tossed me a towel, and raced back to his room, rubbing a towel over himself as he went.

With the door firmly locked, we fell onto his bed, still wet and not caring even a little. "You want to come on my tongue, baby?" I asked, grinding down against him.

"Oh my god," he moaned. "Yes. But actually—" He nudged a hand against my chest, and I sat up, straddling his thighs.

"Hmm?" I asked, caressing his slim pecs and sliding my thumbs along his collar bones.

"You said you've been fucked before. Penetrated, I mean."

"Definitely. Is that what you want?" The lust that had already scorched my veins burned even hotter. "You want your cock inside me?"

Lips parted, Connor nodded. "You don't mind?"

I barked out a laugh as I crawled off him. "Not even a little. Get the condom and lube from my suitcase. How do you want me?"

"Um…" Connor stared with blown pupils. "That was easy." He practically vaulted across the room to my suitcase. "How do you like it?"

I got onto all fours. "Will you fuck me from behind?"

I didn't have to ask twice.

As he pushed into me tentatively, I bore down. "You won't break me," I promised. His cock was a good size, and the burn was absolutely delicious.

"*Fuck*," he mumbled as he thrust harder. His right hand was slick with lube where he clutched my hip. "I'm going to start talking like a porno again."

I laughed. "Do I feel nice and tight, baby?"

"*Yes.* It's so good."

His pubes tickled my ass, and I squeezed around his shaft. He probably wasn't going to last long, but I didn't care. This was about Connor. Another first time I'd been lucky enough to claim.

I wanted them all. I wanted *everything*.

We strained and swore, and I dropped onto my elbows, pushing back against Connor's clumsy thrusts. My cock bobbed, throbbing and leaking even though I wasn't touching it.

"Feels so good," I moaned, loving the sound of our damp skin slapping and Connor's ragged gasps. "Come in my ass, baby. I want you so much. Never wanted anyone like this."

He jerked and shook, his fingers digging into my hips as he came. I twisted my neck to watch his silent, open-mouthed shouts of climax. His skin was red, his wet hair flopping over his forehead. I wanted to keep him inside me, but as I squeezed, he hissed and withdrew, clearly oversensitive already.

Before I could say anything, he tossed the condom at the little garbage can under his desk and flopped onto his back. "Fuck my mouth?"

Kneeling over him, I fed my cock between his lips, and we both moaned. The give and take between us felt like a perfect circle. I came in his hot, wet, generous mouth.

In the end, we hopped back in the shower, kissing and smiling and touching gently. I told him about the circle, and Connor beamed.

"Like an ouroboros," he said. "A snake eating its own tail. But, um, in a sexy way?"

"Very, very sexy," I agreed, kissing him again. "We'd better get out. Get dressed. Being caught by your dads would be very, very, unsexy. And I have a weird request."

He frowned. "Weird how? After what we just did…"

"It's not sex-related. It's weird in that it's probably extraordinarily dorky and will shatter any remaining mystique I might have."

"If you think I haven't figured out that you're a massive dork, you're sadly mistaken."

I couldn't argue with that, and soon, we were out front of the house in our winter gear amid fat, steadily falling snow. Connor bent and made a snowball in his gloved hands.

"It's your lucky day. Perfect packing snow." He tossed the ball up and caught it. "If I weren't so mature, I'd throw this at you."

"Lucky for me Dr. Lis—" I stopped and corrected myself. "Dr. Derwood would never do such a thing when he's supposed to be teaching me a vital task."

Connor grinned. "Lucky indeed. And I like the sound of that." He bit his lip. "Dr. Derwood."

"Me too."

He tossed the snowball over his shoulder. "You've seriously never built a snowman?"

"Never."

"Well, it's the perfect day to start. Nothing says Christmas like building snow people. Get on your knees and roll."

I arched a dubious brow.

Connor rolled his eyes. "Mind out of the gutter! I mean, for the moment. It can go back in the gutter later."

"If my grandmother were here, she'd say I'd lost all dignity."

Connor's expression grew serious, and he kissed me softly. "If she doesn't accept you the way you are, it's her loss."

I took a deep breath and nodded. "Dignity's overrated."

Connor dropped to his knees and scooped snow towards him, and I joined in. When we had a sizeable ball, we rolled it forward, not caring that we were soaking our jeans, our laughter just for us, muffled by the falling snow.

Epilogue

Connor

JOYOUS SHRIEKS ECHOED around the community center as children chased each other and played with their new toys. I wasn't sure how they weren't puking given their full stomachs, but those were kids for you.

I'd been stationed on the waffles, putting them on plates with tongs before pouring maple syrup imported from Quebec over them. Only the best for Reid's grandmother.

Hundreds of people had filed through the breakfast line and met Santa, who lingered and chatted with Reid and Bitsy and a few of her society ladies. Calling her "Bitsy" to her face had been weird as hell at first, but I was used to it now.

I took another bite of the breakfast sandwich I'd made from leftovers of waffles, bacon, and scrambled eggs. My phone buzzed in the pocket of my leather jacket that I'd slung over a folding chair.

Asher was supposed to call from Greece, where he was visiting with his and Reid's mom, but it was Olivia's face that filled the screen. I swiped to answer the video call as I swallowed and put my paper plate on the chair.

"Hey, Liv!"

"Merry Christmas!" She turned her camera to pan over her parents and younger sister having breakfast on a terrace with palm trees and the perfectly blue ocean and sky in the sunshine. "Hello from Aruba, a.k.a. paradise that we're never leaving."

"I bet." I turned my phone. "Hello from the new Utopia Vision Community Hub."

Angela clapped delightedly. She wore reindeer antlers with bells in her poufy blonde hair. "Love all that natural light! Can't wait to see it for myself in March. Did Reid tell you I'll be there for the groundbreaking on the new rental units?"

"Yep. It'll be great to see you."

"How are the solar panels working at the center?"

"Perfectly even though it's been nothing but gray skies. Proving wrong the naysayers who don't understand how solar panels work."

"Are you having a white Christmas?" asked Makayla, Olivia's younger sister, who attended my old alma mater in Boston.

"Not in the city. It's supposed to snow overnight tonight in Albany, though. Reid and I are driving up soon."

"Say hi to Will and Michael for me if you see them," Makayla said.

"They're coming for dinner tonight, so definitely."

"Hi from all of us!" Angela grinned. "I just love those boys. And you tell Reid's grandmama that I'm looking forward to seeing her in March," she added with a mischievous wink.

Angela had been an integral partner in the new branch of Utopia's business: Utopia Vision, a separately incorporated company of which Reid was president and CEO.

"And Reid, too, of course. How's your pumpkin pie of a man? Tell him merry Christmas from the Barkers."

"He's great, and I will."

Olivia shook her head, grinning. "The way your exhausted face lights up just hearing his name."

I rolled my eyes, but I couldn't hide my smile, glancing over at Reid in his slacks and form-fitting red cashmere sweater. His dark, trimmed beard somehow made his bright smile even sexier.

The Barkers whistled and laughed, and I knew I was blushing. Angela said, "You do look tired though, sugar."

"Yeah, it was a busy night. A long week of night shifts, but that's how it goes in residency. Especially since I'm on an ER rotation."

I yawned. I'd decided on neurology, and treating acute cases was more stressful than being on the ward. It was a rush, though. I'd identified subtle stroke symptoms in a young woman the night before, and we'd been able to start immediate treatment.

That rush had definitely faded now. I yawned again. "Sorry. Long night. Wait, I said that already."

The Barkers laughed, but then Angela frowned. "I hope you're eating right."

I didn't tell her dinner last night had been a Twix from the hospital vending machine at midnight. "Yep. Don't worry."

"Well, I know your daddies will make sure. We just talked to them, and they are hard at work in the kitchen already."

"I can't wait."

The thought of being home warmed my chest. I'd moved into Reid's place a few years ago, and it was very much home now too. Reid owned it, but we split the bills equally, and since I'd ended up being refunded the ten grand of debt after a long legal process, we'd been able to make a fresh, even start together.

But there'd always be something special about *home*-home in Albany. I'd worked Thanksgiving, and I'd have to go in New Year's Eve, but at least Christmas Day was mine.

We said our goodbyes, and I slumped on the chair to finish my makeshift sandwich. My lower back was a little sore from all the standing at the hospital and then while dishing out waffles. When I finished eating, I caught Reid's eye, and he nodded without me needing to say a word.

After zipping up my jacket, I lingered near the door while Reid said his goodbyes. He'd just taken my hand when a man called, "Sorry, can I get one more shot of the Cabots and Santa?"

Reid returned to where his grandmother stood by the massive tree decorated in rainbow lights and handmade ornaments from the kids in the neighborhood. Bitsy wore one of her elegant pantsuits, this one in festive green and paired with glittering ruby jewelry. Her version of a Christmas sweater.

"You too," Bitsy said.

She was looking at me for some reason, and it took me a few seconds to understand that, yes, she was talking to me. I pointed at my chest, and she nodded.

Reid *beamed*—I still wanted to lick his entire face when he did that—and held out his arm to tuck me by his side. I put my arm around his waist, leaning into his warmth and smiling for the camera.

The photographer took about twenty-five shots, and my face hurt from smiling by the time he asked, "Name?"

Bitsy said, "This is Dr. Connor Derwood. My grandson's partner."

Now that my name had officially been changed, a process I knew Reid had called in favors to expedite, I loved hearing it. And coming from Bitsy— with the addition of "partner" no less!—it was an unexpected hit of adrenaline.

"Got it." The photographer gave us a thumbs-up. "Are you from the city?"

"Albany," I said.

"Although he is an official New Yorker now," Reid said with a grin. "Got his certificate and everything."

It had been rolled in my stocking one Christmas with an official-looking custom seal. We still made lists of activities to try and both of us had full veto power. There was a checklist on our fridge now, and we'd finally be ticking off skating at Wollman Rink on New Year's Day with Addison and her new girlfriend.

The photographer seemed puzzled, but said, "Uh, great. Merry Christmas, folks."

Reid hugged his grandmother and pressed a kiss to her cheek. I nodded to her. "Merry Christmas."

"And to you." She nodded with a ghost of a smile. "Give my best to your parents."

I fell asleep almost as soon as my ass hit the heated leather seats of Reid's Audi. When Reid placed his palm on my thigh, his fingertips tracing the inseam on my jeans, I jerked awake and swiped the drool from the corner of my mouth. Blinking, I realized we were home.

The old ornament wreath still hung on the front door, and multicolored lights brightened the gray afternoon from the eaves and bushes. It would look beautiful when it snowed later.

"Sorry to wake you," Reid murmured, still caressing my inner thigh.

"S'okay." I rubbed my face. "I wasn't very good company."

"You needed the rest. I listened to that new kidnapping podcast Will and Michael recommended. Three hours flew by." He leaned close and kissed my cheek.

"We didn't talk about this morning, though. That was cool with your grandmother including me in the picture."

Reid smiled, although it was sad. "Honestly the best Christmas present she could ever give me. I know I shouldn't care what she thinks, but…"

I kissed him lightly. "Of course you care. Family can be…challenging, but you still love them. And she's come around. The plans for development sound amazing. Angela's excited."

Now he grinned. "Me too. Did I tell you we lined up our first pick for plumbing?"

"No! That's awesome." I rubbed my face. "Sorry I haven't been around this week to talk about it."

He scoffed. "You're working your ass off saving lives. Don't apologize."

"Your work is important too."

"I know. But I'm not pulling night shifts on hardly any sleep with over-time because of staff shortages. I'm so glad you have a few days off finally."

"Me too," I mumbled through another yawn before slapping my own face. "Okay, time to wake up. Oh!" I straightened with a bolt of adrenaline. "I know just the thing."

We carried in our bags as Logan and Seth greeted us, the house smelling of ginger and pine and roasting meat. I inhaled deeply, a wonderful calm flowing through me as I hugged my dads. *Christmas.* I wished I could bottle it for those long shifts when I needed a break.

I rooted around in the drawer in the hall. "I'm just going for a quick ride while the roads are clear."

"Be careful," Logan said with his usual hint of concerned grumbling. These days, he said it in perfect unison with Reid.

Seth chuckled. "I know you're always careful."

In the garage, I strapped on my helmet securely, jumping when Reid spoke from the open door. "You have another one of those?"

"Helmet? Yeah." My heart skipped. "Wait. Are you serious? You're un-vetoing?"

He tucked his scarf into his pea coat. "I performed another risk analysis, and I'm ready to give it a try."

I squeezed past Logan's truck and eagerly pulled the extra helmet out of the storage cabinet in the corner. Reid waited patiently while I buckled it on him, triple-checking the fit. "Are you sure? You don't have to."

"I know, but I want to."

"Why?"

"Because you love it," he said simply.

I tugged on my riding gloves he'd given me our first Christmas, now well worn like a second skin. "I love you. I'm going to kiss the shit out of you as soon as these helmets are off."

"I love you too, baby."

With Reid's thighs hugging my hips and my bike's engine purring, I drove us around the quiet neighborhood. There were still lots of trees, even though more housing lots were being built.

We should have both been wearing leathers, but there was little to no traffic, and I decided it was an acceptable risk. Reid clung to me tightly, his arms locked around my waist.

"Okay?" I yelled back.

"So far, so good!"

"Faster?"

"Faster," Reid agreed. I turned onto a long, straight, empty road and increased the throttle. The wind was icy, but the freedom and power of riding kept hot adrenaline pumping.

"Faster!" Reid shouted with a joyful laugh, and my heart soared.

But I said, "This is fast enough!"

I could imagine my mom telling me about her dream motorcycle and how important safety was. I wasn't sure if her voice in my head was even what she'd sounded like.

I'd never watched the few ancient videos I had of her on an external drive, old files that had been on her phone when she'd died. Logan had kept them for me, but it had hurt too much. Maybe we could watch them later.

Fat flakes of snow began drifting down, and I turned toward home. Back in the garage, Reid *whooped* as he stepped off the bike and removed his helmet. "Okay, I see the appeal. Consider occasionally riding on the back of your motorcycle officially un-vetoed."

I kicked down the stand and took off my own helmet, not caring that my hair was sticking up. "You want to learn to drive one sometime? I'm getting you full leathers too." I waggled my brows. "You'll look so hot."

Alarm tensed Reid's face. "Drive it myself? No, no, no. I mean, I'll wear the leather, but I'll stay on the back, baby. Also, I believe I was promised a kiss."

He swept me into his arms and almost off my feet, and we kissed deeply until Reid groaned and pulled away, his lips shiny. "To be continued." He nuzzled me, and I rubbed against the scratch of his beard, not caring how red my face was.

I nodded. "Tonight in my room. We'll have to be so, so quiet."

He arched a brow. "Are you sure?"

We'd never had sex in my room when my dads were home, but the adrenaline from the ride had me nodding eagerly before I turned to put away our helmets.

Reid caught me from behind, his arm around my waist and lips at my ear. "We will *really* have to be quiet. Do you think you can control yourself?" He pressed his half-hard cock against my ass. Then, he yanked off his glove and covered my mouth with his bare hand. "You won't be able to make a sound."

I moaned in his grasp, nodding. Merry Christmas to *me*.

We had dinner early around five. Will and Michael brought a tray of creamy scalloped potatoes, and the six of us toasted with red wine at the dining table.

Tomorrow, we'd be playing a marathon game of *Catan*, but tonight, Seth had set the table with the new green holiday place mats and napkins Logan had given him.

The stuffing was always my favorite, and even though Aunt Jenna's was the best, she'd given my dads the recipe before leaving on a cruise with Uncle Jun's family. It tasted almost as good.

I swallowed another bite and said, "You crushed the stuffing."

"And the bird," Will said in that delightful Scottish accent. "This is delicious."

Michael said, "It really is. By the way, I love your tie, Logan."

He wore a dress shirt and this year's tie, an annual gift from Seth. Back in the day, Logan had needed the formal wear for job interviews. He hardly ever had cause to wear a tie now, but he did every Christmas. The ties had become more and more jokey as the years went by, and this one was holiday-themed with Rudolf driving a convertible.

Michael added, "It reminds me of our first Christmas ornament together," giving Will a tender smile.

"Ah yes." Will smiled. "Kevin the surfing koala. We're finally heading back down under for our honeymoon next year. We'll have to see if we can pick up a friend for Kevin."

Beside me, Reid asked, "Do they have Christmas stores all year round in Australia the way we do here in tourist towns?"

Michael grinned. "Only one way to find out."

"Who won the bet this year?" I asked Seth.

He passed over the roasted vegetables without me having to ask, and I scooped more perfectly charred squash onto my plate.

Seth said, "Logan didn't guess Rudolph or a convertible." He pushed back his chair at the end of the table and lifted his foot, pulling up his pant leg enough so we could see his sock. "However, I successfully predicted stripes."

"Only so many patterns," Logan said. "Especially since you won't wear 'em if they're too bright."

"Now, don't be sour just because I'm winning." Seth winked.

After dinner, Will and Michael left before the roads got too bad. I washed, and Reid dried the dishes that wouldn't fit in the dishwasher before flopping on the sectional with very full bellies.

Logan put on his glasses to look at a cruise photo Aunt Jenna had sent to Seth and me, knowing one of us would show him since he'd become even grumpier about not always having his phone with him. Then he turned on the TV while Seth yawned widely. Outside, snow piled up on the back deck.

The worn recliner Pop had always used was still in the corner by the tree even though he'd been gone more than a year now. I missed him with a pang, closing my eyes and replaying the last time I'd seen him sitting there.

It had been just like almost every other time he'd been over—Pop drinking a beer from the bottle, watching TV, and saying little. Hercules had often sat on his lap, though he was gone now too. It was comforting in a weird way that the last time I'd seen Pop it had been so normal.

I fell asleep halfway through *Scrooged*, and I woke curled into Reid's side. Only the colored Christmas tree lights were on, the muted TV casting flickering blue light.

"Hey," Reid whispered.

"Hey. Shit, sorry. Are my dads in bed?"

"Yes. Don't be sorry. It's ridiculous how much residents have to work. You need the sleep."

I arched my back and stretched my arms. "I know."

"You must be tired," I said, stifling another yawn. "We should go to bed." I remembered what we'd said in the garage earlier, excitement sparking to life. "And be very, very quiet." I cupped Reid's dick through his pants. "Silent night."

His breath tickled my ear. "That can wait. Sleep now."

Now I was wide awake. "The hell it can wait. I need you to fuck my brains out. Quietly. *Then* I'll be able to sleep."

"We'll see." Reid kissed me and ran a palm over my head.

"Are you trying to tell me you're going to veto for my own good?"

"I probably should. Doctors are notorious for not taking care of themselves."

"We're also notorious for getting our way."

A slow grin spread over his face. "Doctor, I have a problem. My partner works too hard. How can I encourage him to relax?"

"Hmm." I tapped my chin. "I think I have just the prescription. You might be reluctant at first, but this treatment will work wonders for you both."

Unsurprisingly, I got my way.

We woke late the day after Christmas to several feet of fresh, perfect snow. Tomorrow, Reid and I would have to get back to the city so I could work another shift.

Today, we were warm inside with leftovers, boxes of the kind of chocolates I only ate at the holidays, board games to play, and my dads.

Christmas didn't get better than this. Hell, neither did life. When I was an angry, grieving kid, I'd never have been able to even imagine this kind of peace.

Reid brought me a hot mug of coffee in bed with a kiss, and I could picture even more happiness in the years ahead. In the days and hours and little moments we'd share.

I could imagine *everything*.

THE END

About the Author

Keira aims for the perfect mix of character, plot, and heat in her M/M romances. She writes everything from swashbuckling pirates to heartwarming holiday escapism. Her fave tropes are enemies to lovers, age gaps, forced proximity, and passionate virgins. Although she loves delicious angst along the way, Keira guarantees happy endings!

Discover more at:
KeiraAndrews.com